Jo

THE CUMBRIAN TRILOGY

THE HIRED MAN

Set in Cumberland and covering the period from 1898 to the early twenties, this is the powerful saga of John Tallentire, first farm labourer, then coal miner, and his wife Emily. John's struggle to break free from the humiliating status of a 'hired man' is the theme of a novel which has been hailed as a classic of its kind – as meticulously detailed as a social document, as evocative as the writing of Thomas Hardy and D. H. Lawrence.

'An intensely moving, deeply worked book'
Sunday Telegraph

'A novelist of power and imagination. It is one of Bragg's gifts to create his own atmosphere and so heighten feeling'
New Society

'A magnificently strong and sinewy novel'
Sunday Mirror

'Mr Bragg is a serious writer of manifest integrity. His books . . . have often brought to reviewers' minds the explosive passions of Lawrence and the earthbound bitterness of Hardy'
British Book News

THE HIRED MAN is currently being staged, with music by Howard Goodall

THE CUMBRIAN TRILOGY

A PLACE IN ENGLAND

Set in the years before and during World War II, A PLACE IN ENGLAND is the invigorating and exciting story of one man's attempt to pull himself up by the bootlaces from the degradation of working for others and into a position of some independence. That independence, however, is something hard won and bitterly kept; and the struggle for its achievement makes Joseph Talentire (whose father, John, was the hero of THE HIRED MAN) one of the most interesting characters to appear in a modern British novel.

'Melvyn Bragg's novel places him solidly in the main tradition of English fiction, with an honourable ancestry through such disparate figures as Wells and Hardy, Dickens and Jane Austen to Henry Fielding'

Tribune

'A graceful and confident writer; the little Cumberland town of Thurston during the slump years, the Second World War and after, is beautifully realised, its life, rough and smooth, gathered very naturally around the central figures'

The Observer

THE CUMBRIAN TRILOGY

KINGDOM COME

Douglas Tallentire has at last achieved what his father and grandfather before him fought for so bitterly. Educated and independent, he can carve out his own career and spread his wings. But success, freedom and happiness are more elusive than ever in the fiercely competitive Seventies. From Cumbria to the frenetic whirl of a sophisticated life in New York and London, Douglas, like all the Tallentires, must come to terms with private uncertainty and pain.

'A novelist of power and imagination'

Observer

'Mr Bragg is one of the few British writers of talent with the courage to tackle an ambitious, panoramic novel. His style is unaffected, he has a confident narrative drive, a good eye for detail and a strong sense of drama'

Daily Telegraph

'Bragg knows what he is talking about ... He is worth listening to'

The Guardian

'... he emerges with stature at the end of his convincing contemporary novel on 'the way we live now' ... the book shows range and vision ... Bragg knows about the nuances of dialogue which differentiate character and can maintain nice dramatic irony'

New Statesman

Melvyn Bragg was born in Wigton, Cumberland, in 1939. He was educated locally and at Oxford, where he read Modern History. Since then he has made his living as a novelist and broadcaster. An editor and presenter of television arts programmes, Melvyn Bragg began in the BBC on *Monitor*. At present he is Head of the Arts department at London Weekend Television where he edits and presents *The South Bank Show*. He also writes a weekly column on the Arts at *Punch*. He is a Fellow of the Royal Society of Literature.

Also by the same author,
and available in Coronet Books:

Speak For England
Without A City Wall
Josh Lawton
The Nerve
Autumn Manoeuvres
Love And Glory

The Cumbrian Trilogy

Melvyn Bragg

CORONET BOOKS
Hodder and Stoughton

First published in Great Britain 1969 by Secker and Warburg Ltd. Coronet edition 1977; First published in Great Britain 1970 by Secker and Warburg Ltd. Coronet edition 1975;
 First published in Great Britain 1980 by Secker and Warburg Ltd. Coronet edition 1982. This edition 1984.

British Library C.I.P.

Bragg, Melvyn
Cumbrian trilogy.
I. Title
823'.914[F] PR6052.R263

ISBN 0-340-036150-6

The characters and situations in this book are entirely imaginary and bear no relation to any real person or actual happening

Printed and bound in Great Britain for Hodder and Stoughton Paperbacks, a division of Hodder and Stoughton Ltd., Mill Road, Dunton Green, Sevenoaks, Kent (Editorial Office: 47 Bedford Square, London, WC1 3DP) by Cox & Wyman Ltd., Reading

THE HIRED MAN

To Marie-Elsa

Part One

I

As he woke, the word 'wife' raced up from the fathoms of his dream and broke the surface of his mind as gently as the moonlight met his eyes. And the word basked under the light, rubbed itself against his unnerved flesh, tumbled slowly about the lapping waves of sense before plunging once more down, taking its news back to the dying dream. In marriage he had found life, taken it and given it.

They slept naked, feeling bold. She had drawn the curtains so that they could see each other's bodies. In the deep flock bed, breath, warmth and memory intermingled – but he did not turn to her, had promised not to wake her. Just his hand settling on her belly: no sign when she lay like that: at what exact moment had she conceived their child?

When the church clock struck two, he got out of the bed, his feet cold on the bare boards before the heavy strokes had died away. Framed in the window he looked out and hesitated, turned to look at her partly uncovered by his exit. Her white face sank into a spread net of thick hair, drawn downwards, it seemed, innocent of the charge of life. In his desire was inexplicable pity. For the breasts, docile, lying softly together as she turned on her side: the fingers reaching out to where he had been with fragile disappointment. Why had he to leave her? Even for a few hours.

What more could there be than those thighs which parted sleepily, that waking glance which told him all there was to know, the end of desire in the beginning of their love?

Dawn had not yet come but his way was clear. A child's moon was settled largely and gracefully in the sky and thin bars of cloud trailed from it edged with yellow light, motionless streamers. The tracks he walked could have been currents in the sea, so plainly did they mark their darker way between the still fields. The low wind would intermittently flick the grass and moonlight broke whitely on it as on the tips of waves. The air was raw and he felt his skin beat into it as he went; it left a moisture on his face which he could lick for pleasure. The wind came across the mosses from the Solway Firth and he remembered how he and Emily had walked to its shore in the evenings at the end of the previous summer. The tang of sea air flicked his thoughts to pictures of her running at the edge of the waves, jumping high off the dunes, racing along the hard runnelled sand, her feet slapping.

Alone on the track, memories warming his mind, moving secretly among the sleepers; and on his own now, aged eighteen, married, the slight curve of his child smooth under Emily's white skin, away both from her parents and his. For hire.

In this spring of 1898, John Tallentire was one of thousands of agricultural labourers going to look for employment. In Cumberland there were seven of these Hirings, held twice a year at Whitsun and Martelmas. There the men who wanted to change their employer or the employer who wanted fresh men met and struck a bargain for a term – six months' work. John could have chosen to go nearby to Wigton on the Monday – but he was known in the district and wanted to be in new country where he could set up his family in his own way, be rid of all ties. So he had ignored the Whit Monday hiring and spent the day finishing off the two chairs he had made and stacking up their very few possessions as carefully as he could so that Mr Errington would, by example, be just as careful when he loaded them into the trap. For John was determined to do all at once. Usually, once hired, the labourer was free until Saturday, it was one of his two holiday weeks of the year. But he was going to ask if he could move in immediately. Emily was to come to Cockermouth later that morning – with Mr Errington and the furniture – and they would be away.

He had ignored the objections to this plan. Emily's father, himself a labourer, had been contemptuous at the way in which the young man was so lightly prepared to throw over a few days' rest. Her mother had worried about the practicability of finding a place which would have a 'tied' cottage free that very night. When he had told his own mother she had warned him – strictly – against the foolishness of setting up house where you knew no one, where no one could help you out in the hundred and one things you always needed when you started up. His father had only said 'Try it and see!' And he had made it even more difficult for himself by resolving that he would not be hired for less than fifteen shillings a week – twice as much as he had earned as an apprentice to the blacksmith.

It was eighteen miles to Cockermouth and the decision to walk it was proof of his confidence.

He skirted Wigton and pushed up towards the Roman Camp of Old Carlisle where, as a boy – and that seemed an age ago, isolated behind the reaches of his working life – he had played with his brothers. This play – most often in the scraps of time left over from gathering sticks or looking around his father's snares, collecting dockings or finding roots for his uncle to carve – now seemed like the most idyllic gambolling.

He paused to look down over the moon-shaped mounds and bowls of the camp beneath which were said to be amphitheatres, barracks, walls and defence-works to be had for the digging, and his legs itched to be running about there again with Seth and Isaac and the others. How steep that hill seemed when they had sledged down it – and at Easter the painted eggs trundling to the beck, the gaudy dyes running again, wetted by the grass. Seth had discovered the entrance to a tunnel and they had stored hazel nuts there – and he, being the smallest, had been pushed right down it by his brothers who used him as a ferret to find out if this tunnel led to others. A warren of tunnels, Seth had predicted or, better, a long-ranging system of tunnels, like badger sets, which would burrow down to Wigton and come up in the cemetery, into one of those stone tombs. But instead he had stuck in the rank foisty earth so that every cry seemed to fill his mouth with clamming dirt, though later, when his father had dragged him out, they had told him they had heard nothing. It was his silence which had frightened them so much that they even dared seek out their father for help. He remembered the beating he had received for the trouble he had caused and how he had loved his father who was hitting him. It seemed impossible that once he should have lost himself in there – a place he could walk past in a few minutes.

He went on along the track to Red Dial where he would pass the gates of the farm his father had been hired at for twenty-two years.

Often, on his way to school, he had stopped at these gates to watch the labourers taking to the land. To John, all these men were heroes. Heroes in their work. Labour was their fate and the earth the most demanding of gods. Every year they opened it and every year it would turn its back on them. Every year there would be some things perfect – a ploughed field, hedges, a crop – and every year it would return to what it had been. Only with luck and after the greatest care – 'husbandry' it was called, a word accurately descriptive of the necessary bond of intimacy – would a good harvest come, toss its head, and wait to be mown down, at once the booty and the defeat, leaving its stubbled stalks for pigs to root in. And he would want to jump down and be among them – to go and be part of what he saw, feeling arms soft that had not managed an angry team, legs feeble that had not walked a field a hundred times in an afternoon, his whole self unmade that had not been fired by such work.

At thirteen he had got his wish, gone down to a farm – he could see it from where he stood, a shroud on the pale fields. Winter then, and his wet trousers, hung on the bottom of the bed, often froze, slim splinters of ice crackling as he climbed into them at five o'clock in the morning. His leg chapped raw. The day's work would finish at six thirty and by seven he would be asleep. For that term two pounds were delivered to his mother a portion a week on Sunday afternoon, the only time he had off. A miserable collection of coins – less than two shillings a week – from which she would allow him threepence for himself, the rest to go towards her housekeeping. Nor would that threepence have been allowed – for what, she asked with no irony, had he to spend it on? Only sweets. But his father insisted that he must have something in his pocket to show he had a wage.

Yet his appetite did not sicken. Instead, now that he was among those men he had watched he found even more to admire in their strength, and especially in their tricks. Everything, it seemed, could be made a 'trick' of: there was a 'trick' about holding a scythe, a 'trick' about getting a straight furrow, a 'trick' about pressing the teats – and even in the tiniest things, about making your porridge last or washing your back, there was a 'trick'. These 'tricks' embellished the toil as appurtenances do war. And he became clever with fingers hardened and could plait with nine strings.

His father, after his third term, found a place for him in a blacksmith's at Wigton. He had no alternative but to leave the work he loved. There, starting in springtime he felt at first confined, blowing the roof-high bellows to a fire which scorched the down on his cheeks while the lengths of iron sizzled in the forge and the Smith shaped, holed and hammered them. Soon he moved on to the making of screws and rivets (so difficult that it made his arms shake, his head drum with the impossibility of it), then to the hoops of iron for the cartwheels, the gates and fittings – he had spent his first year in as aching and dreary a time as he would ever have imagined. That he had now three and six a week to take home made no difference. He was shut out, unseen by the world he had been growing to. But as he began to conquer the work, the advantages his mother had spoken of claimed his attention, then his interest. The world came to him. There was never a time when farmers would not need something done to their horses, and soon he was outside on the square, in among the hooves of the beasts, nearly kicked to kingdom come by the first mare he was let shoe, doing all bar the bulls which the smith reserved for himself. It was work, this – no one could deny that – and his hours and labour matched those of any man his age; but also, there was the talk he would only rarely get on the farm. For those who brought their horses would always stay while they were being done and ask and chat without pause. He would have been there still but for his marriage. His father – after the rage which met that declared intention – had told him he would be a fool to leave when he was more than half-way through his apprenticeship. Yet he *had* left and 'filled in' for the fortnight before term. He wanted nothing with work that would not give him that independence he thought essential to a married man.

He put some dry bread in his mouth. Bread a few days old, you could not beat it in a morning, he thought, if he could choose anything in the world to eat, it would be that, with the crusty comb of white crumbling on his teeth, the yeast seeming to rise again as it met the heat of his palate. Then he looked last at what he would leave. By going to Cockermouth he would almost certainly be hired in the fells – and he intended to stay there for time enough at least to gather about him what Emily and himself might need. It was from the fells that the Tallentires had come – at least his grandfather had come from there. But such families as his were merely the numbers to the alphabet of history. 'Labourers – 10': 'Estatemen – 16': 'Foot-soldiers – 17': or more commonly, 'and a number of men'. His path to the fells was paved by no treasured remembrance of things past. Though he would call at his grandfather's for breakfast.

He would not stop to see his father. Their last encounter – after the wedding – would be sufficient for some time. Joseph himself had married at twenty. But it was not a question of age, suitability or anything else: it was a matter of obedience. He, Joseph Tallentire, did not want his son to marry and that should have been that. And he, Joseph Tallentire, a fiery particle, black-haired and cold-blue-eyed like John, a cocky fellow who had quickly become head labourer at the Roberts's and could have had many a better job had he not been so settled in his sports – his cock-fighting and terrier breeding – and the easy independence which his little authority gave him; a man who had made a reputation as a wrestler (Cumberland and Westmorland style), brought up nine decent children and taken them to church weekly, who had hunted on foot in John Peel Country just five miles off with men who had hunted with Peel himself, who knew a horse by teeth, hoof and hide and a man for hire by similar markings: he would not be defied by this boy who had had his behind slashed with birch, his head cuffed hard with a tough palm, his face almost knocked askew with the open hand, and the same who had been comforted when time was, and taught what was for his own good. He would not be defied. But John did defy him and, leaving his father the alternatives of defeat or disgrace, got on with his wedding preparations through the infinitely more pliable parents of Emily. Joseph had chosen that which could be called defeat, but he had not accepted it. He came to the wedding, as he said, 'for your mother's sake': he had spoken once since – on the subject of John's going for hire – and then, as most vehemently at the wedding, made it plain that no future dialogue would happily be sought by him. His mother, though not subdued by her husband, in this matter agreed with him because she, too, thought it stupid for him to marry so young and without means.

But as he walked past the track which led to his parent's cottage, he came to a shed, a black wall from the road, and smiled at his best memory of his father. Behind that shed on Sunday mornings after church was the cock-fighting. Joseph had never once taken his sons along with him. He'd let them feed the birds, shown them how to fix the spurs, but he alone went to the fights. They used to follow him and watch, hidden. Climb on to the shed roof, peep down at the ring of men, watching the high-prancing cocks, flamboyantly plumed, gold on their backs, stab at each other delicately.

It was a stranger that John then saw. Far from the man who had ordered them all earlier in the morning as they stood in a line to be examined for church. When he pulled open their mouths and lifted up their feet. And they, quivering before his regular fury – he hated church – would stay in that line, each holding an article. Then Joseph walked again; taking shoes from one, scrutinized, accepted; a collar from another; the studs and the cuff-links, the tie, the waistcoat and the jacket until he came to the smallest who held the hat. A parody of empire but no one dared think of smiling. Now, here, that same hat was tilted back on a face that ran sweat down to soil the starched collar and the shoes splashed through mud, the cuffs dirty from holding the birds, the murder in his throat dismissed by a loud laugh: waistcoat barrelled and bared, happy as larry. John would have liked him as a friend.

No time for that now. Emily had taken the place of them all.

2

As it was a holiday, Harry Tallentire lay in bed an extra hour. He did not enjoy it. From half-past five until six was just bearable by making the most rigorous effort; but on the stroke of six his patience broke and every other minute he would be shouting downstairs to his wife for the time. Alice replied patiently, but the amused inflection of her words made it doubly impossible for him to quit. So he lay on the rack of his bed for that last half hour – scarcely making a lump under the puffy flock down, a spare, white-haired man, his voice agitated and querulous, wishing and willing the clock to move on but refusing to budge until the time was up; for though his patience might break, his will never would – and he always lay in bed for an extra hour on his holidays.

The small whitewashed room with the scrubbed floor was stippled by a wavering dawn light. Alice had drawn the curtains so that he could see – out across to the fells. He allowed himself to rest his head a little higher on the pillow so that he could look at this view. He was not quite sure about this; for was looking at a view lying in? On the other hand, sleep being impossible, he realized that a mere closing of the eyelids would be worthless. He could have buried his face in the pillow but he always slept on his back – straight out, arms by his side, toes to the ceiling, corpselike. He felt like a corpse, he said, lying there doing nothing. Doing nothing was the thing he hated above all. Yet if holidays were not different they were wasted. So he looked at the view, a landscape he had looked on every day of the fifty-seven years he had been hired at this farm.

Under the weak pulses of light the densities shifted rapidly and the leaves on the trees, the tips of grass, the innumerable pocks and rises, the streams, hedges, even the soft-outlined hills themselves seemed to shuffle in ceaseless interchange of tone and mood, as if the forces below such apparent solidity were ever throbbing, unwilling to be still.

Eventually he heard the clock strike half-past six and then, as always, Harry burrowed himself more deeply into the bed than he had done all night as if, for that second, to find and grasp unconsciousness as a talisman for the day.

Downstairs there was a piece of dry bread waiting for him – no more.

His breakfast was taken at half-past seven – usually after two hours' work – and even holidays could not interfere with the displacement of his meals. He put on his oldest trousers, clogs, collarless shirt, waistcoat and muffler, never 'dressing' until just before breakfast, and took the bread out into the garden to share it with the blackbird he was taming.

He had always kept part of the garden for Alice and this year had laid out even more of it for her. She liked rosemary, bergamot, thyme and lavender, roses for the summer and a few evergreens for the winter; he had brought in some wild flowers which she missed now that she got out less than she used to. But the vegetable plot was his chief concern and he looked at the stitches anxiously. He went to the wall and put a few crumbs on it, waiting for 'Dizzy', his blackbird. Saw him in the hawthorn as still as the bough he rested on; he fluttered and lifted – but only to the lowest branch of the apple tree. Harry waited.

The cottage stood on its own. He had got it when Latimer had made him 'estate-man'. This meant that he worked at the same work as the other labourers but was also responsible for hiring and seeing over jobs, for visiting Latimer's other two farms twice a term and checking things there. Even then, twenty years ago when he had got the job, he had been with Latimer longer than anyone else; slept in the byres there as a boy (his first job at ten had been crow-scaring) seen the farm grow, been married from the farm-house and, over these last years, helped Mr Latimer's sons to keep things going through the hard times by building up the flocks and breeding Clydesdales. Luckily this was not corn-land and so the competition from foreign grain and beef which was decimating large farms in the south was not as severely felt here. Before moving into this cottage he had lived in the row of nine agricultural cottages – two up, one down – which were hidden in a dip to the west of the farm. There his wife had given birth to fourteen children, twelve of whom survived, and now he counted his grandchildren in scores and even his great-grandchildren in half-dozens. Not that he had seen them all, but it pleased him to keep a record of them all – or rather it pleased him to do it for Alice who liked to go through that list, her lips forming the names, her head lifting after every one, eyes searching the ceiling, picturing what they looked like now. Two of his sons had gone to Australia and one daughter to Canada but even then Alice counted on a letter around Christmas to keep her informed. Joseph he knew of more than most of the others, for the two sometimes met at Cockermouth auction and Joseph had occasionally sent his children back to Embleton for a few days in the summer.

In the district he was known for his consistency in all things and his pride lay in keeping that record. Within that tiny locality he was erudite but this knowledge, though different not in kind but only in the material it drew on from that of educated men, he considered as 'knowing nothing' whenever faced by a fact or remark outside his experience. There were two books in the house he had read, *Pilgrim's Progress* and the Bible, and those were the only two books he had ever read. He played the fiddle in the church band and went there not as to peremptory parade once-weekly as did Joseph, but because he believed in it. He had drunk a lot in his young days but gradually eased off and finally become teetotal. In his dress he was as careful and conservative as those 'above' him and always wore a hard hat.

John's first sight of his grandfather that morning was of the old man bent double in the field outside the garden, his head jammed between straddled legs, jutting under his behind. Easily misconstrued. Thus bent, so that he saw the world upside down from as near ground level as made no difference, the old man moved down the field. To help him keep steady, his hands had fastened on his ankles, and to help him keep low, his feet were widespread and so his progress could be compared neither to a walk nor to a waddle but to a performance, one left in the fields by the departing circus. John laughed to have caught the old man like that, but though the laugh was clear enough, the performance was not interrupted until, having reached an intently desired spot in that field, Harry stopped and was suddenly unsprung.

He had been looking through his legs until he could see the top of the tree he intended to chop down. When he could see the top then, at that spot, he could mark to a foot the end of the tree's fall.

Without looking at his grandson who stood grinning at him over the hedge, he pushed a peg in the ground, turned, looked at the tree once more and then, having regarded John in silence for a properly admonitory period of time, said, slowly, as if talking to himself:

'Tell me – thou's been kept at school for a very long time – fourteen wasn't it?'

John was wary; shot was often primed with this powder.

'Tell me – there's a tree in my garden, that ash, theer, an' a fella' wants to lop it down because it's ower dangerous. Now then – use thee eyes a bit mair than for gawpin' at fwolks doin' a job and see that waa.' The wall he spoke of ran along the foot of the garden, stood about five feet high and was a well-kept length of dry-stone walling. 'Now Aa'm gonna cut that ash, and Aa'm not gonna have it fall into t' garden: it'll drop reet here where my feet is. How will that happen widout brekkin' that waa? Tell me that.'

John ran along to the gate, swung himself over it into the field and went to join his grandfather. The resemblance between them as they stood together was startling and both smiled in faint appreciation of this mutual flattery. The younger man looked at the tree, took a few paces forward and back and teased his grandfather with pretence of ignorance, for he knew quite well. It was one of the 'tricks'. After making your cuts in front and behind, you make another diagonal cut across the front, and as the tree started to fall it 'leapt' and, well judged, would clear even that wall.

So he fed the old man's complacency for a while and then said:

'I'd mek a bird-lowp cut, grandfather, and see if that did.'

The old man did not hesitate:

'Thou means *I'll* mek a bird-lowp cut – thou'd mek a hash of it.' Then 'Lookin' for work now, is'te?'

'I am. Is thou not gaan to Cockermouth thissel?'

'Aa've got the men I need.' He paused. 'Maybe Mr Latimer *could* manage another ... know owt about a hoss?' he asked, well aware that John had worked daily with horses for the past three years.

'I can tell its arse from its tip,' replied John. 'On a bright day.'

'Language,' Harry admonished. Then, 'Mebbe we could ...'

'No thanks, grandfather.'

'Aa wasn't through me sentence.'

'I'd raither set up on me own.'

'Mebbe we could do wid – some breakfast I was gonna say,' the old man completed, calmly.

He nodded and the two men walked up the field, over the stile and through the garden into the kitchen.

'Yen o' Joseph's,' Harry announced. 'Set a trough out for him. If he's owt like his fadder he'll eat us oot.'

His grandmother nodded to John happily and got down another basin into which she heaped a ladleful of porridge. There was flat bread, milk and a little sugar on the table as well as a plate of fancy cakes – another holiday concession.

John sat down.

'Stand up to give thanks,' Harry ordered.

John blushed and clattered to apologetic attention.

'Thank you Lord for thy bounty in givin' us this thy harvest. Amen.'

'Amen.'

'Sit down.'

They ate in silence or rather without talking, for the cooling slurp of his grandfather's mouth against the spoon sounded as regularly as the clock. John looked around the kitchen and everything from the black-leaded fireplace which almost covered a wall to the neatly marked jars in which his grandmother kept her stores encouraged him to dreams of his own domesticity which could not come fast enough. He admired the birds his grandfather had carved on the top of the chair-frames: the most he had been able to manage was a cross. And the shiny baking-tins his grandmother had – Emily's mother had given her three but that would not be enough, and they could not afford to buy more for six months at least and even then there would be more important things to buy.

After the porridge, Alice brought them the mugs of tea and then, nodding to John, took down a black pudding and set it in the oven. John blushed once more, for he knew that she had 'likened' it to Emily and himself – as was done with newly married couples – and that she would believe that their life would be happy if the skin held, disrupted if it burst. The idea of his prospects depending on a black pudding made him impatient – and then discomfited him – at the notice being taken of his new status.

And he knew, now that his grandfather was on the less demanding bread and so could be expected to allow speech, that he – the old man – would have words to say on it. He had seen neither of them for a long time. They had not come to the wedding, but he knew that old Harry disapproved, had seen it in the first glance, just as he knew his grandmother was having a hard time bridling her curiosity.

'Thee father's mekin a reet fool of hissel,' Harry began calmly. 'Folk tell me he's nivver off cock-fightin' nowadays.'

'It's only Saturdays,' John countered, half-heartedly.

'A fool can be seen any day of the week. Saturday included.' Harry paused. 'Next time thou sees him, tell him from me to quiet his daft sel. When a thing's been med illegal – thou stops. He could a' been a bailiff yer father, maybe an estate labourer, instead of gallivantin' around like a daft calf.'

'He works hard enough.'

'Anybody can work.'

'Well,' John disliked being his father's defence, but it was impossible to allow an attack to go unresisted, 'Well mebbe he thinks he'll enjoy hissel the bit of time he has over.'

'Enjoy what?' Harry inquired. 'A clown enjoys hissel my lad. That's no mark. And,' he paused and looked on John intently, 'it isn't Saturdays I've heard on. "Six days shalt thou labour" my boy – it's Sundays. Am I right?'

'I don't know.'

'Thou won't say.'

'No. I won't.'

'Well mebbe thou's right. I's'll see him and tell him in me own good time. Don't bother to pass that message on. A son should honour his father – and if you tell Joseph he's a fool, he'd strike you dead.'

'He would.'

John agreed out of respect for his father's reputation, but inside himself he felt better than ever at the remembrance of those two months before when he had done even worse to his father – totally contradicted his authority – and lived.

'Well,' said his grandmother, unable to hold herself longer and tactfully anticipating the severe quizzing which was concentrating in her husband's expression, 'tell us about her, John.'

And now there was no embarrassment because he was talking of her and not himself. But his talk could not describe her. He wanted to tell them that she had hazel eyes that could flare in temper and dare as much as he – but instead he told them what her father did. He wanted to say that the run of her calf, the whiteness of her skin – so white that he imagined he could feel the colour as his charged fingers trembled fearfully on her flesh – that such was his kingdom of heaven – and instead he engaged in the infinite crochet of relations until, by complicated cross-patterning, she was pulled closer to Alice through the husband of a friend who was her uncle. Could she bake? Yes. And turn a collar? Yes. Sew a straight hem? He was certain she could. Manage a house on very little?

'And that's t'first sensible question asked,' Harry said. 'See here. She'll have to mek do, my lad, on next to thin air with the money thou'll fetch. She'll hev that to do, no mistake.'

'I know.'

'He knows that, father.'

'As long as he does.' Then, in case the comment had appeared too surly, Harry smiled and his tone was cheerful. 'Well if she's half what thou says thou's done well. Aa was nobbut nineteen when we were wed.' He hesitated and then, with a shyness which made him look years younger he said. 'No – what worried me, lad, was givin' up a good trade. There'll always be a call for blacksmiths. Yer fedder was lucky to get you in there.' Harry wanted no explanations. 'Thou should hev stuck it, lad,' he said, 'whativver.'

The level tone in which he said that made John shiver – but only for a moment. However well-intentioned, they wanted to rule you. He did not dare tell his grandfather that Emily was to follow him that very day.

'I hev a smoke in t' garden after breakfast on a holiday,' Harry said. 'Thou'll hev time to join me?'

'I will.'

'Thou won't can afford to smoke?'

'No.'

Harry nodded, in approval.

Outside the cottage, they looked over the fields to the small church with the minute tower which just cleared the hedges. John encouraged his grandfather to talk of the old times. To touch on *his* grandfather who had boasted of fighting with Wellington and earning the title 'scum of the earth', of his father who had been a local prizefighter. He got the story of the two-day dance in Pratt's barn and the one about the wild dog of Ennerdale and then, turned eight thirty, it was time to leave.

'The skin never even blistered,' said his grandmother happily as he came in to kiss her good-bye. He was relieved. But refused the black pudding; did not want the bother of carrying it around all day.

Harry, having changed, walked some way down the road with him.

'Thou'll have to have this,' he said, handing him a piece of straw he had brought. 'In my time they twisted it under their hats so it popped out of their ears. They suck it now.'

John took the straw and popped it into his mouth. The end of it jabbed against his palate and he spat it out.

'I can be hired without that,' he replied, over-curtly.

They went up the hill which led on to the road to Cockermouth. They were silent. John's last remark had appeared to the old man to be groundlessly arrogant. It was up to John to atone for it, but he did not want to.

He was afraid of the temptation offered by the old man. Not so much in the hint of a job as in the attraction of his grandfather's look and temper, the contentment of it, the serenity.

About Harry's face and movements there was a veil of serenity – as distinctly to be seen as the spume of fever which hovers around many people today. It was this, perhaps, which sprang his back still spruce-like and gave grace to his work – and the work itself was not met head-on as it was with Joseph or attacked as with John, but done in ultimate service to a Creator who made less demands than men. Harry appeared as a man whose substance was unmuddied, whose life had been spent well, who walked in a serene self-containment out of which John's father had come stampeding like a wild thing and into which he himself could find no entry.

But he was not sure that he wished to find one – and it was this which caused the confusion. For in another glance he saw his grandfather submissive to the place given him by others, with notions which were the crumbs scattered by his masters and manners aped. And he could have knocked off that hard hat.

Yet he loved him more than any other man.

At the top of the hill, Harry stopped.

'So thou'll not work for thy grandfather.' He smiled. 'Mebbe so. Be on thy own if that's the way.' He held out his hand. 'I nivver fancied it meself.'

As John shook his hand, he felt a tide of home-sickness rush into his throat. He was gruff, to conceal it, and the men parted, John watching the small figure return down the hill to the grey stones of the cottage, slate grey like the outcrops on the hills and the steady figure in the watery morning light, as slate as they.

Harry did not go into the cottage, not wanting to meet his wife's question about what he *really* thought of John and his chances. He made for the shed, where he set to carving miniature wooden animals which he loved to carry about in his pockets and give away to any children he met on the road. Gradually forgetting his grandson.

3

Cockermouth was a small town, sandstone, granite and slate which lay as naturally at the confluence of the rivers Cocker and Derwent as a pebble in a palm. Roofs slanted in sharp diagonals of many-toned grey, shields which were never lowered; and nests, lichens, leaves and moss dappled them kindly as if in recognition that they would not be broken, had become, through time, affectionate to that which they obstructed.

He lengthened his stride past the castle, over the bridge and looked beyond the Ring, to the fair which sprang at his eyes, as if he had turned a page in a book from print to a gaudily tinted plate.

Yellow, scarlet and silver were the chief colours, on the roundabouts and swings, the clothes and jewellery of the gypsies, the plates of the potters. Tents had been erected the previous night and they stood before the caravans. The Fat Lady yawned as she sat on her stool pulling her boots on to unseen legs, the magic lantern show had already attracted a small crowd before it; behind the Boxing Booth the men swilled themselves, shivering and muscle-knotted in their straw-tagged long-johns; fairmen stacked the prizes carefully, arranging them on the racks within apparent easy reach. Canvas rippled in the cuff of wind and the fair-people – with their rich scarves and fancy waistcoats, dark skins and chuntering faces, darted incessantly from neighbour to neighbour, the rapidity of their speech making John's tongue feel wooden.

Around, between, among and beside them were the horses

and ponies and dogs. Their noise, the skittering and fighting dogs scudding from booth to booth inflamed by the number of new scents, the horses jostling together or moving over a scattering of straw, ponies forlornly tied to the gipsy caravans, waiting to be sold, had the strange effect on John of making this uncommon dash of activity more human.

Nearer him – the fair was well up the street – was the market. The feature of this was the number of women with their butter, white at this time as the cows had not long been in the fields, each slab with its makers' imprint on it. Butter every few paces, white footstones.

John saw no one that he knew. He noticed a few whippets and a man caging fighting cocks and thought that Isaac, one of his brothers, might be discovered around such sport, but was disappointed. For a second, his solitude clanged against him loudly and he saw the other side of his determination to be on his own, but only for that second. He went towards the Ring.

This was where those went – men and women – who were looking for hire. They did not stand there unmoving but drifted off and back to the market and fair, pulling out together across the street in ones and twos to buy teacakes or look in the windows – emphasizing always, it seemed, that though they would be hired they could not be bought. Nevertheless, the Ring was well enough marked and the farmers left their traps and horses down the town to walk up to it, generally by degrees through the stalls and pubs before they came there to hover around the crowd and ask 'Is thou for hire, lad?'

John went up to it shyly, feeling very much a boy among men. There were all ages there, men of sixty chewing their straw, girls clinging to each other in dragging embrace, slouching in deliberate spite of their femininity clogs clattering on the cobbles. Unless they saw a good friend, in which case an over-hearty greeting buffetted between them and the sudden stroke of companionship drew a space around itself, the men drifted blank-eyed, their gaze fixed on no one, like those abstracted by the sea.

There was little business in that first hour and John took his cue from a much older man who leaned against a wall, as if a mere spectator. But when he heard the words. 'Is thou for hire, lad?' he spun around. To face his brother Isaac grinning so widely that his cheeks were forced back to his ears.

'Aa'll giv thee a hundred pound a year to clean my boots,' Isaac continued, his loud voice attracting some attention, the terms he was offering bringing more. 'Mind you,' he added, 'Aa nivver tek me boots off, so thou'll hev to catch us while Aa's movin'. And Aa can kick – by Christmas Aa can! – last feller had this job med an ivory necklace for his wife and took to wearin' a bucket on his head. Then he couldn't see – bucket blinded. So Aa stamped on it and now he's in a tent over yonder,' he nodded to the fair, 'The Man in the Iron Mask.'

John was so pleased to see his brother that he clapped his arms around him. The embrace was returned with a hug which nearly winded him.

'What the hell, boy,' said Isaac. 'Aa'm thee brother not thee mother.' John stood back from him, but could not take offence so cheerful was Isaac's expression. Seeing that he might have caused his younger brother embarrassment, Isaac immediately moved across to him and flung an arm around his shoulder.

'Seth's in The Bridge,' he said. 'He looks as miserable as ivver. Let's go and show him yer happy face.'

All protests about staying until he was hired were swept quite aside. A lad like him could be hired any time of day, Isaac declared, leading, almost humping him away – while drink would come only while money was in the pocket and there was money in the pocket now. And again Isaac protected John from embarrassment as by saying this he made it clear that the drinks would be on him, knowing that John would not be able to afford them.

'Is *thou* for hire, then?' John asked him as they strode through the parting crowd.

'I'm for owt!' said Isaac. 'Owt there is.'

Isaac was the oldest of the brothers, the second of Joseph's family, the one most resembling the father in his build. He was married with three children and had been at every sort of work since his twelfth birthday. No job was held for long. For what in Joseph was occasional wildness tempered by the unquestioned though often bitter recognition that he could run only so far on a leash which fastened him to his place and type of work, had, in this son, gone on the rampage.

Isaac would go anywhere for sport. Sometimes he left his wife at home for weeks on end, without any warning – 'Aa tell her nivver to worry,' he said, 'there's no man comes home quicker than a dead man' – and the most she would hear about him might be from a tradesman who passed on gossip that there was a gang of men going round after a supposed pole-cat, or taking on all comers at coursing or such-like. For that reason he would always have a jar of money behind a brick near the fireplace, sufficient to last for two months – solid proof of conjugality, for he did not run after other women on these trips nor did he think for a moment that he treated his wife badly. That jar of money was his pledge, never long empty, for he was luckier than anyone John knew. He would win a pig in a bet, butcher and sell it on the spot and have enough for a month. Or turn from his summer sports to hay-making and bargain over every field – a bargain he could count on doing well from, for his rate of work was prodigious and the untrustworthy weather often made fast work a premium. Now he was going to have a go at the men in the Boxing Booth – you got a shilling for every round you lasted with them; and if that turned on him, he was off to the cock-fighting, while Seth had a whippet worth putting any man's shirt on and he thought he might do a deal with a gipsy he knew over some ponies – if the deal could be done fast for he had not cash enough to buy one. And if all that failed – he could always be hired.

Only the set of their eyes showed that they were related, but when John went through the small door of The Bridge there was no doubt about Seth. Though his hair was sandy and his skin almost tallow, the same blue eyes pierced the same slight face.

'Aa's in training for a fight this dinner-time,' Isaac announced, 'so Aa'll just hev a pint. An' another for me brother here afore a cat walks over his tongue.'

He pulled out the four pence and slapped them on the wooden counter, falling into immediate conversation with the man he first set his eyes on. John took his ale over to Seth who had smiled at him as he entered, but now looked miserable, as Isaac had described him, and was bent over his whippet, stroking its slim, bundle-muscled haunches.

In that low room, crowded with farmers and labourers, most of them rawly complexioned, their jaws chunked blood-red, their throats burnt scarlet, hands thick-fingered and brown, smoke from their pipes as steam from jostling horses, Seth looked like someone from another country. He had gone down the pits at fourteen and worked there since, unmarried, energetic with a ceaseless ambition to change the miners' conditions. On this day, he had walked over from Whitehaven to see the fair and maybe give his dog a run. 'Bounty' he called it.

'How's married life treatin' you?' he asked, as John sat down.

'Not too bad.'

'You've put yer head into a hell of a noose there, lad. But here's to it – and your missis.'

He raised his mug and John clinked it with his own. Seth spoke more rapidly than Isaac or himself, as if the urgency of underground work allowed of none of the breadth of vowel, pause and gesture which characterized most country speech. And the dialect, too, was less apparent, though the twang of the words would still have baffled most visitors.

'Why'd you come here then?' Seth demanded. 'I thowt you'd go to Wigton.'

'Father,' said John: for shorthand.

'I see.' Seth paused and then added, gravely. 'He is a gay old bugger, isn't he? I mean, have you ever met such a bloody selfish man?'

'He's not that bad.'

'Only because he can't afford to be.' Seth bent down and tickled Bounty behind the ears. 'He's not as bad as some I suppose – but I'm thankful to be out of that house.'

'So am I.'

'Let's drink to that.' Seth grinned and raised his mug once more. The grin knocked all the severity off his face, and John relaxed. He always felt a little under examination for the first few minutes in Seth's company.

Then he was asked about their mother, about Jane and Sarah, about Emily's family, his own prospects – which Seth heard through very coolly – and finally he told Seth that he had visited their grandfather that morning.

'And he hadn't heard about Ephraim?'

'He said nothing. Why?'

'Ah.' Ephraim was another of Harry's sons and Seth had seen a lot of him. He worked in the iron-ore mines at Egremont, was on the committee of the Co-op and had been trying for years to get an effective union going. 'He's had an accident,' Seth continued. 'I went to see him in hospital yesterday. A crusher fell on him.'

There was only one question John could ask – and yet to phrase it was too bald.

'He'll live all right,' said Seth, savagely. 'But they'll get no more work out of him, so he'll be thrown on the rates – rot the bloody rotten lot of them. A man should have compensation for summat like that. It was their fault – they hadn't the decency to keep the bloody crusher in trim – he couldn't be blamed. And mebbe he'll get fobbed off with a few pounds – less than we'll collect in a hat. It's all wrong.'

'All wrong' was how Seth saw the world. The ideas of Ruskin, Morris, Owen, Engels and even Marx wraithed themselves around the columns of the British status quo as smoke from an ignored fire. But Seth had caught a whiff of them through their popularizers in the threepenny pamphlets his uncle Ephraim bought, and from some of the speakers who came to West Cumberland on their way to building up the Independent Labour Party – and this scent he had followed. For it seemed to him All Wrong that men should slave while others lorded it, All Wrong that the sick should suffer while the rich wore pearls, All Wrong that a man should be ripped from school to work at an age when many of those who would never work were just beginning their schooling, All Wrong that there should be hovels for some and palaces for others, All Wrong that a man should be shut out from learning at the very time he might see the sense in books. All : Wrong.

Ephraim's accident had shaken him; ever since he had begun at the pits, the uncle had been as a father to him.

'Tek this shillin',' said John. It was the only one he had. 'Put it in for Uncle Ephraim.'

'No, lad – you've a wife.'

'Tek it.'

The coin jutted out from the thick thumb and forefinger and would not be ignored. Seth nodded and took it.

'So you're stickin' to farm work,' he said, broadening his accent in appreciation of the younger man's benevolence. 'I thought you'd be cannier than that, our John.'

'It's what I can do.'

'You don't have to be specially bred to work down a pit. Come with me. Even apprentice's wages are better'n you'll pick up.' The idea of having his brother work with him – which had come to Seth just now – affected him strongly and he leaned out and put his hand on John's arm. 'Come with me, lad. Those farmers'll nivver improve things 'til they're starved out. You'll get nothing from them but "Do this! Do that! No, you can't hev Sunday afternoons!" We help each other int'pit. Things'll move there. Look what the dockers did. So can we.' Seth drew himself up, at that moment becoming grand so that his voice thickened and his face felt some colour. 'And when we stop,' he said, 'England stops.'

'Do you really think so?'

Seth reached in his breast pocket to pull out a worn and many-folded piece of paper.

'Read that,' he said. 'I cut it out of a pamphlet. It's word for word as it used to be.'

John read slowly. It was a reprint of some of the evidence given a Royal Commission on the Mines in 1842. Seth had drawn a square around a quotation described as 'The Evidence of a Lancashire woman'. The square was drawn in indelible ink. It read:

> 'I have a belt round my waist and a chain passing between my legs and I go on my hands and feet. The water comes up to my clog tops and I have seen it over my thighs. I have drawn till I have the skin off me. The belt and chain are worse when we are in the family way.'

The last sentence lurched into John's mind like the sick of fear. He thought instantly of Emily and tightened his eyes at the knowledge of her tender pregnancy. Seth took the paper from his hands.

'I thought it would sicken you,' he said, gently. 'But I keep it to remind me how much we've got done already in the pits. There's more, if you want to go on, about kids less than five year old working on their own in the black. Well,' he paused, 'that's been got rid of – and more will be got rid of. But you'll change little on the farms, my lad – especially here where it doesn't take a very bad man to think he can get away with murder. You get out of it – come somewhere where you've got Rights.'

'Emily wouldn't,' John hesitated, realized he had exposed a personal matter and in doing so risked exposing his wife to Seth's criticisms, yet the sentence was begun and could not be left unfinished. 'We're both country people,' he countered, lamely, 'I want nothing with towns.'

'Your work's more important to you than any of that,' Seth replied. 'You'd like it over there.'

John nodded but said nothing. He had been stirred by Seth's words and seen himself working with a gang of men, all friends, all fighting for their Rights.

'Think it over anyway,' Seth concluded.

'Think what!' Isaac demanded, descending on them like a rush of rocks. 'Don't be puttin' bad habits into t'lad, Seth. I knew a fella did nowt but think. Thowt as soon as he wok up. Fed on what other folk thowt. Ate paper like lettuce. Swelled his brains till't sweat of it steamed his hair off. Thowt hissel intil a frazzle so that he couldn't talk for thinkin' that much, wouldn't move for fear o' jostlin' a new thowt. Sat aa day on a wooden bench just thinkin' it aa in – til' his head got that heavy he had to wheel it aboot in a barrow.'

'Well,' said John, 'what happened to him?'

'O, he died,' Isaac replied. 'Just like ivverybody else.' He plonked his empty mug on their table and looked at Seth. 'Yen mair of those, and Aa's game for a shillin' a round wid any man.'

It was John who jumped up to do the honours, however, despite Isaac's frown. He had fivepence in his pocket and after buying his brothers a pint apiece had to be content with half for himself. Which was as much as he wanted, for he saw by the clock that he had been in the pub over half an hour; and Emily was coming nearer.

'This bitch of thine,' Isaac was saying of 'Bounty' as John returned, 'let's hev a good squint at her.'

Seth pushed the shuddering whippet from under his chair and Isaac took her up, opened her mouth, scrutinized her paws. ran his thumb along her muscles, felt deep into the scruff of her neck and then:

'She's a good-looker anyway,' he said, and dropped her back on the floor. 'Thou wants to git a bit of sherry intil her belly, and plenty of raw eggs. And see thou drags a scrap of rabbit's fur through her insides ivery so often. Cleans them out like a charm.' He picked up his mug, raised it to John and spoke solemnly, 'Here's cheers to you and yer bride who Aa hope to have the pleasure of meeting one day. And if she's half as good as thou deserves, old lad, she'll be a rare 'un.' Then the foam covered half his face and he sucked strongly at the lip of the mug. 'That was tip-top,' he said, sat down on a stool which was overlapped on all sides by his behind, his legs planted apart, hands pushed down on his knees – the greatest comfort and display thus being afforded to his belly – and beamed on the world.

'Aa hed a bitch once,' he began. 'And mind Aa thowt Aa was on 'til a good un. She would streak across a field that fast that they had a special patrol of rabbits out to warn ivvrything off 't track. She once stopped to offer a hare a lift. Aa called her Parton after me wife's maiden name. Well Aa fed this useless thing like a babby: black puddings and a cut of mutton – raw, thou knows, bloodied – eggs like Aa was tellin' you, sherry for breakfast – maybe a laal bit o' nutmeg in some broth, just to keep her titillated. Thou's got to spice up a lady dog, John,' said Isaac, 'just like't real thing. Well, this bitch of mine was ready to run. Reet lads, Aa says to missel, El Dorado! So Aa took her up 'til a meet at Moresby. And Aa laid out on her. Ivvery farthin'. There's nowt like jumpin' in wid two feet. And dis thou know?' he paused, 'that daft laal tyke would do nowt but gallivant around wid to'other dogs! It would *not* run. As soon as it was slipped – off it made for t'nearest dog to hev a roll about wid!' Isaac looked as flummoxed now as he must have done at the time – and it was at his expression more than at the story that John and Seth laughed. For the story had tailed away, as Isaac's memory had grown stronger, his bafflement more acute.

'Nowt but play aboot,' he muttered. 'But Aa got a good price for her,' he added, in vindication. 'If she went on rollin' aboot – then she would be a rare breeder – no mistake! Aa selt her for her prospects *that* day.'

They talked on for a few minutes more and then went outside. The sun was still shining, and business in 'The Ring' was much more brisk.

'Look at them,' said Seth, 'like a lot of bloody sheep.'

'Leave them alone,' Isaac retorted, glancing at John. 'They can wag their tails when they come home – that right, John?'

'That's right.'

'Now then,' said Isaac, 'I'll just git missel a couple of pies and then Aa's fit.'

'O, give this bloody lark up,' said Seth, turning to John. 'You want nowt here.'

'Let him be.' Isaac spoke severely. 'He has a wife to look out for an' a life of his own to lead. Let him be.'

Seth nodded.

'But come up wid us and see't fight,' said Isaac. 'That thou *can* do.'

'Aa'd rather get fixed up first.'

'As you say.' Isaac stopped in his tracks, keenly feeling

John's tentativeness about the hiring and yet unwilling to interfere in the other man's life. 'Well mebbe we'll meet up later on.'

'Mebbe so.'

'Grand.' He moved away. 'Come on, Seth!' he shouted, 'and bring that shiverin' bitch o' thine to see some real sport.'

They nodded to John and walked down through the market to the fair. As they went away, John felt as if two pairs of hands had torn bark off a tree and left him the white, trembling trunk. He would have loved to lead the life of Isaac but he did not have it in him. As for Seth, the temptation to accept his offer grew as the sound of the hiring grew in his ears; but Emily would never settle in a town – she was unprepared for it. And he would do nothing, not the slightest thing, which might upset her. To work in a place she would like was the least he could do for her.

She would be here in an hour or so. Mr Errington had explained to both of them where he would set her down, and John wanted to be there waiting, job fixed, luck-penny to hand. He had planned to get her a present – but his money was gone.

He walked over to the other labourers, feeling the heavy ale settling in his stomach. He took up a place beside a small stall where a woman was selling bread, and waited.

4

Emily felt quite queenly sat in the trap. There was little furniture, for which, at this moment, she was glad as it gave her room to stretch her legs. She had never before been this far from home and she tried to store up every detail so as to be able to tell it over to John.

Her features were like those of many girls in that area. Rather broad-browed, strong-nosed, eyes firmly apart, a regular mouth neither thin- nor thick-lipped, and her complexion shaded from the cream of her forehead to that soft redness of cheek which would later harden. Her hair was brown, parted in the middle and laced into plaits under her hat. It was her eyes – hazel with a flick of green in them – which was her difference. They dared everything.

It was she who had urged John to leave the area when he had first, fumblingly, suggested it. She too wanted to be away. So many of the girls she knew were born and hired, married and settled within a mile or two of their own homes. She wanted to be somewhere new. It was she who had been the first to listen to and take seriously those simple daydreams of his – of everything being contented and undisrupted – and encouraged him in them. While, at sixteen, the force necessary to insist on and go through with the wedding amounted to a considerable authority over the circumstances of life as she had found them.

Straight-backed in the trap, only half attending to Mr Errington, she held her hands tightly clasped on her lap, squeezing every drop of adventure out of this journey.

Mr Errington was flattered to have such a pretty young woman for company. One who, but for the ring and the just noticeable child she was carrying, looked as fresh as a girl; as if marriage had whisked over her so lightly that it had not broken the skin of her youth. He put himself in the attitude of gallantry towards her – forgetting (which she did not) that his original offer had been phrased in terms of it 'making no difference to him whether the trap was full or empty as he was going anyway' – and it pleased him to let her stay in the trap as he walked the pony up the hill to Bothel, take her by the arm as he helped her down when they stopped for a drink, have approving looks thrown at him by those they passed.

Errington was a man of about fifty though he looked younger – 'he nivver works, that's why,' Emily's father had explained – who dressed well, kept his pony and trap in good condition and liked to hear himself called (even though the tone was always chafing) a 'gentleman of leisure'. He had inherited a row of cottages in Wigton at his mother's death and the rent from these, together with the rent from his fields – let to other farmers for grazing – gave him 'a modest sufficiency,' he would say. He had never married and kept only a servant girl and one hired man for the limited amount of farming he now did. His leisure was spent driving about the place, to fairs and markets and auctions, to shows, meets and carnivals, and especially to concerts. For he had a good tenor voice and liked it to be heard. And in this busy life, he had acquired the habit of thinking of himself as a clever man, even a witty one, was careful to take many of the thorns off his dialect, read his *Daily Mail* for an hour after each day's dinner and offered an opinion of any subject at all, unprejudiced by the notion that ignorance might be a bar to argument.

After passing Bothel, they had the road to themselves and he began to sing. Emily would have liked to join in, but Mr Errington's tenor was a very self-sufficient organ. He gave her *Harvest-Home* and *The Useful Plow, The Farmer's Son* and *John Barleycorn, The Seeds of Love* and *New-Mown Hay*, holding the ends of each line that touch longer than required to let his tone be fully registered. Emily wanted him to sing *The Farmer's Boy* – John had told her that when Joseph was in a good mood, he would get them up a concert in the kitchen, and this song would bring him to tears. She liked him to tell her of his father being pleasant at times, for she needed it to mitigate the thunderous impression he had made on her and she could not bear to think that there was nothing but that sulphurous rumbling in one of John's parents. Eventually she asked Mr Errington to give it her and he, pleased, prepared its passage by a delicate hawk and a spit, discreetly shielded by his white hand. Then, with feeling, he began:

'The sun had set behind yon hills,
Across yon dreary moor,
Weary and lame, a boy there came
Up to a farmer's door.
'Can you tell me if any there be
That will give me employ,
To plow and sow and reap and mow
And be a farmer's boy?

'My father is dead, and mother is left
With five children, great and small;
And what is worse for mother still,
I'm the oldest of them all.

Though little, I'll work as hard as a Turk,
If you'll give me employ,
To plow and sow and reap and mow
And be a farmer's boy.

'And if that you won't me employ,
One favour I've to ask, –
Will you shelter me, till break of day,
From this cold winter's blast?
At break of day, I'll trudge away
Elsewhere to seek employ.
To plow and sow and reap and mow
And be a farmer's boy.'

'Come try the lad,' the mistress said,
'Let him no further seek.'
'O, do, dear father,' the daughter cried,
While tears ran down her cheek.
'He'd work if he could, so 'tis hard to want food,
And wander for employ;
Don't turn him away but let him stay,
And be a farmer's boy!'

And when the lad became a man,
The good old farmer died,
And left the lad the farm he had,
And his daughter for his bride,
The lad that was the farm now has,
Oft smiles and thinks with joy
Of the lucky day he came that way,
To be a farmer's boy.'

The melody contributed much to its effect.

'Well now,' said Mr Errington after he had finished and allowed due silence, 'it's a grand name you've got for yourself.' He winked at her and ran his tongue around his lips, washing away the frivolous traces of song so that they were clean for conversation – or rather monologue and one which, judging by his delight in himself, he had been working on since the trip began. 'I've been breakin' your name up and brickin' it together again and it'll do a trick or two, O yes, it can jump!'

'Can it?' inquired Emily, politely.

'Indeed it can. Tallentire. Now take its beginnings – "Tall" – not much there you say, none of them's tall, more "short"; that's a mystery for a start. Then "*EN*tire" – entire what? I left off that road. But it's per*nounced*,' this was delivered with the greatest possible emphasis, 'pernounced "Tallent" – like the parable and you wouldn't grudge yer husband that, would you? And again – now this is very interesting! – that last bit "ire" runs back into "Tallent" for cover – so it's more like "Tire" – if you follow. Now hack at that a bit and you get "T'ire" – and your fella's off to be 'ired, that is *h*,' he blew on the H as if to cool it, '*hi*red, has he?'

'He has.' Emily smiled. 'That's clever.'

'I'm not finished,' said Mr Errington. 'The middle of it is "lent" – and I'm lending you this pony and trap – and the back end of it, that "ire", that's just another word for temper – like his father has. Now then, what d'you make of that?'

'I wish it would come out a bit better,' replied Emily frankly.

'So it might if I had pencil and paper and could dig a bit harder,' he answered. 'There's no telling what you might get then.' He paused. 'Oh, I forgot – "Tire" – your man doesn't get tired, does he?'

'No.'

'I thought not,' said Mr Errington, complacently. 'Now you'd never believe what I hacked out of Errington . . .'

When John was not there to meet her, Emily was as startled as if she had found him there hurt. She had seen them meeting and spending the afternoon together at the fair before going on to the new cottage. As well as disappointment, then, she was a little put out. She had never been to Cockermouth Fair and might never again be given the chance. And then both these reactions dissolved under the hot fear that something might have happened to him; reassured on that by Mr Errington's proofless eloquence, she resigned herself to wait and at last felt pity that John should be finding it so difficult to get a situation.

Mr Errington's gallantry failed him. He muttered and looked around, but could not conceal his determination to go up to the fair. Its noise set his feet shuffling like a small boy's to a street band. The place he had chosen was safe, he pointed out; it was at the end of the town farthest from the Ring, just this side of the house in which William and Dorothy Wordsworth had been born (a structure second only to the castle in local importance), off the main street and yet overlooked by some cottages, so that she could always give a shout if she 'needed anything'; there was an angle in the wall, and the furniture could be stacked without harm, and finally, here was a likely-looking boy, now there's threepence for you, wrap it up in yer handkerchief – never mind, hold it in your hand and stand here and look after this woman, she's waiting for her husband, it won't be for long and threepence is a man's wage for the job. There; well, good-afternoon. If I see him, I'll tell him you're here: he won't be long: and good luck.

She hoisted herself on to the wall and looked around. There was not much to see and the noise from the fair, which she had caught sight of for a few moments as they had come up the end of Main Street, aggravated her. She kicked her heels against the wall, pulled off her hat and, to fill her attention, tried to shoo off the small boy. But he had squatted in the gutter, his gaze taking in both her and the bottom of the road (the direction from which danger could be expected to come) and would not move. Nor would he speak. She put her tongue out at him and threatened to jump down and smack his ears, but he stayed at his post unflinching.

Then she forgot about him and pulled out some cakes – only to drop them into her basket and snap to blameless posture as she felt herself being watched. She could see the man looking out of the window – just from the very corner of her eye – but she would not give him the satisfaction of a full glance: nor would she have him watch her eat. So she sat still.

Robert Stephens knew that he had been noticed and sensed that the statue-like attitude was a reaction to his observation, and this pleased him. Her coat had been opened and, as usual with Emily, it tumbled about her and so he could not see the obvious indication of a married woman; by her looks and attitude, he guessed her to be the daughter of a pleasant-faced man who had set her down, waiting while he went to find lodgings – which would account for the furniture. It was not often that he had such an untroubled opportunity to look at a girl like that, and he was going to take advantage of it.

In the downstairs room of his two-roomed cottage, he was preparing himself some tea. A schoolmaster in his early twenties, son of a ship's engineer in Barrow-in-Furness, he preferred to be on his own, even to make his own meals despite the alarm this caused among his neighbours. As he set on the kettle and laid out the table, he wondered if she would accept an invitation to join him. Probably not, he thought. Her father had looked rather a 'proper' man: still, he could take a cup out to her, or, better still, by the look of the weather it might soon rain, and then he could offer her shelter, which would be unobjectionable.

The cloth covered only half the table, on the rest, his notes were scrupulously arranged. He had seen as much of the fair and the market as he wanted during the morning and since dinner-time had been occupied in making a list of the birds he had seen at Monkerhill Lough while at his first school on the coast at Silloth. He taught the youngest class in the Church of England National Primary School in Cockermouth and the list was to be accompanied by his own drawings of the whooper-swans, Bewick swans and long-tailed ducks seen there. Together they would be pinned to the blackboard to be copied. He had also been making ready for his expedition on the following day when he was going with Mr W. G. Carrick, the well-known naturalist, to observe peregrines in their nesting ledges on the red sandstone cliffs at Whitehaven.

But this was forgotten as he bobbed up and down to look out of the window – until he could contain himself no longer and went out to her. Emily was relieved because her back was stiff. The weather, inevitably, provided him with an opening and the two of them were soon talking. He had noticed her ring almost immediately, and while this quenched his ambition (a tiny new flicker, easily damped down) – it did not mar his enjoyment at speaking to her – aided it rather by relieving it of a weight of responsibility he might soon have felt too pressing.

Emily told him everything in one dollop and soon he was as anxious as she about John's future which they were discussing when, unseen by Emily, John rounded the corner as it began to rain.

He had not felt jealousy before. Emily had been his first girl and there had been no question of either of them wasting their precious ends of free time on anyone else. Nor had there been other young men around to tease him by flirtation. He was unknown to it until that moment when it wrenched at him so viciously that he was brought to a standstill.

It was the fear that she could care for anyone else – in any way at all – which shook him; that and the overwhelming recognition of how much his love had led to dependence when such a casual sight could affect him so badly. He was at once outraged, though he realized how stupid it was – of *course* she could talk to other people, like them, be in their company (though he wished she was not smiling so happily) – and depressed, though again, there was some pride to be got from a dependence so entire that only a complete love could have made it so. These extremes stropped his nerves and all he saw salted them. He could have choked her, struck the man, snatched her away, left her forever, given her up to him. Instead he brushed away the tears that had come and walked on, as steadily as he could, feeling that he was stepping out of a pillar of fire still burning behind him.

'John!' Emily exclaimed delightedly. 'O John!' She fell against him and thought his refusal to yield a mark of public manners – so she pulled herself away quickly – which he thought a sign of further rejection. The small boy ran away.

'I thought you would never come,' she said. 'I was just sayin' to this man here – he's a schoolmaster and, John, he knows where Wiggonby is! – that I would leave him to look after our things and come up that town and *make* them hire you. O, I *must* kiss you!'

And then, to John's complete bewilderment, the jealousy which had cindered his affection with tongues of scarcely tolerable flame slid away, and his aching lips filled with his former love as she kissed his mouth.

'Well,' she said, impatient the second the embrace was over, 'who is it? Where are we going? What did you get? What's he like? Come on, John, come on. I must know.'

'If you want to shelter from the rain,' said Mr Stephens tentatively, 'you can use my kitchen.'

'It's nobbut drizzle!' John replied, sharply, again tossed up by jealousy. Emily glared at him for his rudeness. 'Thank you very much all the same,' John added in mumbled monotone of courtesy.

'I should *think* so, John. This man's been very kind.'

Mr Stephens, though he had not sufficient perception to see right through the affair, had at least enough tact to know he ought to depart: which he did.

'Well!' said Emily, as the door closed behind him. 'And have we got so High and Mighty we can be rained on without worry?'

'I didn't like you talking to him.'

'And why not?'

'Never mind.'

'But I do. And I think you're shameful.' She turned away, biting her lip to keep back the tears and not until John had held and gently pressed her shoulders for almost a minute would she consent to turn around. 'Now *that's* out,' she said, 'what happened?'

John stuttered and then stopped.

'It can't be as bad as *all* that.'

'Mebbe not,' he murmured.

'Come on,' she coaxed him, quietly. 'Tell us.'

'I will,' he said, and the blush which had crept around his cheeks retreated as he tensed himself before her. 'There was only one fella Aa got an offer half-decent from at all!' he began, his eyes fierce with the memory of it all. 'The others hadn't this and didn't want that and some of them asked me age and offered *boy's* wages – to a married man! There's fellas down there now hasn't been hired yet and won't be this day. Then came this fella Pennington frae Crossbridge – and he would have me – but for twelve shillings, Emily, *twelve* not fifteen. He laughed at fifteen. And he had a cottage but it won't be free 'til tomorrow. So I took his luck-shillin' – but I didn't spend it. I went to look for our Seth to tell him that I would go down't pit wid him. And I would a' done, Emily, though I know you'd be worried at it. But Isaac had med a lot of money in a fight and taken Seth off to race his whippet and God knows where they've gone. I couldn't go look for them with thou waitin'. And now I can't find Pennington – and his shillin's binding. I must work for him!'

'I would have gone with you to the pits,' she said.

'But would thou like it?'

'No,' she said after a pause. 'No. I think I would have been miserable.'

'So it's just as well, then,' John answered, finding some consolation in that.

'Twelve shillings isn't bad if you've got a cottage,' she said, taking up and heightening his mood. 'There'll be many managed on less,' she added, so sagely that he laughed and swung her around in the narrow street.

'But we'll have to go back home tonight,' said John. 'I saw Errington and he promised us a lift – though he didn't seem ower keen on *my* comin'.'

'I'm *not* going back home,' Emily replied. 'Now say what you want, I'll not hear it. I'm *not* going back home and have ivverybody laugh. I'm not!'

'But what'll we do then?'

'We'll lodge in Cockermouth.'

'What on? I've nobbut this shillin'.'

'I've over a pound.'

'That's thine,' he replied. 'Thine only.'

'So I should sleep inside and you rest out in a ditch?' she asked.

That struck John as a good idea. Then she pouted and he tried to coax her and the rain came down; he spread his coat on the furniture which she took off and replaced by some brown paper which blew away as the wind gusted up behind the rain turning nasty and she chased down the street while he shouted at her to take care of herself; so she stopped to shout back at him and the papers blew into a garden.

Mr Stephens came out and made his offer. He had seen and heard all – though he revealed this most delicately – and would gladly put them up for the night in his cottage, if they thought they would be comfortable. It was this condition, this clause of truly hospitable consideration which finally allowed John to accept an invitation which Emily had lapped up on the instant of its being made. But there was still that scar of jealousy in John and also a sliver of uncertainty – for his experience over the last hours, being ignored and ignored and ignored in The Ring and then approached for such a low offer, being barged around in the fair-crowd and made to ask strangers about Isaac – many of them teasing him and giving him false answers, surrounded and drenched and maddened by the entertainments and goods, none of which he could afford for Emily, not one treat could he offer her – all this made his acceptance easier than it might otherwise have been.

As soon as he said yes, Emily darted into the cottage as if it were made for her, and John went across to take the furniture over into Mr Stephens' outhouse; the rain now slashing down, his luck-shillin' clammy in his trouser pocket, stuck against his thigh.

5

When Mr Stephens went out to buy more provisions for tea – though his excuse offered was that he needed some tobacco – John sat in a chair on one side of the kitchen, Emily stood by the window on the other side, both on their best behaviour. But while he was most conscious of himself, clumsy in uneasy gratitude, Emily was delighted with it all. After seeing Mr Stephens disappear around the corner, she examined the small room minutely, the books on the shelf – reading out all their titles aloud – the three prints on the wall, 'The Education of the Young Raleigh', 'Derwentwater at Dawn' and 'The Drunkard's

Children' – drew her boots appreciatively over the mat, picked up the jug of pencils and finally came to the oven which was next to the sink. Above the sink was a large cupboard which she opened despite the disapproving suck of John's tongue.

'I could make some biscuits,' she said. 'Do you think I should?'

'Leave things be, Emily,' John replied, speaking softly in the new place. 'Thou can't go using other people's stuff like that.'

'He would like some biscuits.'

'How dis' thou know?'

'He would.' She shut one of the cupboard doors only, not to be defeated that easily, and then thought of a conclusive argument. 'I bet he can't make them himself!'

'Well, what's that got to do with it?'

'A lot.' But she swung the second door in her hand uncertainly. 'Don't you think he *would* like some?'

'How do I know?'

'There you are!' She smiled. 'You can't be certain. It'll be done in a minute.'

'He won't want his kitchen mired up wid baking stuffs. That I do know.'

'And who'll mire a kitchen up?'

'Thou's bound to.'

'I am not, John Tallentire! And anyway, it's clean dirt. It's easily mopped up.' She paused. 'He *would* like some,' she reiterated. 'I could make ginger snaps. He has some ginger.'

'Do as you please.'

'Wouldn't *you* like a ginger snap?'

'O, for pity's sake Emily, stop keeping on!'

She slammed the door shut and went back to the window. She glanced at John quickly and then leaned forward, slipped the latch, and pushed it open. Through the rain came the sound of the fair, organ music squeezing enticingly away, unseen.

'So I won't get to the fair,' said Emily – and then, the second she had said it, she covered her mouth with her hand, afraid that her thoughtlessness might upset John. And so before he could say a word, she rushed on. 'Still! I've been to Cockermouth in a pony and trap!'

John got up and went across to her. She heard him but kept her back turned so that she would have his arms around her and then she could wriggle inside them to face him. As he held her she seemed to swell, as if another skin, another body, more calm and perfect than the one she had, grew out of her as token for that love of him which could in looks and words show itself so inadequately. He kissed her on the cheek and her eyes closed to feel his lips breathing so tenderly.

'I'm sorry about the fair,' he said.

'Don't be sorry.'

'We'll come next year.'

'Yes.'

He released her, held her on the shoulders for a moment and quickly turned away.

'There were some logs in his backyard,' he said. 'I'll chop them up for kindling.' Use the axe to cut out the feeling of obligation.

'O! That's good!'

'Emily,' he asked as he reached the door. 'Twelve shillin's *will* be enough, won't it?'

'Plenty!' she answered. 'And if you can chop wood, I can make biscuits!'

By the time Mr Stephens came back, the snaps were almost done, the table was laid, crockery out, a split log burned on the fire, there was a neat pile of sticks drying in the grate, and tea went well. They talked of the market and the fair, and then, Emily having noticed and praised his drawings of the swans, Mr Stephens held forth about his hobby.

'What d'you call a missel thrush down your way?' he asked John. 'Is it a shalary?'

'Yes. That's right. There is a shalary.'

'I thought so,' said Mr Stephens, happily. 'Even in our county it changes its name all over the place. There's storm-cock and chur-cock and shell-cock, shalary and mountain throssel – all the missel thrush!'

'There's something my grandfather calls a shrike,' said John, 'would that be another?'

'It might be. It might be! I'll ask Mr Carrick tomorrow. Shrike! I'll make a note of that.'

'There's something I call a blue-wing,' said Emily, boldly, pleased to be joining in a conversation in which she was proud to see John taking such an active part, 'and my uncle Tom calls it a blue-*back*.'

'That's the "field-fare",' said Mr Stephens. '*Turdus pilaris.*' And the Latin appellation – memorized so painstakingly – crunched between his teeth like barley sugar. 'Your grandfather might have heard it called the felty, or the pigeon felty or even the blue felty – and I think some call it fell fo!'

'Goodness!' said Emily, mouth half-open.

'Oh, that's just the beginning!' Mr Stephens responded. 'Now take the whitethroat – *syliva cinera* . . .'

But after the tea had been cleared, the cups put away, everything tidied, then the three of them sat around in broken sentences. Because of the regular placement of the chairs around the fire, they were quite close together – and yet the small spaces between them quickly became boundaries. John wanted to be in bed so that the night would be over quickly and he could move off the next morning; Mr Stephens had a neighbour who would lend them a handcart and John wanted to be able to push the furniture the eight miles uphill to Crossbridge, settle it, and return the handcart the same day. Already he was worried about their stores lasting until the Saturday when he might reasonably claim a few shillings to tide him over; Emily's mother had given them a box of stuff, sausages, bread, some tea, butter, bacon – but it would have to be spun out. He was burrowing into responsibilities, looking for them almost, for they gave substance to that which bound Emily to him – and still the shock of jealousy pulsed occasionally making him shudder so that he blushed to seem to be shivering.

The schoolteacher realized that his guests were tongue-tied in this strange place and, after a few openings had brought no more than murmurs of self-conscious or self-absorbed politeness, he did what he had found best to do on such occasions. For he was not a man who could slither into any shape required of him. His interests and habits had been too strictly and personally framed for him to be anything less than completely reliant on them. So he did what he was going to do anyway, what would most engage his own attention and invited others to share the preoccupation – which was as much as any man could do, he thought.

He took down a copy of Wordsworth's collected poems. John and Emily sat themselves up to listen, and felt most solemn: but the schoolmaster's plain reading gave them confidence and Emily's hand reached out to touch John's arm.

Mr Stephens was careful to read the short poems and finished up with one set not far from the place at which John was hired. Beginning:

> 'There is a yew-tree, pride of Lorton Vale,
> Which to this day stands single, in the midst
> Of its own darkness, as it stood of yore.'

And John felt Emily's hand tighten on his own as the last lines rolled out:

> '. . . beneath whose sable roof
> Of boughs, as if for festal purpose decked
> With unrejoicing berries – ghostly shapes
> May meet at noon-tide; Fear and trembling Hope,
> Silence and Foresight; Death the skeleton
> And Time the Shadow: – there to celebrate,
> As in a natural temple scattered o'er
> With altars undisturbed of mossy stone
> United Worship; or in mute repose
> To lie, and listen to the mountain flood
> Murmuring from Glaramara's inmost caves.'

That final line itself murmured through the kitchen and they sat silently, the organ music from the streets like the sound from the caves. John looked at Emily and saw a face on which such a keen reverence was trying to settle itself to gaze of understanding that yet again he stirred against the schoolmaster.

He had no such means of casting spells over her. They came from a world out of reach. And he did not want to hear of what was impossible.

When the couple had gone upstairs to bed, Mr Stephens packed his bag for the next day's outing, bolted the doors firmly – for many of the men stayed in Cockermouth drinking for three or four days and would roam the streets at night looking for somewhere to sleep – and then, as if to atone for those first designs he had had on Emily, he picked out *Silas Marner* from his bookshelf and wrapped it up as a present for her. He pushed back the chairs and laid his blankets on the floor to fall asleep, as always, the moment he closed his eyes.

John could not sleep. He had stayed in bed until Emily was settled and then, very quietly, got up. The window in the bedroom was very small and all he could see through it were the roof-tops lit, as the previous night, by a full moon.

He could not recapture the certainty he had felt that morning. And it was not only that he had not got what he had hoped for, nor was it the jealousy which made him feel unsure. In The Ring his pride in being on his own had met with confusion and Isaac and Seth, too, seemed to challenge what he wanted, what he believed in, how he lived – though understandingly enough, he knew. It was as if he had caught an infection which was moving around all men but as yet lighting on few, something which would grow to cause fever where there had been force. He shook his head, abruptly. No wonder you get like that, standing in your bare feet in the middle of the night, his mother would have said. And he remembered Isaac's story about the man who thought too much and smiled once more.

Not until dawn, however, could he fall asleep. He lay in the bed, touching Emily with fingers too rough for her skin, wondering what he could give her that would even approach what he thought of her; waiting to be gone to his own place.

6

John's restlessness continued over the next few days – forcing him to a temper which shocked Emily that all that she had seen in him could be banished by such an unknown mood, or into a brooding alike as alien to her knowledge of him. His work around the cottage soon done, he scattered these unsettled moods around him, seeds which were always covered over by a mutual coveting for warmth, yet waiting only for time to send tremors through the even surface of the life their love played on.

The restlessness retreated when he began his longed-for work; hated work in those few odd moments when inactivity had percolated through the habitual demands of his skin and nerves to give him a rare perspective on his existence; despised work when after telling Emily all that Seth had said to him, the words of his brother spun on his mind – so that he saw himself as a drudge, bound to tread on a ceaseless wheel, eyes to the ruts he trod, unable, unfitted to look about himself as Seth did and see a purpose; feared work as he stood before Mr Pennington that first Saturday dinner-time, hearing his first orders; once begun, longed-for work which served his demands and gave his life a shape, continued that sculpture between himself and toil, filled his day and stilled his questions. If it did not draw from him the quality of response it drew from his grandfather, then it was not for want of trying, for 'work,' he said to Emily, 'is all I'm good for.'

Pennington was not a difficult man to work for, once it was accepted, as John had been trained to accept, that every daylight hour would be squeezed dry of its labour. He had taken over the farm from his father and nuzzled into it as greedily as a calf into its mother's udders; only he was never full. Other life in Crossbridge infiltrated his thoughts and actions, market prices jarred them, his family were invested in them, the seasons were impressed on them, but it was his farm, its every present occupation which had fed and formed them. The world outside the farm was in every way beyond him and by the time the pulses of change and alarm reached him from the cities, they were no more than remarks along a lane, scarcely worth breaking his stride for. He had been left 270 acres of farm and 240 acres of fell for his sheep and not a yard had been added or subtracted, the milkers stood at the same number and there were still about a score of Cumberland pigs which were so fat they could hardly trot but which, once butched, gave bacon whose slim streak of lean tasted, it was boasted, like no other. He kept three working horses, about two dozen hens, fewer ducks and geese and only one of his sons at home.

His tenancy of the farm was far from lifting his circumstances into comparison with those of the few gentry around the village. In outlook and habit he was, to them, not indistinguishable from the labourers but certainly much nearer to them than to any other class. He dressed about the farm exactly as John did, he worked the same hours, did the same work as John did, and he spoke the dialect with no hint of landed advantage in his tone. With education he was less well equipped than some of those hired by him and that great tangible distinction – the money – was taken away to be stacked out of sight and kept for keeping's sake as soon as it had accumulated to a pile of ten pounds. His answer to the bad times was to dig himself in harder; his father had had four hired men and kept two sons at home; he had a single man living in, one married man and three of his sons out earning elsewhere money which would come back to their home farm. That his father had gained leisure-time by a superior labour force did not trouble him; his sights were on survival, his ignorance forstalled experiments or even such changes as might reasonably have been expected to bring about improvements: he made do with less and hung about Cockermouth until someone was forced to take his mean offer of twelve shillings.

One of his economies had been to cut out drink and he was pleased to see that John so rarely bothered with it – though this approval ignored the exigence of his hired man's economy with such lack of understanding as made it formidable. No less. To be able to ignore what he was part cause of and walk around grunting approbation on an abstinence all but enforced by his own miserliness needed extraordinary powers of insensitivity and blindness.

Pennington did not, by this self-denial, miss a great deal – or so he reassured himself, the memory of those evenings in the pub, The Cross, fading as far away as those of his father merely supervising some of the work. Gossip could be gathered over a dyke while on a job.

Crossbridge was a fairly typical fell-village, placed at the first abrupt elevation of fells which, a few miles from the Solway, shuts out the easy passages of the plain and cordons the lakes and peaks in wholly distinctive life and beauty. A church was there, two pubs and a Hall, whose last resident's uneventful branch grew directly from the transplanted roots of Normandy. There were two or three gentlemen farmers, and land agents for the aristocracy who owned far the greatest portion of territory, coming themselves only to flatten it with the hooves of hunters or pepper it with shot. Pennington's farm was leased from Lord Leconfield. There was a school, a carpenter, a tailor, three shops, a blacksmith, a shoemaker – who specialized in the locally notorious 'Crossbridge Boots' which at first wearing seemed to drag alongside the foot like a ball and chain – a band, an occasional cricket team, and the oldest Friendly Society in England. Sufficient people for there to be plenty of room for finely-distinguished classes. Among the local labourers, the names Edmonson, Sharpe, Spedding, Branthwaite, Wrangham, Dacre, Bragg, Tyson, Edgar and Dalzell met, married, and you could warn a stranger – as you could in many villages and at that time in streets and districts throughout England – that care should be taken in talking of someone because you would be certain to be addressing his relation: if you offended one you offended all.

What gave Crossbridge a grip on the times, however, was not this rural net, which had always been and still is, now fatter, now lean, but the opening of iron-ore pits in the village. Haematite had been mined at Egremont for centuries but now the demand for ore drove shafts down all over the area. Knockmirton, one of the fells which looked down on Crossbridge, was opened and haematite extracted from the slate; two more shafts were sunk in the village itself and men who could not find or rejected farm-work were stopped from joining the long drift from the countryside by the prospects in the red, lung-caking ore. Emily heard the buckets whistling down the fields to the railway on the loop, the iron-ore miners passed by the labourers in the fields, and a red stain spread in the streams.

Their cottage stood about a hundred yards from the farm in that area of the loping village which clustered around 'The Cross'. It was one of three, but they were alone, for Pennington used one of the empty cottages as a store-house. The other he left empty in case catastrophe compelled the hiring of another man. As both of them had expected, there was one room up, one down, a very small garden and some outhouses. The space was more than enough for their furniture.

Emily had not reckoned on being so isolated, but after worrying over it for a while, she found reasons to like it and would then have it no other way.

Though tiny, the cottage was not easy to manage. The rent paid by John was so small that it was not worth Pennington's while to make improvements and so if slates came loose or the back wall was persistently damp, if the flags on the floor cracked and the window-frames rotted – it was of no interest to him. Emily either had to do something about it herself or persuade John to disturb himself into further action after his return from the day's work. And the washhouse was in such a state that it took her a week to clean the dolly-tub alone; the mangle was broken and John's attempt to mend it revealed that it was riddled with wood-worm: until a new mangle could be afforded, she had to rely on beating and wringing the clothes.

At the least flush of rain, there would be a trickle as the water from the gutter splashed down into the doorway made sloping by the trampling of feet. The first time this happened she was out, and returned to find mud rising between the flagstones in her kitchen, a puddle collected around the fender, seeping in to wet the only sticks she had chopped, and the second-hand mat she had bought sodden with dirt. The rain had not stopped and a bucket was all she could find to catch the overflow from the gutter; she could not get the fire to start and eventually ran out of matches; cleaned, the precious mat hung miserably from a knob on the oven, refusing to dry and losing all its attraction, smelling like a damp hide; however quickly she scrubbed the floor she could never beat the water coming in and the mud plastered her apron until that too had to be washed. When John came in, he found her crying in a chair, the kitchen reeking of wet and smelling of the mat, wood unlighted in the fire and no supper on the table. He had bricked up the entrance, making a three-inch barricade against the water, and promised to mend the gutter when he got the time. He had not lost his temper – for which she was grateful, but there was an unspoken impatience so obviously charging him that she wished that words *had* flown.

Despite this, once she got the fireplace black-leaded and distempered the walls, picked wild flowers to put in jars on the table and cut her curtains from the old set her mother had given her, ruddied the doorstep and organized her food – the cottage shone for her and she was pleased with herself. Given the money she had, it was not easy to solve the problem of food; tea was an expense, as was sugar, flour and salt. Pennington only truculently kept up the tradition of part-payment in kind and the potatoes he handed over were never enough and often half-rotten; a few turnips could be relied on but he had let his domestic vegetable patch go and any carrots, cauliflower or lettuce had to be bought or found in John's own garden. He had felt compelled to follow his grandfather's example and give a part of the tiny plot over 'to Emily' (though he dug it) for flowers, which left him only a few yards for himself. Considering that the bottom of the garden bounded a field of grass, it would not have been over-indulgent of Pennington to suggest that John take enough ground there for half a dozen stitches of potatoes, but the thought did not occur to him. Eggs had to be bought, as did fruit – there was no orchard and even cooking-apples had to be purchased – but there she was lucky as John did not care much for fresh fruit. They ate fish only rarely and meat no more than once a week. Pennington was apparently more generous with flesh, once offering her a hen, another time offering John part of a sheep, but on neither occasion had these been killed for eating; they had died almost likely of a scabrous disease and both John and his wife had no reluctance in refusing the offers. John planned to buy a piglet sometime and feed it up, but until then he would make do with porridge, broths, bread, jam and meatless hot-pots.

One reason why she soon accommodated herself to being so isolated was that the position made her a friend. Sally Edmonson was a year younger than Emily: she worked at her father's farm – The Beck – three fields away. The youngest of six children, there was no binding necessity for her to stay at home, but the family was too easy-going to demand that she go out as a servant girl and they liked to spoil her around the place. 'Pet lamb', her father called her and like a pet lamb she had been given so many privileges at the beginning that only the most brutal action – which the Edmonsons would never have considered – could have re-set her in the type of her sisters. To her, Emily was a new face, which was welcome; a married woman, which was intriguing; poor, which kept the balance right; almost her own age, which meant they could talk; and above all cut off from everyone else so that trips there did not bring her into contact with the rest of the village who knew all there was to know about her and were perpetually patronizing with their 'What time did *you* get up this morning?' and 'What's it like to do no work?' She could slip out of the Beck by the back garden and be over the fields without anyone noticing. And, finally, though cut off, Emily's cottage was near to the Pennington's – and there lived Jackson.

Both girls accepted and swore friendship after the first meeting and neither was the sort to apply any stingy rules of careful visiting to pickle their affection in a considered regularity. Sally ran up to the cottage whenever she could and Emily would rush through her work to be the better able to listen to her.

Sally brought the village in. All her life she had listened to gossip about those she had grown up with and such interpolation as she had been allowed had been treated as the cue for a joke, rejected as trivial or merely listened to, having no more effect on the general conversation than the wind outside the door. Now she had a clear field and she raced through the uncut grass – did Emily know about Alfred Dalzell's gin? Did she know that Joseph Wrangham had a donkey that could count? And Mrs Dacre wasn't really Mrs – honestly; Jackie Branthwaite had won the ten-stone wrestling championship and the vicar stuttered in his sermons (Emily had not been to church; John worked on Sunday mornings and evenings; she would get there after the baby was born); 'Major' Spedding had stolen a corpse from the pub that belonged to a young medical student and 'Lollop' Tyson kept a pet fox he had found in the woods as a cub. Jo Edgar had not spoken to his wife for fourteen years and Annie Dacre was daft. Joby Stoker had put his mother in the workhouse and Mrs Allan had triplets. Lord Leconfield's son had hunted in Crossbridge that winter and a three-headed calf had been born at Winnah.

The news plumped Emily as surely as the child inside her, and on hot days, they would take the chairs outside the cottage where, while Emily sat knitting clothes for her expected child, Sally would prattle away, dart off to snatch at some flowers, shoo away birds from the stitches, tramp into the kitchen to make tea and come out with some cakes or biscuits she had brought up with her, hidden in her pocket as a surprise. They were very alike in looks, though Sally's hair was darker, her eyes grey; the chief superficial difference lay in their relationship to the clothes they wore. Emily had on her second dress, a dark brown one which she wore on every day but Sunday and whose washing on Saturday night was always done with the worry that it might not be dry by Monday. On top of that, she had a large coarse apron which went from her shoulders to below her knees, with two deep pockets for pegs and her handkerchief. The dress had many underskirts to it and she had yet again let out the waist to accommodate her growing belly. She wore no jewellery and her hair was always parted in the middle and coiled up at the back. Only once, tired out by Sally's pestering, had she let it down for her friend and then it had fallen on her shoulders, over her breasts and down her back like a sudden glorious rush of leaves. Sally had wanted to brush it for her, but Emily had gone far enough and began to plait it up again almost immediately. Sometimes she wore a white blouse with an old skirt a sister had given her, and then Sally would make a necklace of flowers, buttercups, primroses or daisies and set it around her throat.

What caused Emily most shame was her clogs. She had a pair of shoes for such an occasion as never seemed to arise, the boots she wore when she went into the village, and then the clogs for about the house. They had rubber soles with rubber instead of iron corkers, a little brass guard around the toe and the holes for the laces were rimmed in brass; the leather was brown and the entire effect one which in a later age less conscious of the rigid liaison between money of a certain quantity and goods of a specific type, would have been considered chic. Never by Emily. Though she never dared abandon them, she hated them and would take any opportunity to tuck her feet away under her dresses or lean on one foot only so that she could draw the other back. Clogs they were – even though a far throw from those boats of naked wood and iron in which her mother so compliantly sailed – and clogs they remained. The clatter they made sometimes maddened her as much as a can tied on a dog's tail. These clothes then plainly suited her as much as they did a hundred other women; but perhaps because of the clogs, or that heavy line of pegs in the bottom pocket of the apron which swung sullenly before her, she appeared to shake herself free from them as she walked as if making it clear to all that she was but temporary captive to them.

While Sally was a most willing prisoner. No clogs there – except around the farm, to be kicked off as soon as she reached the edge of the yard and the shapely buttoned boots pulled on in their place. Her skirts were mauve and wine and violet blue, the blouses frilled, worked with designs, neat on the wrist. She wore a bracelet every day and the apron was tugged over her head and off as she ran away from the farm. As *she* walked, the clothes made a swirling fanfare for her, and she felt the colour and flourish of them lift her ankles, swing her arms and encourage her hair to tumble down.

The innocence which encapsulated Emily and her new friend was not unlike that simple layer of pure light which in paintings lies across so many medieval ladies like the flattening blade of a chastening sword.

They talked of men as they talked of children – Sally bemused and all-open to her love for Jackson Pennington – and Emily still bound in her first passion for John: the one as ready to be picked as the ripest plum, the other sounding of the complete interlocking of the night. Sally dusted over her demands and desires with a dumb-show of metaphor – now asking Emily who, besides her John, was the handsomest man she had seen in Crossbridge, whether she liked blond or black hair in a man, what she thought of the Pennington farm 'as a house to look at,' skirting her object as deftly as she pirouetted around puddles in the lane. And Emily, remembering the first ecstatic clash of their two virginities, could weave nothing around John but public platitudes: even to herself the details of that intimacy were never admitted and the words which at that time were starting to be used to describe the finest sensations of love would have bruised her like stoning pebbles.

The two girls talked chiefly about Sally's prospects. Being married, Emily's prospects were considered to be closed. But for Sally – the world waited. She could leave home and work in a department store in Carlisle – her mother had said so. Or she could go and live with her sister, for a time, in Barrow and there learn to be a lady's maid. More realistically, she could be employed as a companion by Mrs Arnold, 'but she's such an old mope, Emily! And I would have to read to her every day. And the *smell* in that house – dad says she must have mixed moth-balls in the paste before she had her papering done. She's *shivery!*' or she could stay at home, 'but who wants to stay at *home*' she exclaimed with an admiring glance at Emily. 'I've seen all there is to see there.' Or, finally, and she proposed this skittishly – pawning it on to her father as a suggestion entirely of his invention and one so far-fetched as could only settle in such a ridiculous place as his head – she could get herself married. 'But who would have me?' she complained – and hurried to add 'And who is there that I could put up with?'

As Sally began to recite the rosary of her 'possibles', ticking each one along the string of her self-assurance with a cancelling click of her tongue, Emily tensed herself, for she knew exactly where this would lead and dreaded the subject. Jackson Pennington, son of John's employer, was the village beau: he had run off from home twice and been told, it was known, that the next time would be the last time. Taller than most of the men around him, he would still lean forward into his toes when standing talking, as if every extra inch were a point in his favour. He was blond-haired, good-looking, had totally escaped from the pinching myopia of his father and, within limits, he was dashingly dressed, never afraid to put on his best suit just to go out for a stroll, a scarf fluttering around his neck not, as with John, tucked well into the high-buttoned waistcoat. There was talk that his first disappearance from home had been to go and live with a married woman; that it was he who had set the ferret among Braithwaite's brood-hens and killed them all to get his own back for a lost fight and he *had* been found drunk on a tombstone one winter morning and terrified the vicar coming in to celebrate early communion – but Sally could shut all these stories out of her mind with little effort.

Emily endured the talk because Sally was so eager to have a confidante. And she wanted to keep Sally's friendship; without her the days would be lonely. Moreover she liked her, loved her – and one day she would tell her . . .

She had met Jackson on her very first day. John had unloaded the furniture, and immediately set off to return the handcart – taking a few sandwiches with him to eat on the way; so impatient to be quit of this last link with past obligations that he could not bear to stop and share a meal with her.

Alone, and, she found, glad to be alone in her new house, Emily had spent the first hour sweeping and cleaning. John had brought two buckets of water from the Pennington farmyard where the tap was, but these were soon used. She set off on the first expedition from her cottage – feeling it to be no less than that, the unfamiliar hills bounding the landscape, the short track to the farm unexperienced, and the compound of panic and excitement stirring nervously inside her as she realized that she knew not a soul in the village.

She saw Jackson under the pump, stripped to the waist, dousing himself. When he adopted a flamboyant expression of surprise at seeing her, she had smiled, recognizing the beer which leavened reactions to caricature: harmless, she thought, remembering the clumsy clutches at dignity of those she had seen drunk in her home village. When he parodied gallantry and filled the buckets for her then his attentions were excused, she thought, by her telling him who she was. And when he insisted on carrying the buckets down to the cottage, she had taken his flattery and mock-advances as no more than mildly drunken high spirits. Besides she was glad to find someone so lively and friendly in this new place, while she could reassure herself that her married state made her invulnerable, so she chatted excitably, pouring out her life-story and her plans, constantly mentioning John – the name like a charm to keep her safe – unaware that this openness could be construed as evidence of compliance, her naming of John as deliberate incitement, her excitement as anticipation.

He got himself invited in for a cup of tea and she sliced the loaf given them by Mr Stephens: as she cut it, she remembered doing the same thing for John an hour or so before – and looked at Jackson anxiously. Fingers locked together, arms behind his head, he tilted back the chair and gazed: convinced that he was overwhelmed by this unknown woman, and feeling great freedom in the fact that he was unknown to her, that their being together in this cottage would be unknown, that he would be able to see her whenever he wanted to. She put down the knife and rubbed the palms of her hands down the thighs of her dress – afraid, unable to speak, in case she should be the cause.

Jackson stood up, the effect of the beer returning in that warm enclosed space. And stepped towards her. Her head still flinched as she remembered that first step – but at the time she had stood, rooted, arms suddenly quite forceless. This first rise of terror made her face appear only more enticing, inflamed, it seemed to Jackson, with the same thoughts as his own. He had grabbed her: even in thinking of it long afterwards, her hands crept up to those parts of her arms whose bruises she had at such cost hidden from John. The shock had torn all restraint from her and she had kicked and screamed until he had been forced to use his strength not to subdue her but merely to keep her quiet. A hand clasped over her mouth had been bitten deeply and she still remembered the blood on her tongue and Jackson's yell. He let her go and she took the knife from the table, and stood, panting, outraged – the blade most steadily held, its point firm for action should he dare come near her – which he dared not.

After he had gone, Emily had wept as she had never done before. For at once not only herself, but it seemed her unborn child, John, their love, all that she had grown for, had been violated. It seemed to her that she would never recover from it, that she might as well give up everything at that moment, that she must rush home, kill herself (for she felt that somehow she was to blame and this swelled immediately and spat its poison back into herself) that everything was 'finished, finished, finished,' she had muttered to herself, letting the water from the bucket, which had been knocked over in the fight, soak into the hem of her dress without budging. And then she had heard footsteps, rushed to the door and shrank back to its frame as she saw Jackson yet again – this time meek, apologetic, holding out a chicken in his bandaged hand, as atonement; almost comical, he looked, but there could be no laughter. Seeing him (whom she thought she ought to loathe) now so docile before her, she felt without either will or sense – and took what he gave her, turning silently away from his 'Sorry'.

This strange full-circle had exhausted her. Where his attempt in itself might have shot through her and away this sudden turn on his part sealed his action up and kept it thrashing within her, impossible to respond to, impossible to reject. That she had determined John should know nothing of it made this enclosed knowledge lodge sickeningly in her. When Jackson came around to see them both – she had to be polite and pleasant. When over the next few weeks he brought her flowers – having easily slipped away from his father and John in some distant field – she had to accept them for fear he would ask about them in front of John the next time he came. This torture lasted for almost a month until she could no longer bear it and was prepared to tell John and leave the place whatever the consequences. Jackson heard this threat solemnly, repeated, again, as he always did, that he was sorry and said he would keep away. A few days, a week, a fortnight passed, then Sally arrived and Emily felt almost free.

One thing nearly gave it away. Word came from the Pennington household that Mrs Tallentire might see her way to spending her hours between breakfast and supper within the walls of the farm – to do work as a servant-girl which Mrs Pennington had long required, no one until now being found suitable. Wages, the word continued in a more muted tone, could be arranged.

John thought this a marvellous opportunity – just for a few months until the baby got too 'bad'. He was carried away by the benefits it would bestow; there would be more money – and she could have *all* her wages to do with as she pleased, 'a dress and things': she would have company and get to know about the village; he would see her more often through the day as he was frequently in the farm and the yard; they could walk back together at night . . . Emily was adamant. She would not go. At first out of curiosity, then out of anxiety, then in anger, John asked her why not. At last, when she sensed his suspicions grow warm to her secret, she said: 'Anything that can be done in my own cottage – washing or baking or anything, I'll do for them. But the *two* of us need not be bound to them. Besides, you've given me my own house and I want it kept right for you. I want us to enjoy it – when the children come it'll change soon enough. I'd do without any amount of dresses to have it right for us these few months.'

Spoken so calmly, that, coming after one of John's more heated outbursts, it not only reassured him but reminded him of his love so that he put his arm around her to beg forgiveness for his temper.

Her answer he carried to Pennington with no little pride.

By that, it seemed that she had cut herself off from Jackson, would be no more forced to see him than his father, and somehow, by wishing, even the memory would be shaven down. The more she grew to command the lonely cottage the more confident she became and, to her surprise, she saw herself behaving as before, laughing, kissing John, thinking the same thoughts. By ignoring it completely it would be erased.

Yet there was one further incident which checked that hope – though it did not break it.

An early summer Saturday, John had been out turning the hay since early morning. His supper was warm on the hob, the table laid with a white cloth, water hot for him to bath in, the lamp on, herself tidied up, everything ready. One thing more, she thought, would make it perfect and she took down her shawl, looked out a big jug and went up to The Cross to buy him a pint of ale.

She knew from Sally that many women went there on a Saturday night – to the 'Jug and Bottle' entrance – and that some of them stayed there to 'push a few into theirsels', as Sally had impressively expressed it. Further, by her friend she had been warned that though most of the families at Crossgates were 'as decent as you've a mind,' there were, in that row of cottages built to serve the iron-ore mines 'one or two families,' said Sally 'only one or two mind you, where the women are,' she had paused to whisper, 'Awful.' And that these women were regular visitors to the 'Jug and Bottle.' This Emily remembered, and also she realized that Jackson would most likely have slid early out of the work and be drinking there – but she was not going to let anything stop her – it would take no more than a minute – and she pressed on.

The small corridor which led to this off-licence bar was crowded with women and children, many of whom had been helping in the fields now that some of the farmers (Pennington was behind-hand) were beginning to bring in the hay. The women's faces were red from the sun and redder from the ale; voices loud and assured, knowledge of each other complete, they fell silent as she joined them and despite her resolution not to be afraid she had shivered and her fright had gone right to the nostrils of the fiercest. Emily's smooth and pretty pregnancy and the boldness which fronted the timidity provoked them. At first she was merely bumped, then barged, then accused of barging, then accused of lying when she denied it. When she raised her voice accused of arguing, when she fell silent accused of sulking. When she turned to go accused of putting on airs, when she turned to reply, cuffed. And she threw her jug into the face of the woman who did it. Wiping her brow she discovered blood from a tiny cut made by the jug and the sight of this launched her against the stranger, both hands clawing.

What Emily remembered was that Jackson had come in with some other men and separated them, had held off the other woman with one hand and made her friends laugh at her. Had walked her home quickly and, at the door, explained all to John. And she remembered having been held most tenderly as they had walked back towards her cottage.

Jackson had not exploited this circumstance, and she was grateful. Wove reasons for this into her thoughts of him. For she could not prevent herself from thinking of him – so distant now, she thought, nodding cheerfully as they passed one another; no more.

When Sally spoke about him she felt such a cheat that she could not bear herself. Sometimes she could scarcely contain it, felt as a jealous woman – but always kept the secret; and to Sally's final appeal 'So that only leaves Jackson Pennington. Doesn't it, Emily? Doesn't it?' her reply was given with an emphasis of agreement far stronger than necessary.

'Yes, it does, Sally. Only him.'

7

Emily kept all this from John. She did not want to imagine what would happen. There was some consolation in her conviction that he suspected nothing and this had to be sufficient balm for her guilt.

But without seeing or hearing anything directly, John experienced the effects. The thousand flexible strands which held them together tightened: words meant kindly sounded indifferent, a casual glance would be coloured to cruelty or reproach by the interference of secrecy. Less and less was he able to feel her moods. Once he had known what she would think about everything: rested on it as on part of himself: they had been one.

The flaws appeared immediately.

When, after Jackson's assault on her, she evaded his eyes while undressing for fear he might see the bruises on her arms – making an excuse to go upstairs well before him and have the sheets up to her chin until he blew out the candle, or, pleading cold, retiring down the stairs to dress for bed before the low fire – he felt repulsed. Yet he did not ask 'What's wrong?' in such a way as would once have pulled inevitably on the loose thread and unravelled all the length; if he spoke the words now, they were toned in resentment and delivered with clumsy vehemence. She was also at this time nervous – and for this he was more inclined to blame her at being so weak that a little solitude could make her jump; pale, which he put down to the child, overlooking the evidence he had so far had – that the child had increased her buoyancy, heightened her colours; she looked at him sadly, and in that he saw neither a plea nor a pain – but reproach for the circumstances into which he had brought her. When she was tense he could not leave her alone, as formerly, and allow that splinter to work itself free in the cossetting of his companionship, but he must pester her and drive it in further until the hurt was numb.

As yet, such reactions were not set hard in him. He still felt all his former love on days when he would see her outside the cottage as he waved to her from the fields, or look down on their home from the hillside as he went among the sheep. And perhaps, he sometimes thought, his irritation was simply to do with the fact that they could not make love together so often. He had once heard that the moment a woman became pregnant then everything should stop. Both he and Emily had been unable to stop themselves. But now, the warning pressed into John's mind and he was influenced by it. That he allowed himself to be influenced was an act of spite against himself for treating Emily in a way which made him feel ashamed. So he desisted from that in which much of their communion lay in order to punish himself; which increased his exasperation and led to his treating her worse. Constantly his mind referred to the jealousy he had felt when seeing her with Mr Stephens.

Sometimes he thought he saw the tips of a root of external malevolence reaching into him, possessing him. For after days of peace and quiet, when he would see her smile as it had been and watch her as she stood at the window, waiting to be held by him, when Sally would flutter in with a mouthful of gossip, or he would again polish the ram's horns he had found on Knockmirton fell then, quite suddenly, as if a poisonous root had squirted out venom, he would be unable to stop this feeling of strain and temper and sometimes savagery. He wanted to hit her, hurt, destroy her.

So that, at such times, he looked at Emily as if she were merely the woman who happened to be sat near him in a chair, with no more right to be there than anyone else, tied to him by nothing more than an instinct which would pass – was the first awakening to this knowledge the root which spread the poison? – and there, always there, not to be moved, her enlarged belly fixing her to the spot. Though he caught sight of himself spinning in this vortex he was helpless to aid himself: and even if he remembered the pulse of what had been he was incapable of recapturing it.

The mood would pass, he would feel it go out of him, slip away, discard him, and he would walk like someone taking first steps, amazed at the trivial cause of such a thing, look at what was before him with clarity, the mists of his locked-in fury evaporated.

Emily gave herself the simplest of all explanations for that which shook him so totally. Which was that he worked too hard. Having grown up where men could be made senseless through work, she could reconcile herself to that and would go no further.

His work indeed filled his day, or rather it made of it a structure into which he climbed to ride through the minutes and hours and weeks of toil, full pelt. Never had he felt so capable of work for though his body could be sated, it could not be satisfied. The marriage, the approaching child, the new place, the freedom from those who watched and knew him, the determination to make Pennington recognize his value and so be forced to offer a less insulting price at the next term – all this goaded him into the work. It was not so much that he put everything into his work as that he looked to the work to put everything into him. Labour was his school, his opportunity, the stuff of his imagination and increasingly the object to which his senses reached. He attacked it and wanted his blows returned, to go harder, daring it to give him limits.

It could be seen in the way he did everything. At his arrival at the farm, Pennington's miserly ways had left the biggest field unploughed. A good test for his new man. And John took it up willingly on his first day. He had been round with the horses the night before to brush them (they were so startled at being groomed – cleanliness and smartness had to pay their way on the open market with Pennington – that they almost kicked the stall down) had them harnessed in the morning and out into the lane as Pennington's slow feet shuffled to a stop at the unaccustomed sight of groomed horses, dressed and ready without any of the usual hindrances which necessarily beset such pinched methods as he generally employed. Once out of the lane and on the road to the far field, John swung out his boots, clacked his tongue at the two massive Clydesdales before him and had to prevent himself from flicking them into a trot or pulling them back into a rear of delight. The dawn air chapped his cheeks and clipped his ears – encouragement to go faster: the horses were restless and one was much stronger than the other – but he felt his muscles flex at this extra trial.

The land was stony, there would be many pauses for clearance, he would have to hold the plough deep, the ground would be tough under those stones – but this was nothing as he tied up his team and walked down the curved field. It sat like a shallow bowl upturned so that when he broke off he could see only the heads of the horses. He strode back to them straight up the line he would plough, his mind locked on keeping that line straight as a rod on his return.

As the day went, his back tightened until just to move was to cause pain. Gulls came in from the sea to swoop and turn around his head. A large stone almost buckled the iron tip of the plough. The weaker horse listed over to the stronger at the slightest relaxation of the biased hold. Heavy wet earth fastened itself on to his boots until at times it made a second pair so that he walked in earth on the earth; and a fine drizzle moistened his drawn face until it glistened whitely. But behind and before him lay the straight furrows. As he paused after turning the horses he would look up the hill to them, get down on one knee to confirm their straightness and stiffly rise to stand on tip-toe trying to peer over the brow and be clearly certain that they continued as immaculately on the other side. Then came his pleasure: for the field looked as if it had been waiting to be opened up, the fresh runnels and steep little banks of earth revealed by the plough attending him to put their regularity across the featureless ground. When he closed the gate in the evening, saw the greening hedges holding fast the long lines of dense brown earth, the gulls still turning in the dusk, darkness coming down the fellside to cover what he had done, the curtain to his performance, the field in which he had lived for that day was proof in use and beauty of his work: undeniable.

Unlike love. Feeling uncertain, he turned to what was sure; and it was through work that he reached out to fasten his transient grip on the planet.

There was nothing to stop him – certainly not Pennington who presumed on total service and was only moved to comment when that was not forthcoming. He could work fourteen, fifteen – all the hours God sent. There was nothing to hinder exploitation. Joseph Arch had formed an agricultural union in 1872 and himself gone into Parliament in the election following the labourers' first use of their vote; but the union fizzled out in the damp of the long agricultural depression and Arch saw his work undone. Pennington was in no danger from that quarter. Throughout England at that time, work was pitching so many men into a condition outwardly like slavery that the ugliness of outward forms, such as the new towns, was no wonder; they were sores, wounds, infections on the body of a land groaning with strain. Yet in so far as the condition was *not* slavish, freedom presumed if not enjoyed, work was a source, for some the only one, which could nourish those who fed it.

And there were many ways John could take on the Pennington farm; he could find an endless quantity of work and so strength need never be exhausted for want of application; difficulties he could discover in how to make do with rusting implements and fallow ideas – and this tested him, for the presence of difficulty was, to him, essential. He could achieve perfection in hoeing and win victories even over the weather. While, in his relationships with Pennington, there was the pleasure of a fight.

Pennington never thought of regarding John as an equal, and neither did John. He took a great delight in doing things before the farmer asked for them so that the man was stumped for a suggestion and would glare out of his small eyes vindictively until, after a certain play, John would propose his own next job. Or, seeing the chance, he would not do as ordered, wait until the storm burst then either prove the greater urgency of what he had done or argue once again, often with Jackson's support, about the worth of what had been originally pronounced. He eluded Pennington's table by taking all his meals with Emily just as he sometimes met his criticisms by direct action – as when Pennington had forced him to go out with a ramshackle cart – clearly in need of repair – which John had driven so hard and badly that a wheel had come off half-way to the field. This confrontation with Pennington led to no boasting on John's part and, though it was spurred on by the resentment he felt at being so cheaply hired, it did not express itself in personal dislike for Pennington with whom he would have said he got on 'well enough'. It was essential to him that he laid down his rules: were he not to do so he would, he knew, have been walked all over. For though Pennington was dulled, he would have trodden as hard on John as he possibly could, given a chance: his nature was to wear down things and people until they fitted smoothly into his own proportion. The hired lad who lived in the house would have run up a tree if asked. The only way to prevent that was to obstruct it – and that could be a pleasure.

The cottage and the farm; Emily and the work; what could be and what was; these facing sides made the cliffs for his valley. There was little time and less inclination to join that young gang of men – led by Jackson – who followed the dogs, played football, pitch-and-toss, went to dances and flung themselves into as much as possible before they met their match. And despite his talk to Emily about being 'on his own' and 'starting out again', he was rather shy in the village. As keenly as her he missed the thatch of long-known friendships: those daily minute acts of recognition which seem so transparent as to let in the whole world but which, once abandoned, are seen as walls which kept the elements out. Many a time he sickened to be back at home and had to force this denial of his hope back down his gullet. He was out of touch with himself as he appeared. For he thought that he had become surly, almost a recluse, part of nothing but the farm and the cottage – unaware that people were beginning to know him, note his habits, fit him in: he would have been astonished to know that he was generally regarded as cheerful and contented, that people liked to see him about his work, hear him whistling and singing to himself: he would have denied that he did so, unable to make a real connection with the village, bound by the spell which he had cast over himself.

Emily had encouraged him to go to The Cross about once a week but after her fight there he rarely stepped in the place.

One disappointment which followed this decision was that he missed the company of the iron-ore miners who used it. He admired the way they made as if to despise the work they did – and on such occasion he would sincerely join in with their contempt; that he himself had to be up in the small hours of morning, willing to go out and get ready for a day's scything the hay was quite another matter. He liked also their collective intrigues about wages – what they would do, what benefits they wanted – his own contribution to the Crossbridge Friendly Society appearing in comparison the most fragile camouflage against fortune. And one night, after he had seen them entering the pub as he drove past with a load of hay and rather sadly endured their chafing he determined to ask Emily if she would mind if he left farm work at Michaelmas and joined those better paid, fresher, altogether freer men in the iron-ore mines. She would not answer him at first. He knew that she objected but he thought the objection based on her unwillingness to leave the cottage, to go and live where she might be in daily contact with the women who had fought her, to uproot from the place she daily made more in her own image. None of these objections, when he proposed them to her were confirmed by that particular tone of conviction which he would have recognized as conclusive.

Patiently he waited on her reply. Her silence was objection enough and already, as when Seth had urged him to come to the pits, he was easily ready to pass the chance over if it would hurt her. The moods which had built up in him and despite himself broken on her and the work which had sated him but in his exhaustion made him no more than an object of fatigue some nights – these were now regretted and wished all away. They seemed the twistedness of uncertainty and selfishness beside the love which at this moment flowed between himself and his wife. He felt her resistance and, through that, was allied to her again. He would not go, she need not reply. He knelt down and rested his head against her and his face was broken into patterns by the fire.

It was not until some days later that she told him her reason. She could not think of his working under the ground, she said. She had laughed in admitting it, but the force of her fear was plain. No, as he took her hand and teased her that he would dig a hole in the garden for practice, to let her get used to it, no she could not bear it. This answer aroused such a feeling of gratitude in him – that he could be considered with such tenderness – that far from blaming her or telling her she was silly, as she had expected, he had kissed her and caressed her there in the kitchen.

Later, when he was at the work he most liked – on the hills going round the sheep, checking each one, he thought that perhaps it was because of the child; with one part of her in darkness she wanted the other in the light.

The impulse to change his work left him. Emily's concern again unlocked his feeling for her and he was glad that his work took him on to the hills where he could always see the cottage and watch over her, waiting for the birth. At that time they were beginning to cut down the plantations of spruce and larch and the woods sounded and re-sounded with the ringing of axes on the trees, bells for the birth of his child. Large carts took the wood down to the yards, the horses drawing the huge stacks higher than the cottages they passed, from a distance resembling antique engines of war.

John loved their new place then, the peace at the little tarn of Cogra Moss to which he would take Emily on Sunday evenings, and the strange feelings, at once wild and heavily peaceful, which swept him as he stood on top of Blake or Knockmirton and saw before him range on range of interlocking fells which seemed to shift as purposefully as clouds whenever he moved; and behind him was the plain, the sea. Tranquillity settled on him so drenchingly that it seemed his feet could never move from the spot; every sort of man had passed from the sea to these hills, all as transient as he would be – there was no fear in it; and the landscape seemed to change and swirl in front of him, as the light on the hills; the only thing which rested still was that cottage down there, with Emily.

In October she gave birth to a daughter – May. Soon after that came the term and John forced his original asking price out of Pennington who, urged on by Jackson, eventually allowed the benefits of the bargain to his side impress themselves on him. Emily's mother came up for a week just before Christmas and the child was baptized.

On one of his holidays, John went to Cockermouth and bought Emily a new shawl and May a christening cup and these purchases took all that he had saved from his first term's wages.

8

Just after the New Year, Isaac landed. The money he had won in the fight at Cockermouth had been lost on Seth's whippet, 'beaten by a *real* speed-merchant,' he said, 'Aa'd back her agin any other – but not agin that thing. And there was nobbut a snout in it for a' that. Anyway, she skint Seth and me – so Aa' had mesel hired by Parkinson o' Bothel. A right statesman he is: he's got that many hats it's a wonder his head doesn't get lost and he has hisself bath'd ivery other day! There's no dealin' with him! So Aa moped around theer for a bit – 'til Aa bowt this cock from a feller at Mealsgate – Silas Hocking his name; you won't know him – an' by the Lord he was a good 'un. Old wash 'is fancy breeches – Parkinson – he has spurs all polished up, hanging in his stable like some bluddy ornament. So Aa' clicked them a few times – he wouldn't miss them, ower busy keepin' 'is hats on – and away we went boys! Aa've nivver seed a strike like that cock hed. It could a' ripped the liver out of a sheep – pardon me missis. So Aa' collected a packet on that, fettled up our old lass, filled the jar, John, filled the jar! That's a man's life-work, filling the jar! – and Aa'm gonna hev messel a few months huntin'. Now then,' he turned portentously and politely towards Emily, 'Aa don't want to butt in on folks, if they're busy. Say the word an' Aa'll be off.' He was shy before Emily and attempted none of his jokes, altogether uneasy in any female company but that of his wife. 'An' you've got yersel a babby – they tek some cleanin'. But,' back, with relief, to John, his body shifting direction with the words, 'this Mellbreak pack's havin' a hell of a season, Aa've heard. Hardisty – he's huntsman now. Aa' knew him when he was whipper-in wid the Blencathra – he tacks like a bloodhound, yon fella. They tell me he could sniff them out of a rock face. An' your house is handy for it see? If Aa' could leave me bag here, missis,' again to Emily, 'Aa'd pay for me feed. Thou wouldn't see a great deal of me anyway – but this could be a basis, kinda thing, for me sport.' Putting the sport before himself lessened his fear of imposing on them.

There was no question, he must stay, and Emily was moved to see how grateful Isaac was for this simple offer of accommodation. Moreover, there would be no word more of his paying anything. This he would have protested at had he not realized the mutual embarrassment which would result, so he made a note in his mind to buy some pans for Emily with the money he had set aside for his keep.

The Mellbreak he spoke of was a pack of foxhounds which was followed on foot. No horses could hunt where these dogs travelled – on the fells. And possibly because of the pedestrian effort involved, there was no aristocracy to make the occasion courtly, nor that gentlemanly professionalism of men in love with horses and sport but also conscious of a fine nerve of correctness which gave to hunts such as those described by Siegfried Sassoon the knightly aspect of a personal quest. The Mellbreak hounds were owned by the tenant-farmers and their labourers and kept at home by them through the summer. In the autumn they would go to the kennels for the huntsman and his whipper-in to work into a pack. The huntsman himself did casual work in the summer and claimed huntsman's pay from September: his wage was met from donations by the various hunt committees in the villages from which he would set out, and the food for the dogs was as often as not provided, in dead carcasses and left-overs, by the men – themselves living on very strict budgets – who owned them.

When the season opened, the huntsman, in red coat, red waistcoat, red tie, hard black bowler, brown jodhpurs and thick nailed boots with black leggings going from ankle half-way up his calf would blow the small horn he kept in one of his pockets – and they were away. He would settle in a village, staying free of charge in the pub, and – as still today – hunt around that locality for about a week before moving on to the next spot. At that time his range was not as wide as it became, and most days he would be out around Loweswater Lake, hunting under the dominating cone of the Mellbreak fell from which the pack took its name.

All the men involved were mad on the sport. They would set aside good cuts for their dogs, go without a drink themselves if the hounds needed some sherry, look out for the foxes in the summer, note down bolt holes and badger sets, bet on the staying power or speed of their hounds, and talk, talk and talk of nothing but the hunt throughout the winter. Unlike Pennington such men did not bore on as if all seasons were one but saw where work could be quickly got away for that day, set aside, even neglected if the pack was running well.

The hunt was centred around Loweswater, and as the lake was no more than two or three miles across the fells from Crossbridge, Isaac was wise in his choice of a base. In fact his qualification to Emily, that she would not see a great deal of him, was well advised. As often as not he would be invited to stay with someone he had got talking to after the night's drinking which followed the sport, or the hounds would have taken him so far from Crossbridge that he would find a barn or knock on a cottage door for the night.

In a previous season Isaac had got in with two much older men who clearly remembered Peel's day: they had half a dozen dogs of their own. For a whole winter the three of them had chased everything over the countryside, often dropping with fatigue where they stopped at the end of a long chase, sleeping in their soaked clothes behind a hedge. That time nothing in the world mattered to him but the sport; the three men walked and clambered over the fells until all soreness of muscle gradually turned into a tirelessness of limb which made them capable of what appeared to others incredible endurance. As when they had chased one vixen four days and ended up in Lancashire for the kill; and being laid up in an abandoned cottage near Shap, they had seen the rare sight of weasels packing – racing down the hill wailing with hunger, more terrifying than anything Isaac had seen or heard in his life: that time had been the happiest in his life. He had learnt from the older men and grown to be as knowledgeable as they, he had listened to stories and details every night, he had been freely bound to the sport he loved more than anything, and in the empty hills felt himself as contented and as strong as he could be.

Strength was something taken for granted in the farming

areas; from childhood most of the men had lifted and hauled weighty objects, walked miles to bring sheep down from the fells or sow a field, pulled and heaved against horses and stones – their bodies were not puffed with that lovingly delineated muscle which in the sculpture of Greece imbues the forms of apparent gods with the shades of narcissism – they were often fat and bulky, as Isaac was, or tending to be scraggy like John – but their capacity for endurance above all set their bodies in an unvaunted power which was adamant.

On the occasions when Isaac *was* at the cottage, Emily enjoyed it greatly. He would talk for hours on end and, as he grew to know her better (though he always called her 'missis'), would make her laugh, her laughter warmed by the thought of these, her two men, as brothers. He set snares on Blake and sometimes brought her a rabbit or, once, a hare. Above all, his presence protected her, and she realized how much even now with the baby a few months old, she feared that Jackson might return to confuse her. He had come down once or twice since the birth, but the demands of the baby, or the entrance of Sally, had caused him to sheer off in disconsolate haste.

John, too, was glad to have his brother about the place and he grew to envy those early departures when Isaac would steer off across the field, his arms swinging beside his thick body like short oars on a boat, impatient to be with the hounds. John curbed this envy as best he could and even felt ashamed of it – and he realized that he could never be as adventurous as Isaac – but he could not eradicate it, and as his cold-swollen fingers cut up turnips for feed, or as he trudged up Knockmirton to look over the sheepfolds after a snowfall, he wished that he, too, could sail away on a free morning.

'Well why don't you come?' Isaac asked one night. May was upstairs in bed and the three of them were sitting around the fire, curtains drawn, light from the lamp toning everything in deep browns and blacks like Flemish kitchens, the wind rampaging around the isolated cottages, 'catching its tail,' said Isaac, 'chasin' itsel intil a bluddy fit – stupid ornament' – and John's eyes immediately went to question Emily's reaction and then moved away again, irritated at this dependence.

'Yes, why don't you, John?' Emily said. 'It would suit you.'

'It would suit him as snappy as a garter, missis. Aa can see thy John puffin' along there lad, tryin' to jump on to t' fox's back – it would buck him up, no trouble.'

'Ay, but I just have Sunday afternoons. What use is that?'

'Thous can claim a long week-end – Saturday dinner-time 'til Sunday tea-time – one week in three my lad – and mek no hesitation. How many time's thou taken it?'

'Hardly more than three or four,' said Emily.

'Well git stuck int' that Penitent o' thine. Tell him thou has a brother needs entertaining and tek a *full* Saturday – and t'Sunday to mek up for what thou's owed. He has thou workin' like stink. Thou mun throw some of his own muck back at him.'

'He doesn't drive me to the work,' John interpolated quickly.

'No – thou needs no whippin'. Thou's like our mother – she'll tidy up her grave and pop up in heaven with her pinny on. But that's all reet,' he conceded broadly, 'no harm in any man as likes to stick at it. But – be fair to thesel, John – kick up a bit!'

The challenge was met and after a direct and abrupt confrontation with Pennington first thing the following morning, John got his two days for the following week-end.

The hunt met on this Saturday morning outside Kirkstile Inn. The yard was full of hounds and the forty or so dogs sniffed and scuttered around the outbuildings incessantly. They would be loosed at nine o'clock. Hardisty was in the pub taking his nip of whisky with the landlord, and Isaac – greeted by all and besieged by the dogs so that he had to wade through them to the door – went in for 'a bit of the same'. The bar was full, though few of the men were drinking, and John, tingling from the walk across the fells with his brother, sat down delighted to see so many new faces, luxuriating in the knowledge that he would be two days away from the farm, from the cottage. Yes, even from Emily and the baby. As he looked around and grasped the glass of spirits which Isaac put in his hand, he considered himself in rare company.

The men were dressed in their working clothes, patched jackets dangling open, stained waistcoats lacing up their chests with tarnished buttons, boots and leggings and corduroy, hands thick as bricks, caps containing faces shining red from their beating with the weather. One or two had terriers which would be set down the holes, and John saw something he had not often seen – a bitch terrier and her pup chained together by a short length which led from collar to collar; they would run together all day, and every day until the pup had learned how to work with the hounds. He was like that with Isaac, he thought.

He was soon introduced to the company by his brother, a deceptively easy operation for the prevalent names were Joseph or John and convenience had bred from these such a confusion of Jos, Josters, Jobys, Josses, Joseys, Jontys, Jacks, Jackies and Tonts that the nicknames would have made things simpler – but those could not be assumed by John that came from intimacy or distant recitation only. Though he loved to be in this company he could not rid himself, however he sprawled in his chair, of the belief that what was natural for them was, for him, a treat. As if to emphasize this, the excitement had drawn all his boyishness onto his face and he felt over-young among them – while Isaac, not much older in years, stood there with his foot on the bar-rest planted, part of a generation altogether more substantial and assured than his own. And though he was away from Emily, John could not help remembering her face as she had kissed him that morning, the sleeping child, its arms flung out over its head as if floating in the cradle – thinking of them as if he had abandoned them, not merely left them for a couple of days – so that as he sipped his whisky and listened to the steady mutter of dialect around him he was irritated and bewildered by a sudden desire to return to his home, to reassure Emily that he loved her, to be with May, to tell them – what, he did not know. Nor could he understand his certainty that although there were men here no better placed than he, yet he would never be able to take leave of everything in the way they did: never be able to be out after his sport leaving his wife and children and work to look after themselves. For these reasons also, he was glad when nine o'clock approached and the huntsman moved out, the whipper-in called the dogs together so that they herded as a pack and moved, a jostling phalanx, up the lane. The horn sounded and the hunt began.

They went over to draw Holme Wood, a fox having been noted there on the return from a hunt a few weeks back, and John and Isaac stood outside the wood as the hounds streamed through the trees, their bark echoing the axe-blows which came across the valley from the wood at Mosser. The day was grey but there was nothing to prevent the scent rising strongly and the hounds were as skittish as kittens.

John looked around him. Everywhere the fells rose, their yellow-green winter grass cut across by the dark bracken, the scree grey, a dull glint of mineral which would later glitter under the sun. Even under such canopied cloud, the air seemed to leap at your flesh and bark its shins on your skin. Farms and cottages sat along the valley bottom and on the lower slopes as easily as rock-pools left by the tide; and from the intent scarlet face of Isaac to the top of the Mellbreak itself, the day was made for sport such as this.

Holme Wood yielding nothing, they moved on to a small planting at the foot of Little Dodd. The hounds clamoured – but for no more than a hare, and John laughed at the electric hopping of that animal as its white tail flashed up the fell-side. Hardisty called the dogs back to him and they went up the Mosedale Beck, right into the fells, their sides rising steeply. This was the time for conserving talk and energy and the two or three dozen men tramped steadily through the peáty bottoms, skirted the bouldering outcrops, said little, intent on Hardisty, scarlet, at their head. Before them the hounds fanned out until the bare hillsides seemed to breed dogs out of those cavities and clefts which pocked them. Heads to the ground, feet padding ceaselessly, long tails swaying gently, the brown, black-white patched dogs muzzled for the scent. They went the length of that climbing valley without raising more than a crow. Even the sheep seemed unimpressed, merely scattering a few yards distant and then standing to look on the procession, rigidly still.

It was after midday that the fox was raised – down towards Burtless Wood beside Buttermere. It turned immediately and ran back the way the men had come and John had a view – the fox racing across a skyline, clinging to the ground it seemed, tail straight up in the air to leave no scent. But the hounds had the view as well, and they were after it.

It gave them a hard run. Into Mosedale bottom where it crossed the beck three times, around Hen Comb, behind Little Dodd, back the other direction towards Kirkstile. They lost it for a few minutes there until someone halloed they had seen it slipping up the beck – and they were off again.

John seemed to swoop and roll among the fells as he followed the chase. The field spread out, the hounds themselves strung along a quarter of a mile, two or three of them off on a scent of their own – lost to the day's sport: one hound cut its paw so badly on a wall that it dropped out, the terriers scurried along, the tied pair, like a diminutive canine monster. There were halloos every few minutes and the men themselves became hunters, climbing the heights in anticipation of a vantage which would give them a total view and enable them to race down when the kill was near, cutting up the loose screes and perhaps finding that the valley they reached was already clear of the chase, making for the badger sets down at High Nook which the fox itself could be expected to make for (they had been blocked the previous night), suddenly, by the action of that lush red-brown fox, spread out over a full range of hills and valleys.

Isaac's plan was to stay with the whipper-in. A younger and faster man even than Hardisty who would cut off this and hedge that, he held down his job to a great degree by his ability to stay close to the hounds – even when they broke and raced as furiously as they did now. No man could keep right up with them on that ground – but as near as anyone could get, the whipper-in did. With Isaac at his shoulder and John, sometimes gasping in agony, behind. As if to find yet more use for his breath, Isaac yipped and hooped all the way along – his belly shaking with the efforts he made, the hills riccocheting with the barks and shouts, and on his face an unshakeable grin. 'What a day, lad!' He shouted back at John. 'O, look at yon stupid hound! What a size – eh? Did you see him lad? Did you see that brush – like a bluddy Christmas tree. Eh! Come on! Come on! My God, they're scalin' those screes. We'll slither down yonder, lad, like fish on slab. Yip! Yip! That big hound'll hold out. My money's on that 'un – Bellman it is. Go on boy! Look at him lift! Come on, lad! Come away! Eh! What sport!'

They killed him down near Holme Wood where they had started the day and the early winter darkness rapidly fastened over the sky; the tops of the fells were in total darkness as they arrived back at the pub, lamp-lit windows, the men dispersing across the fields to eat before drinking, a few crows settling in the tops of the bare trees, John's legs shaking unsteadily as he made his way down the twisting lane.

Isaac insisted on buying John the first drink – a pint of ale was demanded and Isaac thrust the poker into it before draining it in one.

'That's more like it!' he exclaimed. He shook his belly. 'Oh! It's swimmin' around in there like a good 'un, John, sailin' home, boys.' He bent forward as if to listen.

'It's a grand property you've got down there,' said the landlord of Isaac's stomach.

'O my lad! This is an investment! There's fellas would queue up to put money into this thing. Aa was once at Appleby an' a fella offered me ten pounds cash for this corporation o' mine. Give us the munny, Aa said, an' Aa'll feed her up a bit wid it. What they call *interest*, see. Thou can watch they ten pounds grow, Aa said. My Godfathers, he was a fool to back out of it! Come on then John – sup up! We must have lost twelve pints of sweat clamberin' up that Mellbreak. Same again!'

'They tell me Bellman was up there first,' said the landlord, opening the tap on one of the large wooden barrels which stood on a ramp behind the bar.

'He was!' said John. 'Thou should a' seen it go into that wood – eh, Isaac? It could have tackled a wolf! It led all the way – didn't it, Isaac?'

'It did, lad, it did. Here,' he handed over a pint 'stick a poker in that – it'll sizzle thee gullet a treat. Fry up his insides – won't it landlord? Now then there's taty pot on if my snifter's correct.'

'It is.'

'Well thou's got two clients here'll dig into it.'

'We'll have to wait of Hardisty. He should be back from his kennels in half an hour.'

'True,' Isaac smiled. 'He did a trick today I haven't seen for a long time, thou knows.' Foot on the rest, elbows on the bar, head squat on his shoulders, Isaac settled down. 'It was just when they came out of that bit of a wood see . . .'

The taty pot was served in the kitchen. Eight of them sat down to it and a full stew-pot disappeared. Then eight apple tarts were brought in and two jugs of custard. Plates of tea-cakes, butter and jam, cheese and cakes followed. The landlady came in to watch them eat as one might go to a circus.

'Well, missis,' said Isaac, whose trenchering capacities had astounded her 'that was a very good tea. Thanks are due. And if you've no objection – Aa'll have a pipe at yer table.'

He smoked and then snoozed for about an hour, head tilted back, mouth open, boots kicked out before him – hugely lodged in the round-backed wooden chair.

John would have liked to sleep – he was tired enough – but he could not. He was too excited, still not quite able to believe that he was to have another day off, still perplexed by his longing for Emily – if only she were with him, he kept thinking, and the fact that he had the thought irritated him more than the thought itself. So he interested himself in the quiet chat of Hardisty and the men around him, afraid of missing a single drop of that day.

When Isaac woke up, the pub was full, the men having had their supper and come on. In the bar above the open fire was a deep rectangular rise in the wooden ceiling, making a platform in the room above on which the band performed for the dance. The women and girls went up by a staircase which allowed them to avoid the bar but there was another staircase, a short wooden flight of stairs in the corner, which led directly up to the dancing room and trays of drinks were taken up by that route. It was here that the landlord recouped for keeping the Huntsman and his whipper-in free of charge – for the knowledge that the Hunt was at the pub brought people in from miles around, especially at the week-end. When John went outside into the yard, he could hardly get across to the lavatories, with the horses and carts, dogs tied to doors, girls swirling around the foot of the stairs – Emily would have loved to dance! – a few early drunk men playing pitch-and-toss by lantern light. The enjoyment and laughter of such a crowd affected him greatly; after his constricted existence in the cottage this was like a blast from a new world; it intoxicated him and yet still, still, he did not know why, there was the feeling that it was not for him – that he had made his choice in marriage and a family and work and this was one of the sacrifices.

Back in the bar the songs were starting up and the men stood as a jostling crowd, Hardisty's scarlet a fiery hub. Again, as in John's cottage, it was brown which ripened all colours, the oak settles and beamed ceiling, the oak clock from which the dead fox hung down, teeth stiffly unclamped; brown was the predominant cloth for the suits, yellow brown the light from the lamps, amber the ale, red and brown the faces; and the dialect in its tone had a matching glow to it, so that as John stepped into the noisy arena, he felt ripened by the richness of it all.

Some of the men knocked the fox so that its blood ran and they collected a few drops into their beer. Isaac was squeamish about that and bellowed to John:

'Some of them would eat the bluddy thing raw if it would bring them a good hunt tomorrow! Don't thee try the blood, lad – it clogs the bladder.'

From upstairs came the sound of a fiddle and piano, and the ceiling shuddered, dipping like a spring mattress as the dancers got under way. John wanted to be up there with the music: the pounding of men's voices, men's faces, the congested hunt of men at their drink and their talk, stifled him. Yet to dance with another than Emily should not be imagined.

'We'll be up those stairs in a bit, lad. Shorten that long face. And don't look at thee breeches! It's nobbut muck. They expect it after a hunt – thou won't be out of place. Eh? Emily? Eh? Damn this pandemonium! Thou's goanna *dance*, lad, I hope! Not run off wid another woman. Eh! What's thee worry? Come away me lad! Come away! Give us a tootle, Hardisty! Huntsman – blow that horn.'

The sound rang out and Halloos sounded throughout the bar. Then from upstairs the dancers echoed it with their own Halloo! The bar answered, the dance once more replied – and the long hunting cry sounded between the two companies in longer and longer wails until it resembled no earthly cry but was like the sucking of wind and forging water in a cave.

'That's better! Grand! Grand! O, my lovely lads one and all!' said Isaac.

'A song! Give us a song Isaac!'

'Ay. Tune that throat of thine to music.'

'Use your bellows, Isaac! Blow us one up.'

'Here we are then,' Isaac announced, game for anything. 'Aa'll even put down me mug for it. We'll start wid a Tragedy. Very short.' He coughed and held out his hands, the whites of the up-turned palms suddenly making vulnerable that stout cask of him. He recited very slowly.

'There was an old woman had three sons,
Jerry, James and John.
Jerry was hung. James was drowned,
John was lost and never found:
And that was the end of her three sons.
Jerry, James and John.'

'More! More!'

'Right lads. A comedy. A bit longer this. Needs a push in the chorus region.'

'There was a jolly beggar,
He had a wooden leg.
Lame from his cradle,
And forced for to beg.
And a begging we will go, we'll go, we'll go;
Come away lads! And a begging we will go!

A bag for his oatmeal
Another for his salt
And a pair of crutches
To show that he can halt
Away lads – And a begging we will go, we'll go, we'll go;
And a begging we will go.

'Seven years he begged ...'

By now the ale had run out and back again through every vein in John's body, and his cares were flushed away. This was the life! He beat time with his mug before him and as Isaac called to another man and then that other to another, the fumes from the ale and the steam from the men infused the singing with such a density of pleasure that hefe lt he could curl up in it forever and wish never to be disturbed.

'A speech, Hardisty, a speech!' someone shouted. 'Give us a speech, give us a blow, give us a song, and then tek us up those stairs Hardisty – there's women like a hunt as much as any man!'

Hardisty nodded – solemn and starched with drink he was. Whiskies brought for him had been slopped into his ale until it was so spiked that one gulp would have set him reeling had he not made certain – his trick for drunkenness – that his feet were a yard apart and his bootlaces loosened. But it was his place to round off the drinking in the bar and so with momentous pomp, he went the three yards to the fox and nudged some blood into his mixture.

'Thou was a good 'un lad. A game 'un.' This spoke most earnestly to the dead fox before he made his slow turn to the rest of the bar. He surveyed all. Caps askew, waistcoats unbuttoned, pipes growing out of faces, the landlord filling the mugs, the bar crammed and tumbling with men as stout and braised-faced as himself.

'A speech, a blow and a song,' he began, thoughtfully. 'Well, as for the song – that'll be John Peel, lads. It can be no other. He was our own man and he was on foot me lads, like we are, and he lived and died his life for huntin'. And may we do as well, lads. We'll sing his song – the best huntin' song there is – and the greatest song ever written about any man, dead or alive. So that's the song.' He paused. 'As for the blow – we'll I'll be askin' Jasper Fell to do that. If I blow now, lads, you'll all be splattered wid ale – because I've a skinful under me this night as could float an armada.' Slowly he half-turned once more, so that the fox was brought into his misting vision. 'As for the speech – I'll go one better! I'll give you a toast. And here it is. To the Fox, me lads, to Fox!'

After an hour at the dance, which went on until three o'clock, John began to sober up – but wish to as he might, he could not bring himself to ask a woman to dance with him. He joined in when they made two circles, one of men the other of women, to do the Roundelay – and Isaac even managed to get him up for the Hooligans which started with the men and women in straight lines up and down the room; but that was all. He did not feel sorry for himself, being happy enough to watch the others, especially Isaac, whose torn and mucky clothes and figure were carried on a most nifty pair of legs, while his gallantry, being rather drunken, escaped buffoonery only by a hair's breadth. John sat near the band and watched the man with the fiddle: the sound of it made him think of his grandfather – and he saw that he, too, must have enjoyed nights like this. As he could not come like Isaac, perhaps he could learn the fiddle and come as his grandfather had done: Emily would be fast asleep: May long in her cradle with her arms flung back: he would have to buy her a present to mark his absence . . .

Isaac woke him up and they went out. There was no hunting on Sunday and the plan was to use the night to walk over into Buttermere where, illicitly, there would be cock-fighting in the early morning.

'They're huntin' down at Lorton on Monday,' Isaac said. 'By godfather that should be real! There's foxes down there breed like rabbits.'

'Aa'm comin' with you,' said John.

'No, lad. Thou said thou'd be back a' Monday.'

'Aa'm havin' one more day's huntin',' John replied, doggedly. 'And Pennington can do what he likes wid his work. Aa'm havin' one more day.' She would have to accept it, he thought, and was irritated at his shiver of unhappiness. He was afraid to acknowledge the underlying thought that he might want to be rid of her.

'But thy missus'll be expectin' thee, lad.'

'Aa'll send a message. She'll understand.'

Isaac's worry ceased.

'Ah. She will! That's correct! She's a real 'un, John. Thou's catched a good 'un.'

There was not much moon, but the two men were not in a hurry. Isaac had a quarter bottle of brandy for when the cold hit them – as it did when they felt the night wind come off Crummock Water.

'Look at that lake, lad,' Isaac murmured. 'Just look at her. She's the finest thing thou'll see in a lifetime.'

They walked along the track, under the dragon-like crags, the lake to their right, the slow tread of their step building up a rhythm against which the sky, the line of fell-tops, the trees and walls, even that strange silver spread of water, could make no attack.

'Stop!' Isaac whispered. 'Listen.' He put his arm around the younger man's shoulders and they heard sheep scatter in a field above them.

'That'll be Fox,' said Isaac, beaming. 'Come away, boy! Come away!' he shouted into the dark. 'What sport, John, eh? What sport!'

9

Emily had been relieved to see John go. As he left the cottage with Isaac she felt happier than she had done for a long time.

Since the birth of the baby, she had been unable to cope with his restlessness as once she had done; at times she feared it might escape her altogether and turn into something which could harm both of them. Isaac mopped up John's spillings of mood like gravy off a plate and she believed that the two days would satisfy at least some part of the mainly unspoken chafing which threatened to bring him to despair.

There was so little for John to do except work. He had not the money nor – it now appeared – the inclination to join in with those married men from the pits who met at The Cross most nights. He had not the time to keep a dog or follow a sport. He had done most of what could or needed to be done around the cottage and though he enjoyed challenging Mr Pennington, it gave diminishing returns. While the way in which he was driven to work by himself frightened her. Sometimes he would come in so riven by it that he could neither eat nor sleep, and she had to pull off his boots, even help him with his jacket and more than once abandon him in the chair beside the fire – so cleft in sleep that she could not hope to disturb him until the morning. If only he would take it less hard. And not be so concerned that herself and the baby should be lacking nothing. She knew that to find the baby crying as he opened the door on his return from the farm drove into him, his face tightened with irritation – and yet he would neither explode into temper nor leave her alone for the few minutes needed to calm the child – but force himself to be pleasant, to relieve her of the baby, to shush away his meal until May should be quietened. And she could see his hands shaking as he nursed the baby. Yet at other times she knew that May gave him the same kind of peace as that which was on his face as he returned from a rare solitary walk among the fells.

Sally came over in the afternoon – bursting to tell Emily that she had talked to Jackson Pennington that morning. And he had said this, and she had said that, and wasn't it funny how some men were *better*-looking close up and others worse? And he had asked her if she was going to the dance the following week! *Asked* her. As if he wouldn't be bound to know that she was going – and so he *must* have intentions. There was a feverishness about Sally's delight which again riled Emily though she did not let it show. She thought that the younger woman was whipping herself on to affection, demanding a Great Passion as her right, greater than anyone's as she was so special. No, she calmed herself, she was just a little sad – though why should she be? – at seeing someone so free. But she would be silly to deny a place to her observation – and Sally *was* making too much of that most casual meeting. Probably, those eyes sucking at his face, poor Jackson had felt forced to ask her about the dance out of self-preservation! It was not that, though, not that! There was a coy vulgarity about Sally's appreciation of her new sexuality, a switching from superiority to over-humble inquiry – truly a fever, which slyly and whimsically mocked that love she herself had for John and May. She was glad when she left. Then she was sorry to have thought so badly of her friend.

It was pleasant to spend the long afternoon playing with the baby, no deadline to meet with a hot meal. She set May on the couch which her mother had bought them in a sale, and tickled her until both of them were laughing, tiny fingers and the softest palm imaginable tucking themselves around her forefinger and tightening there. She shook her hair loose all over the child and tears sprang to her eyes as the baby pulled at it. Emily felt that she could gobble the baby up with love. Sometimes she was so afraid of how much she loved her that she would neglect her for a morning – letting her cry on, not coddling her at all, being strict where she would have been soft – but that always ended up with rushing over to her and hugging her as if she had been away for a week. More often, she wondered that John might worry that there was any love left for him – so much was given to the baby: and then she saw that love was not a capital amount, limited and exhaustible, but a source itself which could feed many streams.

When May was in bed, then she missed John. She took down *Silas Marner* and skipped one or two of the pages of dialect which tired her. She wanted to see Silas alone in that cottage in the woods, the loom working, the gold growing into the earth. She could not read for long – the silence about her unnerved her. Her eyes looked at the fire and the logs' heat burned on her pale skin; her face was thinner since the birth. Soon she was in bed, but unable to sleep until she lifted May out of the cradle and brought her in with herself.

Sunday would bring him back again and the day had a point. She spent the morning cleaning, the afternoon baking, and spread the table with food more than John had seen since his wedding day. She had dug into her savings for this meal and got young John Wrangham whom she had seen in the fields to go up to The Cross and bring two jugs of ale. She expected them at about five.

As the minutes and then hours passed, the table appeared more and more forlorn. Nothing was removed, nothing eaten – but the meal seemed to diminish in size, the fire to glow less brightly, herself to turn from condoning even pleasurable annoyance to worry.

She did not stop to wonder at the knock on the door – Isaac might have come on ahead and he would have knocked – but flew over to open it, smoothing down her apron and, after lifting the latch, reaching her hands up behind her head to comfort her hair. It was Jackson.

Emily stepped back in surprise and this was taken as permission to enter which he did. To avoid unnecessary proximity Emily retreated further, to the other side of the laden table she had set in the middle of the kitchen. Jackson pulled off his cap and stood just inside the open door.

'It's a fine welcome, that,' he indicated the table, 'for any man.' He paused. 'I'll close this door if you don't mind. It's cool out.'

He turned to close the door, very deliberately lifting the bar over the latch and Emily shivered to see the blond hair waving down to his clean collar, the tall, best-suited back of him slender and at ease in her home. She put her hand to her throat where she had just that morning sewed a little frill at the neckline of her blouse – and wished she could tear off the frill before he turned to her. Her fingers tugged at it, then dropped as he once more faced her.

'Yes,' he repeated, softly, 'it's a fine spread.'

'He's a fine man!' she retorted, a little shrill her voice. She was taken aback by its sound.

'He must be,' said Jackson. 'He must be that, Emily, to have thee for a wife.'

'Why did you come?'

'Aren't you pleased to see me?' He smiled gently and she thought – he's drunk; that would help explain it: but he might be dangerous in drink; that would make it worse.

'You – you – are you drunk?' she asked, timidly.

'No.' He laughed. 'No, I don't need drink to fetch me here.'

'John'll be back soon,' she said, quickly looking at the clock. 'He said he'd be here at nine. In five minutes.' He was unimpressed. 'Isaac'll be with him,' she threatened.

'No he won't.' Jackson spoke very slowly as if to lengthen

his time so. 'Word came to The Cross that they won't be back today. They're off to Lorton. They'll be back tomorrow.'

'Oh.' She felt a self slip off her, run off like water – but she recovered immediately.

'So you only dare to come down here because you know that neither of them's about.' She paused. He did not appear chastened. 'Maybe you didn't need drink – but you needed . . .'

'What?' He asked.

'I don't know. O please go, Jackson. Thank you for bringing the message. Please – go.'

'I'm hungry,' he said. 'Looking at that table's made me hungry. I think I'll have some supper.'

'No!' She made as if to dart across to him. 'No,' she repeated, stopping as she saw him move to meet her.

'You wouldn't begrudge a man some feed, would you, Emily? It's a long walk from The Cross.'

'It is not.'

'It seemed a day's journey, lass,' he replied, gently.

He calmly sat down and began to eat.

'Would there be anything to drink?'

Emily's throat was too dry for her to be able to let words slip through. She shook her head.

'What's that there?' He pointed at the jugs in the hearth.

'No.'

'I'll get it myself then.'

As he pushed back the chair she cried out. He looked at her and shook his head.

'I won't do you any harm,' he said. 'I won't harm your little finger.'

She put her wrist to her mouth to stop herself from crying again and he nodded before bringing one of the jugs over to the table.

'Sit down!' he said, sharply. 'I'll do you no harm! If I'd a wanted to force myself on you I could a done when I came in. Nobody could hear us down here. Sit down, woman!'

Emily sat on the couch on which she had played with May just a few hours before. She looked at the ceiling as if hoping to see through it and reassure herself that the baby was all right.

'Don't be stupid, Emily. I'll do nobody any harm. I haven't forgotten.'

'Neither have I,' she retorted, suddenly less afraid through this reference to that first time. It could be no worse than that. And she had survived.

Jackson pushed his plate away from him: it bumped into a plate of teacakes which tumbled down: he pushed harder and more scones and cakes spilled. The table was spoiled. A childish action.

'That wasn't very clever,' she said, gaining yet more confidence from this nervous display of his. 'And if John and Isaac aren't coming back tonight – they'll be back tomorrow,' she warned.

'Do you still want me to go?' he asked, uncertain now that the balance had inexplicably tilted in her favour.

'Yes. Yes I do. I'm married to John Tallentire and you've no business being here in my house.'

'But what can I do, Emily?' He stood up, a hand reached out towards her. 'I can't stop wanting you. I can't stop blaming myself for what I did to you.'

'Well you'll have to learn to stop. And I've long ago forgotten what happened that first time. So can you.'

'You've forgotten.'

'Yes I have!' She attacked. 'I've other things to think about, you know.'

But she had gone too far. The lie about forgetting what happened that first time was less damaging to herself than this over-reaching disparagement. For as soon as she said it, both of them knew that she *did* think about him – and Jackson smiled.

'You still think about me, Emily. However many other things there are.'

'I think about all sorts of people.' She paused. Then with a weak throat she added, 'I think about Sally. It's *her* you should be visiting.'

'I care nothing for her,' he said evenly. 'Does that please

you? Are you glad I care nothing for Sally? Well if that's a way – I'll go further. I care nothing for Mary or Martha or Janet or Jane or for anybody but Emily – and that Emily, you. But why doesn't that make you more glad? Tell me that, and I'll go.'

'I can't tell you.'

'But you must.'

'There's nothing to tell. I like you as much as a married woman can like a single man who's been kind to her –'

'– and terrible!'

'– I *can* put that out of my mind even if I can't really forget it. You've been kind, by staying away.'

'Only by that?'

'Yes.'

He stood silently, looking into the fire, dejected once more.

'Don't you see how impossible it is?' she asked.

'I see now.'

'But it was impossible any time. I'm married, Jackson.'

'But it doesn't matter! I don't give a damn for any marriage. It doesn't change a woman – just gives her a little ornament to dangle in her hand.'

'If that's what you think I'm sorry for you!'

'Yet if you had said any different,' he continued, as if she had not spoken, 'then you wouldn't be what you are. And what you are I love, Emily. There it is. Love.'

'Please go,' she murmured. 'O please, please go.'

'Come with me.'

She shook her head and would not speak.

'And I believe if I stayed and talked and talked,' he said, more loudly than before, almost bitterly, 'and talked and talked to you, and told you enough times I loved you I believe I could wear you down this night, Emily. Even you.'

But she sat rigidly still.

He took up his cap and swept some of the scones off the table. 'Say something!'

She stayed silent.

'My God, I could come across and beat you away with me. *Say* something!'

'Go.'

'You'll give me nothing? Not a kiss, not a kind word, nothing?'

'No.'

'Damn you Emily! And damn your precious marriage!'

He went and the slam of the door woke May to whom Emily ran, crying as unhappily as her child.

10

The subdued and nervous mood in which Emily greeted his return matched John's anxiety. Neither told the other that there was a flaw in the love which had never till now threatened to lose the chance of regaining what had appeared to both of them as an original perfection. John said nothing of that night after the dance when he had wanted to be rid of her and the thought of her for the first time ceased to be there. Emily did not mention Jackson and buried her lips in John's neck to forget, forget that perhaps Jackson was right, she knew that he was right, had he stayed on and on, she would have given in – blaming weariness maybe, but still, O John, she would have given in. In this false mood they told each other that they were happy.

John was relieved when Isaac left – though the sight of his striding off there on his own made him sad at the time. For with Isaac he had lost himself. With Isaac he had thought – why *not* just jump up and leave Emily and May for weeks on end? Why *not* spend life after sport? Why not dance with other women? Why not go off with them? Why work? Why love one alone? But then he realized that what could be limited in Isaac, by the grip he had on his own affairs, would spread further and further in his own softer hold; feared that by following Isaac he would grow to imitate him and knew that he would make a mess of it and end up as nothing.

But being with his brother had defined him for himself a little more. He had been away from Emily and his home – and two days was enough. He had not enjoyed the Monday hunt at

Lorton; all the time he was longing to be back. Back to his work, too, for in the end he felt that hunting on a Monday – a working day – not a holiday in anybody's book – was a waste. Of what? He did not ask, but waste he felt in the day, the hounds, the walking he did, the talking, in the drink at dinner-time, on the fields he walked through and in himself from his dragging legs to his disapproving reflections.

More than this the possibilities spread before him by Isaac made him afraid that the way he had chosen to live – for he had a choice – was most insubstantial, being so easily threatened. This led him to attempts to attack the origins of the fear, to work even harder, to stick even closer to the cottage, to sign on with Pennington again at Whit and again the following November.

Emily, who had been more unhappy than she thought she would be at Isaac's departure, was more than compensated by the relief she felt when, about the same time, Sally told her that Jackson had left home again, 'this time for good,' said Sally, 'he told Jo Dalzell he would never come back again. Never!' And if she felt so happy – and she did, she sang all that day and was lapped in a sweetness of temper she could taste in her mouth – then everything was surely all right again, she thought.

Mr Pennington made a short comment on Jackson's exit and drafted back another son.

In her release of enthusiasm, Emily made her first constructive effort to get into the village. Before now she had excused her disinclination, first on account of having to put the cottage in order and later of devoting all her time to May. She had even begun to blame John for bringing her to Crossbridge – and all Sally's chatter could not make up for that net of relations and born friends she had found such unacknowledged safety in at home. At one stage, she had worried him into considering a move down into the Wigton area – 'not Wiggonby itself,' she said, 'though if you could ... but somewhere around there, John, to be nearer.' 'Nearer *my* lot an' all,' he said. 'Aa thowt thou wanted rid of them all as much as me. There's no need for a great gaggle of friends, Emily. We can stand it on our own, can't we?' Nevertheless she had worried him with her suggestions – and now, when a few months had stamped the certainty of Jackson's disappearance on her and, most finally, she heard from Mrs Pennington that he had gone to London and joined the army to go abroad – now her enthusiasm pushed out its waves to unclog all the silt that had checked her love. It was all that she wanted. In earnest of this, she made her efforts to be more part of the village.

What she enjoyed, however, were those occasions when everyone was part of the crowd – the day of the Club Fair (called a Walk) when the band played all day in the field behind The Cross; or in that Autumn the time the Potters came and stayed for a month – selling their plates and china by organizing fêtes and sports, competitions, raffles, socials, Nights of Daftness when the men would line up with their hands tied behind their backs to try to eat a teacake dripping with treacle and hanging on a string, or push their faces into a barrel of water to eat the bobbing crab-apples; she liked to go to the concerts at Martelmas and take May to the children's do at Christmas eve – willing and happy to go anywhere where there was a crowd and she could nod without having to stop and talk. But for the more personal matters, being in the chorus at the concert, serving in the pub as many of the young women did on the nights of the harvest supper, or accepting the invitation to tea sent by the vicar's wife, so regulating her visits to the shops that she met the same people every time and thus was slowly absorbed into and identified with a particular group – for these she had no taste. Perhaps not having done it right away made her feel awkward, as if her action was saying 'I was waiting to see if you were good enough for me,' or, worse, 'I thought I could manage on my own but I can't' – whatever it was, she felt that she obtruded into any group she met, while in a crowd, she was as happily numbered as the rest. More certainly, however, her meetings with Jackson had left her with the fear that somehow knowledge of them was carried around the village: that Jackson had said nothing she could have sworn – for Sally's ears would have pricked at the slightest wind carrying that name and yet she brought no gossip, not a suspicion. Still, Emily would not be sure, and this made her most wary.

In the winter John bought a hound, but sold it soon afterwards and got himself a concertina. He would play on it every night, no matter what time he came in or how tired he was, he would go upstairs and play and sing to May, and as she heard the thin, lightly-crushed sounds of the concertina and May's small voice laughing and singing out of tune, then Emily felt that such happiness as she had known before was but a girlish affair compared with this.

That summer she was pregnant again but she hardly felt the child, it was so small inside her. Seth came up to see them a few times and she was amused at the contrast he made – so white and serious – with Isaac, but happy to see John talking to him and watch the brothers as they left her comfortable (after the four of them had walked together to Cogra Moss) and went off to scale up the screes on Blake Fell, John pressing Seth to physical action as Isaac had pressed him. Then she would look at the small, perfect tarn in the hollow of the hills and switch from that to the men and then to May stumbling along beside the fence, falling over the bull-toppins or reed-tufted grass. Two boys were splashing in the cold shallows and a man had waded out almost to the middle to fish: she could see John and Seth scrambling, black figures on the slatey screes, and felt the child inside her so quiet. So different from May, as peaceful as the hills around.

But as the time for the birth came near, she could no longer be as peaceful. The child hardly plumped her even, and when she felt a movement it was so slight, so faint that she worried. She retreated from the village and once more allowed the fields which cut off her contact with it to become her boundary. She demanded that John take her down to her mother and then, after he had gone to arrange it with Pennington (for which necessity she despised him at that moment), she would cry and say she was sorry, being silly, of course she wanted the child here, in her own home, with him. She would go to bed with May and let him come in to a fireless kitchen, no supper, no welcome – and then, after listening to his clumsy efforts, rush down to make reparation. The hills which she had looked out on and loved angered her by their unchanging, unyielding, uncomforting aspect. She woke at the first patter of rain on the tiles and felt the pellets of water drum on to her motionless belly.

Ephraim was born in November. The birth gave her little pain, but to make better the malformed, spindly body of her child she would have endured anything. The doctor when he arrived the next day confirmed the midwife's private opinion; that the boy would be lucky to live until Christmas.

That he lived longer was due to the total subjection of herself which Emily made before this child. Throughout the winter and into the spring the cottage was concentrated around that poor body whom the slightest chill would threaten. John took May out of Emily's way whenever he could, but the action was barely noticed as he and May and all about her was barely noticed. Ephraim, Ephraim – she prayed and nursed and willed him to live and grow strong. There was nothing John could do – the bond between the mother and the sickly child filled the cottage and no other feeling could penetrate.

John worked but the work lost its meaning to himself. It was necessary for the money for Emily and the child, but that had not been the wheel which had driven it to become such a provider of life. The work changed its nature and became a weight to be shifted; or he would be crushed under it. What he had thought undeniable did deny him; his labour yielded nothing.

John spent the night of his twenty-first birthday watching over his son while Emily lay forced to sleep on the chair beside them. He kept the fire going and milk ready. A scattering of hail tattered across the window pane. His boots stood before the fire, growing and shrinking before his eyes. Emily's hands were shut and her head sat brokenly on her shoulders, pulling against the shawl he had put around her neck. Afraid of her now, even the help he gave was offered guiltily, almost shamefully intruding on his wife and the baby.

The boy died in June and they buried him on a bright clear day with the noise from the haymaking and the sight in the distance of the big marquee rising behind The Cross for the Club Walk. Emily was frozen at the small grave and she did not return his look but kept her head bent to the ground as they walked down the short path to the church-gate.

He promised her he would leave Crossbridge at the end of his term, in November, but 'It's too late,' was all she would reply.

Days later, on a hillside, looking down at the shut door of the cottage he felt himself to be spent of all life, love between Emily and himself blighted by a birth which should have nourished it.

II

By the end of the summer John was desperate. He could make nothing of Emily, and himself he hardly recognized. Only the work thudded through him with any comprehended regulation, and that now beat inside his body as loudly as an amplified heart-beat, straining to burst.

He finished at tea-time one Saturday afternoon and set off for Embleton to see his grandfather. The twelve miles was mostly downhill and he went quickly and easily, his back to the fells, before him the plain and the sea. There was no clear idea in his mind as to why he should want to see the old man or what he would say to him: he had thought of taking May with him as if to use the child as an introduction – but Emily would not let her go. He wanted to talk to someone, perhaps even just to touch them as sick people needed to touch a saint for a cure: there was no one else he could turn to.

The day was windless, a long white harmless ridge of cloud above the Solway, trees in full leaf, cattle and horses grazing in the field, the sun warm on his face, it would be light almost to midnight even now and the cheerful clop of the horses that passed him, the chatter of two young women holding their hats, long skirts covering the pedals of their bicycles, a vicar in a trap with a bull-mastiff sitting unmoving beside him – all mingled with the ease of the descent, the appeasing rhythm of a walk to lift John's hopes sufficiently for him to look out from the shutters he had drawn on himself and breathe the balm of the long Edwardian afternoon. Privileged. For in an order in which privilege plays such a striking and important part, even those who are its props can yet occasionally be touched by a belief that they, too, are privileged. So, as John walked down to Embleton, he felt that a grace had understandingly permitted him the few hours off, that providence was working for him in the steadiness of his health, the roof he had for his family, the grandfather he would see; that luck was with him, waiting at the end of the golden afternoon.

He knew that the old man had retired on his seventieth birthday and been allowed to stay on in his cottage at a reduced rent. As he approached the place he thought of his last visit and his legs lifted briskly in anticipation through that memory.

There was a silence after he stepped into the cottage, one so marked that it belied the existence of the querulous voice which had bidden him in. John saw his grandfather in a deep chair by the fire. The room was away from the sun and the fire emphasized the shadows, brought coldness to them.

'Well. Who is it?'

'It's me. John.' He stepped across to his grandfather. 'John.' he repeated, wondering why he had done so.

'Have you seen Alice?'

'Grandma? No.'

'She went for some shopping.'

'Yes?'

'She should be back. Go and look out of that back door for her.'

John did so and returned.

'She isn't in sight.'

'Well she should be.' Then Harry looked carefully at his grandson. 'Will you be wanting your supper?' he asked, sharply, then added, 'it's not as easy when you're not working. Shut that door, will you? I'm starvin'.' This last order was given apologetically, as if, conscious of his rudeness – though unable to check it – Harry wanted to be unregarded for a few seconds.

'Thank you. Sit theesel down. Family well?'

As he skipped through the hoops, the old man returned his gaze to the fire and kneaded his hands over it, as if to press its heat into his veins by main force. John answered and rolled back his stock of counter-inquiries, all the time shrinking inside himself; he realized he had come to be given amulets, but the charms were not to be had, the spirit gone.

There were two occasions only during that uneasy visit when John felt his grandfather to be as he had once been.

'Well, they've retired me, John,' he said, suddenly cutting across an answer he had demanded as to the stock on Pennington's farm. 'They used me up and cast me off. Like the chaff, John, sent away from the barns to be burnt.'

'But . . . But thou's bein' well looked after, Grandfather.'

'Who wants that?' The old man's volume and authority returned in the voice which threw out that accusing question. 'Aa can still work. They know that. But it's – "No, Mr Tallentire, thou must retire." "Yes, Mr Tallentire, we want thou to have a peaceful old age." They didn't kick me out, John – Aa could a' kicked back then – they Mothered me off the job! Whativver Aa said against it – they laughed – mekkin' out Aa was a comical old character 'as couldn't think of what to do widdout his work – and wasn't that so *very* comical! But it isn't a question of fillin' time, lad. Nivver was. Not to my way. Aa can't be interested in piddlin' aboot like a soft-bladdered old nag. Aa'm nothing widdout work. Nothing! No man is.'

The other time was after supper – during which Alice had passed things to Harry in such a protective way as caused the old man to groan and look silently at John, as if saying – 'Look! They've convinced her as well,' and John had been forced to assent to the significant nods and looks of his grandmother – a meal in which the clatter of cheap forks on thick china dominated all other sounds in the room and a light was unlit beyond the time of tolerability and left unlit into regions of miserliness – then, thankfully after John announced that he would set back for home, Harry walked with him as before, but this time stopped at the gate.

'Thou mustn't upset theeself about that boy that died,' he said. 'Aa can see it's botherin' you; don't protest. "The Lord giveth and the Lord taketh away," John – and if thou's not as strong in Him as Aa was – and am – then that's a truth can still be spoken.' He paused, and John waited, attending for the word as if his future needed it. The moment seized him. 'Besides,' the old man concluded, abruptly, 'it might be better nivver to be born. Good night.'

He turned away and John let the door bang his grandfather back to the fire before himself turning to go. Emily was asleep by the time he got home and despite his soft-footed care, she woke up and her accusation drew a hasty reply from him. Once more their words hurt each other.

Emily went nowhere for consolation: her only regular visits, apart from a resentful shuffle around the shops, were to the churchyard, to Ephraim's grave. She went weekly on the afternoon on which he had been buried and trimmed the small hummock on her knees. May would be left with Mrs Braithwaite. The vicar once tried to lead her from the grave into the church but was given short shrift.

In so far as her mood broke on to the surface of her life at all, it appeared as slatternliness. In her looks, her clothes, her behaviour, the way she kept the cottage, the way she let May run about in clothes long dirty – there was that willed carelessness which incited attack if only to rebuff it.

In October, John told her that he had given Pennington notice he would quit at Martelmas.

'Well you can go and tell him you're staying,' she said.

'We said . . .'

'*You* said. Maybe I did. But whoever did doesn't matter. I'm not moving from this place.'

'But I could be hired near your mother, Emily. Somewhere you'd have people you know about you. You wanted that.'

'I don't now. I wouldn't care if I saw none of them again.'

'Don't be like that.' He was still too bemused by her reaction to find any anger to match hers. 'Don't be like that, lass,' he repeated.

'I'm not a lass!'

'O, don't be so touchy, Emily.'

'Leave me alone.' Then, with a sudden stab of bitterness.

'*You'll* never touch me again – that's for certain, John Tallentire.'

'What do you mean?'

'You know. And if you weren't such a day-dreamer you would have guessed before now.' She paused. 'I'm married to a man who'll stick in his rut 'til it buries him. And he'll not even notice he's disappeared.'

'Less of that!'

'Truth hurts, does it?' From her expression it was she who looked more wounded than John by the 'truth' she darted at him.

'No,' he answered, eventually, 'it doesn't. But how it's said that hurts, Emily.'

He wanted to go out but did not care to think of her being alone. His back moved against the back of his chair and he pressed until he could feel the wood cut through his jacket and batten on his shoulder blades. He could not look at her, yet he could look nowhere else for longer than a moment and his eyes made ceaseless forays around the kitchen, as if memorizing everything for an inventory.

'Who would look after his grave if I went?' she asked. As if to emphasize the limits of the concession her sentence had contained, she stood up and went upstairs to May.

He did not follow her and soon, from the silence, knew that she would not come down until he was out of the house.

In the pub a glass was a mask for every man's face. He began to drink. In the pub he could stop his crying by drowning the tears before they reached his throat. In the pub he could buttress his solitude with the props of other men's lives. He was there on that night soon after Christmas when Jackson came in, lean and settled in his uniform, home on leave.

John had dulled himself to Emily, but he would have needed to blind himself to miss the change that came over her now. She took out all her clothes to clean and brush them; bought herself a new skirt; she had the house pretty once more, none of it for him. He prised open her new self – noticing that there was a flamboyance in it which was strained, an eagerness which was disconcerting – finding some relief in that she was *not* as she had been with him. There was nothing he saw to charge her with directly. Nor dare he confront her in any way. Afraid of hurting her. Afraid of that startled tension which, he thought, could snap her if wrongly broken. As near as possible, then, he did blind himself, alternately despising himself for it and reasoning that it was the only way – she must be let work out her own life: interference from him would be asked for – and given – when needed; he must be available, no more.

That his love had come to this demoralized him. That their life could come to this. Though now he was too concerned to keep up his present defences to allow the full effect of the reduction to be experienced, he knew it was there, waiting only an opportunity to set on him.

Emily waited for Jackson to call on her. From the minute that John left the morning cottage she was ready for Jackson to call on her. It seemed to her that only he could lift her from the torment of her grief. She refused to recognize that she was inserting more into that faith than its slender basis in her affections could sustain, nor did she let herself think of consequences; her faith was too bound up with fantasy for that. Jackson would save her – she believed that, had felt the knowledge certain from the moment she had heard of his return. Then her body had quickened as it had not done since that age before Ephraim's birth – and, the weight of inertia lifted, she had seen a way to breathe again, again be herself, rid of the despair which was destroying her.

But he did not come to the cottage.

She saw him across a field as she was returning from the shops – he waved, shouted a greeting and walked on as he would walk on from any other woman in the village.

She began to plan so that she would be forced to a meeting with him. She had been too severe, she thought, and he was too honourable to take advantage again – or too proud to come again. Yes. She must go to him.

She went to the Penningtons' for water and, as had not once happened before, used the trip as an excuse for calling on Mrs Pennington whose surprise was covered by an immediately accepted invitation to come and look around the house. John found her chatting to the farmer's wife in the cold flagged scullery and avoided her eyes, embarrassed for her. When Jackson came in, flanked by his father and his younger brother, the three men passed the scullery with a bare nod of acknowledgement and made for the table – for which Mrs Pennington had also to desert her. Emily had no excuse to accompany the other woman's flurry.

John was waiting for her in the yard, holding May by the hand. In his other hand he took the bucket of water and set off in front of her, not looking back though he could feel her body trail behind him, stinging with confusion.

The leave-time passed away until there were only a few days left and yet Emily had managed no more than a brief, pointless conversation with Jackson – one so artlessly and openly begged for that not only John but a number of others in the village observed it. Knowing that his wife had thus become the new juicy lump in the stew of gossip, John did not go that night to the pub. For which she accused him of never leaving her alone. Of pestering her by his everlasting company. Of torturing her by his silence, of murdering her by that never-gone look in his eyes. *She* would go out if he was determined to stay! It was her turn, anyway: her turn for a long time.

He let her put on her coat and watched each button pushed through its hole. He saw her try the shawl and then throw it away to take out the new scarf she had bought for her hair. Into the dark brown gloves her white fingers went like foraging strokes of light and the hooks clipped shut, one, two, three. Only as she went for the door did he move. And she stopped. Still on his chair, he looked at her without equivocation: she would not leave him that night. She ranted – he did not move. She laughed at him, still he watched her, and when she ran for the door he grabbed her wrist and held her, let her free arm beat on him that locked her, forced her back towards the couch into which she dropped, suddenly lifeless.

On the day following, her determination obsessed her. She took May to Mrs Braithwaite, took no notice of the unblushing curiosity on the other woman's face and went back to watch until she should see Jackson go out on his own. When he did, she followed him and caught him as he turned out of the lane and made for the pub. Despite helping his father he daily let it be seen that this was freely done – and his midday drink was one of the signs.

'Let me talk to you,' she said.

Jackson kept walking and smiled awkwardly at her.

'You'll have to come and have a pint then, Emily. I need me whistle whetted. I don't know how your man sticks at it all day and every day widdout a drink.'

'Please. Stop and talk to me.'

No one was on the road but Jackson was impelled to look around him by the urgent pleading of her voice: as if such nakedness should be seen by others as well as himself, covered by a company. Alone, it was too harsh for him, and he turned from her, wishing the lonely road crowded so that she would not go on.

'Don't look away, Jackson.' She caught his hand and held it tightly. 'I'll come into the pub with you. I don't mind. I'll watch you drink.'

He stopped and saw such agitation between wildness and servility in her face that he dared not answer. Anything said would be sucked into her and he himself with the words. Her mouth was a pale mark across her paler face.

'Go on. I don't mind. I won't be afraid in the pub with you there.' She paused and pressed both her hands on him. 'You've lovely warm hands. Maybe I will have a drink. What should I drink?'

'I'm going to set you back home, Emily,' he said eventually, his tone forced – light. 'You don't look well.'

'Oh. Do I look terrible?' Her hands left his hand, flew to her neck, settling there like broken wings. 'I can look nice when I take time to get ready. I suppose you're used to nice-looking women. You must have seen hundreds of them. Tell me about them, Jackson. Oh! don't be afraid. How can I be jealous? I'm a married woman.' She laughed, and the sound drove his head back. 'I mean, I only want to talk to you.'

'We can talk – let's go back and talk. It's cold here.'

'Back?'

'We could talk somewhere warmer.'

'Your hands are warm enough.' Then she looked at him slyly. 'You mean you want to come back to the cottage? I don't know whether I can have that.'

'Well then. Let's go to my place,' he replied, heartily. '*Your* hands are frozen.'

'I just want to talk.'

'I know that, Emily. Come on.'

Cautiously he took her arm and went back the way they had come. She clung to his arm and he wished all his force that *some* feeling could go out of him to comfort her: but he had none for her, nothing but pity. And that, to her wrecked bewilderment, was a lash.

'Well I can say I've walked out with you,' she said as they went into the lane.

'Yes. Yes – we've walked out together. A stupid private soldier and a pretty young married woman.'

'Don't joke, Jackson.' She leaned her head on his shoulder. 'I know you don't love me anymore.' Her head jerked away from him. 'But I thought I loved you. I want to, Jackson.'

'We're nearly there.'

'Don't talk to me as if I was a kid!' She broke free of him. Then once more she took his arm. 'I'm sorry. You're being kind, aren't you. I'm the one who's stupid, Jackson. Worse than any kid.'

It was with Emily still holding on to his arm that Jackson reached the farmyard. Pennington and John were wheeling turnips over to a byre. John lifted the spade from the barrow and went for him. He saw Emily's mouth open but heard none of her shouts – pushing her out of the way, knocking her down as she clung against him.

Jackson had run over and grabbed the other spade. He, too, shouted – but John concentrated on making firm his grip as he walked forward. The two men swung the vicious weapons like axes. John grazed Jackson's cheekbone and charged at the blood. A short chop hit his neck and he dropped senseless.

12

He tied the bed on to the cart and knotted the coarse binder twine tightly. Everything could be fitted on except the settee which he had taken down to Joe Edmonson's when borrowing the cart. He had said that he would collect it sometime but knew that he would not.

John worked very slowly, his fingers deliberating each time they touched a piece of furniture, the object eased along, even the chairs lifted only a necessary couple of inches from the ground so that they would not be scraped. Though it was mid-morning, the sun had made no entrance and sheeted clouds blew over the fells lending their metallic coldness to the wind which bit into the man's hands; the big central vein of the back of his left hand swelled up, purple puffed under the raw skin, a hard blood lump from wrist to knuckles. Looking down from the top of the fells, the cart could be seen small outside the door of the cottages: a capped and corduroyed figure slowly moving in and out of the door with the possessions which, once removed from their place in the small room, took on a strange double aspect; looking at once too many objects to be hung around the neck of any man and yet too few to support him in all but the most trivial afflictions. Seen from that height, the winter fields and trees bare about him, life coming from the chimneys, the whine of the overhead loop with the ore, the pits themselves – all hidden, burrowed as any hibernating creature – he looked minute and forlorn, his gesture of leaving purposeless, and the white linen, which was placed on the top of the cart and was ruffled by the wind, seemed a flag of distress or surrender.

When the job was done he went back into the cottage and squatted on his haunches to look into the dying fire. The door open, the cold found the small area as a trap and his feet and body stiffened against it; but he did not move. Emily had taken May away, he had not asked where, and he waited for their return to prompt him once more.

She had gone to collect his money from Pennington and the Friendly Society and then walked down to the churchyard to look as she thought might be the last time on Ephraim's grave. In her movements and her expression there was dreadful briskness which needs but a light blow to fall off and reveal the desperation it defies, that shell of pride whose hollowness reverberates at a touch.

Jackson watched her leave his father's farm – but remained where he was, guarded by the window. He was no longer afraid that she might cling to him – her step allayed that fear – but yet another circle had turned, and as he saw her now, white-faced in the shroud of the shawl, May trailing behind her holding a disregarded hand, he saw his loss of love for her as the blindness of momentary conceit. He wanted her to stay, to talk to him – he wanted her to love him – but he could not move. She had gone through her feelings for him – or they had been sealed off within her. She would, he knew, look plainly and disinterestedly at him and he would have nothing to say.

In the churchyard she felt panic. The grave was so small and there was no stone. It could sink or be grown over so easily. She looked around the tilting headstones, carved with the names and times of men's lives, and thought that the grass was better than such pitiful chippings, yet this did not reassure her. If she did not mark it well now, then she would forget it. She went back to the gate and looked up at the church, filling her eyes with all details so that she could find her way back without fault in any dream.

John waited until she came into the cottage and then he stood up. He was ashamed that he could not look at her – ashamed because it was such a petty, half-way thing, neither revenge nor understanding being in it, merely a weary spite – but he could not. And whenever he talked to her, the words came through a threat blocked by tears forced back from his eyes.

'Are you ready now?' he asked, quietly.

'Yes.'

'We'll go then.'

'Yes.' She paused. 'You must have *some* idea, John. You must know where you want to go.'

'No,' he said, head bent making for the door. 'I don't know.'

She did not press him, being as incurious as he was about where they would land up that night and what he would do. Only May, silent between their deep retreats, had brought her to the question. She would know soon enough.

Emily heard him lift the handles of the cart and begin to push it out to the lane. Two of the pans jangled mournfully and the wheels bumped slowly over the track, dragging behind them the slow step of her husband. She shivered on the bare flags of the kitchen and yet could not leave it until John had turned the corner – then she turned and was swiftly out, ushering May before her, slamming the door as abruptly as the wind, wrenching the key in the lock.

Pennington was outside his gate waiting for the key and she hurried to get in front of John so that he would not have to stop. But Pennington barred the way, and the pile of possessions slid to an angle as John set down the cart.

'Sure thou won't change thee mind, eh?'

'No.'

'Aa don't know,' said Pennington. 'Just a bit of a fight. Our Jackson's always been a stupid bluddy man. He'll be off where he belongs again on Saturday. Aa means – what the hell – Eh?'

'No. We're off, Mr Pennington.' John picked up the handles and pushed ahead, this forcing the older man out of his way.

'Aa'm greatly put upon by this,' said Pennington, as the family went past and away from him. 'Aa could sue thee, John Tallentire, but Aa's not that kind of man. Eh? Is'te listenin'? Thou can start again this minute.' He raised his voice as the small procession left him alone and went further up the lane. 'Thou always got thee money on time, man. Didn't thou? What else dis'te want? Eh? Answer me that! Eh? Answer me that!'

At the end of the lane he went straight on, down towards Cockermouth, away from the fells.

The hedges lining their route were bare of leaf and bird and it was only May, soon sat on a chair on the cart, whose pecking head and chatter brought lightness to the dour journey. John between the shafts, Emily a few paces behind him, each in limbo, shades of themselves never to stop, it seemed, this aimless walk.

John avoided Cockermouth and avoided Embleton. The early night came and still he did not stop more than for a few moments now and then to rub his forearms – he would not draw in when Emily offered him bread but ate the food standing staring at a cottage across the fields. He was relieved that it was dark. They came to Bothel and passed the place where Mr Errington had offered refreshments to his blushing companion and Emily was so tired she could have fallen to sleep on the road itself. No moon and the wind colder, gusting the trees, silencing the huddled sheep in the fields, whining through the hedges. May was asleep in the chair, covered by a blanket, strapped to the chair-back by a length of rope. Sometimes, when she had been troublesome back in the cottage, John had used the same rope to tie around her ankle and the table leg so that she moved only a yard or so from the care of the table.

He wanted not to stop ever. To do so would mark a place, and he wanted no connections. The jobs he would have to do would throw him into a certain intimacy with Emily – which he could not bear to think of. Moreover, he felt that without the weight of this cart before him, without its frame he himself would fall, be able to do nothing in the world but lie there, inanimate.

'If you go much further we'll be at your father's place,' said Emily. 'Maybe they would put us up.'

'We'll not turn to them.'

She hesitated.

'We'll have to stop soon,' she said eventually. 'Or I'll just drop, John.'

'We'll stop when we can!' He shouted. 'Stop whinin'!'

The anger stoked his energy and he raised his pace. After some minutes he noticed that all was silent behind him, her following footsteps gone. He set down the cart and looked back – to see no sign of her in the black night.

He clenched his fists as a spurt of fury threatened to loosen his mouth to accusations – words he wanted to check, fearing their flight. Finally she caught up with him and stood, a few yards off, a shadow in the dark, swaying.

'Get on the cart with the babby,' he said.

She nodded but did not move.

'Come on then! Get *on*, woman!'

'Yes,' she replied. 'Yes I will.'

But still she stood.

'Let's stay here, John.'

'Don't be stupid.'

'I can go no further.'

'Yes you can – try.'

'I can't try.'

He went to her and for the first time that day looked full into her face. The skin pulled at the bones as if to find their cutting edge. Her mouth was tight, lips pressed together firmly as if afraid ever again to relax to a spontaneous expression.

'I'll lift you on,' he said abruptly and picked her up, feeling her body hard underneath the swathes of cloth, the cheek frozen which rested on his own for a moment before pulling away. She said nothing but allowed herself to be set on the cart, covered with the other blanket, wedged beside her daughter.

'I'll look for somewhere,' he said.

John took the next turning off the main road and looked out for an empty shed or cottage. At that time it was not too difficult to find abandoned cottages pocking the countryside like craters on a battlefield and after a mile or so he came across such a one. The windows were broken – but boards half-hanging from them showed that there had been squatters there before. The door was open and inside there was sacking on the floor, stinking of excrement. Hooks hung from the low, cracked ceiling, there was a hole in one of the walls stuffed up with wood and paper.

He threw out the sacks and secured the windows – and then his energy was spent. The bed he brought in with more sense of effort than he had showed along the whole way. Emily helped him with the rest of the furniture. John realized that he should have found wood and made up a fire, should have prepared against the cold of the morning, helped by more than the lighting of two candle stumps to bring some warmth into the place. But he was without any impulse to it. That mood which had once seized so malevolently on him now merely touched him – and he went under.

The life he lived for the days and weeks following could best be called an under-life. Too much for him, he neither fought it nor ran from it but crept down into himself away from it. His day was set from the first morning when he looked at Emily making the fire. He watched until she was finished and then went to the chair beside it, sat and stared into it. Saying nothing when bread and tea was put before him, making no effort to help as she dragged the furniture into a more practicable position, never moving to be out for wood or to look around. He washed and shaved once a day – did it when he was alone in the room. To May he was indifferent but he was not angry with her when she scrambled on to his knee or made a noise. He went outside to defecate and saw nothing but the short track. One thing he did do – he laid on the table all the money he had in his pockets.

When, about a fortnight after they had come, the owner came, John was alone. His silences were such as the man expected and once he had made up his mind that no money would be got out of these new squatters he made the best of it, as he had done often enough before, the cottage having been empty for years. He noticed the fire and scored that up as something for himself: the damp would be held back a little and so the cottage would be in some condition if ever he wanted to let it again. It was too distant from his own place to be of the smallest use to him and already too derelict to be spoiled. So he left not unhappy at having the place inhabited and rather pleased to be maintaining a squatter whom he could own and display in his daily talk.

The only comfort about the days, to John, was their end. Then his terrible blankness could be used in sleep. In a short time he had exhausted such thoughts as he had on the reasons for this condition. He now thought himself a stupid fool for ever believing in love, and deserving of all he heaped on himself for holding to that faith so fiercely. He did not blame Emily –

for he scarcely considered her now; no lift of her voice, no action of hers, no sight or touch of her impinged even slightly on his retreat. Occasionally on his inward eye would flash a picture of her and himself as they had been – and then his face would tighten, draw as if for tears, but the lines would be hard, squeezing out the memory, rejecting it as foreign to his state. Even more fiercely came memories of those days he had spent knowing that Emily's thoughts were all of Jackson: that painful suspense would now quicken to such a bite of hatred as shuddered through his body until he moaned for it to cease. At such times Emily would touch his arm only to feel her fingers shivered off. John knew that his circumspection had been out of care for Emily: unable to understand her, he had thought that only by going her own way could she be saved from herself. But he also called himself coward.

Having known such a passion as could make a sight alone fill with contentment, one that drove into him until it seemed that everything shone through love, he was now in darkness. He could see nothing but shadows of former shapes and was no more inclined to discover their substance than that of ghosts.

And he thought that the god he had made of himself at work was little but a function of his desire to serve. To a function he had given his spirit. To call what he had done more than a mechanical drudgery was to glorify it. Demanding satisfactions in it he had found them – but such as had ceased when the self-erected purpose had fallen. His work had been a labour to himself and had over-leapt the rewards of absorption in the results. It was his skill and stamina he had loved, not the growing barley or the safely delivered lambs. That in himself he had sought, that was right, he knew; but so to impose yourself on the world is to challenge it to return your force, and the disruption it had returned carried in it the wreckage of labour, flotsam of days and tasks, useless-seeming now – he thought of them with amazement, fingering their recollection, unable to imagine the form which had held them in place.

Finally, with no self-pity, he saw himself as a man whose life would never be fit for anything but manual labour. Whatever was required of the meanest talents and the most blinded mind would be required of him. He remembered what Seth had told him of the farm labourers not many years ago joining and marching for their unions so soon to founder – but the image of those men and their meetings at night on the cross-roads, lanterns shielded from the wind, women and children with them as they listened to their fellows saying 'it cannot last', 'it must change', and thence going to risk eviction and transportation for fifteen shillings a week – such conjoining and faith in a future was not able to draw any hope to him. The conditions might change but the situation would be the same: he would fill in the holes in the ground and then stand aside as the pyramid rose.

These reflections fragmented, elusive, flickered on the walls of the cave in which he now lived.

Happy to be a blank in darkness.

Wishing neither to give nor to resist.

Sat there at the side of the fire, still as a painted man. Old. Shoulders bent, body hunched, petrified by the unyielding reflection of the thing he looked on. In this pagan and beast nothingness, he was immovable.

It was Emily who acted. She was out looking for wood in the morning, fetching water from the beck, spending the little money on the cheapest flour and lard. They ate flat-cakes and drank water when the tea ran out. She kept to the one room as if fearing that an attempt to get him to move upstairs would destroy the last of the small contact they had. Sometimes she was lucky and could persuade a farmer's wife to let her help with a day's washing: she sold her two dresses and with the money bought wool and sold the socks and pullovers she made. For two months they managed on less than seven shillings a week – and then the savings were almost gone. She sold the chairs John had made and bought two hens so that May would have eggs. For one week she had herself hired for stone-picking and took May to help her clear the seven acres for five and threepence. At all costs to herself John must be allowed to come out of that empty waking nightmare on his own. She worked to keep him and May alive, and the fundamental nature of such work restored her as, she hoped, it atoned for what she had done. So as John grew worse, the cumulative effect growing on to him like a scaling disease, she became firmer. The despair which incomprehension had rotted to a frailty like madness was put away from her and she thought of nothing at Crossbridge but Ephraim's grave to which now she could not bring herself to return.

Once Isaac came by, bold as ever, driving a flock of geese. Caught out at the end of a good run, droving had been the best he could find – 'lasses' work,' he said, beaming that he was doing it. The geese were like a drift of snow, magically carpeting the brown track.

Their sound did not bring John from his seat, nor did the information that his brother was there. So while Emily looked after the geese, Isaac went inside.

John was more pleased to see Isaac than he would have been anyone else. But his pleasure was soon spent, having now so little to nourish it: like his appetite, his doings with the world had grown so meagre that a peck served where a bushel had been needed before. Isaac could make little of this exhausted replica of a brother and, it not being in his nature to give more advice than the call 'Get up, man! Come away!' he was soon baffled. John's unhappy appearance, the bleak cottage, the distant acceptance of it all by Emily – all this unnerved him. The best he could do was to wring the necks of two of the fatter geese – for which he would himself reimburse the farmer – and hand their hot, downy bodies to Emily before passing on.

His visit, though, changed John. That passing touch which seemed to come from another world touched on him and, weakly, he began to struggle from the bottom of self into which he had been pitched.

He walked out a little the very next morning – looking at the dull, featureless fields, feebly scanning this bare no-man's-land into which he had brought himself – neither fell-land nor plain, neither lush nor formidable, poor land. He was soon tired. Emily hoped that he might be getting himself ready for the Whit-hiring now only a fortnight off, but soon she saw that even if he had the intention he had not the strength. He was as white and fragile as a convalescent. All that was boyish had gone forever from his face, replaced by lines which age would trace deeper from then on, his cheeks sunk deeply so that his mouth was raised up on his face and stood out from it, a most fragile challenge to the world.

He watched his daughter playing. The child had found games to fill her solitude and he watched her as she built and destroyed, chatted to herself, ran after the birds. He carved a doll for her with his pocket knife.

Then Joseph, his father, came. Up the track and into the cottage and no less directly to the point.

'There's a place for thee at Wiltons,' he said. 'He missed gettin' a good man at Wigton. Got landed wid a stupid calf as couldn't work off steam. Thou can tak ower frae him on Sattiday.'

'I won't go,' John replied.

'Well thou shall have to do summat, my son. This pig-sty's no place for a man. Thee wife's next thing 'til a beggar. Thee dowter looks like an orphan. *Thou* looks like workhouse fodder. Thou shall hev to do summat. Yer mother's sick wid' worry.'

'Don't bring her intil it. Thou means *thou's* shamed. That's all.'

'All! Ay lad, Aa's shamed. But *thou's* bluddy near ruined. Now – theer's a job, he'll give thee fourteen bob a week. Tek it. Git out of this muck-heap. That's what Aa kem to say.'

'And now thou's off.'

'Ay, that's correct. Aa knows better than to stay to reason wid thee lad. A fool can't see his own good. But think o' thee wife and dowter. That's all.'

'Emily hasn't said anything.'

'Then she's dafter than thee. There's no credit in agreein' wid weaklin's.'

'So now thou's off,' John repeated, deriving amusement from that which annoyed his father.

'What the hell dis'te expect? A carnival? Thou's bluddy lucky Aa kem, lad. Ay – Aa's off! Aa'll catch diphtheria sittin' in this byre. What the hell, man! Is this as good as thou can manage for thisel?'

'It's little enough different to what thou's got.'

'If thou think like that – thou's mad as well as daft. There's no question.'

'And that's that! Eh?'

'Yes.'

'Come in – orders and out. Job done.'

'And wasted by the sound of it,' the older man replied, almost jumping from one foot to the other, so furious was he against his son, so irritated by what he regarded as sloth, so keen to be gone that it might be thought he was afraid that to stay would tar him with the same pitch.

'Go then,' John said.

'Ay,' Joseph hopped about – John laughed. 'Tek that smile off, you useless effigy! So the poor little lad got blocked wid a spade. O dear me. Thou needs hittin' wid another to knock t'sense back in. Ay, laugh away, you bluddy ignorant pile. *Thou* was gonna be "on thee own", *thou* could manage – ladida – bluddy mess! Useless! Ay – laugh away. God,' he drew back his arm, 'I would brain thee if Aa thowt it was worth it.'

'Thou can't brain thesel father. Never mind me. Tell Wilton thanks – but no.'

'No? What's 'te mean – no?'

'Well, father – thou can work it out as thou runs back home. It's only got two letters so thou should just about manage by Red Dial.'

'Oh! Oh now! That's it. That's it! Good-bye my lad. O yes! Good-bye!'

'And now thou's off.'

'What in hell's name dis te keep wailin' that for? Ay – Ah's off.'

'Father,' John paused. 'Thou never asked one question – never wondered one thing. Dis te not *want* to know what happened?'

'Aa do not.'

Yet Joseph hesitated.

'What'll Aa tell folk?' he asked, eventually.

'Tell them the truth, father. Tell them thou found me a squatter and near enough a pauper and daft enough to turn down a grand offer frae Wilton. Tell them May looks badly and Emily looks worse – and tell them not to look up from their own feet, because if they do they'll see the same thing I see.'

'An' what's that?'

'*Nothing!* Between here and high heaven – Nothing.'

'Aa'll tell them thou's mad daft.'

He left and Emily, who had listened outside, rushed in and hugged John. He held her up and kissed her flying hair.

'Nothing at all.' He murmured.

Part Two

13

John had taken work in the mines. It was, Emily thought, like coming in from the wilderness.

The town boomed against her senses as the sea sounded along its shore. This move from the countryside to the town – even though the town had a population of no more than eight or nine thousand – was the more dramatic as neither John nor herself had lived anywhere larger than a village: the effect of any subsequent move even to a city would be much less than this first impact of town life.

In the beginning it had seemed to her like a ceaseless carnival. Though approaching the end of another pregnancy, she would still go with May, and Harry – born a few months after their arrival in the town – drawn to the centre to watch the people. She thought she would never tire of that. Streets full of shops, each jostling the other for trade, pushing out on to the pavement with boxes of fish, slabs of meat, sacks of vegetables, an ironmonger littering the street with his implements, cobblers in their windows hammering and peeping, clothes shops deep-blinded in shaded respectability, tripe for sale, pigs' trotters, sheep's heads, a rich cave of carpets – and on market day the stalls stretching up all the side streets, a plantation of canvas and boards loaded with booty for plunder – white pyramids of eggs, geese dangling by their feet – and a swarm everywhere, a restless crowd of women and children, the children scattering around about their mothers like disordered planets, the women scarved and sharp-eyed, by their looks equipped for any bargain, swooping along the shop fronts and trailing by the stalls almost scenting out their goods, so eagerly were the faces pushed forward. In the beginning, Emily had clenched her purse tightly, afraid that once opened, all would go, be bound to, so much there was to be bought. One street's length had exhausted her – the unknown faces rushing past, none carrying a history for her yet each so like herself – she felt the helpless exhilaration that many feel when they settle in new places. That everyone was new excited her, that she had no part in their lives unnerved her. For two or three years, until after the birth of Alice, the sounds and smells of the few streets in the town's centre spun her into this web. Just to go shopping was an outing for them all.

In the first decade of the twentieth century the town, like many others, ran with the juice of many pressings. There was the elite – doctors and solicitors; above them the men who owned the mines and the tanneries and the bank, living outside the town but still dribbling a last flavouring on to it of the aristocracy and gentry. The church was strong but the chapels were fuller. Temperance Halls were as busy as the pubs. The Salvation Army played on Saturday nights and all day Sunday. There were football teams, a music hall, a new bath-house, horse-sales, boy scouts, a workhouse, a cottage hospital, lodgings, slums, schools for the now compulsory secondary education, reading-rooms – and between all this, between the hills which came into the town to meet the slag heaps which rose up on the shore, physical pincers of the society, were the miners, clogged along the cobblestones, black droves to and from the shifts.

At that time, the West Cumberland Coalfield produced over two million tons of coal a year from forty-three collieries: almost nine thousand men worked in pits. Tell anyone that the pits would be closed by the second half of the century and he would not have listened, let alone believed. West Cumberland sat on coal; if you dug too deep in your allotment you would break into a seam. And not content with the land, the coal ran out under the sea where here it was mined further out than anywhere else in the world – some of the men walking four miles under the water to reach the facings, hewing below a depth of over 200 fathoms. The Earl of Londsdale had leased the mines to the Bains who had introduced new machinery, doubled the number of men, opened further seams – and below a hundred square miles of earth and water the miners drove shafts, seams, roads, ripping the coal from the rock and limestone.

John had found a cottage to the north of the docks, in a settlement of terraced houses that ran almost to the edge of a cliff. Below were the coal-dusted rocks and along the shore – north to Maryport – the wheels and workings of the pits like beacons in their aspect but in purpose more resembling the Roman mile-castles which had once guarded the coast – for like them, the workings were both a mark of power and a defence against privation.

He was not as beguiled as Emily by the glamour of the town. He saw more of the empty steep streets as morning rain soaked on his way back from work under a sea that had not spotted him. Where Emily saw the liveliness of the women, John's impression was of their gauntness. The hollowed faces and bone hopelessness of the people Picasso painted at this time were portraits of a continent of the industrial poor. Emily felt the benefit of John's higher wage now that he was out of his apprenticeship: to him, though the extra cash in hand was pleasant and welcome, there was strangely less plenitude about him than there had been on the farm – for all its grinding labour and ignominious pay. When he went out of his allotment to walk along the cliff and look down at the fishing boats, the lights of the town, the sea – even then he felt an absence, for despite the movement of the sea, or perhaps by contrast with it, the shapes beneath him seemed static and angular. He could break it up into squares and triangles, hard solid forms – in a way which was impossible on the land. As if the weight of men below the crust threatened the surface. So that the houses ran in battle-lines, the larger buildings in the town centre making a fortress. Ready to repel an attack from the exploited riddles below. While the cracked walls, the tall chimney broken like a bottle-top, a waste of land between terraces – a void like scar suppurating – the rampage of a Saturday night showed the danger to the town of this strain. And it crumbled to small, racing bodies as the wail of an accident sounded from the sea's edge.

Having made his decision, however, he was not going to let such vague misgivings spoil it. It was, he thought, no more than a hangover from that terrible time of blankness (which to remember made him shiver) – and besides, he had then made his discovery, then found that existence had no needs but a little food and shelter, then felt himself as near the bottom of things as he could be – and survived. That he was stuffing much of his instinct down his throat was painful but it had to be swallowed: for no matter how much he 'liked' the new life, he could not feel for it as he had done for the old. Those innumerable recognitions which mingle around you as you work at something you have done from childhood, the visions that they form, one layered on the other as fantasies, day-dreams, proper hopes and impressions which constantly advance and recede around you – they were gone.

His grandfather had died a few months after he had last seen him: his son Harry was named after him. At the funeral only four of the old man's sons had been able to come and John had been a pall-bearer, walking behind his father. The funeral was attended by over fifty people including those who had employed him throughout his life, and John had felt as old as his grandfather when one of his uncles had thanked the Latimers for 'letting his last days be so peaceful'. He knew that the old man had deteriorated even from the state he had seen him in, and that added to his determination to break from work whose nature so bound men that they could not survive in any way without it.

Now at twenty-six, John was well on that plain which, in his life, was like a table-topped mountain between the rapid steeps of childhood and the swift drop to the grave. If his mind was not made for the mines, his body was, its comparative shortness an advantage in the pits – sometimes he had snuggled into seams no more than eighteen inches high, stripped and running with sweat, lying on his side to hack out the coal, being more than ready to go on into a double shift for the extra money. He worked in Seth's gang but Seth was a cutter and John's marrer was a man called Fred Stainton who had been in the mines since his thirteenth birthday.

That great rush towards work – which had been an expression of himself as much as an act of labour – was now gone. He did not mind it – though he dreaded to hear the cough of some of the older miners and broke his temper regularly as he tried to scrub the black mineral from his skin – but he had no love for it. On the farm, doing the job well had sometimes given a satisfaction other than the job's completion; here, the mark of a job well done was the quantity of coal dug out. There were men who worked as if their lives depended on their skill – some of the big hewers who cut down coal as remorselessly as lumberjacks topple trees – and men of all ages who would take pride in the making of a pack wall or a gateway and lay out their tools like master carpenters, pointing out the old shafts which led to the great columns of coal, twenty-five yards square, which had formerly supported the workings as grandly as pillars in a cathedral. John could not match them – nor did ambition rise as substitute for affection: Seth disparaged his brother's willingness to stay an ordinary collier, but John wanted no more. Only when he climbed into the cage to be pressed against a crowd of thirty or forty men and drop down into the earth, or in the shed when he lined up for his wages and felt each man ready on the same mark – only at such times, being an anonymous member of a crowd, did he feel the smallest enthusiastic stirrings for the work he did and the way of life it dictated.

Seth, who had helped to set him on his feet when he first arrived, had put him on the list for one of the company's cottages. After a few weeks he had got one – such cheap shacks were a small investment for the money that could be made out of them – and John had moved in, with little more than the bed after Emily's forced sales. It was one of the cheapest of those cheap barracks – necessarily so as he was on apprentice's wages to begin with. Even those, however, were higher than the man's wages he had received from Pennington. The settlement of which their terrace was a part was known as 'The Tops'. An easy target for justifiable sarcasm. Anyone looking on the miners' cottages from the air would have seen regular stitches of roof and alley. No differences could have been imagined between them. All had back-kitchen, a kitchen and parlour downstairs, two bedrooms and perhaps a minute extra – little bigger than a cupboard – upstairs, a backyard with a lavatory and coalshed. Alleys ran between the dark backyards like stony river beds after a drought. Washing was strung from wall to wall on Mondays, filling the dry rivers with skeletal linen. A step or two led from the front door to the street and there the children or their parents would sit and watch the world go by on sunny days. Yet within the town there *were* differences – between Kells and Ginns, Bransty, Hensingham and Mirehouse. And 'The Tops', as would be said with such a blindness to the effects of repetition as made originality appear a waste of time, a thing for the children and those without self-confidence, 'The Tops are aboot the Bottom!'

Built before the great expansion of mining at the end of the century, they more resembled those plain agricultural cottages that John and Emily had lived in; but two up, two down, bigger. Some were scheduled to be pulled down – and already halfway to it from the assistance of those who used them as quarry. One terrace was called 'Rat Row' and the men would take their dogs down there on Sunday mornings to bet on the number of rats which could be killed in an hour. Potters lived in some of the houses and treated them with the same respect as they treated any property – open or closed – without their caravans. On the same terrace as John lived two families, the Wylies and the Stobarts, whose drinking and thieving was about to end in their eviction. Yet after John had made certain that Emily was not frightened by it – which she was not – nor worried for the children, he settled down well enough. Like most districts with a bad name, its differences from the others were far less than its similarities.

The parlour was to Emily as the allotment was to John. He had rented a big chunk no more than five minutes from his door – along the back alley, across 'the waste' to the small subbranch of the Co-operative, and from there past the chapel down a little path to a flat piece of land on the lip of the cliff. It took him most of the first year to take the stones off it and break up the ground. He managed no more than a few stitches of potatoes that time. And Emily had got a pair of armchairs for the parlour. Over the next two years, it became a race – he down there most nights when he came back from work, she gambling on the sales like a professional punter. She had to win, for as soon as he got the allotment 'something like', he was away with plans for building a small shed and planting some shrubs – whereas once the parlour was completed – including a piano which had been bought for ten shillings 'and taking away' – it was set, to gather as much dust and silence as any sanctuary. The space in the house, the children about her and the neighbours' business so often made her own, left her with little regret for the village. The time when she had placed herself entirely in John's moods, when they had spun together so that the world about them was no more than a whirl of colours, undefined compared with the power of their own motion, was gone and she was glad of it. For the first time there was something in her which could not be touched by him. While John thought back on that time as one of wonder and intense life, she regarded it as a storm, thankfully blown out.

Though he had regained his temper with his self-respect and she could still feel the tremor of that compulsion which had led her towards a fever of intolerable longing, they were easier with each other than they had been, neither the dead affair of Jackson nor the body of Ephraim turning an accusing face to them, and each too, now aware of the consequence of sinking to that dying selfishness which exhausts those nearest.

The days went in no certainties. There was no great aim, no investment made in the future, no life carved out with care for the calls of a tyrannical conscience or a driving will. At one of Seth's meetings, John had been turned to and described as 'an ordinary fella' – to mark him off from the union members – and he had felt it accurate and no slight. Emily, too, made no extraordinary demands for herself – neither barricaded her doors against all-comers nor lived as much in neighbours' houses as her own, as some of the women did. When a woman was ill, she would take in one or two of her children, just as

May had been lodged out at Alice's birth. She did not go to chapel but gave money to the Salvation Army and May to Sunday-school. She neither drank nor smoked, nor was she extravagant, though she would pinch for herself to get fancy bits of things for the children. The supper was in the oven when he came home and she shoved the children away as she washed his back in the tub before the fire. The Co-op served her for most of her shopping, the stalls at the market for the rest. She settled in and settled down and in those first few years let the routine of house and the demands of the children take her over. What with John entailed rejection and suppression, in her seemed to fit without cutting.

On Saturdays she went to the market, that portion of the previous days' earnings left for the spree itching in the bottom of her purse. She always got sweets for the children and John, for herself she liked to get a little fruit – grapes when there were any – or a bought cake – cream sandwich or vanillas. After tea John went to the pub.

She sat in the rocking chair – smiling at the image of John there just a few minutes before, Alice on his lap, May on the rockers at the back, Harry straddling an arm, John's arm circling the baby and strapped in the concertina as he rollicked the four of them half-way across the kitchen.

'Gee up jockey to the fair
What will you buy me when you're there?
A silver apple and a pear
Gee up jockey to the fair.'

– and with all his voice shouting 'Whoa-there!' and 'Faster boy!', the children hanging on as for life and then released in a squall of laughter. Now Emily sat, the bread fresh out of the oven, the supper ready for his return, all the children well and in bed – trying, as she sometimes did, to get into a book but alerted at every sentence by an echo in her mind which the words caused but could not catch. She was determined not to waste her time on sleep – Saturday being the sole evening on which she could be absolutely certain of being alone – her children not old enough to have friends come around after seven and the women along the row either preparing against the morning so that they could slip to chapel, out drinking, or, like herself, hugging the luxury of a week done, these few hours the slow calm when one week was ended, another yet to begin.

She was irritated by the knock on the door, and made uncertain by its being at the front door. Pulling off the apron, she folded it up neatly without stopping to do so, laying it over the back of the last chair as she left the kitchen.

'Are you Missus Tallentire?'

'I am.' Seeing the caller was a woman carrying a child, Emily was relieved enough to open the door widely, but not yet so confident as to take away the foot that was wedged behind it.

'I'm Sarah.'

'Oh yes.'

'*Sarah* Tallentire. John's sister. Don't you – well you wouldn't. Aa wasn't left school when you got married. Can I come in?'

'Of course you can. Here – let me take that baby. What an awful thing you must think me standing here without saying anything. Come in – do. Bang that door, would you Sarah? The snib's funny.'

'Oh. It *is* warm in here.' The younger woman, relieved of the child, set her large basket down on a chair and rushed to the fire. In the impulse of her movements, Emily recognized John and, even stronger, May. All of them had that black hair and the small hard blue eyes. 'Bread!' Sarah exclaimed – like a girl, clapping her hands over it. She could be no more than seventeen. 'Ooh! Can I have some, Emily? Can I tell you Emily?'

'Of course you can. But have something better than bread. I've a sponge cake in the back-kitchen.' She smiled at the baby.

'Oh. Lovely.'

'What's she called?'

'Veronica.'

'That *is* unusual. But very nice. Here – I'll put some cushions on the settee so's she won't fall off. Would she like some milk?'

'She might. I'll be happy with the bread.'

'No, no. Sit down. You can't have just bread. What am I

doing letting you go hungry like that? Sit there – up at the table where you've got some room. I'll put the kettle on. Now make yourself at home.'

From the back-kitchen, quite guilelessly, Emily shouted.

'And who's the man?'

'A navvy.'

'Where does he work?'

'I don't know. He *did* work at Wigton. He might be in Timbucktoo now for all I know.'

'They get around, do they?' Still from the kitchen.

'They certainly do,' said Sarah – giggling and then crying.

Coming through to the kitchen with the sponge cake on a plate, Emily bit her lip for an ignorance which, though unavoidable, had yet not been guarded by sufficient sensitivity to prevent the pain caused to the girl. She needed no further elaboration of the situation.

'Well,' she said later, having helped Sarah to a quick enough recovery and watched her make a rapid raid on the meal – the sponge cake reduced by over a third. 'You must stay here 'til you get settled in a bit more. You can sleep with May, and Harry can come in with us, that'll leave his bed for Veronica.'

'I knew you'd be kind!' The younger woman launched herself from her chair and flung her arms around Emily's waist, treating her who was but a few years older than herself as one capable of bearing every responsibility which she herself would not carry. 'I knew it was no good going to our Dad. He'd have taken us in – but . . .' She pulled back her head and glared at Emily 'but my God we would nivver have heard the last of it. So I thought – Aa'll just get on that train – and I did, Emily – it goes right to the sea from Flimby, you could lean out and catch a fish – Ooh! It made me seasick, to look at it – and you should have seen this one young man in the first-class compartment – Aa'm sure he must have been a Duke, or a Sir – anyway – *Some*body – his *clothes*! – I could have pulled them off his back and got into them meself – oh! such *cloth*! – and there was a woman took Veronica when she started to cough so that was nice – and I says "There's our Seth and better, there's our John and his Emily – they'll take us in." So I came. I am *glad* I came.'

And Sarah stood up, calmly turned a small circle and went across to the mirror.

'Haven't you got big mirror, Emily?'

'There's a bigger one in the wardrobe upstairs.'

'Can I go up?'

'You might wake the children, dear.'

'Oh. Oh well. When Veronica cries I just put my fingers in my ears. They'll cry for ever if you give in to them, you know. Then you're finished. Do you like this brooch?'

'Yes. I noticed it. It's lovely.'

'There's supposed to be a real garnet in it somewhere.' Sarah squinted severely down at her blouse front. 'God alone knows which bit it is. You can have it if you like.'

'No. Whatever for? *You* keep it.'

'No. I don't *really* care for it.' She unsnipped it. 'It'll look better on you, anyway. Your hair's not so black. Try it on. Go on. Don't be silly. *Keep* it. With my hair you need really bright stuff – otherwise it isn't worth it. There. What did I say. You suit it beautifully. Go and look.'

'It *is* pretty,' said Emily.

'Makes you look younger,' Sarah added.

'But it's too good,' Emily snapped it off as decisively as Sarah had done. 'You must keep it. No! If *you* don't like it – keep it for Veronica. I'd better get that little girl some milk – does she have it sugared?'

'As it comes. Is this a photo of you and John?'

'Yes. That was at Crossbridge. Our first year there. A man called Joe Edmonson took it.'

'Makes you look very young!'

Emily went to fetch the milk and from the retreat of the back-kitchen dared to ask a question that she would have avoided face to face – would have avoided altogether before a less volatile woman.

'How is it we didn't – know about all this, Sarah?' she asked.

'Oh. Well, I ran away with him – see.' She shouted – as Emily was out of the room. The volume gave the words a cheerful, even singing, air. 'And – well Mam guessed but I had to say something so I told Dad I was married. We lived at Garblesby and he came to see us once – just when I was gonna pop – and Jerry knocked him down. What a fight they had! My Jerry said that we were married – but Aa suppose Dad didn't believe us because he didn't tell anybody. He just nivver mentioned it. Then when Jerry went away, I went home – you should have heard the old lad *swear* – mind you, he daren't hit me 'cause I kept tight hold of the baby, see. So I went off again. I'm glad to be out of his reach.'

'How old were you then?' Emily asked, totally unable to resist her curiosity even though she tried to make of the question the merest passing remark as she brought in the milk to the child.

'Fifteen when I left home. Sixteen when *she* came to spoil things. Oh! I mustn't say that. I didn't mean it, darling. Here, mammy'll give you the milk, won't she? Won't she then? Is it too hot then? Well, *don't* puke it up just because it's too hot! Wait a minute, can't you?' She turned to Emily. 'It's too hot,' she said.

Sarah was fast asleep in bed by the time John came back. He was short of being drunk but the ale and the company had done a good job on him and Emily had no difficulty in accommodating him to the situation – particularly as she felt no obligation to repeat all that Sarah had said to her, nor were her own conclusions firm enough for her to do anything but override their reservations as mean and ungenerous.

'Of course she can stay for a bit,' said John. 'She'll be terrified, poor lass, I shouldn't wonder – with our father carryin' on and one thing and another. Of course she can stay.'

14

'Don't worry,' said Seth. 'It's an open meeting. Thou needn't say a word.'

'Are you certain?' John demanded.

'Positive! And even so, you might pipe up summat or other, no?'

'No,' John replied, decisively. 'I would have nothin' to say. It'd be a waste of time listenin' to me.'

'Well. We'll see. I felt like that once. Everybody gets used 'til it.'

John had joined the union, but while regular with his subscription and as solid as the others were in his demand for the Eight-Hour Day, he was, as many were, uncomfortable when faced with Seth's fanaticism.

'Your trouble,' he said to John, 'is that you worked too long on that bluddy farm. At the bottom of you you don't care who you work for or what it is you're asked to do as long as you get your money and can think of yourself as bein' independent. And you think you were independent because you could serve your notice any time. But that's the least of it, lad. You've got Rights. You must claim them. And there's no God Almighty ever said you should sweat your guts out for somebody else's profit. You should have a share in the profits of your work. But you're that pig-ignorant – you can't really believe that, can you? You just can't *think* that you have as much right to a fair share in what you produce as they have. It won't drop, will it?'

No matter how much John protested, he knew there was some justice in Seth's accusation – and felt inferior to his brother both in his understanding of the situation and in the resolution with which he responded to it. Yet as he walked beside his brother now, down the hill to the pub where the meeting was to be held, he wished himself back in his allotment or kneeling in front of the fire making the brass ornaments he had turned to, talking to Emily or Sarah – in any place but this. With other union men he felt easy enough, but Seth had Fight and Unionism written all over his face: still a bachelor, he breathed Tom Mann, Keir Hardie, Burns and Pickard, and would have his brother as committed as he was: chivvied him for the slightest tone, not of dissent – for that he enjoyed, giving him, as it did, the opportunity to smother John with argument – but such as betrayed less than total enthusiasm; John had to be the prize convert, a showpiece.

Slowly, still amazingly slowly, the working classes of Britain were organizing themselves into Unions. The miners had already the largest union and the most potential force. The Taff Vale decision at the beginning of the century had shocked them to greater urgency and in 1906 Union funds became immune from legal action. In that year also, about thirty members of the Independent Labour Party went into Parliament and although they were still the tail of the Liberals, the tail was starting to wag the dog. Old Age Pensions on a non-contributory basis were being fought for, workman's compensation, medical inspection for children, unemployment and health insurance – and the miners' cry for the Eight-Hour Day had grown into a practicable demand. All this is often represented as the 'inevitable tide', the 'logical' conclusion of votes and education. Written down so, it seems that the causes fought for were certain of success. Yet in that first decade no more than one man in seven was in a union; even within those trades which appeared powerfully organized there were many non-union men. Funds were in constant danger of running out: lodges could be strong one year and abandoned the next: there were differences which made large-scale co-operation very difficult; entire unions could perish – as did that of Joseph Arch's Agricultural workers, and only by the most painful efforts did George Edwards build it up again, years later, a man in his sixties bicycling to four or five hundred village meetings a year, himself alone setting it up. The forces against them were at least as well organized as they were and the police and the militia were easily called in to break local strikes. There were Bloody Sundays and bayonet charges, lock-outs and victimization – the crude reactions of a disturbed bully.

And over all this, like the fog in Dickens' London, were the fumes of inertia – a mingling from many sources. For there were men who could not believe that anything could be done, could not believe that they could win more than a temporary victory which would surely carry savage retribution: others who had been hammered so hard that the smoke they gave off was dust only, blinding, clogging, deadening: others who did not care – had not in themselves that capacity for extending their vision of life so wide as to include humanity, preferred to be outside all groups however worthy, felt themselves uneasy and diminished in the corporate clamancy; others who would come and go with the wind and saw the Union as useful to their private purpose sometimes, sometimes not; and men of all kinds who saw no solutions in the Union, whose life was wholly private, seeing no relevance in any organization to their sparrow's flight from dark to dark.

The movement was very far from being an irresistible force. As yet it was more like grit in the swarming jelly of a society which contained modes of life, still lived, from every age and circumstance of the last few hundred years, a society which could see it as but another mass movement – nearer in spirit and appearance to the Wesleyanism of a previous century (on which indeed it fed for orators and moral purpose) than to anything else they could comprehend.

Though Seth had been elected on to the committee, he had been given no distinctive post. As organizing secretary he would have been effective – even as it was he would travel every street every night to distribute leaflets or collect for an accident; he would have been reliable as treasurer, competent as general secretary, dedicated as chairman. But there was something about him which would always deny him those posts. He was too ruthless in his decisions, he would call on strikes for everything, he intimidated the older men by his urgency and depressed the younger men by his calls for 'an endless struggle', 'never, never to stop until we've got everything – and *then* to go on to get more!' In an instant grievances would become bitter. He embarrassed people by the stare-eyed almost possessed manner of his speech which, coming from that white, too-soon worn face, had in it something over-excited, 'like a consumptive curate' some people said. And as in his most neat and sober dress – even for this routine committee meeting he had put on a clean collar and wore his good shoes, gleaming with polish – there was a striking similarity to the puritanical God's-truth-fearing of lean-backed low-church curates, so in the pasty glaze of his face, that black hair lankly despising any wave, the blood-nicked chin, razor too fiercely drawn, there was the relished brimstone of those men, shadowed jaws snapping at purgatory eyes hot for hell-fire.

This too, John was aware of and so beside his brother he felt both inferior, and protective. For there was no doubt that Seth had been overlooked for positions in the Union he could have expected; no doubt that he was not given the same sympathy as the other members of the committee; but little doubt, either, that the day was approaching when his zeal would choke him, stopper him in some way so that he would become a comical caricature of himself. Boys already imitated his walk; the crack about the consumptive curate had stuck: he was already a marker in argument – 'You'll get as bad as Seth Tallentire next,' they would say, 'Now if Seth was here he would have us marchin' to London over that!'

To himself, John explained his brother by reference to their uncle Ephraim. For after the accident with the crusher Seth had taken Ephraim to live in with him and looked after him for those five last years of life when everything had to be done for the maimed man – from feeding him to holding him on the lavatory. All Seth's pleasures were sacrificed in the service: he left the choirs, stopped going to concerts, gave up his whippet. It was during those years that Seth had become infected with this strident fanaticism which had eaten away the youthful muscles of enthusiasm and cancered him with revolt.

John had been to see them often during the first two years of his coming to the town. Emily would send teacakes or broth or some fancies. Ephraim particularly liked rock-buns, holding a shivering hand to his mouth, his slackened eyes weeping as he tried to direct his teeth to nibble the currants. The rooms in the large lodging-house were most barely furnished – Seth having not the slightest instinct for domesticity. There were two rooms and in them the two single beds stood as isolated as the day they had been brought there, sheets lopsidedly trailing, brown blankets fiercely bundled into the bottom to keep the feet warm. It was chiefly boys who occupied the other rooms in this lodging house, and the smell of bacon fat peeled off the walls. Seth had taken these rooms as soon as he had come out of his apprenticeship and never thought to change them for the comfort he could easily have afforded as a paying lodger in one of the colliers' cottages. There was a table and three chairs, a brown corner cupboard, a most hastily carpentered bookshelf which contained all his Union library and literature, even one or two strips of coconut matting – but none of this held together: like the objects in some still-life paintings, the possessions were self-sufficient, each one to itself, and a man seemed but another object among them, crossing the slats of light.

There, at a window which looked down to the well of a back-yard Ephraim had sat, all day. He could have gone to the work-house but Seth would not have it. John would come and take across a chair and sit down immediately to get over the fear he felt at seeing before him the pulverized man: no less strong a description would be adequate, for the accident had crushed all but the essential juice of life out of him. He was now too small for his clothes, his bones seemed too small for his skin – cloth and flesh hung about him. The little control he had over his movements was spent in trying to retain dignity and his face screwed with effort to stop the dribbling mouth and eyes. One hand was less all fingers; he had not enough strength to move across to his bed without lurching, in pitiful burlesque of drunkenness, from one object to another for support. He spoke little, the words shaking him painfully – and in his eyes there was a hunger for life or death, not this existence he had, so that they accused all who looked in them. Often, when John came away he marvelled that any man could survive as Ephraim had done and marvelled the more at Seth's uncomplaining devotion. Only he winced when Seth, in one furious mood, pointed to the old man and shouted 'look what they did to Ephraim! Look at him!' – for then John could *not* look at him. Nothing could persuade Emily to visit him and the fact that the old man's name was the same as that of her dead son did little to mollify Seth, who always held it against her.

Then Ephraim had been found dead in the yard by Seth as he returned home from a shift. He must have thrown himself out of the window; there was no accident about it...

As they approached the pub, Seth became more cheerful and

winked happily at John. The committee rooms were at the back of The Royal Oak but, early, they went into the bar. Seth went over to talk to the secretary and John settled down to watch some of the miners playing dominoes. It was a game he liked to play himself and he was content enough studying the way they dropped.

He was nudged up the bench as two men came over. Like most of the others they wore clothes similar to those they worked in – dressing up was, for most of them, a weekend affair. The pit boots were planted in the sawdust like coal scuttles. Soon, John turned from the dominoes to listen to them, for one of the men, oldish, his cheeks still retaining a faint apple redness, almost magically set on the yellow leather of his face, was telling the other about the interconnection of the seams between the different pits.

'Yes,' he said, 'thou can match them aa' up, if thou's a mind. Tek that seam at Cleator Moor – Five Feet Coal Seam they call it – well that's same as t' Mowbanks seam at Workington, and t'same again as what they call't Ten Quarters' seam at Ellenborough, Ballgill, Flimby and Broughton Moor. And that Ruttler Band at Ellenborough – well that'd go into t' Little Main Band at Workington and then hit 't Banrock Band at Cleator and Whitehaven.'

The list of names went on, and John was fascinated just to hear them. There was something mysterious and also grand in such a list: he remembered the calling of names from the register at school, the excitement which came from his mother when she set off in pursuit of a relation and plunged through forests of names unknown to him, the might which seemed to rise up from the Bible as the preacher read from the Old Testament until the air rang with names, visible and strange as a wheeling flock of wild geese. And in the relish of the old man's voice there was pleasure: John could sit all night and listen to these men talking, feeling less danger then from that nihilistic despair which his self-absorption had burnt into him than at any other time. Healed by this calling of names.

'Up, lad!' Seth said. 'Meeting's on.'

He went into the bare back room and sat on one of the benches which Seth had so carefully laid out earlier in the evening. There were too many. Nothing but a routine meeting, few had bothered to turn up. From the back, John kept looking at Seth – smiling to himself at the fact of his brother's presence up there on the platform with the committee – and then, as if shy, he would look away from him – embarrassed by Seth alternately slouching and stiff-bodied glaring, now beaten, now triumphant and both somehow out of place in the even reading of the minutes, proposing and seconding, short treasurer's report on the funds, a long question about Bain's new provisions for starting times, a complaint about the threat to raise the rent of the cottages ('outside our jurisdiction,' said the chairman – to be followed by such an expletive from Seth as covered even him with confusion and prevented him from making his point at all), the plans for getting in touch with other, more powerful areas (the Cumberland-Westmorland coalfield was not only isolated, as most of them were, but very small, comparatively powerless) and as men rose from the benches each bearing particular witness to the spirit of injustice, John left Seth alone and warmed to the quiet tenacity of the miners around him.

The committee rooms were available for many other organizations and no particular banners or decorations betokened the miners' cause. The walls were dark brown, the ceiling spread with wavering circles of tobacco smoke, gently layered on the cream paint: the platform did not ride across one end of the room like a stage but jutted out from the wall, a precarious jetty. The sacrifices that the men were prepared to make in merging themselves into an organization seemed to have begun in the similarity of clothing. The common mark of the pit boots, the bow of the back as they leaned forward on the backless benches, like sailors bending into a wind. And as the talk went on – the voices echoing in the large room, each word thereby a challenge, flung out to carry beyond those present – he felt secure in the rightness of what they were all to fight for. The days when a man worked as if he was made for nothing else in the world, when he called by 'sir' and 'master' those 'set above' him – those days would never cease to cast their shadow over his own, but for his children he wanted it to be different. However much he had been in awe of his grandfather, to have followed him would have been blindness not forgivable by those following *him*. His grandfather had never seen, but for him who had there could be no looking away. Yes, he agreed with the man who was talking, it was not right that Bains should expect them to work up to the waist in water: yes, he agreed, when there were explosions in the pit then the walls should be inspected by independent observers before work was resumed: yes, it *was* criminal that they should use fewer props than was safe just because the company was worried about the cost of timber; yes, it was a scandal that the widows of the five men killed and the seventeen injured in the last William Pit disaster should be given such insulting compensation. These things should be put right. If only, he thought, he had the intelligence and the guts to see how they could be put right without recourse to actions in which he felt himself to be abandoned to the will of a mass less finely pointed than that of any of its members. But habit or squeamishness, selfishness or stupidity – he did not know what it was – prevented him from moving from the word to the deed with other than timorous, almost grudging reluctance. He would do odd jobs for Seth meticulously, and in the mechanical operation find some satisfaction: when men were to be counted, he was present. Yet always there was the unease – that he was there but not as totally committed as he felt he ought to be, not as completely convinced as the reasoning should have made him, marching, fighting even, but without the scent of the glory of the battle which was there, he saw, in the faces of others. Once, he thought, he would have been capable of it.

He kept such reservations to himself. In the town he was thought of as a solid worker and a solid union man.

He could never talk anyone else into joining the union though: was not capable of even attempting to do so. Yet surely, he thought, if he believed in it, he should have been able to do that.

Into these partly secret, partly guilty thoughts which had, as usual, drawn his concentration away from the meeting, came the voice of Seth, made raw by the cold response of his audience. John was aware that some of them disliked his brother to the extent of hating him.

'An' I say we should *force* them to join!' said Seth. 'Any man working down a pit as isn't in this union is a walking blackleg – yes you needn't laugh, Tom Miller, blacklegs aren't just brought in from outside – they live amongst us – no, Mr Chairman, not here – I accuse nobody at this meeting! I accuse ... now, yes – *all* of them should be in. They take the benefits that t' Union gets for them – when, I say, *when*, Mr Chairman, when we get this Eight Hours through – who'll turn on it! I ask the meeting – who'll turn on it? – and there's many'll benefit as haven't paid one halfpenny subscription to this Union – men who've just sat on their arses – yes I apologize to the Lodge,' Seth's brow had already risen to sweat, a gleaming band, yellow under the poor lights. 'So – who'll object to working eight hours a day?'

'The hewers will,' somebody shouted. 'They'll lose on it if they can't do their ten-hour stint. And thou knows as well as anybody, Seth Tallentire, that the hewers in Durham's *not* for it. Not a bit.'

'That's not my argument!' Seth exclaimed. 'You're muddlin' my argument. Hewers'll have to put up wid' it. They have too much their own way as it is.'

'That's reet!' somebody shouted. 'Aa'll tell Ted Blacklock that!'

'Tell him! And tell him that if he keeps puttin' my gang on them poor seams it'll amount to victimization. He's worse than the bluddy company!'

'Order. Order!'

'Yes. Well – yes. Now – I've lost hold of me bluddy argument wid' all this talking.'

'Harken to t'lad!'

'No – no offence. But a fella should have a straight run ... Mr Chairman. He should be given that. If he gets tripped up ...'

'His face lands int' clap! Like thine, lad! I propose we end this meetin', Mr Chairman, t' business being finished.'

'No!' Seth exclaimed. 'I mean, with your permission. Let me

bring forward me point. I must bring it forward, Mr Chairman.'

'Well sharpen it a bit.'

'Two more minutes then, Seth,' said the chairman, severely looking at his watch. Then he nodded to Seth more kindly. 'Give the lad a chance, everybody. He's got something on his chest – let him get it out – we don't want him to throttle hissel.'

'Thank you, Mr Chairman. Yes. Well? What d'you say? I propose that we *make* everybody come into this union as'll stand to benefit from it. And if they refuse – now listen – I propose we refuse to work with them. Don't work with non-union members.'

'Don't be daft, Seth. It's a free country.'

'No – it isn't. That's exactly the basis of your mistake. If it was a free country – then we would be free to get what we want. And we can't. So there's your answer on that argument. But – listen! – we should not allow men who are not with us all the way to be down there working. Because they're working for the other side. Every man that isn't in the Union is for the masters. That's it! Every man that isn't in the Union is against it. And they know, they work on it – whoever heard of a Union man, a man on this platform, gettin' an easy seam? Answer me that! It's bluddy Ted Blacklock and his marrers walk off down that road. And for why? Because the company favours them – because it doesn't fear them.'

'And they're frightened of thee, Seth, are they?'

'No – well yes! Don't laugh. Yes! They are. Not of me – on me own – no, not of me. But of what this Union might grow to. They give in, they give in – but they give little away. We won't get anywhere until we smash them! And to do that – every man Jack of us must be in the Union. And women, I would have the women in so that they could draw the benefits – and I would have the children in, the day they're born – so that ivverybody's in the Union so that we can take all over – education we can tek over, governing and workin'. I would do away with all companies – parliament – everything – only the Union that is democratically elected by the men on the spot should run things.' He had held his audience when talking about bringing all men into the Union, held them despite the laughter, the chaffing which chapped John's nerve-ends, for it was something with which not a few of them were privately in agreement. But even this small current of sympathy had overcharged Seth and now he lost them all as his voice heightened its pitch, the sweat broke on his brow and he stood, hands clenching and unclenching, tugging at the white cuffs which hung from the short sleeves of his suit. 'There should be *nothing* but Unions,' he said. 'For men can see what they get then – they can see who rules them – and nobody rules them because they rule themselves! The Union would organize the business – maybe not us are clever enough, but we can mek sure our next lot are – and from the cot to the cemetery a man – or a woman, because they're more of slaves than we are – well – listen! – they could carry their heads high – one more minute, Mr Chairman – there would be no injustices and no accidents, there would be no dying of want and no neglect or poor people – and the Unions would care for men's minds because they would *know*. The men would – what a terrible thing it is to have a stunted mind, more terrible than many a bodily affliction – yes! – the Unions alone, on their own, only them, the Unions should take over this country and lead it out to a better place.'

'There's a better place in that bar next door.'

'Propose we close, Mr Chairman.'

'Seconded.'

'Passed. Word of Next Meeting will be circulated.'

'Meeting over.'

The men got up and moved out, taking no more notice of Seth than if he had been a post. He sat there, flushed now, tense on his chair, sitting after the others had started to move, still bound to the words he had so painfully let go. Unoffended by the brutal cutting-off – the bruises which would rise later and be poked and further inflamed by him in the solitude of his lodgings – now a man rapt in a vision. And John, too, did not move, his face riveted to that of his brother, love going out to him in waves which broke before Seth's wall of conviction. My God he was a brave man, John thought, and he was right, right! But why, looking at him, did such a cold sorrow run through him like a deep undercurrent pulling below the warm waves, why did his love chill to such despair at that rigid sight? As all his loves froze now when greatest demands were made: the responses left on the other side of that death-trance in the squatter's cottage.

The room quickly emptied, he walked down to Seth and touched him on the arm.

'That was a good speech, Seth,' he said. 'A real 'un.'

'Yes?' Seth stood up, jerked to life. 'But I think I talked too much.' He smiled. 'You liked it, did you?' He paused. 'I meant it. It's true what I say.'

He walked to the side of the platform and came carefully down the three steps.

'Give us a hand to clear these benches away, will you?' he asked.

15

Sarah had been staying with them for almost a year when they went to the sea-side on a Bank Holiday.

St Bees was only a few miles from the town and in summer Telford's horse-drawn coaches ran a regular service there. It was a fine, clear day, fresh but not cold, and there were a fair number at the beach. Emily found a good spot. To her right was the cliff called St Bees' Head riding out into the Solway like the prow of a ship, fields streaming back from its very edge, full green sail. Behind her were the narrow, steep streets of the village, the public school which was quartered on the lush spread which ran back from the bay, as protected as the pheasant which Kipling mourned as being the 'Lord of Many a Shire.' To her left, the south, more cliffs, lower than the Head, with houses sheltered in the creeks before the land swung out once more to sea and made perfect the arc. And before her the level water, rolling in calmly under the windless air, merely washing the pebbles. She felt completely refreshed, her sensations filled from such a deep spring of tranquil solitude as made her relax entirely, the sound of the sea a soft choir to her pulse.

Sarah drifted off towards the village on the excuse of looking for sweets for the children. Most reluctantly, she took Veronica with her. On several occasions she had announced that she would leave, could leave, should leave them on their own, that Veronica and herself were a burden, a nuisance, a pest.

'But where would I go?' She would invariably conclude. 'Just look at my skin! It must be the stink that comes off those slag heaps; or our John. Who would have a woman with a skin like that? Besides I'm useful, aren't I, Emily? Who did the shopping this afternoon? Who trailed down to the market? And I don't eat so much, not more than anybody else, do I? So I'll stay – I know you don't mind.'

Seth had offered to take his sister in with him – been eager for it, saying that a woman and child would make his lodgings something of a home: but Sarah had paid one visit only.

'Live in that place! You couldn't want to put me there, John. And that chair still sat there – and knowing Uncle Ephraim used to sit on it. I told Seth to throw it out. It's an awful place! No wonder Emily would never go. And there's nothing but boys and old men around. I know what would happen. Soft-hearted old me would be cookin' and washin' for the blooming lot of them with Seth saying it was all part of the benefits of the Union. No, thank you very much. He can find his own woman.'

The question of compelling her to leave – in some unhurtful way – had arisen many times in whispered agitation between John and Emily, the last to be downstairs, hearing Sarah above them land on her bed as decisively as a bag of coals on a pavement.

'But you can't put your own flesh and blood out on the streets,' said Emily.

'It's nobbut by a short head that me own flesh and blud aren't *walkin'* the bluddy streets. Don't start back – thou knows my meaning plain.'

'Well she's a good-lookin' young woman,' Emily replied. 'You can't expect her just to park herself indoors, waiting to be asked.'

'Can't I? Might be better if she did. She terrifies half o' them and t' other half comes wid their tongues out.'

'John!'

'It's true! Now Alf Toppin's a canny lad – she put the fear of God intil 'im. He couldn't walk down a street where she was widdout flickerin' on and off. Like a lighthouse. Yes – No – Yes – No – I will – I won't – she does – she doesn't – at her – back up – I can – I can't – thou could see fowks crashing intil each other all over Lowther Street. He confused the multitudes. An' then Arnold Blacklock comes up – brass wouldn't be outdone on *that* mug – up comes the bold Arnold and remember how *that* turned out! I nivver thowt I'd fight for any woman but thee – but it was that or be taken ower. And him wid' five children – five credited.'

'She's lively though,' said Emily, loyally. 'Good company.'

'Well if thou's prepared to put up wid' it – that's it! The lass has to live somewhere.'

'Yes,' Emily replied, sadly realizing that her regard for that fact would force her to continue to tolerate a situation which often appeared intolerable. She could dull her ears to Sarah's occasional dirges, she *did* enjoy the girl's chatter – was shocked but not outraged at the way in which she chased men and was a woman fully capable of dealing with the gossip that sprouted up around her husband's sister – but the life of her own family was intruded on, trampled over, it seemed, by the restless paces of the younger woman. She was afraid, above all, for John who was mute before her, his outbursts absorbed in polite silences. She had feared the quick rut of his bad moods when they were first married; but now she wished them back, for at least there had always been a return, whereas here she saw a slow freezing, in himself, of himself from her, from everyone; their love was now a grey, protective canopy, hardly noticed from one week to the other.

She sat among the bags and watched him with the children. The beach was stony at its edges but further out long flats of sand were left by the sea. The tide had just turned and would take some hours to reach her. With Alice on his back, May trailing behind him, dragging a stick across the unscratched sand, Harry trotting and splashing through the small puddles, they were making for the fringes of the sea. John had made no concession to the conditions, and his boots, his cap, his heavy flapping jacket all marked him out as a miner – and she could see his like scattered along the shore, a dark company of regulars, resting for a day. She watched his walk, steady and easy, Alice no more than a feather on his back – and he stopped to pick up Harry, carrying both children, the same pace. At that moment she loved him and wanted to shout out, to have him turn and come to her in that way, with that walk. It seemed that the children would claim all that she loved in him – or all the love he could give – she could see it in his stride. As she had done in the churchyard on her last visit to Ephraim's grave, she noted them, concentrating to remember every detail she could pick out, John and her children going over the flat sand towards the ebbing sea. He was too far away to hear her shout.

As always, John had started off with the children full of what they would do together. When the impulse came to him he delighted in the children, they were then like precious memories of his own childhood and every sound and movement they made intoxicated him – just as another twink could see him morose and indifferent to them, even savage. What discouraged him, however, was his response when given a perfect day such as this: then, with all to expect, he could perform so little. He would begin by being determined to enjoy the time with them, almost snatch them to him and run to beat the day: then, by irresistible degrees, an inexplicable paralysis of interest would seize his enjoyment, stiffen his enthusiasm to a drilled series of reactions less and less controlled until he either collapsed into himself in self-disgust or wrenched himself away, abandoned them.

This day, he had tried to forestall it by inviting Seth to come along with them – the two men easily able to form a small republic fit to withstand any number of women and children.

'No. I'm gonna slam through this lot!' Seth had replied, indicating a large volume, a new one, as fresh in the middle of his brown table as a new-laid egg. 'There's not enough of us at it,'

Seth continued, 'and I reckon I'm in a better position than most – having no family – to read. If I get a good run up of a morning, I can nearly always break a good bit of it down before night. Mind,' he winked at John, 'I'm no great athlete, I tell thee.' He rubbed his hands, 'there'll be some jaw-crackers and eye-bogglers in that – I'll bet. Oh, it'll be a reet do. If thou comes past here midday thou'll probably hear it – that'll be me, talking it out aloud to frighten it. No,' he added, sinking as suddenly from this rare pinnacle of frivolity as he had risen to it, 'no, I've promised myself a day like this for a long time. And there's no Union matters to attend to, nothing but folk rushin' off to enjoy thersels – and so they should. I'm all in favour, and many *more* like days say I – so I'll get crackin'! See John,' he concluded, a little sadly, 'When you know what's in these books – folk give you respect. They listen to you – See?'

John had not the heart to persist in persuasion.

Before reaching the sea he had decided what to do. He would not stand and listlessly let them play around him but keep moving. Feeling a little ridiculous at the pressure of determination necessary to cope with three children so much in awe of the sea that the lightest touches would have kept them spinning with delight all morning, he ran the last way across the sand, the two held children joggling about him like army packs and, having set them down, he took off his boots and socks.

'Tek your shoes off!' he commanded. 'May, come away from it wid' those shoes. Your mother'll kill me if they're ruined. Tek them off. We're gonna paddle'.

'Can I swim, dad?' May asked.

'Thou's no bathing suit. Anyway – it's ower dangerous for swimmin'. Swim in a beck if thou must. Not here.'

'But I don't need a bathin' suit. Jessie Collins swims in her knickers.'

'Dis she?'

'Yes.'

'Well, see how't paddlin' goes. But Aa'm no great swimmer, lass. Thou'll be on thee own.'

'Thou means, thou can't save me if I drown?' the little girl asked.

'That's correct.'

'Well maybe I'll swim just at' edge. Where it's shaller.'

'Git them shoes off!'

Alice was too small to be left for long and soon John was holding her again, wading through the shallows, feeling his toes spread over the sand, the spray fleck his white skin. Like May, she had been little 'trouble' – to himself, that is, meaning that he had not been woken up more than a few times, could manage her quite easily – but she was much prettier than May. Harry had been a bloody nuisance: in the first year he had cried almost every night – until John had been forced to go into the other bedroom: it was that or collapse at work. And for the first time, he had seen Emily beaten by one of the children: she had carried little milk and after a few weeks the feeding was torture to her. There was a woman a few doors away who had given the child milk but always he wanted more, his mouth strained open like a ravenous chick, head leaping forward from the neck to clench the gums on the teats. It was only then that John began to compare his wife's lot to his own. She had a hard life, yes. But so did he, and that made it even. It was not a matter of discussion, but something accepted by both of them. Moreover, Emily would have been in no way able to provide for herself and the children without him. Yet with Harry, when he had come home to find Emily making his tea, the boy on her arm, her action the flakings of energy, her body moving with such dilatory fragility as threatened to stop and sink to liquid, so insubstantial was it – then he had been shocked to realize that she had a world more slavish and demanding than he could have endured. It was this, too, which had led him to the act – rare among those he worked with – of taking the children off her; his principal satisfaction was always, as now, to look back and see Emily alone – for then, he thought, she must be relieved and happy.

Afraid of drowning, May did no more than paddle – Harry was soon sitting scraping out the sand and making a castle. John walked backwards and forwards, offering Alice to the waves it seemed. He offered little else. Perhaps the knowledge that this sea pressed down on him when he was working beneath it made him restless: whatever it was, he was soon bored and he felt a darkness, seeping in like the sea, coming from nowhere this fine day, but irresistibly settling on him as it had done in the cottage.

'We'll go and see if we can ratch out some bird nests,' he said, abruptly.

'Come on. Here. Dry your feet on my jacket.'

He went away from St Bees' Head to the lower cliffs at the Southern edge of the small bay, waving to Emily and, with the return of the wave, getting an injection of enthusiasm which led him to organize a race – sending Harry and May well out in front before he himself began to run. Alice screaming with pleasure in his arms so that he laughed aloud and kissed her as he ran, the large boots thudding such footprints into the sand as looked indelible.

Emily had hoped they would come back to her – but when she saw May and Harry run away in front of their father, she let them alone, deciding against going after them. She knew that John wanted to have them for himself sometimes.

A wind came up with the tide and it was too fresh just to sit. Sarah had not yet come back from the village but Emily had no hesitation at leaving the bags and coats unguarded. The red sandstone cliff of the head drew her towards it and she walked towards boys playing among the rock-pools, past women like herself planted in the middle of their family's stores, the sea's edge dared by a few paddlers, only one man swimming, a game of football starting up.

Mr Stephens was returning to his bicycle to get some drawing paper from the bag. This bag sat most impressively on the back mudguard. He had fitted it out himself and it was so built that two dozen eggs could be carried in it without any fear of their being broken. When the breeding season passed, he took out the frame and inserted a minute system of drawers for his paper, his chalk, pencils, rulers and the new geometry set. His 'book of the moment' would fit in there too, still leaving room for the french chalk and glue, the scissors and the patches. His sandwiches and flask of lemonade were in a small pack which he carried on his back. Dressed in stout tweed suit, with his mackintosh strapped on to his handlebars, he was then ready to meet any day.

Emily recognized him but was too shy to approach him. So much so that she was tempted to turn around and be off to prevent any possible embarrassment that might come to him as a result of having to engage himself in the act of remembering – and perhaps pursuing – that encounter they had had when he had given her shelter at Cockermouth Hiring. Though he did not at first recognize her, Mr Stephens was very conscious that a woman was about to pass near him. Still unmarried, that last ten years had encrusted him with bachelor habits which his hobby had greatly encouraged. He was too old now for that willing flirtation into which he had been prepared to enter with any girl – and too young to regard himself as irrevocably single; too aware of his feelings to regard himself as a misogynist, too cautious before their implications to permit himself to trust in them. Marriage was his dream and as yet he was still able to regard it as a happy perfection – no less would do – which one day would slip on to him as neatly as his coat.

The path at the cliff-foot was narrow and he stood aside to let her pass. She looked away from him – but the definite impression of that action caused him to look at her more closely. Then he turned away, afraid to be caught staring. Emily was within a yard of him and had to glance up in order that she might indicate to him that he must step to one side for her to pass – and she was glad to see the evidence of remembering in the concentration on his half-averted face. Aware of the necessity for his small retreat, Mr Stephens turned to her, thus using the excuse of courtesy as a stalking-horse for his gathering curiosity. The nod which she returned to him for his well-mannered stepping back contained a confidence to which the formal and inconsequential nature of this small passage lent no intimacy: his returned inclination was thus the more vigorous – acknowledging, too, that there was more cause than common politeness for them to greet each other. Yet the very vigour of his bobbing head was an unsuccessful joggling of his mind to unloosen the cause. Passing by him, Emily was amused and she smiled; but she was relieved, now, that she would avoid an embarrassing exchange and this forbade her eyes to light at the signal from her mouth. Stephens sighed, too slight a sigh for anything but the incident just concluded, reaching Emily's ears like a plea for more time – as it was meant to – and causing her to hesitate for a moment, wishing that she could throw off the wrappings of this prohibitive sensibility and straightforwardly address him.

'Tallentire!' he said. 'Mrs Tallentire!'

Beaming with pleasure, Emily turned and bowed, slightly but so easily inclining from her waist as made her appear much younger than she was. Mr Stephens clutched off his hat and held out his hand.

'Robert Stephens. You – we met at Cockermouth – oh, ten, twelve years ago.'

Slowly her hand went out to his, she watched it rise before her, saw it coarse in his slim white fingers.

'My sketching paper got wet,' he said. 'Silly of me. I dropped it in a puddle. But I always bring a spare block. How's your husband?'

'Very well, thank you.' Her hand slid out of his, no pressure having been applied by him or her. 'He's over there with the children.'

'Children! O yes – you were – children, eh? Deary me.'

'It was May I was carrying then,' she said.

'And how many more?'

She paused. 'Two more. Harry and Alice.'

'Goodness,' he replied. 'Well. I've often thought about you.'

'You were very kind to us.'

'Oh – no, no. No, no, not at all. Often – thought about you. You were such a – how can I say it? – you were such a – a handsome young couple: so lively,' he said, rather forlornly. Then 'Of course, you still are – as you were – I should have recognized you immediately. But I get so absorbed – there were some shovellers I was trying to get down, and then I saw a redshank – even more unusual around here, you know, must be the weather. And I couldn't decide which to do. That was when I dropped my pad. Still on farm-work, your husband – Joseph, that's it! I've been trying to remember his name – Joseph.'

'John. No, he's in the pits now.'

'John. Yes. In the pits eh? Well,' Mr Stephens looked out to sea, 'the conditions are improving I'm told.'

'They won't be improved until they shut down the mines altogether,' Emily returned, calmly.

'I see – Yes – Well, we must burn wood. Except there are so few trees now. I'm sure that's one of the reasons the fowl-mart has disappeared.'

'Has it?'

'H'm? Yes – it has. And the short-eared owl's becoming rarer now. They think birds can sit on stones, you know. Well so they can – you'll find thousands of herring-gulls nesting on these rocks in season you know: but it would be a dull world with only herring-gulls to look at, wouldn't it?'

'Yes,' Emily replied with great gravity, hoping that she would thus conceal the giggle which ran up her stomach as rapidly as a lizard. 'Yes it would.'

'It would. It would. They never think about what they've got – always wanting more. And they frighten away all the delicate things of the moment. True, Mrs Tallentire, true. Have you seen the golden plover?'

'No.'

'There you are. You should have done. They're frightening him away. Sometimes I think the world's going mad, Mrs Tallentire. It breaks irreplaceable things so carelessly.' He smiled. 'You can tell I'm still a schoolmaster, can't you?'

'Oh . . . where do you teach now?'

'Maryport – ugly place – full of miners – not, of course, I mean – the cottages they have to live in – they *are* ugly, aren't they?' The wistful end of the sentence truly craved an apology.

'They're better than some places,' Emily replied, briskly.

'O yes. Everywhere's better than *some* place – isn't it? I mean – the world's a circle. Never ending.'

'That's something to be *thank*ful for, isn't it?' asked Emily, not at all confident before this method of talking but happy to keep going, having observed that the man had ducked so determinedly into his hobby out of shyness and been more than willing to caricature himself through fear of becoming over-intrusive. She liked him.

'Yes, yes I suppose it is. Maybe this is another period when things become extinct – and somewhere others are growing or changing to take their place.' He smiled. 'Maybe *we'll* become extinct, eh, Mrs Tallentire?'

'Good gracious, Mr Stephens. Why should we?'

'True. True.' He paused. 'But if things keep changing at this rate – we'll soon have nothing left to invent.'

'We can sit back then,' she laughed.

'Yes. Sit back. Yes.' He paused. 'I'm going that way,' he continued, nodding in the direction behind her. 'Would you – I suppose you want to be alone.'

'No. I'll be pleased to walk with you, Mr Stephens.'

'Will you? That's very kind. I'll just get my pad – this one's ruined I'm afraid.' He laughed at her, 'though I could always use it for *water-colours,* I suppose.' His smile stopped on his face, waiting for the response to his little joke. When it politely came, on went the smile, thankfully.

When she thought back on those next two or three hours it would amuse her to imagine them as a flight. For, once on the trail, with gulls and waders and peregrines to point out, Mr Stephens' confidence was restored, and from being restored, it leapt to action. He was gallant and considerate helping her across the rock-pools, taking her by the easiest routes – and soon he began to abandon his dependence on birds and chat to her in a way which freshened her thoughts. Yes, she wondered what it would be like to be married to such a steady, gentle man: not that John was other than steady in his ways, not that he could not be gentle – the defences went up like a drawbridge – but John's steadiness was all in his turning over the weekly money – that done he would allow himself any extremity of mood before her, or merely subdue her by that awful indifference to what was around him. While Mr Stephens, she thought, would be steadily curious in the world around him, not forcibly questioning it as did Seth but ceaselessly prodding this fact, that object, something in him that would spin out a lifetime. And then, because he talked to her so, she relaxed and lost that strain she so often had before John – before most of the men who had ever come to the house with him – when the silences would be stretched by contradictory interpretations until it was rent by temper. Talk made Mr Stephens more open, he was not afraid to remark on his attitude towards anything – and even in that short time, she found herself able to redefine her own feelings because of his statements about his own, whereas with John, things were defined in disruption or left unspoken, so potently unopened that they sank below the soil of the mind to fester and fructify there, hidden.

This flight, then, so unexpectedly come upon, forgot her worries – and when John – trailing the children – discovered her she was sitting on a rock, her bare feet splashing in a pool looking over Mr Stephens' shoulder as he sat beside her, sketching.

'What the hell are you doin' here?'

'This is Mr Stephens, John,' Emily replied, immediately.

'I don't care if ...' then John saw the disturbance on the mild face which turned to his and stoppered his outburst abruptly. 'Alice was mopin',' he said.

'Oh – poor thing. Here. Let me take her.' She came across, her feet lifting wincingly at each step.

'They're so tickly these rocks.'

'Thou should keep shoes on.'

'Yes. There we are. Poor lovely. Did she think mammy had run away?'

'She did.'

'Mr *Stephens*, John,' Emily whispered, 'Cockermouth.'

'Oh!' John looked at the figure scrambling upright, with legitimate intentness, relief coming with the recognition. 'I didn't recognize you – Mr Stephens! How are you then?' – the words were shouted across the short space; perhaps the sea encouraged such volume.

'Oh – very well, Mr Tallentire. Very well indeed.' The hand came tumbling over. 'Thank you. It's so very easy to slip on those rocks. Yes. Deary me. Cockermouth. I hope you haven't been anxious about your wife, Mr Tallentire – I should have thought to tell her the time but you see when I'm sketching ... you must have been very anxious.'

'Not a bit, Mr Stephens! Glad to see you – keeping well are you?'

'Yes. Thank you. Very. I was telling Mrs Tallentire that the black-headed gulls are more numerous this year than I've ever seen them.'

John looked up – and in doing so caught the wink in Emily's eyes – she alone had observed his slipping from forced to spontaneous speech, as the break on a wave, which could not be wholly successfully withheld – and she knew that if she could catch him in this way it would flick him back to her as neatly as could be. It worked, he returned her wink. If only she could have told him how that simple reaction penetrated her more deeply than any thousand hours with Mr Stephens.

'More gulls, eh?' said John. 'Well they must be finding this territory good for breeding, eh, Mr Stephens?'

'Quite so,' replied the schoolmaster realizing that, whatever the danger he had so clearly felt, it was now past. 'It's the salmon boats, you see. Well, all the boats. D'you know, there are about three hundred along this coast now. All from Cumbrian ports. Of course, the bye-laws are very good – but even so, it's too many boats, I think. I have a friend who tells me that they've cleaned the herring out entirely.'

'Have they now?'

'O yes. Scuppered him – if I may use the word. But of course, the boats are useful for the gulls.'

'It's like that song – Ilkley Moor baat 'at, Mr Stephens. You know – t'worms eats t'man and t'birds eats t'worms and we eat t'birds so we eat t'man.'

'I know the song, yes. *Ducks* eat the worms. *Ducks*. Yes. It's very popular in Yorkshire.'

And again Emily wondered at Mr Stephens – that he could be so nervous in front of people as to shy away into part of himself that had been almost entirely absent while they had talked together, him drawing, she dabbling her feet in the water, on the rock.

'Mr Stephens – would you like to come and have your tea with us?' she asked. 'We have plenty.'

'Well – I do bring my – it's very kind of you – but, well . . .'

'Come away, Mr Stephens!' said John, encouragingly. 'Thou's most welcome.'

'Thank you. I *will* come.'

He let May wheel his bicycle and Harry held his hand.

Sarah had got to the provisions first and shook hands with Mr Stephens after a most energetic gobbling of the sandwich and dusting of her palms on her skirt. Soon, she was comfortably settled.

'Don't you find it funny – living on your own?' she asked him.

'It is a little,' he admitted, again relaxing now that he had cleared the introductory hurdle – and innocently finding in Sarah's directness the possibility of airing questions about his bachelor state in a much more serious and satisfactory way than usual. 'Yes. I suppose you would call it unnatural.'

'*I* would,' said Sarah, stretching out her legs, the skirt hem flapping prettily over the small boots, propping herself up on her elbows. '*Most* unnatural,' she added – and laughed.

'Yes. And laughable, too. You know, sometimes I think that I was made to be a bachelor.'

'No man is,' she retorted.

'Exactly. That's always my conclusion. Still,' he went on, 'there's nothing much I can do about it at the moment.'

'Isn't there now?' asked Sarah, thoughtfully.

'Have another sandwich,' said Emily.

'Don't you have even a housekeeper?' Sarah asked. 'Surely you could afford one.'

'Yes. I suppose I could. Well – I certainly could. But – well, I like to think that the first woman in my house will be my wife.'

'That's nice,' said Emily.

'It's *right*,' Sarah countered, as if the distinction were a correction. 'I've known men who never got past housekeepers and ended up by marryin' them – or just pretending you know There should be wives in there.'

'Thou's wise to tek time,' said John. 'Tek all the time there is.'

'John Tallentire!'

'Yes,' smiled Mr Stephens. 'You're a bad disciple of your own teaching.'

'Well – mebbe for me it was different.'

'Yes.'

'It's the same for everybody,' said Sarah. 'They should do it just as soon as they can. Get on with it.'

'I agree,' said the schoolmaster.

'Do you ever come to Whitehaven of a market day?' Sarah enquired, lazily.

'No. I'm teaching.'

'They have a small market on Saturdays as well.'

'Do they? Of course they do. I know they do.'

'It's very interesting,' said Sarah.

'It's exactly like any other market,' said Emily, 'and possibly no better than Maryport's.'

'Maryport's!' Sarah exclaimed. 'If he's been no further than *Maryport* market then he *must* come to Whitehaven of a Saturday afternoon. Maryport's nothing!'

'Well. I might try it.'

'You do.'

John had the greatest difficulty in keeping a straight face before Sarah's relentless incitements and when she added, 'There's ducks and pigeons and geese and aa' that sort of thing there – dead, mind, but there again, it'll give you a better chance to draw them. All that at Whitehaven market!' then he rolled over and picked up Harry to chuck him in the air and have an excuse for laughing.

When Mr Stephens left pushing his bicycle over the grass to the track, waving to them and quite moved that May came to escort him – he gave her threepence – then John was even more entertained at Sarah's defence before Emily.

'What you mean "poor man"?' she demanded. 'He's better off than our John for a start. And he's old enough, isn't he? I thought he was *very* pleasant, anyway – and anybody could see he just needs a bit of encouragement to open him out. I bet he's a different man altogether when he's opened out. Anyway – you could tell he liked me to talk to him – anybody could –

and it's a good job I was here or he would have felt out of it. He liked Veronica as well.'

'He never *said* anything to Veronica.'

'But a mother can tell, Emily, a mother can tell these things.'

(When Sarah did leave them it was not with Mr Stephens – never seen at Whitehaven market – nor anyone prepared for or considered but one who, like the first, came and took her, accepting the baby as casually as he expected Sarah to follow him back to the town he came from. Which she did, leaving as suddenly as she had arrived. Emily was convinced that, had she been accidentally out when Sarah had danced in to collect her clothes and her child, then she would never have discovered what had happened to her.)

That afternoon, however, Sarah brooded on Mr Stephens. Because she recognized that her resentment was caused by just a little jealousy, Emily was more openly affectionate with John than usual. And as they left the beach and walked slowly over to the coach stop, the freshness of the day's sea air seemed to mature on them, and the slowness of the children's steps spoke of a richness of running and seeing which nourished the parents with the knowledge that the day had been well spent. Emily heard her skirt trail on the grass behind her and she wished it could always be so, it was like the sound of the waves. A wind blew in from the sea and she snuggled more closely up to John.

Three children. John steady now in the pits, all silly hopes and uncertainties irrelevant now to the life that was set plain before her.

John was thankful that he had not lost his temper too often or too badly with the children. The thought of being home soon, the children abed, Emily with some work of her own to do, himself away, maybe for a drink, maybe to the allotment – would make it easy to be pleasant enough on the way back. It was impossible to live without Emily and his family; yet to live with them was almost unendurable.

But were these the only thoughts he was to have? This, his life, now settled on this plot, pit-cottage, an outing to some predictable place; was this all? So it was. So, in the beginning; no, it was the same then. But despair came over him when he contemplated such a life. It should have been enough – but it was so much less than enough, he thought. Day by day all he saw was what he threw in his own face, and it blinded him to what could be seen. And before vision went altogether, he wanted to see, he wanted to reach out, and perhaps to touch it with his hands.

16

He read the notice for the third time.

THE WHITEHAVEN CAB & GENERAL POSTING CO. LTD.
COACH BUILDERS, CARRIAGE PROPRIETORS & CARTERS
REGISTERED OFFICE, TANGIER STREET

These stables are occupied by a large stud of well-seasoned, thoroughly reliable horses which places them in a position for supplying on hire at the shortest notice – Landaus, Broughams, Phaetons, Dogcarts and Wagonettes of every description. Hearses and Funeral coaches: Funerals furnished in the most modern style.

'No sudden bereavement, I trust,' loaded with anticipation and coated with self-congratulatory politeness – the cleanness of accent being a matter of great pride – the words came from a small, well-dressed old man who had approached John from the other side of the market and stood behind him biding his time.

'Mr Errington!' John took the offered hand. 'Well. What's thou doin' here?'

'The market,' said Errington succinctly, and coughed. 'No ... bereavement – then?' he repeated.

'Oh – no. Nothin' o' that'

'Ah well,' said the old man. 'At least you'll know where to come.'

'Yes. Still as cheerful, eh?'

'Now Don't mock, John. As a man grows older his mind begins to dwell on his funeral. I saw one in Wigton last week –

and, do you know, they couldn't even manage matching horses! It looked badly.'

'I don't expect t' corpse complained.'

'It was Mr J. T. Ritson. A very respectable fella. I felt embarrassed for him.'

'Well, thou's'll hev to coom here to be buried then.'

'Who said anything about being buried? I'm still fit enough for a man ten years younger than me.'

'Yes. Thou's taken good care, Mr Errington.'

'I have. And I intend to continue in that direction.'

'What's'te think of our market then?'

'Fair to middlin'. I'm glad I came – but I think I'll skip it next time. Your wife's mother's only poorly, you know.'

'Yes. I do know.'

'And George Johnston died last week – did you know that?'

'No.'

'Robert Fell the week before.'

'Yes?'

'Mary Jane Wallace just before him.'

'Ay?'

'Freeman Robinson isn't lookin' good.'

'He nivver did.'

'Well he's worse since his brother died. That was George.'

'It was.'

'And old Frank Hewer fell down a ladder – broke his back: very bad.'

'Sounds like an epidemic round Wigton way, Mr Errington. Thou'd better clear out.'

'All me fields is let,' said the old man, testily.

'I see.'

'Well – you can catch a cold if you stand about. That sea's all very well but it shouldn't be allowed to play on the chest.'

'No.'

'Good day then.'

'Look after yourself, Mr Errington.'

A needless warning. The old man wrapped his coat collar around his throat and battled through the warm spring air No jokes now; John remembered that the old man had once delivered 'witticisms' and riddles as readily as some men give away sweets: he regretted his flippancy, but not enough to pursue his former neighbour through the market. Still, he thought, as long as Errington was getting around the markets there could not be a great deal wrong with him.

He himself had come this holiday morning to buy some brass studs for a small stool he had almost finished. They had been quickly got, but he had made no immediate rush to be away, preferring to dawdle around the stalls, masking his aimlessness and the femininity of the action by a small furrow on his brow which was to serve as evidence of an instantly justifiable search.

There was only enough money in his pocket to buy a couple of drinks. This was no cause of concern. Indeed, John and Emily had considered themselves decidedly well off since his work in the pit. They took no holidays beyond the very occasional day-trip to the sea. The house, once furnished, stayed as it was with Emily quite capable of replenishing knick-knacks, repapering the walls, replacing whatever was broken out of her savings from the housekeeping. John had one good suit. He was not much of a betting man just as she was not concerned to be flatteringly represented by her children's appearance: shoes were a problem but with care on her part and a few extra shifts on his, most of the children could be satisfactorily fitted out at Easter. Though to many their income would have seemed incredibly small, it might be said that they had few financial troubles. All that came in went out and there was sufficient for John to have his few drinks on a Saturday night, for Emily to feel the pleasure of being able to hunt down a small bargain on some Saturday afternoons at the market.

Propping up this attitude was the memory of what things had been like when John had worked as a labourer; though his youth had dissolved any incipient bitterness at the meagreness of the wage yet, looking back, John saw that for Emily those must have been hard times. And for Emily, whose attitude to money had been formed in a labourer's cottage early in life, the terms 'poverty' or 'subsistence-level life' would have seemed insulting as well as inaccurate. Insulting to those before her who had managed on so much less. Occasionally she had to scrape – and when the big strike had been on a year ago in 1912, she had been forced to cuts and stratagems, to skimping on her own food and regulating the number of slices of bread for the children, selling small treasures and taking the utterly distasteful step of asking for credit – but in normal times she had no complaints. She would have been ashamed to give sentence to them, there, where she daily saw real poverty. Where there were families whose numbers had grown so large that the least break in the man's work would crash them all to Homes and workhouses or near starvation. Where there were men drawing the mean sickness pay, made the more ill by the sight of their deprived families. Old people huddled in the corner of a kitchen on the five weekly shillings of pension. People not quite competent enough to hold on to proper jobs reduced to the scraps of labour which took every hour they had for miser's returns. Though a small town, it was large enough to breed that number, almost caste, of the very poor who swirled sadly and dispiritedly about it like sediment in a bottle. On 'The Tops' where they still lived was many a woman who could not give shoes to her children, and each wife, like Emily, with a man bringing in steady wages, was accustomed to the consistent behests of two or three neighbours; thus, daily, as she lent a sixpence or some bread or a pat of lard or gave away something too small now to fit any of her own children – she knew what the grind of poverty was – and through John's job, she escaped it.

Her escape was his confinement. Sometimes he would be overawed by the obligations which made his work so necessary. On a good day, when he was cheerful, working in the backyard making a rabbit-hutch for Harry – then he would feel as if an oppressive weight had been lifted from him: his cheerfulness now not, as before, coming out of the conditions of his life, but at such times as he could forget them. So far he had been lucky: there had been four bad accidents since he had come on to the coalfield and he had been involved only marginally in one of them: that time a piece of timber had torn across his calf – but he had been off work only two weeks. Otherwise, a ceaseless routine into which, at thirty-three, he felt himself settled for life. Without appeal. Now rummaging around the market to appease indistinct murmurs.

As soon as he noticed Emily, he drew back behind a stall to watch her unobserved. All the children were with her, including little Sarah, now just old enough to refuse to be carried, but still too small to walk very far. John smiled at the listless and dutiful expression on Harry's face: if there was anything the boy loathed, it was going shopping, preceded as it was by all the brushing and washing which superimposed a plaster-cast cleaner self on him, so tightly fitted that it took even him a good hour to break it all off. Now, as the stiff chunks of wet hair broke away from the head at the back and one stocking hung slackly over his boot, he was beginning to win through – but John could appreciate the struggle.

The occasion for their appearance in force was May's return. For two years now she had been the hired lass on a farm – she had not wanted to work in a factory or a shop and Emily had discouraged her from going into service. Her wage was four and six a week, and four shillings of this was sent home; thus, as throughout England, the younger children were fattened by their older brothers and sisters. It did not occur to Emily not to take this money, nor did May think herself in poor circumstances: she knew, moreover, that things had been harder since Sarah's birth and, as she loved the baby as if it had been her own child, the thought of her money going towards her made her positively glad. She walked the four miles home each Sunday afternoon to deliver her wage but had never more than an hour to spend with her family on that day. All the more, then, did she want them to move as a group, herself to be constantly among them when, as now, she had her week's holiday.

It was at this time that Emily would buy her a dress, or a pair of shoes, or whatever necessity was required by the girl. May was uncomfortable that so much money should be spent on her; at the same time, knowing that she herself had earned the money, she was determined to miss no opportunity of having it spent on her: yet that secondary feeling made her miserable. She was foolishly generous, giving effort, time, consideration and such possessions as she had to anyone who asked. Mrs Fenwick, her employer, had merely to nod to a pile of darning in the evening and May would take it up – though she had been up since four-thirty doing hard and heavy work all day. 'May this, May that' – yes she would help lift the potatoes if Mister needed an extra hand, yes she would thin the turnips, as she did nothing with her two free hours on Saturday afternoon – it was too short a time to go home in – and so yes, she would help with the ironing. Even out of those sixpences she kept for herself each week, she would hoard enough to bring back sweets for Harry and Alice, a ribbon for Sarah, a piece of chocolate for her mother.

John watched her, feeling tender towards his first-born. She had never recovered physically from the effect of those few months of his despair: she was a lumpy girl – her hair lustreless, her hands fat-fingered like a man's, she wore spectacles, she slouched as she stood – and yet John's eyes were drawn to hers with a wonder which his other children could not inspire in him. For there was such innocence there as reminded him of Emily when he had first met her: though what in Emily had been open was masked in May; what had flicked the hazel of his wife's eyes with excitement was calm on his daughter's face, the one expression seemingly careless amid abundance, the other often forlorn, set in a sadness; but this could not conceal the similarity. Through a gap in the canvas of the stall's side, he looked long at his daughter.

Emily had put on a little weight after the birth of Sarah, but it suited her, drawing the slim frame more firmly upright, giving a confidence to her walk which made it slightly slower, rid of that hustling scurry which had previously threatened to turn it into a run. She wore a hat and the hair could never be so strictly managed that it failed to loosen a little and sink some way to her shoulders, with the luscious thickness of a swathe.

She bought some thread and a thimble from the stall and turned away. John stepped out and came up to them, swept up Sarah and walked along to the shop.

'We thought we'd get May's dress at Studholme's, this time,' said Emily. 'The one we bought last year at the market wasn't much good, was it, May?'

'It was aa' reet, Mam. Honest it was.'

'You said it split after a week.'

'I mended it.'

'I should think so – but it shouldn't have split after a week.'

'Let's get her a hat, as well,' said John. 'She couldn't have one at Easter. Have one now, May.'

'I divvn't like them.' May blushed with the effort of denying her father's wish. Impassioned to further defence by a complete understanding of the love and favour which the suggestion contained, she was impelled to excuse herself fully. 'I look like a silly calf in hats.'

'Thou's look pretty,' said John.

'Nivver that,' May murmured. Then, 'Mam – I can easily do widdout a dress.'

'So we can go home,' said Harry. Adding, 'See, Mam. We needn't 'ave come.'

'You need a frock for summer and that's that.'

John pulled a face at May to excuse her mother's authority and went into Studholme's with them.

'Please go away, Dad,' May implored him.

'No, lass. Aa'd like to see the fit-up. Aa can't bide to be wid' yer mother when she's shoppin' – but Aa'd like to see thee set.'

'If Dad stops, I'm not goanna hev one,' May said, miserably.

'See, Mam,' repeated Harry. 'We needn't 'ave come.'

'Now don't be silly, May. He wants to make sure you'll look nice.'

'I can't git one wid' *him* there, Mam. I just can't!'

'Thou's a simple maid,' said John, affectionately moving over to hold her shoulders.

'I am.' May was but a touch from tears. 'I'm very simple Dad – so please go. Oh – let's all go, Mam. Please.'

'See, Mam,' said Harry. 'We needn't be here.'

As they stood just inside the door with the deep bay of the shop running into twilight, long counters meeting in eternity, a host of assistants hovering, pale in front of the darkly papered walls, they made up an obstructive gaggle, now teasing, now pleading with May, until the shop-manager set off from his control seat deep beyond the children's wear, and bore down upon them, boring his way through the damp air by the propeller action of rapidly dry-washing hands.

Sarah cried and Emily sent John off with the baby – allowing Harry to slip out and join them while she stayed with the two girls to meet the last push of the manager.

'We want a summer frock for this – young woman here,' said Emily, pleased to have turned it so well that the Manager himself was thus obliged to conduct them to the frock counter.

John went home and deposited Sarah with a neighbour before going over to his allotment. Harry had raced ahead of him, changed back into his patched playing clothes, and been out of the house long enough to score a goal in the back alley before his father's arrival.

The allotment had long been as John wanted it and now he had not much interest in it. On principle he kept it neat, for economy's sake he kept it productive, but it gave him little satisfaction. He would do what he had to do and then walk over to the edge of the cliff, sitting down there to look, as now, at the ships, the collieries, the town in which he had spent more than eight years of his life, feeling in its streets as much underground as he did in the pits which ran from it.

If he could not lift himself from the shadows in which his blankness had left him by dwelling on his memories of the glorious light which had once lit his life, then perhaps more action or even movement would provide a first foothold.

When the children were all in bed that night, he told Emily about the sign he had seen advertising the Whitehaven Cab & General Posting Company.

'I was thinkin' of askin' them if they wanted a driver,' he said.

'Whatever for?' The reaction unnerved him: she ought to have known without words.

'What d'you mean, woman? Because I want a change – that's "whatever for"!'

'Well – you change if you want to. We shall have to get out of this place.'

'That'll be no heartbreak.'

'It's been a good house.'

'We can find one just as good.'

'Just as you please.' She paused. 'When'll you be changing?'

'I haven't said it was certain.'

'No. No you haven't.'

She got up and adjusted his boots inside the fender. They needed no such adjusting.

'You would like to work with horses again, would you?' she asked, softly, though not timidly, as she returned to her chair – purpose achieved in breaking the rise of his temper.

'Mebbe.'

'Well I'll be glad. Anyway – I never like to think of you way down those pits, under the sea. It's a fearful job.'

'It pays well.'

'I know it does, dear.'

'This would certainly pay less.'

'I expect we'd manage.'

'I expect we would,' he returned glumly. Then, catching the sound of his dismal response, he laughed.

'What would'te think of us then – Eh? Up on a coach – gee up there! Horses peltin' on – ridin' through t' town – or mebbe I'd get a country run – eh? Git along there! O hell – it's be a *change* Emily.'

'Are you sick of the pits?' she asked, laying aside her work to look directly at him for the first time.

'Who isn't?' he answered. 'No more than anybody else, thou knows. But some mornings, when that cage clangs and that bluddy bell rings, and down we go, cramped together like cattle – and I get out to see t' same tunnels goin' on for miles, ready to smother me up, and thousands like me, that pick-axe the only thing that I've got to fight wid – well it makes me feel I might as well drop dead there and then and be finished wid it. Hackin' and squirmin' about – like a mad thing, Emily – pickin' away at that coal – there's nothing gives, nothing. Thou rips it out – and then there's more. There's nothing grows, nothing answers. Emily; a man could *be* his pick – he's worth no more.'

'Well, go and see them in the mornin',' she said.

'I will.' There was some satisfaction in this final agreement. He felt the reins in his hands, the horses breaking into a trot.

The following morning, on his way to the company, he met Seth and was alarmed the way his brother bundled him into a shop-front and stood there, frightened, his large eyes scanning the street ceaselessly.

'Ted Blacklock's got a gang out for me.'

'Where are they?'

'They were standin' outside t' committee rooms but I came out back way.'

'Did they see thee?'

'No. But they won't wait all day. I heard him say he would settle me first and then beat ivverybody else wid' his whippet this afternoon. I think they're still drunk from yesterday, John.'

'How come?'

'They were in Larry Allen's 'til five. Blacklock got in a card game wid' this sailor-fella and they wouldn't stop.'

'Let's go to t' docks,' said John. 'Come on – we can move around down there.'

John was upset at his own initial reaction. For he resented his brother's unspoken plea for help and could not stop thinking of the job he had set out to try for. He overcame this by taking his brother into his entire protection: willing him to put himself in his hands.

It was equally useless to go to Seth's lodgings or back to his own house. Later in the morning, John saw Harry and told him to tell Emily that he was with Seth and would be out for most of the day. If anyone came – she could say he had gone off to see the whippets.

The two men dodged about most of the morning. John went into the town at midday to see if the gang were still around – and just escaped observation. Blacklock, taller than most of the miners, was there in the streets with four others, hunting along the pavement like a pack of boys in their gestures, wolves more like in the ferocity of their obvious intention. People stepped into the gutters as they approached and the confidence grew on them as they saw the startling effect they could have without so much as a spoken threat. John stood in an alley on the other side of the street and felt their purpose smack into his face. He let them pass, bought a couple of pies and went back to Seth.

Seth's behaviour had often threatened to get him into trouble. It was a pity that it had to come from such a dangerous man as Blacklock. Soon after the committee meeting which John had attended, Seth had caused a nasty scene by standing at the entrance to the pit urging the miners not to work with Blacklock, who not only refused to join the Union but was totally against it. As a hewer and shift-leader he was doing well out of the present system.

He had not joined the Union then, but soon afterwards, when the opinion of the majority hardened, he did join – and Seth, utterly without vindictiveness, ceased to bother him and was annoyed if anyone reminded him of how he had once publicly denounced the man. He gave it little significance. But Blacklock never forgot it; he boasted of that. Then the Union had moved forward through more strikes towards the big one – and Seth, though he never rose above the level of an ordinary committee man, had more and more work to do, was sought out, even listened to. And in the strike, Blacklock dare not touch him.

Now sufficient time had passed and the span of the grudge had given it the quality of an epic revenge in Blacklock's mind. He was after him.

Though he knew that Blacklock would be out with his whippets in the afternoon, John thought it wiser for them to stay away from the town centre – and he took his brother to the side of a slag heap where they sat and looked down on the rocks.

'They're nothing but drunken savages,' said Seth. 'I should really just walk up to them and tell them what I think.' The tone robbed the words of all confidence.

'Thou couldn't,' John answered. 'They'd kill you.' He paused. 'I wouldn't go up to them on me own neither,' he added.

'Blacklock thinks that if he can intimidate me – then he can intimidate all the committee. He wants to smash the Union – I'm just a start.'

'It's nowt to do wid' t'Union. Better if it was. Blacklock wouldn't dare move against t'Union now. No. It's thee he's after, Seth. And he won't settle 'til he has thee. Now he's started, he won't rest.'

'Well I can't keep away from him all the time. He'll have forgotten by tomorrow.'

'If he has, there'll always be somebody to remind him.'

'I'm spendin' no more afternoons on a slag heap,' he smiled.

'Let's work it out a bit.'

'There's nothing *to* work out. He's a stupid, drunken fool, that's that.'

John was silent and sadly he thought of Seth. The violence was all in the words. Even strike action had to be orderly. In his charge for knowledge he ran into the cannon's mouth but he treated his body as if it were of no account. Now, faced with a direct attack on it, he was not so much afraid as helpless. Fighting was not at all uncommon, yet the prospect had caught Seth unaware. As they sat there, John felt for his brother's loneliness. Wished he had provided more of a family for him. The efforts Seth had made had been for them all: all of them now should help him. At least his own family should. This idea of the brothers uniting for Seth appealed to him romantically; a candle to the flame of his own first vision with Emily. Besides, something had to be done; by avoiding them in this way, Seth had done no more than thicken the scent.

'What we do is this,' said John. 'We send to Maryport for our Tom,' (another brother, who worked on the docks there) 'we get hold of Isaac. Fred Stainton'll come in wid' us and mebbe that fella sometimes knocks about wid' thee – Harry Barnes. That'll mek about half a dozen. And we meet up wid them and tek them on. There'll be no rest 'til it's out.' He paused. 'And *that's* certain,' he concluded.

Though such a fight seemed futile to Seth, such a cooperative effort appealed to him. And gradually John managed to get it into his head that the alternative was to run away or be badly beaten. Seth was slow to take the full impact of this – blood could not run through the bandages of his ideas. *He* would not have assaulted anyone. John's persuasion was tempered by the melancholy realization that he was urging his brother to a necessary action which with finer instincts Seth wished to avoid.

In the end, however, it was done, and Seth set off for Maryport to get Tom while John went home to send May for Isaac.

They met the next morning. The four brothers, Fred Stainton and Harry Barnes. John was full of himself. Isaac insisted on sending Harry down to Blacklock's to tell him they were coming. For without due warning they might have caught Blacklock alone and that would be 'poor does,' said Isaac. 'We would be stuck then, lads. We couldn't be six to one. Poor does a'together.' The arrangement was that they would meet that afternoon, the last day of this holiday – and fight it out on some waste, the south side of the Docks, hidden from the town by coal heaps, sparkling with minerals streaked under the bright sun.

Blacklock sauntered up with seven men and after an awkward almost shy preliminary few minutes when the damp sea air threatened to fizzle the whole thing out, Isaac demanded whether they were for business or not and this peremptory question from a stranger was sufficient spark to set it off.

As they fought the children who had gathered around them grew in number and men who had vaguely heard of the fight came up to watch. The fighting spread out over the waste down to the rocks beside the calm sea. All the men were strong from the work they did and the number of those involved meant that even if a man was badly knocked down, he could still recover in time to pitch in again. The only sounds were the grunts from the men, the boots on the black rocks, screeching black-headed gulls. It lasted for over an hour and because of Isaac, Seth's side were winning when the crowd suddenly slid away and the men stumbled and scattered along the waste and rocky shore as two policemen pushing their bicycles came from behind one of the heaps to survey the small groups of men walking off. They stayed until the place was cleared

The fight lost John the opportunity of changing his job, for as he explained to Emily, he could not now leave the pits. It was impossible to think of working anywhere in that town but with those he had fought. That she did not understand his explanation was no cause of wonder to John, who did not understand it himself. But it was much the same as that impulse which forced him to meet up with his brothers soon afterwards and volunteer for the war.

17

Joseph was born soon after the start of the war. He was the most difficult of the children – worse even than Harry had been, and Emily found that she had not the reserves to cope with him. She was then doubly glad that she had moved from the town to a cottage near John's parents, for her mother-in-law was a good help and would take Sarah off her hands for a whole day. Alice and Harry were at school, May had shifted to be close to her family, near enough to come over on mid-week evenings as well as on Sunday afternoons. When May was there she could just about manage Joseph. At other times he was too much for her and she would sit back exhausted on the chair after he had had a feed, with neither the strength to button up her dress nor the energy to whisper protests against his crying. She never forgot those afternoons. As she lay there, she heard her own breath, whimpering in the silent kitchen; and she wondered that it might stop. Then once more Joseph would begin to cry and her face crumpled before this simple assault. Outside was the quiet garden which Harry kept so well for her – already, at twelve, a hard worker. Across a field, for the cottage stood alone, was the house of John's father and mother. Below, on the plain, Wigton, Wiggonby and the places she had grown up in. She should have got protection from all this – yes, May *was* coming that evening, *was* coming, *was* coming – but the baby would not cease its cries and she could not move from the chair to the cradle, there was no strength in her. A particular dab of distemper on the wall would fascinate her and the shape would rivet her eyes so that all in the kitchen led to it, that senseless shape, that meaningless shape, and tears came down her cheeks as she weakly tried to pull her gaze from the shape which was the only hard thing about her, the rest insubstantial as the air which threatened to withhold its benefit from her: she closed her eyes and once more saw the shape printed on the screen of the black lids.

She remembered the long enchainment to her son, Ephraim, and the lock which Jackson's assault on her had put on her emotions; like a magnet this shape of despair drew to it all the filings of unhappiness. May's cold, stunned face when they had settled as squatters in the abandoned cottage. John's impenetrable misery at that time, his face, dead. Images of horror came to her and sucked at her bare breasts, scraped the stretched belly, clawed the slack, lifeless thighs and she could only wait for them to pass for she had no power to make them go. No John to help her, and as Joseph grew and that terrible first year passed, it was on John's absence that she laid the cause of her terror. She heard of other women pining for their husbands and by the line of comparison slowly pulled herself once more above that shiftless fear.

In this situation, May thrived. Her bulk seemed ablaze with premature mothering energy. She could not think of her father at war without tears – yet his absence relieved her of the strain of appearing well before him, which, undertaken as an impossible burden, had oppressed her to a stunted representation of what she might have been. Emily longed to hear her singing as she walked across the fields, marching along, her clogs like army boots – and she loved to see that broad, innocent face beaming in at the window before coming in; immediately to pick up little Joseph. Soon he was called Little Joseph to distinguish him from John's father, who was very pleased at this first repeating of his name among his grandchildren. Emily had done it to please – grateful for the way in which the old man had found her a cottage and helped her to move there.

Joseph was not only pleased at the christening of the last boy, he was delighted that John's family were near him. He had seen his own children scatter away – more often than not blessed by a well-delivered 'good riddance' – and none save

Sarah; who, as he told her, he could have done without, had brought their children to him on more than the most perfunctory and fleeting visit. The outbreak of war had changed him. After a drunken evening to celebrate it, he had gone off to Carlisle to volunteer and though he had lied emphatically, his true age – fifty-eight – had been winkled from him. The laughter which had then met him, as he was pushed back by the dozens of younger men impatient to be in, and the solitary afternoon he had spent adrift in the city – seeing everywhere men who would be accepted where he was refused admittance, feeling the thunder of war over the calm sunny skies of the medieval market city and himself no more than able to shake his fist at it, shrinking away as he thought he heard someone or saw someone who might recognize him and so bring him to relate his stupidity – a desultory, shambling figure, his very stockiness and strength making the cringe in his eyes the more pitiful – all ending with the dark of night slinking home, this had taught him more than his age. For though his life had been cut off from many things – all turnstiles opening to wealth, privilege or breeding being closed for a start – he had never been excluded from that in which he had seen a part for himself; until now. He saw that he would be left in the countryside with the children and the unfit – and the old men, he thus marked as one of them.

This self-pity had been strong in him when he heard that Emily was finding it difficult to manage in the town: another child was due, May was too far off, the money was scanty; and the self-pity had watered the roots of generosity. He had restored an abandoned cottage, settled for it at a month's rent and even gone himself to bring her over. Until then, the war had been a permanent Sunday; and the spirit quite lacking from his conventional Christian obeisances had found a faith in that observance; for *this* could not be done now because of the war, cock-fighting was out because of the war, you did not drink to drunkenness on the side-lines of a war, you watched every word and gesture in Wartime.

But Harry had mocked that glum observance on the first day of his arrival when he had sworn back at his grandfather and catapulted the old man to a chase which had lasted for half an hour ending with Harry near the tip of a long beech branch and Joseph holding on to the trunk, cursing and threatening him, afraid for them both if he tried his own weight on the slender arm. Emily had seen the beginning of the pursuit, the small boy scurrying away before the stout old man, diving through a foxhole in a hedge-bottom, wriggling through the bars of a gate, the two of them galloping along the skyline like comic opposites held together by an invisible rope which would never let them apart – she had seen this and laughed at it, but worried that the earlier reputation of Joseph might rise again through his newly assumed responsibility and regretted the panic which had spurred her to move to where she would be so dependent on him. She need not have done. That invisible rope became visible as the boy and his grandfather became inseparable: through Harry, she and the others were permanently accepted under Joseph's protection.

May would not go up to see her grandfather no matter what the order or the temptation. Even Alice, whose childishness made her less liable to persecution, and Sarah whose prettiness gave her a certain immunity, were far more pleased to come home than was polite. For May saw in Joseph that domination of children which often ran to real persecution – and it reminded her of her father in his severe moods. She expected not to speak at meals, unless spoken to, she expected to stand in the line while Joseph finished his dressing and hold out the collar, to serve on him at table, to clean his boots, to fetch and carry for him, to be controlled by him in all matters of dress, manners and fact – this she had learned to do for John: but she could not accept to be hit, to be sent out of the room, to have her supper taken from her, to be blamed for nothing just because he was in an accusing mood; she never forgot being tied to the table leg with a length of rope, her father leaving her there all evening, and while she had not the power of answering back which is given to many rebels, she was sufficiently independent to fight as she could by avoiding what she did not approve of. She stayed with Emily.

The older woman was glad of her company. As Sally had done

when they had lived in Crossbridge, May brought gossip to the isolated cottage, and the premature oldness of the daughter matched the mother's last lingering with youthful looks and ways, making them sisterly in their interests.

When letters came, that was a day of talk and re-reading, remembering and prayers. For not only did she receive John's letters, but Seth wrote to his mother, and Isaac's wife would send over letters received from him and from Tom. When a letter was received from John, Emily would have Harry go over to where May worked so that she could slip down in the evening. The girl always read most carefully, and then skipped through it again, still not permitting herself to utter a word, and then she would return it to her mother, blushing as she remembered the 'Dearest Emily' which had begun it, and wait for it to be read aloud to her. As her mother read, the most marvellous parcels would float before the young girl's eyes, parcels stuffed with sweets and socks, black puddings which he particularly liked, magazines, chocolates, tobacco, parcels which she would the next morning begin to save for until Emily would check their size and off they would go, the nights of posting being the sweetest in May's life, as she thought of the brown paper being torn open by her father and all those good things there to cheer him up. After once more looking through the letter, she would play waltzes on the old gramophone and dance around the kitchen floor with her mother, happy in the proof of their father being alive and determined to let that happiness be enjoyed by Emily before the inevitable withdrawal to fear and sadness

The first rush across the Channel, created by the widely recorded zeal of the volunteers, broke on the rocks of the German artillery, and telegrams of death washed back to England like flotsam from the wreckage.

'I'm with Jackson Pennington,' Isaac wrote. 'John knows him. Ask Emily about him – John and him had a fight! Last night I piled up some in tin drums and slept seated on top of them. Mud's worse than Wedham Flow. Our Sergeant-Major was killed last night by a bullet that bounced off Alan Pape's helmet. I tell you, I get sick of sitting in these holes. You would think that Cumberland would disappear when you're so far away but it doesn't. There is never enough news. A man must be the easiest thing to shoot at in the animal kingdom, my love. But don't worry – they say it'll be over soon. And tell Emily not to worry about our John. It was nothing but a flesh wound and I saw him before they took him off. He was happy enough. He might even get sent back! Lucky him!'

John had been slightly injured in the leg. He was taken to a base hospital and just as he finished his convalescence, sent back across the Channel, but only to the Isle of Wight to be a blacksmith there.

'It's my own fault,' he wrote. 'I couldn't bide doing nothing at the hospital so I used to get down to one of the forges and help the fella there. Norman Allen he was called, from Staffordshire. Then some Captain seen me and asks a lot of questions and the next thing I know I'm in the Isle of Wight. It won't be for long though, I hope. They promised me I could go over with the next big lot. It's nice working with horses again.'

Sarah arrived on the day of Seth's long letter. She had another child with her, a boy, Reginald; apart from that indisputable evidence she appeared not a day older nor a jot different from Emily's last memory of her.

'Where's your man this time?' Joseph's first question.

'He's fighting, like everybody else!' She shouted at her father, hitting him unwittingly at that point most vulnerable in his temper's frail armour. As before, the choice was to have her roam the district as a vagabond – a travelling advertisement of his hard-heartedness – or take her in. Which he most begrudgingly did, knowing that the two children would be left with his wife while Sarah pranced off. He managed to slip a bridle on her this time, however, for he would only agree that his wife look after her children if she would enlist as a land-girl. After spying out all other possibilities, Sarah declared herself willing and was posted to a neighbouring farm.

The war settled to those two armies separated from each other by a few waste yards, the trenches, two long cracks across the face of Europe.

'And sometimes,' Seth wrote, 'when we're back from the lines, me and two other fellas go up on this little hill – mont, it's called in French, no higher than a slag heap. They're both from London. We lie on our backs and just look at the sky and talk all night. They can talk about anything – they talk about why we're here and where we're going. It's an education just to listen to them. And you can see the battle going on in the distance, the flares like shooting stars. The ground shakes when the heavy artillery let fly and you know what it's like before an earthquake. I've never heard talk to match these two. They can go on for hours and never repeat themselves. One of them said that "War is the way men revenge the sacrifice of their cheated instincts." I copied it down then and there.

'Come on!' Sarah urged.

'But I'm tired, my love. May'll go with you,' Emily replied.

'May's staying to look after the children, aren't you, dear?' returned Sarah firmly. '*You* come. You never get out and you've still a good figure, Emily. You should walk it or it'll turn fat on you. Nothing looks worse, especially when you're married. They think they can pick you up like an old cushion. Look at how I've improved since I started on that bluddy farm. *You* must come.'

Once Sarah had set her mind on something it was impossible to deny it her unless you were prepared to be violent. For no protestations could be offered which were stronger than straw before her mowing will, no excuses could be invented that could not be challenged, no rebuffs that would not be returned with no hard feelings: she would stand and insist and, unless picked up and thrown out, have her way. Emily was certainly no match for her.

The two women walked across to the road and went some way south along it. To their right about three miles away was that first drift of fell which marked the perimeter of the Lake District in the north-west as the fells around Crossbridge did to the south-west. To their left, Wigton, the plain, the Solway, the Scottish hills, as clear as the fells this soft summer's evening. Sarah had not even bothered to put on a cardigan and her brown arms were bare. Emily had taken her shawl and this, with the hat she wore, strands of grey hair filtering around her neck, flashing white as the low sun caught them, made her appear rather stern beside the gallopy walk of the younger woman.

At first she had been irritated at being dragged from her book but as she walked she sensed the air, the view, the memories of country roads, nourishing those buds in herself which had been without sustenance for so long. She breathed easily and the nightmare of those moments when she had sat and seemed to see the air hovering before her mouth unwilling, unwilled to enter, could be thought of without fright. With Sarah on this summer evening all was well.

She wondered at that. The country was turning into a Machine for War, so the papers said – and the lists of killed and wounded spread over a page every week in the *Cumberland News*. She saw the photographs of men leading wounded away from the battle, of broken weapons and soldiers ready to kill and, most movingly to her, a group of men cheerfully posing for a photograph, waving and smiling to the camera as if they were at the sea-side. Yet here, in a country at war, she could feel calm and cheerful – even though her own husband was away from her. As once she had learned that she could contain many loves, for parents, husband, children, friends, so now she saw that she must contain many contradictions within a struggle: for the clouds would not roll over in fallacious thunder, the roofs would not split in agony at the desolation of the empty beds beneath, the people did not wring their hands and shut out all but grief: though only a total surrender to sorrow would have portrayed what they felt, yet they could still smile and talk of other things. And here she was herself, on a little outing with Sarah, enjoying it.

'They came yesterday night,' said Sarah.

'I heard tell of it.'

'Mary Franks saw them. She said they looked like murderers. She got the creeps and ran home.'

'We must go past as if we were out for a normal walk,' said Emily, firmly. 'Nobody likes to be stared at.'

'But they're *Germans*,' said Sarah.

The prisoner-of-war camp was no more than a mile away, and as they approached the gate of the huts which were set in a small pine copse, Emily was embarrassed to discover that they were not the only ones inquisitive. There was a small crowd, some of them had biked up from Wigton, pressed around the wire; retreating no more than a temporary yard when barked at by one of the guards.

'Let's go back,' said Emily. 'We won't see anything.'

'But we must look,' Sarah returned. 'There's no harm in looking – and we've come all this way now. What would we say to folks if they knew we'd come all this way and seen nothing?'

'We could say we had seen them.'

'That would be a fib, Emily,' said Sarah, unctuously.

They were rewarded by the appearance of the prisoners as they came out for their evening air. All were silent as the strange men moved around most normally and even laughed once or twice. They looked at the sky and commented, perhaps, it was later hazarded, on the weather; they moved with a listlessness proper to that institutional dogma called Exercise; one of them spat – but in the opposite direction – and another made a mild face at a little boy who was clinging to the wire top and fell down to the grass in immediate terror. All these actions were carefully noted down and when, on their return to the huts, the men began to sing amazement and satisfaction competed for attention in the response of those outside the wire.

'They look all right,' said Sarah. 'Nothing special. But did you see that big one, Emily? The one who winked at me. Didn't you see him wink? The one who had the cap on the back of his head. He was *nice*.' She paused – and then made her declaration. 'I don't expect they're much worse than anybody else. Hm. What 'you say? Emily? Emily, you're crying. Emily! Don't. You know I always start up as well. Don't cry, Emily. Please.'

'I was thinking – John could be shut up like that in another country. He could be shut up just like that.'

'Oh, Emily,' Sarah moaned. 'That's started me off. Don't say things like that. It's not fair.'

'They said I could go over with the big batch,' John wrote, 'and I got out of the smithy to get ready for it. Then the day before embarkation some blacksmith breaks his arm and I've got to stay. Why can't I get back there? Sometimes I think I'm selfish to complain. I mean, a lot of men would be pleased with my job, and I should be glad I'm needed. But it isn't any good, especially since our Tom was killed. I wanted to get a gun and murder the lot of them.'

His railing against the fate which had landed him in a safe spot appeared touchingly comical to Emily; but that was the easier interpretation of it. She knew that his frustration at being away from the battle would be once more savaging the contact between his actions and his feelings and feared that this time the line would be irreparably cut. And she, too, felt his anxiety as a cruel privation and found herself wishing that he could be back on the front, despite the danger. When she caught herself wishing for that, she wondered that her feeling for John could be called love – for it was without doubt wishing him nearer death. Yet she was not ashamed of her sympathy for his situation.

'Some of the men here are sick of it all,' Seth wrote from a hospital in Surrey 'and I agree with them. We just sit there and kill each other. Nobody moves. We could be in those holes the rest of our lives. It isn't the ordinary man that wants war on either side. Generals and Politicians and Big Business make wars to please themselves. I saw some German prisoners before I came here – they were just like us. We gave them some biscuits. If they'd been three hundred yards away, we'd have given them bullets. It makes no sense. One night me and Fred Stainton was out on patrol. We crept about through no man's land: when we put our ears to the ground we could hear the tunnelling: there was gunfire everywhere. We found a man hanging over some barbed wire. He was a German. *He'd* been out on a patrol, I suppose, and caught it. I wanted to see him and waited for a flare. His face was all shot off.'

He recovered and spent his leave in London before going back.

'I suppose you've heard about our Seth and his carryings on,' Isaac wrote. 'He thinks that if we all stop – that's an end to it. And so it is. They would just walk all over us then. Do you remember me telling you about Jackson Pennington? He got killed last night – the bravest man I ever saw. He was our Sergeant that got Seth recommended for a rest – battle-fatigue – and he deserves it, really, he's been out here since it started. Jackson caught it out on a night patrol: he always liked to be in among it. He'd been an army man most of his life, you know.

'Here's a coincidence – soon after our Tom got it I saw that another Tom Tallentire had caught it. He was an Australian and I found out that his father was the brother of our father – Robert that went to Australia with Jim. The same man told me that there was two other Tallentires about – Tom's cousins – I would like to meet them because they must be my cousins as well – but doubt if I will. Things are much the same here.'

'It looks as if I'll never get away from here,' John wrote. 'I might as well be at home for all the fighting I see. But never mind, I must make the best of it. I might go back to a smithy when I come out – or I would if I could afford to set up myself. Some of the men say that horses are finished. I can't see that. They'll always be needed on the farms. Ted Blacklock's here. He isn't so bad when you get to know him. He says he's never been happier - no wife and kids to bother him. He drinks like ten.'

Harry was now past his fifteenth birthday and his life with Joseph had helped to make him look older. He had taken work on the same farm as his grandfather and the bond between them, which had now lasted for three years, prospered. Joseph took the boy into pubs with him, he introduced him to all the men they met; on his fifteenth birthday he had given him a gun that he had acquired second-hand, an old weapon, but still a gun. He called on him on Saturday afternoons to go out somewhere just as a young man might call on a friend. He delighted in Harry's aptness on the farm and took more care in teaching him how to do things than ever he had done with his own children. Harry repaid these favours by accepting them – for he thought it was important to be with his grandfather and relished the old man's talk of times past, of the tricks they used to get up to and the way they had to do things. They were inseparable.

Emily wished sometimes that the boy would take some friends nearer his own age, but when she saw the flush on his face at night as he set off for some poaching or smiled at the swagger in his walk as he came back with a few rabbits after an evening's shooting, then she saw that he was content and did not interfere.

Indeed she could scarcely wish him differently, so husbandly did he care for her. Since their first arrival he had made himself responsible for the garden – laying it all to vegetables, not a flower-seed sown – gone out to collect wood for the fire, taken upon himself to regulate the conduct – even the dressing – of Alice who was only three years younger than he was, but 'so that she's off thy hands, mother,' he explained. He would run a mile to the shop at the slightest request and dauntlessly play truant from school on market days so that he could go down into Wigton and make himself useful for sixpence or a shilling brought back to her untouched. Emily had never been able to chat to him as she had done to May and Alice and as she was beginning to do with Joseph, but she saw he was straining to make himself her protector, and she loved the authoritative scan of his eyes each time he entered the cottage. 'You're my man, now your father's away,' she wanted to say – but she shrank away from it, knowing that he would find such affectionate sayings distressing.

In all matters proper to his love for his mother he was scrupulous and undeviating – but he lacked that playfulness which can make affection nourish itself on its own regard. She knew that he did not lean on her as John did: Harry's support had an independent foundation – and though she was relieved by that and admired it, she found that she would catch herself saying: 'I wish him no different. He's right as he is,' with as much regret as pride – for she wanted to be closer to this son whose constancy and daring offered her so much love. Though she hated him to go out with the gun, she would often choose that afternoon to take the air herself, hoping to see him walking with his grandfather in the fields, the gun so casually hung in his hand –

and the action so quick and definitive when he pulled it to his shoulder and fired. Or when she went to the farm to collect the washing that she took in, she would deliberately dawdle back with the big basket, selfishly pretending that it was too heavy so that he would notice her and tie up the horses or drop his sickle and race across to her – and that eager, considerate expression on his face was one she would have made any pretence to see.

She still smiled at the memory of the night Joseph had got him drunk, how he had stayed out in the washhouse, ashamed to come to his bed and she, worried into going out to look for him, had found him there, asleep on the wet flags, shamedly groaning that he had let her down and so must leave her. He was so far gone that he had been obliged to put his arm around her neck as they walked to the cottage, and she hugged this rare physical intimacy to herself, his lean body now just a shade taller than her own, pressed against her, dependent. But mostly she had to be content to observe at a distance, and when John came back on leave Harry quite disappeared – so overawed was he by the sight of his father in uniform and so shy before the open affection between the man and woman who were his parents. Then she wanted to call him, to have John call him, to let him share with them what his guardianship made so easy – for he had left school before fourteen and every penny from his work went to his mother which, with May's wage and the bit that John could send and she herself could earn took them way from the scanty scrapings of the opening two years of the war – but he would not be called.

When Harry spoke to her other than on domestic or local matters, it was about the war. Lloyd George was calling on the chapels to give up their congregations, the entire country was becoming a factory, the Germans were caricatured as beasts and monsters who must be destroyed at any cost and the bitterness and doggedness of those at war infected the boy with an ambition to be fighting; and no poultice of Emily's could draw it out.

Later, she realized that she had known what would happen and been unable to do other than ignore it. That week, two letters had come – both of which upset him. One was from Seth who told them that he was being discharged 'on medical grounds' – and Joseph's sneer at that brought Harry the shame of having an uncle who was perhaps running away. The other from Isaac whom he idolized: in it, Isaac wrote that he had had a leg blown off and his back was peppered with shrapnel, 'they come in and hack a few more bits out every day,' he said, 'just like as if I was a pit and the doctor was a miner. Still, it means the fighting's all over for me, I'm afraid.'

When Harry failed to come home for his supper that night she was annoyed – but it was not unusual for him to eat with his grandfather – though it *was* his habit to let her know whenever he intended to do so. She covered the plate and put it back in the oven and sat down to read. Alice, Sarah and Joseph were in bed, May would not be down that night – she had looked forward to spending the evening in Harry's company. He was very deft and would sit with his feet inside the fender, carving a piece of wood into a toy for Joseph or Sarah, the yellow shavings blown on to the fire, one by one. His knife moved so silently through the wood that her pages rustling was the only sound.

She could not settle without him.

Word would have been sent her immediately if he had been hurt.

She started a letter to John but had no heart for it. She took up the darning basket, put it down again, checked the plate in the oven, lowered the pulley to feel the washing, and wound the cord around the two hooks with meticulous attention to the task.

All this was losing time. But she did not want to believe that he had gone and she willed herself to maintain her illusion. She went out to the washroom and discovered there sufficient kindling chopped for a whole month. That was conclusive.

Joseph borrowed a pony and trap from the farmer and they set off along the night road, the lantern bobbing on the trap, an indistinct beacon. She had put on her coat but the finest drizzle soon made it sodden and the cold clothes soaked her frigid flesh.

'He'll have med for Carlisle,' said Joseph. 'We should catch him before he reaches it.'

She nodded and concentrated on fighting against the shivering fit which came on her. There was no moon and Joseph was forced to drive carefully. Through Thursby they came upon two soldiers walking back to their camp: Joseph gave them a lift and Emily looked at their uniforms, her silence chilling their friendly chatter. The slow steps of the pony were like the ticking of a clock, relentless.

They did not pass him on the road.

'He'll be sleepin' out somewhere to be at the Recruiting Office first thing,' Joseph guessed.

'We must drive around and look for him.'

When the pony became too tired to go further and Joseph weary of moving through the empty streets of the city – the pony and trap bumping over the cobbled stones lit only by smudges of palest yellow from the few gas lamps – even then Emily would not stop. She left Joseph with the trap under an archway near the town-hall and walked about the streets until the morning, the drizzle turning to steady rain, the cold set white her face until it was strained numb. She had little chance of meeting him but there was nothing would stop her looking.

They had some tea in a café near the recruiting-centre. The hot liquid scalded Emily's tongue and that first sip was all she could manage.

Joseph kept his eyes to the window and he saw Harry arrive, well before the office was due to open, walking almost shamefully down the street as the morning workers hurried along the pavements. His grandfather brought him in and produced him before Emily with pride.

'He slept in a barn at Cardewlees,' he said. 'We went right by him.'

'You look tired,' said Emily to her son, 'have some tea to freshen you up.'

She waited until the tea had been brought and Harry had drunk from the cup before further speech. In truth, she knew that she had to store her strength, for the night had penetrated her and she ached with the wet cold.

'If thou teks us back home, Aa'll just run away again,' he said, quietly – and Emily wanted him to look at her so that she could win or lose him with full face, but the boy's head was bent down over his cup.

'You're too young,' she replied, very low. Then her voice rose, 'You're not yet sixteen, Harry. They won't let you in.'

'There's younger than me in,' he said. 'Arnie Barwise told me that they're desperate for anybody now. I can pass for seventeen and a half.'

'I could go and tell them your real age.'

He shook his head, still refusing to look up.

'Thou wouldn't do that, mother. Thou couldn't do that.'

'I could.' What was meant to be firm was frail.

'No,' he smiled confidently to himself – and had that smile been given her directly, had he looked at her when the knowledge of his mother's love brought that smile to his face – then she could have said no more. Even the few words spoken had wrenched more from her than she thought she could bear.

'Oh, you shouldn't go,' she said, 'it's wrong even for you to think of it.'

'Why's that?'

'Live while you can,' she replied. 'Please. Wait the two years.'

'It'll be over then.'

'So it's just the killing you want!' This, her one flaring. 'You want nothing but that. You just want to be there to fight. It's nothing else!'

'But what else is there to do?' he asked, eventually, his face drawn up, made anxious by the vehemence in her words. He saw the tears in her eyes and looked away once more. Her crying was his only fear. Knowing it, Emily drew a breath which racked the aching of her body and forced herself not to cry.

'I shall miss you,' she said.

'Aa'll send all me wages,' he returned, eagerly – and that she could not bear. Her feeling broke and she wept.

The two men regarded her uncomfortably. Other voices in the café were lowered and Emily's sobbing alone was heard.

Harry put out his hand and touched the clasped fingers of his mother. She quietened at that and stopped as his hand gripped hers more tightly.

'I'm sorry I was so silly,' she said, abruptly stopping, reaching in her bag for a handkerchief.

'That's all right,' he replied.

'There. I'm better.'

'So thou'll not mind?' he concluded.

It was Joseph again who brought her down to Carlisle some weeks later to see Harry off at the station. This time she did not weep.

On their way back, Joseph said:

'He's better there, Emily. Aa said nothin' – remember – nowt that mornin' thou talked to him. It wasn't for me to come between you two. But he's a lad won't settle 'til he's doin' what he thinks has to be done. Once it was in his head, Emily – that was that. There's nobody on earth could have shifted it out. And if somehow thou'd forced him to stop on – if thou'd pleaded and tormented him – thou would nivver have been forgiven. And his spirit would have broken. Thou must just hold up, now. Hold on, lass. Thou can do no more.'

The pain in Emily's side, which had begun after that night of searching for her son, grew and developed into pleurisy. When Seth came back, ravaged and stunned in his expression, she could speak to him for no more than ten minutes and then she was exhausted: yet there was so much she wanted to ask – about what it was *really* like there, what chance Harry had. Isaac's 'performance' on his wooden leg raised only the pretence of a smile in her. As Joseph mooned his lonely way about the farm, Emily scarcely left the cottage, for even when the illness passed she had no will to stray from the sanctuary that Harry had made for her.

He was killed three days before the end of the war. When John returned he found her set on leaving the cottage. The land around it reminded her only of her son and John took her back to the town, himself returning to the pits.

18

The year after the war ended, the Crossbridge Friendly Society had one of its greatest days. Founded in 1808, the Society had served the village as an unmilitant co-operative, labourers paying in a few pence a week as a guard against sickness and accident. It had never been sufficiently militant to attempt to raise the standard of wages or improve the conditions of work of its members, its inclination was rather to provide a safety net below the wires of paternalism. The fifteen-piece band was its real pride – among those instrumentalists, committee men flourished serenely; an oligarchy of sounding brass – while its joy and to many its purpose was this day, the last Friday of June, the day of the Club Walk, that Walk being a formal affair from the pub to the church and back: the rest was sport, food, entertainment, drink, gambling, racing, competing and fullest debauch.

John decided to go up to it. He was now in the privileged position of being able (with sufficient notice given) to manipulate his work to such an extent that he could get a specific day off. May was not able to come but he kept the other children from school so that they could enjoy the outing. And it was a good occasion for tempting Emily out of the house, getting her into the fresh air, reviving that body which had begun to retreat from all life.

They went from the town on one of the omnibuses belonging to the Whitehaven Cab and General Posting Co. Ltd. A favourable morning, money in the pocket, nothing to do but enjoy themselves. John took Joseph on his knee and they counted the number of horses they could see.

Indeed this day was a wake for many dead. The foam of welcome at the war's end had soon been licked off and it was only now that the deep spring of relief could cascade in the dry fountains of peace. In some parts of the country this led to whirlpools of near-revolution – soldiers refused to obey their orders, strikes were mounted. In others, as here, there were times of calm: the pool already being re-filled. Throughout the land memorials were being erected in the churches forever to display the long list of English dead. Tattered banners leaned bedraggled in the corners of the altar; in France the acres of white crosses stretched across the flat fields, a harvest barren of seed; and as yet the folly of the peace settlement, which was such as could insult even the stupidity of that war, was unperceived, its retribution uncomprehended. Nor would there be many more of those Walks, for the Government had taken upon itself to insure and protect all citizens, offering better terms than the Friendly Society which, pierced at the root, was to lose its members.

In 1919, however, its funds and functions could still claim to be firm. If the days when men came up and stayed the week, sleeping out in Lund lonnin, spread over the village like a sacking army, if those days were gone – then *the* day itself had still the power to attract crowds and legends. John breathed more happily as the coach went through Frizington and saw the fells very near. He bounced his son on his knee and was rewarded by a flush and a smile from Emily as she told him not to be so noisy in front of everybody. But he took this as his cue to increase his exuberance. All on the omnibus were going to Crossbridge and the air was a curtain of rough tobacco, cleat leaves or aniseed which some of the men still smoked for economy's sake.

John, looking at the hills, imagined that he could see the shepherds coming down for the day's events, the cowmen leaving the fields, the labourers hurrying through the milking, and once again, it seemed, the character and form of the country he had grown up in could meet in celebration as if the war had been not a severe operation on the people – one that would change its face and form – but a wound only, deep, to the bare bone, but capable of healing with new skin grown from the old.

In his fortieth year, John was at his prime: whatever despair and frustration he had, it could not be seen on such a day. If it had given him little else, his work had brought him indisputable strength, the rhythm of it beating now as the very pulse of his life and his days cast in iron through that ceaseless, intense throb. While any release from such toil could not but be furbished with all the ornaments of delight – no baubles scattered through the evenings of many leisured days – but the spirit of festival, bottled up through the most of the year. And he knew there would be the sports he had enjoyed before the war, the men with the stories, the dialect and tricks and feats: he joggled his child impatiently, longing to be quit of this slow conveyance so that he could push himself among it.

Emily was very pale, as always now, and she wore the black dress she had worn at Joseph's funeral. For the old man had survived the news of his grandson's death by a mere six months: he had been knocked down by his own horses while ploughing but there was little doubt in anyone's mind that he would never have let himself in for such an accident or, even so, would have been well able to recover from it, had not Harry's death so affected him. To please John she had stitched some white lace around the neck and on the cuffs but these added more to the frailty of her appearance than to its gaiety, and in her bag was a pair of large scissors, secretly packed, with which she would trim Ephraim's grave. She made an effort to be cheerful, for John's sake, and also because she could not but think herself self-indulgent: others had greater troubles . . .

Mrs Sharpe had just that year come into The Cross and this was to be her first big Club day. She was a pretty-faced young woman, a farmer's daughter, used to catering for large gangs of men after harvest or hay-timing and after her marriage she had rushed at the chance of taking over The Cross which she managed through the day as well as looking after the small farm attached to it while her husband continued to earn his regular wage in the iron-ore mines. This day, however, he too was one of her many helpers.

The night before all the furniture was taken out and Jo Howe the carpenter came to board up the stairs. Sawdust was put on the floors. Forms and barrels were set out at the back for people to sit on. The Cross was in the corner of the field where the day's entertainment took place and all the back windows on the ground floor were opened and used as bars. Mrs Sharpe and her helpers not only did for the pub but for the marquees which rose overnight in the field. As a sole peg to those insubstantial tents, The Cross took the weight of the day.

She expected to feed at least 250 people for dinner at midday and well over 500 for high tea. The food arrived at this small country pub much as the wagon-loads of feed must have come to a castle at the time of a great feast. Ninety pounds of beef, ready cut, came up hot that morning from Cleator-Moor Co-op. Six hams were boiled and carried off the waggonettes to be stacked in the small kitchen. Over a hundredweight of potatoes had been peeled the night before. Mrs Sharpe herself, with Miss Graham and Mary Edmonson, had roasted two legs of ham, two of pork, and prepared more than a stone of green peas, two dozen cauliflowers, two dozen cabbage and a stone of split peas. Eight hundred teacakes had been baked around the village and more were to come from the ovens throughout the day, as well as bread and cakes and biscuits. Dozens of jars of home-made jam were got out, pints of cream and preserves. For the puddings, she had the help of the older women – Mrs France from Crossgates, Mrs Jackson from Bird Dyke, Mrs Parker from Hoodge Cottage, and Miss Graham: twelve plum puddings were made, twelve rice puddings, rum sauce for the plum puddings, ale got ready for the Crossbridge Pudding (buns steeped until soft in hot ale and served with seasoning and spirits to taste) and twelve herb puddings. The children had collected for a week the ingredients for the herb puddings: rhubarb, nettles, blackcurrant leaves, cabbage, cauliflower, leeks, sour dockings, barley, Easterman giants – twenty-one different ingredients topped by whisked eggs. Before the dinner, the eight carvers came, each bringing their own knives and steel, Tom Wrangham, Harry Edmonson, Joe Wood, Jo Stoner, Joe Jackson, John Dalzell, Tom Cowman, John Eliot, and the rasp of steel on steel cleared the throats of all who heard it.

At nine-thirty the band assembled outside The Cross, among the horses and wagons, men moving in with food, women rushing about with pans, Jo Branthwaite stacking up the crates of bottled beer which would fortress-fill the small back-room for the length of the day. The coachload of Licensees arrived from

Workington with the Brewery's compliments and at the Brewery's expense from the coach straight into the field – the church service would be full enough with local people. Children panicked with pleasure running around people's legs like chickens avoiding capture – and the President of the Friendly Society, Harry Wilkinson, brought out the silk banner from the pub – gold and blue it was – unfurled it, presented a pole apiece to the Secretary and the Treasurer, nodded to the bandmaster – and led off for the ten o'clock service.

They were standing in the aisles as the vicar went through the short office. The band accompanied the long hymns and the packed congregation settled back as comfortably as they could to attend to the sermon for which the vicar received a guinea from the man at the Hall. A new family there. The old one which had been there since it was built, now died out, the last son killed in the war, the last act of the father being the erection of a cottage, called Le Plantin, to be lived in rent-free by a poor widow of the parish.

The sermon done, the band lined up once more and the vicar marched with the President back to the field for the day's entertainment. As she heard the band leaving the church, Mrs Sharpe put the potatoes on to boil and five women in nearby cottages did the same. They would be boiled, mashed and put into earthenware pots with a blanket tied around them to keep them warm.

In the field the President gave his address – embracing the membership list, the funds, thanks to the creator for the weather, and to Mr Tyson for the hurdles, a throwaway reference to a new cure for sheep-scab, a remark on the founders and the official opening of the Club Walk.

John and Emily arrived just as the President began his address and after it, with the rest of the crowd, they walked over to watch the sports. In the late morning there would be the terrier racing, whippets after dinner and the sheep-dog trials, fell-racing and field sports in the late afternoon, hound dogs in the evening, the band playing continuously except at meal times, and hawkers, gypsies, bookmakers, side-shows, displays and old friends, monkeys on barrel organs, a blind man with a fiddle – all the day long. Now, however, was the start of the wrestling – Cumberland and Westmorland style, supposed to have been left in the two counties by the Romans. The men stripped out in woollen vests and long-johns, black trunks, soft black plimsolls, crouching crab-like against each other, each chin on the other's shoulder, one arm above one below that of the opponent, swinging up for a grip against his back which, once held, signified the start of the contest which ended when one man broke the other's grip.

Emily took the children away to see inside the big marquee and John settled down to enjoy the sport. He had already nodded and talked to many of the men from the village, the conversation always the same mixture – beginning with references to those dead in the war, continuing on the present condition of the bereaved, from there to the improvement of life in the village since the doubling of labourers' wages in the war years and concluding with tips for the races – and stayed for a long chat with Mr Pennington who had given over his farm to his two remaining sons, living with them in his old age. John told him what Isaac had written about Jackson and Pennington was so grateful for this praise of his son that he treated John to a complete appraisal of the prospects on the farm, no meagre or easy confidence from one to whom nothing but that land had held real substance even during the war itself.

Now John sat and watched the wrestling – more than glad to be joined by Isaac. Their first remark was to express mutual amazement at Seth's sudden marriage – an arrangement which had prevented him from being here this day: both knew the woman, both had heard gossip of her, both disliked what they had heard, both thought Seth a sad fool – neither said so.

Isaac was working 'like old Nick, John boy. Nickerdemus himself!' – setting up in a butching business, 'for it's the best Aa'm suited for now, me boy' – but still he would not miss such an outing. Indeed, the false leg and the back even now embedded with bits of metal, had stopped him from doing very little that he wanted to do. He had made up his mind to ignore his injury. His years in the trenches had lost him some of his weight – which helped – and the broad face was cut by lines like faults on its grainy surface. 'If Aa sit down and mope – Aa's finished!' he said. So, as soon as he had felt well enough, he had gone off on a hunt. All day he had stuck at it though the other men, seeing the blood come through his breeches, had tried to send him off. He had spent the night 'wid' me stump in a basin, lad, like a bit of raw meat hanging in a dish' – but the statement had been made, the tempo set – and three days later, 'bandaged up to me belly, lad' – he was off again with the hounds. Since when he had hunted regularly, sometimes prevented by the considerations of his business but never by those of his stump.

'Aa fancy Alan Stott,' said Isaac, looking at the two heavyweights now slinging up their arms for a grip, 'Aa fancy him to win it.'

'What price is he?' John asked.

'They'll give thee four to one now. They'll shorten when he wins this round.'

John went across and put on a shilling.

The two men were still wrestling when he returned, which was unusual as the contests generally lasted for no more than two minutes, often less.

'Stott can't git his buttock in,' said Isaac grimly. 'That other fella must have a double-jointed backbone.' He looked intently at the wrestlers but continued to address John. 'Aa've tried to git back into wrestlin' myself,' he went on. 'But fust time Aa did it Aa vanyer brok t'other lad's toes – wid' me stump. T' umpire sed Aa'd a "unfair advantage." Ay. Aa hed to drop owt on it aatogither. There! He's got him. My Christmas – Aa thowt they were ganna cuddle up agen each other aa day. Well, if he can beat yon rubber-bones, he can lace anybody else.'

They all had dinner together in the marquee, where Isaac's wife revealed herself with her children and agreed to look after Sarah and Alice while Emily took Joseph down to the church. The men were beginning to lay into the drink and devoted all time apart from that to talk and inspection of the dogs.

John walked Emily and their son to the gate.

'I could nip down and hev a look ower it,' he said.

'No. You stay. I won't be long.'

'Don't go, Emily,' he said, abruptly. 'Thou'll just be upset.'

'I'll be fine.'

'Thou looks for trouble,' John continued.

'You just go back and enjoy yourself.'

'How can any man enjoy hissel when thou's mopin' and crying down yonder?'

'I won't mope.'

'Sorry. But thou looks so lost, Emily.'

'No I don't. I'm enjoying it.'

'The way that's said goes against the words. You look so miserable these days, Emily.'

'I don't! But I will if you keep on at me.'

'Dis thou remember when we first came to this spot?'

'Yes. I do.'

'We used to walk up to Cogra Moss.' He hesitated. The dogs were barking for the beginning of the races. 'If thou wants, I'll tek thee up there now.'

'No. You want your sport.'

'We could be there an' back in an hour.'

'No. Go back.' She smiled at him and touched his arm. 'Thank you, John. I'll get better – just – let me do it my way. Please.'

'Well don't be long down there then. I'll expect you back for tea-time.'

She nodded and watched him go back into the field, soon hailing someone, laughing with them. She wished that she could throw off this burdened, gloomy atmosphere which had settled on her. It made John restless and she thought it unfair of her to impose that on him. Sometimes she caught sight of herself in a shop-window and almost laughed at the enclosed dreary reflection which was returned to her; many, many were in worse position than she was – this she kept telling herself so often it became her only weapon to alleviate her despair, yet the weapon more often worked against than for her, hammering her down into her unhappiness. She thought of Mrs Kemp, a widow, a husband and two sons lost in the pits, a brother killed in the war, a daughter who was backward – but this piling up of comfort by contrast was no good; Mrs Kemp would appear to her as someone to be pitied, yes, but also someone whose list of disasters over-weighted the pity until it broke into helpless detachment. Seth she was more sorry for, who ailed nothing but had come back from the war frightened out of all his former certainty: and still she shuddered at the way in which he had once 'claimed' old Ephraim, allowing none of the other relatives to take any charge of him, drawing on to himself by main force the one member of that large spread family who had been so fated, planting him in those bare lodgings like a living note to himself. Emily had never been able to take much to Seth.

If only, she thought, as she left the field behind her and walked down to the church, if only she could get rid of this pain in her side. For things were easier for them now – and she ought not to drag them down. She was afraid to admit the pain – afraid that she would be sent off for a long operation and the family split up. It was this greatest fear which made her move and act in such a self-constricted way: for she was sure that once her illness was declared, then she would be taken up with it entirely – and there would be no alternative for the children but to send them out to relatives. She would never have that.

In the churchyard now, she called Joseph away from the graves and took him along the narrow path which led to that of her first son. The small hummock had been shorn by the caretaker at respectable intervals but she wanted it, this once, to be perfect. The noise from the Walk came down the fields to her on the wind and she worked quickly, afraid that bodies might follow the voices and she be found clipping the grass with scissors in the empty cemetery. Afraid, afraid, afraid of her own shadow.

Yet the more she worked at the grave, the calmer she felt: and saw clearly through her confusion a glimpse of order and simplicity, or a rule behind the disturbances which drift on the surface of life. That same impulse which sends anthropologists to lost tribes to discover the mould for all subsequent castings, and thinkers to myths and legends to find codes and correspondences, that which makes the Golden Age of all times so persistent a legend, however vulnerable – an understanding, come to some through intellect, to herself through her senses; that clarity and beauty were there beneath all that men piled upon it; – and yet the feeling which this insight gave her was one of sadness only. Those hills around seemed mournful.

She insisted that John and herself stay on in the evening for the dance in the assembly rooms. Many women took their children into the dance and so she had no qualms about that. And Alice, awed by the occasion, guarded the sleeping smaller children while Emily danced with John.

John had been well set for a drunken day when she had returned to tell him that she would stay – but so pleased was he with this evidence of her willingness to try to 'come out of herself,' as he said, that he steered himself away from that port. They danced until she was exhausted but John, inflamed by drawing her to him once more, mistook the colour in her face for excitement and easily persuaded her to dance some more. The room was packed with those from the Walk and the thick air made all the children tired so that soon the three of them lay across chairs in a corner, warmed by their coats, oblivious to the noise of the band, the shouts from the men as they whopped at the tunes, rocked by the shaking of the wooden floor.

'I can dance no more, John,' she said, finally. 'I couldn't go another step.'

'Thou mun come outside for some air,' he replied. 'Don't worry about Alice and them. Charlie'll keep an eye on them. Won't you Charlie? There, see. Come on. Thou's startin' to look pale again. Let's have some air.'

They went from the assembly rooms, manoeuvered their way through the coaches and bicycles and walked a little way up the road. The crescent moon could have been papered on the clear sky and beneath it the tops of the fells were clear. The air was chilly but John held his wife around the shoulders, her head lightly against his shoulder, their steps matching.

'Would you like to come back to farm-work, John?'

'I was just thinkin' that myself. Just that minute! That very thought.'

'Well?' And in her, too, was a tremor of pleasure that they were once more close: like copper through rust, the vision flashed.

'It's a better feelin' here, isn't it? Better for the children an' that.'

'You must – what about yourself? John?'

'Me? Oh – I'm easy, Emily.' He laughed. 'More true to say I'm finished, really.' He wanted her contradiction.

'That's not true at all.'

'O, it is.' He paused; why could he not go on, catch the vision? 'It is,' he repeated, lamely.

'But – you've got all the time you want. You could do whatever you wanted.'

'Don't be daft,' he grinned, further to disarm the gently delivered rebuke. 'My alternatives is work or work. Well that's all right. There's many got no choice.'

'What other people do doesn't matter,' she protested, vaguely recognizing a direct echo of her own encircled reasoning. 'You shouldn't be bothered about that.'

'No,' he answered. 'Mebbe so.' He hesitated. 'Let's stay where we are,' he said, 'mebbe – mebbe, later, we'll change.'

'But what d'you *want*?'

'Want. Yes, I've thought on that as well. But my Wants come up so fast that they throttle me, and the next minute they're gone, as if they'd never been. I've wanted many things – but I've seen that they could be done widdout, just the same. When I was in that army – I wanted to fight, and got over it when I couldn't. I want thee to be well, lass, but if thou's not so strong – that's how it is. There's Wants that's never seen the light of my day – and how glad I am they've stayed out of sight. I want nothing, Emily.'

She bit her lip to hold in her reply. It could not be that he, too, felt himself hollowing, emptying. He looked so well, so strong, surely that was not the shell only.

'Oh, John,' she said, 'John.'

He paused. 'Yes, Emily?'

But she did not know what to say: why did he not know? 'Take me back.'

As they walked back to the dance, she leaned heavily against him. She needed him to be the same; they had grown apart, and neither would speak of the chasm at their feet; they had the power to touch only, not to heal. She began to cry.

'Thou's taken ower much out of thissel,' he said, reproachfully. 'Come on. We'll go home. We must be careful now, eh, Emily? Cut our coats.'

19

John felt that he had failed. Emily's illness worsened and a tide of persistent consideration swept quickly over every other feeling in the house, making it impossible for him to reach out sharply to her for fear of jarring the fragile hold.

In that quiet terraced cottage, with Emily lying upstairs, refusing to leave the house, May back with them having thrown up her job at the farm to come into the town and work in a factory so that she could manage the home, himself taking Joseph down to the allotment when he finished his supper so that the place would be quiet, removing his boots in the backyard, the carrier of news of his wife to all who met him so that he walked the streets like a muted cryer, his information known to all but all who knew him concerned to indicate their own concern at his changed circumstances – there he thought he would go mad. Never to talk directly to her again, never to be able to show her how he felt except by the lap of small attentions.

'Blind, blind, blind amid the blaze of noon.' This he was. Feelings uncomprehended, undirected, feelings alone, it seemed, had been given him – and blinded him from understanding. It was as if, shorn of the training of reason, deprived of the leisure for speculation, and no believer in the strictures and aids of a dogma – all that he was had been forever churned into those impulses and sensations which rushed through him and left him unaccountably. Now he wanted to claim Emily back to himself – but though he talked to her and reached out for her, it would not work: and he knew as he sat there beside her bed that he had lost. Between the blindness of his own volition and the necessity of his daily life had been formed the inevitability which he had finally acknowledged.

On his return from the war, sprung with the resolutions and energy which his frustration had generated – he had been ready for anything as never before in his life. The bloom that was then on him had survived Harry's death, held to the year following, been there still that day of the Club Walk, now a year past. But the fruit had not followed. For Emily had bowed herself over her grief – and he had let her alone: alone he had tried to mend the hopes, fragments of a vision. In a few months only it seemed of no more substance than the declarations of a schoolboy. He got into his pit clothes and latched the front door behind him, walked down the middle of the street to be joined by all the others, nearer the pits indistinguishable from them and like them taken into the earth and along the dark roads under the sea. It seemed a fool's fancy to have ever thought that it could be otherwise.

There was no one for him to turn to for he needed not an intermediary but a past self. So he sat there, reassuring her, and sometimes she would be strong to come downstairs and he would find her there on his return, and once, even so ill, she had set out to meet him, getting only a few yards down the street before Joseph had to run and fetch a neighbour to help her back, and she looked at him with such a look as filled him with helplessness and wrung him, for though he could return it, he could not secure it.

May came home to prepare the midday meal for the three younger children. Afterwards, she took a tray up to the bedroom for her mother. May, unmarried, plain and heavy, had assumed maternal command over all material matters with a determination which slowly revealed that she intended to keep it so when the worst happened. Always the one most concerned with family, she worked against the dread of having them split up. To prevent this, she did everything that her mother had done – and then more – feeding the three younger children, seeing to their clothes, their cleanliness, their manners, keeping the house spotless, employing all her energies in stratagems to ensure that there would be a cooked meal waiting for her father when he came back from the pits, all in the shadow of her mother's approaching death and in fear of the disintegration which she was sure would follow. The girls who worked with her in the factory – most of them younger than she was – thought her devotion passing praise, formidable in its single-mindedness and for that reason difficult to bear. May was aware that she was becoming increasingly isolated, excluded from the gossip and practical jokes, spoken to with special consideration as if she herself had been the invalid. It was she who wrote letters to other members of the family – a practice which had never been more than desultory among them but in her attempt to underpin the household, May contacted aunts, uncles, cousins and grandparents all over the county – merely to give them news. Wanting the letters to be evidence of her capability and intent. She even managed to overcome the dread she had before her father – though this victory was never more than a mask – and would sit to be attendant on him while he ate and after he came down the stairs from seeing his wife: knowing that he had always liked to have Emily available for talk, making herself so available, though she would not sit in her mother's chair.

None of this was easy for her. For she had always discounted herself – Sarah was prettier, Alice more clever, Joseph the boy. Harry had been admired for qualities she could never have: she had always had to fight for a place, first between her mother and father and then among her sisters and brother – and she alone had carried the weight of knowledge of her father's retreats which had been expressed towards her in unendurable sullenness, and her mother's words which had cut even more deeply into the daughter. Indeed, May was compounded of memories which bruised her whenever she thought of them: she was as sensitive as the princess to the pea of people's feelings towards her, towards each other, towards their circumstances – and this made her life a continual stumbling for she imagined herself to be intruding continually, leaving on the wrong note, forever breaking across the current of emotion which conducted life between those she loved, and those from whom she would always be somewhat excluded by the fact – the principal fact in her life – that she was taken for granted, by herself, by others, and, she thought, rightly.

What made it possible for her to come through was a temper, an anger which had rarely much play but in private rendings of herself when she would cry or shudder into her body: physically taking as blows the words that barbed her mind. This anger now was that her mother should be ill. She idolized Emily: she loved to watch her move, even now, when the wasting disease had rolled away that first slight thickening of early middle age and Emily was as thin as she had been slim as a girl – she loved to watch the delicacy of her mother's gestures – delicacy of all characteristics being the most desired by May and the most adamantly denied to her. A thousand panics swept the young woman each day, in her stomach, in her throat, before her closed eyes until she thought that from anywhere, rooftops, streets, the sea, a thunderbolt would come and destroy her, destroy them all – and to combat those terrors she found that her teeth clenched, her hands tightened as if in a fight and she fell upon the forces which dared threaten her so. Her mother was not to die, and that resolution released positive forces in May long repressed or channelled to the swamp of work – and the anger that such an event might occur gave her all the strength she needed to work, to look after the family, to nurse Emily and attend John, and to contain her own fear which woke her in the dark, bottling up her mouth.

Emily vowed each night that she would get up in the morning, but when the dawn came she had no will – only the wish that John would not slide out of the bed beside her, would stay – lie with her all the day so that she could lean against his strength. She said nothing, but when he heard the first ring of the alarm and banged his hand on to it so that it would not disturb her, then she prayed that he would put his arms around her, not go, not go as he gently did, easing out carefully, holding down the sheets and blankets so that a draught did not come on to her – taking away what hope of life she had. He brought her a cup of tea and a slice of bread and jam which he placed on the bedside table before bending to kiss her brow – and she, eyes closed to bless this kindness, would counterfeit a calm awakening.

Downstairs he sat before the fire to fry his own bacon and toast his bread. He liked the kitchen to be his own at this time, the only moments when he was alone, and the senses opened in sleep would fill his mind with sweet thoughts – even, occasionally, now, despite his wife so ill above him – while the kettle boiled on the fire and the frazzled bacon crunched saltily on his palate. His toes played against the edge of the fender through his stockinged feet and the shirt and trousers, warmed by the night's fire, sat comfortably on him. He remembered the frozen wet trousers he had climbed into at his first job on that farm and the memory always made him feel a lucky man.

Now, as ever since Emily's condition had worsened, his fingers were reluctant as they pulled at the laces on his boots. He had heard May get up and dress all the children upstairs with many a shush! and stricture to silence: she would not bring them down until he was gone. But whether to go, whether this would be the day – he pushed his legs out stiffly in front of him and pulled on the long laces as if they had been reins. He closed the back door quietly and turned, at the bottom of the yard, to wave up at the children whose faces were pressed against the back bedroom window. Then into the back-alley, immediately walking over to the middle of it, his head looking down at the scoured stony ground. When he came out of The Tops on to the streets, his pace quickened and he hurried as if to encourage the day to go faster.

Often, as he pushed back a tub of coal along the seam, he would want to abandon it and continue that walk back to his house. It seemed madness to be working so when he could be spending time with her – and yet he accepted that he would and should work each day, saw nothing remediable about the day's absence.

May brought Emily a second cup of tea before she went off to work. Then the children came in to kiss her good-bye before school – and the house was her own until mid-morning when one or another neighbour came in to take a shopping list from her, build up the fire, make yet more tea – almost all the nourishment Emily had, for she ate sparsely – and chat about her health. 'How's your chest, Mrs Tallentire?' 'How's your breath, Mrs Tallentire?' 'How's the pain today, Mrs Tallentire?' until Emily thought that she was no more than a combination of ailments, each demanding a child's consideration. In this time, though, after the children had gone – before the neighbour came, she tried to get up. She would relax for a little while, culling back what sleep there had been in the night, trying to make tranquil the tensions in her body, and then get out of bed and begin to dress. She made herself do this at her former speed, not allowing the illness to grip and drag at her, thinking to cheat her body back to its former self by observing all that she had been. And every morning she had to sit down on the half-descended stairs, sit in that gloomy staircase feeling her cold sweating break against the cool air, her lungs fill and almost choke her with coughing, fingers wrapped in on themselves, her only thought to get back to bed so as not to be found so weak. She had to crawl back up the stairs, her knees catching against the long skirt, pulling it from her waist until her blouse came out.

After dinner there was no chance: the children began to arrive home from school and sometimes the doctor came. Emily would not have allowed there to be any chance of the children seeing her distressed. John had shifted the bed so that she could prop herself up with pillows and look out, through a gap in the opposite terrace, to the allotments, the sea and across it, these fine summer days, the Scottish hills. Then she would read a little or knit, or, occasionally – as a treat with which she rationed herself most carefully – look at photographs and re-read the letters John had sent her from the war. There was a photograph of Harry with the Londsdales, the men in shirt-sleeves, one of them holding up a shaving brush, his face lathered, and Harry, arms folded, a cap squarely on his head, a slim pipe self-consciously clasped between his teeth. He, too, had sent her a few letters from the war.

As she looked out, at the red-bricked terraced houses – so

neatly laid out when seen from this height – under the clear light the bricks and lines, the white window frames and occasional black-coated women moving in the confined spaces – she experienced a feeling of gratitude which she would neither explain nor reveal. For the noises – the few cars on the streets, the sirens at the pit, the more daring talk of the young women as they came back from the factory – came up to her window like tremors from a new world. Her own world had been one which, with few enough digressions, went back for centuries on the land in villages so that whatever changes occurred they had not shifted the central hub of a woman's life – the cramped conditions, large family, carefulness in all things material, the rhythm and obligations the same. As she lay and looked out, she was grateful to be protected from what was coming. Yet she had never been afraid before now of what might be unknown before her: had as much led as followed John to that village unknown to them, to the mining-town foreign to her. But this gratitude soaked her body as the balm to the illness; and as the tuberculosis sapped her so, to slow surprise, she let go, let go without fear – and even the pain of not being able to tell John, and the sudden clutching in her throat when she knew that soon she would part from her children, these passed: she lay, palms down on the blanket, hazel hair well mixed with grey, long over her shoulders, falling on the black shawl, and looked past the chimney pots to the grey sea.

It was towards the end of the summer. John had now lived for so long in that narrow vein of subtly changing hope and despair, each week shortening the distance between them but still the extremes oscillating like a compass needle that will tremble between the very closest points, that he was not more than usually troubled by the doubt as to whether or not he should go out to work that morning. He took her the tea and kissed her forehead: it was once more damp though he had wiped it clean and dry only a few minutes before as he had got up. He parted the curtain a little and closed the door quietly behind him.

And in the pit, that afternoon, when there was a small rush a few yards up the seam from where they were working, he remembered later that he was calm enough. Even more calm, perhaps, than the five others as they sat down and extinguished their lights. It was too dangerous to try to dig out through the slack fall but Alec Benn, who had been nearest to it, said that it was nothing but a small rush. They knew that a rescue party would be there in a matter of minutes and themselves released, they thought, not much later than their normal time.

When Joseph came from school, he would come into his own house and go upstairs to change from his shoes into his clogs. It had become a small conspiracy between Emily and her son that he go into her bedroom to do the simple change. She was often asleep and this time, as others, he sat on the edge of the bed, changed, and then waited for her to stir at the interruption which his pressure on the bed gave to her breathing. This time she did not stir, and he sat, waiting, slowly numbed by the cold and fear of his own stillness. Found there shivering with the full sun on his face, holding the dead hand.

As the men went into the seam they discovered that the fault ran right back. To dig there, however carefully, would bring the roof down on all of them. They had to go down another shaft and cut in from a parallel seam. The miners cycled quickly across to the next pit where the seam was cleared of work and from there they pushed towards the trapped men.

At midnight, frozen in the dark, with the water running down the walls as if the sea above them was beginning to seep through, its immeasurable weight taking this chance – as it had done before – of crushing those ceaseless workers beneath its bed, John could scarcely keep still. He knew that all of them had equal troubles, all were in the same danger – and this communality alone restrained him. But, in the dark, his mouth opened wide in soundless cries for help – to get out and back to Emily – to see her once more.

With the women at the pit-head was May. She had helped to lay out her mother and dumbly allowed the children to be divided out among the neighbours. Now she waited for her father.

The trapped men had soon guessed that they would have to go out through the other seam and the realization had silenced them completely. As the morning came, however, they began to talk to each other, all speaking with very deliberate casualness about football, their friends, the town – the gossip of the day. Alec Fisher, the oldest man there, had been trapped three times before and that was a distant comfort to all the others: his 'luck' became the centre of their talk, the one thing always referred back to, chafed about, encouraged as they drew out of him other instances of this 'luck'; at cards, in growing leeks, in every smallest matter that would yield. John was the second oldest man, the other four were young, two in their early twenties, two in their teens.

When they heard the picks in the other seam they cheered and knocked back at the wall. That simple knock brought a small rush down on them and they were prevented from digging to meet their rescuers. John was furthest away from the sound. As the men came nearer the falls in the trap grew more frequent. Alec Fisher felt for an area that could be propped up, so that they might make a small shelter for themselves within their hole. For by now it was obvious to all that the nearer the rescue party came, the harder their blows – the more certain it was that the crumbling roof would crash down on them. But there was no timber for the propping – nothing to do but wait as they were.

Joseph had run down to the pit-head directly after his breakfast and he wriggled through the crowd to join May who took his hand, made no reproach.

Warned by the silence of those within – for Alec had ordered that they stop hammering back at the oncoming party – the rescue party slowed down and stood back to allow one man alone to work and he most carefully, making a path less than two feet high and propping all the way. Almost all the men in the rescue party were related to those within: Seth was there for John.

Patiently, almost delicately, his nerves more wracked than his bruised bare body, the miner picked at the last few feet. With no more than inches to go he stopped and listened. He could hear Alec, who told him what the trouble was. But the only other way in was by another seam entirely, would take another day and meet the same problem. He passed the message back and was dragged out by his feet to let in someone fresh to make the last cuts.

A small hole was made. Within, the falls had become so steady that it seemed to pour slack and small pieces of rock. Those nearest went out first. John would be the last. Each one had to crawl over to the hole, and the movement of each caused another, heavier fall. John gripped the wet coal about him, bracing himself so that he could lift himself from his position with as little disturbance as possible. Alec Fisher went. It was his turn.

He pushed his hands on to the floor and so levered his body clear. Then he placed his feet out and used both hands and feet to crab himself forward. As he left what had been his seat, a fall descended on it. Slowly, patiently, he moved forward. His feet went into a pile of slack. He would have to stand. The hole was about five yards before him. He eased himself upright and dived for it. His head caught a low sagging piece of roof and it came down on him. The fall was heard and Seth, who had come to the front waiting for John, slithered through the narrow shaft and right into the hole – another man behind to grab his feet. He saw John's hands and the top of his head and shouted to be held as he leaned in and pulled, heaved his brother out of the rubble, pulled him clear.

John was still unconscious when they buried Emily. Unconscious as Seth over-rode May's cries and sent out the children to various relatives. His head injuries were severe, his back lacerated.

No one told him of the death of his wife, even when he did come round. It was thought better not to. But as John felt some strength come back to him, he thought only of her. The mumbled reassurances to his questions about her did not satisfy him. He was allowed no visitors but Seth those first two weeks. May accepted that she could not go as she would not have been able to conceal her mother's death.

After two weeks John was out of danger but still extremely ill, often delirious. That night, however, he did something he had tried to do each night since he had collected his senses. He got out of the bed.

He was in an isolated room and luck came to him – for he found the place where his clothes were and slowly put them on. His forehead was bandaged, more bandages wrapped around his body – and every noise he heard came through thick walls of cloth, each movement he made went slowly through a dense curtain. Standing, holding the door ajar, his boots held in his hand, he waited until the sister went past his room into the general ward. Then he went out. The night air cut at his face and he could remember nothing of what followed. Nor, afterwards, would he have it spoken of in his presence.

He had to see Emily and thought that she was at Crossbridge, in the first cottage they had had, waiting for him. They had put him in Whitehaven cottage hospital and he came down the drive on to the dark streets where he took his only bearings – for then, turning his back on the pits and the sea, he began to walk towards the fells. There was a moon, a dry night.

It was more than eight miles to the cottage and he did not stop. When his balance left him and he staggered across the road or into a dyke, then he would right himself immediately, calling on himself to go on, to see her, the only woman he had known, the woman he had to see before she died.

He collapsed a few yards from the old cottage and there he was found at dawn, as if dead.

He left his mother's house in mid-morning. Taking the back road to Wigton, he passed Old Carlisle and saw the boys playing among the grass-covered mounds of the old Roman Camp. He stopped and looked for Joseph who had sat alone by Emily when she lay dead; but the boy was too absorbed in his play to notice his father.

He turned away when he heard the clock of St Mary's church strike ten. The Hiring would have started now.

As he walked down the hill, he felt his jaws clench at the reply that would have to come through them when, soon, he would stand in the Ring looking for work. But the jaws would have to unclench – work had to be found.

'Is thou for hire, lad?'

Yes; he was for hire.

A PLACE IN ENGLAND

To William and Violet Ismay

Part One

The Big House

Chapter One

Joseph's eyes opened with a blink of fright. Only the first bird in the garden: a thrush. The nightmare slid out of his mind.

He swung his bare feet onto the floor and went to the attic window. On the ledge, in the lid of the cocoa tin, was a butt; a third of the cigarette. Lighting up, he smoked with careful pleasure; short, thrifty puffs.

Still the thrush whistled alone and the young man grew impatient of looking at the tones of grey: lawn, lake, mist and clouds, as heavy and dense as the fells he would see the following morning.

His bag was already packed, even though he had another day and night to endure before his holiday began. He had thought of nothing else for weeks. The bag was pushed well under the bed. It would not do for an intruder to see this eagerness. There were times when his eighteen years needed protection. The cigarette was drawn to its last millimetre, held to the hot skin of his lips by the tips of his nails. He squashed it between unhardened thumb and forefinger.

First the dawn light touched the bark of the silver birch trees, then the mist above the lake, the water itself – all the birds now singing – until he saw clearly this plump Midlands parkland, so gentle and secure. He both liked it and loathed it and could not fathom the contradiction.

To give himself something to do, he made his bed, dressed and splashed his face with cold water: no need to shave. Then, as a treat, he took out a whole cigarette and decided to smoke it through. The huge house was still silent; he would not be called for an hour.

She hid the cake awkwardly in her uniform. It bulged above

her belt and she kept touching it as if pointing out her guilt.

But for her brother she would do anything. She repeated this to herself; the members of her family were her rosary.

Though she had been at the house for five years, May still sneaked through it. Huddled her neck into her lumpy shoulders, screwed up her eyes behind the putty-framed glasses – hesitated before every corner. The maids were in a different wing of the house and she had to come down and cross the main gallery: and though she had polished every inch of it, the place frightened her at this half-lit quiet hour. Yet she knew that if she did not see Joseph now, there would be no chance for the rest of the day.

The moment she entered his bedroom she envied him the place of his own. Never in her life had she had that. It took a physical act of swallowing to repress the envy.

'Here then,' she said, taking out the large segment of apple cake, 'get this inside you.'

Joseph was lying on the bed. He had found an old newspaper and now pretended to be absorbed in it. Having scarcely acknowledged his sister's entrance, embarrassed by the openness of her emotion, he played the lord and without lifting his eyes from the page, held out his hand.

May raised the cake as she walked towards him – she always needed to be reassured that he liked her; teasing made her furious. Joseph looked up just as she was about to slam the juicy segment onto his palm.

'Thanks, May.'

She lowered it gently: his eyes had been kind.

'You had a narrow escape, lad,' she was pleased to say.

Tenderly she watched him raise it to his mouth – still standing sentry over him – and sighed with pleasure as he smiled.

'Oh, May. One of your best. Just – grand – really.' And his tongue cleaned his lips of juice.

'I thought it was maybe a bit heavy.'

'No – light as a leaf, May. Nobody can make pastry like you.'

'Hm! Them apples were nothing special – are they sugared enough?'

'Perfect.' Then because he knew that she would be more

pleased by a small, even unjustified criticism than by any praise, he added: 'Maybe they are just a *little* bit sharp.'

'Don't be so stupid,' she replied, 'they're too sweet if they're anything.'

'They're not too sweet.'

'Give us a taste.' She nibbled at the bitten cake. 'Hm! That pastry *is* a bit heavy.'

She sat on the wooden chair and, as always, folded her arms, jerked back her head, and reflected.

'My Christ, lad, thou even gits a chair.'

'It was here when I came, May.'

'There was damn all when *I* came. An' there'll be damn all when I go.'

'Now, May – it isn't my fault that you share a room.'

'*Share!* Is that what you call it? Oh – *you* don't know Lily hoighty-toighty Peters, my lad – she'd make her own mother feel a lodger.'

'You're older than she is, May, you were there first – you should stick up for yourself.'

'Aha! But my face doesn't fit, see. I mean – I won't say it.'

'Why not?'

'It's your last day.'

'I'll be back, May.'

'Oh – eat your cake and shut up!'

While he obeyed her she wrestled, visibly, with her temper. She loved her brother so much she could have hurt him for not recognizing it. In every action of his she saw their Mother whom she had worshipped: Joseph had held her hand as she had died; an incomparable privilege.

'It's good then, is it?' she shouted, suddenly.

He pointed to a full mouth and shook his head; her relief at this most gentle mockery was great and she rushed out of the chair and bounced onto him, he wriggling further down the bed as she called up half-invented memories of childhood to protract the game.

'Now then,' she warned, as Joseph escaped from under her and advanced, aping threats, 'We've stopped.'

Later she said, 'Trust you to get an afternoon off the day before your holiday!'

'It's just the way it goes, May.'

'Hm! *And* you have good weather.'

'It could rain tomorrow.'

'Anyway, you'll have a better holiday than me.' She paused, then with an attempt at malice which injured her more than it could ever have harmed anyone else, she added, 'Our dear step-mother saw to it that I had a bad time.'

'Now May – that's just your imagination.'

'Imagination be buggered – she made us sleep three in a bed!'

'What's wrong with *that*?'

'She could've offered me the sofa. She'll offer it to you – just watch.'

'Now May . . .'

'You're too young,' she retorted – and for the ten thousandth time went on to say 'You can't remember what your own mother was like.' Then her broad face puckered, became anxious. 'That isn't meant as a criticism, Joseph. Don't think that.'

'He had to marry somebody, May.'

'Why?'

'Well – somebody had to look after us all. We were split up long enough as it was.'

Again he gave her the cue she desired – could do no less – so plain was her longing.

'I could have looked after you, all of you, *I* could.'

'I know May. I know.'

'Just because our father never liked me – no he didn't, now – don't shake your head – after that time when he went to bits – *you* won't remember.' The mystery gave her some comfort for however hard Joseph had pressed her to tell him about the time their father had 'gone to bits' – she had refused.

'Well speak as you find,' said Joseph, firmly, 'she's always been good to me.'

'Oh – I'm not saying anything against her.' May hesitated, and found that the sentence she had spoken misrepresented her position. She made it plain and added, 'Except that he should never have married her.'

'You can't say who he should have married.'

'No.'

With another sudden change, May became sad and defenceless. As he glanced at her – overlapping that wooden chair, thick-bodied, fat even, padded with clothes – he was caught, as always, by the sweetness of her expression at these unaware times.

Near thirty now and made to be a wife and mother, May had never been asked.

'Anyway,' said Joseph, aggressively, 'I'll be glad to get that bloody Garrett out of my hair for a bit.'

Garrett was the butler, Joseph's immediate boss.

'What's wrong with Garrett?' May demanded, knowing full well, but needing to question as he so often questioned her.

'If you can't see that, you're blind.'

'Oh – am I?' she answered, coolly. 'Well if you'd open *your* eyes for a minute, you'd see how well off you are in this place. My Christ!' her control never lasted long, 'you haven't been here ten minutes and you've a room of your own. Look at me! I'm no further than second cook and my prospects is nothing. I would leave this place if it wasn't for you.'

'I know, May: but Garrett's such a slimy character.'

'Ignore him. You're doing very nicely.' She approved of his success. 'He's Nobody.'

As Joseph still looked dissatisfied with her, she added: 'It's better than farm-work.'

'I know, May. It was good of you to tell us about this place. I only got it because of you. I know that.'

'I didn't say it to get your thanks, Joseph.'

'I know you didn't.'

Looks soothed with words.

'Never let it be thought that anybody's doing you a favour by letting you work here, my lad. You do them a favour.' She was solemn.

'It's only Garrett that gets on my nerves,' her brother replied.

May was to be trusted – especially with a secret. 'I keep thinking I'll end up like him, May.'

She breathed very deeply – glad to her heart's core that he should have such confidence in her, tears already primed for the bed that night where she would weep at the recollection.

'Never in this world,' she answered, most tenderly. 'He'll never be anything but a bloody butler.'

'Me neither if I stop here.'

'Oh – you'll go some day.' Decisively said, then put aside. 'Some day. But for the moment – think yourself lucky; there's thousands with no work at all.'

'I know I'm lucky,' he groaned in exasperation. 'You're always telling me I'm lucky.'

'Am I?' she said, accused. 'Just ignore him, Joseph. No wonder he gets mad with you – you're really cheeky with him sometimes. You should be polite – even if he is an old – I won't swear on your day off. Ignore him – just like I ignore cook.'

He had not the heart to point out that a score of times a day she was bruised for all to see by the sadistic little rap of that Irishwoman's bog-bitter tongue.

'But how *can* I ignore him? I hate him.'

'That's nothing,' she said, disdainfully.

They sat for a few moments in silence and in May's mind began the inevitable fantasy of what she would do to Mr Garrett who upset her brother so much.

'It's after six,' said Joseph, taking the pocket-watch from the old chest of drawers.

'My Christ, he has a watch as well,' May muttered.

'You bought it for me.'

'I know.' She sighed and left his room on tip-toe; as if she had been on an immoral visit.

It was the hour when the butler retired to his pantry. Throughout the house a sigh of relief came from the servants, a gentle hallelujah sounding down the corridors. Mr Garrett was charmed by the murmur: each whisper but a comma in the long sentence of his authority.

Feet pointing like the hands of a clock at ten to two, he

lorded it across the hall, savouring the juices which seeped into his mouth in anticipation of the glass of port and lump of Stilton. And there was young Tallentire standing by the pantry door as requested: Oh – the pleasure of settling a small score!

The unlocking of the door, like Garrett's accent, manner and vocabulary, was immensely mannered and Joseph was almost unbearably irritated at the way in which the butler hauled up the keys from a pocket which reached from stomach almost to knees: they were pulled up so slowly, as if they were to unlock treasure, and then regarded and assessed individually, as if Garrett were on too high a level to make such simple distinctions and did not comprehend such base tools.

Inside, the butler sat on his stool and the pneumatic murmur was used to disguise a discreet belch: he had caught sight of the Stilton. Joseph leaned against the door, legs crossed, arms folded – well aware that this would annoy the old toad.

A trick that Garrett had learned from their employer – Colonel Sewell – was to wait, allow a pause. He noted Joseph's attitude and it confirmed his secret decision, nevertheless, he would go through with the charade. Joseph was concentrating his gaze on the thick black elastic suspender which gripped the butler's waxy calf like a tourniquet.

'First things first,' Garrett began, in the manner of Colonel Sewell – even letting his voice die away at the end of a phrase – 'It isn't your business to tell young William' (the hall boy) 'what to do. When you were him – not so very long ago – you listened to me – so does he.'

'He likes cleaning the silver.'

'That's not the point.'

'What is then?'

'He does nothing without my say-so – see?' The officer gave way to the boss.

'What else d'you want me for?'

'I haven't finished with William yet.' He paused. 'You won't rush *me*, Tallentire.'

Joseph shrugged and Garrett interpreted silence as surrender and began to enjoy himself. A glance behind the tins of polish reassured him as to the proximity of the stolen port and he eased himself in his seat, tugged at the knees of his trousers.

'Remember what happened to the fella who was footman before you.' The boss gave way to the tyrant. 'He thought he could tell me what was what.'

The footman, dismissed for stealing port though denying all knowledge of it, had been a friend of Joseph's and he blushed to remember how impotent he had been to prove his friend's innocence.

'That's right,' said Garrett, approving the rush of blood into the cheeks, 'stick out your neck too far and – chop! – off goes your head. Not that *you* stand accused of the sort of thing *he* went in for ...'

'I *never* believed he did it,' scarlet, over-dramatic, Joseph forced his sentence over the butler's bullying tone.

'It was proved.'

'Not to my satisfaction.'

'Your satisfaction, Tallentire, is neither here nor there.' He began to imagine the cheese yielding to his teeth.

'Is that all then?'

'One more thing,' the tyrant gave way to the philosopher: he could afford it now. 'You're too free with the Family.' The Family which he himself served without question; or answer. 'If you want to keep your place – keep it, savvy? You might *think* they're friendly but they're just playing you along. Step out of line and one day – chop!' Neither gesture nor change of expression accompanied the word which fell from the bland face as smoothly as a guillotine from the blue sky. The warning was lost on him, Garrett noted. Chop.

As Joseph went for the bicycle – there were two old boneshakers in the shed and the servants were allowed to borrow them in exchange for maintaining them – he heard the splash of oars from the lake. Lady Sewell was teaching William how to row: it was an accomplishment with which she endowed all her hall boys. Joseph waited to see them when they came from behind the island and remembered his own lessons.

Near the farm where his father was now hired there was a small tarn and Joseph had pinched or borrowed a rowing boat many a night to go fishing. Yet he had been grateful to Lady Sewell for taking the trouble and too confused by her invitation to admit this competence. She had assumed he could not row and planted him down in the stern, herself taking the oars in a well-demonstrated grip – and off they had gone. She rowed skilfully – which added to his confusion, for though he could row well enough, he was not as graceful as she was. Indeed as she stroked the long blades through the still water he wondered if he *did* know how to row; properly. So he had kept his mouth shut and followed her instructions. These were so numerous and precise – particularly with regard to the wrist movements – that his embarrassment had flushed away all his confidence.

He had been learner enough that day – even pleased when told he had 'no done *at all* badly for a first outing'.

It was a matter for smiling when someone else got the same treatment. 'Shallower, William. Shallower!' The light voice carried across the water and as the boat came into sight he went towards the bicycle shed, the uncomfortable suspicion following Garrett's interview dislodged by his own, stronger recollections.

What he liked to do on his afternoon off was to find a quiet place, settle there and let what might come into his mind. He was rather ashamed of this, thinking that he ought to turn the fortune of the free hours to better advantage. And he had once gone to the nearby town – to the swimming baths, to the park, to the shops – as if he had to amass points for some score that was being kept somewhere. But always he had found himself day-dreaming and the drifting time had spread as the dutiful activities became more perfunctory. Now his method was to race down the drive as if some urgent appointment waited for him; continue that farce through the hamlet and beyond for about a quarter of a mile; then turn off down a lane, make for the river, find a favourite spot and lie down.

The way he kept in touch with what was around him was by concentrating on one object and playing with it all afternoon. Sometimes tree branches; or when it was dull or cold he would huddle against a tree trunk, wrap himself round his knees and look across broken clouds; then he could look up and measure the gap between the clouds and the sky, seeing them now as parted in the blue, now suspended from it, now bringing the sky near, now emphasizing its distance. And in the silence he called up his fantasies; allowing them a furtive liberty in that solitary place.

The fantasies would be of perfect lives: of rescue, adventure and victory in war, sport and love. Scenes barely related to any part of his experience in their content; coming mainly from comics, Hollywood, women's magazines and the football pages of the Sundays: but fed by the impetus that is given when light appears after long darkness. The darkness was also his early life which he remembered only in images; a crack in the wall, a gap between two houses, the wheel at the pit-head, a cliff of slag sheer against the sea. His mother had died when he was seven – he had been holding her hand, yet he had sunk all recollection of that. And his boyhood with his father as wilful as the Old Testament God, their means limited by utter dependence on an oppressive, broken-backed rural economy. But somewhere in there were moments when he had felt things could change – an awareness, a light, a recognition – when he had felt himself open to chance in a way his father was not, perhaps never had been. It was that which had enabled him to accommodate himself to being sent to the Sewells as Hall Boy. The notion of being a servant had been transformed into the idea of being a servant in disguise.

But when he thought about the work he did he squirmed. Despite being in no different a position from his father who was a hired farm labourer, the fact of working inside the house stripped off that essential appearance of independence which outdoor work gave his father. Besides, 'work' was too good a word for this cleaning of shoes, laying of tables and serving of food: yet it would be unthinkable to complain; it was too easy.

This afternoon he was too restless fully to enjoy the peace. The return home brought up so many questions. Had he been educated 'properly', he would say to himself, he would be able to identify the questions and answer them. As it was, they came as a harvest of sensations which he could not gather in. Occasionally he thought that he might 'really' take up reading and get to know a few things: he had unobtrusively borrowed books from Sewell's library. It had not really worked. Once or twice he had found a story he liked; but the books of knowledge annoyed him by their density and his boredom. He fell back on intuition, cultivating an awareness of what the people around him were feeling; so that his most refined exercise was to measure exactly the 'state', almost the 'atmosphere', of others. With May, for example, this morning he had got everything right – including that pretence of ignoring her when she first came in: had he not been preoccupied she would have assumed that he had expected her to arrive (which he did) and this would have led her to conclude that she was being taken for granted, which would have distressed her a little.

As he knew, and he got up, stiffly, gave up the attempt to lull himself into day-dreams – abandoned the football matches, deserted the South Sea Islands, withdrew from the Film Stars – he knew now that Garrett intended to fire him and there was nothing he could do to prevent it.

Lady Sewell looked so unhappy that Joseph felt sorry for her, although his sympathy could understandably have been reserved for himself.

'You see, Joseph, it's one of those times when we all have to make sacrifices.'

The carpet was so deep you could have slept on it; the distance between Joseph and Lady Sewell was more than the length of every house the young man's father had ever inhabited; the velvet curtain would have been considered 'far too good to use' by his step-mother – and folded away in a drawer for ever. The Sewells liked to think they were not rich, but that water-colour which Joseph had always liked would have sold for his year's wage.

'I'd hoped to postpone it – but just this afternoon Garrett said that it would be better to tell you before you went on your holiday. He said that – as it happened – you'd mentioned that you might be looking out for another place: nearer your family.'

'I never said that,' he answered. But she never attended to objections.

'No? He said you'd *implied* it.'

'I didn't say anything about it. I don't want another place.'

'Joseph: I'm terribly sorry – and you've always been so cheerful and helpful – quite the most – *vigorous* footman we *ever* had – but' and now, her duty clear, she was firm, 'someone *has* to go – we *must* cut down. The whole country has to pull in its belt with all these men out of work – it's dreadful. And I *do* agree with Garrett in this – it's much better to tell you *before* you go away – I consider that was most thoughtful of him.'

'Do you want me ...' He stopped. Then, rather sharply, he said, 'You won't want me back after this holiday then?'

'Well. It probably *would* be easier – for all of us, *especially* for you – if you *used* your holiday time to look for something. Colonel Sewell and I have talked it over *most* carefully – believe me, Joseph, *most* carefully – and we decided that we could do without a parlour-maid, an under-gardener and the footman – yourself.' She smiled. 'I must tell you that my husband made the observation that if anyone *had* to go it might as well be someone with your initiative as you would be much more likely to land on your feet than the others. Garrett's been with us for years of course; William is too young and Evans, as you might have heard, has an Unfortunate Past.'

All this was said in a 'public-speaking' tone of voice which seemed to seek applause and in fact Joseph only just held himself back from saying 'thank you'.

'Now then,' she said, briskly, 'I will give you the highest references and wish you the best of luck.' She held out a long arm and most clumsily Joseph touched her hand which grasped his fingers and squeezed them. 'The Colonel will see you in the morning. And Evans will drive you to the station of course as usual. Good-bye, Joseph.'

He nodded, said nothing and went out.

He had no cigarettes.

Garrett's quarters were away from the house, and by the time Joseph reached them he had lost his enthusiasm for a row. Besides, the curtains were drawn and the glow from the window was so cosy that the young man would have felt more like an intruder than an antagonist. And when he considered it, he wanted no more of Garrett.

As he walked around the lake for the eighth time, he heard the chimes from the village church – ten. It was a warm night, he would stay out. Instead of the cigarette, a piece of grass had to make do between his teeth. He remembered that his father had once had to smoke cleat leaves.

His mood surprised him, for he was not distressed or upset but rather excited, as if his dismissal was a pleasant and unexpected present. He was happy to be leaving the place. From the way in which Lady Sewell had said 'the Colonel will see you in the morning,' he guessed that the old man would have one or two families for him to write to. At this moment he hoped not; he would like to be out of service altogether.

He had enjoyed it well enough, he told himself; *and* been good at it. That needed to be emphasized at this particular time. He had taken as accurate her complimentary remarks about his work: if there was a conceit in him it was this; that he could do any job he set himself to – as well, at least as well, as any man. And he repeated that to himself in the dark, blushing at the boast.

But now he was out of work. In the letters from home he had heard about the thousands unemployed, particularly in West Cumberland, and felt even more lucky and even more isolated than he usually did. One of them now, he was glad of it.

It was May who kept him out of the house, circling the lake as if unhappy. He did not know how he could cope with her; for she would be waiting for him in his room and he was moved that she would be so dismayed by his leaving. She would cry and, imagining her tears, his own began to press into his eyes. Somehow she would feel that she was being let down and he would feel as if he were leaving her deliberately. And it made him angry, finally, though he would never have confessed it: why should he have to face her when he wanted to savour all this alone?

What to give her? That was the difficulty. The only thing of any value he had which would serve was the chain he had bought for the watch she had given him. He would gladly have made a present of both watch *and* chain but that would have offended her. The chain – and a letter – saying how grateful he was to her – he would leave them on the hall-table where the morning's post was laid out. The watch-chain would please her.

At eleven he left the lake; reluctantly, but he was afraid that May might panic and raise an alarm. Walking towards the black house his feet were springy on the turf, and he felt more alert than he had done for months. At the house he turned to look a last time at the lake, shivering under the half-moon. 'Shallower, Joseph,' she had said. 'Much, much shallower.'

Part Two

Waiting

Chapter Two

The train stopped at Carlisle, from there he took another train to Thurston and from Thurston he walked the few miles to the village. There *was* a bus, twice a day, but he was unsure of its time of departure and preferred to be on his way.

His case was not heavy though it contained all he possessed. He went under the railway bridge and set off up Station Hill; like most of the smaller railway stations, Thurston's was on the edge of the town and once he had climbed Station Hill, he was in the country. It was a cloudy day but brisk, and he walked quickly, his mackintosh flapping below his knees, the light wind freshening his face.

A few horses and carts passed him by and a black Austin Seven, racketing along the middle of the road – he nodded to them all and turned off into a lane which would take him through the fields to the village. Always as he walked his eyes went over to the fells which began about six miles away, and the outline of the hills made him feel cheerful. He whistled and kicked his way through the grass, feeling certainty as well as relief at having lost that job. The walk shook off the stiffness of the journey, the land was bare, leaves turning yellow and brown in hedges and trees, he had his pockets full of presents and everyone would be as pleased to see him as he to see them. He skirted the village itself for fear that he would meet someone who would pass him the gossip he wanted to listen to in his own home.

This cottage was the biggest that John, his father, had ever had. During those first few years following the death of his first wife John had never stayed at one place for longer than a term. The birth of children, the protestations of his second wife, the bother of being re-hired and moving and re-settling –

none of this had stopped his wandering. But now he had settled.

The place stood two or three hundred yards away from the village, over the railway bridge (the station had been closed down the previous year) in the lane which led to the small mere. A large, most plain building, it had been erected as the house for a farm never completed. It had no running water, no gas, an outside lavatory and forever rising damp.

Although Joseph had scaled that scraggy beech tree in the yard to hide from the schoolmaster after he had led half the school away to follow the otter hunt; set off to school, work and play from the place, climbed onto its roof, jumped from a window, scrubbed its steps and cleared the gutters, it was not the house he thought of as he looked at it but his father.

Whenever he came back to Cumberland he remembered his father so intensely that the images came at him like hail, settling finally to freeze him in admiration – he thought of his working in the mines and living through the pit-accident which should have killed him; the envy of his time spent with Joseph's 'real' mother; and the awe of his strength which would never leave him. Since his childhood, Joseph had been his father's subject: hauled from house to house by him as the man's restlessness had taken its course, worked from the age of eight, disciplined with hand and belt from the age of sense and allowed only flight as an expression of protest. Then, if he could keep running for long enough, his father's temper would break into laughter and they would be more friendly than at any other time, the boy tacking across the field slowly, his wariness diminishing the more he grew sure of his father's affection, even a hand on his shoulder.

Most times he did exactly as he was told. As once when John had taken a foal away from its mare. He'd given the mare to Joseph to hold, warning him that she might be 'frisky'. As John began to take away the foal – pulling it into his arms and easing it from under its mother – the mare had begun to throw her head, squeal, buck and try to snap at the small boy who was frightened almost out of his wits but not quite, for still, as he was jerked up and down, his feet clearing the ground, there was the awareness to hear John shout – 'HOLD! Hold on!' And he did.

For two or three years of his boyhood he had always sidled past his father, his right arm crooked in front of his face, ready to parry the expected blow. Yet the ferocity of some of the beatings did not kill his love. And now as he waited behind the dyke, he shut his eyes and immediately was soaked in scenes in which the man spun all around him. Nights when John would get out the concertina and they would clear the stone-flagged kitchen, send out the younger children as runners to announce that 'there's gonna be a dance at oor house – to-neet!' The girls would be frantic to make sandwiches and raid the loft for cooking apples that would be baked and stuffed as a treat. Between the women's preparations and their bossing, Joseph would weave himself as his father's representative; setting this right, finding that, as handy and finicky as his stepmother – the laughter and the interest warming the kitchen until it seemed to have a score of lamps and not just the two. And when people came! Oh, when the place was full! The Lancers, Three Drops of Brandy, Quadrilles they did! Everybody shouting with that ring of honest happiness he had never heard since – to do with relief from work and poverty and worry and frustration, burning all in one flame of communal pleasure: and conducting it all, playing there, his blue eyes slits of fun, his father.

Joseph saw Mary in the yard. She was running over the yard, her small wooden clogs banging on the flattened earth, the hen she was after tippling drunkenly as it raced away. His eyes prickled with tears seeing her: it was always so when he came home, though never when he left. And this was another reason for his careful approach. He liked to get the tears over before he met anyone.

He had come by the field on the other side of the lane. Only upstairs windows looked over it and so he was safe. He could see into the yard by standing on the small bank on which the thinning hedge was set. He had caught the early train in the knowledge that it would enable him to reach home just before the children came back from school – and he waited for them, still watching Mary the smallest.

He ducked when his step-mother came out to make sure that the little girl was safe, and, a few minutes later, almost gave his position away to run out and comfort her when she began to cry; but the crying stopped, as inexplicably as it had begun. A meagre trail of smoke came from one of the chimney pots: he heard the open-engined report of a rare tractor a few fields away, herons from the mere, a few crows – but most of all the sound of his breath pushing against the silence.

The school-bell had gone – and soon he saw them coming across the field. None of them his full brothers or sisters: of those, Sarah and Alice were married and away, Harry had been killed at the very end of the Great War and May of course was in service. Yet Joseph could not have loved them more. Frank was first, running ahead; he was to leave school at Christmas. Now he was racing to get on and finished with the jobs their father would have laid down for him to do. Donald, four or five years younger, was trotting well behind him but obviously drawn along by his elder brother; he would inherit the jobs soon enough. Finally, Anne and Robert who had just started school, climbing the stile with immense care, trailing to the cottage with such diminutive weariness of carriage as made a small caricature of the homeward plod of labourers coming from the fields. He watched them all into the house, then picked up his suitcase and went across there himself. Tea was on the table and so he could have a place from the instant of his arrival.

For his step-mother there was a package of scented soap, for his father (who would come in two or three hours later) twenty Gold Flake; wonderfully complicated knives for Frank and Donald, games in cardboard boxes for Anne and Robert, and for Mary a doll which shut its eyes and sighed when you laid it down. As he handed out the presents (total cost, over two pounds: four months of hard saving) he fought against the pleasure in giving which threatened to take over all his feelings: not to enjoy the distribution of the presents would have been impossible but there always came a point where he felt that he was showing-off, in some way flaunting his virtue and his luck in front of the others. So he switched the conversation immediately and refused even to look at the gifts – all still spread over the table – afraid that the merest glance would be the occasion for another attack of gratitude.

'And what's Frank going to do?' he asked. Both his step-mother, Frank and himself accepted that the subject could be discussed as if he were out of the room.

'Your father wants him to go into farm-work.'

'That's no surprise.'

'I would like him to stay on at school,' said Avril. She nodded to Joseph as if to show that she shared his memory of a similar wish being expressed on *his* account. 'But that's impossible,' she continued briskly. 'He didn't pass for the grammar school, like you, and the only place he could go would be Workington. Your uncle Seth said that he could lodge in with him – but,' she paused, 'well; we need the money. There's no shame in it,' she added. 'You see your father had to take a cut when he was made groom. But I made him take it. He was working too hard just labouring: he will drive himself, your father, and sometimes he'd faint. We didn't write to bother you. It was that thing in the pit, you know: it's more serious than he'll allow. The doctor said he could live to be a hundred if he stopped knocking himself out with work – but if he kept on ...' she hesitated. 'I made an apple cake,' she said, smiling, 'just for your tea – and I've left it in the scullery – Donald – go and bring it – and don't *pick* at it.'

'Where would he be hired?' John asked.

'Mr Dawson told your father he could take another boy on. He could still live here, then.'

Joseph felt a rush of jealousy. *He* had not been so cared for. Though he had passed for the grammar school he had not been allowed to go. At fourteen he had been hired to the best bidder. But he forced the feeling away – long ago he had accepted that while she was always fair to him (though not to his sisters) his step-mother could not but favour those children she had borne herself. She had been good to him though, he knew that, and he had no difficulty in calling her 'mother'.

'And what do you want yourself?' Joseph asked of Frank.

'Aa divvn't know.' Frank blushed and twisted violently in this undesired limelight.

'He's interested in motor cars,' said his mother.

'Aa would like t' be a mechanic,' Frank rushed out, hopelessly proclaiming his ambition. 'Aa would like to work in a garidge.'

'Your father went to see Harry Stamper – but he can't take anybody else on,' said Avril, 'and there's nobody else he knows that has a garage.'

'What about George Moore in Thurston?'

'Your father doesn't know *him*,' said Avril, with such emphasis as implied that George Moore was beyond all knowing.

'Our Alice courted Edward. *I* can always ask him.'

'Can thou?' interjected Frank. 'Can thou just go up and axe him like that?'

'*Any*body can ask him,' said Joseph, moderatingly.

'Not me,' said Frank. 'Aa couldn't axe nobody nothing, nivver.' And he stuffed some bread into his mouth to stifle all further confessions.

As Joseph had once done, so Frank was approaching his fourteenth birthday as a ravine which, if leapt badly, could result in the near-fatal accident of 'getting a wrong start'. In a few days following that birthday, he would have a man's work laid on him. From about the age of six, he had been training for it, doing more and more work around the house and garden, helping his father, spending his holidays on the farm, the summer evenings haytiming, his autumn weekends potato picking. It was as if the severity with which the children were brought up and the insistence that was put on their working, far from being a harsh expression of affection, was the most considerate way in which such parents could arm their children for what would follow. And the boy was watched for his work, his ability at it, his constancy and interest, watched and talked of as someone about to go out to battle so that the men would say, 'He's about ready for work now', 'He's shooting up a bit, he'll be all right now', 'He wants nothing at home, now, let him get to work,' and, most commonly of all: 'Can he work yet?'

Avril, like many of the mothers, accepted this until those

few months before the actual transfer took place. Then she tugged against it, counted the savings she had, regretted all sorts of missed opportunities, resented the lack of other opportunities, vowed that he would be the last to go in such a way, turned this way and that to rescue him, failed and watched him go – over the top.

After tea the children scattered. Remembering May, Joseph refused the offer of the sofa and went up to the room he would share with two of his brothers. There were some books on the window sill – five volumes of the 'Today and Tomorrow' series which he had won over a number of years as school prizes: in all of them a great future was promised, with everything in every way daily getting better and better. He had not liked them much and now used them as a prop for his feet, to keep his shoes off the bedding, as he lay back and smoked a butt.

Had he not carried in him the news of his lost job, he would have basked around the fields in the plenty of his homecoming. But now he wanted to be alone before the revelation. Already he felt that he had cheated them all by holding it back: it must be said before night.

As he lay there he was washed by a misery which seemed to rise from nowhere. He had long heard May and his step-mother talk of his father's 'moods' – and experienced the effects of the foul ones directly. Somehow he had never thought that he too would be enslaved by them. John had had such a hard life compared with his own, and even when his father had once told him that he had been unable to rid himself of this possessing blankness since a young man, he had found reasons for it which did not apply to himself. Yet here, with his family around him, a soft bed, a cigarette, nothing to do, he was swept over, drowned in a despair which was neither pity for himself nor a lament for others but a meaningless thing, opaque to any analysis he could bring to bear on it, an irresistible closing up of the pores of his mind, his body and his senses which submerged him and left him powerless.

The sound of his father's voice pulled him out of it. He had lain there for two hours. He went down the stairs hesitantly, always over-wrought at seeing his father after a long absence –

and as usual covering this beneath an appearance of cocky cheerfulness.

He opened the kitchen door and for a second looked full at the older man before going across to shake his hand. Now fifty-one, John Tallentire was as lean and stiff-backed as ever he had been. His clothes hung baggily on him, the thick wide trousers dropping over the boots, the buttoned waistcoat, collarless shirt and scarf, jacket with full pockets swinging against the thighs like weights balancing his precise walk, cap shoved back from his brow. His face had been cut up in the pit accident and the left cheek was divided in two by a scar, but the scar was deep in the skin and the effect was to bunch the upper cheek, making it rosier, merry under the blue eyes. There was another long scar just below the hairline on his forehead – hidden by cap or hair – and a dry pucker of skin at the right corner of his mouth twisted his lips when he smiled – but again the harm was masked by its consequences, for that twist made his slightest smile irresistible and you could not but smile back at him. The real damage had been done to the base of his skull and his back which was crossed with thin blue welts as if he had been lashed with a cat of nine tails tipped with coal. When he saw Joseph he nodded and held up the new packet of Gold Flake which his thick fingers were fumbling with – and offered his son a cigarette as soon as they had shaken hands.

'Good to see thee lad,' said John. 'Ay. Good to see thee.'

'Good to see thee an' all,' Joseph replied.

'He's grown, mother!' John shouted, though Avril was but two paces away. 'Ay,' he repeated more gently to Joseph. 'Thou's just about filled out, Aa would say.'

'He might shoot up some more,' said Avril, loyal to Joseph's possibilities.

'Nay,' John contradicted her. 'Come on, back to back, lad. Back to back. See thou keeps thee 'eels on't carpet. Theer.'

'Take your cap off, dad,' said Avril.

'A cap's no advantage. Squint a bit on my side woman.'

'I'll get the poker.'

She laid it across their two heads.

'Exactly the same,' she said.

'What did I say?' said John. 'He's filled out and finished.'

'He might be taller than you yet.'

'Nivver!'

'Well,' Avril smiled as she looked from one to the other: they were very much alike. 'He's a real Tallentire, anyway.'

John laughed and took his son's shoulder to lead him into the garden. 'A real Tallentire.' To Joseph the remark gave a thrill: no-one but Avril ever said it and she did it to please his father, John thought. Yet the idea of being a 'real Tallentire' appealed to his romantic imagination: not that it was an appeal which had much of a hearing. The only other Tallentires he knew were his uncles Seth and Isaac and his aunt Sarah; little consistency there. Joseph's real pleasure was that the remark contained the implication that he was like his father: which suited him well.

After watching Frank working in the garden, with Donald at his brother's heels like an acolyte – John crooked his finger mysteriously and led his son to a hut he had put up halfway down the next field.

'Pigs,' he said grandly. 'Two. What dis te think o' that?'

They watched the pigs scour the bare ground and Joseph, like his father, regarded the fat, roinking beasts with great pride.

Then, as he had hoped, his father began to tell him of the Shows he had been to that summer with the horses. He talked of each horse individually, of its moods and temper, how he dressed it, how calmed it, how led it, how managed it, the cups they had won, those they had missed, the journeys in the horse-box, 'me snuggled in a bale of straw, Joseph, and oot at yon end like a scarecrow. I always took me best suit to lead them in. Some said it was daft – wearing a good suit like that. But what the hell – I've hed her since I got married and she does no service anywheer's else. And mother can still git her squared up for a funeral or whativver. *Your* mother was just the same as me for that. If thou's got summat to wear – wear it, she would say. And I parcel it up again as soon as I'm through.'

The fact that these shows put hours on his day, doubling some of them for very little extra – and then only if the horses won – was nothing compared with the pleasure John took in them.

Joseph could see the horses in his imagination, tall, powerful silk-maned greys with polished hooves and finely combed hair draping them like tassels, thick gleaming coats and plaited tails, flowers sometimes in the manes and straw in the tails – beautiful horses that could pull a plough a long day and trot as delicately as ponies. He knew, too, John's care for them – could see the older man working to make them shine, working hard as he always did as if in endless combat with himself not only to see that every job was well done but also to prove to his constant though invisible foe that application alone, though a minor quality, could also draw towards perfection.

While this talk went on, Joseph's pleasure was increasingly spoiled by the knowledge that he would have to tell that he was out of work. After a time it again appeared to him to be cheating not to tell, as if it meant he was getting all his father's confidences on false pretences.

He blurted it out.

John paused a while.

'Thou wasn't fired for badness?' he asked severely.

'No.'

'Thou did *nowt* wrong?'

'No. This butler wasn't fair though.'

'Why not?'

Joseph told him. Again John paused, then: 'Ay – bugger that sort of a man.'

The two men walked slowly up the field.

'But thou's gonna find it gay tricky up here,' said Joseph thoughtfully, 'there's more men out of work now than I've *ivver* seen. We've had poor work, lad, and we've had slave-work. But that was better than no work.'

'Was it?' The two words came without forethought.

'What do you mean – was it?'

'I mean,' said Joseph, unafraid of his father now, however much he admired and loved him, 'I mean sometimes it might be better not to work at all than to work like a slave.'

'Thou's *got* to work, lad.'

'Mebbe so. But . . .'

'No buts.' John did not want a contest with his son. He knew how easily he lost his temper and did not want to crush the younger man in any way. 'Thou's lucky to hev a week's holiday to start lookin',' he said. 'There's many a man widdout that.'

In bed that night Joseph found it difficult to sleep. He tossed about and then forced himself to lie still – he was in the same bed as his two younger brothers and did not want to wake them. All his fantasies were of jobs. Work had to be found and this night's sleep stood in the way of the search. Yet somehow, he whispered it to himself uncomprehendingly, it was not so important, this Work.

His movements disturbed Frank. Awake, the boy felt his elder brother close to him and wanted in some way to express the gratitude he had for Joseph's interest in his ambition. He thought hard for something intimately appropriate: to thank him again directly, in the dark, would be too weak. At last it came to him.

'Joseph,' he whispered, 'Joseph?'

'Yes?'

'Has thou ivver stripped a gear-box?'

'No.' He paused. 'Nivver.'

'I have,' Frank replied, happily – and turned to sleep.

The first thing to be done was to get Frank fixed up. That he was no relation at all to Joseph but a 'brother' by marriage (the one child that Avril, a widow, had brought with her) had always made it the more important to Joseph that he should be scrupulously cared for. He wasted no time, set off for Thurston the following morning and went to George Moore's garage.

He found Edward, George Moore's son, under a tractor – and immediately told him of what he wanted. Edward told him where his father could be found and Joseph went up to see him.

The garage was built on two levels – the bottom level opening on to Station Road, the top level backing on to New Street. Between the two was a wooden ramp and on the top level a shop for crystal sets, the new wirelesses and toys. Joseph found Mr Moore in the shop.

'Interested, is he?' said Mr Moore, the matter being explained.

'Well now. Interested.' He spoke slowly and paused often between words, sometimes between syllables.

'Yes. He's done a lot of messin' about with engines a'ready.'

'Messin' aboot eh?' said Mr Moore, ruminatively. 'Now then. Messin' aboot.'

'You know what I mean.'

'Oh aye. I know. Aye. Now when did he want to come?'

'New Year.'

'New Year eh?' said Mr Moore, meditatively. 'That's reet. It *was* t' New Year thou said.'

Which reassured him, it seemed, as to Joseph's basic honesty.

'Well,' said Mr Moore, after a silence. 'It's bad to git work these days.'

'It is.'

'Yes.' He paused. 'It is.'

'But a boy's wages are less than half a man's,' said Joseph relentlessly.

'They are.'

'And he's not frightened of work.'

'No?'

'No. Me father'll vouch for that.'

'Thou knows, Aa've heard tell of thee father – but Aa've niv-ver met him. Is he a big fella, raither blond, wid a tash?'

'No. He's shortish, black haired – works at Dawson's.'

'Now yon's a particular customer.' To make it clear that he was referring to Dawson in his personal not business aspect, he added, 'He brings some work here.'

'Well Dawson can vouch for him. He's worked at Dawson's.'

'That'd be farm-work?'

'Ay.'

'Not the same thing,' said Mr Moore, tutting slightly as he shook his head. 'Garidge work and farm-work's different basics a' togither. Direct oppisytes, Aa would say.'

'But he's worked on Dawson's tractor.'

'On that John Brown he has?'

'Yes.'

'Aa wondered where that hed got 'til,' said Mr Moore, rather annoyed. 'So this laddo's been tinkerin' wid it, hes he?'

'Ay,' Joseph smiled, 'thou'd better git him in here – then Dawson 'ud be forced to bring it to thee.'

'He would, ay. That's correct. He would. Aye. Tinkerin' eh?' He paused. 'She's a bloody awkward machine, yon John Brown, it's aa te buggery inside, thou knows.'

'Frank keeps it going.'

'Frank, eh? That's his name then; Frank.'

'Ay.'

'Well then,' said Mr Moore – and if he had been cautious before, a new word must be invented to describe the wariness, the ambiguity, the care, the non-commitment, the seizure in the tone which informed his next words: 'Send him along,' he said, 'Aa'll hev a look at him. Then – we'll be like Mr Asquith – we'll "wait and see".'

Down the ramp Joseph had the following exchange with Edward.

Joseph: 'Do you need another lad?'

Edward: 'Thou can say that again.'

Joseph: 'Sure?'

Edward: 'Certain. We're cluttered up. And he won't pay a man.'

Joseph: 'Thanks.'

On the whole he was pleased with the morning's work. There was nothing promised, and he would not be satisfied until Frank had actually landed the job – but as he biked home for his dinner, he felt that he had made a start.

He would have liked to work in the garage himself – and a 'lad's' wages would amount to much the same as he had received as a footman. He had not allowed himself to think of it until now: but it was not only too late, it was impossible. Frank had to be given a decent start.

Chapter Three

Over the next two months he spent six days a week – all hours – looking for work. On Sunday he met others like himself and they played football from light until dark, breaking only for a few sandwiches and cold tea. Some of the men who had given up all hope used to play all week. The energy which went into the game and the pleasure which came out of it made the forlorn apathy over unemployment seem uncanny at times; and though it was a very rare man who would admit to enjoying this necessary idleness, many discovered leisure for the first time in their lives, and privately relished it.

Though this was in some direct sense true and was felt more by younger, single men, the frontal fact was unemployment and the consequences were ugly and often desperate. In those weeks, Joseph saw it everywhere and was frightened by it. For all over the country, at that time in the early 1930's, there were workless men moving ceaselessly; largely ignorant of the system which had brought them to that state, largely ignored by those who ran that system; good men, mostly, who turned anger on themselves rather than seeking to inflict its results on others, who tried to nurse discontent with good humour and kept going because of those who depended on them: women and children first: the man to take all the punishment necessary.

Fear settled on him slowly, like drizzle, soaking, soaking, gradually penetrating the confidence until it touched on the quick of his self-esteem and there lodged fast. In the Sewells' house he had not realized how it was – not at all: and to his shame, he longed to be back there, at times, snug in his attic room, footman's uniform neatly over the chair. Shame because when he was at the factory gates or the pit-head with all the others, waiting to be told there were no vacancies, then there was no doubt that he was himself without any equivocation: even, after the luxuries of the big house, there was something welcome in the knowledge that there was no further to go; this queue for the dole, this shuffle and saving of single pennies, this pinched stomach, these melancholy streets and overcrowded rooms, barefoot children and old men grimacing at the cold – at some times these were firm as a board beneath him.

But whatever the compensations – and their nature as benefits appeared only passingly, not to be truly accounted until later, in reflection – whatever the incidental happiness from seeing his step-brothers and sisters – especially little Mary, through delicacy and a certain poise become the darling of the family – when Joseph got up and when he went to bed he thought of his failure and slowly began to think it really *was* his. Began to fear that he was not man enough to get and hold a job; and as much of his own sense of himself was defined by his work, he would feel the cramps in his stomach and know it was not just the longing for more food. Though he did not believe in labour as his life's purpose – as his father did – yet he was unable to find anything which even began to take its place.

They waited for work, those men, thirty per cent and more of the adult male population; some fought, some begged, some hunted, some crawled, but most waited, circling the system with caution; as if the sea in which they had all once swam had thrown up a monster which lay there, beached, not known to be dead or alive – which might destroy them all.

Two months: eight weeks: he counted the days.

It was Colonel Sewell who got him work. Someone quite near Thurston wanted an 'all-purpose chap' (so the Colonel wrote) 'someone like yourself – willing for anything and pretty capable. Go along and see him immediately.'

The house was no more than twenty miles from Thurston: he was employed on the spot and told that he would be charged only one pound for the uniform left behind by the previous footman: it would be taken from his first month's wages. Oh, and after Easter they might need him no longer – and did he mind sleeping in a cupboard next to the cellar. And smoking was not allowed. Did he smoke? Do him good to stop.

Joseph had met Mr Lenty in his first week at the house – when he had taken the shoes down to be mended – and since then had seen him regularly. Lenty's shop was in a side street of the nearby town and he sat in the window, watching the world, talking incessantly, and mending shoes. He was full fat, the long leather apron truly like a hide on that bovine frame; 'Sitting', he explained, 'sitting makes you swell. The skin closes on you, Joseph, the muscles sleep, the limbs stiffen, the sweat is retained. Any man who retains his own sweat is swollen by it, Joseph. But who can sole and heel walking about a room? No man. Never retain your own sweat!' His face was red as was his neck, his hands and all the hairless surface of his head.

'Hair,' he said, 'was given to man for warmth, Joseph. And now we live indoors and do not need it. Soon everyone will be bald. And the appendix will finally disappear if not in my lifetime, then in yours. Teeth and toes will most certainly follow and I would not be surprised if our nose and our ears were reduced to holes in the head. I won't live to see that.' A man who prided himself not so much on his knowledge nor on any innate powers of reasoning but on his affection for words – 'for running them together, Joseph, and scattering them abroad, for knitting them into patterns and stitching them into shapes: I don't seek out the strange words, Joseph, those that check a sentence and trip the ignorance of men – those are scholar's words – and I leave them to that distinguished body to enjoy in exclusivity. Mine are the everyday, a few Sunday words mashed in like gravy to the potatoes but no Bank-Holiday expressions – if you follow my line. I like to prattle, Joseph, to prate and patter and for every tack I drive through leather I must drive a word in with it.

'A collection of books has been my salvation, Joseph, and education. Had my grandfather on my mother's side not bought that job lot at a church auction – an act of charity, Joseph, and there are none better – had he not paid two shillings and sixpence for Lot 121 – I still have the ticket – I would have been dumb. Speechless. Silent.'

And there they stood – job lot 121 – on the window sill beside him, battered calf-bound volumes, about two dozen – Dickens, Thackeray, the Poems of Hogg, some of Carlyle's Essays – incessantly revised and reviewed by Lenty. Joseph had borrowed and read some of them.

Lenty had always talked so, his wife said – and she put the blame on his left leg. This was much shorter than his right leg and the debility had confined him to bed for most of his youth, 'and there was nothing for him to do but talk and read books,' she said, hopelessly. 'His father had a small public house and they brought him downstairs when he was eleven and made a bed for him in one of the snugs. That was where the talking men went. He caught it then and now he can't get rid of it.'

Lenty had one child, a daughter, Mair. 'My own mother was Welsh,' he said, 'and Mair is Welsh for Mary. In England they put a "y" on the end, having removed the "i", in France they put an "ie", in Spain they juggle it about with your Maria, as in Italy: I am told by Mr Kirkby, the schoolmaster, that the name occurs in every language known to man, Joseph. He takes it as proof of the Garden of Eden. I questioned that on the grounds that in Eden the lady was called Eve. He then proved that he was using a symbol.' Joseph had had a brief flirtation with Mair as much from the overspill of his affection for Lenty as from any real affection for the girl. It had come to nothing and they enjoyed a pleasant acquaintanceship. She, he knew, was 'walking out' with a junior gardener from another House. Joseph came on his free afternoons.

Lenty expected Joseph to make himself useful. Before long, the boy would find himself with a last, ripping off worn soles and heels, tapping the small nails into boots, even cutting out the leather. This did not bother Joseph much. He did not like to be idle when someone else was working: it was a privilege which he could not bear easily. Moreover he enjoyed the work – the smell of leather was as rich as the smell of bread; he liked to carve a sole from a sheet of the stuff and fill his mouth with the bright tacks. He had watched his father mending shoes often enough to be able to pick up the tricks quite easily – and at first, Lenty had taken some trouble to instruct him. Such a master-like position had soon bored the older man, and the moment he had seen that Joseph was passably capable he had allowed him to get on with it.

Lenty was no great craftsman: he had no song about leather and delivered no speeches in praise of the well-made shoe. At times he made a complete mess of it and it was not unusual to see him ripping off a new sole to start again. 'I was not called, Joseph,' he said. 'I heard no voices, felt no divine impulse, in short had no vocation. Yet – strange – I had all the time in the world to think one up. Lying in that snug as a boy I would consider my vocation: even after the elimination of the athletic pursuits (due to the leg) there was still considerable choice. The callings of man are as various as his desires, Joseph – and there were many courses open. But however much I made my mind as a clean slate – no hand inscribed thereon the letters of my future. So when one Tommy Black said he needed an apprentice at a sitting-down trade – I took it. Or rather my good father – bless him – did. I was tired of the snug by then. Wider fields, Joseph, even in mice there is a search for wider fields – hence the field-mouse.'

The one room served as workshop and selling shop. Whenever he entered it, Joseph felt cheerful, for besides the sight of Lenty framed by his window like a beaming goblin, and the smell of the leather, there was the effect of that brown suffused jumble – lengths of freshly tanned leather hung on the walls like tapestries, strips of it on the floor, the work-bench littered with it, the peeling cream wallpaper melting (through dirt) to its colour, the heavy books a leather line on the window-sill, boxes of nails, tacks, rubber heels, caps, clips, corkers, toe-plates, laces, eyes, polishes and ointments on the bench which was semi-circular, Mr Lenty sitting in it as if an arc had been carved out of a rude dining table to comfort his stomach – and everywhere shoes, sandals, boots, slippers, clogs, all shapes, sizes and colours, new, finished, gleaming, battered – it was as if the clouds had opened one day and showered footwear on Lenty. This had on Joseph the effect that all such jumbles had – especially those conglomerations which had consistency, which served one end, as this did the shoe: delight.

'Ah, Joseph,' said Mr Lenty with relief and great pleasure. 'Ah, Joseph!' He paused and wiped his mouth on his sleeve. He spat, just a very little, as he spoke, since his upper teeth had been lately reduced to four molars and two rather fangish canines: it was not dangerous to sit near him – but it was as well to keep at least a yard away. 'I was beginning to despair of company this dreary day when the rattle of your back mud-guard alerted me to the remembrance that this was your after-noon off. Those cobbles are like an alarm. I have asked many customers if they could think of a link between cobbles and cobbler but it stumps them all. Where was I? Yes. I cannot re-member the last afternoon I had off – which is to say I can though I prefer to forget it. The left one, yes. Good.

'I had not taken an afternoon off since my daughter's con-firmation when I went to hear the bishop speak – very poor it was, not enough quotations for a bishop. Mr Kirkby gives me more quotations when he brings his slippers in. That being five years past, I thought – use *that* strip, Joseph, I know it has a hacked look but you must do what you can; it is a very hacked shoe – that I deserved another such but waited, Joseph, for a few months, to let things take their course. The *small* hammer: very well, use the large one.

'Then one day Mrs Lenty said that *she* proposed to take an afternoon off: I was astounded.' (Here he held his hammer above his head and paused: the quality of the silence was re-markable: then he brought it down firmly just to one side of the nail, bending it badly, and resumed.) 'Mrs Lenty *never* takes an afternoon off, never, never takes an afternoon off, not to see the bishop or I dare say prince, king, Pope or emperor, Joseph: *you* know Mrs Lenty. Well then, I said nothing – for a moment – and then, without jumping in to question her decision with the impetus of a nanny-goat, admitted to her that I too, was think-ing in the general direction of taking an afternoon off. It was her turn to pause, Joseph, pass the number 5 nails. She, too, good woman, said nothing of an enquiring kind and it was my turn to suggest that we take the *same* afternoon off – to which she assented in a state of great relief – and only *then* did I slip in, most casually, my question. I moved like the slow-worm,' said Mr Lenty, 'and said – Did she have anywhere to go? "Yes," she replied, "a funeral." Did I? No, I said, a walk would be good enough for me.

'The day came, Joseph, make a good job of that, I've just remembered who it's for – I know my talking loses me customers, Joseph, but those are the sort you can do without. Anyway, I have about two thousand pounds in two building societies, besides what Mrs Lenty has in the post office and the cash-box and the large blue jug – I could sit back and live on that, Joseph, if I could get time off. But I can never *finish*. There have been occasions when I was down to a few shoes – no more than four pairs, I remember, once: and I said to Mrs Lenty – "those done, up go the shutters." Up they never went, Joseph, because that cheeky hall-boy arrived the very next morning – the one from Pinkleys' – with twelve pairs to be soled and heeled: twelve! I've been no nearer than ten since that day. Sometimes I think I don't *want* to retire because there surely must be other ways to break free of this vice, to turn this downward spiral into an upward course leading to rest and peaceful free pastures – but I can't see it. And what you can't see you can't want, Joseph – being yet another of Mr Kirkby's quotations, though he called that one "hidden".

'The day came and I prepared myself. Mair had painted a card with the words SHOP SHUT THIS THURSDAY AFTERNOON. FIRST TIME IN FIVE YEARS. MANY APOLOGIES. BEST WISHES. G. P. LENTY, ESQ. – there it is, I keep it by me for a calamity – copper-plate lettering, very distinguished – and I hoped all morning that the usual pattern would be observed. That is, a few first thing in the morning, a few at dinner-time, and a few late on – hardly a soul along the afternoon, Joseph, and despite all sorts of guesses at it I've never been able to really work that out – it's a normal enough town in all other respects – and after dinner, with Mrs Lenty gone about her business, I closed that front door which, as you know, is open every day on the calendar from nine until nine except when it's raining but even then I keep it on the latch.

'Then – good boy, sandpaper the edges of this for me, would you? Yes, a good job you made of that – then I made my preparations.' (Here Mr Lenty having disembarrassed himself of the material of his trade by passing it to Joseph, also set down the tools and his two small white hands rested on those bumps beneath the leather apron which were probably his knees.) 'I changed,' he said, lifting the hands from the bumps and patting himself from navel to neck as if testing his resilience, 'from skin to skin. Washed completely. Did not stint. And out of the front door.

'I decided to go to the main street which I had not seen in weekday daylight for five years, and set off. At the Co-op, before I had turned the corner, I met Mrs Charles – would I put irons on her husband's boots and by the evening please as he was walking to a mass-meeting? Back I came – changed, throughout, once more – irons, you know, are a dirty job and those boots were old, very – it took me almost an hour. Still time. Again' (he lifted his hands to the ceiling) 'skin to skin. This time I turned left and decided to make for the park which I have not seen day or night for twelve years at least but I know the keeper – a customer – and hear that his stocks are beautiful. *In* the park then, sitting down, watching the children, very summery, waiting for the keeper, always a good talk in him, when Eric Hetherington comes up. All white because of his cricket flannels. His cricket boots *had* to be re-studded for a friendly with Cockermouth that evening. I looked at them. There was no doubt about it. They *had* to be re-studded.

'I was no more than ten minutes in that park.

'He stood there (where you sit) – talking – all the time I did the cricket boots. I had not changed, but with that talk and the white polish which flaked off all over me I found myself at 4.30 p.m. dirty, exhausted and, in short, defeated. I changed back for the last time and have never had an afternoon off since. Nor a morning. Now then, what was it I started to tell you?'

He was interrupted by Mrs Lenty who came in to announce tea. The men went through to the kitchen for it. An apple cake – which Mrs Lenty had soon discovered to be Joseph's favourite and stuck by as his relentless treat ever since – stood in the middle of the cloth, newly baked, the light brown crust ready to melt on the palate. Bread, scones, jam and fancies stood as at the four points of a compass and the crockery spliced the principal bearings.

At tea Mr Lenty ate well and said nothing.

'This is what I started to say,' said Mr Lenty when they returned to the shop, unfolding a piece of paper before him as if preparing to read out a sermon. 'That is, this is what I meant to start to say when driven off course by an undercurrent of reminiscence, as I remember, just as I am always threatened by what might be called Trade Winds (the customers, Joseph, you see – think hard!) and, to keep the thing at sea, I ask you to regard this piece of paper as a chart, an explorer's map, a map of the mind but no less interesting for that.'

He handed over the piece of paper. On it were the numbers 1 to 20, written out as numerals several times, and beside each numeral, there was the word of the number recorded, as Joseph thought, in several different dialects. 'The sheep-score,' said Mr Lenty. 'Brought to me by my friend Mr Kirkby the schoolmaster after I had mentioned to him your reciting the way the shepherds count here in Cumberland. I was invigorated by that performance and also by the reminder of that particular lump of information,' he went on, battering the heel off a boot, 'and as you know I'm not a man for information – generally. Facts are facts people say, and so they are, but in my experience too many of them clutter up the throat – throttle you, hard things, no give in them. But that stuck – most likely, Joseph – that's right, the large nails in the cocoa tins – because of the way they sounded. Say them again.'

Any embarrassment which Joseph might once have felt at responding to such abrupt demands had long gone. There is a certain fear underlying embarrassment and it was impossible to be afraid of Mr Lenty. So Joseph rhymed off the count from one to twenty, in his own, the West Cumbrian dialect, singing it almost, as the words demanded:

'Yan, tyan, tethera, methera, pimp, sethera, lethera, hovera, dovera, dick. Yan-a-dick, tyan-a-dick, tethera-dick, methera-dick, bumfit.'

'Bumfit!' Mr Lenty interrupted ecstatically. 'Oh, thou Bumfit! My Bumfit. Now why can't we *still* say Bumfit. Fifteen doesn't hold a candle to it. Bumfit! Oh – go *on*, Joseph.'

'Yan-a-bumfit, tyan-a-bumfit, tithera-bumfit, methera-bumfit, giggot.'

'Giggot!' said Mr Lenty. 'Twenty. And-the-days-of-thy-years-are-tethera-giggots-and-dick. Now isn't that better than three score and ten? Tethera giggots and dick. It *sounds* like a lifetime, doesn't it? I could hear you repeat that all evening – but pass the paper back and listen to *my* count.'

He took the paper, held it at arm's length (a short distance as his head tracked down the shoulder to bring his myopic brown pupils nearer their target) coughed, smiled most mysteriously at Joseph and began:

'Now Mr Kirkby wrote this out for me. Remember that. Mr Kirkby. I'll take this one. Yes. "Een, teen, tother, fither, pimp, een-pimp, teen-pimp, tother-pimp, fither-pimp, gleeget (yes, Joseph: I too prefer "dick": but forward): een-gleeget, teen-gleeget, tother-gleeget, fither-gleeget, bumfra ("fra" for "fit", you'll observe, but same base – bum): een-bumfra, teen-bumfra, tother-bumfra, fither-bumfra, fith-en-ly." (Twenty. Rather slippery along the tongue.) Well then. So what? – you might ask?'

Here, Mr Lenty really did tremble with excitement, even to wiping his brow, calming the nervousness, unable to bear the strain of it all.

'Joseph,' he said, solemnly. 'Some of those other lists you saw on that piece of paper were sheep-scores taken from different parts of England and one from Wales. You will admit that they were most remarkably similar to the one you say, ours, in Cumberland. But the one *I* read to you, Joseph, and one *other* on that list, Joseph, now listen, hold the nails for a moment, yes, the one *I* read, Joseph – that one is used by the Indians in North America.' He paused to let this revelation have its full effect. 'Indians of the Wawenoc Tribe,' he said, 'and it was recorded there in the year 1717. In a land 3,000 miles from our own. Joseph, across that mighty ocean, there, over there,' he pointed, 'are Indians and Cumbrians counting sheep in the same way – give or take dick and giggot. It says something about man, Joseph: but what? That was my immediate question to Mr Kirkby – and he traced it back to the Garden of Eden. *Extra*-ordinary though, isn't it?' he continued, delightedly, 'really, as information goes, that's the most extraordinary specimen that's come to me for a very long time. And I have you to thank, Joseph. And I do thank you. I've asked Mair to make a copy of this for you. It's something you'll be able to keep all your life.'

Joseph had not the heart to hazard the possibility that the Red Indians might have learnt the count from the Welsh or English settlers. And indeed, though this suggested itself to him, he dismissed it as a piece of unnecessary cleverness. For he, too, *wanted* it to be true, wanted there to be this tangible yet mysterious connection between different peoples: and besides such a desire, his observation appeared as a trivial irritant. The two men sat in silence, feeling the world spin them about, deeply content that all over it there were men counting sheep with the same numbers.

After he had left, Mr Lenty took advantage of the shop being empty and came into the kitchen to take up what was obviously a well-worked topic:

'Yes,' he said deferentially, standing at the kitchen door and thus halfway between his domestic and industrial self, 'Yes, I think I shall most certainly ask him after this Easter holiday. He never speaks of the House with a *great* deal of affection and he is already fairly useful in the shop. He could be a prize cobbler. I shall ask him.

'And he can live in,' said Mrs Lenty. 'He's very useful about the house. He can have the spare bedroom.'

'Do you think he *will* come, then?' Mr Lenty asked – for the thousandth time.

'I'm sure of it, my dear,' replied his wife. 'We'll all be really snug together.'

'Good,' said Mr Lenty. 'Then it's settled. I'll ask him on his return.' He smiled happily. 'We'll have some good talks together.'

Joseph had worked for Lenty for two months when Mair got

married. The marriage, once announced, was rapidly concluded and it took only another three months to explain the rush of it all.

In these circumstances, Lenty was forced to offer his new son-in-law both shelter and a job. He accepted both and Joseph was again out of work and parted, probably forever, from someone whose geniality had secured him most happily.

May also married at that time and he was glad he had some money saved to send her a decent present.

Having lost after having had was worse than never having had. He felt the pressure of John, his father, on him, who could not face a man without work, and tore around the district between panic and despair. Nothing, nothing to be had. And once more he left his own County, this time on an impulse come from fear.

Chapter Four

Twenty now, thin-faced, small-framed, watchful, having lived through the first pangs of real hopelessness and yet managed to retain a capacity for pleasure – the blue eyes suddenly wincing, the laughter ringing out in the industrial Midlands, Joseph was out on his own.

After leaving Lenty, his only regular work had been with a road gang – mainly Irish – who had started to dig a new route between Walsall and Birmingham and then stopped after two months. 'The money ran out' was the extent of the explanation granted to those who had done the labouring.

The gentle fantasies had retreated, yet their romantic imprint remained on the pattern of his ambition. This was 'to be his own man'. The phrase had been overheard casually and instantly fixed in his mind. He wanted ease, yes, and time for play, for thinking and dreaming – but they were on the other side of the wall he was building for himself: first, to be his own man, first, first and last.

Because of Stoddart. The Foreman. Tall – over six feet tall – big-boned, heavily muscled, gaunt from his longing for violence which clashed ceaselessly with his will to control everything; he had taken Joseph on and then disowned him, the very next day, for mimicking him in front of the others.

He had neither fired him nor hit him. Kept him there to torment him. Called him 'Runt'.

It was a big coal yard: Briggs Bros. had more than twenty lorries and they delivered over most of the city. Joseph had been taken on to work in the yard where the coal was stacked from the mines and loaded into the lorries. His job in the first week was down the 'hell-hole' – that is, under the grating which covered the loading bay. Here the coal dust piled up and had to be shovelled away and put in sacks. Until Joseph arrived, the way of it had been for half-a-dozen men to dig it once a fortnight – on a Friday when there would be some lorry drivers around after short runs, and the drivers would put the stuff in sacks. A new boy was always sent down there first, of course (everyone accepted that brutal necessity) and made to work in it for a week. But after that, he was put on normal work and the usual routine re-introduced.

Stoddart set up a new 'system' after Joseph's first week. One man alone was to be responsible for the 'hell-hole' to get in there every day and shovel; to do the sacking himself and also sort out the useful small lumps which had fallen through the grating so that they could be sold directly at the gate with the cheap 'slack'. Joseph was to be the man.

'Yes, Runt, you! Any objections, Runt?'

The insult had been swallowed at the beginning when it could have been a joke. There were worse nicknames than 'Runt'; Joseph had not smiled but he did let it pass. Even that day he regretted it, and soon Stoddart was using the word like the lead tip on a lash: forever flicking it at the younger man, enjoying the fleck, the blood.

And 'Runt' became his name to the others in the yard – who used it in a neutral manner, though, and he did not mind so much; except that it was always an echo of Stoddart.

The man began to obsess him in a distressing way.

In that first week, unused to such concentrated work, Joseph's hands had given way. The blisters on them were like pouches and he could press them so that they wobbled from side to side under the black membrane of skin. For him, hands were grained with coal; and to get them clean meant bursting the blisters.

The lodging house he lived in – and which took thirteen of his twenty-one shillings for two meals a day and a bed – had no bath and a very erratic, always limited, supply of hot water. Washing averaged two hours a night that first week; on top of a ten-hour day and one hour's travelling. And alone in the cellar with the two tin basins – one full of cold black scum, the other a black sludge of tepid grit, there on the damp flagstones, he cried to himself as the blood came out of the raw blister patches.

Lonely there. And every other thought of Stoddart whom he dreamed to smash and murder, garrot and flay; and feared to confront.

He was not afraid of a beating; of that he was reasonably sure. It would be a severe beating because Stoddart would not fight unless he really meant it and then would have no hesitation in using to the full all his physical superiority. He was not afraid of that, he would tell himself, perhaps a little too often, too emphatically.

As he saw the face, the jaw, the hands, the walk, the look of Stoddart; every other second. Slept and woke on him.

The only impulse which had any power at all to interrupt this spell which was cast on him was the regular droning of his hope 'to be his own man'.

Stoddart terrorized him. Down there in the hole, his mouth and nose most pitifully protected by a length of rag which he tied at the back of his head, he would look up and there would be Stoddart, feet astride on the grating, bending almost double, sometimes squatting, so that he was thrusting himself into Joseph's face. And always 'Runt'. 'Runt.' 'Give over, Runt, there's a lorry coming.' 'Is that the best you can do, Runt? I've seen a sparrow spew more than's on that shovel, Runt. Runts have to work, no?'

The shovel was broad; he could have been out through the tunnel and up the steps in a few seconds; Stoddart would not be expecting it and go down; for good if the thing was swung hard enough. Why did he not at least attempt that?

It was his indecision which helped to paralyse him. For he had never had much cause or opportunity to hesitate before.

In one way he felt that Stoddart would have loved him to lose control of himself and try to fight; recognizing this occasionally gave his passivity the colour of obstinacy; and the more he was provoked, the more he could regard his self-control as tenacious. But though Stoddart would have enjoyed seeing Joseph break, he was quite willing to torture him without the bonus of such an outbreak.

The work itself was terrible. Besides the muscular exhaustion, there was this dust which, after a few weeks, felt as if it coated the inside of Joseph's body, When he coughed, the spittle was black: when he breathed, his lungs felt caked and clammy. He lost weight, could scarcely find the energy to wash, spent all Sundays in bed – nor would he have eaten on that day had not some of the men brought him up a plateful from the table.

In another room in the lodgings were two men who worked in the pit and were active in the unions. Late in the evenings, when he had half-eaten his supper and almost crawled up the stairs to bed, he would listen to them arguing as he tried to forget how he ached, to forget Stoddart squatting on that grating 'Runt! Runt!', to obliterate that face from his mind. They spoke of 'action' and 'comradeship' and strike-funds, protest, hours, benefits, Rights: it all sounded so strong, so worked out, so fair. He envied those who could be in unions: no one in the coal yard was; no one in the Big Houses had been, nor on the farms, nor in the road gangs. If you had a job that took you into a union, he thought, then you would have no problems: you could complain about being in the 'hell-hole' for ten weeks if you were in a union; that was the sort of thing you *could* do there. And they would listen.

'Listen – Runt, you work there or you work nowhere.'

The other men grumbled and one or two even worried about the young man now literally almost staggering around, blood-shot eyes, hands bandaged in oily rags. But what could they do?

He knew what it was, in the end; what it was that kept him at it. His father – John, yes. John would say 'What's a bit of hard work? What the hell. Stick it.' And he couldn't lose another job. 'You can't just quit, anyway,' John would have said – Joseph heard him now. Him and Stoddart talking: never arguing against each other – just one talking after the other as the lorries backed onto the grating and the dust fell down onto the heap. 'Call that a sackful, Runt?' 'Good God, man, it's only work.'

Joseph could not say 'God' nor 'Christ'; not aloud. But whatever it was he could swear by, he did – but it was neither an oath nor a vow he swore. 'I'll work, I'll work all right. But it's because I'm bound to. When I'm not – I'll forget it. I'll set up on my own.'

He got a very bad cough which kept him shivering in bed for three days. Then he got up and went back to work.

Stoddart had replaced him.

Chapter Five

Once more at home, he settled for a desultory drifting. He had been hurt by Stoddart and needed time and a little peace to attempt recovery.

Thurston was well placed to sustain him. There were slabs of days numb with boredom but ... gradually ... it was an interesting time. He spent almost all of it in the town. He had not stayed long in one place in Cumberland since childhood, and discovering the town, gradually sorting out the names and relationships, becoming familiar with the gossip and private histories, this street-corner study was to be remembered as a happy time. It seemed a town so packed with life and yet so comprehensible. You could walk from your house to any important building – church, school, pubs, auction, shops, post office. There were about four thousand lived there – a manageable number.

Because of its position, just in from the coast, it was much less badly affected by the depression than the mining towns of West Cumberland. Thurston had been a very plump little town at the end of the nineteenth century when its location – as the natural centre of that mid-western part of Cumberland – had made it such a successful market-town. It was still fed by those farmlands, but the increased use of trucks and lorries was taking trade to the bigger centres – Carlisle, Dumfries, Hawick. Yet though decay was slowly making its way through paint and prospects, there was still layer on layer before the bare bone of a West-Coast Maryport where 85 per cent were unemployed. Only between 15–30 per cent unemployed and of that percentage, a fair proportion of unemployables.

It sat very well, the town, and only to the west did you leave it down-hill. Otherwise you dropped into it from Howrigg

Bank or Standing Stone, Station Hill, Longthwaite or Southend. Two main streets which formed a T at the Fountain in the centre: the cross-bar was West Street and King Street; the upright High Street. There were many versions of how it had come to its nickname, 'The Throstle's Nest'. The one which Joseph favoured was that of Gally Wallace who said that his father and some other Thurston men had come back after the First World War and found that the train from Carlisle to Thurston was delayed: so they walked the eleven miles and as they came over the hill and looked down at the churches, Highmoor tower, the town with fields and auctions in the middle of it, with farms just a few yards from King Street and all shapes of courtyards, alleyways and passages – Gally's father had thrown off his pack and declared: 'Away, lads – it's the Throstle's Nest of All England.'

Though knowing people in the town was a matter of pride to most of those who lived there, Joseph had little clear idea of the middle-class lot: the solicitors, bank managers, teachers and doctors; those who owned and ran the small clothing factory where the women worked or the paper mill where the men were employed – these drifted around the edge of his landscape, suits of tweed and white weekday collars, high black prams and changes of clothes.

He was on nodding terms with some of the shopkeepers; with George Johnston who had a large shoe-shop and bred Basset hounds, Toppin the butcher and Pape the ironmonger. With Mr Harris, one of the three clock-makers in the town, a white-haired, waxed-white-moustached man, courteous and thoughtful, who sold no watch he could not mend and served voluntarily in the public lending library. He knew Joster Hardin who was a carpenter and old Mr Hutton who took most of the coffin trade; Harvey Messenger he knew who had a paper-shop and was never once seen by anyone out of temper; and Ginny McGuffie's bread-and-cake shop, the best vanilla slices he had tasted, so fat with sweet custard that just to touch them was to make them ooze. Soon he could run around the town in his mind, marking it by shops and houses and faces – see the old women in black who would greet each other by two

Christian names 'Hello, Mary Jane,' 'I saw Sally Ann,' and the old men on the wall of Tickle's lane, carving wooden ships and daggers for the little boys; and he would deliberately not go to sleep at night so that he could see again the faces of the men on Water Street corner, the women coming out of the covered market, the farmers beating their cattle to the top auction, small boys everywhere running around the town in endless chases.

He hoped for work at the paper-factory, but so did about two score others. While waiting and doing odd jobs which brought in the extra few shillings, he began to make friends: there had not been the leisure for this since early childhood, for at eight or nine he'd become his father's apprentice. He did not find any special friends, though he would have liked a 'best friend', a man to whom he could have told anything, from whom he could have asked anything; but had to make do with acquaintances. Decent at football, game for any scheme, useful at all sorts of work, he was not short of company. And when his father shook his head and regretted the solitary trudging of his son from no to no, the son would like as not be living, as John thought quietly himself, the life of Riley.

Early in winter he took up with Dido and his gang. In Thurston there were many like Dido, called 'Potters' or 'Squatters' or 'Gippos' by ordinary people; others called them rascals or criminals or vagabonds; respectable old people who feared and disliked them referred to them, if at all, as 'wastrels' or 'scavengers': children who idolized them, daringly whispered that they were the 'boyos' or the Hard Men.

For generations, an important gypsy camp had been set up near Thurston every year – at Black Tippo, just beyond the cemetery. Hundreds of gypsies came, for weeks, sometimes for months, and the women would sell their pegs around the district and accost people with demands for silver on the palm; the men would trade in horses and dogs, be accused of every crime and accident there was, and move around with their animals and children at their heels as wild-looking as a tribe of Red Indians. Romany words came into the Thurston slang – 'scran' for food, 'mort' for girl, 'parney' for rain, 'duckel' for dog and 'cower' for anything at all – already the local dialect was notorious for its impenetrability. And some of the gypsies stayed, to squat in abandoned houses; to live as free as they chose, it seemed, as daily they scoured the countryside for the leavings which sustained them.

Among them were all sorts, from the Hard Men who were up regularly for theft, fighting and assault and sometimes sent down to Durham Jail; through all the sports and boasters to those near to jokers, like Dido and his two pals, Lefty and Glum – who were yet clever enough to float where others were sinking.

Joseph had been walking back from Waverton after playing football one night when Dido had come up in his pony and trap and stopped to give him a lift. Then instead of going Joseph's way, Dido had turned off and made for the Wampool, for a part which he'd heard was full of salmon. On private property they had poached, Joseph keeping a look-out while Dido walked into the river with boots, socks and trousers on, and tried to tickle them by moonlight. Something relaxed and careless about Joseph at this time had sealed an attraction which he had always felt towards the boyos, ever since he'd first heard tales about them. And their nicknames were never to be forgotten: there was a Diddler besides a Dido (and to each other as to the world in general they appeared to have no other name but this, none) Patchy the brother of Lefty; and Gripe the father of Glum; a Nimble a Nosher and a Tont: Bloss, Tuttu and Swank; Muck, Fly, Old Age; and Kettler, the star – way out of Joseph's reach. In some families there were three generations of single-minded unemployables, now the clowns, now the villains, but all, to Joseph at that time, a great relief.

They were outside the struggle and he too wanted to be detached, for a while, for a rest.

Chapter Six

He had first taken notice of her when coming back from Mickle-thewaite with Dido. They had cleared some old byres belonging to a Mr Purdom and the trap was high with broken mangers.

It was evening, about half-past six: February, dark, snow-covered; hedges and roads black threads on the downy surface. The moon came up as he turned on to the main Carlisle–Thurston road and the cold rays lit the snow so that he could see clearly. The pony walked steadily, the mangers swaying perilously on the cart. Joseph and Dido took alternate puffs at a cigarette and they went slowly through this level spread of snow.

He heard the voices, the noise of the bicycles, and then the bells as they came up to pass. It was a gang of girls who worked in Carr's Biscuit Factory in Carlisle and cycled the eleven miles there to start at seven in the morning; now on their way home. As she passed the cart, Betty turned and smiled at him. Her face was white, pinched, would later, in warmth, smart back to life; her headscarf had come loose and her black hair blew around her neck: she rang and rang again her bell then pulled ahead of him, the others following. He could hear them free-wheeling down the hill, the rubber tyres crushing the crisp slush, and the laughter as they straggled up the next rise until he saw Betty again, cresting the skyline, circling on her bike, a silhouette waiting for the other girls to catch up. They straggled to join her and all seemed to stay still for a moment until, with shouting and more ringing of bells they swooped out of sight and finally out of hearing.

Betty's mother had died a few weeks after her birth; unbalanced by this her father had left the town and gone south where he was killed in a fire without ever seeing his daughter again. One of his brothers had given a sum of money to Mrs Nicholson and she had brought the girl up.

Mrs Nicholson had then two sons but no daughter: she so longed for one that she gave Betty her own name and treated her as a daughter – quelling every reference to the girl's real parents in those early years.

Betty was bright, active and amiable: Mrs Nicholson took in washing and the girl used to deliver it for her when she grew big enough to manage the baskets: she did the shopping for the woman she always called 'Mother', and in various ways got to know and love Thurston – every alleyway, house and row of steps, the halls and arches, yards, side streets and shops. She was a pleasant girl, not at all shy, and soon became well known, well liked. For the rest of her life she remembered those childhood years in the town as a capsule of perfect happiness.

Mr Nicholson, whom she always called 'Uncle', had worked at a factory where he had had an accident; there was no compensation and for two or three years while he recovered and then looked for work the house was in trouble. His wife decided to 'take in' unwanted children; not uncommon as a source of income. Many mothers who could not afford to or find the circumstances which allowed them to take care of their own illegitimate children would pay a married woman a weekly amount to do so. Mrs Nicholson took in three.

The illegitimate children arrived when Betty was eleven; the fact of their illegitimacy frightened her, for though the town accommodated ten different churches from Catholic to Quaker, people of Betty's sort – the respectable working people, the majority – were united in a ferocious puritanism. The little girl cared for the new arrivals as devotedly as if they had been lepers.

And when she herself was told that Mrs Nicholson was not her real mother, she nursed this knowledge secretly for almost a year – and throughout that time she daily believed herself to be one of the paid-for children. When she could no longer contain it and burst into terrible sobs one night, her 'mother' corrected her mistake but the new information, that both her parents were dead, only deepened the wrong and the damage was confirmed.

About a week after she had 'been told', Betty who was a strong swimmer, got into difficulties in a dammed-up part of the river and almost drowned. She ought not to have found herself in such trouble – she had swum there many times.

Later as the girl became more timid at the edges of her experience, more fragile, Mrs Nicholson smiled to herself with relief: she saw it happening to all the girls of about fourteen, this preparation for the leap into courtship. She was relieved to observe that the business of discovering her real parents to be dead had had such a temporary effect.

The first time they were alone together was just before Easter after a Pea and Pie supper and social in the Congregational Hall. Betty stood at the top of the steps leading out of the hall, waiting for her girl friends, and glanced sharply at Joseph as he bounded up towards her, the look accusing him of trickery in catching her so on her own. But he was as surprised as she and stood away from her, leaning against the railings, trying not to shiver in the cold night.

He had first hunted her in the expected places, circling the town on his bike in the dark evenings, seeing her come out of her house, the pictures, a friend's, the Guides – and at that stage she had accepted to be the prey and run away from him, slipping down an alley which he would turn into to find himself bumped off his bike by steps or jammed against a wall with the escape wide enough only for one. And when he left his machine to race after her he would always lose her in this town riddled with tiny sideways, interjoined and dark.

Then he had joined the male gang which was the counterpart of the female gang in which Betty concealed herself; but here she was no longer single prey, and gave every appearance of her preference for numbers. As immediately as she had sensed the weight and urgency of his first intention and manoeuvres, as sullenly now did she seem to have no notion of it. Any attempt he made to single her out was instantly defeated.

So they stood outside the Congregational Hall and looked

down Water Street, waiting for the others. Nor was it until a full five minutes had passed that they realized that a plan had been made to leave them alone.

Each recognized this at the same time and, answering together an unuttered question, Joseph said, 'I'll go and tell them to hurry up.'

But she shook her head. To be the girl who had demanded that the others give up their scheme would be far more shameful than an accommodation. Already she could hear the giggles from the cloakroom at the bottom of the stairs. 'I suppose we'd better go,' she said gloomily. 'But just to the end of Water Street.'

He wheeled his bike in the gutter and so kept to the outside of the pavement: she walked beside the house-fronts: the street had no lights and they were guided by the lone gas lamp at the end, where it joined the High Street.

And they came to that High Street without having exchanged a single word.

'Well,' said Joseph sternly, as one who has kept his faith, 'you said just to the end of Water Street and this is it.'

'Yes,' her tone was penitent.

'Good night then, Betty,' he said, and slowly but decisively he wheeled his bicycle out into the middle of the road and prepared to mount.

His use of her name gave her no option but to use his if she wanted to call him back. She watched him bend over his back wheel to put on the red light.

'Have you ever thought of going *away* somewhere for work, Joseph?' she asked, timidly. He turned and smiled at her. 'Or the army,' she asked, more confidently. 'They always want people – why don't you go and join the army?'

'Well, others can, that's all,' she said.

'And some others can't.'

Betty was not interested in argument. Most men in Thurston had jobs: it made her uncomfortable to qualify references to Joseph by saying that he was out of work. Had they lived in Maryport where unemployment was almost universal, it's likely that she would have been just as uneasy if he had been *in* work. As in dress, manners, ambition and tastes, so in this matter also, she would not have anything out of the ordinary: would not do anything to draw special attention to herself.

'Look,' he would say. 'What else can I do? I say I'll go south – but you won't come with me.'

'I should think not. We aren't even engaged.'

'If I *did* join the army I'd never see you.'

'They have holidays sometimes.'

'But Betty . . . !'

'And you should think better of yourself than to go around with Dido and them.'

'Why?'

'They're dirty.'

'O God!'

'Well they are. Nobody's *that* poor. Soap's cheap enough.'

'It isn't that important.'

'Is it not? Well they pinch things, Joseph Tallentire, you know they do, and it doesn't matter if they don't do it when you're there, it's not right.'

She hated any hint of illegality and thought Joseph was determined to see Dido and the others a few more times, to maintain his dignity, her clear opposition confirmed some of his own inclination and he knew the roaming was at an end.

'Well I'll try farm-work again.'

'Not *farm*-work!'

'What's wrong with it?'

'Nothing.'

'Well?'

'Once you get started with it, you can do nothing else,' said Betty, rather desperately.

'So?'

'*I* don't want to be stuck in a cottage in the middle of nowhere.'

'Ah! So that's it.'

'Yes it is.' She hesitated. 'I'm sorry, Joseph; I'm not much help, am I?'

'Never mind.'

One of the proofs of love, he thought, was to serve; and though Betty seemed demanding she wanted little. To stay in Thurston with those she had known all her life, engaging her, protecting her; he could give her that at least.

He would have given her much more. His life until now seemed a procession leading to her: the figures along the way no more than those who had to be passed by on his way to this ...

He decided on the big rayophane paper factory. The managing director lived in a most spacious and grand manor house set in its own large grounds in the middle of the town. Joseph stationed himself outside there every morning and every morning followed Mr Lancing through the town, down to the factory. It was a walk of about half a mile which Lancing used as his constitutional. Joseph kept about three paces behind him, having looked him blankly and silently in the face as he had come out of the large wooden gates. In the evenings, Lancing was driven back, and when the car stopped for the chauffeur to get out and open the gates – there would be Joseph, standing beside the right-hand pillar, making no attempt to help the chauffeur, looking directly into the car at Lancing.

After a fortnight, the director's curiosity awoke, or his nerve broke. He got out of the car and came across to the waiting man.

'Who *are* you?'

'Joseph Tallentire.'

'Why do you follow me about like this?'

'I want a job at your factory.'

'So do a lot of people, young man.' Mr Lancing's use of 'young man' was cutting: he himself was just in his early thirties. 'I think I could do a good job,' said Joseph – the words forced out, throwing off coils of embarrassment and self-consciousness.

Mr Lancing smiled. 'Do you indeed?' He paused. 'I suppose you'd better come and see me on Monday. Eight o'clock sharp. And *don't* follow me down the bloody street again!'

Joseph swallowed all that.

He began work on the Monday as a junior slitter, and in that factory found his place in industrial England.

At that time the machinery was antiquated and the men needed to be mechanics as well as do the job they were paid for; the conditions of work were foul, with chemicals clogging the air, long barely lit sheds, rarely cleaned corridors, freezing in winter, broiling in summer. A noise whose first impact must have sliced most of the more tender nerves leading from the ears and after that hammered at the mind until it was a wonder the men did not come out with pulped brains dripping from their nostrils. All had the knowledge that the job must be held to at whatever price, whatever humiliation because there were plenty of people ready to take their place and they were lucky to be in work.

To this place Joseph came for eight eight-hour shifts a week, one every day but Wednesday when he did a double shift, and his going in and his going out were attended by the punching of his card into a machine which registered to the minute his daily span of servitude and rang a bell.

When he went there you got the same rate (in his shop) for the job – 4d. an hour – whether you were a boy or man. The foreman got 5d., otherwise differentiation according to ability, output or age was unknown. There was much talk about the injustice of it – but no action. There was no single union which embraced all the skills in the place and such union members as there were knew that to call in their branch secretary would be worse than useless: there was nothing he could do in such a place of varied trades. Not one shop steward was there in the entire place. Troublemakers were fired and no questions answered.

Joseph almost enjoyed the work for the first year or so – enjoyed getting to know the machines, enjoyed being in work. He had a flair for mending the big machine he worked on and made two improvements on it. One was to invent a roller which worked in synchronization with the feeder and so enabled the paper to roll along steadily in even lengths, thus making the slitting much simpler; this saved time, increased production, cut out a great deal of irritation and passed without notice from the owners. The other thing he did was to make a much more efficient passage for the rolls of paper from the machine to the stacking bay: this involved the simplest mechanical adjustments and gained its chief effect from a reorganization in the system of stacking itself: for this he was given five pounds.

Now he could start courting Betty, slow and hesitant it had to be, but her need for him showed itself often enough for him to forgive the reluctance.

At the end of the year, Betty found a job in Thurston's cloth mill, starting at 9s. a week; top wage (after five years) 23s. a week. She gave 8s. 6d. of the 9s. to Mrs Nicholson and to supplement her pocket money worked in a bakery for two nights a week.

Her move gave them more time together.

Chapter Seven

They met on Sunday mornings beside the Fountain at about eight. This fountain was a gift to the people of Thurston from the man who had given the town its swimming baths, helped found its boys' grammar school, restored its Anglican church, sat on many boards and helped many people, lived in the huge and fantastical house on a hill to the south of the town, kept a deer park there always open to the public and died bankrupt just after the First World War.

The base of the Fountain was like a tomb and it was defended by black, pike-topped railings. Small gaps to east and west led in to wizened heads of bearded old men from whose black bronze mouths water dribbled when a large button was pressed on their foreheads. Above this funereal base, there was a shape something between a thin pyramid and a fat spire – about twenty feet high; a stumpy cross had been stuck on the top. It stood in the centre of the town, at the junction of the three main streets, and was the natural place to meet, especially if you were on bikes. You could circle around it, hold on to the railings without dismounting, do any last-minute checks and repairs on the triangle of space which lay to one side of it like a parking place for its shadow, and watch for the others coming along one of the three ways, cheering at them in the distance, the full sound like a reveille along the empty morning streets.

It was not a cycling club but a gang who liked to go biking together. People Betty had known all her life – John Connolly and Jack Atkinson, the Middleton girls and Mary Graham. They were ten this June morning and Betty and Joseph, like two of the other couples, rode a tandem. Sandwiches, a big bottle of lemonade, capes and a football in the large bag which rested on a frame of its own over the back mudguard: they were set for the day. The bicycles circled the fountain, waiting for the church bells to strike eight, and then they peeled off down the main street, down Burnfort along the Carlisle road, making for Whitley Bay, the East Coast, about seventy miles away.

Within a couple of hours they were well on the road which ran parallel to the Roman Wall: bound straight as a ruler for Wallsend, but dipping and rising like a switchback. The tandem was an old model, bought second-hand and built for survival rather than speed. It required heavy pedalling, for if anything was to be got out of the day, they could not loiter. Nor did a slow pace appeal to any of them: the idea was to go as fast as you could without breaking your back.

Now that he had been at the factory for over two years Joseph could claim one Sunday in two in winter and one in four in summer: he took them all, luxuriating in the strange dimension of a full day with Betty. Strange Sundays they were too at his home. Frank stayed in bed – the garage being closed. Joseph got out the tandem to bike into Thurston and collect Betty; only John went to work – to the farm where he mucked out the stables and helped with the milking.

Joseph rode in front, Betty behind. He preferred it that way – because he could set a steady pace and stick to it. When she led, they would be forever drawing ahead and then dropping back; sometimes she would decide to get off at quite a small rise, or she would accelerate as they approached a big hill and he knew that there would be no stopping her until they got to the top of it. You could not forget yourself and day-dream or look at the countryside or chat comfortably to someone riding alongside you: not when you were liable to lurch forward any second or suddenly find that she had decided to free-wheel. In none of their time together, despite the usual quarrels and disagreements, had anything even begun to approach the irritation he experienced on those rides on the tandem. What made it worse was that she appeared tireless. There was never the prospect of calm which could have rested on a knowledge of ultimate superiority. He had tried to exhaust her once or twice and ended up blowing hard, turning on his saddle to meet such a mischievous and pleased smile as made him want to dump the damned tandem in the nearest river. But he could not do that, nor could he sell it – to do so would be an admission of defeat.

At the time he bought it Joseph had thought it a romantic idea. He had seen them spinning along through country lanes, bound together, the idea of two in one symbolizing and strengthening their affection.

> Daisy. Daisy.
> Give me your answer do,
> I'm half crazy,
> All for the love of you:
> It won't be a stylish marriage,
> I can't afford a carriage,
> But you'll look sweet
> Upon the seat
> Of a bicycle made for two. (Ta-ra-ra-ra-ra ...)

But from that point of view it was a disaster.

What it did do was to refine Joseph's attitude towards Betty. Again, he thought it ridiculous that she should learn about her through a tandem – his fantasies had told him that he would learn about her as they sat side by side on a river bank, or in 'the nook of an inn-parlour' or they would be given knowledge of each other 'on fairest days under whitest clouds'. But it was on the tandem that discoveries had been made.

They biked along the desolate road and stopped at Housesteads, the Roman cavalry camp, to have a breather. There were a few sightseers looking over the site but though Joseph urged the others to go up and have a look, he was outvoted. It would take up too much time. He insisted a little and so was howled down. As they set off, Betty slowed the tandem's pace so that they fell back behind the others a little.

'What did you get so worked up about?' she whispered to the back of his head.

'I wasn't worked up.'

'Well?'

'You should see things like that. *You* would have liked to, wouldn't you?'

'I might,' said Betty after a little hesitation. Then, honestly, 'Yes, I would. But nobody else wanted to go.'

'We'll come on our own one day.'

'Yes,' she replied, unexpectedly. 'I'd like that.'

He twisted around fully towards her to make confession of a dream private to himself for years until this moment: 'I would like to have been a village schoolmaster, you know,' he said.

Betty smiled and he leaned back to kiss her. 'Watch out!' The bike swung towards the ditch and he only just managed to get to the handlegrips in time to swerve away from it.

Through the towns along the Tyne they went, and quickly, silently, for there, writ large, were circumstances but a thread-snap away from their own. The towns were as in mourning – Jarrow, 'the town they killed' – and at this late morning hour the streets were lined with miners waiting between the shilling for the football match the previous afternoon at St James' Park and the threepence for a gill when the pubs opened, for many the span of their week's entertainment. There was an injustice and shame about it which Betty felt as directly as the cold. Such misery as could plainly be seen oppressed her and she was made sick by it, so that her stomach tightened, her hands sweated and she bit at her bottom lip nervously, feeling ashamed to be biking so carefree past these men. Joseph turned around to say something to her, feeling the drag on the pedals, but seeing her expression he guessed precisely what she was thinking and this sympathy overwhelmed him with love for her. He changed his remark.

'It's terrible, isn't it?'

'Yes,' she said. 'They should be shot for letting this happen.'

The words brought the relief of anger to her and the thought of what should be done to those who were responsible for governing the country helped to displace the weight from her feelings. She wished that she were old enough to have a vote: when she was, she would throw it down for Labour like a weapon for them to use.

They raced the last mile or so to the sea, heads down, rubber handlegrips warming to the clenched fist – a spontaneous rush for the coast. The weight which had clung to their legs over the last twenty miles fell off as they sprinted towards the holiday resort, along the front to the grassy banks at the northern end of the town where they turned their bikes upside down on the ground – to keep sand and dirt from getting in the chain or hubs – and lay down to eat their sandwiches.

After the sandwiches they went to the beach and played in the cold North Sea. There was only one way to go in – full speed and altogether – and they joined hands and raced across the wet sand right into the water, running until they were thrown forward by the pressure of water around their legs. They splashed each other, the men duck-dived and grabbed the girls' legs, heaving them clear and throwing them up into the air. They swam but a little way from the shore and kept as closely together as a school of dolphin. The beach was filling up; it was the afternoon and all along it were thin white bodies, men in black woolly swimming trunks, women in full covering bathing costumes temporarily balded by their white rubber bathing caps, children paddling along the edges of the sea, grandmothers deep in sand and packets of food, bundles of clothes, the whole a shivering exposure to freedom as if they were not holidaymakers so much as refugees, the very movements jerky and over-strenuous as if the most had to be made of this day for there might be none like it to follow.

So the gang from Thurston, having dashed along the seventy miles, bolted their food, bashed into the unenticing waves – now raced from the water and started a game of football with the girls as energetic as the men, and then a form of handball, men against women.

Afterwards when they had changed and dried themselves came those embarrassing moments when they split up. For an hour or so they would wander off in pairs, alone with their girl-friends – and yet the hesitation and false starts involved in bringing about this uncomplicated and unexceptionable situation gave them the appearance of being set on an insoluble problem. They hovered around the bicycles, the women wrapped up what was left of the meal and put it in the bags, a bottle of lemonade was passed from hand to hand, it became imperative to move a few yards away from each other and look out to sea unblinkingly, broken mutters and glances tore at the even weave which had held them together all day and eventually it became a matter for courage. Who was going to make plain what was on the minds of all, and make himself the target for mumbles and jokes by over-heartily announcing that he felt like going for a walk on his own, and did she (his girl) fancy coming along? Before this happened the men and women split into two groups and the bicycles between them were like a magic line – once crossed new laws would operate.

Joseph always held his peace. He was irritated at this procedure and would have seen that it did not even begin to happen had he had his own way. The situation was clear and obvious and it was stupid to waste time in this way. But he had learned his lesson: when he *had* gone first and abruptly to propose to Betty that they should go off on their own she had said no. Which had turned muted awkwardness into an open argument, with *everyone* feeling in an impossible position. So he waited.

At last alone with Betty he feared even to put his arm around her so much did he want her, so afraid to frighten her. More than just accepting her strictness about making love he believed it intrinsic to her attraction. But even in his kisses he feared to bruise her. Lying with her, there, in the high grass in a hollow of the dunes, his body melted to hers and a slow intoxication suffused him, the world became this deep drift of coloured, tasted love and all that was hidden and trapped in him broke free at this time and found a place in the pressure of his lips on her cheek.

Though they were not yet engaged, they intended to be and Joseph wanted her to be seen. Boxing Day was just right.

Everyone was waiting for them. The smaller children in giggles, Frank determined to see that Joseph was given fair play, May, who had come with her husband and baby for the day, trying rather unsuccessfully to forget the sharp clash she had just had with the 'step-mother' as she always called her. John had his good suit on and was looking very conscious of his 'smartness' there in the kitchen.

Joseph had wanted to come out on their tandem – but she had insisted on walking.

She got as far as the end of the lane, saw the cottage, felt the eyes peeping through the windows and refused to move further. Nor would she go back. Joseph argued – but: 'I *can't* go there,' she said. Then, half-derisively, allowing room for her to see that he would have no objection to being followed, would quite welcome it, in fact, if she cared to come along with him, he drifted down the lane alone; and was still alone ten yards from the cottage. He turned and saw her stuck to the same spot as if her feet were in cement.

Smarting under this – for he had *seen* as well as felt the eyes at the windows, he marched back and lectured her on her responsibilities to herself, to him. 'They'll think I've taken up with some half-wit,' he said. 'Good God, Betty, if thou's frightened of this – how'll we ever get married?' 'Well I won't get married, then,' she said, 'not if it's as bad as this.' It was a cold day: she had on her only coat, bought the previous spring and intended for the summer. Her face was beginning to turn blue. 'My mother's *expecting* you,' said Joseph. 'I'm sorry,' Betty wailed '– but I *can't move*.' 'I'll bloody well push you then.' Joseph went behind her and pushed. She stumbled a few yards forward and then stopped. He pushed again. Again she trotted a few steps and then halted. Once more. 'We must look right fools,' he said. 'I'll walk on my own,' she said, 'but don't hold my arm, now *please*, Joseph, *please* don't: it makes us look like an old married couple. And not like that. That's not what I meant at all.' (His arm had gone around her waist.) 'Now just walk normally – and I'll go without pushing.'

'Mebbe we should march,' he suggested. 'Don't be silly,' she answered, speaking out of the corner of her mouth. Joseph imitated this and put on an American accent: 'Do you think they'll shoot before we can draw, baby?' he asked. She giggled. 'Don't make me laugh, please,' she said. 'I'll whistle, baby, to throw them off the scent.' He began to whistle *Dixie* and marched in time to it. 'If I had a handbag, I'd clatter you with it,' Betty muttered. 'I'll buy you one for your birthday,' he replied. 'Ooh! You're awful, Joseph Tallentire.' 'Ooh! You're lovely, Betty Nicholson.' They were now but a few yards from the cottage, Betty as stiff-shouldered as a guardsman. 'Give us a kiss,' he said. '*Joseph*: please!' 'Just a quick one. To show everybody how much you think of us.' 'I'll show you what I think when I get you on your own.' 'I can't wait,' he replied. 'Let's just walk right on and go down to the tarn.' 'Do I look alright?' 'Smashing.' 'But *really*?' 'Really?' He paused, they went through the gate and were almost at the door. 'Really,' he replied slowly, 'there's a bit of soot on your nose. Mother!' He opened the door. 'We're here!'

And she looked so solitary, so fragile in her determination as she entered the kitchen before him that it was all he could do to stop himself folding his arms around her and holding her to him.

It was May who ran to meet Betty and in that action was both a generosity to see the girl of her brother's choice properly welcomed and a pointed declaration of the fact that she stood closer in relationship to Joseph than his step-mother. May, even plumper now, took Betty's hand cordially, scrutinized her quite frankly and nodded three or four times with unmistakable significance. Having *seen* her, the younger children bolted until tea-time. Mrs Tallentire took her coat, Frank took her gloves, Joseph took her scarf, May took it from him and, in very plain dumb-show indicated that Betty ought to be found a seat. John had already found a seat, May's husband searched for a match, Joseph gave him his box, and as the waters of the Red Sea closed over the Pharaoh's army so that where there had been movement there was none so as Betty sat down all sank into their positions and there was a deep silence.

Then. 'It's quite mild,' said May to the rescue, 'for the time of year.'

'T'lass looks frozen,' said John.

'Put some more logs on't fire then!' May rapped out to Frank who leapt up – and obeyed.

May nudged her husband, wanting him both to help her at this time of need and to show his form.

'Is thou any relation to 't Nicholsons o' Warwick Bank?' he asked.

'Shurrup dad!' said May, buffeting him with her elbow this time and glaring at him for taking his cue so crassly.

'There was a fire in our garidge a fortneet ago,' said Frank, clearing his throat, manfully.

'I heard about that.' Betty turned to him with gratitude.

'Just small,' he said, his effort spent. 'Nowt to talk aboot.'

'Tea'll be ready in five minutes,' said Mrs Tallentire.

'Aa'll gaa and see what Aa can do to bring it on faster,' said May striding out to the scullery.

'That's a very nice dress,' said Mrs Tallentire. 'Did you make it yourself?'

'Yes,' Betty whispered.

'I wish I could make them like that. Where'd you get the material?'

'Studholmes. They were having a sale. One and a penny a yard.' A reasonable price; already colouring that she might appear showy.

'*Very* good quality. Can I touch it?'

Betty nodded and went across to the older woman who felt the hem with unaffected admiration.

'That *is* nice. I've never seen such nice material.'

'*What's* nice?' May demanded, hands on hips, filling the scullery doorway.

'This material,' said Mrs Tallentire.

'You'll waste it if you keep rubbin' at it,' said May.

'I don't mind,' said Betty.

'Hm. They'll have it off your back if thou's not careful lass. Off thee back!' and she turned back into the scullery where she could be heard haranguing the jelly. She blamed herself for her twistiness, laying all manner of strictures upon herself, but she could not bear the other woman to take her mother's place; again and again she came back as full of good resolutions as a New Year choirboy and – within minutes – she was lost to her temper.

Tea made things easier because there were things to do – but even so it would have been a poor do had not John taken the matter in hand. He spoke to all of them, but looked at Betty, and they took to each other from then on. Of what came most easily he spoke to her – the work he did with the horses – and described the big Shows he had been to that autumn.

After tea May claimed her, and did it so sweetly and skilfully that Joseph, who recognized the effort involved, was moved that she should be so concerned about him. His mother took the smaller children and May's baby for a breath of air; his father took off his stiff collar, poked the fire, stared a while at the flames and then fell asleep; he himself went with Mary's husband to see the progress of a van which Frank was building from scrap.

The two women talked over the dishes: May washed. 'You'll not be used to such a gang,' said May, using a delicate tone and using it tentatively as if she were handling the very best china.

'Oh, there were a lot of us at home – at Mother Nicholson's –' The girl paused and May scrubbed a plate severely, already furious with herself as the apparent cause of Betty's distress. But Betty felt the woman's kindliness and rushed to heal the breach she herself had made. 'When anybody else came we had to have two sittings.'

'*Did* you?' May was delighted. 'So did we.'

Later, May said, 'It doesn't matter if you have money, you know. We had nowt – Michael and me – we had nowt then and we've nowt now but we got married.' She paused and then, blushing, added softly, 'Mind, I was older than you.'

'Where did you meet him?'

'At this big house where Joseph used to work. Michael was assistant gardener – he came after Joseph went away and it was just luck that I'd decided to stop on a bit because I was that mad the way they got rid of Joseph, he was the best footman ever! And *smart* . . .!'

'So Michael came to work in the gardens . . .?'

'Yes. Well you see I'd been told he came from Cumberland – "a native of your county, May"' (a mincing imitation – so off-key that both women giggled, though quietly, not to wake John) 'and he came from Wiggonby, see, that's where Joseph and my, our, that is, *real* mother was born – not meaning to be nasty to anybody but that's where she was born. Mind, he's older than me, Michael.'

'But that right,' said Betty. 'I'm glad Joseph's older than me.'

'Ay, but *considerably* older.'

'He doesn't look it.'

'No?' May smiled proudly. 'I'll tell him that,' she paused, then frowned. 'Mind, it'll make his head swell.'

And as they stacked away the dishes, 'Now look after him!' For the first time, May spoke sharply and Betty drew back.

'No, no, please, don't take offence.' May put out her arms, took the hands of the younger woman in her own. 'But, you know, I helped to bring him up, you see.'

Though rather frightened by the urgency of May's emotion, Betty was impressed by its sincerity and making an effort, she stood her ground, even let her hands lie in the grasp of the other woman though she longed to pull them away.

'I know,' Betty smiled; but her lips were dry and so the smile restrained.

'If you love him,' ignoring her own nerves, May broke from the knots which so often bound her – 'if you love him, look after him: and if you don't, tell him. He's a good man, Betty, and he deserves that.'

'Yes.' Betty nodded, eased her hands free and then had to glance away, away from May's open gaze.

At first, Betty was reluctant to talk about the visit; or rather she was reluctant to talk about it as incessantly and at the length demanded by Joseph's 'What did you think of father? and May? and Frank – isn't he a *good* man, really? and May's husband – he'll be right for her, don't you think? she gets hurt so easily, he looked a kind man, didn't he? He works in the woods up near a place called Crossbridge, in the fells – we could go and see them. May says it's marvellous – and our *real* mother lived there once.'

It was his innocent reference to his 'real' mother which unsealed her reticence. And it was that missing woman who marked that visit as something final in Betty's mind; for Joseph must have suffered too and yet he kept his face open to the world. She would marry him.

* * *

As the time of their wedding approached he was conscious of all sorts of impulses which had been forgotten or never before appreciated, and walked feeling that his legs, his eyes, his taste, his body, everything about him was freed and tingled as freshly as if he had just raced out of the sea. Merely to walk that summer, and see the sun slant down between the trails of cloud, a blackbird landing on the tip of a bough of hawthorn, springing the bough, the leaves waving, the pulse beneath the feathers – with his mind creating its senses and then slow-plunging back into them, that was enough and a wonder.

These sensations drew on his past, thickened his present, obscured the future. And at his father's cottage he culled the pauses in the routines of activity, watched the small children play unawares, drew from his father not the positive claims on circumstances which he liked and admired but that dedication which threaded through the older man's tussle with life like gold through a dull tapestry.

Sometimes he thought he was walking in a waking dream and was surprised to find that he did things, that he set off for a place and reached it, that he talked and made dates, that he played cricket and went biking. So static did he feel, so slumbrously, voluptuously still – and there was no guilt, no worry – no concern other than his own living. I am here now. That underlay all he did. Without stress or accent on any of the words, each one the simplest declaration, murmured softly when alone – I am here now.

He saw a man walking with his child towards the town, and slowed his pace, would have stopped had that not brought attention to himself who wanted to be unseen before this sight. The man was a labourer, old, possibly the little girl's grandfather. She held up at his hand and skipped, using the hand to steady herself. Then she wobbled away from the man and went through the long grass on the verge, pushing her bare white knees against the long sheen-backed blades of sweet grass, picked up a dandelion, trotted back with it to the old man and made him stop and blow the time away – until only the dry bleached heart was left, and the shrivelled petals. Joseph saw this and it rolled into his mind like the slowest wave which had travelled across a long ocean and still would not break but forever curl around his senses.

He began to look out for such moments, for expressions on people's faces, for the shape of a cloud, for the wind in the candles of a chestnut tree, the glide of a perch in the water, drizzle cold on his warm face, muscles pulling so slightly in his legs, the light on Betty's face, the moon quartered against the empty sky, a dog curling slowly on its tail before setting its muzzle on its soft paws. There were times when he felt like a man who had contained all the earth's feelings, times when he felt that each pleasure was a gift loaned him, a nest half-hanging over a gutter, beer sliding through the froth to part between his lips – he must look for them and remember them from the past and make a store of them, not as a miser, to gloat, but as a man who had discovered that if so much is necessary, then there is so much more unnecessary, for merely in looking and feeling he was conscious, and the more conscious he could make himself, the more alive he would be.

And in this mood, which sometimes weighed him down with such a surfeit of pleasure that he thought he would never move from that spot for fear of breaking the spell, with this and Betty's love and her to receive his own love, then nothing more from the world could be wanted. So he swam, floated, drifted, was still, and the matters of the world struck him not as challenges and exclamations, demanding a spark from the flint of his desire, but lapped him around and made even more intense the richness of his perceptions. Later, he was to look back on this time and wonder that he could have passed so long in such a state, and at times he could not understand it – thinking that he must have entered a long dream.

It was the same feeling which had gathered in him as he dreamt through the summer afternoons while the sounds and smells from outside the school had intoxicated him as he sat at his desk, his legs weary of idleness under the coarse weave of his patched trousers; which he had drawn from the land he grew up in and dragged out of it as he had worked at the farms in that first eighteen months; which had spun at the back of his mind while he cleaned the heavy silver in the gloomy big house.

Now his love for Betty made it so powerful that he was convinced that this was what his life would be, that marriage would intensify it still more, that he and Betty had found the perfect way and so would keep to it.

Late autumn, 1938, married for about a year and a half, Douglas six months old. She had insisted on that name though it was most uncommon in the district; it came from the fictive world of films and magazines which had nourished Betty's secret, repressed feelings: in the naming of her first son she planted her groping claim on that world.

Joseph had changed jobs and worked in the 'Stores' at the new aerodrome about six miles away; a five and a half day week and now, this Saturday dinner-time, free for the longest regular break he'd ever in any job enjoyed. But he ate his egg and potatoes with no pleasure and at each sip of tea glanced across the dark kitchen to the corner where Betty was feeding the child, bottle held firmly against his mouth, such a bitter silence about her that the sound of his eating was a taunt and the child's suck a provocation.

It was dark enough to warrant putting on the gas – but it always made Joseph feel uneasy to have a light in the day.

He still did not know what was the real cause of the row, but he would have to get it out of her for it would just sink deeper and deeper, the longer he left it, become increasingly difficult to discover, result in one of those marks of their life, like the white trace of a scar. Though his own temper was quick, it was short: hers seemed to ignite areas unknown to him and they would feed the temper exhaustingly, sometimes against her will. 'C'mon, Betty,' he said, as lightly as he could manage. 'Get it out.'

She said nothing. He hesitated and then imagining himself to be making a heroic effort (it was this which tired him – so soon did her defences demand the very last ounce of his attack) he repeated.

'Come *on*, Betty.'

But she would not.

He pushed his plate away, the food he had eaten already

heavy and disagreeable. There were no more cigarettes in his packet – Betty did not smoke. He needed a smoke, he thought, to settle down for the fight – to sustain himself through all the tedious sparring necessary if she was to be drawn. Yet to scramble about the kitchen for a stump would undercut his position.

(He liked to think of it in such terms; to pretend it was a contest which he enjoyed. For a contest had an end, and if he pretended to enjoy it then the despair which fled into him would pass.)

'What did I say?' No answer. '*Was* it something I said? I said nothing.'

She took the bottle from the child, sat him up in the correct position and began to pat him for the wind. The half-bald head joggled uneasily in shoulders hidden under two mounds of white knitted wool.

There was nowhere he could go but the back kitchen: the house had no sitting-room. And to go upstairs would be to sulk. 'C'mon, Betty. You know you'll tell me sometime – tell me now. Eh? Will you?' Gently said, those last words – a final effort.

And though realizing this, understanding that Joseph would now move beyond patience, recognizing that his cautious approach invited some reply and feeling rather foolish now that such a situation should have arisen from what at this moment appeared a mean cause – still Betty could make no answer. Something inside her luxuriated in the sullenness and would not be revealed.

'Well,' he said, jumping up, his eyes rapidly scanning the top of the mantelpiece to see if there were any stumps (there was one behind the clock), 'I might as well go and talk 'til a stranger as talk to myself.'

He took his jacket from the back of the chair and pulled it on. Betty still patted the child who had not yet passed wind. 'No wonder the poor bloody thing can't burp,' said Joseph, using this facetious observation as a bridge to bustle him over to the stump behind the clock, 'it's got a mother that's dumb.'

'And a father that's selfish!' she returned.

'A-Ah! – it can talk!'

'Don't be nasty.'

'I wasn't being nasty.'

'Yes you were.'

'No – I – was – NOT!'

'All right then – but you were.'

And later, as always after such occasions, Joseph would be unable to explain how such childish altercation could lead to such murderous feelings.

'I – WAS – *NOT!*'

'You'll upset the baby.' Calmly said; uninterrupted, the patting.

Joseph felt himself urged to go forward, his arm pulled to be raised and smack down some compliance into her.

'Don't you dare, Joseph Tallentire,' she said. 'It'll be the last time you *do* touch me.'

He put the stump between his lips: some of the tobacco flaked onto his tongue immediately and, in his nervousness, he spat it out, spat too forcefully; it landed on the child's clean wool cardigan.

Betty stopped trying to wind the child and for the first time looked directly at Joseph.

'Get a towel,' she said, 'the one next to the sink.'

He went through to the back kitchen and did as he had been told, hovered around her while she cleaned the garment, took up the scarcely blemished towel and returned it to the sink.

'I'm sorry about that,' he murmured politely, as he re-entered 'but it doesn't change things.'

'Oh – go to your football match.'

'Who said anything about a football match?' It dawned. 'Aha? George Stephens has been round pestering to see if I would go and see Carlisle this afternoon – hasn't he? And you thought I'd hop along and forget I'd promised to let you have time off to do some shoppin' – didn't you?' He was smiling now. '*Well* – didn't you?'

The child burped.

'*He* knows what's what any road,' said Joseph.

And she used the child once more as an excuse – but this time to slip out of that sulky imprisonment.

'*You* hold him,' she said. 'You can always make him laugh.'

'Does he burp better when he laughs?' Joseph took his child and cradled him in his arm.

'I wish you wouldn't say "burp".' She stood up and smoothed the front of her cardigan and the skirt she was wearing. 'Are you sure you had enough to eat?'

'I didn't but let it be. I would have choked myself with you glarin' like that.'

She cleared the table while Joseph had the satisfaction of feeling this child warm on his arm and against his chest: he gobbled at the face which peered back and then opened into a laugh, a sucking sound accompanying it which, if simply heard and not seen could have signalled pain as well as pleasure.

'Why *don't* you go to the match with George?' she asked in as earnest a tone as she could manage.

He stepped aside to let her carry past the tablecloth which would be shaken in the backyard: there was so little space in the house that unless you were seated you were invariably in the way of someone walking around.

'I don't feel like it,' he replied; and to the baby he sang while he joggled him:

> 'Gee-up jockey to the Fair
> What will you bring your man from there?
> A silver apple and a pear
> Gee-up jockey to the Fair.'

'I could do what *I* have to do in half an hour,' said Betty, helped in the easier expression of her generosity by the song which half-hid her words.

'No – you have your afternoon,' he insisted, not to be outdone – and indeed the current changed and both now were charged with affection for each other.

'It's no good my going with George anyway. He *talks* all the damned time. When I go to see a thing, I like to watch it in peace and quiet and enjoy it in my own way.'

'His *father's* a quiet enough man,' said Betty. 'Old Mr

Stephens. "Old Father" he used to be called, by the boys.' She paused and then, as a confession, she added 'He wanted me to sit for the Grammar School you know. He thought I might have a chance of passing.' She tailed off, confused by what might be interpreted as vanity. 'Anyway I liked *him* – he did beautiful drawings of birds and flowers – I would have loved some of them to keep – they were worth framing.'

'Well, George is a blabbermouth,' said Joseph, addressing his son.

'Blabbermouth, Blabbermouth
Send him back to Cockermouth.'

'Oh – George is all right.'

'There's worse,' agreed Joseph, now shuffling into a dance with his child:

'Georgy Porgy Pudding and Pie
Kissed the girls and made them cry
When the boys came out to play
Georgy Porgy ran away.'

'When does he get teeth? Twelve months is it?'

'About then, I think.'

'You should *know*.'

'I'll know soon enough; so will you.'

And when George came, boy-like standing on the step asking if Joseph was coming to Carlisle, Betty said 'no' with a warm heart: Joseph was upstairs rocking Douglas into his afternoon sleep.

She shopped and took her time about it – but the streets were not full and she did not meet as many people as she had hoped.

Her life since the birth had changed so much that even now she could not quite believe it. The child chained her to that dark and damp little house: the loss of her wage had meant a severe domestic economy. She could never go out in the evenings and though her friends dropped in to see her it was almost as if they were visiting an invalid: while she herself, even given such a completely free afternoon as this, would soon be tired, have to return home, feel even that small heap of provisions she had been able to buy too heavy.

Joseph made a cup of tea for her – a rare and tender treat – and she insisted that he go out and watch Thurston play, at least. He needed little persuasion: they had a good team this year and he liked to watch a game on Saturdays. He himself no longer played.

It was about half-past three and the town was dead. He passed the shop which had bought the tandem from them – still not sold – even though the shopkeeper had knocked down the price to £3; past the pub where the bus used to pick up the aerodrome men in the mornings, past the church – a glance at its clock and above to the scudding clouds. It began to rain. He pulled the mackintosh tightly round his neck and with difficulty did up the button; shivered a little, stepped out. And in the house Betty huddled over the child and tried not to think of the future.

Chapter Eight

Joseph ran up to the top. The thinly ridged rubber which covered the diving steps pressed damply and pleasantly on his bare feet, almost tickling them. There were two others on the top step, tussling, each trying to push the other in; Joseph got behind them, rested his arms on the back-rest, heaved up his feet and shoved against both of them. With mock-death cries they fell off and down into the water. A cheer went around the swimming-pool, damp and booming, and Joseph took a pace forward and clasped his hands above his head like a boxing champion, bowing and nodding to the applause. But someone had crept up behind him and the next second he too was hurtling down, to land on the choppy green water with a skin-smarting belly flop.

They were at Blackpool for square-bashing. He had applied for air-crew and been sent to a place near Edinburgh for the written examination. Five hundred of them had gone, two hundred had passed, and he had come seventh overall. To say that he was pleased with himself is to describe only the reaction he felt it proper to register. There were men there straight from school, college and university, from office jobs, the civil service and business – and in those tests he had beaten almost all of them. Nothing in his life could ever be the same, he thought, for now all the threshing in the shallows was over – he was out on his own, had found his way.

Although in common with the others he had adopted a dismissive and downbeat style with regard to the business of being in the services – effing this and effing that until the word performed grammatical miracles and was waved like a magic wand; making a bee-line for the NAAFI as soon as duty was done, cards out, drinks in; sceptical of the society of most of the officers and of the sense of most of their orders; trooping around Blackpool of an evening with a deliberate though furtive slouch which cocked a snook at the rigid shoulders of drill – in fact he was enjoying himself enormously. He worried about Betty and the children – but qualifying the anxiety was the certain knowledge that he was doing more for them by being trained to fight than ever he would do by staying at home with them. Besides – that was what happened in war-time.

You waved to everybody on the street in war-time, you pooled the pocket money you allowed yourself and went around in a gang in war-time, each one prepared to battle for the other, and some even sought out the opportunity to display this physical loyalty, you knew exactly where you were in war-time and forgot all those self-entangling days of brooding, you had an aim and an honourable one, a place and that set, a cause which could draw on all your instincts for romance, and a sense of active justice in war-time.

Joseph now clearly saw the Germans as the Enemy. He had never so totally and unreservedly had an enemy, not even Stoddart; it gave him clarity. And now that he was actually doing something – even though it was only training – he felt a duty to the rights he saw that England was defending. Rather shyly, in secret, he felt that there was something to be fought for greater than any cause he could have imagined. As the news came of German victories and advances, and he felt the shock waves as things began to grow worse, so his belief n the liberties he was defending grew stronger and he wanted only to be safely through this preparation and out there, among it.

He had decided to try for navigator. He would have preferred to be a pilot but that seemed to be pushing too hard. He could not, he thought, be that lucky. A navigator or a gunner. As long as he was in the plane – that was what counted.

In the pool the men – all of them naked, their bodies very white and boyish – flung themselves into enjoying the last quarter of an hour which was 'free time'. Some soared in dives from the boards, others, like Joseph, clowned around and jumped into the water in freakish poses, a water-polo ball had been thrown in and a game had started up across the shallow end: everywhere the men ran rather self-consciously, as if enjoying the nakedness but not absolutely sure that it was quite right.

Some of them started to try to swim a length underwater. Joseph watched them stroking silently beneath the surface, their short hair swept back from their scalps, arms and legs moving with a slow-motion effect which gave to the white bodies a strange, attractive appearance in the green water. He went down to the shallow end where they were lining up to try it. All along the length of the bath, heads bobbed through the water like lifebuoys suddenly bouncing up from behind a wave.

Joseph took a huge breath which swelled his chest and dived in. Under the water his hands seemed to draw through thick feathers. The chemical in the water stung his eyes and he closed them. It was marvellous this easy weight to be displaced, his legs kicking against the faint resistance, his arms drawing through as if massaged by their contact. His head was under pressure, he opened his eyes, his ears sang, he felt the breath come into his mouth and push against his lips. He saw the wall at the end. Pulling with all his strength he felt himself surge forward to touch its white surface.

There was a terrible pain in his ears. He shot up to the surface and shouted out in agony. His hand went to his right ear and he felt something trickling out of it.

He spent the rest of the war on non-combatant service.

Betty posted the letter in time to catch the 5.45 collection. She wrote to him every day.

The streets were already dark. Douglas walked beside her. Harry, almost a year old, was in his pushchair: they made a bustling compacted figure going through the town. Harry was the son of one of her 'brothers', a professional soldier who had been killed at the outset of the war. His wife had died of pneumonia soon after the birth and Betty, remembering her own beginnings, had taken the baby in and would adopt him, already thought of him as her son.

She collected money for an organization which sent gifts to the prisoners of war in Germany. People gave a certain amount a week, a shilling usually, sometimes sixpence and the subscription was entered in two account books, her own and theirs – each entry concluded by a double signature. At the end of the week she took the money to the post-office, got a postal order, and sent it off to an address in Liverpool. Tuesdays and Thursdays were her collecting nights. On occasional Wednesdays she went to the Labour Party meetings in the late afternoons, and on Friday she made up her weekly parcel to Joseph.

Wherever she went, she took the two children with her, even to work. She cleaned for people who had big houses, two mornings a week for two of them, and two whole days – Mondays and Thursdays – for Mrs Rogers, who lived three miles away. The other two houses were away from the town also, and she went there on her bicycle, with Harry in a small basket affair at the front and Douglas behind her on the carrier-seat. She loved to ride so, Douglas commenting on all that took his notice, herself safe and protected by their presence, freer than ever she felt when alone. As now, walking up the street with them, secure, free and contented. They were very tidily dressed. Faces washed, noses blown, hair combed, socks straight. And however hard Douglas would try to make himself untidy, he would be kept neat until they had visited all the houses and collected all the money.

She went around the dark town like a secret messenger, bringing proof to all that things were still going on, help was still needed. Throughout the country at this time, penetrating each hamlet and city side-street, nosing out solitary farms and reaching even to the centres of labyrinthian slums, came such messengers coaxing more and ever more for the war. At night, in their homes, in factories, people worked for the war – and each day in the battle their work was spent and more was demanded.

Mrs Askew, Mrs Graham, Mrs Sharpe, Mrs Hetherington, the Misses Snaith, Mrs Ismay, Mrs Wilson, Mrs Beattie – she left Mrs Bly to the last and had to be firm with herself, reiterating all Mrs Bly's good qualities as she walked down the street to her house – she *was* a good woman, gave to everything, was very nice, was very nice, nice, yes, yes. Betty detested setting foot over the woman's threshold.

Mrs Bly lived in squalor which, as it was patently avoidable, Betty abominated. There were old people in the town who had neither the will nor the means to clear up after themselves – but Mrs Bly was in her forties, her husband brought her in a decent wage, there was no need for dirt to be thick on the floor, meals left on the table, a stink throughout the house. Mrs Bly liked a gossip – but again, Betty told herself, there was nothing wrong in that, she herself enjoyed talking to people, in fact one of the compensations for the embarrassment of such an obtrusive job was that she was building up her connection with the town once more, unafraid of it, loving all the details and nuances in it – yet Mrs Bly's gossip was a deliberate search for malicious reports. Betty was almost afraid to open her mouth, so aware was she that Mrs Bly could spin whatever she said into a reflection, a sour or damaging one, on the person concerned.

Finally, Edwina Bly was dishonest. And that was awful.

Betty took a deep breath of the cold air and knocked. 'Always come right in,' Mrs Bly said. 'You needn't knock.' But Betty always knocked. She pushed the children in before her.

Mrs Bly stood beside the fireplace, a tea-caddy in one hand, in the other a spoon dropping treacle on to the mat.

'I'm making treacle tarts,' said Mrs Bly. 'Do you want one?'

'No thank you,' Betty replied, over-quickly.

'I'll give some to Douglas then; Douglas'll eat it: won't you, Douglas?'

The boy stepped forward. Despite the gaslight, the kitchen seemed dark. Behind him he could feel his mother willing him not to go: before him was the tipsily enticing figure of Mrs Bly now holding a treacle tart between her long mucky fingernails.

'Thank you,' he said and bit at it. Mrs Bly watched him bite, saw the pain go across his face as the hot treacle touched his tongue and then said:

'They're hot, Douglas. Be careful.'

Betty wondered where she had got the sugar.

Douglas let the treacle cool against the soft flesh of the inside of his cheeks and then he slid it painfully down his throat: he held the tears at his eyelids.

'Oh dear, I can't find my purse,' said Mrs Bly.

The purse was on the sideboard, clear to be seen by all. Betty did not like to point it out.

'It's there,' said Douglas.

Mrs Bly shed a small smile and put her hand on Douglas' head as she passed him: as if wishing to screw it into his neck.

'He's going to be a clever boy,' said Mrs Bly. 'You'd better watch him, Mrs Tallentire.'

'I will,' said Betty, abruptly – then, realizing that she could have sounded rude in that she made retribution. 'Mrs Beattie's back's bad again,' she offered, and regretted it immediately for Mrs Bly turned on her, holding the unopened purse, and pounced on the news.

'Did she say *why* it was bad?'

'Is it – because of the rain?' Betty faltered.

'Ha!' Mrs Bly replied. 'That's what she would like you to think. Did you see Ted?'

'Yes.' Ted was Mrs Beattie's lodger.

'You mean you saw Ted and she said she had a bad back and you thought it was because of the rain! I wonder she has the face! Fancy trying it out on a woman like you, Mrs Tallentire. You wouldn't think badly of anybody, would you Mrs Tallentire? That's not like you, is it, Mrs Tallentire. But *I* can make two and two of what you've said, believe me.'

'Now then, Mrs Bly,' Betty replied, 'I said nothing.'

'That's right, my dear. But it was the *way* you said it. Oh, you can't kid me. I know you'd be the last person to cast blame, but the *way* you said it, Mrs Tallentire, I could *tell* you'd been upset by that woman just the *way* you said it.'

'What way?'

'Now then, Mrs Tallentire.' Mrs Bly shook her head. 'Enough said.

Betty was without an answer.

Next, Mrs Bly got on about Mrs Hope, and so on as before with others, each time prying through keyholes seen only by herself, winkling out secrets secret only to herself until Betty felt like the Dutch Boy trying to stop a whole dam from bursting with only his thumb as a defence: and yet so ruthless and swift was Mrs Bly that Betty was completely thrown, for at times she thought that she was merely imagining all the badness, that Mrs Bly was simply chatting away as normally as anyone else would. 'Well I'll have to be off to put them to bed,' said Betty, indicating the children, so determined to be gone that she cut right across Mrs Bly's speech. Which did not go unnoticed.

'Oh, rushing off, are you? I thought you might stay for a cup of tea.'

'No thank you.' She took out her collection book. 'I'll just enter it in and then I'll be away.'

'I haven't given it to you yet,' replied Mrs Bly in a tone which might have been teasing.

Betty smiled and took out her pencil – indelible ink – which she dabbed against her tongue.

'It's poisonous, you know,' said Mrs Bly, 'that stuff in pencils. Poisonous.'

'Is it?'

'Don't they tell you that?'

'No.'

'*Don't* they?'

'No.' And again Betty felt that somehow she had betrayed someone.

'Well now,' said Mrs Bly, 'you'll be wanting a shilling, I suppose.'

'Yes please,' said Betty, brightly.

'I'll see if I can make it.'

The coins were tipped on to the table and she sorted through them, very slowly.

'I'll tell you what,' she whispered. 'I can give you it in eggs.'

'Oh.'

'Here.' With her first rapid movement of the encounter, Mrs Bly turned, bent down and came up with a large cardboard box. Inside were a dozen eggs.

'Oh,' said Betty. 'You're lucky to get hold of them.'

'Lucky?' Mrs Bly laughed. 'You need to be better than lucky in this world, girl. Four do?'

'Do what?'

'Four for the shilling?'

It was reasonable. Betty could easily put in the shilling herself. The eggs were new-laid. Two each for the boys. Of course four would do!

'I have to take the money,' said Betty, speaking as if through a lump of wool in her throat.

'*You* put in the shillin'. And you get the eggs. Hard to get, believe me.'

'I know.'

'Tell you what – Five.'

But there was the book and a shilling had to be entered. Mrs Bly's book and a shilling had to be entered in that. Though it would not be cheating – it would not be right. As soon as Betty felt that word come to her, she felt much more sure of herself, everything became much clearer.

'I'm sorry, Mrs Bly,' she said, 'but my job is to collect a shilling.'

'All right my dear. But after you've collected it, would you like to buy four of the eggs for a shilling?'

It was all perfectly in order. The shilling would be handed over: handed back.

'I'll do without the eggs, thank you, Mrs Bly,' Betty muttered.

'Will you now? Mean to say you're going to deprive those two little boys of fresh eggs?' To Douglas. 'You would like an egg, wouldn't you?'

'Yes please, Mrs Bly.'

'There you are. I'll wrap them up for you.'

She reached out for the newspaper and began to wrap up the eggs. Betty hesitated.

'I've some eggs coming,' she said, eventually: not a lie, at some time she would get some eggs. When they came, they would validify the statement.

'Oh,' said Mrs Bly. 'Who from?' She paused, an egg half-wrapped in the photograph of a tank.

'From – *some*body,' said Betty, faintly.

Mrs Bly grinned.

'Good girl! Don't tell! I knew you had it in you. Still waters, Mrs T., still waters. Here's your bob! Sign the book. Small handwriting. But clear – very clear. Good girl. Mrs Rogers, eh?'

Back in her own house, Betty washed the children and put them to bed.

'One kiss from me, and one from your dad.'

'Is he coming back?'

'Yes. Of course he is.'

'When?'

'When they've finished the war.'

When she felt particularly lonely, she brought the two boys into the double bed with her. One on each side, rolled down against her.

Easing himself out of the hard narrow bed, Joseph swung his feet on to the cold floor and waited. All the men were asleep. Outside he could hear the booming and the whines. In the dark he reached out for his socks and pulled them on. He took a blanket as a dressing-gown and walked quietly down the long room to the door. Sometimes he woke up Norman, his mate, but tonight he wanted to be alone. He felt rather selfish about it, but he was more able to dream, alone.

Up the back stairs and into the attics. He had brought a torch. It was a big house they were billeted in – rather like the Sewells'. The sergeant had put them on the top floor. Joseph had two stripes now and argued freely with him: if a bomb drops the top floor's bound to get it most badly, he said. The sergeant would not be convinced. Perhaps he thought that others might be coming and wanted to establish superiority over them in the most undeniable way. Whatever it was, they were billeted on the top floor.

Joseph pushed open the window and got out on to the roof. It was cold and he pulled the blanket around him. Carefully he walked to the turreted edge of the roof and sat down – looking across to London. He got out a cigarette and lit up.

An air raid was under way.

He saw the lights raking the sky, like shimmering scissors snapping at the aeroplanes. Fires, the red glow, a furnace in the night. Flak, deadly morse, flicking rapidly through the dark, shrill silent screams of protest. All he could hear was hollowed by the distance: as in the swimming-pool, the sound boomed strangely. Sometimes an aeroplane came back in his direction and he ducked, for occasionally they off-loaded any remaining bombs. He saw some drop about two or three miles in front of him. Again, it was like a display.

Nothing of screams or human agony: to see and hear that he had to shut his eyes and remember the photographs in the newspapers, and then he saw London burning, the cranes and ships in the docks like eerie models, looking artificial in the bleeping light; imagined the Thames stained red and yellow-white: saw the houses crumbling as if the stones had suddenly rotted, and people surging to the shelters, ambulances like refuges in those uncertain streets, the grey, smouldering desolation at dawn. He was safe from that: he twisted his body on the stones, jabbed by the word; safe. The stars were obscured.

They could not be seen in the sky, the enemy planes. Like the plagues which had come to London in the past they struck the people down with crude decimation: you were spared by luck which flung itself from street to street.

It was terrible – like a sight of the end of the world or a distant pattern of hell. Yet – he would not admit this to another soul – there was something compelling about it. It was a dream and he was part of the dream.

He sat there and smoked a full packet of Woodbines. The cold settled slowly on him and he did not move, becoming as fixed on the turreted ledge as beneath him were the crude, Victorian gargoyles.

When he did go to bed it was about dawn.

He woke up, startled, as a bomb dropped in the grounds. All the windows of the bottom three floors were shattered. Doors were blown in, furniture inside the rooms smashed against the wall.

But the top floor was untouched. Not a pane of glass cracked. The sergeant took full credit.

Douglas was Montgomery. Jackie Paylor was Rommel. Harry (3 now) and Lionel Temple were the Eighth Army: Jackie

Paylor's two sisters were the Germans. William Ismay was a Soldier.

The battle was fought between Station Road and New Street with Moore's garage where Frank used to work as the bridgehead.

Douglas was tireless. Up and down the ramp, the wooden machine gun raining a forest of bullets before him – 'de-de-de-de-de-de-de-de-de-de-de-de-*de*! Drrrrrrrrrrrrr – de-de-de-de-de-de-de-de-de-*de*! RRRRrrrrr – you're dead, William Ismay! And your Mary's been dead since it started.' 'I'm not!' 'Yes you are. De – de – de – de – de – de! There! You're dead now, anyway.' 'That wasn't fair.' 'It doesn't matter.' 'I wasn't ready.' 'You should have been.' 'De – de – de – de – de – de. There *You're* dead.' 'All right,' said Douglas lying down. 'Count to a 100.' 'In 10's?' 'In 5's.' '5 – 10 – 15 – 20 – 25 . . . Harry! You were supposed to stop in that tyre.' 'Mr Moore said go away.' 'But it's our headquarters!' 'De – de – de – de – de – de! You're dead again – and you can count 200 this time.'

The songs on the wireless which made him wince when they said 'love' – turned away from the wireless and looked at the wall, sure that everybody must be as embarrassed as he was – but at night he murmured the words to himself, licked them in his gob, shuddered at their power. The town seethed with strangers – evacuees who used the school and came in buses; orphans at the convent, girls, cropped hair, green dresses, walking down to the park two by two, the nuns fore and aft like the daughters of Noah; airmen come to the local airfield to work on the maintenance of the planes. Douglas moved through a shimmer of love, people shouting hello to each other on the streets, songs from the pubs, the horses coming in scores to the horse-fair, the organ at church and the words at Sunday school. Football, cricket, running, running everywhere, catching tiddlers in jam jars, getting lost in a field a quarter of a mile from home and the man he asked the way was an American who carried him back on his shoulders and gave him some chewing-gum. His mother gave him tea.

Then the war. On the news, at the school – 'will children whose fathers are in the war stay behind?' – swollen with pride

– war against the Southend lot, war against Michael Saunderson who thought he was cock of the form, fear of the older boys who could turn when he gave them cheek and then he had to run through the riddling side-streets, right through a shop once, for fear of being caught and hit. Picking up stumps in the gutters in imitation of Alfie Coulthard who was ten and fought at the matinees. War on the news at the pictures. Coming out sick with fear, running home for the wooden gun – de – de – de – de – de – de – let them come here, he was ready. His mother's father had died and they had moved in with his Grandma. He had been taken to see the man laid out in the parlour. Musty, dust risen. An aunt had taken him to see. His grandfather's face was the colour of porridge: and lumpy. He had wanted to touch, dared not.

His uncle Frank had been killed in North Africa. That was why Douglas was always Montgomery.

So they had moved out of the cottage and lived now with his Grandma. His mother's mother: he had to say it slowly at first until he had practised. The house was full of people coming from the war, coming from work, lodgers, relatives, people put up for a night: Harry and himself slept in the same room as their mother. Deeply calm there – and yet in that calm the coldness of his mother's tears at things that had happened. He was sent to that room to be alone when he was bad. Not locked in – but he could not go out.

Tanks came, one dusty afternoon through the town, real tanks, scores of them. Soldiers were always there, left-right, left-right, marching in the gutters; but these great long-snouted tanks which shook the very ground – they came and fastened a menace and awe on the town. One of the soldiers let him have a ride. They left the tanks on Market Hill and the men went to drink. Like all the other boys, Douglas followed the men, asking for sweets and chewing-gum. He saw his aunty Helen with them – and that gave him the confidence to stay out much later than he had ever done before. She had Lester with her and pushed him across to play with Douglas – but Lester was about a year older then he was, beyond Douglas's childishness.

He stood around the pub doors and heard the men laughing

and singing. His father was in the air-force, so was his Uncle George, so was his Uncle Donald, his Uncle Pat was in the army, so was ... The black town was full of enemies and loved faces. Oh, he rolled about that town the boy, blind and drunk with the endlessness of it. His mother did not keep him in. There would always be someone who would know him, someone he could talk to if he felt anxious.

Later and later he played, exhausting the others – daring himself to stay out longer.

Before going home he went down to see the tanks once more. Cold and massive in the dark. The Jerries could never win. He touched the tracks of the tank, hard, impenetrable under his soft, shivering hand. De – de – de – de – de – de – de – de – de – de – *de*! You're dead! You're dead! You're dead!

Helen was Joseph's cousin. The daughter of Seth, she had been brought up in Maryport and after her mother had run away from Seth, been spoilt by him – turned into the little darling of Socialism. Her interest in his politics had died when, aged sixteen, she had taken up with a married man and refused all pleas, resisted all pressures, staying with him long after he had grown tired of her. Then there were others.

She had arrived in Thurston just after the war started: with her was Lester, three years old and carrying her name, Tallentire. She had lived with the man for two years and then he had gone back to his wife. She had tried to force him back to her, going around to his house, fighting the other woman, screaming, promising – but he had stayed with his wife and found another sweetheart. Then Helen had broken down, shifting around the West Coast like one homeless, though Seth had followed her devotedly, patiently. During that time, her reputation became a public joke in the mining towns and so Thurston was a retreat.

There she had married George Stephens, son of the schoolmaster, a damaged man who failed to match the sweetness or scholarship of his father and insisted on attempting to be one of the 'boys', the 'Hard Men', working at the factory when he could have found an office job or been articled. George had known Betty since childhood and she'd always felt sorry for him especially as his father was so widely admired. Having been taught by old Mr Stephens, she was full of affection for him; but this reinforced her feelings for his son. And she worried when he married Helen who saw him off to the war with relief and turned to a boy-friend again.

This time, she said, it was serious. She was going to go steady with this man and tell George straight out when next he came on leave. But would Betty look after Aileen for a few days? Lester could stay with the Cleggs but Aileen needed mothering still. They were just going to go to Blackpool. He had leave and he wanted to take her to Blackpool. She had never been. Would Betty, please?

Aileen was indisputably George's daughter and this may have had something to do with Betty's immediate acceptance. But she could not blame Helen: nobody could blame her after what had happened to her. Yet it was not right, not at all, to run around while George was away: just not fair. He had no chance.

Helen's reputation in the town was bad. No one ostracized her partly because her retorts and her liveliness were too good to be deprived of. Betty would never tolerate any gossip about her, went out of her way to see her, talk to her: the two women got on well – both were fiery though with one it was on the surface, with the other below it, both liked to laugh, both were energetic and had definite opinions about what they thought good and bad, right and wrong. That in one area these opinions were totally contradictory provided occasional trailing silences in their talk ... but a recovery would soon be made. Helen cleaned the lavatories for the parish council and also scrubbed down the offices five mornings a week. She was a great one, too, for organizing herself when there were rose-hips to be picked or raspberries, hazel-nuts or potatoes: she managed well and if Lester was scruffy, it was after he left home that he got into that state.

Yet was *she* not deceiving George, also, by looking after Aileen and so making it possible for Helen to rush off to Blackpool? The question posed itself to Betty as badly as the riddle which precedes the solution of a thriller. She wanted to laugh at this rattling interrogation – but not for long because it sank into her mind like a cold needle and could not be withdrawn. For days she thought of little else but Helen: more of Helen than of her children, her husband or her work.

And when Helen returned with the announcement that 'it hadn't worked out', Betty felt even worse. The more so because there was no way out. Having given her affection to Helen, she could not nor would she withdraw it.

Yes, Aileen had been very good. She had played with Harry. Had a fall – but been more scared than hurt. She listened to the tales of Blackpool's nights. Betty hid her confusion in work.

Both the boys were at school now and she had taken on the cleaning of another house. She liked working in these houses if the people were pleasant. The new woman was not, alternately snobbish and over-confiding, curt and over-possessive. Betty dreaded going there but would not give in her notice. She could not bear to break with people, to allow the possibility of having enemies. Alongside that was another feeling – that she had openly taken the job on and was not going to give it up: not going to look like somebody who could not stick out a difficult bit of work.

Alone in a room – with a duster and polish – then she would bring it to life: what was dirty became clean, the dull shone, the messy became tidy, the disordered ordered.

She was scrupulous but not fussy. She did not run after muddy feet with a dustpan. The houses she cleaned – as her own – were cleaned for their own sake, not as an example to those who lived in them.

She liked the furniture and the space in these houses. The large and deep armchairs with flower-printed coverings, the long dining tables, the pictures on the walls, the lovely china and cutlery; yet she felt no urge to imitate this when she thought of her own ideal house. This was not at all to do with the notion that she must 'keep her place': on the contrary, her own tastes were firm and inclined to what was neat and easy to clean and modern, light, simple-lined.

But work could not solve everything. Lying awake on hot

summer nights, the windows wide open behind the blinds, no sound from the town but occasionally a dog barking, she grew conscious of the forces which held her so rigidly to the town. She felt, as much as saw, that they grew out of the fearing part of her and she was tired of them. Now that she had the children, now that she had 'paid back her mother', there was no reason why she should not leave the place altogether.

If Joseph again asked her to move – she would.

At the new place, the Stores were in chaos. The Sergeant met him at the door, gave him the keys and told him to take over: he was off to England. For a time Joseph lived almost as a recluse, never called to parades and drills (sometimes he thought it was unknown that he was there at all: one day in the canteen he heard a Flight Lieutenant say, 'There's a man called Tallentire supposed to be here to do our stores.' 'No need for that,' someone replied, 'chap called Joe down there, working like a beaver.' Joseph said nothing) and at the end of two months the huge buildings were clean and organized, their contents checked and catalogued, the method of withdrawal regularized and efficient.

For that he was offered sergeant's stripes. The condition was that he should sign on for another five years. There would be a house provided for him in Germany, and the Air Force would pay for his wife and children to come across. He was very tempted but did not write to Betty about it. He knew that she would not move and saw no point in upsetting her by relaying the offer.

John was silent. With Joseph he had walked from the cottage towards the road that Joseph would take back to Thurston. The afternoon was hot and Joseph had suggested that they sit on a hedge-bank for a few minutes to relax.

He had seen his father the day after he had come home, but this was the first occasion on which he had had time to talk to him. Talk they did along the road, the chat that concealed the real statements while yet allowing them to be pointed to, but there was a severity in the old man which nothing but straight talk could do justice to. A severity in his manner, in his tone, in the way he refused to look at all about him on this bright day but walked with his head slightly bent; he was past his mid-sixties now but the years seemed to make him only more hale, bright-eyed, deft in his movements.

Now they sat on the bank, Joseph in his still unfamiliar 'civvies', John in the same sort of working clothes he had worn his life long. He lit up his pipe, having silently refused the cigarette Joseph offered him. A car passed by on the main road. There was some wind that day and the full-leafed trees shivered gently. Near them was a chestnut and its large leaves seemed to Joseph to be cut out of foil, so exactly were the lines shaped. He watched the leaves, supply lifting on the slow shifting branches. When John spoke it was all of a piece, very quiet, as much to himself as to his son.

'Frank went.' He padded the rising ash of his pipe down with his thumb. 'Just like that. He was driving his tank, thou knows. Always was mad on cars. In the letter *we* got they said he hadn't a chance. A direct hit. So mebbe he didn't know much.' He screwed up his eyes. 'He wasn't me own, you know, Joseph, nowt to do with me really, but I thowt a lot on that lad. Straight as could be.' He paused. 'Then Donald. What can a man mek o' that, eh Joseph? There's a lad went right through – and then he dies of food-poisonin' two days after it's all over! It would mek you laugh if it didn't mek you cry. And he was a real warrior, Donald, a bit like our Isaac – your uncle Isaac. Frightened before no mortal thing.' He murmured once more. 'Food-poisoning.' Then, more steadily, 'All of them, our Isaac, Sarah, Tom that was killed int' last war – one of his lads – they've all got somebody gone or hurt for ivver. And we've lost touch. There's brothers of mine I wouldn't recognize, and full cousins o' thine thou dissn't know exist. We're blown like chaff, man: there's neither sense nor purpose in it.'

Part Three

The Throstle's Nest

Chapter Nine

He slid into the peace, half-dazed, half-heartedly euphoric. That a few months before he had been prepared, if given the chance, to shoot at and drop bombs on people now appeared as an unreal hiatus in his life. Yet he knew that it was part of him, and that he wished he had been given that chance. The only way was to forget it: but the act of forgetting was numbing.

When in the services, he had thought of his demob as a release from a bow: he would soar with unrestricted energy, driven by the clear knowledge of what he did not want, straight to the target. But he had slipped out almost reluctantly at the end, sad to leave the chains which were also supports. Arriving in Thurston on the double-decker bus he had looked at the streets half-nervously, wondering that he had lived there and would live there. It seemed a stranger place than the foreign country from which he was returning. Stepping off the bus, the people in the streets were in a glass, he knew them all but would have to break the glass to talk once more to them. More than ever he wished he had taken the offer of the sergeant's stripes. There had even been a hint of an eventual crack at a commission.

He went back to his job at the aerodrome and within a few months felt as if he'd never left this treadmill and never would. As usual, he looked outside the job for more driving interest but his glance went no further than the old crowd, George and Norman, John and Lenny – a few drinks, a little gambling, some sport. The real interest of the town was in community efforts – and Joseph was always rather detached from those.

One of the things which was clearly a drive, seen in Thurston as elsewhere, was that the children should be given their chance. The Butler Act legislation had made it possible for children from poor homes to go right through university, the

National Health system would see that they were fit, school dentists would check the teeth, school milk and school meals see that they were looked after, all over the country homes were endowed for those orphaned or deprived, articles about child-rearing appeared in every sort of magazine, films were made in such a way that the majority could 'safely' be seen by young children; though far from being a stampede a movement for 'giving children their chance' was well under way.

Directly out of that came the vivid, post-war carnivals. In Thurston after the war, you could whistle up a carnival in a week. There was little money spent on the dresses or the organization of the affair, yet by sorting through old cupboards and by borrowing and 'all piling in together', these carnivals became, for a few years, occasions of marvel and excitement. Made for the children, on a shoe-string, corporate and yet neither hierarchic nor informal, they wove together many of the strands of the post-war mood – and everybody turned out for them.

There was a man called Kathleen who was to lead it this year. It had all been a mistake, Betty explained to Douglas. His mother had wanted a girl so much and everything had been prepared for that: little dresses made with 'Katie' embroidered on them, Kathleen painted on the brand new cot, K on every handkerchief and even on the panties – yes – Douglas need not laugh – it was all true. And the woman was broken-hearted, but she would not give it up. Kathleen he was called, and as Kathleen he was dressed until he went to school: it took a terrible threat from her husband to get the boy into trousers for his first school morning. Douglas, who was now eleven, suggested point-blank that the woman had been a 'stupid old fool': Betty clattered his ears but later admitted that perhaps it *was* a little too soft of her. She ought not to have burdened the boy so.

Douglas, who had immediately fantasied himself into the situation and saw himself walking up High Street being called 'Kathleen' (writhing with embarrassment at the image but hugging it to himself again and again) persisted through days on this questioning about Kathleen. At night, he looked out for him and followed him through the streets.

Understandably, said Betty, Kathleen had grown up very quiet: too quiet really: in fact, almost completely silent. He grew very tall and people got used to the name – people who had known him all his life – but there was always somebody who found it a joke or children (she glared at Douglas, demanding a confession and at the same time daring him to make one) who thought it clever to run after him and shout his name. Douglas closed his lips firmly: the chanted taunt rattled against his teeth – he wondered that his mother did not hear it: only last night, he and a gang had pursued him, shouting:

'K – K – K – Katie!
Ain't 'e a matey
His mother couldn't tell
A knob from a door!'

The lyric was now traditional. It was shrilled in cockatoo – film-cockney – and the boys longed for Kathleen to turn and look at them – then they would scatter, the terrible consonant – K – K – K – Katie – kicking through the streets. So, Betty continued, it was no wonder that he didn't talk to anybody. But if you said Hello, nicely, then Hello would come back. Or Nice Day, or whatever it was: back would it come. Always pleasant. A very good worker. Very *strong*. (This, too, said with admonitory emphasis and Douglas swallowed and nodded.) Always did labouring jobs and always did them well. Never short of work. Handed his pay packet over entire to his mother. People had occasionally told him to get his name changed (you could do it, though it cost a lot, said Betty) but he just smiled and did not answer.

But, recently, aged about forty, Kathleen had begun to open out. He had started to drink a little, to go to hound trails, was seen at the local football matches, smoked cigarettes. This metamorphosis had reached its climax the previous year when Kathleen had appeared in the autumn carnival dressed up as Mae West. Where he had got the idea, the nerve, the wig or the other things, no one could guess. But there he was. Immaculate.

A long cigarette holder and high heels, silk stockings, the lot.

Of course he was put at the front. A position which he had accepted very calmly – almost as of right – and then the walk! The works. Talent stared everyone in the face. He got first prize for Gentleman Individuals and shared the Certificate of Originality with the woman who came dressed as King Kong. Many considered he ought to have won it outright.

This year he came as Two-Ton Tessie O'Shea. Tessie O'Shea's bulk was always balanced by a lightness of foot, slim ankles, and her fatness was jolly, almost a prop. Kathleen was six feet two. His legs very heavy. (For Mae West he had worn an ankle-length gown in silvery material.) Moreover he had increased his bulk by employing some of the methods of mummification: sheets had been wound around him and pillows used, though sparingly, between the sheets. In outline he was a circus Fat Man – grotesque. But such was his talent that there *was* a recognizable likeness of Two-Ton Tessie O'Shea peeping through. *He* needed no card on his back. And to allow for no misconstruction, he had a ukelele which he strummed continuously, singing Tessie's songs. He could not play the ukelele and made no attempt to. The instrument was held firmly and his right hand swept across the strings without pause. He knew about half a dozen songs and these he sang through and then began again immediately with the first one. When the organizer asked him once again to lead the procession, Kathleen nodded without interrupting his performance, and took his place in front of the band. His mother who was again with him as she had been the previous year stood nearby on the pavement and prepared herself for the long walk to the park.

It was a silver band – about twenty-four piece. Uniforms navy blue with silver buttons. Music on small rectangles of cardboard stuck into a holder on the instrument so that each man marched rather myopically, head hunched over mouthpiece, eyes peering six inches in front of them. The bottom half of their bodies strode in time. Johnny Middleton played the big drum this year, temperamental but unrivalled at twirling the large, mop-headed drumsticks. He had found a leopard skin and already, before the procession had begun, was swelter-faced.

Another speciality of his was the slow march of Guards where one foot paused as if to touch the other as it moved forward. He had not been tall enough to get into the Guards himself but had learnt it all the same.

The carnival was in a way a fantasy. That this was constructed out of very limited means only made it more poignant. In the four years after the war it became a very popular affair, calling in competitors from villages and towns all around the neighbourhood made it more powerful. The town was not too big (Carlisle could never raise a respectable carnival) nor was it too small (the village carnivals always resembled fêtes). And in these years after the war, relief at having passed through the thirties, triumph at having been victorious in battle, dread of the Atom Bomb, carelessness encouraged by the ominous warnings of future struggles, all perhaps were combined with a half-mythical memory of community display, of those sun-bursts of earlier times when the festivals were explosions at the end of a thin and narrow trickle of months of dry-powdered existence.

For though there were no great traditions such as have part institutionalized CARNIVAL in many countries – carnival day in Thurston did disjoint the town: people set out most purposefully to get drunk; those who dressed as conservatively as all England did at that time suddenly put on wanton plumage; others, like Kathleen but not only him, played out a personal vision or desire at once harmlessly and at the same time challengingly. For many it was a day of outrageous expense to be saved up for like Christmas; for others it meant a very rare Saturday morning off work. Children abandoned themselves to it, shops closed early, pubs stayed open late, traffic, such as there was, was diverted and overnight the men who had organized it became Officials with a large brass badge and the word in green letters. The park-keeper mowed the long stretch which would be used for the sports and did what he could to station a few boys around the more important flowerbeds. Shopkeepers gave prizes, farmers gave sacks for the sack-race. Where the procession passed there was bunting so that the upper stories of the street were rigged like a ship and all morning the man with the Tannoy tested his equipment beside the tennis pavilion.

Behind the band were the dancers and following them the procession proper. First, those on foot, Walt Disney was a great influence and so were the Nursery Rhymes – Donald Duck walking with Old Mother Hubbard, Three Men in a Tub and Mickey Mouse, Snow White hand in hand with Little Boy Blue: people of all ages, though children were in a majority. Hollywood provided much inspiration – Indians were very popular with boys of about nine or ten who loved to be covered with brown boot-polish. Occasionally, personal likenesses were traded on: there was someone who looked exactly like the Prime Minister, someone else who did Max Miller. The Arts were under-represented, though there was Robinson Crusoe, a Laughing Cavalier and an idiosyncratic attempt at Fagin. Sport was strong with boxers and footballers numerous among the boys. There was a Pope, an Aristocrat ('The Duke of Knowall'), Al Jolson, a farmer with his dog, policemen, apemen, and various circus stars like the Trapeze Artist and the Strong Man. These formed the backbone of the walking procession – to be judged according to known and established standards in relation to their known association with reality. Threaded through them, like ribbons through a mane, were the surprises. A girl dressed as an Ice-Cream, a man who was the News of the World, a Lamp Post, a Tree, a family who were London under the Blitz, a Tin of Corned Beef, the Spirit of Charity, a Tea-Cosy, Songs of Praise, a Haystack, a Fiddle, Man of the Future, a Grandfather Clock, the Evils of Drink, Heroism, Mount Everest and Poverty. And, finally, there were a few people bursting to dress up, incapable of fashioning an idea to fit the costume they had made, roving about the edges of the procession, as novices to the priests who bore cards.

There were about twenty wagons. Even at this time there was an annual horse-market in Thurston which lasted for three days. The horses without exception were well-dressed. The rear was brought up by four lorries – two coal lorries and one from the West Cumberland farmers and one from the Co-op. The wagons and lorries became small stages on which were groups from streets or churches or clubs. There was the Old Covered Wagon, of course, and Beside the Camp Fire; the Grand Piano, as usual, with the boys in black and the girls in white representing the notes, jumping up and down while a woman played a real piano. The Carnival Queen and Attendants, the Flower Queen and Her Maidens, The Darby and Joan wagon. And then, again, the free-wheelers: In the Trenches – the lorry stacked with sandbags and mud, the men in their uniforms singing 'Pack Up Your Troubles'; a Packet of Woodbines – a truly colossal piece of work, the wagon made up entirely of small woodbine packets built up to make one monster carton, with four people in white tubes, their hair powdered brown, poking out of the end; English Heroes (the Methodist wagon): Jonah in the Whale; the Old Woman who lived in the Shoe; the Test Match; Heaven and Hell; the Bank of England; Alice in Wonderland (C. of E.); Inside Big Ben and the Spirit of Labour (on a lorry provided by the Co-op). Neither Catholics, Quakers, Methodists nor Salvationists had an individual wagon but the Congregationalists had their own carnival. The winning wagon was 'Liberty or Death'.

What made it the stuff of fantasy was not so much those of the entrants who had thought up unusual costumes – but the thing itself, stretching for three-quarters of a mile along Low Moor road, the hedges dull green just before autumn, the town which they would march through a grey, rather battered place, with little new paint, only the very smallest marks of any prosperity, where five pounds a week was a very good wage and the long reach of the war had stretched even so far from the battle to pluck lives and cancel ambitions. Thurston was no place for tourists or day-trippers, too mournful even for some of the inhabitants who wanted only to leave it, with the clouds grey and the people watching the assembly of the carnival almost all dressed in navy blue, black, clerical grey, brown – in this place the fact of the procession was like a dream made tangible and quite unexpectedly laid over a normal waking life. The colours were bold – yellow, red, green, purple, orange – and the whole fragile, well-ordered noisy procession could have descended on Thurston from another age and climate. Yet the faces were the same as those in the crowd and this gave the dream its lush substantiality.

Betty was in charge of the dancers. There were about thirty girls, dressed in white, with four bells on a white handkerchief, bells on their wrists and bells around their ankles, small, on grey elastic, shining like little bubbles of silver. The girls walked in pairs directly behind the band – jangling in the wind – and danced every four hundred yards when the band stopped. The dancing was called Morris Dancing but had long lost any relationship it might have had with the Maypole and yip-haw, the dialect and sticks of those revived original dances which are a mixture of pedantry and Swedish drill set to slender melodies that often shudder at the impact. No, the girls danced a very formal, very simple, skipping and chain-making dance nearer to a Scottish reel than to the pure source of Morris. The band accompanied them with Scottish tunes, 'A Hundred Pipers', playing slowly, being the most appropriate.

It was only this day, the actual day of the Carnival, which made Betty nervous. During the war, particularly through the Labour Party, she had become quite used to organizing things: because everybody else was mucking in, that had been all right. Even when proposed as treasurer of the party she had not objected. It was the war – the men were away and everybody seemed to be on some committee for this or that. It was the same with the collecting of money, and when the Carnival Committee had asked her to take charge of the girls, she had agreed immediately. A hand-written notice in Harvey Messenger's shops and it was done:

> Will all girls between the ages of 7 and 15
> who would like to be in the Morris dancing
> please meet at the West Cumberland Farmers
> Building at 5.15 next Monday.

Everything about it appealed to Betty. The girls took their places in accordance with age, the younger ones leading – and so it was fair. The dance was so easily learnt that there was little nervousness. The business of getting them all to move at the same time was difficult enough to make it exacting work, but not so difficult as to make it hard work. Most of the girls had white dresses and if not, they could easily be made – while J. & J. Airds sold the bells for a penny each – so few could possibly feel barred through poverty: and if there *were* girls from large families who came along rather sadly after the announcement about the white dress and said they could not afford it, then it always proved possible to get hold of some material (from somewhere) and run one up in an hour or two.

It was pleasant down there during the rehearsals, beside the West Cumberland Farmers, on that quiet, narrow road, this horde of little girls, all known to Betty, their mothers and grandmothers known, dancing away, singing the tunes to accompany themselves, grey cardigans, loose ribbons, ankle socks. Sometimes Douglas would come down with her (Harry would never go near the place) and sniff about like a wasp for pollen. His mother's position gave him a reason for being there – but he could never quite believe his luck, at large among so many girls. He fell in love with most of them on sight and his Monday evenings were powerfully intoxicating. Almost eleven now, he had just passed the scholarship for the grammar school, but interest in the new uniform he was to get, the satchel, even the two weeks of extra holiday, waned before this occasion. He soon picked up the dance and so further established himself by being able to teach it to some of the more tardy girls. And when a set was one short, he would fill in. Had one solitary boy ever appeared, as once did happen, then no matter if he was totally unknown to Douglas – that particular boy was very well-known to him – he would shrivel with embarrassment and run, not considering even looking back until he was well into the town where he would halt, abruptly, shove his hands into his pockets and kick something into the gutter.

At six o'clock the factory hooter went and she could see the first men on their bicycles going up into the town and it was then that they stopped. For Joseph's bus came in at six-thirty and she liked his supper to be hot and the table laid.

Those early evenings there, with the girls, like herself when young, remembering the Girl Guide evenings, seeing the moving phenomenon of well-known characteristics inherited by yet another generation, the quiet town up Toppin's field, the clothing factory where she had worked, and about her the fields she had played in and dared in and courted in, these times gathered together her love for the town which she had never lost, though fear had overlaid it and misery had once seemed to dissolve it. She loved the knowledge that at the end of this road there would be Hill's showrooms and some of the same furniture would be in the window as had been there before the war. And there was still the black corrugated-iron of the shed, with one panel loose, which she had crawled through, and her feelings lurched as she saw Douglas crawl through it. Truly there were countless places, expressions, smells, tones, tableaux, intonations and memories all crushed and contained with ease in this town. Such a small place – but still she loved to go along Bird-cage Walk with Joseph and the children in the evenings, still loved to look towards the fields and watch the clouds move across them, see those luridly painted sunsets drawn down a few miles away to the Solway Firth. The town was her life but it was also like a grand, endless and deeply thrilling book. For not only did she live there, she saw herself living there: not only met the people but appraised them; not only heard of what they did but felt for them. She had never lost the absolute love given to the place in her childhood. Oh the steps at the end of market hill where she had played with Anne Bell's dolls and the smell of the Co-op, wheaty, bacon, musty vegetables, of the bakery in which she'd worked, the girls arm in arm singing as they came from the factory – sometimes she could have hugged them to herself as she wanted to hug the two boys: but only rarely did so, fearing that she might spoil them.

Gone, now that the war was over, was the desire she had felt to leave Thurston. To have been tired of it seemed now, to Betty, to be tired of life. There were so many people to talk to, weddings, births, gossip of all kinds, shows, sports, carnivals, meetings, auctions, markets, strangers, a new building, a new vicar, a story about one of the boyos, a breath of legal tattle, and herself able to go back to cleaning in the mornings now that the boys were at school. Just approaching thirty, she could still enjoy dances – when they could get Joyce Ritchie to come in and baby-sit – could still feel the flounce of a new dress as she walked up the street on Easter Monday; though not vain she was pleased with her figure which had quickly returned to its slimness after the birth – and the lipstick red, bright on her lips, the hair waving on to her shoulders – dare she try the New Look? Sometimes it was as if she were taking part in a story. Betty at this time moved in a world heightened and made more dense by its relation to that rhythm in her mind which took pleasure in extending what she saw and did into a form dependent on but different from the accepted reality – fictive, dramatic, sometimes fantastical, sometimes tragic. And Douglas was charged with this feeling of hers.

The preparations over, the day arrived, and then Betty was nervous. She had to walk at the head of the girls – lead them in fact. However hard she tried to walk very closely to the crowds on the pavement or drag a little behind, there was no doubt that she was prominently in charge and this upset her. This doubt transferred itself to everything and What to Wear? became an enormous problem – all the more disturbing because her wardrobe was meagre and she never otherwise hesitated for more than a few seconds. But 'Would a dress be too showy?', she would ask a totally indifferent Joseph – or 'Would a coat – the black coat, the wine one was for going to shop or cleaning in – would this black coat be too formal? or too hot? or too gloomy? or too short, anyway?' And should she wear 'sandals or shoes – what do you think?' 'Whatever you like,' Joseph replied from behind the paper – his response to many of her questions. 'Whatever you like.'

This day she wore her second-best dress, the green and white striped one – which did not suit her as well as her best dress, not even as well as her everyday dress. Despite it she looked lovely: eager, sparkling at the thought of so much enjoyment about to be had, the tension giving a little glow to her skin.

And she felt so well about this carnival. There was nothing 'laid on' about it, neither from hands of the mighty dead nor from the hands of the rich living. In that way, Betty thought, it was like the Labour Party which proclaimed that people were now equal with regard to their health and their basic livelihood, and more equal than before in regard to education and the systems. She would respond emotionally for the Labour Party on any subject – but especially now, at this time, when they were in power with Clement Attlee as Prime Minister and 'making a really good job of it considering the mess there is to clear up after a war'. Somehow, the carnival was directly related to the Labour Party's term of government – but more importantly it was related to people peacefully enjoying themselves. She loved to be in crowds but feared it terribly when the slightest ripple of nastiness stirred. Here was a time when there was none.

So, grasping her handkerchief in her left hand – for this dress had no pockets – she did her best to forget her feelings of unease – (she was *not* showing off, she had a legitimate reason to be there – and nobody noticed her anyway – who did she think she was?) and nodded cheerfully when the official came and asked her if the girls were ready. The bandmaster muttered 'Men of Harlech, quick march tempo, get them going, plenty of cornet in the chorus,' lifted his baton, turned his back on the band, prodded Kathleen – and away they went.

'O'er the hills, thro' night lies sleeping,
Tongues of flame thro' mists are leaping,
As the brave, their vigil keeping,
Front the deadly fray;
Then the battle thunder
Rives the rocks asunder
As the light falls on the flight
Of foes without their plunder:
There the worsted horde is routed,
There the valiant never doubted
There they died but dying shouted:
"Freedom wins the day." '

The music stirred Douglas to uncontainable excitement. So clear the sounds from the silver band, with the drum-beat lifting his feet in time and so much to look at! Douglas had never yet been in a carnival. Each year had been the same: overwhelming intoxication at the thought of it, a thousand ideas as to what he could be and, in the end, almost drowned in his multitudinous waves of emotion, tears and the decision to 'go as nothing'. He loved dressing up: in the choir he closed his eyes with pleasure as he slipped the pleated surplice over the long buttoned black cassock, and when the vicar had introduced ruffs he could hardly bear to take his off, would have worn it in the street if he had dared. At the primary school, also, a new teacher had set them all doing plays in the last year and the doublets and hose, the sword and Wellingtons for top-boots, the character to be assumed and the lines remembered, all put him in a daze comparable to that which came on him when he felt that Pauline Bell was looking at him with interest. And each time he read a book or went to the pictures, then for at least a day afterwards, he *was* the hero: either a quiet, strong, honest schoolboy with deep talents, too profound for the superficial observer – someone from the Fifth Form at St Dominic's – or he was Errol Flynn or Johnny Weismuller going O-o-o through the streets, calling the elephants to his rescue. When his father took him to watch Carlisle United, then he was Ivor Broadis for the rest of the weekend, and in the cricket season he was Denis Compton. He was forever imitating the gait, expressions and attitudes of those boys older than himself and longed to wear long trousers so that his roles could be further extended. Douglas had a hundred masks a day, swung between ecstasy and despair hourly, ran everywhere – even going up the street to do the shopping – was now the leader of a gang, now excluded from it, lived in a daily pageant of bonfires, Christmas, Easter, football matches, films, the Cubs, the choir, the auctions, the horse-sales, exams, swimming, hounds and hares, fishing – he was played on by the town and its images each day of his life.

When it came to squashing all this into one costume for one carnival day – the effort was beyond him. Besides, he liked to be alone, watching, hovering, out of it yet marching perfectly in step with the band, seeing all the people, alternately proud and ashamed of his mother being so pretty and so prominent, looking at the new people come into town for the do, hugging it all to himself, lonely and at the same time feeling himself to be almost the spirit of the carnival, for he had been down to the park every night that week to see them get it ready, had stood outside the Temperance Hall to hear the band practise, had explored the yards to catch a glimpse of the wagons being decorated on the Friday night, had asked practically everyone what they were going as, had dreamed of the carnival, entered and won the races, won the hearts of the crowd, met a beautiful girl, had his mother smile and congratulate him.

Sometimes he had to close his eyes and look away, for it was all too much, too many people he knew each carrying a different scent which he breathed as he passed them by, too many alleys and lanes, walls and doors he had played in and done something he would never forget or never be forgiven for. So he was charged with his past and flooded by his present, his moods winking as rapidly as morse, and sometimes he had to dive down a side-turning to be alone in the empty street and hear the carnival in the distance because it was too much to bear.

Harry had dressed up as a boxer. He had wanted to be Joe Louis but Betty said it would be much easier to be a white man. Joseph had suggested Bruce Woodcock but Harry was not convinced until he had started to rub soot on his legs. The sight of his legs turning black had unnerved him. So he was Bruce Woodcock. A pair of shorts, his goloshes, Douglas's dressing-gown, a pair of boxing gloves which Joseph had sent back from Belgium and, last demand of Harry's, a black eye. The costume was not inspired but Harry felt very pleased with himself and was quietly convinced that he would be among the prize-winners, though when he arrived and found five other boxers, he was prepared to concede that he might just miss the award for originality. He was a little chilly because he insisted on the dressing-gown being open so that people could see his shorts, and he rather resented having to stop every so often while the girls up front did their dance, but on the whole he was very happy about it all. He wished that he had not been put quite so far back because he liked to hear the music and could not be sure of keeping in step when it was so faint; that was his only complaint.

In the Lion and Lamb, Joseph was keeping an anxious eye on George. He was annoyed that he should be doing so, but by now it was a habit he could not break. Even while playing darts, he would find as he pulled his arrows out of the board that his first glance was for George, sitting in the corner of the room, almost drunk, belligerently arguing. It was impossible to avoid being with him, for George clung very tightly; and even when Joseph had been directly rude, George had bounced back – into the welcoming arms of Joseph's regret at his loss of temper. Moreover, since George had married Helen, Joseph felt obliged to be somewhat responsible for him. Helen was treating George so badly now: she drank around the place, most probably slept around, no matter how many the evasive constructions Betty put on her actions, she was careless about Lester, her son, and always short-tempered with Aileen, and George's only defence was to pretend to be ignorant. For he always loved Helen and it was that which bound Joseph to him.

As he heard the band approach he, too, as Douglas, felt the rhythm penetrate his skin. He finished off his drink quickly and went out into the street to get a good view, George tagging along behind him.

Kathleen passed to ironical cheers which he acknowledged gaily by even more furious strumming on the ukelele. Then the band stopped, bumping into each other like a falling pack of cards. An official ran ahead and tugged Kathleen to a halt.

The girls held their handkerchiefs in the air, the bells tinkling lightly, and the bandmaster nodded at Betty who turned and by the most unobtrusive of gestures, informed the dancers that they must be ready. Joseph was near her but did not try to catch her eye, knowing it would unnerve her, though she looked so cool, so tranquil in command. The music began, the girls dipped forward, sweeping their handkerchiefs to the ground. Joseph looked for the boys.

He saw Douglas on the other side of the street, squeezed between two stout women with shopping baskets, his head just above one of the baskets so that it looked as if he was being carried in it, live, as a turnip on top of the groceries. He was staring at the girls, so completely absorbed that he looked almost shocked to attention. His hair was mussed up, tie askew, cheeks red. When he did notice his father, he gave him a most peremptory nod, and though Joseph knew that this came from the annoyance many boys of that age feel at *having* a father – especially one who was to be seen in public – and understood that this was compounded by the intensity of his concentration on the dancing, which could not tolerate even the temporary intrusion of a brief recognition – yet he was hurt by his son's lack of need for him. The hurt came and went no more painfully or powerfully than passing muscular twinge, but it added to the muggy isolation already encouraged by the beer: his wife there, and his son, untouchable. He looked along the line for Harry and eventually spotted him, standing quite still, looking up into the sky as if praying for an aeroplane to pass to give him a diversion while all this dancing about was going on. Joseph smiled, and forgot the hurt he had felt.

The dancing over, the procession set off once more, passing the fountain, turning into West Street and going down the hill towards the park. Joseph stood and watched all of it and was delighted when Harry saw him and waved a glove.

More pleased, however, with the gang at the very end, behind the lorries and wagons. For after the procession had left Low Moor Road, this gang of boys – aged between eight and fourteen, about twenty of them, all very poorly dressed – had joined on and wagged like a tail. Lester, Helen's son, was the leader, and he carried a stick on which a large square of cardboard was nailed, with the words 'THE CADJERS', written in charcoal. Some of the boys wore trilbys, others wore old scarves around their neck, most, even the smaller boys, wore long pants and boots.

Joseph did not quite know why they pleased him so much, this gang. The cheek of it was something, for they scattered whenever the band stopped and with threatening and barefaced determination held out their hats to the crowd, taking a collection for themselves. Perhaps, also, after the artifice and work of the walkers and the wagons, this higgledy piggledy – 'Let's see if we can get away with it' – mob of boys came as a relief. That they came from very poor families made poignant their rapacities over the coins – usually pennies and halfpennies – which were thrown at them. These were the children of people as poor as you could be without deserving the description 'destitute'.

Most of all, Joseph was glad to see Lester out there in front. He had taken to Lester ever since Helen's arrival with him and lost no opportunity of giving him a treat or bring him along to Hound Trails and football matches. Lester repaid this by never wavering in playing out his own part which was that of a reckless, daring ceaselessly active boy. Whereas Douglas sometimes got into trouble, Lester went out looking for it. Whereas Douglas seemed to plunge into himself on occasions and be inaccessible, Lester appeared to act on every impulse that took him. He had not passed for the Grammar School and only longed for the day on which he would leave school altogether. Then – he had plans! Joseph threw him sixpence and Lester caught it, beaming and, waving at the others to join in, began to sing a currently popular cowboy song which came out from those twenty liberated throats with shrill jest and menace.

The procession passed, Joseph went back into the pub, He would get down to the park later. Or perhaps not at all: there were three races on the wireless that afternoon and he could not really miss them.

Douglas became magnetized by a girl with long corn-coloured plaits whom he had never seen before. He schemed to stand near her and yet be unobserved: tailing her like a 'private eye': jostling with others so that he could stand behind her on the steps to the banana-slide and touch her; rewarded by a smile; then together on the American Swing – love, marriage, at last; her father called her, and she ran away nameless.

Harry saw a man who had been in Thurston the previous year with a small company of repertory actors who had taken over the parish rooms for the autumn. A very lugubrious, rather paunchy, myopic man. He needed chatting to, Harry thought, and cheering up. So he went and stationed himself nearby, edged closer, explained things, asked him how he made himself look different on the stage, and finally asked what he had withheld for fear of a negative answer – whether the actors were coming again? They were. Harry was struck dumb with pleasure and allowed himself to be bought an ice-cream.

Betty took charge of those girls whose mothers had not come, went around the wagons with them, looked at the costumes, encouraged them to enter for the races, looked out for Joseph who did not arrive.

Lester ran in every possible race and when they were over began the intensive operation of finding empty lemonade bottles and taking them to the stall to claim the twopence return. Single-minded in this, he was also light-fingered, and many a mother placed a bottle neatly beside a tree and found it gone at the next glance.

The girls did one final dance on the lawn just before they were given their tea and then Betty's work was done. She had five of the little ones hanging around her, but she knew their older sisters or brothers and could disengage herself from them whenever necessary. For it was now that the husbands drifted down; not the dutiful or interested kind who had been there all day, nor the fellas who would never be caught in public with their wives, but the ordinary type, who'd had a drink or two in the afternoon, or been to a match, or worked on the allotment. Not Joseph.

He had gone into the back room of the pub to listen to the last two races and drunk more than usual because it was rare that he was in with the clique who drank out of hours. When he came out, even this early autumn sunshine made him feel a little dizzy, and by the time he reached the top of Ma Powell's field and looked down at the park, he knew he needed a little snooze. He went back home for it. Besides, it was one way to get rid of George.

Having given up hope of Joseph, Betty felt lonely. Douglas was not to be caught nor stay for longer than a minute anywhere near her – plunging through the dying carnival in a state of exhausted over-excitement, he was too rootless even to wait while she searched her handbag for a promised threepence for an ice-cream. Harry was not to be seen anywhere, but Betty did not worry because plenty of people knew him and the boys had been able to find their way home from anywhere in the town ever since they had started school.

Though there were other wives there without husbands, she

thought it mean of Joseph not to put in an appearance – if only for the children's sake. He never took them for walks or anything like that; the most he managed was to let them trot beside him as he went to the bookie's or along to a match.

She had come to expect so much during those years alone while he'd been away. They had not been all that easy, despite the children to take her mind off things. There had been too much time to think about herself; to listen to the radio and think; and wonder about Joseph and indulge frightening thoughts. She remembered the kitchen, the blind down, not a sound from the town, news of war and the consequences of war, the pulley heavy with clothes which would never dry out in that damp weather, the gas mantle which needed renewing, blistered brown paint on the corner cupboard. At least he could have stripped or scraped those cupboard doors since his return; at least that. *She* would have painted them.

When she got home, she was so disgusted to find him snoozing on the sofa that she had not even the energy to wake him up. The boys had not come with her but she did not expect them until dark.

George came before Joseph woke up and his presence was a stopper to the argument which silently tore between them; as the men went out the boys came in and Betty got ready their supper, determined to wait up for Joseph and face him with his life.

Chapter Ten

He came back after closing time full of beer and guilt, gave the door a slight kick to show his independence and caught it with his hand before it banged against the wall to show his consideration.

Betty was in the corner pretending to read the *Women's Illustrated*; she had knocked off the music on the wireless as she had heard his step down the street.

He turned his eyes aside, pretending that after the few minutes between pub and house the gas-light was hurting them. Already the cheerful memory of the evening's roving – with the tailpiece of the carnival trailing enticingly through the pubs and dark streets – curdled to a thin trickle which might have been fear; and so he deliberately 'lurched' forward to provoke an accusation of drunkenness. None came.

O this silence of hers! He could have murdered her just to hear the sound of it.

He sat down 'heavily' opposite her, thrusting out his legs as if wanting her to get up and trip over them. She did not even glance over the top of her page. Joseph then glared at the fire and behind the over-masculine gestures cringed, then reproached himself his weakness and willed his real feelings to match those assumed.

Betty had begun to read the while and one tired part of her mind was quite interested in it, curious to turn the page. What was the use of arguing?

'Do I not get a cup of tea then?' Joseph's right foot kicked at the air as he shouted this question.

'You'll wake the children.'

'You always say that.'

'I shouldn't have to.' She had glanced up but now looked back at the magazine and with loathing added: 'Coming in drunk.'

'I'm not drunk.'

'Well stop acting it. Anyway you are.'

'I – am – not,' quietly emphasized.

'They just have to whistle and you go wherever they want.'

'Who?'

'Anybody.' The pause was her burden and having lost the advantage of her silence, she was too irritated to bear it long. 'Look at George – he just has to come and you're away.'

'You could come with us.'

'Who wants to go drinking every night?'

'Nobody *goes* drinking every night.'

'You might as well for all we see of you.'

'Put that bloody paper down.'

'There's no need to swear.' She lowered the magazine but did not let go of it. 'Sometimes the boys wonder if you still live here.'

'I can't help that, can I? I'm up before them ...'

'I have to drag you up.'

'... and when I get back they're out playing.'

'And when they get back you're out enjoying yourself.'

'Why shouldn't I? You would do the same.'

'Don't be ridiculous – I need the nights to keep this place in order.'

'I've told you before – drop one of your houses and use the time for this: there's no need for you to work so hard.'

'You don't say that when I buy Douglas a new suit out of my own money.'

'Betty!' Far from being offended, he used her tentative reproach as a means of gaining sympathy for himself. 'That's a nasty thing to say. Really nasty,' he added, complacently.

'I'm sorry.' She put down the magazine and went into the back kitchen to make a pot of tea. To get there she had to step over Joseph's legs and as she did so he made a grab at her. His touch restored her disgust and she pulled away so forcefully that he knew it would be asking for trouble to hold on:

but he hummed to himself and still rested on his little victory.

'Anyway who would look after the boys,' she asked, hidden from him, 'if I came out with you?'

'That's stupid, Betty. You can always get somebody in. Anyway, they're old enough to look after themselves now.'

Betty nodded to herself – her point proved – and stood beside the gas cooker, waiting for the kettle to boil. She heard Joseph pull off his shoes and then take the poker to riddle the fire, over-energetically: that would be another shovelful of coal which could have been saved.

The tea mashed, she brought in the two cups and handed his to the outstretched hand – he was lying out on the sofa.

'Is there a biscuit?' he asked as she was about to sit down.

'Yes. There's a full packet.'

She had the cup on the arm of her chair and went again to the back kitchen, found the biscuits, brought them, handed them to him, sat down, still holding to his words 'they're old enough to look after themselves now.' Watched him sip his tea and felt a passing regret that he should so be letting himself go that at his age he had a beer belly; if only he knew the effort she was forced to make time and again as he took off his clothes for bed – there was a lack of delicacy about his undressing; and the clothes were left where they dropped – but that was unimportant, she told herself, doggedly, appearances were unimportant: though she lived by and for them.

'Harry was upset this afternoon,' said without apparent provocation. 'Hm?'

Betty did not press for the moment, concerned to control the anger which bobbed into her throat. Joseph, cigarette, tea and comfortable displacement of stomach, blew unsuccessful smoke rings at the ceiling and relaxed in anticipation of a Sunday lie-in.

'I said Harry was upset this afternoon.'

'Was he?'

'He wouldn't say why.'

'Can't have been much then ... they usually say, kids, don't they?'

'Do they? I shouldn't have thought you knew much about them. Kids.' Still evenly delivered.

'I helped to bring up four brothers and sisters – remember that! – I could change nappies when I was ten years old.'

'Yes, I've heard all that. It seems to have sickened you for life.'

'O now don't *start*, Betty. Just when we were peaceful.'

And there was some justice in his complaint, she thought. 'But if *I* don't say anything – nothing ever *gets* said.'

'That would be a relief sometimes. Everything I do's wrong.'

'I only said that Harry wasn't himself.'

'I know. But you meant that it was my fault. I should have come to the car-niv-al – oh, deary-me.' He blushed at his own meanness, shifted uneasily on the sofa as if something was sticking into him. When he began like this, he could not stop himself; yet all the time, a calm voice was singing inside his head the incongruous sentence: 'You love her more than you could love anybody: if you left her you'd be lost.' He turned to her and accused her face to face. 'So what was wrong with Harry?'

'I don't know. He wouldn't tell me.'

'And what do you expect me to do about it now? Go and wake him up and ask him a lot of questions?'

'Don't be silly.'

'Well why drag it up then?'

'Because these are the things that people do bring up,' she said, desperately. 'Those that don't spend every night out drinking.'

'Once and for all you could have come with me!' He swung his legs off the sofa and saw them land on the carpet, soft under his woollen socks, knitted for him by May: that fact reminded him of how unquestionably he was appreciated elsewhere. 'You're welcome! You know that. You're welcome to come!'

'I never ask where you've been,' timidly. Betty darted to the glow of another suspicion, once warned by a whiff of gossip.

'I always tell you.'

'But you needn't. I don't want to know.'

'What's that got to do with it?'

'It has.' Her face set, defying what, she was not clear, but defiant. 'It has.'

'You can't carry an argument – that's your trouble. It puts years on anybody talking to you. You've no idea.'

'If I was clever you would find something else to shout about.'

'I'm not shout – O, I hate all this. I do. I really do. I come home, it's been a carnival day. I've had a few all right so I've had a few, and off we go into arguments. What a bloody life it is. It is! It really is.'

'There's no need to swear.' Upright on the edge of her chair, her back straight, the cup and saucer poised in her hand as if she were being observed at the very politest tea-party: miserable.

'I mean, I saw you this afternoon,' Joseph had moved himself rather deeply by his previous speech and wanted to consolidate the feeling of noble suffering it had given him. 'I did – just outside the ... District Bank ...' his tone sentimental, he stopped to let it take effect.

'You mean opposite the Lion and Lamb.' The sentence popped out and then her lips snapped shut, as if they had suddenly parted to allow her tongue a rude gesture and, too late, were shocked at what they had done.

'All right,' Joseph groaned and eased himself back into the horizontal position on the sofa. 'Opposite – the – Lion – and – Lamb. That's what I mean about you! I've forgotten what I was going to say now because of your stupid interruption! And where did it get us? Eh? Eh?'

The challenge fell between them and grew cold in the silence. His voice had sounded so querulous and old; Betty was a little frightened by it.

Some dream broke through and in an entirely different accent and manner, thoughtfully, as if speaking for someone else, Joseph said:

'This is what happens to you if you haven't been educated, see? I *feel* all these things, but I can't explain them. And *you* certainly can't – no, I didn't mean to be nasty, really, I didn't, really. But if we'd both of us, if we'd stayed on at school and maybe gone on from there – we would always have something to talk about. Something sensible and interesting to talk about instead of these arguments that don't get anywhere. I mean, I would have read an interesting book or something and I would tell you all about it and you would be interested to listen to me talking because I would know how to put it, see? Then we wouldn't – I mean I wouldn't *have* to go out, at all. No – but –' he closed his eyes and the beer seemed to be stirring around inside him, soaking through him as through paper and in his mind he saw the papers, the comics and magazines and self-declared 'rubbish' which served his large appetite for reading matter; and felt ill at the thought of it. 'What we read is trash! It *is*. Trash! Like that – that thing you're reading now – I mean, what's in it?'

And again, though he had made her sympathetic to him, there was something too demanding about it all.

'There are some very nice things in it,' she replied, promptly. 'Patterns and things –'

'Patterns! Who could have a conversation about patterns?' 'You're not supposed to talk about them – you're supposed to knit them.'

She smiled: Joseph would start to laugh at her, she could see the beginnings of it in the corners of his mouth. 'And anyway, there's the serial.'

'And what's in that?' he demanded.

'Well ...' She had forgotten. Her mouth opened, and realizing that it could be comical, she took care to parody herself, lightly, hoping that Joseph would be affected by it but would not notice so that she would find a way out of this trying argument without having been seen to seek one.

'Sounds a great story if you can't even remember it.'

'O yes. There's this young doctor. And he's working for his exams.'

'What's interesting about that? That's what they all do.'

'Ah. But there's this nurse as well.'

'Don't say it! Don't say it!' And Joseph lifted his hands as if he was beating off a wasp. 'He starts to go with her but he can't see her often enough because of these exams of his and she thinks he's running around with another nurse and so she sets herself up to another doctor who isn't as clever as number one but has more money – what's wrong?'

'You've read it!'

'No I haven't.'

'Why did you ask me what it was about when you'd read it?'

'I – haven't – read it. I just made that up.'

'You can't have done. That's the story.'

Joseph giggled – very well pleased with himself. 'There we are then. Your husband's an author. That's another reason you could do without that magazine.'

'You *must* have read it.'

'Don't you believe me?'

'But that's the *story*?'

'I tell you I DIDN'T READ IT.'

'You'll wake the children.'

'You always say that.'

'You must have read one just like it.'

'Maybe so ... maybe so.' He was tired now. 'You give me credit for nothing.'

'Why? What have you done?'

'You would drive anybody crackers, Betty. Really. I mean, we started by talking about education.'

'I'm sorry.'

'Never mind.'

'I'm sorry though.' She hesitated. 'Well then?'

'Yes?'

'Well?' She nodded, smiled encouragingly, 'let's talk about education then.'

'What about it?'

'Douglas is always top,' she said.

'*I* was always top as well.'

'Hm! I didn't say it proved anything.'

'Why did you say it then?'

'To get us started.'

Joseph shook his head and tasted his tea, pulled a face: 'See? This tea's cold now.'

'Oh blooming heck!' Betty stood up, took his cup and went towards the back kitchen. 'Anyway, Harry wasn't himself.'

'I'll talk to him in the morning – Oh! That reminds ... can I borrow your bike for Tommy Mars tomorrow morning? His own's bust and I said he could borrow yours.'

'Why?' She resented lending her bicycle; partly because she depended on it so much for her work, but also for some of the same feeling which made her unable to drink out of someone else's cup.

'What d'you mean – why?'

For goodness' sake, Joseph, stop taking up everything I say! No wonder you're bothered about education if you don't know what "why" means!'

'Keep your hair on.'

'I hate you saying that.'

'I know.'

'There's your tea: drink it hot this time.'

'We thought we might go to Bothel.'

'For cock-fighting. Don't try to kid me, Joseph: everybody knows what goes on in Bothel on Sunday mornings.'

'It's a good job everybody doesn't.' He laughed; a forced and unnecessary laugh.

'You'll have a fine lot of chance to talk to Harry, then, won't you? By the time you've had your lie in and read your blessed *People*, it'll be Tommy Mars and Bothel on my bike.'

'I'll talk to him.'

'It doesn't matter.' Her tone was sensible and calm: as if she had realized this all along but thought it not worth mentioning until now. 'He wouldn't take any notice of you anyway.'

'What a thing to say!'

'Well he wouldn't. You never talk to them about anything so why should you talk to him about this? No – I'll get it out of him sometime. Then I'll tell you.'

Much relieved, she sat back in her chair and took up the magazine, quickly finding her place in the story. Joseph looked at her, looked away from her, considered shouting, considered soothing, then shook his head with mock-bemusement and lit a cigarette, the last one in the packet: he must be sure to nip it so as to have a stump for the morning.

She read on.

'Well,' he said, his voice rather nervous – he didn't know why, he wasn't in the least nervous – 'aren't you going to tell us about the carnival, then?'

'You said you saw it.'

'I did.' His curiosity gave him patience. 'But who was there I mean. Who did you see?'

'Everybody was there except you.'

'O for Christ's sake, Betty, give us a bit of chat about it!'

'It's nearly bed-time.' Still her head bent to the page; which she turned over. 'And don't swear.'

'I would've come if I could.' He tossed restlessly on the sofa. 'This bloody – sorry! – this damned sofa's neither one thing nor the other.'

'Damned's just as bad as anything else. Neither one what nor the other?'

'You know – it's too short.'

'It takes up that wall. What else do you want?'

'Was Harold Patterson in charge of the sports?'

'Yes,' her hand went out, unerringly, for her cup.

'He would be. He gets on my nerves that fella. Sets himself up in charge of any mortal thing he can lay his hands on.'

'I think he's nice.'

'Oh – maybe he's nice to you. But you should hear him down at Kirkbride. "Do this Tallentire", "Have you got that, Tallentire." *Yes*. No "Joseph" – and he just went to the National school like everybody else. Every bloody – well I *feel* like that! – any blooming job I've been in, somebody's bossed me about. And look at me now – STORES! What sort of a life is it being in STORES?'

'Well change it.'

'How can I? What am I good for now?'

'You're as good as you've ever been and don't whine, Joseph Tallentire.'

'But it's true, isn't it? Even when I was at that factory I was the slave of that machine. I *was*. The Slave of that Machine.'

'Don't be so soft.'

'Why don't we have beer in the house?'

'What d'you mean?'

'Well you see them – on the pictures and that – "have a beer", "have a drink" – *they* don't have to go to the pub for a pint of Ordinary do they? Why don't *we* keep stuff in the house?'

'It wouldn't keep long with you around. You've a belly like a balloon as it is.'

'Who's got a belly? Who has?'

'Well if it isn't a belly, it's an illness – I'm saying nothing.'

'You've said enough as it is.'

'I never say anything,' said Betty, most sternly, 'that's my trouble.'

'Trouble she says ...'

But warmth had come into her tone and he luxuriated in it – how could he tell her how he felt, that there was no need for anything else? Once he would not have needed words.

She yawned and stretched: her arms were thrown to the ceiling and in the act her body was tightened and thrust towards him: had he not known her as he did, he would have thought it provocative. But had *she* not known that he knew her well, she would never have yawned like that.

'Bed-time,' she said. 'And don't you be too late. You promised to speak to Harry in the morning, remember.'

'They've got bikes – they can come to Bothel with me.'

'You wouldn't have them back in time for Sunday School.'

'Promise. Cross my heart.'

'Anyway. What do they want cock-fighting! No.'

'*They* won't have to fight, mother.'

'Don't call me mother. I'm not thirty yet. Look to yourself.'

'I'm no mother either.'

'I can't make you out sometimes.' Again she yawned. 'You say you wish you'd been clever,' yawned again, 'but you say such soft things.'

'Who said he wanted to be clever? Eh?'

'I can't be expected to remember all you said off by heart, can I? You said something like that. But I can't repeat it all back to you like a blooming echo! You're not *that* important.'

'All right. All right. Keep your hair on.'

'I *hate* that ex—, ex— that way of talking.'

'At least I don't take on words I can't finish.'

'No need to be so nasty.'

'Who was nasty?'

'You don't even know you're doin' it. Good night. And don't be long.' The final phrase – though its effect was intended to hasten him to bed – was so far from an invitation to pleasure as to be a parody.

'I can't wait,' he muttered.

'What was that?'

'Nothing.'

She went up the short staircase quietly.

Joseph was happy. He reckoned that he'd got off lightly. Oh – he knew she was disappointed in his laxness but she couldn't know of those unhappy feelings which had been pressing onto his mind for the last few years. Sensations which could not be mentioned: dreadful feelings of his mind in shipwreck, not only hope but instinct adrift, which frightened him and found relief only, only in drink. The times he felt the swell inside his head – as if all that had been ignored and brutalized in him, unused and unacknowledged, suddenly used his uncertainty as the opportunity to show their strength. His head was rocked with fears he could not name.

Chapter Eleven

He thought he had made his 'real' break when he left the aerodrome and got a job with the Insurance. But after a very few months he knew that it would satisfy only the smallest part of him; he worked longer hours than at the aerodrome for much the same pay, and though the hours were more under his own control and though this collecting insurance and selling it in the town and the neighbourhood appeared more interesting, he was soon bored, took pleasure only in the unexpected and looked for it outside of work.

When the big opportunity came it was only because he was feeling ashamed of himself that he took it. He had been to see his father to try to convince the old man to give up work. John was in his seventies now and his wife had asked for help to persuade the old man to retire. With small contributions from their children and the old-age pension they could have about as much coming in as his present wage packet. His father had been so contemptuous of Joseph's suggestion that he had lost his temper, and weakly argued from the effect it had on other people – that for example and most importantly his wife suffered because he continued to drive himself so. None of his business; get back and sort his own life out. He had biked back to Thurston, smarting at the accusation and angry at the effective rule his father could still impose on him.

No one at home: Douglas, who was now fourteen, off to Oxford for a week with three other members of his class and the history teacher, attending a series of lectures arranged by the Grammar School and the Church of England. Harry away playing Rugby for the same school's Under-Thirteen side. Betty shopping in Carlisle. Joseph had stamped around the house, unnerved that it should be empty when he wanted to tell someone what had happened. As if someone were present to be impressed by his action, he had begun to lay the table for tea, slamming down the crockery, barging his way about the kitchen, rattling the slow kettle on the timid gas-ring, muttering to himself, banging the wireless to clear the crackle and only making it worse. He broke the best tea-pot. It had been given to Betty by one of the women she had worked for: not a cast-off, but something gone out and bought – a special thing. Joseph gathered the pieces, guiltily looking at the door in case Betty should come in. When, eventually, she did he could not conceal that though the destruction had been accidental it was somehow intentional, both symbol and retribution for a stupid attack of temper. Betty had winkled that from him in a matter of seconds and from then on he flapped around her hopelessly, until it became obvious to him that he had touched the fuse which fired off a dense and impenetrable mood in her and the only thing to do was to clear out.

It was in the Blue Bell that he heard about it. A pub, the Throstle's Nest (known as the 'Thrush') was to change hands and the Brewery were looking for a new tenant-landlord. In the general mood of the last few years, Joseph would have let it pass. But with the set faces of his father and his wife before his eyes, each in different ways having made him feel feeble and centreless that afternoon, a spark of his former optimism flared, his self-assertion was lit up, remembered, invoked once more. Without telling anyone, he went home that night and wrote a letter applying for the pub. He had nothing to lose. Nothing at all.

A week later, he received a reply asking him to come for an interview. The letter arrived when Betty was out and again he did not tell her, put on his best suit on the nominated morning, caught a bus to Workington where the brewery had its works and offices.

There were five others there – he being the only one who *lived* in Thurston – and the interview was much longer than he had anticipated.

He had thought of the questions they might ask him and rehearsed his answers on the bus. All done secretly, rather desperately, as the red double-decker swept out to the coast road and twisted past slag heaps and pit-heads. His insurance book was heavy in the pocket of his long, belted raincoat. The bus was almost empty. The interview seemed a simple affair. Nor was it much different from what he had imagined: but longer, and as he came back he felt that he was in with a chance.

The Throstle's Nest was the least flourishing pub in the town. Before the first war, when the town had been a prosperous market centre, there had been about forty pubs. Now, with the population shrunk to less than 4,000, there were only sixteen. Yet most of these were run by landlords who made a living from the pub alone and did not have to take a day-time job to supplement their income. The Thrush was badly placed – about two hundred yards from the nearest neighbouring pub, and away from that central cluster which made it so easy for drinkers to change location; in High Street, for example, there were seven pubs on a stretch no longer than fifty yards, which made for concentrated evenings. It required an effort to go down to the Thrush and few at this time thought it worth making. A man called Archer had held it for twenty years; he was in his sixties, his wife was dead, he drank a good deal, the pub was never re-decorated, his beer was poorly kept. It was a difficult pub to run; built as a small inn with several rooms, it required a staff. For the habit then was that unless you were in the bar itself, you did not fetch your own drink: the publican, or a waiter, came for your order and served you. To run the Thrush properly on a busy night would need at least three waiters, which knocked up the overheads and was only worth it if a good trade could be relied on; not to have waiters discouraged trade. Mr Archer had a woman who helped him on Saturdays and Sundays and left it at that. The brewery were grateful for his retirement.

The understanding – and the contract – was that once a tenant-landlord was installed, then he could not be fired unless he broke his contract or broke the law, by serving after time, giving incorrect measures and so on. Once installed, he paid a weekly rent for the house to the brewery, paid rates to the council, was responsible for all his own accounting and ordering and had only two obligations: to buy all his beer from the brewery, and to sell it according to law. Thus, though a tenant, he was very much his own man – remembering Stoddart he was glad of that. Profits came as a percentage of the gross takings. There was no possibility of the tenant's ever being able to buy the pub from the brewery (unless by some misfortune or unexpected change of policy they decided to sell off the pubs) and as very hard work was needed to make a decent living, the brewery were commanding all the energy and worry which goes into small businesses while bearing none of the direct responsibilities. Yet once their choice had been made, then, beyond a little chivvying, there was nothing they could do to force the landlord to work at a pace other than his own.

In the week following the interview, Joseph was very subdued. He came to regard this as his very last chance. Past his mid-thirties – the boys too settled in school to move, this was the best he would do in Thurston. Secretly, he fed it with all the old dreams: that they were still there unnerved him for he realized with what effort he had repressed them. But if he got that place ... then he would be able to run his own house, organize his own life, be his own man.

Still he did not tell Betty – and there was more than pride in that recalcitrance: he knew that she did not like pubs, did not really approve of drinking, would be afraid of 'setting herself up', putting herself even so marginally in a position to be envied. For there was no doubt that the landlords of Thurston were envied. As some did quite well, so all were thought to do, and their income was doubled in the imagination, trebled in the gossip, and finally turned to treasure by a consideration of the potentialities of their situation. That Mr Archer retired to live with his daughter and had nothing but a few hundred and his old-age pension made not the slightest difference to this: and if, as sometimes happened, a man came out of a pub and went back to his former job, swearing he was better off so, he was thought devious, incompetent or both. Landlords did all right – that was the proposition, which was unchallengeable – but the nod and wink which accompanied the words would, he was sure, be distressing for Betty. Yet he knew that she would follow him.

The fact of the Thrush being in poor condition and reputation would help him there. And if the boys were going to stay on at school and even go to university (he dared hardly dream of that) then any possible extra money would be a help. At the moment they managed by not much more than a hair's-breadth and trips like the one Douglas was taking had to be long (though privately) considered, the fourteen pounds involved being no easy sum. That, too, might sway her, though again he knew that she was rather pleased with the fact that they managed on so little and were yet able to get school uniforms for the boys, allow drinking-money for himself (though he supplemented that by odd jobs as always), even, the previous year, take a week's holiday at a seaside resort instead of the usual staying with relatives in other parts of the county. And money worried both Douglas and Harry: Douglas did not want to go into the Sixth Form because he knew that the expectation was for him to be bringing in about £2.10.0–£3.0.0 a week and giving most of it to his mother: Joseph had been forced to argue with him at length on that and Douglas now treated the school as a job, tearing into the work until he exhausted himself. Harry insisted on doing a paper-round before he went to school in the mornings, and the six and six was handed over regularly. That it was as regularly handed back did not disturb him at all.

Yet whatever Betty's objections were, Joseph was determined that he would overrule them. If he got the pub, he would present it straightforwardly. As soon as he recognized his determination, he became self-righteous in it. He would go around the streets, his insurance book under his arm, muttering to himself – 'She *should* agree. I can't be expected to follow her *all* the time; if I think it's right to do it, she should see that.' Overhearing himself he would become rather shamefaced. After all, he could not force her to do something against her will. Yet was not one of the facts of marriage that you accepted to do things against your will? Or at least tempered your wishes and opinions? Again he checked himself, for marriage to him was as 'natural' as work to his father; suddenly to invoke it was proof of a serious nervousness. So he would forget about it. It mattered little whether he earned six or twelve pounds a week, what was that to Betty's peace of mind? He had married her knowing and accepting that she would need protection against certain things: now to abandon that was almost to go back on his word. Well, he thought, he was allowed to change, wasn't he?

What a time he could have there! To make that broken down ruin of a pub into a good 'house'. He saw, or imagined, in the flux of the pub – in the people who came in, the customers to be satisfied, the ordering to be got just so – chances for employing himself in ways prohibited now. You sold an insurance and were glad if you saw it come in useful and that was all. On the airfield and in the factory and the forces, he had got to know his job and then become bored. Yet he had not now the energy or confidence to turn that boredom into dreaming or scheming. Neither of those had pleased him for very long anyway. He had felt that if you came to be so on top of your job that you were detached from it, then there was need of iron somewhere else: some men found it in a hobby, or in drink, women, books, music, talk – none of these gave Joseph sufficient return. He imagined that he wanted a discipline which would, like a magnet, attract the filings of his mind and let him live parallel to his earning life. But he could not find anything outside the job which was strong enough, he thought; or which could truly warrant so much effort. Though he liked to think himself different from his father, he too could not escape work though, unlike the old man, he tried to. He read Harry's comics and lounged around the town supporting the teams, following the dogs, following the horses, following the days. In the pub he would have little free time – he intended to try to get a living solely from it – for there was not one day of the year when a pub was allowed to close and the opening hours consumed the day and there would be an empire for him, as his father's empire was labour.

When the letter came with the news that his application had been accepted, Betty caught at once this longing of his for the possibilities which the pub promised. She did not want to go – for more reasons than Joseph had thought of; but she repressed her objections, dismissed her fears and did as he wanted.

As the arrangements were made – Joseph had to borrow £40 to cover himself against his first order – he had to go through to the brewery and learn about cellar-work for the beer, he had to organize everything just so because there is no closing allowed when a pub changes hands: one man goes out, another comes in, changes of furniture and all the carry-on no matter – so Betty went more and more energetically into it, and her misgivings hardened. Though she would have flinched at the word and most probably denied its accuracy, she was making a sacrifice which disturbed her desperately.

It was not so much that she was well-settled, though the disruption of a way of life which she found both agreeable and full might have helped to lead her to the identification of her disturbance. For she liked the small house – neat now, much the same as it had always been but emboldened by a new set of chair covers, bright flower-patterns, a brass lampstead, two rubbings made by Douglas and framed by Harry strangely peaceful on the busy wall-paper, a new strip of carpet in front of the fender – and she liked to go to the other houses about her work in the mornings and return to have the place to herself in the peaceful early afternoon hours, to arrange it so that all three of the men were well and equally served.

Moreover, she realized how much the present settlement mattered not only to herself but to Douglas whose engagement with his schoolwork had become a battle, following rigid rules, plans, timetables, long spells of solitude each evening in the parlour; and she sensed his fragility beneath the effervescent, prize-winning bumptiousness; knew that he was constantly pressed by the doubt as to whether it was right that he should stay on at school while his mother worked, knew, more, that he could find no secure relationship between the world of his books and that of his daily life and was undermined in his confidence through doubts as to his own value in this new world. A change might throw him badly. His approach to the work often thrilled her by the passion which caught both old and new in vivid articulation, often saddened her by the clash and pull which was in his expression, dogged, almost sullen, as if he thought it all fatal but necessary.

But Douglas was only a part of it. She was nervous at the prospect of standing there serving drink to people, some of them scarcely known to her, seeing some of them get drunk, becoming a 'legitimate' target of envy, tight-lips, and even abuse in a town which, as Douglas had said, 'packed a stiff bible-and-respectability combination punch'. She realized all that and decided she was prepared to take it for Joseph's sake: it wasn't asking much of her. Prepared also for a change which would make it extremely difficult for her to go to church on occasional Sundays (because of the clearing-up after Saturdays and the relentless opening hours), difficult to have friends drop in and see her in the evenings, difficult to be as free as she now was in her movements around the town.

The deepest cause of her misgiving, as she worked it out, the power before which the sacrifice was made, was something she was never in her life more than intermittently and vaguely conscious of. It came from her own feelings but was fed by scraps read, by remarks made by Harry (whose first dawn of adolescence made itself known by a dogmatic belligerence on the subject of politics) and most consistently nourished by statements from Helen. For Helen was very much the carrier of her father's convictions and as her boldness became less of a strain, she found more edge in the notions heard promoted so vehemently throughout her childhood. Fragments rather than statements, to do with the Working Class, the Struggle for Power, the Revolution, Oppression, the Proletariat, the Masses – words which Betty only partly understood, which clarified her feeling rather than her thinking but moved her to considerations of what had for so long been taken for granted. Helen spoke more freely to Betty than to anyone else and her views were expressed with more force and accuracy than Betty had heard at any Labour Party meeting. There similar words had stirred her – but to reassurance. She was not at all reassured when Helen spoke. She realized in a twilit way that there could be more than Reform as an aim, that such changes might even suffocate the real end with good intentions.

And somehow while they were not better off than anybody else, while they were near the brink of their resources all the time with nothing left over for savings, herself obliged to scrub and polish for others every day to make it possible for the boys to stay on at school and so on – still she was on the proper side. To take a pub meant to change sides. And that frightened her most of all.

What succeeded in repressing any show of this misery was her belief in Love – once and for all given – and the commitment of her own love to Joseph.

She moved, she moved, and loaded the handcarts outside the small house (it was no distance from their place; and this way was the cheapest) and scrubbed the floors of the new place, laid fresh lino, planned to re-paper the walls, quietened Douglas, relied on Harry, in public was pleased, in private was compliant, with Joseph was often thrown high by his pleasure and intoxicated by the rush of enthusiasm and fire which came back to him, with those who murmured against her was firm, to her friends who welcomed it all, was grateful: alone, was silently desperate and at a loss.

Chapter Twelve

For the first year or two the pub was even better than Joseph had hoped. He had always done jobs well and been proud of that: this one he did supremely well. And the factors involved were so many and so changeable that most of his resources were needed to make of it what he wanted.

He had a clear idea of what that should be. He wanted it to be the best pub in town. An enormous amount of the desire for this was a matter of sport: the customers were out there, the pubs were open, the race was on: for the first time he had a job where his competitiveness, so far enjoyed vicariously, could have free and fairly harmless play. For he would not do anyone down to get trade. No under-cutting, no over-measuring, no disparagement of others: within the rules. It would be like a fight. Thurston had always been a hard-drinking town and its central position meant that people came in on market days and weekends from miles around. There were plenty of good pubs already: which only increased his determination.

Handicaps: lack of experience, an out-of-the-way situation, small rooms, little 'good will' or tradition of good trade, and certain prejudices (for example against swearing when there were women present) and convictions (that it would not be an area for fighting as many of the more successful pubs were over the weekend) which, in that rough town, would weigh him down. And of course Betty, who thoroughly disapproved of drunkenness.

Advantages: through his many jobs in the area, he knew almost every single person for miles around. Moreover, he had always been exceptionally good at remembering names. And it seemed that the jobs he had done in the past now served him as he had once served them; for there were many who would come out of interest or curiosity to see what he was making of it and that was a start. There was the fact that he was chancing his arm, trying something most of them would have been unable or too timid to attempt – that was worth following. While from his time on the insurance (when he had also run a 'book' for a while) and from all the stories known about him he was scrupulously honest in all money matters and fair with regard to his opinion of others. Indeed, part of the reason for his barely suppressed thrill of those very first days was that his qualities, as his acquaintances, seemed to come out and proclaim themselves. It was a little like a wake, and again that added to Betty's sense of a 'passing-over'. She was glad he was well-thought-of and felt sure he would not change: he had held to himself as he was in many conditions and regarded this as a change of circumstance merely, imposing no mutation of attitudes. Finally, he was fairly young, enthusiastic and as always had nothing to lose. While Betty would keep the place spotless: everybody knew that.

The first thing to get right was the beer. Like every pub in the town (except the Crown and Mitre which, standing near the auction, had the full benefit of the flusher agricultural trade on market days, and sold as much whisky as lemonade some afternoons) the Throstle's Nest was virtually a beer-house. Spirits perhaps for a final fling on Saturday night, a toast to sabbatical superstitions the following day, perhaps after a good win (at weddings, marriages, funerals and 'eighteen' of age parties of course) always at Christmas, necessarily at New Year but for 255 days of the years, the spirit bottles stood, neck downwards, so inactive that when you did take a measure you automatically glanced at the bottle to see if the precious level had left a rim. Sherry, egg flip, advocaat, port – a little for the ladies, very few and a very little unless the occasion or the lady was ripe. So beer it was, and hard work to make a living from – a very steady number of pints to be served before half a crown profit showed: between twelve and twenty, depending on the type of beer and the room it was served in. Mild was the staple – two kinds, light and dark; a tender beer, ideal for long nights of drinking, for slow-accumulating richness of the stomach, sternum, heart, lungs, tongue. It had been kept very badly by the previous landlord.

The bitter had not been kept much better, which was more serious as it was more expensive. Also, this brewery's bitter had a good name and people were inclined to judge the full stock by it. Finally there was porter – less and less sold but still, at the beginning of the fifties, popular enough to be worth a regular order. This porter was rather like draught Guinness but less sweet, less creamy, smacking more of wood and less of peat, heavy, like Guinness, but not as thick in the stomach.

There were bottles of course: pints and halves, light ale, old ale, sweet stout, Guinness, export, lager, brown ale – but there was nothing a publican could do about these. They arrived in their crates, capped and captioned, requiring only to be poured. In this there was a little skill, for it was easy to spoil a bottle by pouring too quickly and making too much froth, or by pouring too slowly and making too little; and there was the question of dregs – for some customers thought that the lees contained 'the goodness' and wanted them in, others wanted them in whatever they contained because they had paid for a full bottle of beer, the more discriminating recognized the bottom as powder, undrinkable, and would frown if they saw the sediment floating down *their* glass. But this was simply a matter of hearing preferences and remembering them. The bottles could be nicely displayed and individually wiped with a cloth – for dust settled quickly on them – they often arrived on the brewery wagon covered with dust – and Joseph insisted that each one be cleaned so that people did not get their hands or clothes dirty if they bought them to take out. It all helped, he said.

Despite the fact that some of these bottled beers were lauded on their labels for having won prizes at Vienna in 1894 and Paris in 1910 and so on, it was not these which attracted custom. Trade followed the barrels.

These came every Friday and were lowered down the cellar on ropes which guided them down, a man leaning back into the ropes, padded, tattered leather gloves to keep his hands from being burnt, the barrels thundering down into the cellar like cannons rolling down a slope. Harry loved to be there to help the men in the brewery wagon. They were big, very West Cumbrian, both had worked in the mines, both played professional Rugby League for their town and had been given a job in the brewery through local fame (for it was regarded as a cushy number) and they had taken it because they could swing the hours and give themselves time for training and the occasional mid-week match. Harry, thirteen, was neither undersized nor puny yet they would pick him up and throw him around like a parcel of laundry.

Once they were in the cellar the two men rolled the barrels across the floor and then lifted them on to the ramps: there were two little boards they could have used for this, to roll the barrels on, but these two kicked them away just a little ostentatiously, gripped the barrel, crouched tensely and then heaved it clear of the ground and set it in position without even the suggestion of a bump: the wedges were put in place and the barrel was set. The very smallest barrels, nipins, empty, Harry could just roll from one cellar to another.

The cellars opened outside the pub, in front of it, a large trapdoor, and he would stand at the bottom, as of a pit, and see the wagon towering with barrels and crates, one of the men stalking over it like a warrior among plunder. The way they swung down the crates was beautiful to watch. Each crate held two dozen bottles. One man on the wagon would pass them down to the other, two at a time. He would stack them around the edges of the trapdoor. Lift one, pause, lift another, swing around, the man below took the first, the second, turned and stacked them, turned back, two more waiting, a slight jostling thud each time a crate was placed. The way a stack of crates was reduced was like seeing someone scything down a field of hay. Then the man who had been on the wagon jumped down into the cellar and the crates were slid down the long ramps, two at a time, and again the coordination. Harry – who was mad on Rugby League and went to see these two play whenever he got the chance – was sure he observed in their actions the same rhythm and balance which entranced him when he saw fast open play.

Sometimes when he was off school and his father was away at a trail leaving his mother to look after the pub, then he would make their dinners – that is, go and buy four fish and two shillings worth of chips, set them out on the table with buttered bread and cakes, make a pot of tea and then have every right in the world to sit and watch them eat! And listen to them talk about Rugby. They rarely spoke of anything else.

When they had gone, Joseph went down to the cellars and checked that all his order had arrived. The making out of this order – done on Tuesdays, phoned through, confirmed by post – was tricky, and here he benefited from having worked in stores. Yet another part of his past which actively contributed to the present: he had thought of all those jobs as so many pegs driven uselessly into the ground – but now they held the guy ropes of his working life. The difficulty about the order (not a great but a real one) was, of course, to get it right. For to order too much meant that you risked having beer on your hands which had been untapped for too long and so was in danger of getting flat: to order too little was unthinkable. Yet to estimate on the amount sold in each department – mild, bitter, the bottled stuff, etc. – especially when you were improving trade and so could not refer to the previous week's figures and were not yet sure of the effect of seasonal variations (Christmas, Easter and Bank Holidays were comparatively easy to judge – but what about August when most men took their holidays in the town, more precisely, in the pubs? – or September when the coach-trips might or might not stop? or a week when there were three darts matches?) this took judgement which, though it might be of a limited order, yet shared with its more interesting relations all the intricate problems of nicety.

The order checked – there were three cellars, good-sized rooms – Joseph would relax and prepare to organize everything to his satisfaction. He liked the smell in the cellars: dank beer. A strong, plain, unvarying, unmistakable smell, which carried in it wood, hops, yeast, and the damp odours from the walls of many years the same. When you breathed in, deeply, the taste of beer swept into your lungs, and when you came upstairs you could feel it settled on your face. The organizing was quickly done: the crates piled in groups, some prepared for the empties, spirits and cigarettes locked in an old Welsh dresser, and then the barrels.

First, the cellar had to be kept clean. Archer had left it as he had found it and there were so many layers of cobwebs on the walls that they were like fish-nets slung there for effect. They had to be scrubbed down and then whitewashed and treated like that twice a year. The flagged floors were hosed and swept out every morning, in hot weather the barrels were sprayed with cold water and covered with damp sacking. It was important to know how to tap a barrel correctly: when, that is, to drive in the iron snout onto which were fixed the pipes. It had to be driven in with a mallet, preferably with one swing bursting the small brown ring which sealed the barrel. A slim peg in the top of the barrel – like the hole a whale breathes through – ventilated the beer and, at the same time, by the froth which came from its edges, indicated its temper.

Cleaning was the main thing. You had to rest on the assumption that the beer had been well-brewed. If Joseph thought it 'off', then he had no hesitation in knocking off the barrel, reporting it, and facing the consequences of an inspection. At that time there were few houses left which served directly from the wood, and few men who would go out of their way to have their beer thus served. For if the pipes and pumps were well attended to, the difference in the taste was unnoticeable to all except those rare men who really did sample beer as consideredly as connoisseurs sample wine.

The pipes were like hose pipes. They went from the barrels through the ceiling to the pumps – snaking up the middle of the cellars like tropical weeds which thrived in the dark, damp place. To clean them you unscrewed them, put them in a bucket of water and went up to the bar to draw through until the water was perfectly clear. Long and laborious work. The pumps had to be stripped down like any other machine: each part scrubbed, polished, re-fitted. It was not inspiring work, nor could it be rushed, but without its being regularly done, the beer suffered. Joseph knew that none of the landlords in the town took as much trouble as he did and, while never mentioning that to anyone, he felt good about it – for it was a fair triumph.

Moreover he hated the thought of anyone being served a pint which was 'off'. At the beginning of each day, he would examine the first glass by the light from the window and if it was not clear – throw it away: not into a slop bucket which would later feed low barrels on careless Saturday nights (funnelling in the profits while the moon shone) but down the sink. There was mileage, of course, in so public an act – for to see a pint of beer poured down the sink would certainly be remembered by the thirsty man who had ordered it, whose hand was still hanging out to receive it, whose gullet had opened in anticipation – but it was for his own satisfaction as much as for his public reputation that Joseph did it. He knew that he could look after beer properly and would not accept less than the due his work owed him.

Finally, he disliked serving a pint which had been over-pulled: which had as much beer on the outside of the glass as the inside. He taught Betty and everyone else who helped, including Douglas who looked near enough of age to pop behind the bar for an hour or two, how to pull a pint so that it would not spill. Glass well into the snout of the pump, angled about 45° towards you, first one long firm steady pull which should yield about half a pint, then straighten the glass slightly and with two shorter pulls, top it up, bringing the glass to a vertical position as the last bit went in. About a quarter of an inch of froth, starting just below the rim and then heaping above it, a lovely convex layer to cushion the lips.

Within a week, the beer was better: in a month it was good: after three months it was generally recognized so.

A day.

Late to rise, latest ever, a guilty eight o'clock for Joseph, perhaps even some minutes later, seven thirty for Betty for the boys' breakfasts: the other three moving around while he turned over once more. That lie-in until eight a real expression of privilege: the buses had pulled out with their workers on board, shifts long since started at the factory. The girls clattered up to the clothing factory, farmers coming for their breakfasts after first milking, Gilbert Little, Stan Oglonby and Henry Sharpe long since back from Carlisle with their fruit, the butchers taking in their meat, Arthur Middleton, Bert Toppin, confectioners ready to open, Miss Turner and Noel Carrick, papershops long in business, McMechans and Messengers – and himself still between the sheets. The luxury of that lie-in never palled and for it he traded in the rest of the waking day as work. The bedrooms, sitting room and bathroom were upstairs, the kitchen and pantry downstairs and the scent of razzling bacon filtered through the beer and house smells, the polish and flowers; his favourite smell, and he favoured in bed.

It was a pub-kitchen – licensed for drink though used by the publican and his family. Betty got the boys away, shouted for Joseph and then prepared breakfast for the two of them. Already she was a little tense. Before eleven-thirty – opening-time – there were the rooms to scrub, seats and tables to polish, the lobby to clean and the lavatories, four fires to get ready. Harry chopped a box of sticks every night. The steps to be ruddied. Douglas swept the front before going to school: sweat-breaking, people from the same school passing all the time, unfailingly moved to crude shouts which just missed retributive abuse by being tossed in the tone of wit. The upstairs to be dusted, beds made, perhaps the laundry sorted out. She had accepted to send sheets and clothes to the laundry after a struggle: the decisive argument was that there was nowhere to hang the stuff to dry, for though the pub had stables and outbuildings, these were all cramped around a tiny backyard – a catch-well for soot and also the area containing the Ladies and Gents – no one, Douglas insisted, wanted to dodge through a line of damp laundry to get to the lavatory.

Glasses, which had been washed the night before, were to be polished, the shelves dusted and tidied, brass to be rubbed – the coalman came; she had to slip across to Minnie's for a tin of something – and a dinner to be put on. Helen helped her from nine until eleven. But Betty's mind fled at the notion of someone helping *her* when she had spent years cleaning for others, and she went so far out of her way to make Helen's work light that it would have been marginally easier for her to have done it herself. (Helen stood back: she did not sympathize at all with Betty's passion for cleanliness which was becoming more determined under pressure.) In fact Betty was relieved whenever, as quite frequently, Helen pleaded a minor ailment and did not come. She went through the work at express speed. Joseph liked everything spick and waiting at eleven-thirty prompt: and she agreed with him principally because she did not like to be seen in the old and tatty clothes she kept for cleaning. So she raced and scudded around the pub, carrying before her two small rectangles of rubber, like prayer-mats, on which she kneeled. Upstairs quickly when the doors opened, to wash and change and be down by twelve-thirty so that she could relieve Joseph while he had his dinner.

His morning, though less frantic, was no less busy. Cellarwork, crates to carry up, bottles to put on, bar counter to be polished, backyard swilled, the arranging and re-arranging of teams for this and coaches for that. He had started up a darts team but as yet it had no great reputation (later he was to run two) and it was difficult to get people for away matches: transport to be arranged if the rival pub was not on a good bus route. The Thrush had also become the centre for the Hound Trailers: Joseph had known that they needed a pub. None of the other landlords in the town had sufficient patience to put up with the demands of hound-trailing men who needed impracticable-sized coaches at inconvenient times for all but inaccessible destinations. Or if the landlords had, their wives objected to the dogs which, starved before a race, would howl and quiver outside the pub or, brought inside by their indulgent owners, clamber over the seats without a chastening word, licking the polish off the table legs in their hunger. Or if the husbands had the patience and the wives the tolerance, then more likely than not a member of the executive committee of the local branch of the Hound Trailing Association would have an objection, a grudge wrapped up in a principle. In short the football team had a pub, so did the cricket team, the tennis lot went to one place, the Rugby club was very particular with its favours, so was the Round Table, the pigeon men found a home (in the British Legion) – but there was no place for the Hound Trailers. Joseph was promptly made secretary. This entailed collecting the subscriptions and doing the accounts because the treasurer was nervous about dealing in money, calling the meetings and often taking them because the chairman was either on night-shift or *at* a trail, going around to the houses of the committee members who found it impossible in season to break the training routine of their dogs, and, finally, laying on the coaches necessary to take men and beasts to sport. The recompense by way of increased trade was slight. But the chance the post gave him for legitimate attendance at a sport he loved was the real reward.

Betty was touched that the Labour Party decided to hold its committee meetings in the kitchen of the Thrush. And she was made to realize that she ought to be touched by receiving a copy of the pertinent resolution: 'Seeing that a former worker for our Party is now in a position to offer us a place of meeting at no expense, and seeing that the Temperance Hall costs us five shillings a time with proposed increase to six and sixpence, and seeing that the aforementioned former worker was a loyal worker and is the only landlady in this town who can be said to be openly in support of the ideals of this party, it is proposed in future to hold the Alternate Monday meetings in The Throstle's Nest kitchen. The Annual General and Extraordinaries will be discussed as they arise. Proposed C. Nye. Seconded. D. Muirhead.' Joseph suggested that she frame it. A private word with D. Muirhead beforehand had led to the understanding that there was no *obligation* on members to drink.

Bar and cellar work done, bills paid, coaches booked – all before eleven, Joseph changed and went up the town. There was always a reason – or excuse: the bank, bills, a word here, a chat there – but, like the lie-in, this walk up the main street, dressed in collar and tie, smoking a cigarette, unhurried, unpressed, was its own reward. It was not that he triumphed in not being at work – or perhaps, just a little – but the real satisfaction in that walk was that he gloried in himself. In being alive, cheerful, independent, walking, the sun, the clouds, hello, yes, there, now. On these strolls once more did he experience that ravishment by the external world though not now of things and shapes, colours and animals, but of people, their voices, gestures; and of the town itself.

When the doors did open it was here comes everybody. 11.30 a.m. prompt and he stood on the steps before his prize. Slight attitude of a pirate aboard a captured treasure ship: the engine-room below overhauled, decks swabbed, fresh stores, under his feet the swell, in his eye a twinkle of conquest.

Lunch-time trade – 11.30–3.00 – was slack. Even so he would see about a dozen or twenty men he knew, chat to them, have time to let their characteristics fasten on to the bottom of his mind. Some of the boyos came in and through payment for one pint got access to the dartboard where they practised carefully: a good darts player could keep himself in drink four or five evenings a week; go out, buy a first pint, stay in the pub all evening, never pay for another, play each game for drinks. Dido came and, older, slower now, decided it was as good as any and better than some and chose to stay. Sometimes a few of the men got out the dominoes – in time the domino school became quite regular at lunch-times and Dido became compulsive about it, his first indoor sport. The chief activity, however – for mid-day drinking was low-powered (except on market-day) more a passing tribute than an act of dedication – was in studying the racing pages, assessing the form and placing bets. A 'runner' came down twice, and if someone was stuck, Joseph was always prepared to nip across the street to the phone box and ring the bet through. He himself had a bet every day.

He began to carry around in his mind the people who came into the pub. They were in his house; his job was not only to give them drink but to see that they were happy there. Which is not to say that he played Mine Jolly Host; like every other landlord in the town, he had no time for that sort of affectation. When on the wireless or later on the T.V. he heard or saw such a Jolly Host, he was ashamed for the man. But the fact remained that he stood in a peculiar relation to those who came in. For many the pub was their parlour, they sat in the same seat, had the same type and number of drinks, said the same things, laughed at the same jokes – the pub had become an extension of their own houses. For others it was a place of liberty – where butts could be dropped on the floor, fantasies aired, opinions practised. There were as many reasons as customers, yet within each reason was a willingness to come to another's house: the phrases 'he keeps a good house', 'a poor house that', 'a quiet house' were accurate indications of this attitude. Pubs were 'houses' – and when a man came to your house you could not but be involved with him most closely.

In time, every single person who came was so well known to Joseph that he became a confidant, sometimes a confessor, often a source of material help, sometimes a scribe (particularly for income-tax forms which often caused a near-paralysis of panic) and always someone who could be talked to. Strange that from men who, as a rule, were dour and tight-lipped, who would often use the phrase 'I'm saying nothing: nothing,' and mean it: who found great difficulty in replying to the question of a doctor because they resented his interference and would go through weeks carrying an unspoken burden, who hibernated before icy blasts which might feelingly persuade them what they were – strange that of these men, not a few would tell to Joseph (to a landlord) facts and incidents withheld from wives, brothers, children, even mates. With no nervous demand of its being kept confidential: that was taken for granted.

There was, of many, a retired carpenter who came in at midday every weekday for a light and mild, ten Woodbines, a box of matches and a packet of crisps (on the counter before he had reached the bar, his stick-aided step clearly heard a few yards away): in the matter of the actual buying of drinks, there need have been no talk at all after the first month, for Joseph remembered what they had and few ever changed. He sat in the corner seat beside the fire, unfolding from deep in his coat a copy of the *Daily Express* which he would bend over, putty-rimmed glasses sliding to the tip of his nose, for all the world in his manner, and in the fine mould of his unindulged face, like an ancient scholar breathing life into yellowing parchment. After about half an hour, he would re-fold the journal, stand up at the bar, ask for a sheet of notepaper and then, in meticulous copper-plate, black ink, make out his bets. Never more than four and six (except for the Derby, the Oaks and the National) and all broken down into sixpences, so that with each-ways, doubles, trebles and accumulators the finished sheet would be crammed with names and figures. Had all his fancies come home, it would have rained sixpences for a fortnight.

To describe Mr Hutton's actions and moods would have taken Joseph a week: for he came to know every lift of the hand, the different moods of it as he raised the glass, knew what Mr Hutton was worth, what preoccupied him, what he had done, what he still wanted to do and who was in his will. Moreover, in imagination he could follow him through the town on his way home, knew how he acknowledged greetings, his feet shuffling to a stop, right foot turned outwards; could go into the butchers with him, worry about his dog, follow him home, see him in his blanket-covered armchair – the curl of one of the hairs on his left eye-brow like a lamb's tail. He knew the slight check in his expression when a remark was made which he disagreed with, quite another facial gesture when a remark was made which he both disagreed with and was incensed by, yet another when a remark was made with which he disagreed, was incensed by and moved to reply to, and another when a remark was made with which he disagreed, was incensed by and moved to reply to in tones of anger: yet another when all the foregoing forewent and his reply was phrased ironically ...

Three o'clock close, half an hour to sweep out, mop, dust, bank up the fires, check supplies, tea, read a little, shave again, wash down. Five-thirty open. (Unless he went to a Hound Trail.)

There was one thing in particular which he was consciously irritated by, yet, in that first year, incapable of doing much to remedy. He was too open. It was sometimes said that he was too honest. That is, when some of them asked how much he was making he would tell them. He was doing quite well: very well, in fact. He would never give any actual figures away but after deductions for fuel, light, waiters, help and so on, he and Betty together, from about 160 hours work, cleared between ten and fifteen pounds a week in that first year. Before tax. More than they'd ever had.

He had not been used to hiding his opinions and in his new situation saw no reason to change the habit: instead of pussy-footing about politics or religion, he said what he thought. In this he was unique among the town's landlords. In all things – about someone's action, a buy, a theft, a statement, a beating up, a piece of devious dealing – he always said what he thought; prided himself on it. But, being a landlord, he was particularly vulnerable to challenges to his openness: and there was a pressure to make it outspokenness, bombast, opinionated, a caricature. He never successfully dealt with this, however much he practised silence, turned a deaf ear, concealed not by deceit but by omission. A little grit there was, and could not be rubbed out.

Betty was in a similar position in that she was constantly being told (by her woman friends) that she was 'too nice'. This was said with more than a touch of criticism. Yet she acted in no way differently from the way in which she had acted before. Less tough than Joseph, she sometimes felt that her removal to the pub had unleashed a Pandora's box of jealousy, spite, mutterings around the town: and she could not but think that this was the necessary price to be paid. Yet her spirit flared up against the injustice of some of the direct criticism she heard; and in some way, thrown to defend herself (which she was timid of doing, but not afraid to do) she came to entrench herself more positively in the pub and the way Joseph had chosen. To be committed to it.

Which was as well, for her evenings as her days were spent working in it. She either waited on in the kitchen or helped behind the bar. And she looked for ways to reconcile herself to the new life. Certain phrases, often clichés, which bore on their backs much of the weight of what she thought, fitted her need perfectly.

'Nobody's different' – that merciless egalitarianism which could sound almost brutal and yet somehow accommodate and approve of distinctions in style, manner and behaviour (for the Queen had privileges which Betty would defend day and night and yet, co-existing with this, there was a deeper belief, though but secretly referred to, that even *she* was not 'different'). 'Nobody's different' therefore everybody had to be treated alike – 'whatever you think of them'. She did not like some of the people who came in, would, in private say so plainly and, however hard she tried to disguise it in public, reveal it most patently to those who knew her. But the principle was practised despite challenges which sometimes threatened to overwhelm it, and in the struggle she became firmer in her attitudes. Far from being persuaded that such a turning of the other cheek and blessing those who cursed was impracticable, she saw that without such an idea she would not be able to go on for a day in such a job; while there were always sufficient examples of people changing their attitudes and behaviour to show her how much more supple was the principle than any number of decisive 'practical' judgements. There must be no favourites, and no swearing. Here Joseph objected for her. There was little she could do about it: she hated swearing and always had. It made her feel dizzy, the blood thinned: and again, she did not see why people had to swear in public. If they wanted to, they could do it at home.

Most of all, she was against fights and trouble. Joseph did not like them either. They upset the entire pub, left a bad taste on the evening, frightened people and were bad for trade. 'For every hard man that walks in,' he said to Harry, 'two good customers go out!' Again there was the underpinning of what he believed in by what was good for business; which appeared as a contradiction.

Stopping those fights was a nasty and dangerous business. The town was full of people who went out on Saturday nights expecting trouble and looking for it. There were quarrels between families: there were often gangs of men (sometimes Irish, sometimes Geordies) working on the roads or building the new Secondary Modern school or doing a season of farm work in the area – and they moved in a bunch, challenging attack. Moreover, Carlisle's pubs were state-controlled and at this time allowed no singing: a singing-room was essential to a pub in Thurston, with a regular pianist, Fridays, Saturdays and Sundays, and gangs used to come through from Carlisle for the singing. Again, Thurston had a large, generally rowdy, dance on Saturday nights with quite well-known bands: this attracted a lot into the town, and tanking up beforehand was essential. On Saturdays, Thurston rang and shook and it was a very rare publican who did not take four times as much as on any other night.

Douglas watched these Saturday fights, tense and entranced. After the first house of the pictures. Too young to go to the dances yet. And wanting to be in the pub, to be frightened out of his skin. In bed. A supper tray. The meat and potato pie which they sold at weekends, an apple, some sweet, wireless on, fiddling for pop on Luxembourg, ready at any moment to flick down the volume and rush to the top of the stairs to see what was going on. If seen there, white-faced, pyjamas baggy, full of thoughts of murdering those fighting – then sent back: to peep between the banisters or run through his room to the window where he could see the fight go on across the road, on to the hill. Harry slept through it all.

Betty too was terrified. Yet because of appearances, she would not allow the one thing which could have helped them. Joseph wanted the telephone in. For the bets, for business, especially for Saturday nights when he could then phone up the police. She would not have it. Under no circumstances, yielding to no argument: a telephone, like a car, would, she thought, be a clear and justified object of scorn and envy. She wanted neither. So they were locked in the place when trouble started; for Joseph could not leave to go across to the phone box, nobody volunteered. It marked you – calling in the police. People were afraid to be the one who had called in the police. Nor was Joseph happy to have them around; it would always be held against him that he could not control matters himself, had to get in the Law. *His* authority would be the weaker for it. In that respect, though it contradicted common sense, he was glad that Betty was so adamant about the telephone: for had they had it, then for her sake he would have used it. It was a relief to be able to deal with it himself. Of course, if one of the three policemen who were on duty on Saturday nights happened to be near the pub and came in – that was fair, all in the game. The odds against it were high; sixteen pubs, a dance-hall (two needed there), drunks and the shop doors to check; more than twenty to one.

It was something that he had to deal with himself. In two ways, he was handicapped. Firstly, if he himself got into a fight and was brought up for it, then whatever provocation could be proved, he risked having his licence taken away. Secondly, he knew the men too well. He had been among them until a few months ago. Not as a trouble-maker, and very rarely in the fight; but certainly around. And because of that they thought they could get away with it. Pubs did not change hands very often in Thurston, and most of the younger men who started the fight had been brought up with the present landlords already in power. Authority rested in them from being those who drew the fathers away, pied pipers, magicians, whatever; important men. Not so Joseph. The very circumstances which assured him of an early inquisitive influx also made for a feeling that you could do what you liked down at the Thrush. Moreover, despite the strictness, even severity, of Joseph's 'rules-to-himself', he was a very easy man to get on with; since the age of ten he had knocked around and worked with men and survived with his own ideas about himself bruised but not flattened. This ease, again, invited exploitation. 'Good old Joe – remember when he ...' 'And that time we all went to ...' And *he* remembered and he had been, but there was a different choice now: if he let them have their way, they would take over. That was the fact.

When the fight began, like a glass container under Betty's skin the phial of security and decency broke into fragments. Panic powdered her veins. But Joseph would *not* be driven away from the pub. She cried and dreaded: to herself, but he who loved her had no need of tear-stains on pillows to know. Neither would *she* be driven away. It became a test of her faith in Joseph and her own sense of justice. It was wrong, she thought, for people to come and upset everyone: and if you gave in to them, they would think they could just get away with it with anybody. So though she shivered and had difficulty in keeping herself from fainting – she would not leave for this trouble.

Usually it started in the singing-room. Often over a woman. There were women who came in worse than the men: harridans from the times when it was common in working-class pubs to see women waist-stripped fighting each other, men in a circle egging them on. Times thought to be past: here, only just submerged, like fire in peat, ready to flare again any time. Three or four of them mothers of the men who fought: the men, often in trouble, one or two of them been in Durham jail for three or six months. More stupid than malicious, Joseph maintained: and how could you expect anything other the way they were brought up? Betty excused, with dry bread and jam for all meals. Kicked through the Catholic school and left to roam ever unattended around town and country – often truly looking for food out of hunger.

In the singing-room, glasses break, a woman starts to scream, the music stops. Joseph out of the bar instantly: locking Betty and the two women waiters in it, behind him. With Frank and Tommy, the two men who helped to wait on, straight into the singing-room. Helped by the room being small. Not much real fighting could be done in that space. Girl-friends, people pushing them away; pushing out: furniture baulking, and checking when tables full of drinks go over. Two men in a corner, one holding the lapel of another, bashing his solar plexus with the free hand; the other an arm around the man's neck, trying to grab the striking fist.

Smile, laugh, joke a bit as you go through. Always around the fighters the two or three trying to 'stop it', half-waiting to get in it, a hindrance. Joseph – trying to lighten it – come on lads. One sentence very clear: 'If you want to fight – fight outside.' Repeat. Repeat. As a proposition without a flaw. 'If you want to fight, fight outside.' Clear the room as much as possible: a passage. Then – suddenly dive on them, pull them up together, shout – 'You're going outside! That's that! Now come on!' Dangers: – pub might think it unwarranted interference: if the dive makes your man lose his grip, liable to be dived on yourself. Also, fighters might like excuse to combine and turn on someone else – at this stage everybody hates the landlord: – because he's stopping it; or because he isn't.

Joseph was not going to stand back and let them wreck the place in front of his eyes. A bubble of hubbub from the corridors. What's happening? Who's winning? Tom, a tough little fella, who waits on in the darts-room, used to box – flyweight – in the army: a contender for Northern Command title – wants a crack. Joseph has to leave two men, now humping and swinging more freely – more room now – and warn him off. Tom would make it worse.

Easy now to lose his temper and swing in: so they might hammer him: so what? His body had been hammered many a time. At least there would not be the strain of knowing that everyone might just possibly think he was a coward: and that he might just possibly agree with them. Get right in and *join* in. Want to. Want to now. Hell! – enjoying watching the fight. There'll always be fights. If he took one, Tom would have a go at the other. But consider – a second this – less than – consider – a real scrap: and then all the hard men from miles around would come in to have a go. You can't beat all of them. Nothing friskier than a scrapper for a landlord: like a man on a high-wire: everybody rolls up to see the fall.

He, Tom and Jack, together, grab the two men, leave them locked together, push them to the door – blows, on his face – don't retaliate – push, push. Into the corridor – friends coming in on both sides: bottle-neck in the corridor. Now, like a scrum, turn your back to the pack, bar door locked, slam the door of the darts-room – no escape – only the front door, bend your legs and push. Enjoyable again, wink at a fellow watching it all, maybe strike up 'Yo-o-heave ho' – people laugh – the street outside waiting for the fighters – push, push, heave. Out on to the street, down the steps, a big fight now – slam the door and bolt it.

The sorting out of the pub afterwards. Douglas at the window above, curtains flung back, white-faced looking down, fists clenching, his mind shuddering.

Then the men responsible had to be barred. The publican had the right not to serve. Knowing this, the men would make it their business to come down soon afterwards, usually early Monday evening when it was quiet. 'Just a minute, Joe, just a minute.' The two of them into an empty room. Sorry. *He* started it – never again. Another chance. And, depending, sometimes Joseph *would* give another chance. Or he would merely bar the man from going into the singing-room. In those first months, however, he barred more than twelve from ever coming into the pub again. Eight more were barred for six months. It was even more delicate a situation than the first time he had gone into the singing-room. For the men involved in fights were rough, they had a way of fabricating combative tension out of very little. Joseph, small and sturdy like his father, was patient unless long provoked. To stand alone in an empty room, early evening grey outside the windows, the men in the bar silent, listening, and Joseph determined not to give in – it was not something to wake up in the morning looking forward to. And always it ended in the same way: somehow Joseph avoided a fight on the spot and the man would slam out with the words that he would 'get him'. Neither an empty nor an idle threat. The pub was broken into three times in the first year. Walking up the street when the gangs were propping up the walls, late morning, passing them, very much like running a gauntlet, mutters, attitudes, a shout when he was past, spit on the pavement. Douglas saw him walk this way, was himself buttonholed by some of the men – 'Tell yer father he'd better tek us back,' 'Why's yer father barred us then, eh? He's a sod. Go on, say it. He's a sod.'

Joseph scarcely if at all considered the effect all this would have on the two boys. It did not seem to him to be unduly rough. He had expected it, seen worse. But Douglas saw his mother shiver when she got up on Sundays to clean out the Saturday mess, and he shivered with her: Harry knew that his father had not raised a fist, understood, admired, and then despised, condemned him. Whereas if he ever even thought of it, Joseph could not but remember that on his fourteenth birthday he had been sent away to labour, up at five-thirty, a fourteen-hour day: men around to perform brutal circumcision.

Many times, of course, both of them, Harry in particular,

loved the pub. Harry especially liked the early weekday evenings when he whipped through his homework (never a long job for him) and went down, leaving Douglas in sole possession of the upstairs part of the house, locked in his bedroom, lashing into his books as if knowledge could be flailed out, like corn, whipped away from those stems of learning. Most nights for four, five, even six hours, Douglas would be there, muttering poetry, blasting against Latin, singing at the top of his voice sometimes as he discovered something he liked or wrote a passage which had gone well, alternately ecstatic or miserable; slightly mad.

Joseph most liked the early evening. Here the work came at a relaxed pace. Later, when it grew busy, he would accelerate and move very quickly, for he never liked to keep anyone waiting for a drink. As with the keeping of his beer, this was inspired by a regard for a personal standard: people must be served right away. Working behind the bar with him at a busy time was hectic; hellish, sometimes. He demanded the same speed from everyone – and the same rapidity at adding up the figures: furious at delays when someone else was pottering about at the till and he was there, waiting to change a note. Betty often turned her back on the bar, pretending to sort through the glasses, really to regain her balance. But it was exciting working with him – the movement in the tiny bar-space was like dancing when they were busy, rapidly dipping for bottles, pulling the beer, swinging around to the till, knocking the small glasses against the spirit measures, loading the trays.

One thing Joseph had privately dreaded more than a little did not happen. The clinging attitude of George. But George did not want a home, he wanted a base. For the first time in his life, he now had one. He could surge around the town alone, or even with Helen and be secure everywhere – because there was always Joseph's place to go back to for comfort and supplies of confidence. He would never get drunk in the Thrush – such was his fear of being barred. If trouble threatened – he would hop it quick. Besides, he could not monopolize Joseph's attention when there were other customers there, and as he continued to see his friendship with Joseph as being very special to both of them, this rather affronted him. Yet there was nothing he could do about it. Therefore by being rather sparing in his visits to the pub, he thought to emphasize his uniqueness, to assure himself of a warm welcome, to claim legitimate personal attention for a while and to confirm his unchangeable rolling-stone independence.

It was a great relief.

Lester, left school, driving a lorry for a lemonade firm, was someone Joseph could not see enough of. Lester had taken up sport professionally and went all over the place to run, often cadging a lift in the Hound Trail buses as sports meetings were often held at the same place as the trails. Joseph and he enjoyed each other's company: he found that if Lester did not come into the place for a few days, he would miss him.

The pub closed at ten, swept out, glasses washed, Betty away to make supper – then Douglas would come downstairs, taking ten minutes off from his own work to help his father count up. Count the sixpences, threepenny pieces, the silver and the copper, neat piles, ten, twelve, eight, forty. Knowing that this was the boy's tribute, Joseph let him help – though he disliked anyone but himself having to do with the money. Strange, this silent counting, miserly in appearance yet neither of them at all moved by the money. Joseph pleased as he did the day's accounts if the sum was greater than the week before – but the pleasure came from the figures which represented work and victory: not from the cash which was the reward. The bold figures in those small blue cash-books – almost a diary.

A cup of tea, sandwiches, Betty reading her 'book' – a magazine – Douglas, hair long and tangled by his hands, face nervous and exultant at once, his mother's fatigue pricking a tirade of bloody remarks the effect of which brought replies equally lancing. The bursts of argument, the pits of silence, Betty soothing them by reading from the personal column or from an advertisement in the 'book'. The pub in darkness now, top dirt off, waiting for the morning clean. In the town almost all the lights off.

Leadenness along the veins in the legs now. Betty quite

suddenly white-faced and drained. Joseph sat holding a cup of tea, reading a novel, alone in his own family. This was all. And if what had seemed new territory now looked like any other stretch of land, this was all he could do. His stand, his yes, his no to the world.

Chapter Thirteen

Betty could not be bothered to put on the light. She sat there in the upstairs room – called the living-room or the lounge or most frequently, the upstairs room – almost huddled in the sofa, watching the dark clouds massed outside the window. She sat as if trying by an act of will to *make* this room into the centre of the house. The downstairs kitchen was a thoroughfare, people coming in to see Joseph while they were having tea, staying, table quickly cleared before opening time, no centre, no focus. She wanted them all to be together as once they had been: though even before there had been lodgers, half-'brothers', friends staying, but yet for a little while the four of them had lived as an ordinary family. There was a piano there and Douglas had played; gone to lessons, sat for examinations set by the Trinity College of Music, collected certificates (at his insistence, unframed) and then suddenly stopped playing. No one could persuade him to go on. Couldn't even play the latest tune now; couldn't even help out if a wedding party arrived without a pianist and needed entertainment. Waste of money, Joseph said. They both said, to be fair.

Also in the upstairs room, the tea-chest with broom-stick and thick string which Harry pretended was a double-bass when he played in a skiffle group. Sitting there in the corner; could be used as a packing case, hint of moving.

The room had nothing 'lived-in' about it. Joseph never set foot in it. She had hoped he might do his accounts there on Sunday afternoons, but the bathroom was large and he preferred to work in there. The boys had made dens of their bedrooms, small forts they were, and they never thought to come into the upstairs room for longer than an obligatory minute – both of them realizing that their mother so wanted them to come in, neither enjoying it. There was an electric fire, both bars on, a rather stern three-piece suite, a bookcase, a sideboard, the piano, not much room to move in and everything rather badly placed, clean but spiritless. A gloomy room. Betty felt that she was saving it from death by coming in and sitting there. But when she got in she was intimidated; this neglected, heartless room was so like the life which faced her, and whispered intimations of that life came from the walls. She had come into the room to calm herself, to pin-point her anxiety and dispel it – but she found that her mind drifted quite aimlessly.

She would have liked a more ordinary life. More people had better wages now: Joseph served men in the bar who made about as much as he did after fewer hours of work. She was relieved at that; a balance had been in some measure restored. Friends of hers from school now took regular holidays, one or two even had cars, the women would get a new winter coat, wages coming in from the children made a tidy heap on the kitchen table Friday evening. If Joseph had stayed at the airfield or even on insurance, then they would have had a quiet, pleasant life.

Maybe the boys would have been less well off and Douglas might have left school: but she would not have minded that in the least. She would have preferred him to have been an engineer, something like that, where he mixed with everybody else and had a wage, maybe a motor-bike, got out to dances more often. If he wanted to stay on at school, it was fine: but she wished he had wanted something else. Even when the result had come through the last year – that he had won a scholarship to Oxford: even then, behind the pleasure, there was pain that now he would irrevocably be lost to what she did not understand. And Harry was determined to leave school at sixteen anyway, whatever happened. It would not have changed him at all to have had less money available.

Weary, weary she was. As if her life was over though in years it was little more than half-way done. Girls on the street outside, and the heavy shoes of the men walking up the pavements into the town. This town she had run through, retreated from, embraced again – now it came into her house and there was no escape but to this empty upstairs room.

Yes, the old men from the Home which used to be called the workhouse brought her the oranges they were given at Christmas. Joseph let them sit in the bar throughout the lunch-time, often giving them free the one half-pint which was all they allowed themselves so that they could have the fire and the company before trudging back up to the beds in the communal wards. Very clean it was up there; they were given good meals. Well looked after. So why did the thought of it stop her mind like the clang of a broken bell? Such nice old men, some of them – wanly she saw their faces superimposed on the dark window – all well looked after.

The young tough guys who would risk everything in fervour of their sense of victory or vengeance – it was to her they came for advice about their girl-friends and their parents. Alone in the kitchen, low-voiced – 'but really, Mrs Tallentire, when I get a few, I just feel like killin' them all. I nearly killed her again last night. She says she'll leave me, Mrs Tallentire. Talk 'til her, eh? *You* talk 'til her. She likes comin' here. And I'm nivver any trouble in here, am I, Mrs Tallentire?' Maybe because she called them by their full Christian names when all others spat out the nickname or a handy truncation. More likely because she had no advice to give. Trapped, they came to another likewise trapped: smelling out the one who could not help but, who could not refuse.

So she had never done any one thing dishonest on any day of her life. Was ill at the thought of Harry leaping on the trains to Carlisle as they moved out, and ducking out at the other end to avoid the fare. Sent him to the station with the money. Yet Douglas had rounded on her – 'There is no God, it's all propaganda to keep you in your place. Your place is wherever you want to be, mother. Don't let them cheat you.' Weary this load of honesty, fairness, truthfulness, duty, cheerfulness, loyalty, carefulness, self-reliance now seemed. But dreadful and terrifying the abyss with those bridges burned.

She tried not to think of her body. Lying in the bed: Joseph making love to her. That was too secret, too sacred, perhaps.

But the skin was still firm, and when she walked it teased her to push through, push through this self-spun web.

Would not go through. Watched Helen now in fascination and saw the freedom – saw also the sacrifice, the daughter Aileen dumpy, desultory, refusing to follow her mother but unable to find her own way. Fattening as a resistance, a disguise – slowly obliterating herself in heaviness of mind and body. Tailing around Harry most hopelessly with a cringe in her eyes, never erased, made more poignant by his kindness.

Would not go through with the loneliness in the room now. Adrift, feeling so old that she now had boys who would soon be leaving her forever; and this body curled on the couch would soon wither. Looking at her hands – bruised red by the work – she could remember when they were slim-fingered, dainty, that day in the park when she had caught her finger-nail and it had come off. How old then? Nine? Eight? She could see the black finger end, feel the numbness and the pleasure come from waggling the dead nail, like rocking a loose baby-tooth. Dashing back through the town, the pain long gone, holding up the hand like a flag. Yesterday. And tomorrow? – the *weight* of tomorrow.

She heard Joseph calling her. It was not so much that he needed her to help at this hour, but he liked her there. In this working together perhaps he had found a communion. Whatever he had found, she must see that he kept it. And get changed. Stand – it was as if she had to command herself to do that. Stand. Put on the light. Close the curtains. Go to wash and change. Remember Harry's rugby things, remember there were the pies to order for Thursday's darts match, remember the blue glint and laugh in Joseph's eyes as he had swung up to her house on that tandem, remember Douglas crying to have a bandage on his knee though he was not hurt – why had he done that? – remember Mary, her best friend, who had left the town a few years ago and lived down south, going on holidays even at Christmas, it was her birthday soon, remember how often she had longed to talk to Douglas and found no words, remember how she had trembled as she put on lipstick for the first time and Joseph had said – 'better than Gloria Swanson' –

remember her 'mother' who in due measure had loved her, and the way the church looked before they cut down the trees, remember Joseph's father crying at the memorial service after the war, Douglas crying when he lost his first girl, herself crying when Joseph was away in the R.A.F. – would Douglas have to go and fight now in their new war? – and why are you crying here, woman at the mirror in the cold bathroom?

The first hour of the evening. Rare for anyone to come in for longer than a few minutes. The bar smelling of polish, brown wood shining, the oak wall-clock ticking slowly, deliberately. The rubber mat behind the bar still damp from the afternoon swabbing. Shelves full. Joseph pulled himself half a pint: he had all but stopped drinking since taking on the pub, the work demanded a clear head. There was a high green stool which he had had made for him and he sat on it, reading the paper. On the front, the headline that the British army was going into Suez.

He read the news once more – turned to another part of the paper, but again and again came back to it. Harry had already made up his mind – raged against Eden and the Tories for doing this and tried to quench Joseph's flickerings of patriotism and that low crackle mixed of patience and inquisitiveness with which he approached it. Douglas, now in Scotland occupying himself on National Service by shooting blanks, could well be involved if things dragged on as they often did – yet Joseph could not see that, could not see it being more than a skirmish though the hollowness of the prediction ran back through many such and had always been mocked. But Betty would be upstairs, worrying about him.

Joseph could not honestly claim to be worried about Douglas's personal safety. He was more uneasy than anything else: he felt no excitement, no sense of a cause, and yet you supported your own lot if they needed you, didn't you? Not if they were wrong, said Harry. And he had little defence but reciprocal rhetoric just as over-reaching and generalizing as Harry's.

Chiefly, he felt sickened. Another war, more men to be killed, and most of them the ordinary people who'd no hand in the big decisions and all of it played in the shade of the atom bomb. He did not like to feel that the world was mad – hardly any other description had force before the facts. He had met his father in the town in the afternoon – seventy-five John was now, still working, perhaps a little more open to the temptation of retirement but prepared to consider it only if he himself raised it – and there had been no question. Yes, we should go in. Give them a good thump. Hope Douglas and the lads got a crack at them. In a hurry. Quiet nod and away. And then Joseph had realized how myopic he was – between the blind certainty of his father and the wide-eyed convictions of his son.

Like weary dolphins the old question heaved through his mind. Why did men fight? Why could there not be peace? What was the point of anything if there would always be war to destroy all points? He realized now that he had felt this when he himself had gone to war – but had disguised it under timid reflexes of jingoism, buried it firmly underneath his own needs – to get away, start again, trod it down in the name of justice. But, if called, and if he believed in the cause – as in 1939 he had certainly done – he would go again. Which was why those questions came through his mind so exhaustedly, for there were no answers.

He knew his feelings but could not direct them on to a way or thought of life which satisfied him. Between, between; that was his fortune. Between necessity and ease, ignorance and knowledge, confusion and clarity. The past and the future, father and son, met in him and threatened to eat him away.

Patrick O'Brien came in. Liked the full Christian name used. Pint of porter, ten Woodbines and a box of Swan Vestas. Red scarf around his neck. Trilby back from his brow. Builder's labourer. Five children of his own, two more of his wife's from the times she had left him, and now was another such time. To which he raised his glass. Joseph saw the light broken through the froth which lined the top of it. Douglas's last letter – a mate sent to the glasshouse for pinching spuds. Patrick did a stint of tatie-pickin' in the season. Did anything. Believed very seriously in formal conversation. Stood and supped and thought of a formal remark. Did Joseph know that despite hundreds of years of research there had been found no cure for the Common Cold? Had to say no. Yes or no would have been the same, for Patrick ignored the reply and asked for the racing page – his self-respect another day intact. 'The Common Cold,' he added, as he picked up the paper, and he used the two words to feel his way into the palm of fortune as he looked at the runners, 'the Common Cold. Yes – done it again – a mare, "Cold Comfort", 12 to 1.' That was the bet. And a cover on the favourite. No complaints.

Mr Wallace, a Guinness for his health (he was 83) and half an ounce of Brown Twist because he didn't see why he shouldn't. Every day this challenge was thrown to the gods, still unanswered. Joseph grinned as he turned to serve him – that white moustache, like cat's fur, combed and petted for the flattering thing it was. Mr Wallace would shrivel away, but still, he imagined, the moustache would be silky and fat until at the last it would lie across his face like a well-kept smile. Lucky. Same again?

Now Teddy Graham, worked in the estate agent's office, just a quick one, just a quick one, light ale, light ale – close, isn't it? close – how much is that? how much is that? same as yesterday? ha-ha, ah, tastes good, very good, just another, just another, same as yesterday, same as yesterday? and ten Seniors, ten Seniors. Tweed suit: collar too tight: horn-rimmed spectacles: small feet. A man to be impressed, Patrick thought, to be engaged in conversation – now take the Common Cold . . .

Farmers from the market, a group, loud, booted, walking-sticks and whisky; a little boy for two packets of crisps with three empty bottles and the men from the Old Folks' Home – the news? The news? – Take two days, Arabs – they are Arabs aren't they? can't fight, with them in the desert – make it a light ale this time, light ale, light ale, – how much is that? Same as yesterday. Same again?

Yes, the Hound Trail bus leaves at 3.15 for Rowrah. It'll be a walkover exercise for my lads. Betty – Betty – hurry up, need a hand, a rush on.

Joseph whirled around the three occupied rooms, serving out

the drink as expertly as a gambler shuffles cards. Betty came down, smiling. One flesh. Lucky. Joseph nodded to her. Brushed his fingers across her arm. Knew she was worrying about Douglas. It would work out.

Same again?

It was easy to reassure her in the pub. The fact that the private gesture took place in public made it easy. For alone together they rasped against each other ceaselessly: they were compelled to live and act in the same place and condemned by custom, habit and the fear of others' judgements to be united; like twin ball-bearings set in motion with oil to lubricate them but the oil had run away. In the few private moments they allowed themselves, each nudge or pulse of mood, each gesture and attempt scraped.

Only in the public place could they show affection and then there was the bitterness of knowing it needed others to help them even like each other. Joseph saw it everywhere: dozens of men had no more than passing remarks to give to their wives: between bed and the bus; between work and the pub; between the house and the match – at the necessary junctions an inevitable sign, the more unthinking the better. It was a desolate expression of the effects of matrimony and he comforted himself sometimes by thinking that you only saw the failures in the bar, those who'd run away: for he wanted to think there was a Happy Land and Marriage had once been that place. Where now?

It was words which failed them, he thought. They could not speak but to remind each other of hurt and disappointment and the misting of the vision which each, as orphans, had polished so brightly in the silence of a chaste adolescence. They could bear neither to be with nor to be without each other. Only moments remained; sometimes weeks would pass and then a light would cause an ember to glow, perhaps a spark would flicker and be extinguished, and that was all that remained of the love into which they had poured every hope and ambition. Having no other deposits and being unarmed with the resilience and irony of self-knowledge, they had tried to capture and claim instinct.

Even Douglas who might have brought them together only defined yet again their separate arenas: in him each of them scored out a territory and declared it a total and private bond; and he was so used to the division that he needed it and went to seek metaphors for it within his mind and in the world. His only reply to them might come in the fiction he was trying to make: this necessary lie his weapon to attack their fears which pulled at him or lay on his face, quivering, smothering.

As with the pub, the town, the news, the customers, the world and their son they found most joy and most relief (the two becoming synonymous) when least personally engaged. They had stretched themselves fully, as they thought, in the marriage and were left outstretched by it. To this exhaustion they attributed a cause – their overwork – and were saved by it as it wore them out.

There came the time when they could not even remember the candles on the chestnut tree that had shaken so violently in the wind when they had looked up after making love in the rain; could not taste the earlier skin, the mouth, nor see the shy glances of desire; shed the other in dreams and in sleep went further back to those root rejections and disruptions which they had sought to correct and heal but failed.

Silently they stripped each other, privately they attacked, publicly held firm and talked of Douglas and Harry late at night in phrases so mild as to lack all passion: but had they said what they wanted they soon would have said nothing. And there were still some matters worth the sacrifice.

Chapter Fourteen

Harry was in his glory. Mid-afternoon, a Saturday in summer, bringing in the last crop of hay. A hot sun sucked the smells from the earth: he could have fallen on his face and let it suffocate him. He had taken off his shirt and the white, rather wandy body rose smoothly from the clammy blue jeans, the thinnest coat of sweat smoothing the skin still more, emphasizing the fluency of his movements.

He was seventeen, been left school almost a year now and had worked on this farm throughout that time. It was where his 'grandfather' John was hired, about three miles from Thurston. He biked to and from work daily, unwilling to sleep at the farm as he would have done even one generation ago. The prospect of spending long evenings in the farm kitchen had been his only reservation about the job. It had not been difficult to find a place nearby. John had recommended him – and that was that: a short meeting with the farmer (it could not be called an interview) where each had stared at the other in embarrassment, terminated by Mr Dawson's abrupt 'So thou's set on it?' and Harry's 'Just about.' He had been hired – though that word stuck in his throat and when asked what he did would never use it: 'farm-work' he said.

Betty and Joseph were a little bewildered by his choice, but kept it to themselves. Since telling Harry they were not 'really' his parents, they had felt shy and, unaccountably, a little ashamed in front of him. Sometimes it seemed to Betty that he had taken the work on as a challenge to their love; for occasionally when he returned from work his very entrance would seem to demand 'tell me I've been wasting my time' – longing for this to be stated so that he could refuse it. But she held her peace. She was not in the slightest worried what job he took, as long as it was honest work. For neither of the boys had she any pecuniary or social ambition whatsoever. She saw that Harry was generally cheerful, looked well on this outdoor work, had plenty to say for himself and was always left with enough energy after a day's work to gobble down his tea and be out in the town. It was this energy which reassured her: given that it was allied to a character which was not harmful – and Harry's was transparently such a character – then she believed that it could be relied on; more than any other characteristic, energy was a virtue, she thought.

It was agreeable to her that both Douglas, now back from his National Service and preparing for university, and Harry – by working at a long learning job like farming – shared somehow in the outward form of apprenticeship.

The tranquillity of her attitude had affected Harry and helped erode the bravado which had led him to farm-work. This was the first hay-timing he had done as a fully paid worker on the farm: and it would be the last.

But it was marvellous to be doing the work. Stabbing the fork in the shuffle of hay, twisting the prongs to grip, lifting with a quick scoop and long swing on to the wagon where Sheila took it and pressed it down. He had never felt so well in himself and almost resented the impulse which was leading him to change his job. Yet, after a year of it, he had realized the inadequacy of doing something in order to contradict a reasonable expectation. So this hay-timing was a valediction; and yet he wished it was not so.

There were seven of them in the field and they moved without rushing, indolently it might have seemed. In the case of John, and Vernon, 'the married man', the indolence lightly masked a very concentrated effort; they displayed with ease what had been gained with difficulty. Among the others, there was real laziness. The day was too fine to squander in toil: there was just the one field left and no worry about bringing it in dry; and once the edge of urgency on such a job was blunted, then laziness was almost demanded by the nature of what was being done. For if you did not drive in the fork fast and whip the hay over quickly, ramming the dead grass into the trailer like coals into a steam engine – then the next best thing was not to do it just a little more slowly but altogether differently: the same jab and scoop certainly, but with pauses between to chat, look around, watch the others. Watch Sheila.

Harry loved to emphasize the lotus-eating pace of this work: for at home, in the pub, it was all bustle and rapid actions, snatches and quick additions, the drive to get the customers served because 'people must not be kept waiting'. Here the waiting had been done in the rain; and now that the sun shone, the hay itself would wait. Unless you were used to fierce and economic work, as his grandfather was, then it was much better to go as easily as possible. You lasted longer. And there was something grand in going about it so slowly. The day was hazy and in the distance the first line of fells could be seen a soft blue-grey: from the mosses a few miles north came the smell of sea; tractors puttered as cosily now as the smack of leather on willow this Saturday afternoon.

Dawson himself drove one of the tractors. 'Young' Dawson. He had taken over the land from an austere and hard-working father with whom John had been hired for over twenty years and was fat, genial, spoilt and 'bloody useless', John pronounced, as much in admiration as scorn. Sheila was his daughter, fifteen, reluctantly girdling herself for one last year at school: Dawson thought that the easiest way for him to keep her occupied during that leap in the dark, which promised to be short, between gym-slip and wedding white. Harry had seen her at the farm for years; he had often worked there in his school holidays. But the week before this, she had walked down to the field in which he and Vernon, 'the married man' (it was almost a surname) had been clearing a ditch. He had watched her walk from the top of the field, every step seeing her, as he later told Vernon 'for the first time': the tight red jeans stuffed into shiny black wellingtons, the white shirt open-necked holding breasts so soft and steady that the slightest movement trembled them while yet the most active movement could not disturb their firmness; he had watched and seen her long brown hair lift and fall at her shoulders, a cloak to her white neck, and he had felt himself go dry; only Sheila could quench such dryness.

She had agreed to 'go' with him a few days later, and this Saturday night was to be their first real date – at the early show in the Palace Cinema, Thurston.

He had had a number of girl-friends. Letters in school, S.W.A.L.K. pencilled hurriedly on the back; a code to puzzle no-one. First he had gone with Marjorie Barton; then been keen on Lena Brown. Contact – negligible; averted glances in the corridors, giggles from the girls at the milk-crate, forlorn appointments kept by himself alone, speculative bike-rides ending at a row of terraced houses with the house number forgotten, lace curtains drawn against the Sunday-afternoon silence. Occasionally a few kisses after a dance, disturbed petting in the pictures, a brief partnership at a social.

Until now, Harry had not launched himself at girls as Douglas did: perhaps the rapacity of his elder brother had pushed Harry towards the other extreme. For though Douglas had been settled with the same girl for two years now, at Harry's age he had made forays enough to become a passing lordling, limited, but in local regard, a legend. Harry had sometimes felt that he was taking the blame for this when his turn came. But it was more than that. For whereas Douglas could articulate an impulse immediately, Harry burned more slowly and often when the flame showed through the wind had changed and it flickered out in the cool air.

Like the lady of the lake, Sheila had raised her arm through the waters holding the promise of knowledge by conquest. Many times, in those few days, Harry had married her and taken her to a cottage; and his body leapt towards her in reality and dream, so that he was convinced, rightly, that all around not only saw but heard the love he had. In his own head she was celebrated each second, each fraction of a second: she was in the smell of the hay, the beat of the sun, the wind, the leaves. And he hung his head slightly as he walked, overwhelmed by the richness which was in his possession.

The tractor drew away, with Sheila on top of the haycart pressing herself down more to feel the hay pushing up into her body than to achieve any useful effect, her eyes gobbling at the long gaze of her new boy-friend. Vernon, as usual, banged him in the ribs with the back of his hand and chortled in a tone compounded of all the experience which a long life of incessant lechery had secured for him. At twenty-one Vernon had married the first girl he had courted: they had two children now, and if a single woman ever held his eyes for longer than that time necessary to a formal greeting, it was he who blushed – though afterwards he would be intoxicated with the remembrance of his own brazen flirting. Like many, he was a once-and-for-all-cracked virgin whose fidelity captured prizes in adulterous dreams – randy, rapacious unlicensed dreams rocking him through night and day as gently as a baby in a cradle – and for these dreams he demanded ransom from mere 'unmarried men'.

'Thou'll be all right there,' said Vernon, said Vernon, said Vernon, Vernon said, again and again and again. 'Thou'll be all right there. Clamourin' for it, she is. Clamourin'. I would be in there messen but – fair do's – *thy* bit. She'll be hot, mind. Thou'd better git a haircut. Go to t' barbers,' he emphasized the point most carefully. It was the only proof of his sexual life, this downcast purchase of 'two packets' every other Saturday morning at the barber's. 'An' she'll ride well,' Vernon continued, generously, ruminatively, 'she's a good bum on her and a fair pair of bangers.' Then, to business – with a little asperity, 'She'll be worth a bit when old Dawson kicks it. Thou's on 'til a good thing theer. Worth a fair scrap.' He nodded rather severely, for he could be a grandmother matchmaker as well as a guide to the cesspool of lust. 'Git stuck in,' he concluded imperiously. 'My trouble was I was ower fast. The four effs, Find 'em. Feel 'em – Do t'other and Forget 'em, that was me. Don't thee be soft, lad.' By another transformation he was the old wise man around the camp-fire. 'Thou's ontil a gold mine. And she's not bad, Harry, not bad at all.'

He returned to work. Harry had long ceased to react to him. He, too, returned to work, shuffling the hay, raking it into a heap, waiting for the second tractor to come over the field to join them. He knew all there was to know about Vernon's own sex life: knew that there had been one woman only, would in all probability be that one woman only for the rest of his life.

Yet he did not use his knowledge to contradict Vernon's authority. He enjoyed being talked to by a man of the world, as much as Vernon enjoyed being the man of the world. And Vernon knew he knew. Moreover, Harry liked Vernon too much to injure this innocent conceit, and it was because of this affection also that he did not object to the crudeness of his friend's language. For he could well have objected, had he for one moment applied Vernon's words to Sheila and himself. Douglas – he knew, he had seen it happen – went half-mad when people talked of women and sex in that way: relating it directly to himself and feeling himself fouled by the muck of such sewage. To Harry, it was all apart from himself. Indeed, from the bawdiness of Vernon's talk there came most strongly of all a feeling of tenderness. His eyes belied the mouth's contempt.

So the afternoon. They finished the field before tea and went back with the last cartload. The hay was pitched into the loft – enough stacks had been made on the previous days. They sat below the loft and drank from the small white china tea-cups which Mrs Dawson brought them. She had prepared an outside meal and honoured her plans though they could as well have had the meal indoors. Harry soon found an excuse to chase Sheila and they dashed across the yard, in and out of the stables, finally closing to a long, sweet, body-charging kiss, himself pressing her against a white wall.

John watched them play. He squatted on his haunches – the habit remaining from his time as a miner – a short pipe, stem deep in his mouth, a thin wisp of smoke from the Black Twist coming from the small, carbonized bowl, one side of his lips opening slightly, popping gently, as the smoke was released. The pipe emphasized the scar and twist of his face which had ever since borne witness to the accident in the mines which had forced him back to farm-work. He watched them play and remembered some time when he had gone to see his own grandfather – also called Harry – and the two of them had stood that morning in the cup of the fells looking at a couple of hares frisking, mating in the corner of a long field. It had always fascinated him to see birds and animals playing: to see the swallows wheeling to no apparent purpose and swinging across the sky, fox-cubs wrestling with each other outside the den, the hares that distant morning and his grandfather beside him, smoking a pipe, air of a churchwarden in those early months of his retirement. No, he was not as dignified as his grandfather – though he, too, could afford the pipe. Could afford many things which his grandfather would have thought the right of landlords alone in his day: but he had not made himself the man his grandfather had been.

John was just short of eighty now, surly about revealing his age. He feared that he might be 'laid off' work and thought that by keeping his age to himself it might gather around it the protection of secrecy. Everyone knew, of course, and some admired him for it, pointed him out as one of the 'old type', seventy-nine and still going strong. He hated that, totally avoided those older people in the village who sat and counted their years as victories and were kept almost mummified by relatives who loved their age more than their bodies and pointed out with vanity what had been gained, most frequently through modesty.

Harry had already told him that he would be leaving the farm and John had received the news sadly. For though he had daily warned him against the life he was letting himself in for, he had been flattered by Harry's decision to do farm-work. He saw clearly that it was out of love for himself that the seed had been warmed; none of his own would have anything to do with it – Robert was away in the Midlands, an engineer, Annie and Mary had married and gone to towns, one on the west coast, another to New Zealand and so the children from his second marriage had scattered, as had those from his first. He had always regretted Donald, who might have followed him, bold and careless, cut down in war.

Harry had promised a continuation of himself. It did not matter that he was not Joseph's true son: to have been brought up in the family was enough; to have known the boy his lifetime. He liked to listen for the bicycle in the morning. Harry left it at his grandfather's cottage and they walked together to the farm. John slept little now, and would wake before dawn, and came to listen for that bicycle bumping over the cobblestones before the cottage. He liked to talk to the boy, to teach him things – to teach him how to do a thing properly, the pleasure he received from transmitting that knowledge easily as great as that experienced by Harry in receiving it. In all things he liked him to be there – to hear the name 'Tallentire' called and know that there was another to answer for it. He loved the boy *as* a son : and yet had told him he was glad he was going from farm-work.

For there was nothing to farm-work now. Machines did this, engines did that, electricity did the other, you were a mechanic, not a labourer. He knew that one of the reasons Young Dawson had not questioned his right to continue to work there was that he could do things which most younger men had simply never learned to do. And had the patience to do well what they thought irrelevant to their real function. He had accepted that : to be a patcher and mender – well at the end of a life it was something. But there was nothing here now for men to gather to themselves as private strength. Any fool could drive a tractor, he thought, but it took more than a key to drive a pair of horses. It aimed at being a factory now, did a farm, and would end up by being one. Then there would be little to be learned, little to hold interest.

Harry laughed at the vehemence of his pessimism. Just as he frequently laughed when John told him some of the facts of his own first years as a hired man. And seeing that perhaps only with humour could such unknown experiences be transmitted to one who could never really know, John had often found himself telling his own story as a comedy. Surprising Harry by some incident from it and himself catching the smile immediately. A comedy. It was a word which had crept into his head in the early days of talking with the boy – and it stayed there. Rubbing itself carefully over the past like a lucky charm. So it had been that. A comedy.

He knocked out his pipe and stood up. The farmyard was half-shadow, half-sun – hay scattered on the ground, the men propping themselves against the wall, a few hens parading warily at a distance. The open door of the farm-house letting out the chatter from a television set. His thigh-joints ached as he stood up. It was as well that things had become easier on farms. He was slowing down. In a past time he would have been left way behind. Now he could keep up: at this pace, he assured himself, he could keep up until he dropped dead.

Sheila and Harry walked out from behind the stables, she leading, himself most carelessly following. John nodded to the others and set off for home, relying on Harry to catch him up, which he did.

As they walked together through the village, Harry glowed in his grandfather's company. They came to the cottage and he stayed for a while to watch his grandmother patting the butter she had made. The wet slap was like a sweet metronome in his mind, counting the heart-beats.

He freewheeled down the hill and lifted his hands from the handlebars. The bike swung under him as he swayed from side to side. He would see her in two hours and then walk her home in the dark. The air whipped into his face and he shouted, senselessly, back into it; his shouts became a song to the sky.

The table, which he had once called his desk, was placed in front of the window. He could see over the roof-tops of the short-boundaried town, beyond the two chimneys – of the gas-works and the swimming baths – out on to fields drenched green or yellow and the hills under the sun. Neatly on the table were the books he had been gutting but now abandoned: *Roman Britain* by R. G. Collingwood and *Anglo-Saxon England* by Stenton. Two of the books on his reading list for Oxford. He would be going 'up' in a few months. The books were stacked on top of three files, each of the files marked by a small white label which described their contents. This was a fortress on the table, moated by pens and pencils, a severe imitation of the life he had let himself in for.

Now he was scribbling with a biro in an old notebook, curling his left arm around the top of it as if to hide it from the scrutiny of those serious works. His arm was a barricade, and behind it, the pen dashed and paused on the page, crossing out words, changing their order, until the verse he was attempting appeared as a cluster of blue stringy letters. This table was too low for him and the front of his thighs pressed against its edge: the steady pressure, which had once been used by him as a pretended trap to keep him there working, was now become a necessary physical pleasure. As the images lit up his mind and he waited for the word which would describe them, the weight of the wood on his legs was now a body against his own, now a tree, a rock, a hand: at that point the words were sounded. Outside the fresh, warm summer afternoon: it made no call on him.

In these notebooks there were many attempts at verse, and a few pages of prose. He had made an agreement with his father to work for him a certain number of hours each day – in the pub and the cellars – in return for two pounds a week, which was as much as he needed; and spent as much time as he could on the reading list sent him by his college and in attempting to write something of his own as now with these lines. He had just written 'Contemporary Dilemma (1)':

> What to do and why to do and who to do it with.
> Where to live and how to live.
> Whether this or this.
> The true fakir relaxes on his bed of nails.
> He knows what's good for him.

The last line impressed him greatly: such poetic cynicism had scarcely been known before now, he thought.

Somewhere in the notebook he had made a distinction between poetry and verse, deciding there was only verse and prose – and poetry wherever it occurred: an early and elementary distinction but one which pleased him constantly, became like a favourite toy. A knowledge of metre at school had seemed like a magic key. Then he had read Cummings and Pound and Eliot and now his lines sprawled or were contracted at whim or will, he was never sure which.

While he worked at the verse, he would use the pauses to write imperative notes to himself. 'Must read all Shakespeare this summer.' 'Must get Baudelaire *in the original*.' 'All art is *unceasing* practice – Blake.' 'Comfort is next to stillness and so death. Accept chaos.' 'The Marchioness went out at 5 o'clock –

Remember that!' 'Before writing, sit perfectly still for ten minutes.' 'Bodily grace and strength are allied to mental and spiritual power. N. B. Tolstoy rode horses, did work-outs, ploughed fields, fenced, chopped trees.' Commands which he would strive to obey, forever charging into the arms of failure. Choppy sentences which appeared embarrassing on the following day but crucially important at their moment of inscription.

He was aware of a necessity for secrecy. Everybody he knew in the town would think such urgency directed to such an end as writing as proof of conceit or senselessness. Many times he felt himself merely self-indulgent, and when he went up the small streets and stopped to chat with people about marriages and injuries, births and alliances, local crimes, deaths, football and trade, the gossip seemed so substantial that its solidity had a moral force and seemed good while his own scribbling by comparison appeared unnecessary, a waste of effort and so no 'good'. Yet somehow there was the hope and sometimes the certainty that the shadows in his mind would take on substance.

There were other times when he feared himself a stranger to all, to everything. A stranger to the way the fly knocked itself against the window pane, how that slip of wind cuffed the empty packet of crisps, stranger before a hand trembling between caress and blow, to the turn of a face in the dark, the stone of the pavement was strange to him, that it should be hard, grey, yet closer, ash-surfaced, old sugar. And in strange dreams at night came the air-raids from the endless past; sirens blew in his ears, bombs of guilt dropped on to his mind, the ack-ack of the present fled whitely to the skies in defence, ambulances carried excuses through the tunnels of consciousness, and all around lay wounded hopes and dead ambitions. All clear! – he sat up in bed, wondering at the silence in the house, that the noises he had heard had not blasted the whole town awake, but there was only a lorry changing gear at the bottom of the hill. Then, most strange, the eye of his mind would slither from his head and regard what remained: like an eye in a painting by Picasso, it would be detached, now like a marble, now a fish, now the beam of a lighthouse swivelling around with its one cyclops' shaft to illuminate the blackness, all forms shadows –

and it would sit there, in the corner of the room, mesmerizing him to unheard cries, unsounded, rending only himself who had no matter.

Being Saturday, Harry would be back for tea at five and his father would open the pub at five-thirty. No peace then.

He left off the verses, could never concentrate on them for very long and picked up another notebook in which for some time he had been outlining, most tentatively, a novel. Not a page was yet written but he regarded it as much more possible than the verses. It was to span three generations and concern a family much like his own. The more he read, the more he thought that his sort of people appeared in books as clowns, criminals or 'characters' and it offended him. Everywhere, it seemed to him then, on the wireless, on television, in films and magazines, ordinary people were credited with no range of feeling, no delicacy of manner, no niceties of judgement: and women like his mother laughed at as 'chars', their opinions and attitudes thought to be trite because their expression was, often, commonplace. One reason for writing the book would be to set that right.

He looked through some of the notes already made. 'A family history which concerns a family who do not consider themselves a family (unlike The Buddenbrooks or The Brangwens) and have always been strangers to history, even their own.' Notes beside that: 'e.g. my father tells me absolutely nothing of his life – considers it lived, but not worth telling.' His grandfather, also, did not talk about his past: at least, not to Douglas; from what Harry had said, it was obvious that the old man did talk there – and Douglas was jealous of that. 'People such as my family are the numbers to the alphabet of history: the words, sentences and Proper Names are outside their scope/hope.'

Another tack: 'Epic – pre-grandfather: Heroic – Grandfather: Silver – father: Decadent – self.' Afterwards a note – 'too facile'. Again 'Grandfather was entirely bound by circumstances and to a great extent controlled by them once initial choice, very limited, made: in short, *moulded*, something *inevitable*: father – the mould breaking but petrified by the flow of lava: self –

attempting to break it deliberately, start anew and yet keep the old – What?' More. '1st generation – the forging of the weapons: 2nd – attempt to use them: 3rd – attempt to do without them – unwanted.' 'Who from the working-class – really from it, no school-teacher-mother-literary-uncle in the background, has spoken accurately and lastingly? Good mad John Clare. If only Lawrence's mother had not been so classy.' He had tried more particular themes: '*Love* – Grandfather had never once mentioned the word love. The most hē says: "I think a lot on her." Could not mention the word to him. Father – affectionate to mam, but mention of Love makes him nervous. Completely paralyses mother. Self – uncomfortably use the word "sex" and am either intolerably prudish or unrestrainedly licentious.' Or: 'Grandfather's life "closed" at eighteen: father's at about twenty-two – in both cases with marriage: marriage being like the reverse effect of dynamite, as if a rock had been blown open and then the film were run slowly backwards – and all the fragments came to home in it.' And 'How far can you make the history of one family that of a country?' (Later – 'not worth trying'.) Another: 'Could have a line going through the book about WORK: as important as Love.' Note in margin: 'More clichés': Note under the note: 'Clichés are the midwives to new discoveries.' (Later, next to that 'Christ!')

He had tried to write something down, but the instant that someone known in real life came to mind he felt that it would be intrusive to write on such a basis. What he knew deflected him and yet without it he was without everything. Then he would feel desperate – as desperate (though it would appear to pass soon) as the time he had been told that Harry was not his 'real' brother. For what seemed totally secure would become completely estranged: as all the 'brothers' and 'sisters' of his mother had done when he found out about them, as his father's 'mother' was not 'real' and so yet more 'uncles' and 'aunts' and 'cousins' changed. If only he had the wit and confidence to make a comedy of it all!

And it was embarrassing to write of people who might recognize themselves: what right had he to do that?

So he would decide to tell it all metaphorically, inside the head of a man who was dying. Or he would write out such as he considered 'the facts' and finding that two pages was enough, leave it at that for a few months. Sometimes he thought that the writer of such fiction was a dinosaur: but this was a pose, adopted from intellectual essays in which most things he wanted to do were described as decaying, disintegrating or dead: he had to ignore that or forget the whole thing. He had too much confidence and too little sophistication to do that. And while he waited for the words to start, he filled in the time by filling out his notions on the book.

Was it about social man, my friends, or political man? Who had ever distinguished them? There was the question of 'Rise and Fall': his grandfather considered (obliquely was this stated) that Douglas had 'done well': therefore – risen? One look at that old man convinced Douglas who had fallen. Rise and Fall was useless. Perhaps the nearest he came to satisfying himself was when he wrote – 'It should be a series of pictures. Flat where little is known. Dense where more is known. Icarus is the attempt: Narcissus the enemy.' But that seemed pretentious, like everything done at this damned table turned desk turned table – five pieces of wood arranged in one horizontal plane three foot by thirty inches supported at each corner by four vertical columns, three feet high – One generation, two, three: one-two-three: 1-2-3, 'play the ukelele': 1-2-3, 1-2-3, as old as a waltz, that point equidistant between manners and desire.

That was the trouble, whenever he made these notes. He would start off with a feeling or an image which was solid in his mind and in the act of writing it would catch words which came from a foreign territory. And there was the choice: the town versus the school, parents against teachers, friends against books, movement versus stillness, ease and strain, living and writing and the one somehow betrayed the other or fought against it. But what did it matter, this writing, what could it matter to anyone he liked or even knew?

Unless, perhaps, he could draw them in by Naming them. Using real names, real places. He would find a Cumbrian name for his family and have a fictive self both appear in the book and write it and so he could both know 'everything' – as the old novelists did – and have a partial view as would be necessary. If he *did* write it, he would use these notebooks – but tidy them up – he always enjoyed making better sense of what he had once done.

These matters were clearer in his head than in the notebooks, for when the page was down – then ... then he could scarcely describe how a smile passed from mind to lips across to other lips which returned the smile within a world of transitory privacy. And he let himself sink to the silence which would give him the written words.

How was it that his mother, who was afraid of leaving Thurston for more than a few days at a stretch was yet ever willing to dash off and see a sight, a parade, a show, a shop, a display? Would take to irregular country buses and the lonely terminals of urban pleasures with constant enjoyment while his father who could have settled anywhere and had wanted to settle anywhere but Thurston had to be prised from his seat for any expedition not to his own selfish satisfaction? This afternoon, for example, Joseph had whipped off to a Hound Trail, leaving Douglas and his mother to clear up. To explain and describe that: to make fiction of it and use that truthful disguise accurately ...

He hated to watch his mother working, though she moved with unforced rapidity and was far from complaining, he hated the idea of it. The idea possessed the reality and he hated to see her working.

There was a debt to pay there. He would have to see that his parents did not suffer for the help given him. Money would be important: the pub job did not carry a pension and his father was rightly determined that such slender surplus as there was should be given to his wife or spent on the boys. Sometimes Douglas saw his father as the man in those sketches put out by an insurance company at that time: four portraits of the same man, at 25, 35, 45 and 55 – driven grey and anguished by the knowledge that he had not taken out an insurance policy. Nevertheless Douglas would not take on a regular job while waiting to go to University: nor would he ever, he decided, in his later vacations. A hand had been offered and no tip required.

If his hand could later be offered in return – so much the better: if not, then at least he would have given these books their proper chance.

He got up from his chair – not to pace around, for in two strides he would have been out of his bedroom door – but to stand merely, to stretch. The bedroom was his record. Timetables, that bamboo cross made when he was confirmed, walls plastered with the history of music, literature, religions, maps, a wind-up gramophone with a cardboard box of 78's, commandments to himself pinned onto the flowered wallpaper, in the chest of drawers his clothes neatly laid out, everything in its place. He opened the door of his wardrobe to look once again at the brand-new three-piece clerical-grey suit.

His mother had taken him to Carlisle for it. He had not insisted on going alone, his inevitable embarrassment – even suffering – weighing lightly in the scales against her anticipation of his pleasure. Together on the upper deck of the bus. The conductor knew his mother, of course, as he used the pub, and let them travel without buying a ticket – which threw her into a terrible flutter. She would not insist because that would offend against the (borrowed) grandeur of the conductor's gesture; but to travel without a ticket was cheating. Douglas had teased her – advising her to tuck the money in the seat, throw it out of the window, give it to the poor – but she had quickly found a way out by deciding to buy a return ticket on the way back, and throw it away after the single journey. Then justice would be done by the Cumberland Bus Company.

To the best Men's Outfitters in Carlisle. The Very Best. Gloomy depths of lustreless cloth. Douglas had always been a dandy – within such financial limits as made the purchase of white socks and black jeans a most extravagant raid into the world of fashion – and this dark chamber of finespun was a disappointment. He tried to keep the detachment offered by that disappointment firmly in his mind as the ceremony got under way. The man who served them was (of course) despotically obsequious and Douglas rocked on his heels counting to ten, then to a hundred and ten, to prevent an incipient assault. Suit after suit had to be tried for the best to be seen in the long mirrors to be the best.

A solicitor from Thurston came in, who knew them slightly. Had read of Douglas' scholarship to Oxford. Used the acquaintanceship for heaviest patronage. These are 'friends' of mine, he conceded, to the supposedly unbelieving shop-assistants old and young. I know these people, see that they have the best of everything. An intimate whisper in his mother's ear – they'll serve you well now, they know me here. Coquettish confidence which made her blush for his vulgarity. Douglas glared. O, Mr Carstairs let us meet when we are naked or alone. And Good-bye – good-bye – the best here, only the best, the sheep are fed on rhubarb leaves.

Savagely through the suits. One, a tweedy model with a lime waistcoat to set it off. Very smart. He fancied himself in that. Forgot the assistant whose nails were bitten and eyes poached grey, ascended to pity him for this lime green waistcoat was very smart indeed. A glass of sherry? Certainly. His idea of Oxford, though tempered by wisps of information from the front, was still founded in *Tom Brown at Oxford* – and men would say 'the port is with you'. 'Be careful not to spill it on my lime green waistcoat bought at Dunnings and Callow, Carlisle. Port stains.' But in the glass he saw his mother, who, though she nodded at how smart he looked, nevertheless communicated her fear of its being too showy for the sobriety of upper-class scholarship. Her eyes were on the clerical grey. Hand-stitching like the vicar's. Quiet. *Three*-piece, not, like Douglas' grandfather, because it was the old-fashioned habit but because it was the way of the world Douglas was about to enter. And grey had never been flashy. Never.

Nineteen pounds ten. More, he knew, much more than she had got married on. Paid over-hurriedly, a bundle of notes in an elastic band. She had brought twenty-five, to be on the safe side.

Mother. Thank you.

Harry's bike rattled over the grating and he battered at the closed pub's door. Douglas heard his mother's slippers flap on the tiles down the passage as she went to open to him. Why did she wear such battered slippers?

He laid aside his pen and put his notebooks in a big tin box that locked. The key was hidden in a sock in the drawer.

Chapter Fifteen

Joseph arrived back from the Hound Trails at twenty-five past five. He had missed the Old Dogs' trail to be in time for opening. Saturday night: must be there on the dot. Time to pant upstairs, having kicked off his wellingtons and thrown down the old mac (Betty would pick it up).

'Did you win?' Harry bellowed.

'Broke even,' Joseph replied as he took the stairs two at a time.

Twenty cigarettes a day. Too many. Impossible to cut down – impossible to stop. Why should he? Enjoyed it. Good-bye sweet breath and clean lungs. Amen.

Stripped to the waist. Farewell to control of the flesh. White arms thick – though some muscle from the work in the cellar – no shape. The rapid second shave of the day. A trail of trousers, shirt and socks from bathroom to bedroom. Kicking into his suit. He would not make it.

'Betty! Open the front door, eh?'

'I'm untidy.'

'Well get Douglas to do it.' An irritating vision of the three of them sitting there around the tea-pot, exclusive, content. 'He's old enough.' Softest sarcasm. There would be no tea for him – yes, now he was sorry for himself, totally forgetting that he had taken his afternoon's sport at their expense.

'It's half-past five!' he shouted.

He heard Douglas move along the passage with a deliberately lazy step.

'It won't kill them to wait,' Douglas said and the volume was loud enough for the sentence to carry upstairs.

'That's not the bloody point,' Joseph muttered to himself, strangling a clean white collar with a wine tie which would not, never would, settle properly but must always have the thin end longer than the fat end which hung like a flipper on his chest. Too late he noticed that the shirt which had been laid out for him needed cuff-links. 'Betty! Give us a hand with these cuff-links!' What the hell she wanted to buy him shirts which needed – then he remembered: *he* had bought them, at an auction, six for a pound, unworn by Mr Edmonson (farmer: deceased).

Again he visualized the scene. Betty and Harry would be giggling together as the noise of his dressing reached them. She would mime his shouts of 'Betty!' and even, perhaps, do so on cue. Douglas would laugh but reluctantly, half-wishing to shout back at his father. And Betty would most defiantly take another sip of tea. 'Betty!' No laughing matter. A cry of misery. The world would falter a little on its axis if he was not down to meet the first customer on a Saturday night. She ought to understand that. Yet it was also ridiculous.

'Let him wait,' said Douglas, lightly, to pretend it was a joke.

Immediately his mother frowned and got up from the table. Went nimbly across to the stairs, the slippers which had flapped most dolefully now almost rattled on the lino.

'You're not his servant!' Douglas bellowed as she had left the room.

Harry looked at Douglas; decided against it and poured himself another cup of tea. Ate in silence.

Douglas sprawled on the sofa which, two hours later, would be occupied by three stout ladies from Dalston who came every week to 'The Thrush' because they liked the landlord's smile and the sing-song coming from the other room. At this time, it was his, and he desecrated it, shoes heeled into one arm, by his fidgeting ruffling and crumpling all the covers, a cup of tea balanced on the edge of the seat, his face buried in a book. On some days, reading was a fever, and print from sauce bottles, newspapers, books, advertisements, anywhere, would fly to his eyes, never appeasing them.

Harry turned on the television.

Douglas groaned.

Harry turned it up.

'Turn it down.' Douglas.

Harry whistled and watched.

'Look,' said Douglas, in imitation of patience, 'you can *see* a cricket match. You don't have to *listen* as well.'

'*I* have to listen.'

'Moron.'

Harry waited – and then, hearing his father on the stairs, quickly reached out and knocked it off. He, too, was part of the protection for their mother. He knew that if Joseph saw the cricket then he would be so annoyed not to be free to watch it that he would call on Betty to hurry to get changed, hurry to come down, hurry, hurry, so that he might pop in and see it.

'What was the score?' he asked, having first taken a look in the bar to confirm that it was empty. As nobody had popped in off the Carlisle bus, nobody would come until about ten to six. But he had to be *there*. The others did not understand that. Neither did he.

'183 for seven.'

'Pathetic!' Joseph replied, angrily. Then he glanced around, parodying a burglar to excuse his truancy, 'Switch it back on,' he urged, 'I'll get an over in.' He went to the door, glanced again into the bar, then came back, laughing to himself as if in a happy conspiracy with the boys who did not look at him.

But Harry understood the peculiar grip of the disease his father suffered from. At times to himself, also, it was most important, naggingly essential, to know the result of a match or a race, a fight, a game. So he was obedient, turned it on, and Joseph poured himself a cup of tea, another accusation.

The picture came on and he saw the white-flannelled sportsmen and stood perfectly still, concentration wholly given over. The state of the wicket, the form of each of the players, the gossip in the newspapers, his own hunches and favourites – above all, the marvel of the game itself, so slow and gentle-seeming and yet full of cruelties, a ball keeping low – unplayable – and the batsman whose drives and cuts had begun to orchestrate his innings into a great movement was out.

Yet even so Joseph listened for a customer coming up the steps, heard Betty upstairs and regretted the untidiness which caused her back to bend and bend again, felt the bitterly strong rather cold tea on his tongue, softly made comments to Harry and received the answers understandingly. With Harry and Douglas he could be happy watching sport – with no one else could he be really at ease. He demanded not only words – those, least of all, but the right tone, the same assumptions, similar stores of information, and an appreciation of silence.

'He caught that on the bottom of the bat,' said Douglas who had soon been drawn into the others' spell.

Joseph nodded, put down the cup and fiddled in his pocket for his cigarettes. The players changed positions as another over was prepared. The three of them waited as the new bowler and the captain re-set the field.

'*Right* round the wicket,' Joseph murmured.

'Look at that,' Harry answered, though after a pause. 'A suicide point.'

'One good belt,' said Douglas.

'And he'll lose his head,' Harry concluded for him. Unnecessarily, but to show, to touch.

Clearly, as clearly as the picture before him, Joseph remembered the time he had taken the two boys to Headingley, Leeds, for the Test Match between England and Australia in 1948. Betty had gone also but each morning been left with the wife of Arnold, the friend they were staying with: Arnold and Joseph had met in the R.A.F. and written the two Christmases since. At 6.00 in the morning on this holiday, the family had got up – the women to make the breakfast and the sandwiches, the men to chivvy the boys ready and string together the stools which would take the weight off while waiting for the gate to open.

Joseph remembered the taste of the air as they walked to the ground. Men moving out of silent streets, likewise taking their week's holiday for the Test, the easy, unstrained march towards the ground until, even at that early hour, it was a mass of them moving as to a factory – but what a difference! The shoes and boots could have been striking a song from those pavements.

Outside the ground, a queue already – and souvenir programmes for sale, score-cards, rosettes, autographed photos, miniature cricket bats, lemonade and crisps, hot tea and sandwiches, prices very reasonable, the stuff provided decent; everything reasonable and decent that day. So into place with Harry scouting back to see how many were behind them and Douglas counting how many were in front. The boys looked shiny and tidy: white shirts and green V-necked pullovers, short grey pants, grey socks and brown sandals. The two men smoked and chatted about the war: that is they followed up incidents and people through whom they could strengthen the sympathy between themselves: both knew that the friendship of war would die very quickly but each felt more free in it than with those they saw more regularly. Indeed, had not Joseph sensed that there was impermanence he might never have come: not even for the Test. He jibbed at close friendships.

But he was here and the weather was so good that only the very old or the very cantankerous could remember a better summer for cricket than 1948. The crowd would be enormous and on that day, as on every one of the five days, he betted, the gates would close before the game began, all of it adding to the treat.

Then the queue had shuffled through the high gates. Play began. The giants out there – Bradman and Miller and Lindwall: Hutton and Washbrook and Compton. Two of the best teams that ever faced each other in a Test. (And England should have won – Joseph maintained – but for Yardley, their captain: an amateur: at that time England had to be captained by an amateur.) The boys were alternatively riveted or caught up in the peripheral excitements. Now craning forward all but touching Denis Compton fielding on the boundary: now slipping up to the lemonade booth while a particularly intense period of defensive batting filled the strip of green with apparent inactivity. For *five* days they went.

Game over, the slow-jostling-happy crowd through the gates released to the streets: home to read about the day's play in the paper and listen to a discussion of it on the wireless. Perfection was that week: the solid core of his sentimentality and a touchstone for many things since.

'Do you remember that Test I took you both to at Leeds?' he dared.

'Yes.' They replied simultaneously, but did not let that disturb his mood. Both of them now knew that they had been thinking of that holiday while watching this match on the television.

'Neil Harvey made a century. His first Test,' said Douglas.

'I thought *you* might have been useful at cricket,' Joseph answered, half-turning towards him. Douglas shook his head, his eyes still on the screen.

'Well!' said Joseph, suddenly snapped alert. 'This won't do. This won't do.' He patted his pockets; straightened his tie and fussed towards the door: he *was* becoming fussy, Douglas thought, despisingly, despairingly. Douglas tried to repress his reaction but looked at Joseph. The contempt in the glance was venomous. So when Joseph braced back his shoulder blades it was not simply to loosen the stiffness he often felt there: Douglas's darts could stab him.

Harry did not see his 'father' go out, nor did he allow himself to become entangled in the bindings of intuition and assessment in which Douglas often seemed to truss up the whole family. He stared at the television, willing time to go so that he could get out and see Sheila.

At ten to six, Dido came in. With his entrance, the evening began and Joseph's mind turned to his business. Without a word, Dido received his pint of mild and bitter – sucked half of it away in one draw, paused for a few seconds to look at the damage, and then finished it off.

'Now I'll have a drink,' Joseph muttered to himself. 'Now I'll have a drink,' said Dido.

Joseph took the glass and bent his head over the pump to hide the smile.

'She's sittin' well, Joe, sittin' well to-neet,' Joseph murmured.

'She's sittin' well, Joe,' said Dido, patting his beer-barrel belly, 'Sittin' well to-neet.'

He sipped delicately at this second glass.

'We'll be wanting to crack a fiver.'

'We'll be wantin' to crack a fiver,' said Dido.

Joseph brought him the change and gave up the game. You could go mad like that.

Dido would drink steadily from now until ten-thirty by which time he would have taken in about fifteen or sixteen pints of mild and bitter. There were many men who drank seven or eight pints every night of the week : some drank more : all drank more on Saturdays. Dido would take at least a dozen every night he came in which was most nights in winter and summer, fewer in spring and autumn.

He was in love with Betty – though the nearest he came to a declaration of it was at Christmas when he claimed a kiss under the mistletoe and gave her a two pound box of Black Magic.

On account of her he drank only in The Thrush and had made himself its unofficial protector. Joseph had had little trouble over the last four or five years – touch wood – but once or twice he had seen Dido in action on his behalf. And appreciated it. 'This pub,' said Dido, 'looks better than many a house. She has it better than many a sittin' room, Joe. This *bar's* better than many a parlour, Joe. Some of them let their bars go – who can blame them, Joe? *She* keeps hers up though, man, by heck she does. Better than many a sittin' room, Joe : I-tell-you.'

He placed himself in the corner of the settle so that he would glimpse Betty the moment she appeared through the bar door – and looked at the large gallery of photographs – of famous Hound Dogs – which covered two walls of the small bar.

Joseph pulled himself a half of bitter, as much to make sure of its quality as to enjoy the drink. He drank so little nowadays. Yet, strangely, though he had been so much among beer – he still thought there was still in it something grand. Drunks, he had noticed, except stupid drunks who piddled out their feelings like bladderless pups, drunks were treated with respect even when they lost all control. And those who drank deeply – like Dido – and held it, they had a position which they were conscious to maintain.

Lester came in for his one drink of the day. A half of shandy of which he drank two-thirds at the very most, being in training. He would have preferred not to drink at all, just stand and feel at ease with his Uncle Joe (the reason for his coming) but that, he thought, would have been unfair on his Uncle Joe (he liked to repeat the two words in his mind, often) who had a living to make after all: though he knew that his Uncle Joe would not take offence, indeed had hinted to him that he need not drink at all; but 'fair was fair' and a half-shandy was evidence of that fair. He could have drunk orange of course, but that would have emphasized that he was in training rather more flamboyantly than he wished; he was not quite fast enough to drink orange.

Lester specialized in the mile but would have a go at anything. He ran as a professional at the many meetings held throughout the Border districts in season, for comparatively low prize money but real opportunities of gain through the betting. The system was well-controlled and (except for the fell-races) organized on the basis of handicapping. Lester had not been conspicuous this season because of his success the previous year, his handicap had been too great for him to have more than an outside chance of winning and so he had concentrated on seeming to try hard at important meetings, taking great care never to be among the prize money and never to have his name in the lists which were sent off to the handicappers. It was a dull and dicey business but it was his only way of preparing for 'the big killing' which he was determined to make the next season. If they would reduce his handicap, it would be certain.

He trained five nights a week by running to Carlisle and back. Twenty-two miles. He would do occasional sprints and time trials between the milestones along the way. On his head, just planted there it seemed, was a crew cut: the short hairs stood at attention, emphasizing the slim face, smallish skull: less resistance to the wind, and a feeling of sharpness, readiness; a spiky crest.

He radiated cleanliness: as a woman can radiate charm, so Lester radiated hygiene. It seemed he had sculpted himself out of soap and let the resulting form bone-dry in a cleansing wind. It was the cleanliness of The Thrush which impressed itself most strongly on him, next to the character of his Uncle Joe, whom he wished had been his own father.

It was Joe who had encouraged him to run, taken him to meetings (there were always Hound Trails as well as races), bought him his first pair of spikes, advised him to invest in a track suit, supported him in those first two seasons when nothing had gone right. Joe always put a bet on him even when both of them knew he was running to lose. Always had. Always would. This 'always' raised his uncle from goodness to greatness.

It was Joe who had always understood his mother. For Helen's frequent departures, her affairs with other men, her occasional drunkenness and the fights she had started or, more miserably, failed to start – this could have isolated her completely in the small town, Lester thought: but due, he was sure, to Joseph's straightening this out, seeing to that, squaring the other, talking to this man, braving another – she had escaped much of the effect of her own life. Now she was changing: the death of her father, Seth, had sent her on a bender as violent and determined as that of any man: but she had come out of it mildly, lamb-like even, shorn. Now she rarely drank, stayed close to her husband, was no warmer in contact with them all than she had ever been, but seemed abandoned by that demon which would forever be throwing them off. And Joe, many a time, had appeared in Lester's mind to check him as he prepared to slaughter his step-father. George existed now with no bones broken thanks to Joseph alone.

Joseph knew of the affection, even the passion, that the young man had for him and somehow he managed to avoid exploiting it. Perhaps he did not know the extent of it – that even the crew-cut was for him. That Lester was not this lean-boned young man. That he badly wanted flesh to cover him; but this he had made himself, for in this limited certainty he would be sure of finding himself satisfactory enough to present to Joseph. Both of them knew the layers which had been rubbed off in the last two years: where Douglas had become a 'local legend' with the girls through activity which had never broken the skin of virginity, Lester had been a layer, cutting down the women within reach until they lay across every path he took, like sheaves on the side of a road. Where Douglas had 'knocked around with a gang', Lester had really hunted for trouble – three fines for fighting, one stretch of twelve months on 'good conduct' – another offence in that period and it would have been Borstal. The Army will sort you out, the magistrates had announced with relish: but the army had rejected him for flat feet. A blank insult, filled in by those who wished to taunt him for whatever amount they dared to draw. There was the wheeling and dealing also: driving a lemonade van wasn't much and he wanted money – poached salmon, helped Joseph in the cellar while Douglas was away, traded with the farmers, looked everywhere for extra: drainpipes then and a long jacket, velvet-collared, bootlace tie, Elvis Presley hairstyle – deep sideboards and a duck's tail at the back – Teddy Boy: smart.

It was when he had begun to win a few races that he had changed. There could be real money there if he could only get his hands on it, maybe a few hundred, buy a lorry, push off somewhere: just to have it in his hands. And as he homed to the sport for the prospects it seemed to offer, the urgency of his attempt was directed by those long bus rides with Joseph when they chatted about this and that and worked out the tactics for a race.

Joseph recognized his family, his father, his uncles and his own brothers, much more easily in Lester than he did in Douglas. For though Lester was shrewd, he could not hide his intentions and looked what he was: with Douglas there were the distances imposed by the space he demanded for himself – and in that distance it was difficult to tell.

Lester came close to the bar now to take his glass – and winked most heavily when Joseph asked him where he was going. 'You'll get caught one of these times,' said Joseph, uncertain before this fact – as always, and again he could do no wrong for Lester thought that his uncertainty came from a most delicate regard for his privacy, rarely encountered in affairs like this – the fact, well enough known, that Lester went through to the village of Kirkby every Saturday night to sleep with a woman who had three children and an avaricious husband who did night-shift at the week-end for the double-pay.

'Nivver,' said Lester, calmly.

And Joseph hoped not – for the other man's sake. How could he tell Lester he thought badly of this? When only part of him did feel so.

'It's all above board,' said Lester, certainly following Joseph's hesitation – though attributing it to different motives. 'I telt her to tell *him* and she telt him, I'm sure o' that, Uncle Joe.' He paused. It was not quite enough. 'An' I always see she puts them kids to bed – fust, thou knows.' That clinched it. He could afford to spread a little now. 'Grand kids they are an' all, Uncle Joe. There's nowt I wouldn't do for them kids.'

Joseph saw the husband about the town, cheerful enough. It wasn't the first time this had happened to him. Nor was it the first time Lester had set up with a married woman – 'they never miss a slice off a cut loaf,' he said.

Once a week only. Would not have it interfere with his training. This was yet another sacrifice which would have to be paid for, Lester thought to himself most grimly: one way or another.

'I've been thinking,' said Joseph, 'maybe you *should* run at Ambleside next week.'

'*I* thowt that meself!' exclaimed Lester, delightedly.

'In the *half*-mile,' said Joseph.

'Oh.' Lester considered. He could find no solution and so he waited.

'You need to go flat out for once,' said Joseph. 'I don't like to see you messin' yourself about. You can give the half-mile everything you've got and still do no damage.'

He waited. It was their only point of disagreement – the way in which Lester was nursing himself this season. Joseph saw every reason for it – the handicapping was haywire and Lester had been unfairly clobbered the season before; moreover, given the system as it was, there was absolutely nothing else to do if you wanted to continue among the winners and not just have the one good season: and he would excuse Lester a great deal – not merely because he liked him a great deal but because he understood – clearly – the lust the young man had to get some money together and launch himself. Yet it went very hard against Joseph's principles: he liked to see good running and would follow Lester anywhere – but really he preferred the amateurs because they did it for nothing. When people exerted or stretched themselves 'for nothing' or 'just for the love of it' he was entranced.

'I might git a ticket,' said Lester, half-cautious, half-proud.

'It might start to look suspicious if you didn't pick up at least *one* this season,' Joseph replied.

'Ay, there's that.' He paused. 'I was thinkin' of t'mile. They'll all be there. If I was well back in *that* field, an' it looked good – well – there's a chance.'

'Them fellas'll be too canny not to notice, Lester. There'll be Michael Glenn there. He knows when somebody's loiterin'.'

'I can mek it look good.'

'They'll smell it out.'

'Think?'

'Yes. Have a good go at that half-mile. Give yourself a treat.'

Lester drained off his shandy.

'Reet, Uncle Joe: that's settled. Half-mile she is.'

He nodded, happily, nodded at Dido – and left.

Joseph knew that he had leaned on this nephew and regretted having had to. He would have liked to be able to talk to him openly about anything – try to go through all the points about this running business, the woman, the search for money, the contempt Lester expressed for George – liked, in fact, to have known him as 'a friend'. But it had not happened like that – and the way in which they met allowed no great liberties on either side, however intimately they might appear to talk and act. If he was afraid for Lester, he could do no more than place signposts before the areas he considered to be dangerous: he could not follow him in.

In a few moments the other two buses would arrive back from the Trails and the pub would be full to begin the Saturday night. He walked out of the bar and stood at the bottom of the stairs. 'Betty!' He shouted. 'Are you ready yet?'

* * *

It was the interval. They had seen 'Look at Life', a cartoon of 'Tom and Jerry' and the trailer for the next film. Now was the time for ice-cream.

Harry got up uncertainly, much surprised that his legs would carry him, and went down to Mrs Charters who sold the refreshments. Thurston cinema was small. Capacity downstairs – 120: upstairs – 48. Upstairs they were of course: two shillings each. He wished it had cost more. Lucky. Not a back seat but only two rows from the back and on one of those truncated rows – of three seats – the third seat empty. Only half-full. Harry knew them all and all, it seemed this night, from the greetings and winks, wanted to be known to Harry. Sheila was a country girl, a stranger, and her preliminary blushes had helped to keep her anonymity. They had sat most correctly through 'Look at Life' and he had taken her hand only at the end of it. In 'Tom and Jerry' he had squeezed and nearly left his seat at the force of the squeeze returned to him. His knee had shot out to jam against hers and both had slid forward a little way so that they sat ankle to ankle, calf to calf, knee to knee and half her thigh to one third of his. During the trailer she had taken off her cardigan and casually he had slung his right arm around her shoulder. Then the interval and the arm had jerked back as if on a piece of string, bumping her head.

Too soon the two tubs of Strawberry Favourite were bought and he had to turn and walk up the red-carpeted steps towards her where she sat so calmly. He was overwhelmed with admiration at her self-control, sitting there, managing to look even a little bored, now turning quite at her ease to examine the lucky couples hunched in the back row with the flagrantly unnecessary raincoats draped over their knees – even raising her white arms to her hair to put a slide in place, so calm while his legs tottered up the few steps, his stomach lurching to an imaginary ship's roll. What a girl! Just sitting there as if nothing had happened!

This bit would be difficult for he knew that despite the ice-cream and the small wooden spoons which most thankfully employed the tongue – conversation had to be made. Otherwise he would feel a fool. He pushed back the waxy circle of cardboard, laid bare his frozen pat of pink and scraped the small spoon rather disconsolately across the surface. Douglas would have chuntered away with no trouble: made her laugh – without telling jokes – just made her laugh.

He decided to tell her something important.

He had got a job on the *Cumberland News* as a cub-reporter. Three pounds seven and six. She nodded and dug into her ice. Of course there would be his National Service to do in a year or so but that was why he had taken the job – when he came out it would be too late. He looked for applause at this cunning and brilliantly calculated stroke of prescience: to himself it appeared even Machiavellian so rarely, he thought, could anyone so excellently have organized their future. She licked the waxy circle of cardboard and laughed at his stare: then thrust her arm through his – locking it, he wondered, or encouraging him? Which? Which? Then, most determinedly, she asked him about Douglas: about Douglas and his present girl, about Douglas and the other girls he had been with. Harry answered her willingly: rather proudly. As the light dimmed and a certificate came on the screen to declare that *Singing in the Rain* was fit to be seen by everyone, Sheila sighed and said 'He's so smashing looking,' squirming as she said it. Harry was shocked: as if his brother had been insulted.

The film began and her head slid on to his shoulder. He felt her hair thick on his neck and let out his breath so carefully – she must not be disturbed – that he almost choked and did, in fact, splutter, had to turn away. But the action had released his arm; he could not have done better had he done it on purpose. No hesitation this time. His arm went around her shoulders with an experienced swing, a swagger in the elbow. She sighed once more and this one, he knew, was for him. He bowed to peck at her brow and was met by her lips, reaching ravenously up to his own: they clamped against his mouth and her tongue rushed between his teeth rapid as a terrier, searching furiously. He responded by thrusting his own tongue into her mouth – though never before had he employed this sort of kissing – 'French kissing' they called it, and they foraged away while

Gene Kelly went liquidly through a routine. Parted, gasping – and immediately set to once more. Below, from a lake of longing, Harry felt a rise, like Excalibur. To balance this his hand slid down from her shoulder to clutch her under the arm. The fingers touched the bottom of her breast, pouched in cotton. They lay there lightly, numb. She leaned herself down on to his hand and made a cup of it. His feet pushed against the ground and the breath went out of him.

The pub was at high-tide. In the singing-room, Jack played the accordion and Ronnie Graham whistled *In a Monastery Garden*. A woman squeezed her thighs together against the emotion engendered by the stinging tone of his whistle and against the bladder about to weep in sympathy: not wanting to run the gauntlet down the man-blocked passage to the Ladies in the backyard: a change from lager to a little drop of port would do for the moment. Many thanks. Such good sing songs. 'If I were a Blackbird' (with imitations) would be his encore.

The Hard Men in the darts-room played on despite the crowd, and the arrows thudded into the board. Shanghai they were playing and a bull to finish on. One man was trying for it: thud, thud, thud, the arrows streaked towards that central black, feathers brushed back along the shaft. Douglas was serving there.

In the corner of the bar sat Dido – like an immense turtle overturned on the sand. Mild and bitter *if* you don't mind. Mild and bitter. Crowded here as everywhere and a stranger making a bit of a nuisance of himself in the corner, Joseph keeping a steady eye on him.

John was in the kitchen in his corner seat drinking brown ale. Grand when your son was a landlord. And Joseph always saw him all right. The three ladies from Dalston sat, wadded in satin with deep décolletée, plump as Christmas geese, breast to breast on the sofa with gins and the little red cherry on a stick, listening to Ronnie in the singing-room, murmuring the word of the songs to themselves: swaying together.

There were almost a hundred people in those four small rooms. The waiters called as regularly as porters 'Mind your backs, please,' 'Mind your backs, please,' and the trays of drinks were held on high passing through the crowd, the ark of the covenant.

Betty and Joseph managed behind the tiny bar, serving the waiters, serving the bar. They worked together like a music-hall team, even an act, so expertly did they swing the bottles and pull the pumps: a family act – at once moving and intriguing. Rapidly, rapidly the orders came and it was now that Betty abandoned all attempts to add up the cost of long orders and Joseph did all the calculations while yet he served as quickly as she did. They seemed perfectly matched but Joseph felt her resentment beneath the cheerfulness like a cold current under warm waves. The pub bored her and she defended herself by working harder and tiring herself. And she had no liking for him, Joseph thought, was lost in a concern for the boys which she could not share, even with them. But it was this double-act which upset him: to the customers cheerful, to himself bitter – moods following each other as rapidly as pictures in a reel; Douglas could be like that too.

'Mind your backs, please. Mind your backs; your bellies won't save you.'

Lester watched her get out of bed. He saw her pull on the dressing gown and blush a little when she felt his look on her, yet he had clambered all over her body minutes before. She put her fingers to her lips and went out. He kicked off the bedclothes and looked down at himself. Muscles thin, relaxed; white body with deep brown neck and forearms, like the marks of chains. In his thoughts, Lester struggled between the decency he wanted to have and a stronger force which, now bitterly, now with satisfaction, he recognized as being nearer to himself. She was a good old thing. She made no complaints – just as well. She put up with a great deal on his account: that was her business. She demanded nothing: had no bloody right to. She took risks for him: her own look-out.

He waited for her. Straight to bed he had come on arrival and would leave it to go straight home. The kids had been asleep. He raised his knees and prodded the calf muscles with his fingers. Yes, they were supple: mustn't stiffen up. One more season – and then this life, these people, this god-forsaken spot wouldn't see him for dust.

Along luxurious lanes pitch-black and rustling with known sounds, Harry cycled very slowly. Sheila had biked into Thurston alone but he had insisted on setting her back, and that gallantry was the bow on the new parcel of feelings which had just been delivered to him. They had kissed and held each other for an hour outside the gate of her farm and he went very carefully now, as if carrying a bowl of water brim-full, afraid to spill a drop.

The day behind him appeared so large that it was only by a miracle that there was room for other days to exist. The hay-timing, how she had looked then, the stolen kisses behind the stables, the long wait for the pictures – and then, as if all his life had been but a trickle of powder leading to this keg, the silent explosion of every nerve end, blown to the wind, collected there and swept back on him.

He got off the bike and pushed it, to take more time, to let it have all the time he could.

It was at night that John felt most odd. Then the darkness shrouded him and made him no more than a ghost to the present. And about him, in lanes and away to the hills and the coast, he could sense the free run of the young on this Saturday night: money in their pockets, not tired by work nor afraid to lose it, heirs all to the titles of choice, leisure and liberty: sons of his sons yet, it seemed, hardly of his breed at all. If only he and his brothers could have delayed their birth!

The men who had given him a lift home had dropped him off just before the village and he walked up the hill very slowly, pulling his collar around his throat though it was not cold, clenching and unclenching his fingers in his pockets for they were stiffening with arthritis and he had to keep them moving: long since had his concertina been wrapped up in the bottom of the wardrobe. His knees, too, were painful as he pushed up that slight rise – and he remembered when he could have skipped up there like a buck – and after a full day's work.

They could not understand. Sometimes he told Harry about what it had been like; but it was always the same. It sounded either comic or tragic, and himself a clown or a slave: he could never get it right, show that it had to be in those times, that there had been real pleasure in loaded toil which mingled with the pain and drudgery of it. No. Harry believed him, of course, but could not understand.

Nor could he: sometimes, looking back on himself, he would see the man he had been, see that man loading a cart or in the pits and shake his head as his eyes passed him by – uncomprehending.

Joseph knew. Joseph could understand. But then Joseph had begun in farm-work himself: and had always been a toiler. But these others ... they were all doing well ... nor was it a cause for wonder ... Things had changed, things, things, which daily deluged him from television and papers . . . and men must change with them.

Now on the flat, his shoes the only sound in the village, he walked even more slowly, for this night it was of Emily his first wife and love that he thought. They did not understand: she was there in his mind as young and fresh as ever and he in that mind reached out and took her with ease: only the bodies ruined it all, cold or caged. He was still the same. Still felt the same anger – still felt the same pleasures, more, more in the ease of his eye these days, wanted the same, same lusts and even, strangest of all, the same hopes: yet, being old, he could admit them to no one, would be called a fool and deservedly thought one – and, being old, he had to see each impulse shrivel at the wrinkled exits of his skin – no longer could they be released and fling themselves on the world – forever must they be imprisoned now, and he the jail to his own freedom.

God, God, the feet pushed on: he who had at least never hesitated before his own body, never spared it, never hoarded it, used it as his weapon for life and with it battered down doors of need and desire, stumbled maybe and seen little but felt enough for any man – now to be slowly stiffened, and not to go mad, refuse even to show.

Look at the sky – a hard young moon. And the garden, flushed with blooms. And the door of his house with the key under a stone.

Douglas counted the midnight strokes and when they had stopped counted once more, trying to keep both tone and rhythm of the strokes in his head. On that church-tower he had stood, many a time, shivering for fear the caretaker should come up and catch him, intoxicated by the battlements and at the same time shadowed by the feeling that to jump, to float down to the gravestones, arms outstretched like a bird, a hawk he would be, to do that would be possible if only he dared.

He was sitting on the wall of a garden on the Syke Road above the town and eased himself off it, suddenly aware of the preciousness of his solitude, not wanting an accidental sound to disrupt it. Yet he would have welcomed such an accident. He was going to walk the three miles around the Skye Road: there was a clear half-moon and so it was cheating slightly; for this walk was a test of his capacity to bear the solitude he dreamed to inhabit but which, met, threatened him with disintegration. But he was calm now, felt strong, could take the test and thus appease the slavering chops of self-detraction for some more time.

Still he stood, near the lightless house and lit a cigarette. Few sounds below in this town he hated to leave. There the faces he knew, the people he loved – and would never leave, he told himself, would never abandon – he protested too much did he? an incision would be made and the limbs would be sawn off unless he went on his knees to stitch every gash. He would do that.

He tried to think of something written on paper, to give himself a hold on both words and an object, to uncoil a lifeline which would draw him safely through that moon-shadowed walk. He saw the scribblings he had made about the novel he wanted to write, and in the stillness they seemed yet more unreal. But the thought of writing was at least something: the only thing to counter this terrible, inexplicable and desperate emptiness. He remembered that he had read somewhere that only a blank page, an empty canvas or a silent instrument could be a valid response to these times: and here he understood it, for he was overwhelmed by the variety and multiplicity and fear in his mind and felt the madness of skull-bound yet ever expanding desperation; but that way led to Nothing. Better to attempt a 'just representation of general nature': for though the mirror might be tarnished it should never be broken. Should it?

He thought of his parents, set in the town, he thought, like a vein of ore. Was it because of them alone that he was what he was? If he could be good, as he saw his mother good, then he would be glad. How easy it seemed for some to do good actions – for Harry, who never lied, was not underhand, was not led to spill over his faults into harmful effects: but you could not side-step it like that. Even if it were not possible for him to be as good a man as he would like to be, it was certain he could avoid being as bad as he could be. The words 'good' and 'bad' – they came to his mind like places once loved as a child. Yet he could not forget them: sometimes felt himself crippled because he could not forget them. Good and Bad. They appeared 'irrelevant': and he had laughed at them with others: but irrelevant to what? Not to behaviour, nor to purpose, neither to manners nor to thought. Irrelevant, perhaps, to clarity, to will and to ambition: yet perhaps these were an empty count if there was no moral reckoning.

His mother would be sitting on that low stool beside the fire nursing her tea. Her feet half-in those old slippers, too tender even for those old slippers, sore, aching feet. Now, at this distance, he wished he had once had the courage to bathe them.

'Bed?' asked Joseph.

'Hm?'

He knew that she had heard. The distances now between them were so vast: only work united them: yet how long could they rely on that?

'What about bed?'

'You go if you want.'

'We could both go, eh? Eh?' The tone tried to have the colour of light.

'I'll just finish this tea.'

'Come on. Let's go together.'

'Don't keep on, Joseph. Leave me in peace.'

It was often like this now. And as he looked at her, the waste blacked out his mind. They *had* loved each other; now their affection scarcely touched, could hardly co-mingle in the boys who led their lives for them, only met now and then in a person of this town which was all he might ever know until his death, this town which was locking him in, this town which was calling up his last effort, which would be directed to escape.

All he thought of now was getting out: the grass was indeed greener on the other side of this fenced town. As they sat there in the dead hour around midnight, when all but a few in that place were tucked up and those active were at work on the machines at the factory, then he would weigh his chances, prod here, dig there, shake some rubble, make a mark, prepare for when he'd have the confidence to attack. The timing was easy: Douglas's going.

Why was it, though, he wondered, in pain at the thought but unable to repress it, why was it this woman, this love, this Betty, now appeared ugly before him, unlovely and even hateful?

Chapter Sixteen

At the trail his dog failed to come in and he had to wait for it. He had watched all the other dogs come in. Every one. Then the bus driver had sent word it was time to go as the others were getting impatient. The bookies packed up and left. The Crossbridge Committee took down the tent and piled it onto a trailer with the stakes and the ropes: a tractor came to pull it away. Somebody who had offered Joseph a lift in a car and stood with him only after a short while grew nervous; once Joseph noticed this he persuaded him to leave and was annoyed when he did so.

In less than half an hour he was alone in that field: dusk coming on: no sign of the dog. He blew the whistle and waited. There was nothing else he could do. It would be worse than useless to go out into the fells and look for it. If a farmer found it caught in barbed wire or otherwise trapped, he would release it and either send it back on the trail or bring it back to the field. In an hour it would be completely dark and he did not know his way among the hills well enough for that.

He turned up the collar of his raincoat and moved around to keep his feet warm. Now that there was no alternative he almost enjoyed it. Betty would be told and understand there was nothing else he could do. There was something restful about a situation in which there was no choice. And the pressure building up in him to make such a choice about his own life was becoming difficult to bear. He had had enough of 'The Thrush': it had served its purpose. But what else could he possibly do?

From time to time he blew the whistle.

May had thought he might come to the trail and put in an

apple cake for him; put on a clean pinny, ordered her two youngest to be back and scrubbed on time – and tidied up the cottage. When the children had returned to tell her that their Uncle Joseph *was* at the trail and had given them each ten shillings (May took it from them for their post-office books) – she was as excited as she could still always be at the prospect of seeing a relative: especially Joseph. She wished her husband had not gone across into Ennerdale with their eldest son to help with a late harvest: it would have been better had all of them been there for Joseph to see.

And when the trails finished and she heard the cars roar away from the village she put the kettle on. The children had come back before the end of the trail to be clean and tidy as she had demanded – and so they didn't know the reason for Joseph's non-arrival. May wanted to send them out to look for him but she was afraid they might get dirty or run away and play: besides, she did not want to seem to beg.

Eventually she let the children change back into their ordinary clothes and go out: gave each one a fancy cake – the apple cake was unsliced.

So when he did come, she had been alone in front of the fire, nursing her chin in both hands and the cheeks which he kissed were lightly scorched.

'I'll take it some bread, May. I've tied it up against that bit of railing. We don't want it howling its throat out.'

'Here. Give it some of this.' She cut a large segment of the apple cake. 'They starve those poor things – not you I mean – everybody else. Go on then!' Happily, she shooed him out of the door he had just entered. 'I would make them owners run around fell tops on a cold afternoon if it was left to me: and let the dogs sit cosy in motor cars.'

'When's there a bus?' he asked as he re-entered – his first question, May noted: then she reproved herself for being so eager to find fault. 'There's a one at seven to Whitehaven and you can get one to Thurston from there.'

'I won't be back 'til about half-past-eight then – maybe later.' Joseph took off his coat. 'I'll have some tea then. It's too late to bother.' With May he could pretend to this fine carelessness;

convincing both of them that he was capable of forgetting the rush there would be in the pub.

'Aye. You just settle yourself, lad. You must be cold.'

'I kept movin'. And then it just trots up to me as if we'd been out on a little walk. Come up behind me. Next thing I know, its nose is in my coat pocket looking for its bait tin.'

'Well!' May reacted as if she had been given a description of something rare and wonderful. She poured fresh water into the tea-pot and waited on her brother at the table.

'You always could bake, May,' Joseph said, later. 'Haven't eaten apple cake like this for years.'

'Betty can bake.' May would not be counted before his wife.

'Not in the same class. Not – in – the – same – class.'

'Oh – don't say that, Joseph. Last time I came to see you there was some beautiful sponge cake. Don't say that. Another cup?'

'You're very comfortable here,' said Joseph, in rather a lordly manner.

'Why shouldn't we be?'

'No reason, May.'

'I've lived long enough to be comfortable, haven't I? My Christ, I've still got to make do with all sorts of job lots and pass-ons.'

'Now don't get like that, May.'

'Like what?'

'Oh dear. And I've had such a grand tea.' He paused, then smiled at her – 'D'you remember when you used to bring us apple-cake at the Sewells?'

May's expression – which had been perturbed – cleared instantly and she replied.

'We had some good times then, didn't we, Joseph?'

'Sometimes I think that, May: then again I think they were bad times.'

'Now I agree with you, they were. Bad times.' Her brow puckered, indecisively – 'But like – I enjoyed some of them.'

'So did I.'

'They should have been shot for sackin' you,' she declared, warmly.

'Best thing that ever happened.'

'Was it?' She shook her head. 'Bein' *sacked?*'

'Well, if I'd stayed on, I'd have just stayed in service.'

'You would, you would. You were tip-top at it. That's a tongue-twister, Joseph! Like in a Christmas cracker. TIP TOP AT IT.'

'If you say it fast, it's rude,' said Joseph and groaned to himself the moment the observation passed his throat – May would – there it was – blush for him. 'But what I mean to say,' he rushed on, 'is that I'd've looked daft as a butler nowadays.'

'O, you've done very well.' May was on a theme which gave her no doubt. 'Everybody says you've a lovely house – they do, and it's not just because they know you're my brother because most of them don't. And Betty keeps things beautifully – as soon as I set eyes on her I knew She'd Be The One. I knew it. Oh – you've done very well, Joseph. And so have Douglas; and Harry,' she added, carefully, justly. 'Him an' all. All of you.' She hesitated and then, lowering her voice, said, 'Douglas wrote a letter to me from Oxford, you know. He did. Told me all about it.' She waited, not wanting to presume, but Joseph's attention reassured her. 'You wonder where he got his brains from, don't you? I mean – you were clever, you were now, you were: maybe he got them from you. But Betty's clever as well, isn't she?'

'How's David and John and Emily doing then?' Joseph asked, abruptly.

She told him about her own children, defensively, relaxing to praise only when she had weighed his interest and found it sufficient. But to give herself every protection, she cleared the table while speaking.

'Just think, eh, May? – not being able to eat it all up.'

'Aye.' She smiled sweetly. 'Our dad would have knocked our heads off if we hadn't finished everything in front of us.'

'And *he* wouldn't have seen that much food in a week of Sundays.'

'We must be getting old, talking like this,' said May.

'We are,' Joseph replied. He leaned back on his chair and patted his belly. '*That* wasn't just delivered this morning. Took time.'

'You *are* a bit fat. But it suits you. It does! You were a bit thin.'

'I started to put it on in the Forces you know. All that beer.'

May shook her head.

'Aye. No good for you. Oh: I mean – having a pub's all right, but drinking isn't – it makes you fat. Mind – I'm fat and teetotal so what the hell!'

Joseph laughed at her confusions; she ran in and out of them like a rabbit playing round a thicket.

'A pal of mine just now retired from the R.A.F.,' said Joseph. 'Went all through with him. He came out a Squadron-Leader.'

'Goodness me!'

'A tidy lump sum and a nice pension for life. And I was in charge of him when we were in together,' he said and could not prevent the lurch of envy in his voice. 'That's the funny part.'

'I don't think it's funny. You could have been a sq – squaw – what was it?'

'Squadron-Leader. No – I couldn't. Not in Stores. He was *fit*, see. A marvellous footballer.'

'Aren't you fit then?'

'Fit? Fit enough, May.'

'Sit on an easy chair – not that hard-backed thing.'

'You don't half take things literally, May.'

'Lit – what?'

'To heart.'

'Aye well. It's as good as any other spot.'

Later, she insisted on walking him to the bus stop. This puzzled him until she took a short cut which led near the churchyard and he understood; their 'real' mother had been buried there, brought to lie beside the first of her sons, who had died soon after his birth. On her stone was mention of another boy, Harry, who had been killed at the end of the First War. May wanted him to see the grave.

They stood there in the cold, the two of them bulky with clothing on heavy bodies. Tinker sniffed at the close-cropped grass and his breathing sounded too loud. Joseph was moved by his sister's sentiment and knew, as he put an arm around her shoulders, that she was having a quiet cry. He, too, would have liked to cry but could not; was beginning to worry about Betty and the pub, beginning to see the customers file in, the faces in the public bar went singly through his mind.

In the bus on the way to Whitehaven, he joggled impatiently on the leather seat. Would Betty remember that the mild had just been changed? Would she have collected the two pounds' worth of coppers from the bus station? Would she tell Michael Carr that his brother wanted to see him and of course she would forget to check the bulb in the back cellar.

Blank outside, past slag heaps and terraced houses, the bus seemed jubilantly lit. He could not get back fast enough. Tinker was under the seat. He knew the conductor and the man had tried to persuade him to sit downstairs so that they could talk: had said, over-loudly, that he would 'forget' the rule about Dogs Going on the Top Deck. But Joseph had insisted on going upstairs. He wanted to be alone for a while: to look at his reflection in the black windows and beyond them to the landscape he had known all his life. But how he wanted to leave it! His skull would crush his mind if he could not get out.

They moved south soon after Douglas left University; in the summer, when Thurston was most hopeful. And Joseph became tenant-landlord of a large working-class pub which once again needed 'improving'; the work concealed the wound for a few years.

Part Four

Arriving

Chapter Seventeen

As if in preparation for his father's arrival in the morning, Douglas checked through what he had just written of the town he had called Thurston. Deliberately using real names, deliberately allowing his own sentimental feeling about the place to find expression, it was, he thought, a message to his parents.

An evening at the end of summer.

'In the park the braver children have the swings to themselves and dare each other to hang by the legs. In the Showfields the keener rugby players turn up for pre-match training. Harry down there – a useful centre – travelling back from Newcastle to play; and Peasa and his four brothers, the two Bells and the two Pearsons – Taffy surprising everybody with his play at stand-off – Eric Hetherington with his style and mimetic confidence in all things, Keith Warwick the untouchable full-back and Apple the uncrushable trier – there in the green and white hoops they train beside the beck, white shorts against hedges as the twilight comes and Hammy races up and down beside them, urging them on against non-existent opponents, brandishing the net to fish the loose balls out of the river. Across the road there's the shuffle and click of bowls on the pampered green and grave men are thoughtful about their attack on the jack. Beside the green, a few loyalists show face in the Tennis Courts – the Mann girls, Wilson Bragg and Dr Dolan – "to keep the club alive"; the doctor in long trousers because of his bad leg, still hopping shrewdly through a good game. Nearby on the putting green Mickie Saunderson practises the golf shots he's seen on T.V. and does about three an hour – the rest of the time spent looking for the ball. While from the park and the Showfields couples drift along tenderly or tensely, making or breaking the dreams of past and future which whisper most insistently in this still and leisured hour.

'The people *I* know mingle with those my parents knew – for Joey Mitchinson walking along the Wiza, square-shouldered and meticulous, a hard, working man with ginger in his hair and in his character, he who started Infants' school with my mother (when it was behind Market Hill where a garage is now) – in his face I see Margaret his daughter who was at school with me – her wide, magnificent smile – and the same teachers for both, Miss Ivinson, Miss Moffat and Miss Steele – with George Scott the headmaster, in his late-eighties now and still reading the lesson at church, developing his own photographs (and hand-tinting them – nothing was too good for the town he had taught in since the previous century) making lemon cheese and remembering the name of every pupil, every single pupil, not one ever forgot – grandfather, father and son. Stern he had been, quick-tempered – but it soon passed – and believed in Courage, Honesty and Loyalty.

'Of course there was snobbery, bullying, meanness, hypocrisy and despair in Thurston: that is to be expected in any civilized community. What was moving was the warmth of feeling the place evoked. It was in some measure by talking of the town that they talked to each other – and warmth, especially, was transmitted through this knowledge of the people in the place.

'Further up the Wiza, Vince Wiggins would be trailing along watching for trout – and when seen he would stand in the beck and wait for them, "tickle" them, throwing them out onto the bank – something once seen never forgotten.

'Through the gate of the last Show-fields onto Longthwaite Road where Willie Reay would be going for a training run – scarlet satin shorts, the successor to Lester who'd now shot away from the town to a life in Liverpool, rumours coming back half-enviable, half-sinister. But Will Reay pounding away now and through his head the names of famous athletes rolled on a never-ending scroll, their ages and times and weighty remarks – and Geoff Byers just in front of him on a black racing bike, timing him with an ancient inherited stop-watch and using coaching terms with great aplomb.

'On the Syke Road they would be walking the Hound Dogs – Freeman Robinson and Joe McGuggie, Andrew Savage and Old Age – friends of Joseph all and the lean dogs yelping at the end of the broad leashes, the men leaning back as the dogs strained forward, the town they were half-circling, silent below.

'Everywhere small farms in a fold of ground: buildings cuddling the rise of earth, pegged to the landscape.

'Lowmoor Road where they had began to build new houses and the Baths with the boom and shrill of voices coming through the open windows. The Nelson School silent and empty; in the school-house Mr Stowe re-checking the new term's new timetables for the last time and occasionally dreaming of France. Hope's auction as empty as the school, pens and classrooms bare, hall and auction ring, cloakroom and byre. The church, too, all the churches empty, all but the Catholic where the nuns – Sister Frances, Sister Philomena and Sister Pat, the three that Joseph knew best, the three who most employed themselves about the town – where these smiling brides of Christ in antique dress filled the house which was theirs with flowers and chanting. Empty the banks and the shops at this time – Oglonbys, Middlehams, Toppins, Bells, Johnstones, Thomlinsons, the Co-op and the Co-op extension, Studholme's, McMechans, Jimmy Blair and Jimmy Miller, groceries and fish, Lunds with their light bread rolls and Norrie Glaister for pies, Willie Dodd, Radio and T.V. and the Pioneer Stores destined for a brief life against the Co-op, Graham's, Pearson's, Sharpe's, Christies, Morgan Allens, and Miss Turner's. Francis' sweet-shop and Noel Carrick's, the only one still open if you didn't count Joe Stoddart's in Water Street which would open any time you knocked on his back door. Empty the three tearooms and the big new car-park they'd destroyed an interesting street for, people out in the fields, in the pubs, in their gardens and allotments, the younger ones at Cusack's café down Meeting House Lane with the giant juke box penetrating the cinema next door which now was a Bingo Hall. And deserted even those mysterious warehouses which stood about the middle of the town. Silent the slaughterhouse, and the Market Hall.

'Dried blood now in the gutters of the slaughterhouse where

many a time Douglas and Harry watched the still or squealing beasts shot and seen them slump and shiver before being hooked by the throat and slit open – always the steam and the lardy skin, like white frozen jelly, which should have been bloodied but stayed white and gleaming – and then the man would plunge his arms into its belly and bring out the pouches, stomach and intestines and the slaughterhouse reeked, the waiting cows moaned and the small boys were dumb at the sight of it all. While nearby, around the corner in that town where everything was around the corner – the covered market stood idle, no mid-week dance, no social, no amateur theatricals, no speeches, just the stalls pushed back and that lovely, deep rather rotten tang in the fish-market.

'There, in the main hall, on Tuesday afternoons would come the slick operators from Newcastle and rhyme off such a gobful of patter that drummed up a crowd just to listen to them. One black-haired fellow selling sheets who never stopped and insulted them all in ways they did not understand – "I could sell more outside a synagogue on a Saturday," he'd say, and bursting with alliterative delight, add "sell more outside a soddin' synagogue on a stupid Saturday, I could; sell more outside a stupid soddin' synagogue on a soddin' stupid Saturday – really, ladies, please!" (But only one in twenty of his audience would ever be *really* certain what a synagogue was. And the Saturday part of it left them all completely cold.) "*I* won't ask you 80s., *I* won't ask you 70s., *I* won't ask you 60s., *I* won't ask you 50s., feel the flannel, madam, who needs a husband with my sheets? *I* won't ask you 45s. and I won't ask you 40s. – now go to Carlisle, go to Carlisle! Go to Binns and go to where else is there in Carlisle? Go where you want and get me a pair of first-class-quality-guaranteed-flannel-sheets-unmarked-and-unspoilt for 40s. – do that madam and I'll give you 60 for them – you cannot buy what I am giving you – and I'll tell you what I'll do I'll tell you what I'll do – one towel, one face-cloth and one sponge – there, free, gratis and for nothing – rob me ladies while I am weak – there – Not 40, not 39, 38, 37, 36, 35, 34, 33, 32, 31 – 30 bob the lot! 30 bob the lot! 30 bob! 30 bob! Thank you, thank you, ladies. Thank you all!"'

He would try to finish it in the morning. He had always wanted to use the real names of the people there. But would they object?

He got up at four-thirty to be sure to finish the work in time. Though he had snapped down the alarm button just a few seconds after it had begun to ring, Betty too had woken up. He could feel her awake there: the breathing shallower.

But she let him go down on his own. They had agreed that she should sleep on until six, and she did not want to change that plan now, knowing it would upset him. Listening, breath-held, she smiled in the dark as she heard him clatter through his breakfast. She had laid it out for him before coming to bed, of course. Less than four hours previously.

She dozed, as pleased as Joseph himself that this day should be so.

He liked to work alone in the silence. Then he had the measure of everything and nothing was rushed though he went quickly. As always, when going away, he ordered matters on two assumptions; one that every possible disaster might occur, the other that Betty would not be able to cope with any of them. It entailed an elaborate system of stacking and securing and always reminded him of those Western films where the people inside the fort prepare to meet the onslaught of the Indians.

He was going to the World Cup Final. Wembley – Yes! With England playing and Douglas taking him – and which of these two facts gave him most pleasure he did not know. He *had* to be up at 4.30 to spend the hours alone, to weigh and balance his excitement.

England In The Final Of The World Cup At Wembley Playing Germany And Himself Being Taken By His Son.

Maybe they would go out on the town after the match: maybe have that long talk he longed for, he'd dreamed of in sentimental moments, when father and son would emerge from the chrysalis of blood and memory and be friends. Now he was certain of one thing. Douglas liked him. Certain. He'd asked him to come and spend the day and given him that one free ticket he had. Joseph fully appreciated how much the young man would have preferred going with one of his own pals – maybe one of those people he made films with or was on television with – but he'd offered it to him.

Pile up the bottles of light ale by the hatch; open all the barrels; fill the drawers with cigarettes, load the shelves with whisky. If England should win . . . !

He put down the typescript and drank some more coffee. The draft of the novel was scattered all over his table. It read so awkwardly that he was embarrassed to put his eyes to it – and he groaned to think how many times it might have to be rewritten.

He had published two novels which had been 'quite well received'. The one he was working on now – *The Throstle's Nest* – was an attempt to bring his past directly into fiction in an effort to connect it with his present. Perhaps the only way was not to write it as fiction at all but to make a confession and perhaps the best way to do that was in a screenplay for television or film where the nature of the medium would inevitably colour what he was saying in the tones of his present mind. The act of writing a novel seemed to put on him a habit from the past which aided but contained him: yet only in fiction had he felt that he was recreating that density which sought release; taking the load off his mind. At present he wanted to lay dynamite around his inheritance, stand back, look around; and then plunge in the handle – like himself plunging into a woman, like his feelings plunging into his past, like his mind plunging into words – to plunge and blow himself into the instant that is Now.

And so *The Throstle's Nest* – so tentative and reticent as to be foolish compared with his expectation. But you could only go at the pace that was yours. He finished the chapter.

'The pig market empty, the old Armoury and the Primitive Methodist church, and Redmayne's factory closed for the night.

'Only the Rayophane still going. There, where Joseph had once been exploited as many a man in Thurston had, unexpected changes had brought expansion and wealth to the place. Royal Dutch Shell had taken it over and decided to invest heavily in it – and to their surprise in a way, those working there were told that they were more efficient, considerably more efficient than, say, their chief rival in St Helens – which was full of "graduate types". None of these at Thurston, only local men who had joined from school and as well as doing a full day's work, had flogged themselves through night school year after year and were now running the place, young men, George Stephenson, Jimmy Jennings and Billy Lowther. It was becoming a centre of great and justifiable pride now, this factory, and they built the chimney higher and higher to take away the poisonous stink of chemicals.

'So down there in the factory fields there was new building and men moving between the "shops" – running through it still the river Wiza, technicoloured by the discharge, oily and fascinating – changing the feeling of the town this extended factory now sweeping across the bottom of Union Street where further up Dickie Thornton had also cut a swathe to extend his colony of pumps and garages.

'The British Legion would be filling up at this time – they were modernizing that, bringing in the old Drill Hall – it would take a lot of trade from the pubs.

'As the pigeons wheeled above Bird-cage Walk and flew out over the Stampery, the double-decker took the new bloods to Carlisle for the disco-dance (Tues., Wed. and Thurs. 3s. 6d.) in the Casino Ballroom. Into the town came the farm labourers on their heavy old bikes, needing the pint they had measured out their money for; and out of it went Ronald Graham, the hairdresser, the man with the most infectious laugh in Thurston, full of news and tattle, who'd made a "turn" of an illness which would have depressed most people for life – there he goes, carbound, nosing his way to the latest village pub of his delight where he'll stand at the corner of the bar and market the day. And out of it too, George Johnston, thoughtful and preoccupied, exercising his basset hounds and in his mind assembling the book he has to write on them, dreaming of the small dogs at the courts of the French Kings, finding perfection in a paw.

Into Thurston came the boyos, the Hard Men from the villages and estates, to lounge in the corners and take an occasional drink – the darts players loosened up in the rooms as yet empty of all but them. And out of it went Mr James for a walk, maintaining a fast pace, concentrating on Collingwood's Idea of History, breaking it down and re-assembling it, preparing to introduce it to the upper sixth in autumn.

'Most of all in the town there are these men like you, Father,' Douglas wrote, 'because Thurston is full of men like you. Who've been hauled into work and have recoiled into play. Who've been drummed out of childhood and dragooned into a society which had dug itself into them like the man at the slaughterhouse and pulled out your entrails for its own use. Who've come not to expect though they've not stopped demanding, not really to hope though desire can't be killed – "ordinary decent people", the phrase writes you off too glibly and yet you would take it as a compliment. But you saw what might be in the war and in your sons all of you, and pushed for it, and won a little. So now we see each other in sentimental stereotype half the time – but that's all right; it's the dry men who flinch at sentimentality and the timid men who are afraid of stereotypes, not understanding that you can be type and individual, both unit and man without contradiction or surrender.

'The centre of the town is very calm: you could walk up the middle of the road without too much worry. Keeping to the pavement, is William Ismay, having closed the shop and arranged the next day. And in him, for me,' wrote Douglas, 'both of you, the town and myself meet. Approximately the best man I ever met – *well* met in Will, we are . . .'

He read through what he had written and wondered about the embarrassment but decided he had not lied nor romanticized, only omitted and there was still time.

His father would soon be at Paddington and he'd promised to meet him at the station. Why did he need so much looking-after when he came to London. Already, annoyance was assault-his intended placidity and even though prepared for it, time was needed to drive it away.

He made his bed and cleared up the breakfast stuff in case an accident brought his father back there.

He lived in the bottom half of a four-storied Victorian terraced house in a street which had been decaying badly for over thirty years; he had got the down-payment from a film script and his formerly regular television job helped him secure the mortgage. His parents could not understand why he had not gone straight to a suburban semi-detached and sometimes when he came down the steps as now, and stepped into a half-eaten wad of chips, shuddered at the lorry which churned past the new flats being built around the corner, saw the cracked fronts of the houses, the long-peeled paintwork, the broken steps and damp walls – sometimes he agreed with them.

But not as he turned at the top of the street and walked down towards the underground, towards the centre of London. Then this part of town seemed ideal – a place he *had* to live in if he was to keep alive in the present. Otherwise there was nothing but retreat to Cumberland which could no longer be merely a memory – must be the past or a living place.

He walked down this hill of North London and saw the spread of city before him, the place for 9 million people. To the south and south-west, the parks and commons of Wimbledon, Richmond and Ham and the deep domestic luxuries of Surrey; to the south-east, docks and Dickens, Greenwich and the Tower Blocks covering the cinders of the blitz; and slung between them the bricked undergrowth of London, from Wandsworth to Barnes. And on the North side of the Thames – the City – even of wealth still, sucking sterling gluttonously, fattening those who commanded the centre of the town and lived in Westminster, Belgravia, Knightsbridge, Kensington and Chelsea. Then the dreaded Inner London Area of which his was part, where Victorian property threatened disaster to those who colonized it as they themselves had once been colonized – Jamaicans, Pakistanis, Nigerians, Barbadians, Irishmen and Indians – joined by those, like the Duke of York, who were 'neither up nor down'; the continental exiles and the provincial adventurers, all faces, all colours, all hell or heaven depending, a place becoming as dense to his adult mind, he sometimes thought, as Cumberland had been when a child.

And more, more. Because as he walked towards his father and tried to think of the Final, the Cup, the Excitement he forgot it all and saw only the face of Mary whom he could meet this night; her blue-grey eyes soft and serious, her smile as sweet as any happiness, her hair in his fingers, draping his wrist.

Lester had travelled all night. He had scented the gang's intention before they themselves had really tasted it – left the club instantly and snatched the few clothes he kept at Moira's place. He'd caught a bus to the edge of the city. His own car was being repaired and he had only a few pounds cash.

Besides – who would think of looking for Lester Tallentire on a 32 bus or making for the A6 to thumb a lift south? He'd made more of himself than that! And they'd never have dared turn on him if he hadn't had such bad luck lately. Succeed and they'll jump in a lake for you; fail and they find an excuse to turn. Best thing to do was this, best thing was to go south, let things quieten down, get something together and then come back. Or maybe stay south; he'd often wanted to – put it off – no need – now there was no choice and that always helped.

The lorries wouldn't stop – the lights seemed to make straight for him, examine him and then pass on rejecting him. He would not hold out his hand and waggle his thumb like some sodding hitch-hiker! They must know why he was standing there at this time of night with a suitcase between his feet and his hands jammed in his trouser pockets. He wouldn't beg! He had no coat – couldn't endure them – but it was a warm night and he was in no hurry.

It took him over an hour to get a lift and he was lucky even then to be picked up by a fat little prattling Welshman who always looked out for company about this spot on his twice-weekly run of 350 miles south. 'Company keeps you con-cen-traat-ed,' he sang – and the alliterated refrain, invariably employed, it seemed, was meant to be the slyly jocular seal on this transitory acquaintanceship. He could have been excused for passing by, for Lester presented no sympathetic sight: in a well-cut dark suit, white shirt and dark tie, with black hair, dark skin, good looks, he seemed the last man to need help; while his aggressive manner – apparent even when standing at the road-side – was too much of a risk. But the Welshman had his rules and stuck to them: nobody in the cabin for the first 100 miles, then the first one you saw – never been let down yet; many a grand crack. He might have broken the rule had he known about the knuckle-duster in Lester's inside pocket; highly polished and wrapped in a clean handkerchief. But Lester fell asleep and even at the transport café said little; ate his bacon sandwich and looked around, so obviously bored by the Welshman that even the prattle faded.

It was not until he had walked about a mile through the town which was the lorry's destination that he firmly decided to call on his Uncle Joseph. He had heard of their move south and been only mildly surprised: his aunty Betty would resent it, he knew that, but in the end she would have to follow Joseph and his uncle had often said he would like to get out of Cumberland where he was too well known to be himself.

He went to the railway station to have some breakfast in the buffet and clean himself up. It was too early to call on them yet. While Lester was in the Gents impatiently waiting for the hot water to prove itself, Joseph passed by outside, unseen and unseeing, on his way to the London train.

When he saw the sign he stopped to gaze at it.

JOSEPH TALLENTIRE Prop:
LICENSED TO SELL ALES, WINES, SPIRITS
AND TOBACCO.

He remembered how in Thurston he used to stand outside 'The Throstle's Nest', transfixed at the sight of his own name up there. And how, the time he'd been had up for that robbery he'd cut the report out of the paper to look and look again at his name in print.

He stood and felt himself checked. There had always been so much to look forward to in going into his uncle's previous pub that he had deliberately delayed doing so to enjoy the anticipation. Something else, though, as well. Despite the unchanging warmth of the welcome he had always been afraid that he might be imposing, 'putting on' Betty's generosity and Joseph's interest: occasionally he'd turned away so as not to presume too much. These feelings were from a past which seemed so distant – for his last years had been such a chasm after the plateau of his earlier life – that he wondered at his own memories; they were so unexpected, like a rope bridge which hangs across a ravine. What he had been and what he now was! If they knew all he had done they would not even let him in.

And that last thought pleased him! For so often had he come there doubting himself good enough to enter: almost rubbing off his soles on the door-mat so as not to dirty aunty Betty's scrubbed floors: all but introducing himself to his uncle Joseph as if convinced the older man could so easily forget him; always feeling that he had to be on his best behaviour and burdened with a sentimental gratitude towards them for their understanding of his times in 'trouble'; a passionate feeling of thankfulness which he thought would never die but had died. He was glad to be going in carrying the last few years secretly, to be received as a prodigal when on the run from a beating-up because of a botched job. Oh – they knew he'd been in trouble while a teenager, but nothing could be held against him in Thurston since he'd left: he'd been acquitted of the robbery charge; not enough evidence. Witnesses were hard to find.

So he went in with a swagger and pretended to be unmoved by Betty's delighted surprise: agreed to stay the day so that he might see Joseph on his return from the match and looked around appreciatively. They were doing very well, these two. A few bob had been spent on the place – you could see there'd been money spent, not big but some. And the till clanged busily.

What more can be said of that day of glory when England won the World Cup?

The drink they had before the match was excellent – Douglas took him to a quiet, rather exclusive little pub in St John's Wood where they had home-made steak and kidney pie (and

Joseph regretted that Betty would never go in for catering – 'doesn't like the idea of Staff, see, Douglas? Puts her right off, telling people what to do'); where they had a couple of pints of bitter to which Joseph conceded some points; where of course he introduced himself to the landlord and itched to get into details about the nature of the trade and the size of the takings, always letting it be understood that if the place was attractive enough he might keep his eye on it and watch out for future developments; where there was the silence when they realized they were to be alone together and the glancing at each other tentatively, to prise the face of the stranger from the presence of the son and father.

Then outside the ground itself – that twin-domed yet most ordinary place which had supported so many fantasies of so many ordinary Englishmen as teams had come up for the Cup and gone down fighting: the touts there shouting £5 for a 15s. ticket (soon to be sold at 'fair price' – they overestimated the public's willingness to risk missing the match which was to be certainly seen on television by 500 millions was it? Some unimaginable number of intent eyes and 100,000 people actually there) and the Refreshment Tents – as at Agricultural Shows, said Joseph, programmes, balloons, team photos, colours, and everywhere that chant which had become England's Cheer as the series had progressed.

Inside the ground, among a crowd of miners from Barnsley. There were about 30 of them and they worked together at a pit in a village near Barnsley. They'd made 'a reet do out o' this World Cup'. Somehow – Joseph never asked them if the pit had been forced to close down – somehow they had taken two weeks off work together, as a gang. Hired a coach for a fortnight: booked themselves into boarding houses in Liverpool and London, organized tickets for the most impressive number of games and sailed up and down England in a trance of football. Joseph watched Douglas talking to one of them in particular – a wiry little man who kept referring to The Party and was soon launched on a description of Oswald Mosley's meeting in Barnsley Town Hall in 1936 and how the Party lads had tried to break it up. Phrases came over to Joseph – 'those Blackshirts wore knuckledusters, you know, under their gauntlets' – 'we plastered Barnsley wi posters' – 'the People was being fooled – they were – they didn't know what a Fascist was'; and he saw Douglas relax in that old man's company as he did in John's; and was jealous in a way, puzzled in another because these fellows who followed one path undeviatingly were *not* the strong men they appeared, Joseph thought: it was easier in many ways to hold than to let go, to stick than to change, to keep than to give. He wanted to tell him that.

But he was away with one of the miners who'd spent some time in the West Cumberland coalfield and worked with people he knew. And from the swapping of Cumbrian names, they went on to the names of those in the World Cup – now become as well-known as neighbours: the brilliant, delicate Brazilian Pele; Eusebio the oak-thighed star of Portugal and Yashin the Russian goalkeeper, black and gloomy. They laughed about the 'little North Koreans' who had surprised everybody, and agreed about the bad luck of Argentina. If only the Americans really played Association Football, Joseph thought! And suddenly he remembered Mr Lenty, the cobbler, and that time they'd chanted the sheep-count and the old man, dead now, had sworn that the American Indians counted in the same way.

It was strange the two of them sitting there in the back-kitchen watching the game on television, their dinners on their knees. Lester had helped in the pub and carried up the cases from the cellars with such efficiency that the man hired for the job had been rather put out until Betty had mollified him by emphasizing the word 'nephew'; family gave privileges. But 'nephew' was far away from the feeling between them now, the blue plates heavy with fried food humidly pressing onto their knees as they sat in armchairs side by side and watched the game, the one because he was an enthusiast for football, the other because she loved an Event.

For Lester had already made up his mind what he would do and in some flicker of his feeling Betty had guessed it. The grit rubbed between them, as yet infinitesimally small but already it was growing. Yet Lester had been all smiles; charmed the ladies, impressed the men. He had lost his sharp-boned rawness and become 'really *hand*some!' as Betty thought to herself with pleased surprise. And there was something very 'manly' about him – in the bar there whether playing darts, talking or just having a drink, there was a confident, certain-footed, easy command about him. He knew what his life was worth.

What was it then? He could not have been more attentive. Got up to help her with the tray. Made sure she wanted to see the game. Brought her a cushion 'for her back' (unnecessary – but both of them enjoyed the charade in the same way, she thought) and explained things to her about football, quietly, simply, not shouting like Joseph or making a complicated fuss like Douglas. Yet ...

As if facing up to a puzzle-picture in a newspaper, Betty leaned back in the chair and closed her eyes and tried to think of every single thing that had happened involving Lester since his arrival. Something there was which she not only disliked but feared, she realized. A real though slight shiver went across her body. She *was* afraid of him and half-opened her eyes to make sure he was still where he ought to be. His plate by his feet, the knife and fork neatly crossed, sitting back, legs crossed, with a cigarette, an ash-tray held thoughtfully in his free hand, absorbed in the match.

She closed her eyes again and nestled her head into the arm of the chair, imitating sleep to stop thinking about it. Time and again she was plagued by such feelings: such strong reactions to what first appeared as nothing at all; the invisible end of an invisible thread which she picked at and picked at and sometimes *did* unravel.

Perhaps Lester reminded her too strongly of Thurston. Somewhere inside her there was a sob – as heard in her mind as if it had been declared out loud. In the end Joseph's arguments had exploited her own frustrations about matters in general – and she had come to think their cause was the town, its abandonment the cure. But now she felt more isolated than ever in her entire life. She did not know how strong the net of acquaintanceship was until it was no longer under her; nothing now to break her falls. And though she loved people from

Thurston to drop in on their way to London or to Cornwall for holidays – loved it and would celebrate their arrival with a release of gaiety otherwise now preserved in measured form for the self-satisfaction of a job done well or coincidences chiming – yet she feared these reminders too. They were too harsh. As she plundered the visitor's gossip her mind's eye swept up and down the main street, patrolled the alleys and courtyards, inspected shop and market and church – then rushed back to the box made so strongly for it by the old imperatives of duty and loyalty: but really bound by necessity. There her love for the past would be locked up until, again provoked by such direct contact, it would escape once more and bruise itself in taking pleasure.

So she appeased herself, that is for the few painful minutes during which she willed her memory to be dead. That passed, however, she found her doubts unresolved and was worried yet again. Because what had the lad done wrong? Why did she take against him so? For it was no less than that now; she could feel herself turning against him, all the positive, welcoming expressions of her body and emotions were being blocked by this silt of doubt.

A loud roar from the crowd brought back her attention to the match. Lester turned and grinned at her – widely baring his teeth. 'We've scored,' he said, 'we're in the lead,' and she pretended to be only half awake so as to disguise her shiver as a yawn.

'When it was fully realized that the Fête was to be on such an important day, such a day of days for some of the menfolk – I refer of course to the Final of the World Football Cup Competition – then it was too late to change. Mr Wolfers had lent his garden, Mr Russell had allocated the small marquee (free of charge, as ever, our thanks to Mr R.) the Women's Institute had issued rules for cake contests of, let me say, all shapes and sizes, and pleas had sped forth from the Mother's Union for Jumble; the A.Y.P.A. – our brave Young People – had begun the sixpenny raffle with the greatest enthusiasm and one heard stories of strangers importuned on top of Knockmirton Fell itself with the request to buy a pink ticket for Mr Wheldon's kindly donated *Pair* of Chickens – in short, our annual fête was under way and, after a fashion, I'm proud, yes – that hoary old sin crept quietly in – proud, I repeat, to say that not even a World Cup Final can stop our parochial activities. Mr Whitehead at the gate tells me that we are only a score down on last year when, you might remember, there was a freak thunderstorm the night *before* which worried some of the mothers.

'Of course we all want England To Win. And here's where we *score*, as it were. For not only can you enjoy the fête – and I earnestly beg you to spend all the money you can rightly afford; believe me the church tower will benefit enormously and everlastingly – remember, only £9,625 to go in our grand slam for the £10,000 – but not only can you contribute to the mile of pennies – the white line kindly painted by Mr D. Jones to whom our grateful thanks – or catch the piglet (loaned by Mr Duncan, one of 9, I'm told, all doing well) or guess the weight of the lamb (our thanks to Mr Copping – a pet lamb this belonging to his daughter Joan), not only, say I – to use the tricks of that man on television who introduces all the old music hall stars, I forget his name – thank you, Mr Odges, I'll make a note of it – not only can you do this – and don't forget the treasure hunt behind the garden shed – a shilling a peg and a pound for the crock of gold – (Mr McGahern's annual donation) not only (I mustn't forget Mrs Bomford, must I?) not only can you guess the number of raisins in her four pound fruit cake – who else is there? – ah! Mr Hamilton has brought his Hoop-la once more, genuine Victorian Hoop-la – and Mr Farrer's presiding over the Dub-Tub and the sisters three (forgive me ladies but fitting it all in makes me a little light-hearted, not to say headed, we *all* appreciate your endless devotion to St Jude's) the Misses Powell are there once more with the exquisite embroidery on handkerchief and – head-band is it? That other thing? – Art from a long lost past preserved for us only by the devotion of those sisters and quite reasonably priced. Yes, as usual, tea will be served by Mrs Strawson and Mrs Bloomfield boiled the water – sandwiches by the W.I. and cakes by sundry: *so* – not only do we have all this – but in Mrs Wolfers' conservatory – that is behind the house – there is a specially installed television set (thank you, Mr Mapplebeck) on which our more sporting brethren can watch the efforts of their fellow-countrymen in their fight against the German.

'I now declare the 1966 St Jude Garden Fête and Fund Raising Afternoon to be officially open.'

The Rev. Duncan, a young man but centuries-fat with a happy complacency which had begun as a good-natured bantering of 'the natives' and resolved itself into this unctuous facetiousness redeemed however by his undoubted generosity and constant hard work – in clerical grey now padded across the deep green lawn and came to Harry with a copy of his speech.

'You'll find all the names mentioned there, Mr Tallentire. All you'll need are the prizewinners: I could give you those now if it would help you for your dead-line.'

'I think we'll manage, thank you. And I *have* to stay. They want a colour piece on it this time.'

'Ha-ha! "English Life goes on while England fights Again for Victory".'

'Well – I suppose so. They do one a year, you know – for all the ads you fête-people put in. This year it was you.'

'You're a football fan, Mr Tallentire, I can tell that. Slip round to the conservatory – I'll give you plenty of colour. It's my trade, you know.'

'No, I want to do it for myself – no offence.'

'None taken, my boy! Please – say whatever you like about us! We can take it.'

Thus do heroes bare themselves to the elements and the Rev. Duncan felt no less courageous as he paced towards Mr Hamilton's Hoop-La, having dared the *Cumberland News* to do its worst.

Harry had been unhappy about the job for several reasons. There was the match, of course – but now he'd be able to see some of it at least. No – it was this complicated business of the assistant editor who liked him and was always trying to help him and Harry wished he wouldn't. He did not really want to be helped. He was very happy. Very happy to collect names at rugby matches, football matches, socials, prize-givings, fires, anniversaries, meetings – wherever there were names to be collected he was more than happy to copy them down and worry that they were correctly spelt in the final edition. And like all good provincial newspapers, the *Cumberland News* was well aware that every name was a guaranteed sale – and they had the special provincial pupil-distorting small-print to meet that situation. *More* than happy. He loved to motor around Cumberland in his second-hand Mini – going to villages he'd never visited before, finding out more and more about this dense and endlessly interesting county, its names in his notebook ready for the press. He was known as 'the reporter' in villages and sometimes addressed as such by vicars or small children. That suited him fine. He wanted no more. And when he married he wanted to live right here and do exactly the same thing for the rest of his life. The job paid as much as most – less than a foreman at the factory – but pleasanter work altogether. And the *pleasure* in knowing everybody, having all those names in his head. If a slight pride was there it was just in this authority and when arguments developed in the pub about who it was and name of what? – Harry would pursue the matter like a hound until he'd tracked down the correct name and then feel great relief and a sense of accomplishment.

But this assistant editor thought he was made for Better Things; kept tormenting him with encouragement to do full match reports for Carlisle United Reserves or interview Mr Simon who bred racehorses or this sort of thing – a 'colour piece'. And gamely, Harry took on these jobs, not wanting to disappoint the man's expectation of him and thinking himself somewhat greedy, perhaps, in keeping the easy work (though everyone else in the office regarded it as the slogging bit) and feeling, hopelessly, that a 'reporter' ought to be able to turn his hand to a 'colour piece' or a full-length report just as easily as a Scout Rally (how he loved to copy down the names and numbers of all the troops – Wigton St Mary's 2nd Troop – Bothel 1st, St Mungo's 4th, Aspatria – and get the patrol-leaders and seconds and scoutmasters just *so*).

He was no good at this other. And it took him hours.

Now, feeling his stomach clenched in dismay at the prospect

of interspersing the names with 'descriptive passages', he wandered across to the wall – nodding to the many he knew as he passed them by – and looked across the fields towards Knockmirton Fell, its cone-shape clear on this bright afternoon. He loved this part of Cumberland – just where the plain went up to the fells which ringed the lakes: those bare hills, boulder, bracken and scree, figured by sheep or now the occasional hiker. It moved him more than he would ever be able to say. As did this fête, in its way; people making do, enjoying themselves, coming together for company, yes, but for a decent purpose outside themselves as well. He could not understand how anyone born and bred in this place could ever willingly leave it.

Perhaps his affection for the place was due to his grandfather, John, with whom he now lodged. In that meticulous, old-fashioned household there was peace and certainty; restlessness was dismissed as weakness, alternatives to present settlement – mere fripperies.

There was a shout from the conservatory! England must have scored. Briskly he walked back across the lawn – he would labour at the piece through the night. Perhaps they would soon realize he wasn't good enough – that was his hope – and leave him in peace.

The game. Of those at Wembley and others all over England watching television many linked football inextricably with working-class conditions of life, where prize dribblers were nurtured in narrow back-alleys; in the Depression when 'it kept you going' and the War when 'there was nothing else to do'. And the team which stepped out for England was somehow of those times. This was 1966 and there had been Beatles, Swinging London, Trendiness and self-conscious Pop Culture – but this England Team were short-back-and-sides, hair with a parting, soberly dressed, modestly spoken, rather serious – a few beers and a quiet life, cautious, a good job done and no excuses Englishmen. They had come out of the bad times, this team – typified by the stern-faced Charlton Brothers from a mining village in an area so hard hit it was a wonder it had not revolted – but there was no revolution, just perhaps a more open belief in the notion of the dignity of ordinary men. Intimations of such thoughts passed through Douglas's mind and as far as he could tell, similar feelings and others yet more insistent were present in the minds of those around him.

The final brought the Prime Minister flying back from Washington – to his credit.

The actual game was not as good a game of football as the semi-final when England had beaten Portugal; there was good fortune in playing in your own country and at your own stadium; but the chief aim in a cup competition is to win it – which England did; well. Nor did the fact that the victory was gained over Germany detract from the sweetness of the triumph. London rang that night with car-horns and drunken singing and twelve names were ceaselessly invoked: Banks, Cohen, Wilson, Moore, Charlton (J.), Stiles, Peters, Hurst, Hunt, Charlton (R.), Ball and Alf Ramsey, the Manager, soon to be knighted; no less.

They travelled back into London in the Barnsley coach and by closing time Douglas needed a rest. He had taken them all to a big, friendly pub near his house where he knew there was room to move, entertainment later on in the evening. (Piano, drums and occasional double-bass.) The amount of beer sunk in the first few hours was awful to think about. When he got back home – his father insisted on coming with him – Douglas had time only to make a swift postponing call to Mary (he was in no state to see her anyway; and perhaps, for once, he would connect with his father – only that). He asked Joseph to wake him up in two hours, hit the settee and was out. Joseph, by no means empty himself but steady enough still, regarded his prostrate son most tenderly: it was the first time they had got drunk together. Betty had half-expected him to stay the night and he had every intention of waking Douglas up just after midnight and going on to one of those drinking clubs he'd told the Barnsley crowd about. He phoned her and was pleased Lester was there to look after her – had always liked Lester: liked everybody tonight: the whole world.

He saw the words 'The Throstle's Nest' and was glad to think that Douglas was writing about the old town: then he read bits of the novel – it was not very long, that first draft: took him about two hours – fitted in well with Douglas's sleep.

Later, in the drinking club (which Joseph did not think much of) he found himself sitting in a quiet corner with his son and told him he'd read the book.

'Did you like it?'

'That's hardly the point, is it?'

'I suppose not, no.' Douglas hesitated. 'I'm glad you read it. I'd never have shown it to you.'

'I read your other two. I would have read this when it came out.'

'Yes. But maybe I would have thought I ought to have shown it to you *before* it came out. So that you could object if you wanted to. I mean, if you think there's anything to object to. I'm a bit drunk.'

'No. I follow you all right,' said Joseph. 'And you *sound* sober enough to me.'

O Christ, another silence! Another of those empty spaces which had pocked his life with those he ought to have loved.

'Well?' Douglas asked.

'Well. I quite enjoyed it, Douglas. You think you've got me weighed up – and you're wrong though you're entitled to your opinion; and you can't talk straight about your mother – but then you never could. There's a lot left out of course – I appreciate that.'

'What d'you mean "appreciate"?'

'Now then, Douglas.'

'No. What do you mean? Are you thanking me for it?'

'Should I?'

'You know, dad, I know less about your private life than I do about Bobby Moore's.'

'That's not unusual, is it? I mean – your mother and me aren't famous, are we?'

'No. O God, this is getting nowhere! Have another.'

They drank off and Douglas unnecessarily went to the bar himself for the drinks. Joseph anaesthetized his son's irritation with sentimentality. 'You don't seem to realize,' said Joseph, smiling as Douglas sat down, 'that I'm still a bit sideways – it isn't everybody has a book written about him. Not a bad book either ... you got your mother in that part with the eggs. Straight as straight she is. And although *I* can see things in it – I doubt if others will. Cheers.'

'What do you mean?'

'You've been very careful, Douglas. A bit like a detective, I thought – you've covered up where it mattered most. *That's* what I mean by "appreciate". You haven't got me, though.'

'No. I had to invent *you*. I don't know you well enough to describe you.'

'Now what does that mean?'

'It means I don't *really* know what you feel about anything: say about what you've read. A little, a lot; mild, or murderous; flattered, or furious; a bit proud or a bit disgusted – I do not know.'

'No, Douglas. And you'll never get to know, either! And I'll tell you another thing – you haven't said the half of it about yourself, either. Not the half!'

'Dad. Let me tell you this which will, might, just surprise you. Do you know that because of your dreams of Perfection – all those lies about Perfect Love and Perfect Heroes and Perfect Marriage and Perfect Honesty and Perfect bloody Worlds – because of that I've been slithering about with a view of the world which is about as useful as a wooden leg to a sprinter? And the violence between you! And what you would not say and would not *let* be said! And –'

'Hold on, lad, hold on. We all have problems. But they're our own private business, Douglas. *Private*. Now you rang Mary was it? Mary, yes – tonight. Well two and two makes four, even to those that never went to Oxford, son, and you know that I am curious – but it's *your business*. Right? And I want to tell you something – I want to tell you this.

'You've got a chance. No. Don't shake your head like that. You have a real chance.

'Now what I'm telling you is this. Let her rip, lad! Bugger everybody! You just put down whatever in God's name you think's right! Don't ask, don't worry, if you're all right in yourself and you're not after hurting somebody – you can't go wrong. Just get it down – that's what you've picked to do. Get it down!'

Betty had let the woman go home who'd been so carefully commissioned by Joseph to spend the night with her should he not return on the last train. Lester would be staying, she thought, and though her unease had developed into suspicion as the evening had gone on and he'd charmed his way boisterously through the customers – yet almost as an act of penance, she had dismissed the unspoken and unproven charges. Moreover, and giving her strength, the more worried she became the more convinced she grew that Joseph would return: he had not phoned which he would have done had he been staying. And Douglas would have enough to do in the evening without trailing around with his father. They'd never spent an evening together yet. Once, such a hunch would have been tied to a feeling like instinct, but perhaps more prosaic; that mixture of observation and experience based on intimacy and affection which can come to seem like instinct: frightened now, she relied once more on it – but the tie had been broken and the hunch was wishful only.

When, just after 11 o'clock, Joseph *did* ring up – rather drunkenly, she thought, which coloured her reaction, and said that he was staying on, she could have shouted to him to come back – but Lester was no more than a yard from the telephone and she dare not, pulled a face at Lester, as if to say 'aren't husbands terrible!' and pleasantly informed Joseph that his 'nephew' was here, emphasized the word gaily as Lester had once liked it – but who *was* this confident, sprawling man spread out in the best armchair? – yes stay, of course stay, no Anne had gone home but Lester would look after her – looking well, yes, he was looking *very* well.

She put down the telephone briskly to overcome the trembling and walked to the back-kitchen to 'wash-up and tidy up and then upstairs' humming a sentimental pop song under her breath and listening to Lester turn the pages of the evening paper as a scared child might listen to thunder.

In bed, light off, she bunched up her knees to her breasts and clenched her eyes tight shut hoping to press sleep on herself; hearing every creak and breath of the house. A large house this, the biggest they'd had, and the pub itself huge, too vast for them really, but a good living. Tried to think of Thurston which was what sometimes helped her to go to sleep. She'd start at Burnfoot and go up the street, looking out for people to stop and chat with, say hello to: and how she missed that in this new town! To spend an entire afternoon at the shops and meet not one soul you knew! Godless. In Thurston, when she'd gone to Carlisle for the shopping trip, her first gossip on returning had been, always, to tell them all who in Carlisle she'd met from Thurston. But they couldn't go back – could they? Once you'd left you never *could* go back – could you? It would be to admit that once they had thought Thurston second-best. And having *chosen* to leave (though she'd fought it; silently in the end but so obstinately that the withered roots of their love had been wrung utterly and were dead forever) but having seemed to have chosen to leave – that irrevocably altered your relationship with the town, made you above it, lost it to you. Deep in these unhappy but easing reflections she relaxed and was not startled when she heard Lester come up the stairs.

But he did not close the door of his bedroom.

Now, tensely awake, between panic and tears, she waited. After two o'clock he moved most carefully and in stockinged feet crept down the carpeted corridor and into the upstairs sitting room, over to the sideboard (he'd measured the distance and removed the obstacles in the afternoon) and there were his uncle Joseph's takings where they'd always been in the black tin with a gold canary on a silver tree worked on the lid in some sort of wire. He ran his thumb over it as he'd often done when putting away the money his uncle had been pleased to trust him with to show where *he* stood after Lester's early troubles. There was a little satisfaction in this reversal but more of disquiet and he was most careful to put the note face up.

Dear Uncle Joseph, [it read]

I know this will make you a bit mad but I'm in trouble and I'll pay you back. You know I keep my word when I say. I'll pay you back no two ways about it. But I've got to keep moving and anyway this is a bit much to ask you for to your face. Sorry.

Best regards,

Lester.

There were the takings since Monday, including Friday and Saturday – well over £350.

Strangely, as Lester went down the stairs he *knew* that his aunt Betty had heard him and yet was forced to pretend she had not for fear of the complications which would arise from the admission of the knowledge. Similarly, Betty understood that he had divined her attention – the catch of a footstep was as loud as a street greeting – but she willed him to ignore it and felt happier with him than she had done all day when he did that and let himself out – almost noisily, the forms having lapsed and strode across the gravel outside their back door to clamber over the wall (thoughtful that, too, knowing that while she might dare leave her bedroom to re-bolt the downstairs door, she would never find the courage to go outside and lock the backyard door after him) and then away.

The shoulder of relief became a trembling and that helped the fear to the surface of her mind where it leapt in monstrous shapes, seizing on her imagination with horrible force and terrifying her.

Alone, alone, she hated to be alone. The walls would come in, the door would blow open, the ceiling press down, her mind abandon her body, her body dismember and dissolve, alone, alone and yet with this grit of embarrassment which would prevent her from going out to find a friend, going out to seek help, going out to admit the terrible fear into which all her thoughts and feelings now trembled and fell, were sucked down and drowned until faintness and exhaustion left her to sleep.

It was mid-morning when Joseph got off the train and he decided to walk to the pub though it was about a couple of miles from the station. Along the Kennet Canal he walked, slowly, re-living the match and thinking about Douglas, looking at the swans oil-spattered from the pleasure boats.

Down the canal to where it joined the Thames – at the gasworks – and he smiled to himself at the cartoon nature of this pub-besides-the-gasworks-with-customers-who-still-took-snuff, smoked Park Drive, drank Mild, insisted on a Ladies Bar and organized all their own teams and the Outing to Brighton in Summer. What a game it had been! And the way England had come back at them in extra time – marvellous.

Lovely morning. And in these tiny gardens – what flowers people grew! The roses that bloomed here in six feet square of soil! He stopped to pull one to him, a large yellow rose with some dew still on it, still now at this time.

At the pub he looked above the door, as always: JOSEPH TALLENTIRE Prop: LICENSED TO SELL ALES, WINES, SPIRITS AND TOBACCO. What *name* would Douglas use in his book?

Before he went into the pub he dreamed: that he would save enough money to buy a house for himself and Betty – just an ordinary little place, but really his. That they would live there and he would do the garden, she dust the rooms, grandchildren arrive, a swing on the lawn, drinks with his sons, chats in the sitting-room, discussions in the 'local'. With all his might he tried to think that this would work for Betty and himself.

But it ignored the facts. Inside that place before him was a life which had to begin again if it was to be lived at all. He could serve and wait: no more: which called for love or need and the one seemed as far away as the other this bland morning.

Without any premonition, he went to the door and stopped before opening it, under the sign of his name, took out a cigarette as if arming himself with it. Over thirty a day now; have to cut down. He spent more in a week on cigarettes than his father had earned as a living wage at his age – much more; yet Douglas would spend the same amount blithely on an evening's pleasure.

He inhaled deeply and went in.

KINGDOM COME

To Alice

PART ONE

I
Going Back

(1)

Lately, Betty had begun to wake up much earlier than she needed to. It was not traffic which disturbed her—for although the bungalow was in the middle of the town it was situated in a quiet side street, one of the old streets. Nor was it any animal which brought her alive. It was just past midwinter, the early mornings were black, dogs were kennelled, cats indoors, the farms, which had once probed deep into the centre of the market town, were now denuded of barns and beasts, overrun by the new estates. She just woke early, that was all, there was no reason she would admit to: dreams to a woman of her age and background were of no account and she kept her restless night visions private. It would not do to talk about them, or even to confess they existed.

Her husband, Joseph Tallentire, slept heavily and, he asserted, very badly. He did not stir when she got up, and the sudden creak of the door—so loud and suspicious that she paused like a child—did not disturb him either. She went through to the kitchen with a clear conscience.

It was very pleasant, she thought, this early morning time alone in the neat pine kitchen. Her son had helped to pay for it. It was as near as she would ever get to those American kitchens she loved so much in the nice films they used to make once upon a time. It was something, anyway, at the end of a lifetime. She put on the water for the tisane which eased her asthma and drew open the curtains, even though it was dark.

There were three men who would come to see her that day. One, her son, she loved but increasingly worried about, as he seemed to lose himself in preoccupations foreign to her. Another, her adopted son, she saw every day, he lived in the town, he was a great comfort. Sometimes she thought that she liked him more than her natural son. The third, whom she had also helped to bring up, she feared, he had the power to terrify her. All of an age, brought up in the same town. All bearing the same surname. Like her own. Given to her by the man she had married thirty-seven years ago. Now upstairs asleep— almost a stranger.

She had taken the snout off the kettle so that it would not whistle. When the steam came out of it, she found pleasure in just looking at it. A light frost on the window panes. Scalding steam within. For a few moments she felt herself suspended between the two, the ice and the heat. There was a pleasure in it which she could not articulate—just being there, alone in that minute space on the planet, darkness, frost, glass, steam and the electric light. Once she had feared being alone—now she found herself savouring the condition in which memories and impulses rose into her mind like the scent of the tisane breathed in to soothe her weary lungs.

In this solitary time she found that she was thinking and organizing her thoughts as there had never been the leisure to do before. At a time when she ought by custom to have been thinking more of death, she surged at life. She read more, now that all the boys were well away from her home. She listened to the radio, liked the plays and enjoyed the drama and the documentaries on television. At the end of her life she had found the time and opportunity to begin to educate herself. In a quiet, indeed a secretive way, she grasped this. But she kept it tight to herself, as if she were ashamed of it, and in one way she was. She would have hated any of her life-long friends to have thought that she was "putting on airs" or "getting above herself". She had cleaved to the norm, the average, the anonymous, the decent, the tolerant, amused and only apparently passive role assumed by many of those of her class, age and sex. Bingo, shopping, an occasional trip, film, outing, "dance", "do"—that was the camouflage. But inside her was this secret store, this hive where she fashioned patterns out of the books she read and carefully laid up stocks of knowledge and perceptions which she longed to have released. It was as if there was a place, late formed in her mind, which needed just the touch of a sympathetic nature to open it and bring it to life, like a lost garden in a fairy story. Douglas, her son, could have done it if he had wanted to; if he had noticed; if he had tried. But she would never bother him with such silly ideas. She would go further and overact the safe old mother she thought he wanted: safe and plain and without complications. That was what he needed. She knew what all of them needed, she thought, and she was prepared to be wax to their impressions of her. Without regrets. It was too late, at her age, for regrets.

(2)

Cumbria was 39,000 feet below. So definite and clear, it seemed, full of strength, ancient and enduring. Up in the jet, Douglas was incubated like a sickly infant—a body in a capsule, babied with piped pleasures, instant food and drink—totally at the mercy of a machine he did not understand.

He leaned forward for a better view and the stranger beside him gave a gentle, sensuous groan as the light disturbance rippled across her mind. Douglas let her settle herself and then concentrated on the sight beneath him. He had spent half his lifetime down there and half out of it. The two halves nowadays appeared to cancel each other out. He was uncertain, fragile, in a state of violent self-distrust and high as a kite. After a slight pause to register his awareness of the sentimental nature of the gesture, he raised his glass to the scene below and drank to it. No one was watching.

All his family had been born there, even his son. His grandfather's life, save for the interlude of the First World War, had been totally circumscribed by those hills and plains, by the crops and beasts which fed off them and the coal and iron under the tough crust of earth. It was not the earth, though, but the waters which caught his glance. The sea, a final tongue of the Atlantic, licking a firth between Scotland and England, and the lakes, scattered so poetically about the bare fells, glistering brightly on this clear morning of the year. From his god's-eye view, it was all like a charming model in a natural history museum, this place which had borne and supported so many lives and contained so many deaths of his name and kind. He himself, he thought, would probably die in a motorway car accident, an aeroplane crash or of a heart attack in a side street of a foreign city. With luck.

He had begun to think about his death. Most mornings now, when he woke up, he found himself counting the years, weighing up the odds, trying to sift the worthless from the desired, and, as yet coolly, contemplating the sure fact of that return to the dark.

Douglas thought that he spotted the town of Thurston, his home town, to which his parents had returned for their retirement. "The last lap" was what Joseph, his father, sportingly called it, "the last lap". They would be waiting to see him that evening and later he would take his grandfather a bottle of whisky, as he had done the last few years, just after midnight, to celebrate another New Year's Day. His wife and son might be there too, although there was no guarantee, no agreement had been arrived at. Had he finally hurt her too much? He strained to pick out the fell village in which he had recently bought a small cottage, but snow had fallen on the tops, making the landscape unfamiliar.

As the Jumbo dipped towards London, Cumbria was pulled away from under him and she murmured, "That's right, that's right," in her sleep. She put an arm around his neck. He let it rest. Her brown hair smelled rich and sweet from some herb he could not identify. He loved it pressing so lightly about his face and took care to move gently as he drank yet more of the stiff spirit from the plastic glass. Home again, home again, jiggety-jig!

He still found some wonder in this flying. He had drunk champagne after the massive plane—carrying more people than lived in that Cumbrian village where he had his cottage—had hoisted itself up from Los Angeles. Over the North Pole, at 600 m.p.h., he had eaten *Boeuf Stroganoff* and taken two half-bottles of claret. Into a 160 m.p.h. headwind, above Greenland, he had watched a movie about a shark while listening, on headphones, to Beethoven's Fifth and then the Best of the Beatles. Now, with the temperature outside at less than zero centigrade, he was keeping warm on his fourth large scotch, mulling things over, and trying to remember the name of this woman who was half embracing him.

To his grandfather, John Tallentire, at this moment brewing his tea in the cold council Old Age Pensioner's flat in which he insisted on living, though alone, Douglas' whole trip would have appeared as an hallucination or a marvel. To his son, John Tallentire, at this moment banging the buttons of an empty television in a centrally heated metropolitan Victorian living room, it would all be as commonplace as travelling on a bus. Douglas was between the two; between the earthbound life of his grandfather, whose work linked him directly to the shepherds in the Old Testament, and the space-age of his son, who would see God alone knew what.

Douglas was half-cut—in that cradled, voluptuous state (which always had to be paid for) in which life seems either slow motion slapstick or a penetrably profound drama. He found the button and successfully employed it. Then he readjusted his neighbour about his left arm and shoulder and neck. His nose dipped deeply into her hair and he lingered. Why could he not identify this herb? He had helped his grandmother make herb puddings. He had followed her down the lane beside the old Jacobean cottage, so cosy and redolent in his mind (recently bulldozed to the ground—"unfit for habitation"), and helped her pick the herbs. She had patiently told him all the names in those sweet, unharassed days. He had prided himself on learning them. So why could he not identify this strong, delicious smell? His knowledge of nature was now so slight. So much forgotten, ill learnt, jettisoned by his memory—a trail of lost information forever trickling out of his brain, an invisible thread which would lead him back only to ignorance. Danger! Soulful Celtic twilight approaching! The new drink came just in time. Johnnie Walker, a brisk confident Briton on the label!

"C'mon," he encouraged himself, the blood and alcohol in equal and still companionable competition (one of his observations on travelling: capacity increases in direct proportion to length of flight). "C'mon. Pull yourself together and go to pieces like a man."

"I left my heart in San Francisco," the song said, on a sudden loop in his head. What had he left there? He had spent only three days in the place this time: little sleep, tense work, drink, the exhilarated exhaustion of that irresponsible hedonism which is aware of retribution. What had been left in L.A.? As he hummed he tapped his right foot and it nudged the airport toyshop present which was crammed under the seat in front of him. A clockwork whale for John's bath: it squirted water half a metre in the air. He had resisted a large rubber shark—though John would have preferred it, he guessed—but it would not have fitted under the seat. She moved again, snuggled even closer and murmured "Yes . . . well . . . yes . . . hmm." To whom was she talking?

He had promised himself he would make some resolutions on this trip. After all, the last day of the year was the time for it. That long abortive litter of diaries begun, drink stopped, exercises taken up, reading lists copied out . . . At the very least he could sum up the decisions waiting to be taken. Decadence was breaking promises to yourself. A message came from the steward—"Please refrain from Smoking." He finished the scotch.

She woke up and stretched herself most amply. She was a fine figure of a woman, as they used to say, very satisfactorily, and she knew it. By the time she was through with the long, loosening yawn, the arched back and the plunging heave of bosom, Douglas was powerfully aware of it. As she intended. Straight flirtation, Douglas thought, was the purest sex, undeniably.

"I slept?" she asked, throwing him a long, perfectly dentured smile, with just a tremor of helplessness about it. Douglas felt as if his feet were being skilfully tickled by a feather.

"You did," he confirmed.

"Are we here?"

"We are here."

"Is it raining?"

"No. Clear but cold."

"I thought it always rained in England."

"Mostly in summer."

"You made a comfortable pillow."

"Thank you. I did my best."

"Do you always drink so much?"

"Not always."

"I need the john."

"I'm afraid you'll have to wait until we land."

"What if I can't?"

"I hate to think."

"Do you really?" She smiled and turned full towards him and the chat they had enjoyed before she had settled down to sleep rose up from the immediate past nostalgically, somehow hinting at intimacies long past, brushed by this feeling of latent flirtation. They knew enough about each other to become a phone number in the book of future possibilities. In the moment she smiled and her lazy-merry eyes flicked over his face, both knew and were aware, and Douglas decided that his New Year resolutions might as well begin here. He would not, in any way, follow this up.

"Why don't we exchange telephone numbers?" she suggested. Her face was a perfect oval: healthy, open, American and unreadable; he had no idea what she might do or not do. She smiled again, this time with less teeth, more purpose.

"I was hoping you'd say that." He lobbed a return grin.

"I'll be in London a month. Maybe more. *Saint* John's Wood. You know it?"

"Quite well."

"Nice, huh?"

"Nice, very." He hesitated. "Can I ask you something—it's rather personal?"

She looked perturbed. A pace, an order and a progression had been established—the phone call in a few days' time, a good dinner—he could see she feared that he was going to be clumsy and spoil it. Her reaction stripped away the flirtatiousness—and added a few years to her age—and he saw a tough cookie inside the American pie. But the question had to be asked.

"Go ahead." This time her smile was on Automatic. He paused, drew it out.

"What shampoo do you use?" he asked. She grinned.

"It's pine. Pure pine." She ducked her hair into his face. "Take a breath."

"Of course! Damn! *PINE*!"

"Pardon me?"

"I should have known." The pine woods next to the shore where all his childhood treats had taken him—and the tentative walks with girls, nesting on the prickling ground, hurried kisses, fumbles, heads pressed in smell of pine. And he had forgotten even *that*! Thinking too much of Grandmother's herbs: too much piety over Cumbria.

"Can I ask *you* something?"

"Of course."

"Are you married?"

"Yes." He felt happy admitting that.

"Children?"

"One." There had been another, a girl; now dead.

"I like to know the score," she said, and her businesslike assumptions put him off her for ever. But politeness rolled on.

"We could share a taxi. I live near St. John's Wood."

"I'm being met. I hope." She showed him her perfect teeth, but it was not a smile this time.

"I'll keep out of the way."

"I'll expect your call." She tucked a small piece of paper in the top pocket of his jacket, kissed him lightly on the cheek, and then utterly devoted herself to preparations for the landing. These included wrapping herself up in highly unbecoming ski-clothes, which made her look like an Eskimo. He would not have recognized her.

Later, as the taxi screwed itself irritably into a long morning traffic jam on Hammersmith flyover, Douglas recalled that for three days now he had slept little, eaten little, drunk a lot and been in a state of almost constant enervation. Twelve thousand miles had come and gone: half way around the world since Monday, and now he was stuck in London W.6, beside a sign advertising Lucozade. He could have sunk the monstrous advertiser's bottle. His system might not have noticed. It was odd how these vast leaps across the globe could see you refilled with energy as quickly as you were drained of it. The taxi moved somnambulistically in the slow traffic and Douglas, suspended between sleeping and waking, experienced a rush of tranquillity.

He was calmly aware of being embarked on a course which would change and possibly ruin his life, and yet his instincts urged him not to resist that course. The outward pattern was much as it had been over the last few years; reasonable employment as a television freelance producer and reviewer; some writing. Yet he was isolating himself inexorably—from his friends, and from his ambitions in preparation for an action for which he despised himself—leaving his family.

When he was most alone and most respected himself, he thought that he wanted above all things to be a good man. But his character was against it.

Often he would tell himself that this was no more than a pose or a vain attempt to dignify the pointless scramble of his life. He suspected himself so critically that anything which tasted of piety appeared false. But the desire remained, however derided or dismissed. He accused himself of evasions and ill-thought-out reasoning. But the urge remained, and whether this was a hangover from an adolescence intoxicated by Christianity, an insurance, an affectation, a superstition, a counterfeit of strength, a lie to himself, a way to ennoble his life without doing much—no matter—it persisted. And however many darts he pitched into it, it kept bobbing to the surface of his mind. Why did it matter?

Sometimes it seemed to Douglas that his life was not so much punctuated as punctured by questions which were either unanswerable, or meaningless, or both. The question was, what was the question? It was important to know.

The taxi was hauling itself towards Chiswick and soon the driver would be able to leave the commuters, boring themselves into the city, and dodge through the cross routes which would take him to North London through all those Victorian side streets built for a colonial empire and now filling up with Commonwealth citizens come to roost.

He looked out of the window as the cab bounced him through St. John's Wood. He would have liked one of those villas once. Now he knew he would likely never be able to afford one and the longing to own one had left him. Which one, he wondered, would take in the pine-crowned American beauty? He touched the slip of paper inside his breast pocket and stuffed it deeper down. Forget it.

Back onto a big road now, with flats and shop-frontages and

traffic patterns like that of hundreds of other large cities the world over, and up the Hill. There would be no time for sleep. He went back into gear, the metropolitan man took over.

Letters to answer, calls to make, check back at the B.B.C. "The filming went well—yes—well enough—needs careful cutting—yes," pay one or two of the bills—those printed in red—that was the rule—how could he be broke on what he earned? How did you accumulate the capital to take the time to do what you wanted to make the money to live by what you wanted to do? Answer that! There would be, what—three days—about thirty letters to answer: lectures (no), talks (no), requests for charity (yes and no), and bills. One or two particular phone calls to make, a review to write: good clean work. John's whale was safe. Cigarettes for her—a poor gift, though welcome. Then the launderette. Set off for Cumbria immediately after lunch. Go to Bank. £9.50 taxi fare. For a ride from the airport! The pavement was littered as usual: the dustmen must have been.

He paid up, using his money as if he owned it, turned and there she was, at the top of the steps, in her old maroon dressing gown, watching him critically.

"Home?" he asked. She smiled a little wearily and nodded.

"Yes. This is it," she replied and came to help him with his cases.

(3)

"You think you're *so* bloody marvellous."

Lester did not reply. He was getting dressed rapidly and he was concentrating on the job.

"You think you're *so* bloody marvellous."

Emma's voice was full of despair and self-pity. She sat up in the bed, the expensive hair-do (she was blonde again) collapsed about her tired, mussed face, pecking at the ivory-imitation plastic holder which held the first of the fifty cigarettes a day she depended on for dear life and feared were killing her.

She's like a great fat doll, Lester thought, stepping smartly into his new trousers. A monster doll. One of those you see at the big fairs. Walks, talks, blinks, squeaks. He smiled to himself. That was it! *And*—she was like one of those blubbery big sex-shop dolls, "the sailor's friend", they were selling up and down Tottenham Court Road. Yes! She was a half-breed between one of those Kewpie Dolls that blinked (*her* eyes were blue as well) and one of those rubber gals the poor sods carted off to bed with them! The thought cheered him up. He laughed.

"What's so funny?"

It drove Emma mad the way he refused to answer. She felt her head choking with anger as, physically, her throat choked when she vomited. The comparison was easy to make because she was often sick these days. Little food, lager, vodka and lime, cigarettes, no exercise: and the baby. Slowly being formed, silently, secretly there, stalking her relentlessly. She thought of the baby now: she saw it curled and peaceful somewhere deep in her large stomach, safe, slim, white, sucking its thumb. Although she knew that Lester hated it, she began to cry and the mascara came down her cheeks like the markings of a clown.

"You don't even *like* me," she cried.

He speeded up. But all his clothes were new. He had to be careful.

"You don't even *like* me." Emma thrashed around the bed, truly in despair.

Lester looked at himself in the mirror. Not bad at all. Late thirties, but you would take him for late twenties by the body. (The lined face was the giveaway, despite the youthful cut of the hair—still thick, thank God.) Good quality clothing. No more than three or four extra pounds on him since he'd stopped racing—when?—half a lifetime ago. He could still run, though, he kept fit. He examined himself carefully. He inspected himself as if he were about to go on-stage —professionally, without self-consciousness.

"How do I look?" he asked her.

"Pig."

"C'mon. I want an answer. I'm serious. Do I look all right?"

"Give us a hug. Just a hug."

"I've just got dressed up."

The look of distaste on his face almost made her howl—but, by making a great effort, she repressed it. He really did hang on her approval and she had never been able to resist him, or refuse him anything, though he had come and gone like the wind and treated her like dirt.

"You're beautiful," she said passionately; but to Lester it sounded like mockery. He was impatient with her.

"I'm *not*—what you said! Have some sense! C'm*on*!" Lester's need was serious.

"The clothes fit very well. Brown suits you. Give us a hug. Please, Lester."

"What else?"

"Your hair needs a shampoo—but it's just the right length."

"I'll wash it on the train. Shirt?"

"Lovely!"

"Goulding House. Twenty-eight quid!"

"It suits you. Just a little squeeze then?"

He turned back to the mirror and pushed his hair this way and that. She was right about the shampoo. He went to the bathroom to see what he could find. What a pigsty it was!

As soon as he left the room, Emma did what she could to restore herself. She licked her fingers and wiped her face, using the sheet to dry it off. She rolled over and hung over the bed to look for her brush which, she was sure, was on the floor. The action lifted her shortie-sexy pure nylon pink and black lace nightie and revealed the full and tender moons of her large, firm, innocent bottom, trussed about with a suspender belt. She had slipped that on when she woke up to help him along a bit in the morning but he had not even reached out for a quick feel. Lester came in with his egg shampoo as the huge bum juddered with the strain of reaching out for the brush. It was one helluva bum. He went across to it, took a cheek in each hand and gripped very fiercely, digging in his short, newly manicured nails. This was extraordinarily satisfying: he had not a clue why. From beneath the edge of the bed, a happy face screwed round and beamed at him from under the hair-stack which now looked like a drunken Restoration wig, but was, in fact, like everything else about Emma, all her own.

"Jig-jig?" she said in that baby voice which turned him right off. "Lesty jig-jig wif Emmy?"

He dropped her: the red finger marks were as clear as paint.

"I'm late for the train."

"Just a liddle-iddle jig-jig for auld lang syne wif Emmy? Emmy-wemmy."

The middle-class nursery endearments—so gentle, so nicely silly, so sweetly harmless—thudded into Lester like insults. That was a sodding vicar's daughter for you! They were all the same.

"I'm off."

He had already packed his case. It was rather battered but covered with airport tickets and labels. All authentic. That would also impress them in Thurston. After they had digested the story of his travels, Majorca would seem like Morecambe. He still had something to play with.

"Take me." She swung upright, again reminding him of an object with clockwork inside.

"I'm all dressed up."

"I mean to Cumbria. To see the New Year in with you. You and me. I can't stay here. Can I?"

The last two words were rapped out. She gazed tragically around the bed-sitter. It was a small first floor room in a terrace of mid-nineteenth-century jerry-built houses in Kentish Town. Emma had draped it with the debris of her progress and, latterly, her decline. Revolutionary posters from what she called "my student bit" (which had been rudely aborted). Psychedelic posters from what she called "my flower-power bit". Cheap Eastern mats, junk and joss-sticks from "my transcendental bit"... and all the records, paperbacks, cast-off furniture and small, personally precious objects of a lifetime's utterly careless accumulation. Most things in the room looked as if they had merely drifted in for warmth, as Emma herself had. She had come down a slothful, selfless and, as most of her friends thought, stupid spiral which had gradually drawn her from a good university with good pals and good prospects to this, as they saw it, trashy, out-dated "bohemian" existence on National Assistance. Lester used her as a hideaway and boarding house. She was also, he would tell her honestly from time to time, "one staggering screw". Whenever he said that, the little girl inside her wriggled mightly and the large eiderdown of underprotective flesh shuddered.

He would be gone in a moment.

She took her life in her hands.

"Lester." The word was marred in its delivery as she had automatically and compulsively begun to light another cigarette. The smoke was huffed out of her rather thin mouth like steam out of an old railway engine—a little instant cloud. "Lester." She found the exact jolly tone. "What would you say if I said I was pregnant?"

"You're not, are you?"

"If I said I was?"

"Are you or are you bloody not?"

"What if—"

"I haven't time for this crap."

Emma was as brave as she could possibly be.

"But what if . . .?" she whispered.

Lester did not hesitate.

"I'd say for one—whose is it? For two—get rid of it. And for three—it won't be the first time you've done that."

She was very still. She said nothing.

"There's a fiver on the sink," Lester said. "I'll see you."

He was gone.

She paused for a moment and threw back the grubby sheets decisively. In her shortie nightie and the black suspender belt, she walked over to the sink, picked up the fiver and tore it into four pieces. She went across to the phone and rang Geoffrey's number. He was a solicitor. She had known him since they were children and he wanted to marry her. Despite it all, he had stayed loyal and, equally important, he did not laugh at her and use her for amusing anecdotes. He was not in.

"If you stay here, old girl," she said in her real voice, a surprisingly firm, English Home Counties, old-fashioned, ruling-class voice, "you'll go potty. Can't do the wee 'un an injury, can we? *Right*!" She marched across to the fridge, took out the open bottle of Pouilly Fuisse and had a very good swig. "Better." She had another for luck. And then, because why not, she finished the bottle. "Must remember to cut down on it for baby's sake," she said. "O.K., girl. Pack bags. Back to Daddy and Mummy." The ugly, gaunt, unheated vicarage in Suffolk which her mother hated so much that, winter and summer, she spent every possible hour in the three acre garden. "Be a sensible Emma now. Deep breaths. You're keeping this one. God! Help me this one last time. Please."

She burst into tears and then looked for the sellotape to stick together the five pound note which would take her home.

As Lester paid with the Barclaycard he noticed that it would run out at the end of January. He had done quite well off it. Two complete new outfits—choosing his shops shrewdly, as he had done in the old days, never going for the most expensive garment, not buying on Fridays or Saturdays, which made them nervous. Fewer shops were taking credit cards without other identification these days. This annoying mistrust had caused one problem but he had walked out of it: literally. For cash, he had had a stroke of luck at the dogs when he most needed it. He was set up for about a month. That would have to do.

"Sign," the ticket man said. He put the card on a little turntable and spun it round.

Lester Tallentire signed the name James Harrison, with a flourish. He had never given a thought to who this man might be. He'd bought the card from a friend.

"Twenty-six quid for a Second Class return!" said Lester.

"Robbery," the clerk agreed. "Soon all the trains'll be for the Shah of Persia and his missus—nobody else."

"Happy New Year," said Lester.

"Watch the Scottish lads," the clerk said, gloomily. "They generally wreck the trains on the way up to Glasgow this time of year. It's a Scottish thing, isn't it, New Year, with the haggis? They're all on it already. Drunk."

Lester felt a lurch of fear. He smiled, stepped away and walked slowly, considering whether or not to go back and change to a First Class ticket. This would put him out of reach of the drunken Scotsmen, who would inevitably go on the rampage up and down the train, which only made one stop on its three hundred mile journey to Lester's destination. He was in a bad enough way already and needed peace to work things out. As he went over to the First Class ticket window, though, he veered away. It would cost more than thirty pounds, which he thought was the upper limit on a Barclaycard. Besides, it might draw attention. He would get a seat a long way from the buffet and bar. He would set himself up with some beer and sandwiches here in the main hall, which they were trying to look and run like an airport lounge. Lester disliked the style: too modern for trains, he thought. He was worrying too much, wasn't he?

No. There was little point in denying it. Lester attracted trouble as he attracted sex. For about ten years now his life had swooped from one to the other, as he had hung around the Pop world and a few smalltime criminals with increasing desperation, trying to get his hands on some of the bullion. Even now, though he had been part of it, though he had managed five groups, one of which had almost got into the Top Thirty, though he was thought of, back in Thurston, as a Mr Big-Shot who knew all the Superstars—even now to give himself a profound and cathartic thrill all he had to do was close his eyes and think of the money to be made in the Pop Business. Five hundred thousand pound advances: two million dollar recording contracts: old pals from tacky clubs on Merseyside pulling in seven hundred and fifty thousand dollars per man per year for zero. Oh God! He sweated over his lust for it. Flat, sodding broke, with a bunch of Glasgow hooligans on the way to the cold North for the New Year! And reduced to stealing again!

No miracle intervened. It was just as Lester had feared. The Scots, determined to get to their hameland skin-full of Scotch, were soon carousing and then merely yelling: the real aggravation started at the worst possible time, as the train was going up Shap Fell, which would take it into Cumbria. The next station to be made for, where there would be any possibility of getting some police onto the train, was Lester's station, Carlisle. There were about forty-five minutes when the driver's only option was to drive on.

Lester knew he had been picked out. They had passed down his compartment as they moved up and down the train—Hoplites, Cowboys, Warriors in their own eyes: vandals to the mothers who clutched at their children and herded together their possessions: castrators to the men, most of whom, like Lester, had the sense to burrow intently into their papers or paperbacks and attempt to blot it all out. But they had picked him out. No wonder. He was, after all, one of them. And, however much he tried, when that "hard man" stare came at him—he did not flinch but returned it. The leader—in filthy, baggy jeans, clown's boots and a pink, thin shirt, slit to the waist—had turned to the five others with him and said, "He's our boy! He's our pal. Hello, Jimmie. Remember us? He's our friend. Eh, Jimmie?" The gang honked with laughter and stampeded back to the bar for more fuel.

Six to one was hopeless. Even one to one now . . . you got soft. He was in no shape. He looked good, but he was soft. Exercises kept you fit but not tough. There'd been all that trouble with the Law in November. Then the boys around Fulham. Big Emma had been very useful over the last two months. None of his kind knew her—neither the mob from the time he'd first hit London—a hard man on the run from a Liverpool gang—nor the scene he'd crashed into—the Rock lot—Emma wasn't somebody you could take around. Besides, he thought, you had more chance to find a winner if you were on your own. A lot of the Rock lads were bi- or right out gay and there was no point not obliging, Lester believed.

Lester was known to the Rock sophisticates as a scrubber, a tart, bad luck and an ageing joke. To the criminals, he was a fringe labourer. He was unaware of this.

He had run to Emma because he had been scared. He had been scared often enough in his life, but this time it went on for days and then for weeks. He had been out of luck before, and on the run before, but never so frightened. That was why he had treated her so badly. She understood that, even though he did not.

The long train went steadily up the mountainside, steadily hauled over the rock, away from cities, towns, even villages. These hills were quite bare. And inside, half a dozen youths, fighting drunk on about a quarter of what Douglas had absorbed on the aeroplane, looking around for an excuse to start smashing up people and things and themselves.

Lester, tuned in tensely, had awaited the change of tone since the first visitation. He heard it when they were two compartments away and moved fast.

He took his case with him but left newspaper, beer can and uneaten sandwiches there. That might gain him some minutes.

The thick sods might even wait for him to come back for his sandwiches. Which they would have eaten.

He got into the toilet at the very front of the train just as it reached the top of Shap and cruised for a few moments before it plunged down to the plain, averaging about 90 m.p.h. It was due at Carlisle in thirty minutes.

Lester tore off the lavatory seat for a weapon and jammed his suitcase between the locked door and the basin. He opened the small window and looked out at the snow-draped hillsides. Once upon a time he had run up and down those hills—raced to the top of them and back again. His career as a professional runner had failed, like everything else—but there had been one year—with his Uncle Joseph's backing ... He tried to keep himself calm by this thinking of the past. He had taken off his new jacket and folded it carefully on the top of his suitcase. He jogged on the spot and did some isometric exercises to warm himself up. The wind from the snowy hills was bitter. The train rocked from side to side like an old piece of fairground equipment. They went through Penrith and the train leaned over to the right. Only fifteen minutes to go.

Somebody knocked on the door.

He did not answer. Caught, stupidly, unawares. If he had answered, he realised, a moment too late, he could have gained another minute or two. He put his shoulder to the door, dug his feet against the opposite wall, set himself, then relaxed, and waited.

"We know you're in there, Jimmie, you wee bastard!"

There was only one voice. A boot made the thin door shake.

"We'll get you, Jimmie!" The Glasgow city slang, the gang cutting whine of menace, spun out the words sadistically. "We're goan tae hurt you, Jimmie. Eh? Eh?"

Lester had seen the guard. A cheerful old man, coming up for his pension by the look of him. A handsome grey moustache, clean uniform, deferential manner, a loud "Thanking You" for everyone; and panic in his eyes at the sound of this mob. He would be locked in his own cubby-hole, praying, as Lester did, for the train to hurtle down yet faster to the city.

"He's in here! The wee bastard's in here! Pissin' hissel', eh, Jimmie?"

The Scots drummed along the bare compartment floor and then came the blows and kicks and the almost insanely repetitive oaths which accompanied the kicking and hammering and built up the rhythm.

Lester did not say a word. He braced himself but he did not yet begin to spend every effort he had. They were uncoordinated and, though the door was splintering and bulging, no serious breach had been made. Yet.

He was even starting to think he might get away with it when the regular thud jarred the door. They had got together and were ramming it rhythmically. He anticipated it and strained against it with all his force. His insides were dissolving, he felt the stink coming out of him, he was starting to shake from the stress: he must not lose his nerve.

"Together—c'mon lads! Don't say the Glasgow lads were beat!"

Thud! The locked door shuddered.

"Aa' together. Aaaa . . . eee!!"

Thud! The obscenities disintegrated into a howl for blood.

"We're on our way, lads! Stand back—and now!"

Thud! The hinges buckled. The suitcase slid down to the floor.

"We are the champions! Celtic! Cel-*tic*! Cel-*tic*!"

Thud! *Thud*! "Cel-*tic*!" *Thud*! *Thud*! "Cel-*tic*! We are the chaaa-mpions!!"

The door was smashed but he held against it as the brakes came on and the train slowed down for the station. Fists came in to punch his head. A hand grabbed his hair and pulled until the tears raced down his face but he kept his shoulder down, his feet against the wall. "Mother," he heard himself gasping, "Christ!"

"Bastard! Bastard!!"

They were screaming now, scrambling among themselves to get at him, scuffling and slithering in the small space, hysterical with violence at being denied their victim, who was as rigid as a corpse in his small keep.

The train drew into the platform in a leisurely fashion. A bottle, its edges jagged, suddenly appeared a few inches from Lester's face. He jerked back his head and the door fell. They stood there. Teenagers, faces bloated with hatred, screaming to destroy this stranger before them.

Lester picked up the lavatory seat and scythed it at their faces, catching the leader square on the bridge of the nose, which broke. So exhausted he had little sense of what he was doing, Lester managed to lever up the door with his right foot so that they had an obstacle to get over before coming to him and he stood in the corner, between the lavatory and the small window, swinging the seat with all the strength he had. He wailed and gasped as he fought. He was kicked in the groin. His shirt was ripped off him. He was smashed in the head. He felt blows on his chest and bootcaps bruising his legs.

The police came. He was standing on the platform. They told him to wait to give his story. He went in one side of the Gentlemen's—cleaned himself up desperately—put on his coat—came out of the other entrance and quickly left the station. He wanted no trouble.

(4)

Harry was badly winded. He felt embarrassed, bent over like a collapsed marionette, while the trainer pumped him up and down. He did not like drawing attention to himself.

It was a big crowd for a Thurston rugby match—getting on for three hundred and fifty. New Year's Eve was the date of the traditional fixture with the nearest town, Aspatria. There was always needle in these Derbys. Harry had been late-tackled. Around him, the other twenty-nine players waited without fuss. It would take a miracle to change the result now. Thurston was winning twenty-seven–eight and there were only ten minutes to go. The only tension now came from the fear in the Aspatria side that Thurston's backs would gallop over for more tries and run up a cricket score; and the fear in the Thurston side that they might not do so. The men—lightly clad—moved around to keep warm, this freezing midwinter afternoon.

The evening was closing in. Grey deepening to charcoal, drawn tightly across the sky. The rugby pitch was outside the town, built, characteristically, away from the centre, in that short burst of Sixties affluence and self-confidence, when there seemed limitless room for both expansion and exclusivity. The land was owned by the Rugby Club and most people came there by car. It was not handy for those who had to walk from the old town centre or the new council estates. The new Club had changed the social life of the town. Squash courts had encouraged a host of fanatics for this previously minority sport. There were tours of France with the rugby team and, at the Saturday dances, visits from nationally known jazz bands and up-and-coming Rock groups. Wives and girl-friends came to those dances in expensive dresses, the latest styles. The Clubhouse was purpose-built, open plan, rather like a ski-lodge in the Alps, people said. There was talk of building tennis courts and the plans were being drawn up by one of the architects who played for the team. Scruffiness was discouraged and a full-time barman had been hired. An ex-President had unearthed a Seventieth Anniversary and a short "History of the Club" was on the cards. Someone had suggested butts for archery.

Half a dozen brief handclaps acknowledged Harry's return to the game and the players spread out for the penalty. Beyond the pitch were open fields; rich farmland stretching to the sea on the north and the same distance, about eight miles, to the mountains on the south. The young men in shorts, bright shirts, hooped socks, fit and with intent faces, looked as if they had been sketched onto the landscape. It was the light layer of snow, perhaps, which made everything a little fanciful. The penalty was missed: too short.

"Come on Thurston!"

"Come on Aspatria now, lads, there's still time. There's still time, lads, now." The voice was clear: like a farmer calling to his dogs in the neighbouring fields. There was a lot of shouting, but it came from individuals. On the whole, most people liked to savour these games privately or with their friends. Only very rarely did the crowd call out as a unit and then it was soon over.

Harry pressed his fingers into his waist, bent forwards and took some deep breaths without, he hoped, anyone noticing. He had almost scored his second try.

The kick-off again. Thurston's neatly drilled pack took the ball, held it, brought in the Aspatria forwards and then let it out. A long pass to the stand-off. Harry was a few yards outside him, running steadily, gathering speed. The stand-off dummied, almost got through but was caught by the wing forward. A ruck collapsed as the ball refused to come out cleanly. Harry trotted back into position on his diagonal line. He was the inside centre three quarter.

He loved this game. He loved his team-mates. He could think of no better way to spend an afternoon than this. None! Other people could take anything they wanted. Just give him this. "Come on Thurston!" he said, under his breath. The players moved across the field in patterns and formations which delighted or frustrated the initiates.

The ball came at him rather high. He was forced to check his stride but he caught it, turned out of the tackle and made straight for the line. One of his faults as a player was that he was a little over-eager to pass the ball. He did not like to appear to hog it or to appear selfish in any way. But this early passing was often unproductive. No one doubted his courage, so they put the fault down to poor tactics and agreed that it was the chief reason for his not being picked for the county side. He had always played well for Thurston though: or, as the committee phrased it, grown into new authority as organizers of the most successful side in the district, he was, "a splendid servant to the Club".

Harry was now travelling fast, reaching out with the ball between both hands—he would have to dive, the defence was coming in quickly. He began to fling himself forward. A big wing forward lifted him with his shoulder, hoisted him into the air and Harry was grounded. Sixteen pairs of studded rugby boots scrambled above him as the two packs of forwards foraged for the ball. To anyone unused to the game, it must have appeared that the life of the fallen man—whose rugby strip included no protective padding whatsoever—was in real danger. But Harry wriggled out, sound but for a few scratches and bruises, preserved by the conventions which somehow drew a line between ferocity and brutality.

"You should have got that one," the stand-off said dourly as Harry ran back into his position.

Harry nodded. He would have got to the line a couple of years ago. He had lost half a yard. Thirty-three was ageing for this game. Still, he would play for as long as they wanted him to, in whatever team, in whatever position. The Thurston side was still pressing. The ball came out again, the pass low, awkward, fumbled: he dropped it.

"Wake up, Thurston!"

Harry cringed a little and chivvied himself harshly. He was getting slack. The Aspatria side won the ball from the set scrum and tried a break around the blind side. Harry crashed their winger into touch with a hard tackle and then helped him to his feet. He felt better. Defence had always been the soundest part of his game.

The whistle blew. Three cheers from each side. Handshakes. Clapping the visitors into the Clubhouse. On the note of polite and formal amateurism these thirty players finished the game which had absorbed so much of their skill and energy—teachers, accountants, shopkeepers, one or two farmers, civil servants, a couple of mechanics, local government employees, young engineers and junior management from the big factory, a firm stratum of that rising generation which was well entrenched in well protected and well supported jobs, responsible, affluent enough for all immediate purposes, as secure, apparently, as could be imagined. They were a group to whom the words "privileged" and "middle-class" would be anathema. All of them were convinced that, in *their* world, class distinction had dissolved. Yet, perhaps unwittingly, they were building up once again the old structures of exclusivity which they would swear were over and done with forever, and of no interest at all.

Singing in the steaming showers. All the talk of Rugby, Rugby, Rugby. Harry drank a quick pint of shandy in the bar, which was bulging with supporters and players, who were conscientiously putting down a foundation for the drinking which would go on way past midnight and well into the New Year's Day. In Thurston they prided themselves on the way they brought in the New Year—"Scottish style," they said—the Border was only twenty miles away—and bagpipes were at a premium. Harry bought his round and then slipped out. It was dark.

He was going to see John, his grandfather, who was not his

"real" grandfather, just as Betty was not his "real" mother—but they had adopted him so completely that it was only recently, on the plateau of his adult life, that he had faced it as a possible problem. His conclusion had been to love and respect them even more for what they had done. He felt no pain or anger at the implications of his adoption. After all, he had had a real home, real love and "to all intents and purposes" (this was the phrase he used to himself) "a real family". He was glad that he could do something in return, these days, truly pleased at the opportunity to show his gratitude.

Though he had a car—he needed one for his job on the "Cumberland News"—Harry enjoyed walking. He liked to look around the place. It was as if he were checking up on it, or rather, giving it his care and attention. He had lived in the town all his life, he was perfectly contented there and had only once wanted to leave it. That was when he had considered emigrating to Canada with three of his friends who had moved to Toronto. He had joined them, spent six months happily finding his feet, come home for a holiday and somehow never gone back. Now he was settled in Thurston, as he told himself, "for good".

He walked along Low Moor Road, glancing at each of the new bungalows and houses which formed one of the latest little suburban tentacles of the town; noted the still unmended crack in the large end wall of the secondary modern school, which had lately become part of the Comprehensive; looked in the two farmyards which had, even in his lifetime, been separated from the town by fields and seen their fields suddenly sprouting bungalows; went through the Kissing Gate up towards Highmoor, where the old mansion had been turned into luxury flats and the Deer Park was now a private housing estate and the council had made adequate provision for old people. He liked visiting old John and knew his visits were welcome, which was pleasing.

The compound of old people's flats was built, three storeys high, around a small green (once a walled rose garden). The Warden's House had a dining room and a television room to be used by the pensioners if needed. Old John preferred to eat on his own (except on Fridays—a compulsory communal supper was imposed then) and watch television alone. He was a little deaf, hated to show it, and would rather miss a programme in the Common Room than ask his neighbours to be quiet. Joseph had bought him a nice little portable for his own flat.

Harry went in without knocking.

John was mending a shoe. There was a fire in the grate, the television was on with the sound well up, the apparatus of high tea made a trail from the larder-cupboard to the armchair—an open biscuit tin, the bread tin, the pan in which the beans had been cooked, a plate, a bag of fancy cakes—everything looked in disarray—an old man's careless domesticity—and yet the overwhelming impression was of calm, a rather bleak tranquillity, as the old man huddled over his shoe, hammer very carefully tapping in little bright nails which he took one by one from between his teeth.

He nodded to Harry—indicated that he should help himself to refreshment—and continued with his job. Harry poured himself some tea and sat down on the hard-backed chair beside the table.

"You can knock that damn thing off!" The television vanished to a pinpoint and that too went out.

The sudden silence made them smile at each other, then John nodded and went back to the delicate tapping of the short slim nails into the sole of the shoe. Harry waited and unobtrusively massaged the bruise on his thigh.

When he had first left school and gone to work on the farm, Harry had been recommended by his "grandfather", who worked on there long after Harry left for journalism. Eventually the old man had been laid off—well after his eightieth birthday. John had taken to the idea of retirement very badly. However, as always in his hard and unyielding life, he had settled for what was inevitable. There were hedges to be trimmed around the lawns of nearby private houses. He established a routine—his own meals, his own shopping, a drink on certain lunchtimes and certain evenings and a visit to Joseph and Betty for Sunday dinner.

Above all, though, at the end of this enormous life, which had taken him down the pits and under the sea to hack coal in conditions known to Roman slaves and onto the land to plough with horses and work like one, into the First World War, to be used as indifferently as any footsoldier in history, and back to his hero's home to face the death of his first wife, the breaking up of his family, the death of his favourite son, more hardship, more labour, unemployment, eventually drifting up to a ledge of affluence on the mid-century tide, John found pleasure in what had previously seemed nothing but a chore: walking. He walked along the River Wiza and noted the banks where the trout might hide; he walked around the few remaining lanes in the middle of a gutted and modernized Thurston; he walked to the park to watch the children on the swings. Once, near his ninetieth birthday, he had walked to the village in which he had been born. It was three miles off. He had gone without telling anyone. But someone from town had seen him, offered him a lift in their car, been gruffly refused, and reported the curious incident. Curious, because John was beginning to be widely known as "old" (ninety in a man was quite rare) and also because, as the motorist said, "You could tell he was tired out, flaked, jiggered, you could tell—but the old bugger wasn't going to have a lift—'No thanks!' he said, like he was telling me off—just 'No thanks!'" John had gone to look at the cottage in which he had been born. It had been painted and improved and embellished, after the taste of a couple of dentists who commuted from the village to their practice in Carlisle. "They made a smart job of it," he said, approvingly. He had passed it by once and then returned alongside it, not wanting to stop and stare in case he was seen and caused alarm.

His barrel-bellied father, who always wore a hat—bullying—his mother—distant now, an anxious lock of hair on her brow, blue, bluebell eyes, slim face, quick shy smile, red knuckles—his numerous brothers and sisters—they had played beside that stream . . . there used to be an orchard where the new double garage stood . . . all the shops were gone and the forge where he had first worked . . . and Emily, his wife . . . he could not find the place where she had lived . . . there were too many memories, he thought, too much crowded in. What was he to do with it all?

That had been in the spring.

Harry idolized the old man and idealized him. When John was silent, as now, Harry would respect it, know that silence was preferred for a while, be happy just looking at John, small, very lean, still a head of hair on him, though thinner, and still the unexpected blue eyes that struck out of the browned face. John kept his head low, being more than usually careful over the job. Shoes were expensive, Harry thought, approving the thrift; they had to be looked after.

"Did they find out who that lad was?" John asked the question without looking up.

"Yes. He was local. He'd been to school with Douglas."

"Do they know why?"

"Nobody knows."

A young man had just been found dead in some woods a few miles from Thurston. All the indications were that he had lived there for some weeks, until he succumbed to hypothermia. One or two people now thought they had seen him about the woods. Nobody had reported him. His body had been found by a couple looking for a place to lie.

"Those two must have had a queer shock," John said, and he turned his face up to Harry and smiled grimly, the remaining two nails in his mouth giving him a rather bizarre appearance. "Tea's cold, I'm sorry."

"I didn't come for tea. It's all right, anyway." He took a large mouthful.

Awkwardly in his pocket there was the ounce of twist Harry brought up every Saturday. It was always a problem, getting it out of his pocket and onto the mantelpiece where he always left it. Whichever way he manoeuvred seemed flashy, somehow, as if he were throwing charity in the old man's face.

"You won then."

"How do you know?"

"You haven't said anything."

"It was a bit scrappy."

"Aspatria used to hammer Thurston. Used to be miners, Aspatria, all of them. Up from the shift at dinner-time—into their togs and on with a game. I never played a game, young fella, never once. We worked Saturdays. There. That should hold." He held the shoe before him and examined the neat job.

Harry was uneasy. There was an inflection in John's voice

which perturbed him, but he was unable to diagnose the source of his apprehension. He waited.

"They should see you through a few more hundred miles. Eh?"

There was no answer. Harry was uncomfortable now. For some reason, the proportions of the small room had changed. The single light in the middle of the ceiling appeared to illuminate a much more limited area. The undrawn curtains, flower-patterned, green, appeared short, doll's house curtains. The few pieces of furniture were so cramped Harry could have stretched out his leg and touched John, who sat very still, vulnerable. The young man could not bear that vulnerability.

Harry glanced about him as if some visible threat were in the room. His throat was dry. He could not understand why the old man's mood was so fiercely silent and sorrowful. Once again he took refuge in cheerfulness.

"Joseph was telling me you used to make all their clogs when they were little. He said you used to shape the wood to a bit of paper you made them stand on—and then buy the wood and leather to cut for yourself. He said he's never worn anything more comfortable in his life! He can still feel them on his feet, he says, when he puts his mind to it."

John did not react to any of this. As the silence began once more to grow and thicken, Harry felt panic come over him. He feared things that were unclear. He could not endure them.

"What's wrong?"

There was a slight shake of the head.

"C'mon, Grandad! You can tell me."

Without glancing up, or moving at all, John spoke, pausing between almost every sentence.

"I was coming along that bit of field just behind here. Just now. Just walking. I hadn't done much. I hadn't gone far at all. And my legs gave way." Here he hesitated for a full minute, wondering at his own words. "They buckled. They just packed up. It's happened before but I took no notice. Except, this time—I had to crawl back here like a baby." He repeated the sentence, amazed. "I had to crawl—like a baby. If anybody'd come up I was going to say I was looking for a button. I got myself here along by the fences and using the walls." He looked up, quite suddenly, and the blue eyes stared through the swell of tears. "I can't walk, Harry." He paused. "It's all finished. It's all over." He wiped his eyes with his shirtsleeves. "You won't tell anybody," he said harshly, and Harry nodded.

Finally, they looked at each other directly, and Harry was pierced by the old man's terror.

(5)

It was not at all as Betty had hoped. She had wanted them to meet up as a happy family. She wanted there to be easy pleasure and harmony. She wanted cheerful bustle and companionableness—the spirit of Christmas and a New Year. Instead she got a fraught assembly which crashed and jarred through the bungalow, uncaringly, she thought, uncaringly. They made it seem small when it could have seemed *warm*. Even Harry was not reliable, not his usual self.

Lester had arrived first, looking "dreadful", she said to herself, and vowed to say it to no one else and to contradict flatly anyone else who said it. His mother, good old good-time Helen (Joseph's youngest sister), had not left the key under the stone and Lester was in no state to go around the early evening pubs looking for her. He wanted something to eat and he wanted a wash. Betty gave him a clean towel and asked him where he had got the cuts and bruises. Silently, she absorbed the lie about falling down the stairs at the station and went to make him, on request, egg and chips.

Joseph, of course, was pumpkin-packed with curiosity, but he too had the manners not to ask directly. Remarks like, "They should see to those bloody stairs" and, "You used to be quick on your feet" and, "Maybe he needs a breathalizer before being put in charge of egg and chips—just joking! Just joking!"—these and one or two other searching, intimate invitations to confidences were ignored by Lester, who locked himself in the small but well appointed bathroom, relaxed for the first time in hours, opened his coat, removed his ripped silk shirt, stripped off his battered trousers, shivered violently, felt the cold sweat on his forehead and was noisily sick. The sound travelled through the thin walls and silenced Joseph.

There was a desperate merriness about Joseph now. Either that or he was crushed in unfathomable melancholy. His life, it often seemed to him, had come, in all senses of the word, to nothing. He used activity to beat down thought.

As Lester came out of the bathroom—to a fully laid table—the meal all set out—Douglas, Mary and John came in. The lounge was instantly overcrowded. They grouped in the middle, the backs of their knees pressing against the arms of the three piece suite. Betty pushed the few pieces of furniture here and there to make more space. Joseph immediately engaged Douglas in the intense interrogation least likely to be tolerable after a three hundred mile drive—what was he exactly doing? What was Hollywood like? Who did he meet? How was the film going? Betty herself swung between irritation at Joseph's relentless tactlessness and amused sympathy for his understandable curiosity. She too wanted to know those things and Douglas would tell her in his own good time: in time, he would lay his adventures at her feet. But now—tired and fussed after the car journey—he fretted and strained, half wanting to satisfy his father, half aching to be let off the leash of this paternal-proprietorial interest. Between her husband and her son there could still be a tension as competitive and bare as between two boys. Lester watched them with exaggerated interest, as if he were at a ping-pong game: he had always taken Douglas for a fool and, despite Douglas' success, Lester had not changed his mind. Indeed, he had added another dimension to the son of the man who had helped him more than his own father: Douglas was a phony. All that highbrow talking! Phony, Lester thought, junk! Yes: that was about it. He went on with his meal, virtually ignoring the new arrivals.

Betty noticed that, too.

Douglas and Mary had come to leave John for the night, so that they could go out on the New Year's Rounds. Betty insisted on this, even though Mary thought it unfair on her, but—"enjoy yourselves while you can," Betty said, urging others to the self-indulgence she had always denied herself. "Besides, I like having him to stay, don't I, John?" She smiled at the boy and hugged him, but he did not make much of a response. With his hands in his pockets he was staring moodily at the large print of Constable's "Hay Wain" which dominated one wall, and yawning. He had slept in the car and Douglas and Mary had been able to argue undisturbed. "Have some tea," Betty suggested, although she felt, surely and sadly, that her son and his wife wanted to be away as fast as they possibly could be. "Lovely," Mary said, summoning real enthusiasm to sink the scum of selfishness and ingratitude which floated above her mood. She wanted to stay with Betty for a while. "Lovely; let me get it." "We'll get it together," Betty countered, "leave the men with a bit more space."

Harry came in.

By this time, Douglas and Joseph had edged, thankfully, into talk of local news. Joseph was sometimes a little impatient of Douglas' interest in this; Lester thought it was just another example of Douglas' phoniness: the "I've kept my feet on the ground bit", as Emma would have said. (He smiled as he thought of that big bare bum—and the smile hurt his face. Thank God Betty and Joseph liked him for what he was and no questions asked.) But Harry, who loved Douglas as a brother should love a brother, even though, or perhaps because, they were not related in blood, saw that this concern was genuine and was happy to join in and feed it. He respected Douglas a lot. He could imagine how hard it was in London.

Yet, when Douglas was there, Harry felt that he had to alter his behaviour. Although this bungalow was more familiar to him than it was to Douglas, although it was he and not Douglas who had helped Betty and Joseph move in, and although he came regularly and did the heavy work of turning over the garden, re-siting the fence, planting the fruit trees (the garden was disproportionately large)—yet, despite all these daily bonds of help, loyalty and affection, Harry felt it right and natural that Douglas assume precedence in all things whenever he crashed in from London for a few hectic or strained hours. Douglas recognized that and deliberately held back from over-much family attention when Harry was there.

"There was this business of Alan Jackson's death in All-hallows Woods," Harry offered, and gave the same brief details he had given his grandfather, ending with the lonely self-destruction in the woods. "You knew him, didn't you?"

"Yes." Douglas felt suddenly desolate, full of pity for Alan Jackson. "I suppose I knew him as well as anybody, once."

Alan had been a peculiar man. In one illumination, it seemed as if he saw the whole of the life of this man he knew so little and yet, in truth, *did* know "as well as anybody, once". There and then he felt a powerful, instant sense of loss. He wanted to go over it privately. The man was gone from the earth: a man his own age—school—a man he had shadowed in some way in his childhood.

"It seems he was rather the solitary type," Harry suggested.

Douglas nodded. He wanted to concentrate in silence on this death. It was almost as if he needed to be left alone, to grieve over it. And yet the man had been a stranger to him in the years since school. And even then there had been no shared sport or dances or girls, they had not even been in the same form. But Douglas felt that he knew the man to his soul; he could sense the sad parabola of the life which had taken him back to those particular woods; he could understand, he thought, why this lonely individual had died in the way he had. He wanted time to think about it. It marked him out in some way he could not fathom. It was as if the man's death met a need in him.

"Thanks!" Lester shouted his appreciation, pushing aside his empty plate. "Just exactly what I needed." He burped but kept it inside his mouth. "Any apple cake?" He tilted back his chair and took out a cigarette.

"There's always apple cake in this house," Joseph said, sentimentally. "I love apple cake. So does Douglas."

It must be possible, Douglas was thinking, to envisage a soul, or a life after death, when he himself—though in this over-crowded room—could now be so heavily, almost wholly, engaged elsewhere. His thoughts, his imagination, his sympathies were with Alan Jackson—he saw the clumsy young man stumbling about in those damp, thin woods, blindly trying to fend off the in-crushing world—and yet he was also here, in the flesh, in the touchingly spick and span lounge, brightly lit, newly dusted and polished, here he was, one of four men of the same name. What was this sudden cessation of existence?

"If you would take your apple cake on your knees across in

that easy chair, Lester, we could organize everybody else around the table." Betty was making the best of it.

With Mary's help the table was set out once more, this time for four—Douglas, Mary, John and Harry. Betty had wanted to have a proper High Tea for all of them and she had cooked and prepared all day for this. But it was clear to her that Mary and Douglas were impatient to be gone. They had arrived so much later than they had said they would. Then Lester and Harry being here as well made it impossible. So she postponed the High Tea, with the crackers and the sweets, the best crockery and the napkins. There would be another time, perhaps.

Even so, there was enough on the table to feed the four of them three times over. Tongue, veal pie, ham, a salad, fresh bread, teacakes, scones, rum butter, cheese, jams, apple cakes, gooseberry tarts, trifle, cream, "to keep you going until you can get something," Betty said, stubbing the rising cries of appreciation, putting the meal in its place as she poured the tea and hovered, watching them eat.

"I'll just have a bit of that apple cake," Joseph said from his chair beside the fire.

"You've had yours before."

"Well, I'll have some more again, thank you. This is my house."

"Oh dear," Betty smiled: she knew it irritated him when her tone implied his absurdity, but sometimes there was nothing she could do to prevent it. Joseph felt the ice in the silence of Douglas and thought, mistakenly, that it was a comment on himself.

"Well, it is," he insisted. "And I've always been fond of apple cake, now, haven't I? John knows that."

The small boy was appealed to in a situation where the cross-currents were far too many and too charged for him to be at all able to disentangle them. He sensed that there was an argument going on—indeed, sadly, one of the better learnt lessons of his life was the understanding he now brought to the many different arguments between his parents. He could gauge their level of seriousness as well as the adults themselves. Most often he forced himself to appear calm, and the effort of repression often gave him a misleading appearance of being indifferent to what was around him.

"Don't you, John?" Joseph wheedled away at his grandson. "John and me's mates," he announced.

"Oh, have some apple cake and be quiet!"

"I won't if you feel like that."

Douglas chewed very slowly, counting the number of times he was chewing this thankfully thick home-cured ham. Why was it that over such trivial exchanges as this one about a slice of apple cake he would feel that he wanted to kick the house down?

Harry ate as if all life but the digestive system had taken time off. He was unhurried but thorough, going from plate to plate like a platoon engaged in a scrupulous mopping up operation. Lester, sprawled in the chair opposite Joseph, felt himself totally relax for the first time since he had got in the train. Now that he was through it, he felt almost lightheaded at his survival. Douglas would have been pulverized. And Harry?

"What weight do you carry now?" he asked Harry.

"Twelve-six."

"A hundred and seventy-four pounds," said Lester in his Mid-Atlantic drawl. "You carry it well, pal."

"We train three times a week now. Commando courses and weights, they're all very keen, these days."

"We got our training digging ditches," said Joseph, suddenly grim.

"Win today?" For the second time since he had arrived, Douglas deliberately heaved the conversation into a local area. But this time it was to give himself space, so that he could freewheel inside his head. When had he last seen Alan? Had he wanted to die? What did it mean, this plunging helplessly about the woods?

"Yes." Harry admitted the victory reluctantly.

"Who's in the team now?"

"The First Team?"

"Yes."

"The lot?"

"Yes."

"Well . . ." Harry had pronged a piece of tongue, a piece of pie and a pickle; he put them into his mouth and crunched them up before he settled down to list the team.

"Apart from you, there's only two others I know," Douglas said.

"You're lots past it, lad," Joseph said, standing up to hand his empty plate to Betty, "past it. Thank you for the apple cake. I enjoyed it."

"Football lads stay the same," Lester announced, obscurely feeling that this got in a dig at Douglas. "Younger brothers, or lads who are the sons of the lads I played with. Mind you—football lads always did stick together. Didn't make as much of a song and dance as you rugby toffs."

"They don't play football now." Joseph was suddenly angry. "It's all kissin' and pussy ball. Nobody can dribble today."

Douglas wondered where his father's lurches of anger came from. They were like clouds appearing in blue skies—up they came, these black moods, and clearly he could not cope with them. He must, though, he resolved, be more patient. When he criticized his father he was very often criticizing himself: he had realized that only lately.

"What was different about it in your time, then?" Douglas asked, by way of making amends.

Pleased to be able to preach, the floodgates opened and out came a list of great footballers of the Thirties and Forties—a knowledgeable and comprehensive list which ended in a discussion of the respective merits of Stanley Matthews and Tom Finney. Lester and Douglas had just been old enough to see these players and appreciate them and, for a few moments, with the three men jostling opinions good naturedly and Harry and John appreciating it all, Betty felt that there was this thing called a Family, that it did wrap you around in warmth, that it did make sense of everything. If only Mary had not seemed so distant and so tired. She looked worn out.

"There was one Thurston lad," Joseph said, now sure of himself and in command, "now this is true, this. It was just before the War. What a player! All the talent scouts used to come and watch him. Archie Robinson. What a player! I've seen him beat a man and then take it back, just to beat him again. That ball was tied onto his boot with a bit of string. But he wouldn't move from Thurston. He-would-not. He wouldn't go to any of those big clubs. He-would-not. And do you know why? Eh?"

They all did. He had told the story many times. Nobody spoke up.

"Because he would only get changed in his own house! He would only change in his own house!" Joseph began to laugh loudly at the idiosyncratic nature of the man. For him the story was rich in meaning. It meant that individuality still existed: it meant that the Big Money Boys (his idealization of the few sad ex-professional footballers in flat caps who travelled Third Class to remote towns looking at "prospects" in the rain) had been spurned: it meant that the ordinary person had gifts on a level with the highly applauded. It meant he knew a great man known to few. "He wouldn't change," Joseph explained, aware that his own enjoyment of this story was not as infectious as he had hoped, "anywhere else except in his own house. You see? That was the sort of lad he was. Only in his own house. And *that* was why he wouldn't join any of those other clubs, see, John? It would have meant him travelling and then he wouldn't have been able to change in his own house. What a dribbler!"

Douglas choked a little, held it back and tried to catch Mary's eye. She was far away, though, eating her meal as placidly as could be, he thought: perhaps a little tired, that was all. Could she switch on and off like that? In the car on the way up they had all but agreed to a trial separation. Yet there she was, deftly collecting the plates, helping his mother, taking part, more part than he was.

Harry was finding it difficult to carry out old John's request that he tell nobody about the collapse. It seemed to him that Joseph and Betty and Douglas had much more right to know than he had. Yet how could he let them know without breaking the old man's trust? He felt as if he were telling a lie by omission, keeping something hidden which should have been open: it was a rare and most unpleasant sensation and it made him subdued.

The conversation died down again. Mary was too exhausted

to make any effort—but she wondered at these lulls, this recurring blankness. She was a stranger to their class, their town, and their private and shared memories and yet she felt that between them there were sometimes such chasms that she could not imagine where they had come from. Douglas occasionally claimed to derive such a tight and fruitfully cosy strength from this background of his—and indeed he was loyal to it and it was as clear on his life and work as the print of ferns on ammonites—yet, here they were, all met together after months of different lives in diverse places—stone silent. She let it be, saving herself.

"Tick-tock. Tick-tock. Tick-tock," Joseph said and then, staring at John, he began to sing:

"My grandfather's clock was too tall for the shelf
So it stood ninety years on the floor.
It was taller by half than the old man himself
Though it weighed not a penny-weight more.
It was bought on the morn of the day that he was born
And was always his pleasure and pride.
But it stopped, short, never to go again
When the old—man—died."

He sang it to the bitter end, waving his arms before him as if conducting the massed bands at Wembley; when he finished, the silence resumed.

Harry made his effort.

"I just called in to see Grandfather," he began.

With relief, all of them turned to him.

"He seemed a little bit under par," Harry replied, in answer to their enquiries after the old man. Surely "under par" wasn't breaking trust?

"He's a marvellous old man that," Joseph said with a full sweep of sentiment. Here at last was an opportunity to unite the room in that deep good-fellowship which the presence of all these loved people made him yearn for. "Do you know: that old man. Once . . . do you know? He was down the pit, Number Nine Pit, I believe it was . . ." Another familiar story, another respite.

It was no surprise, Douglas thought, that they should be at sixes and sevens. He was hung-over, sucked into self-concern and oddly upset by the death of Alan, his old schoolfriend. Mary, he thought, was in neutral, engines off; no wonder, poor love, the hammering they gave each other. Lester had clearly been in a fight and had rushed here, probably to hole up: he had crash-landed on Douglas several times in London for loans and cover, until the last time, when Douglas, who admired his reckless cousin, had summoned up the sense to say "no more". Harry was in a world of his own, Douglas thought, which was not uncommon. He envied Harry, whom he saw as somewhere out there with the Good and the Contented, in a land he himself would yearn for all his life without being able to visit. John, his son, was not looking forward to being without his father yet again. And Betty—the centre of the family—was disappointed. Douglas wanted to go and put his arms around his mother to cradle away the years of hurt and fill up the emptiness, live up to the expectations ... and, on top of that, Joseph, who was sensitive to all, fully realizing the unevenness, the disinclination and the fatigue, determined to bury it all with those blasts of anecdote which somehow, unfairly, set Douglas on edge.

"And so this other fella and your grandfather," Joseph pointed almost accusingly at Douglas, "were in this shaft."

"The accident," Douglas said, referring to the pit-fall which had gravely injured his grandfather. "When he walked out of hospital bandaged up."

"*Not* the accident! *Not* the accident! This is another time. An old fella told me this, that I met at a hound trail a few months ago. I haven't told you this. It's to show how *strong* they were then, do you see?"

"More tea anybody?" Betty had gone out to brew a fresh pot: she stood at the kitchen door, unaware that she had arrived like an actor on a false cue, smiling hopefully at the roomful, still prepared to work at it.

"I was in the middle of a story!" Joseph complained.

"Yes, please." Douglas pushed his cup forward.

"Mary?" She shook her head and then began to clear away.

"Strength's as much a knack as anything," Lester declared. "There was a fella I knew in Liverpool—they were all terrified of him—big fat sod—sorry—beggar—type of man who could eat one more potato than a pig, you know, great big belly hanging over a leather belt, but hard as concrete—well, for all that, there was a little fly-weight, Johnny Calford, he was Northern Champion—he just clipped him—right on the point of the jaw—his fist can't have travelled more than six inches—and this gorilla was down. Timing, that's what's half the battle." He duffed his own chin, lightly. "Just clipped him like that. Bang!"

"When we had the pub," said Joseph, "just a bit after the war—no, later, never mind when, we seemed to get a run of little drunken fly-weight and light-weight boxers down from Scotland, mainly from Glasgow. And bantam-weights—I bet you'll never see a bantam-weight in England in your day—I hope you don't anyway—they're for starvation times—I've seen two or three come in one year—two or three—these little fellas—some of them top of the bill as well—white-faced little fellas. And do you know what I think ruined them? The wasting! The wasting! All that grub they weren't allowed to eat. That ruined them. Poor little buggers. They'd all been famous once and we knew their names—we were proud to shake their hands—but there they were—on the sharp road down hill. Wasting! That's my theory!"

"What was the other fella like after your battle, then?" Douglas asked Lester, whose eye he had avoided until now.

"Oh! He says he fell down some stairs," Joseph chuckled. "At Carlisle Station. Didn't you, Lester? He thinks we're all daft, you know." Joseph looked around the room roguishly and Douglas felt a stab of warmth for his father.

Lester kept his mouth tight shut and let it pass.

"I was just thinking," Harry began, searching for a way to bring the conversation round to old John once more.

"Never," said Douglas, toasting Harry with his tea-cup. Then he clicked his tongue in annoyance with himself. The silly nervous joke had shut Harry up.

"Your *big* Christmas present's on the bed in the spare room," Betty said, to give John the chance to leave the table and the room. "We didn't send it when we knew you were coming."

"Can I go and see it?" The boy addressed himself not to Betty but to his mother.

"Of course." Mary got out her words quickly: she realized she had been trying to display her right to be the person in authority over the boy and blushed as she caught Betty's troubled reaction. "You know your grandma always gets you such lovely presents."

"We don't want to spoil him, though." Betty was anxious not to push herself before the mother. "We've enough to answer for, spoiling Douglas."

"It's just that I was wondering," Harry took advantage of the slight pause, "I was wondering what the arrangements were for, er—'grandfather'—tonight. I mean, just wondering what —what the arrangements were."

"He likes to be on his own," Joseph declared emphatically. "He's independent-minded. I'll try to get up after midnight and so will Douglas. We got up there together these last two years—didn't we?" This coincidence struck Joseph as positive proof of the strength of family feeling. "Aye. All three of us—three generations there—four with little John here—he can come next year—three generations bringing in the New Year very quietly, so as not to disturb his neighbours. I don't know why we had to be quiet. Most of them are deaf in those flats. But he insisted on that, didn't he?"

"I don't remember," said Douglas. "I don't know whether I'll come into Thurston this year. I'm tired." He looked at Mary: there was no reaction. "We both are."

"You're always tired," his mother retorted. "I don't know why you bring it on yourself. Why do you clash yourself?" she asked, slicing to the centre of her worries—but then she turned away—not wanting to unbalance the company.

"You'll be coming down to The Crown for a drink though, won't you?" Joseph asked, cajolingly. He liked Douglas to turn up in his local.

"I don't know. If we come, we might drop in at the Rugby Club. Mary isn't too keen."

She forbore to protest against this shifting across to her of the responsibility for unpopular decisions. They had made all manner of local promises on their previous visit, but the most constant was that they would turn up to the Rugby Club New Year's Eve Dance. Douglas, she knew only too well, was genuinely tied by such promises: it was almost neurotic, she thought, this compulsion to keep faith with his past. Obligations to a few old schoolfriends could take precedence, as threatened to happen this evening, over the very future of their marriage. Insofar as she understood this, she despised it.

"No," she affirmed, helping him out. "Douglas has just come back from America. I've been busy these last few days —we've driven three hundred miles in hellish traffic. It doesn't seem unreasonable to say we might not want to go to the Rugby Club."

"They're expecting you," Harry said.

"We *might* turn up," Douglas replied. When had he last actually seen Alan Jackson? Three years, four years ago? The face was so plain in his mind now, looming there, steadily in focus.

"I don't suppose any sleep'll be lost either way," said Lester, "whether you turn up or not."

"John can still stay here," Betty tried to find a form of words which would express her meaning precisely. "So that you have the—option, is it? Option!"

"I've got no bloody option," Joseph said. "If I'm not in The Crown by eight-thirty sharp, there'll be three fellas there'll want to know the reason why." He looked around, triumphantly, glorying in the fierceness of his bond to the "three fellas" in The Crown.

As soon as the women had cleared away and left the room, John, who had waited for this moment impatiently, popped through the door dressed in his new present—boots, hat and the gun which, in his imagination, slaughtered the lot of them. He was inspected and approved—but not without both Joseph and Lester commenting on the comparative paucity of Christmas presents in their youth. Douglas had always done well.

Lester now felt bullish. The fear had subsided; he wanted to boast of his fight but the earlier lie prevented it. Yet he was full of himself. Nobody was going to grind him down. He would go back up to London and take them all on! *Luck*. That was all he needed. And he was due some. Overdue. John, abandoned in his expensive rig-out, squatted Indian fashion on the carpet in front of the electric-log fire and pretended to be intensely intrigued in the workings of his gun.

Lester suddenly lifted himself on his arms, swung himself out of his seat, knelt on the carpet and gripped the cumbersome armchair by one of its short, thick legs. He tensed himself and then lifted it, held it steady, paused—John was fascinated by the vein which quivered in the middle of his forehead, Harry noted approvingly the whippet leanness of the man's muscles—and then stood up, the big armchair at arm's length. Full of strain, he reversed the process neatly but quickly. A thin line of blood came from the cut at the side of his mouth: he licked it off.

"And that's a heavy chair," said Joseph, who had always been a fan of Lester's physical prowess. "There's many a man twice your weight couldn't budge that."

"It's to do with balance as much as anything else, isn't it?" Douglas asked, amused at the way in which this trick had absorbed him as much as the other three. "And there's a knack for clearing it off the ground initially, isn't there?"

"*You* do it," replied Lester, who dearly wanted Douglas to fail.

Douglas tried, heaved, joked, tumbled over, kicked his legs in the air, assumed the pose of an All-In Wrestler and chased John around the room as he diminished the occasion from Lester's point of view and made the real achievement seem nothing but the crude accomplishment of lumpen sinew.

When this was done, Harry, who had never tried it on such a large chair before, took off his jacket and came to take his turn. He considered it carefully and then, in one swift movement, lifted it, hoisted it, himself stood up and held it out before him as if it were no more than a torch. Lester grimaced and slapped him on the shoulder.

"I'll have you on my side," he said, "any day."

As Mary and Betty washed up in the kitchen, they talked about how similar the three young men looked. It was against the odds that they should. It was even a little "creepy" (Mary's word) that Harry should be so like the other two. But all were very dark haired, light eyed—hard blue in the case of Douglas and Lester, a soft blue-grey in Harry's case. They were about the same height—just under six feet—Lester the shortest but the strongest looking; Douglas, soft-featured, soft about the jawline, contrasting strikingly with Lester's tough profile; Harry disguising his considerable physical power in a manner of diffidence.

"One's kind, the other's not a bit and Douglas is half and half," said Betty. "He can be violent."

"Harry's good, Lester—worries me—" Mary stopped. Was the book called the Good, the Bad and the Beautiful or the Good, the Bad and the Ugly? And who was what? That line of speculation would only upset Betty. She suppressed it.

"Douglas is all head, Lester's a labourer at heart and Harry's nicely balanced," Betty continued, rinsing the plates swiftly, enjoying this game.

Mary thought of a rather brutal comparison on sex but she instantly repressed it: Betty did not like the language of the recently liberated women. Mary had to concentrate. Soon she would be in her own cottage and be able to relax: she badly needed some moments to herself: so much was unresolved.

"The three brass monkeys," said Mary, turning to smile at her mother-in-law, who looked worried, she thought, and a little lost.

"The Three Stooges!" Betty laughed. "They're certainly *that*."

"The Three Blind Mice!"

"The Three Men In A Boat!"

"The Three Musketeers is how Douglas would like to see them," Mary guessed shrewdly.

"They never had much to do with each other as boys," Betty said. "It's a miracle to get them together really. You would think they would have so much in common. But apart from rather looking alike—there is nothing much. Not really. And they could go from one year's end to another without seeing each other, without really missing each other. Except, of course, Harry always likes to see Douglas. But he's a bit—over—what is it? Not 'put-out'—"

"Overawed?"

"That sort of thing—by him."

"Douglas always speaks very highly of Harry."

"In London? Yes. I'm inclined to think he likes this place and everybody in it far better when he's away from it."

She regretted the tartness in that remark, but did not apologize for it. She was feeling a little put out by the speed with which her son and daughter-in-law were passing through her house. Everybody was so harassed these days. Where had all the time gone? The time for talking and just sitting about. The time she had once had to spend with friends and relations. Nowadays you had to make appointments to see each other and when you did meet you were hemmed in by other appointments. Too many appointments, so much happening, nothing caught; so much activity, no repose. She did not like it and at times it seemed a waste of time to spend so much energy on pretence.

When they went back into the lounge, John pulled the trigger of his gun and the bang caused Mary to clap her hands to her ears with an involuntary gesture and call out, "For Christ's sake! *Stop* that bloody noise!"

The boy stopped, the gun drooped sadly before him. To his school blazer and short trousers had been added a large stetson and plastic calf-boots which were sprinkled with silver paint like the gun and the hat. Mary's outburst embarrassed everyone.

"I have a terrible headache," she lied, despising herself more for this evasion. Why not say she was in a state of tension and could not take even the playful shock of her son with a toy gun? They had talked of separation—for Christ's sake—*separation!*—herself and her husband, so blandly quizzical there. Parting for life! How could he just tuck it away?

"You can add to it," said Joseph, coming to the rescue and tapping the stetson. "There's the pants and the jacket you can get, and there's a lassoo and—what else was there, Mother?"

"Everything you can think of," Betty replied. She saw how the boy's present had been spoiled for him. Somebody should rush over and comfort him. He needed it. *She* could not do it with the mother here. And then, in the way he had which would always take her breath away, Douglas reached out, gently lifted his son onto his knee and, without any fuss, began to examine the gun. Soon the room rattled again with the unpleasant banging of the imitation weapon.

They left as ungraciously as they had arrived. Lester to his own house and a watchful night about the town while he took stock. Harry to the flat he had insisted on finding for himself, despite Betty's declaration that he would be "always welcome" to live with them. It had been a difficult decision for Harry to take but he was sure now that it was better all round. And finally, in a flurry of embarrassment, half-promises, some regrets and some impatience, Douglas and Mary, who clipped herself into the safety belt even for the short trip up to the cottage in the hills. Joseph followed them out after a few minutes and went to his hallowed drinking ground.

Betty felt so tired: "As if I'd fed the five thousand," she said to herself. It was all worry, she thought, and it should not be like that. It should be calmer, pleasanter than that—after all, they were part of each other, they were part of the same family. They were all well enough off. Times had improved out of all recognition. So why so tense? Maybe, she thought, hoovering the room as John sat in the bath playing with the American whale, maybe she asked too much. Maybe life was just like this now. Surely not, though. Surely those people she saw in the street or heard in shops or saw with their families—they were happy, they felt helped and loved by each other—did they not? This desolation could not be everywhere the same, could it? She hoped not: she longed to find a hub of life in the family. She ought to speak out.

Come on—she beat down these miserable reflections. It was just her mood, it would pass, life was a bit complicated at the moment. Douglas and Mary, she had seen directly, were not hitting it off at all. Douglas was always extra-polite to her in public when things were bad. Sometimes she could not make out her son.

She knocked off the Hoover and put it away. She would lay out glasses and cups and saucers later, in case anyone dropped in after midnight to bring in the New Year. Then she realized that there was no sound coming from the bathroom.

She went in. The boy was sitting upright, goose-fleshed, the cheap whale in his hands, broken, refusing to respond to his attempts to mend it. His expression was so unhappy she felt her heart lurch in sympathy. He looked so neglected. And she had been so self-pitying! How could she give in like that? He looked up and shivered fiercely. There was plenty to be done, she thought, starting here and now.

"It wasn't my fault," he said, "I just wound it up."

"I don't know anything about those things either."

"I daren't take it apart in the bath, in case the water gets in."

"Give it to me. You can fiddle with it while we watch a bit of television. Your grandfather's bound to know somebody who can fix it."

"Will he?"

"Oh yes." She was beside him now, soaping the big yellow sponge, about to wash his back. "He knows all sorts of people, your grandfather." She looked at the toy: cheap, she thought, and far too young for him; a gift with no thought in it.

"Daddy brought it from America."

"Did he? That was nice of him." She rubbed him vigorously to warm him up. "It shows he was thinking about you."

"He was in Hollywood."

"Was he? Where all the film stars live. When I was about your age—just a little bit older—all of the girls wanted to end up in Hollywood. We used to daydream about it."

"I think Daddy wants to live there." The boy paused: Betty felt a tremble in him which was not to do with the cold, nor yet the effect of her sponging. She knelt beside him and put her arm around his shoulders. Though she assumed full knowledge of her grandson by right of family, Betty sometimes found herself confronted by a well-mannered stranger. Not now, though: his sadness brought them together.

"If he goes," John sobbed at last, "he'll take me with him, won't he? Won't he?"

2
Resolutions

(1)

The story had to be resolved. Perhaps it was the tiredness and the recent dramatic changes of location which had upset his sense of proportion. Or, more simply, there was an urgency to make a shape of something which was an instinct as deep as greed and fear. Whatever it was, as soon as they reached the cottage, Douglas carried the suitcases to the door, excused himself unconvincingly and inadequately, and went up the path onto the fells to be alone with his thoughts, by now obsessive, on the death of this friend. He had to put them in order.

It was a picture-book midwinter night, the sort of landscape which appears impossible or artificial only to those who do not know the country. The moon was up, clear, crisp, luminous. The stars glittered in their thousands, the Milky Way an easily discernible gauze, the Plough, the Twins, the Pole Star—simple to believe that these were God's spy-holes in the stretched black canopy of heaven. In the moonlight the snow-ridged hills stood clear as Christmas cards and the loudest sound was the scrunch of bracken beneath his ruined city shoes. When he stopped to listen, he might catch the scurry of a sheep, the rustle of a fox, a hare's light lollop. The silence caught his heart and, for the first time in weeks, he felt a breath of ease.

For a few moments he looked along the coastline, picking out the towns and villages he had cycled to, circling empty Sunday streets for girlfriends who had no idea he was within ten miles, racing away to swim all day; there, the pits where his grandfather had worked ran out under the sea. Born, bred, familiar smells, names, places, memories, history, sounds, shapes, air. He felt earthed.

Why had Alan gone into the woods and perished; allowed himself to die?

When he had known Alan Jackson, at school, the boy had travelled in from the country to the local Grammar School and, though he was a year younger than Douglas, a friendship had been set up from the beginning. This might have been to do with Douglas' missionary desire, at that time, to help those who appeared to most need it; it could also have been to do with the fact that Alan was generally thought to be the best scholar the school had taken in for years and Douglas wanted to keep an eye on the front-runner—but those reasons would be to deny the force of Alan's part in the affair. He, after all, had returned the friendship. Nor would it do to underrate his own action. Almost alone in the school he had sought out Alan and truly cared for him: talked, spent time, been interested, felt affection. It was less selfish and possibly more accurate to call it simply—a friendship.

Alan was exceptionally shy, exceptionally withdrawn, from the first, somehow, trapped inside himself. He was unnaturally neat, extraordinarily conscientious, altogether modest, a scholar to the ends of his long, white fingers. The dead languages which caused so much trouble to everyone else opened up to him without effort; mathematics, physics, chemistry—all the "tough" subjects were calmly understood. He was no good at all at sport but, because of his authority and his calmness, no one teased him over this: soon some fabricated agreement relieved everyone of his entirely useless pursuit of rugby balls, cricket balls or tennis balls. The teachers got him out of it, despite his embarrassed protests that he enjoyed games even though he was no good. They assumed he was merely being helpful in putting up what must be a token struggle. They rejoiced in his singularity, which they treated as eccentricity, forever referring to it with affection and driving the boy to blazing flushes of embarrassment and ignored disclaimers. Although he spoke slowly and chose his words after obvious consideration, he held on tenaciously to a broad Cumbrian accent which wavered not at all throughout his schooldays. No more did his hairstyle, no more did his routine. His background was poor, rural and entirely unprepared for such an intellectual oddity as he was: yet he strove fiercely to keep loyal to it. He was not handsome, but he was not bad-looking; his face was large, rather gaunt, but not grim. He was broadly built but carried little fat. Above all he appeared self-contained and seemed to need no one, although Douglas, perhaps alone of the boys, sensed that this appearance was false. Alan wanted affectionate attention and careful friendship, like everyone ever born.

There was, though, about him, occasionally, a smile of great inner delight, or it could change and appear to be a terrible detached and puzzled sadness. Douglas had noticed this. Even now, willing himself to assemble his thoughts on this man, he could summon up the memory of that smile. It seemed to say "what a place this world is!" and hesitate between joy and despair, between a question and an answer. Douglas was mesmerized by what he now thought of as the profundity of Alan's awareness. For there was no doubting that his sensitivity matched his intelligence; he knew how the world worked. Perhaps Douglas' attraction to him was the perennial pull between the philosopher and the clown. While Alan spun his own web, forever ravelling and unravelling in his mind the meanings and vanities of the life he saw, Douglas would be strutting out his hour, now boldly, now hesitantly, now anxiously full of questions, now ridiculously over-stuffed with answers. Douglas saw Alan as one who ruminated scrupulously over life, and though his own questionings were so erratic as to make all comparison vain, he felt again as he had felt then—deeply attached to the quiet, isolated figure.

But how would he tell the story? All he knew about Alan's background was that it was poor—then a bearable and decent post-war poverty which would now be classified as destitution. He had been brought up in an abandoned hamlet—once a row of miners' terraced cottages—beside the woods he had died in. There had always been illness in the family—the mother. He saw the thoughtful and obedient boy helping silently about the small, illness-stricken house. He had never spoken of it. No one from school visited his house, ever. But his mother's illness became "known". His father had worked on the council, as a caretaker or cleaner in the offices; the job which Alan himself had gone into, a year after that unexpected failure at the school.

For, having walked through one examination after another, Alan had suddenly failed in the final examination—the pre-University tests—but failed in such a spectacular, such a disastrous manner that all sorts of reasons had been introduced to explain the lapse. His father had died a few months before the examination but surely *that* would not have such a drastic effect? Alan had simply left school, taken on this job, which he could have easily taken on at fifteen, without any of his qualifications, and faded into the town as a young, lonely eccentric who "hardly spoke", "bothered nobody", "very quiet", "goes for terrible long walks", "keeps to himself", "no friends"—sometimes went off for a few days alone—"simply disappeared". His mother died soon afterwards. He moved into a terraced cottage on the outskirts of Thurston.

Where had he gone on his days off? What had he thought about on those long walks? Douglas thought he might have to invent cruelty in the childhood—not physical battery, but the battening effect of humble service both to an invalid and to someone who did not understand. All the childhoods that leap from one class to another share the same pains. Here, though, was someone who had refused to leap. Looked but walked away. Now, Douglas saw that as an enormous strength. Perhaps there could be a double life somewhere; perhaps this unworldly abstinence could be counter-balanced by spasms of excess or, worst of all, failed attempts at excess. Alan had aged while Douglas was on the rampage he called his life in London and abroad and lately he remembered seeing him across the street—the same neat Fifties belted raincoat, he could have sworn, now oily with dirt, the same tidily tucked-in school scarf, the expression more fixed but, when he turned to Douglas' honking "hello!", still that same rare, lovely, profound smile. What was in that expression? He teased out his memory of it. Fear? Resolution? Clarity? Understanding?

Why had he failed the exam? That would have to be invented. Anxiety of continuing and being a burden to his mother. The obvious wanting to "help at home". But more, perhaps—a sudden disillusionment with the work? Exhaustion from the battle he must have had (who had not?) with the flesh—as far as anyone knew, a battle fought alone. Or had he arrived at a sudden crisis of knowledge, as some very intelligent youths do? One teacher said that Alan knew too much to put it down at the swift, plausible length which had become second nature to Douglas; he said he was writing something of his own and did not swot for the exams; he said he had learned all they could teach him and someone reported they had once heard Alan say: "Nobody knows the answer to anything. That's all there is to it. Nobody knows a thing really."

That stuck in Douglas' mind. For he was certain, the more he thought about it, that he had been in touch, in slight contact, with a "rare spirit", with someone who "saw into the heart of things". All the more desolate, then, that life had taken him on such a parabola: from a home in the woods, through his many gifts to scholarship, to a settlement for his father's occupation and then back to those childhood woods on a quest—for what? Certainly not for continued living. He had been ignorant of all survival techniques, it appeared: his shelter was the crudest hole in the ground inside a large holly bush. He had moved about, Harry had said, they could tell that—and Douglas strained to imagine the search and the desperation in the man's mind as he had blundered alone through those insubstantial woods. What did he find? What had been concluded?

It might have been the stress of the last few days, but Douglas discovered that he was crying and under his breath he heard himself murmuring "the poor man", "poor Alan", "poor man". What a waste and a loss! What a hateful enemy death was! Yet at times, he recollected, lately, he had thought it would not be such an enemy to him.

So, so. He had worked something out, roughly thought it out. He would like to write it to make it appear as a memoir—that could be his lifeline back to writing the stuff he could respect himself for. He must let it rest longer in his mind and then work on it, find a shape, but now at least he knew its weight in his mind. Using Alan? Yes. That would have to be faced too. "The Death Of A Friend", he could call it. Sentimental, melodramatic—yes. That was the starting point. He would try to reclaim him.

Released now from the peculiar thrall in which he had been held by will or by need, he came down, shivering violently, from the mountainside and jogged along to stave off the cold. Down indeed—to a wife with whom his life was unresolved, to problems filial and paternal, to difficulties financial and emotional, facing a year in which there was no certain prospect of a job. Yet, through some blessing, feeling emboldened and somehow cleansed and optimistic, after the tryst kept alone with the memory of a dead friend.

(2)

He tripped over his own suitcase, which was where he had left it—on the doorstep—and, as he picked it up, he knew that war had been declared yet again.

Mary was kneeling, as if in prayer, before the fire in the downstairs room of the small cottage. She must have heard him coming in but did not for a moment interrupt her reverential huffing and puffing into the bottom of the grate, as she strove to stir up some life in the dampish twigs.

Douglas bit on his tongue and headed for the stairs with his suitcase, taking hers also, by way of appeasing her (but she could not see as she did not turn to him). "I'll take yours too then," he said, unable to do good by stealth. Upstairs there was the "big" bedroom and the box-room John used—one and a half up and down it was, enough for their occasional needs, with the outbuildings standing ready to be restored and inhabited later (if the cash flowed in)—promises of future settlement. It was in a remote hamlet, about eight miles south of Thurston, neighboured by a few farms. A small, stone-built, seventeenth-century cottage—firm-driven into the hillside for warmth; no views. He unpacked rapidly, kicked his empty case under the bed and came down to find Mary sitting on a small stool, poker in her hand, rapt in the puny flickerings of flames which tottered about the coals like a child taking its first steps.

"Drink?" he asked, still on the crest of his sudden optimism. "Oh blessed drink! Ice-breaker, match-maker, embarrassment-diverter, acquaintanceship-sealer, pact of friends, arm's length of enemies, godmother of parties, goddess of social intercourse, consolation of solitude—and much else; someone ought to write a book about it."

"We have none," Mary replied, not without satisfaction, he noted; and yet he was easy on her.

"America," he announced, glad to have the chance to surprise her. He held up his large duty-free cartons. "A long way to go for your scotch, I agree, but beggars can't be choosers. Half and half?"

She nodded. He poured two stiff ones, topped hers up with water and then came to sit near her on the comfortable old sofa which, like the rest of the furniture, they had purchased from the local auction. "Cheers." Again she merely nodded.

"It's marvellous outside." He heard his enthusiastic tone: it sounded emptily hearty; and yet he could not be more sincere—it *was* marvellous outside. Why, then, did it seem phony? Mary thought it was phony too. She sniffed. He was sorry she did not believe he meant it.

"Cheers," she said, and took a large drink, cutting off his attempt at conversation.

"There's a letter of Malcolm Lowry's to a young man who wants to write a book but complains that he can't because for one thing he doesn't know anything about nature. Lowry replied that *not* knowing was enough of a subject. I liked the answer. I thought I knew what he meant. I've just been out 'not-knowing' about the stars."

"Could you pass an ashtray?" He did so. There was another pause. So it was this variant: O.K. After a few moments, she said—

"You could have asked me if I'd wanted a walk."

"Did you?"

"Yes."

"I wanted to be on my own," Douglas said.

"When are you anything else?"

"Can't you understand that?"

"You didn't answer my question."

She had not looked at him, even taking her scotch and the ashtray in an outstretched hand, at right-angles to her gaze, which continued, intent, on the fire struggling to be born. Douglas let the silence gather about them. There was still enough resilience and optimism in him to relish the quietness so enwrapped about the thick-walled building.

Mary was red-haired; deeply, lusciously, Forties-Hollywood-dreamy-red-haired. It waved and tumbled about her face and over her firm, square shoulders in abundance. It was like a dowry, something to be remarked on, worthy of a psalm of David. Whichever way she wore it, she suited it, and the wealth of it would often move Douglas to bless his unaccountable luck, even now, almost a dozen years into a scarred marriage. For with the richness of the hair went a character just as rich, which their marriage-war might have impoverished irreparably. He did not know. Nowadays they spoke over a no man's land of hurt.

Her face was open and intelligent with eyes not quite hazel, a nose that ended in a little, sharp, defiant tip and a large, calm mouth which fell away slightly at each end, not sadly but sensuously. Her figure was good, waist still slim, bust firm, stomach flat. And the hands quite ordinary. Yet, when he met her, she had been on the brink of a career as a pianist. Her first concert at the Wigmore Hall had been well received. She was poised for triumph. The marriage had robbed her of it. They had been very deeply in love at the beginning, and then again, two or three times, but the periods between had been cold, often bitter and once before (as now) malevolent and destructive.

"There are no faces in the fire," she said. "The three of us"—her sisters and herself—"used to sit for hours at the fire. Wherever we went we had a fire—even in South Africa."

Her father had been an officer in the R.A.F., stayed on after World War Two and trailed his family half way round the globe and back again. Douglas had once been convinced that this had given Mary a privileged, middle-class life which he had used against her in times of argument. Even then, though, he would concede that it had made her the woman he wanted to marry. Now the gibes were irrelevant.

Douglas wished that he had not given up smoking. Even though he had stopped for five years now, he still wanted one on most days. He could, this moment, see a packet of *Disque Bleu*, the soft, rather slippery packaging, the malleable cigarette with the black spiky tobacco looking as if it had been packed raw—what was the actual taste like? He had not a clear enough recollection. He smiled to himself. In order to describe it properly, he would have to smoke again.

Mary smoked steadily.

The fire had caught now. She put on a couple of logs, wedged them firmly exactly where she wanted them. Douglas watched the flames miss her hand.

Outside the stillness, snow, hills there long before man and most likely there long after him, the sea a few miles off, a few farms surviving on the hillsides, and, down in the towns, the process and procedures of entertainment well under way.

Lester on his way to a pub to meet some old pals who would protect him and take him round the town as their mascot, thinking him a millionaire and believing his answers to their questions about pop stars and sporting personalities. Harry meeting up with Aileen, Lester's serious-minded sister, who had so successfully "taken herself in hand" and got away from the influence of her mother, to London, then to a training college, and now she was a lecturer in economics and on the list of Labour candidates. She would spend the evening with Harry, whom she liked more than any other man she had met, even though his politics were primitive! Joseph deep in a serious school of dominoes. Betty and John watching a "galaxy of international talent" preparing to see off the Old Year on the television—the boy flushed now, a little feverish, she feared, but at least cheerful with his bottle of pop and a packet of crisps, sitting in his pyjamas and his cowboy boots, still nursing that cheap whale. The man whose name he had taken, old John, asleep, his infirm legs clumsily splayed out on the fender before him, the fire dying. Had he, too, the grudging but still genuine faith that on this particular calendar night, as custom ordered that one year be gone and another take its place, it was a true moment for change? Was the habit of New Year Resolutions a cry for free will? In the bleak midwinter, stocks low, land dead, nature withdrawn, was it then, when everything seemed against a man, that most of all he had to stand up and say "no—I *will* do this, I *will* do that, despite the fact that life looks unimpressionable"? Or were resolutions no more than a handful of dust flung in the face of fate?

"What are you thinking about?" Again it was Douglas who had to break the silence. Mary stared into the fire, almost hidden by her hair.

"Us," she replied, eventually, dully.

"What about us?"

"Yes. What about us?"

"This is a bit like serving lobs at Wimbledon."

"Want some coffee?"

"Have some more scotch."

"O.K." She held out her glass. He waited. She got the message and turned to look at him. Her expression was so hurt and beaten that he wanted to gather her in his arms and nurse her; but it was too far gone for that. "What were you thinking about when you were on your own?" she asked.

"This and that." He poured out a large, splashy measure. She could hold her drink.

"What?"

"Well. Money for one thing." He lied easily. The story of Alan Jackson had to be kept secret, or it would lose its potency in his mind. He sipped slowly at the scotch: taken six thousand miles; returned six thousand miles; still tasted the same as ever: looney. "I can't understand why I'm in such a twist about it. I've never been deprived of it, I've always had enough for my needs. It's this freelance caper. I've been brainwashed against it. Why the hell am I in such a comically painful panic about it now?"

"You went up a mountain and thought about money?" Her scorn for what he thought were his valid anxieties about earning a living was something which irritated him greatly: which she did not understand. "I don't believe you thought about that. You're a poor liar, Douglas, sometimes."

"Why should I lie?"

"Because you want to keep to yourself what you are really thinking: therefore whatever you tell me is untrue."

"You should be in New Scotland Yard."

"Life with a moral criminal makes you act like a policeman."

"Heavy."

"You're still high." Mary lit another cigarette. "You're still on that plane, or in Los Angeles or in London—you've been in neutral for the last hour or two—only talking because you can't bear silence."

"Who can?"

"Who *is* she?"

"Who?"

"Never mind." Visibly, Mary pulled herself together and turned to her husband without rancour. "So why don't we work out the bare minimum we need to live on and go on from there?"

"Who is who? Whom?" He paused. "O.K."

"Do you want to live in London or in the country?" she began.

"On the one hand," he did the "Fiddler On The Roof" act, "metropolitan getting and spending: on the other hand, rural sitting and stewing: and vice versa: on the other hand, city—superficialities: on the other hand, country—pedantries: and vice versa: urban flash, rural blankness: ennui and accidie." He registered her boredom and stopped. "There is no other hand. They are the same."

"Is that what you really think?"

"We have good friends in London and I have old friends here. Yet you like this cottage probably more than I do—I suppose I'm a bit worried about being cut off from the metropolitan plug, from the odd jobs for freelancers down there . . ."

"Frightened of having as much time to write as you'd like to."

"Below the belt."

"What is the bare minimum we need to live on?" she went on.

"Well. We have to sell the cottage anyway." Douglas was relieved to be able to announce this in a suitable context. He had held back for weeks. She took his news calmly. "We borrowed seven thousand five hundred from the bank, we have to pay back a hundred pounds a month, plus fourteen per cent interest—it's too much. We'll have to put this on the market, hope that prices are holding up and we can get what we gave."

"I see." She paused. "That's settled then." She loved the cottage very much. Her childhood travels had made her long for roots and this was her place in England.

"Virtually. Unless you can change your job and find a comparable post up here—which is highly unlikely with teaching in the state it's in, and I can set myself up with an advance and maybe—*maybe*—a regular review space to keep us jogging along—again highly unlikely with publishing and newspapers staggering along the brink: we can't run two slum properties at either end of the country."

The cottage had been classified as "unfit for human habitation" by the council when they had applied for a grant to improve it. In London their maisonette was in a very down-at-heel street, thought of as a slum by Douglas' mother. Mary's parents insisted it was "quite pleasant".

"O.K.," she said, "London." She took a pencil. "I'll note it down."

"Mortgage and insurance—say seventy-five—say eighty pounds a month: say a thousand a year."

"Yes."

"Rates—three hundred; electricity—what? two hundred and fifty; gas heating—two hundred and fifty; telephone—madness now—three hundred; running of car—five hundred and fifty, say. Food?"

"Allow up to a thousand. That'll include wear and tear inside the house."

"What else? Well, I'm going to cash in all those small Sixties insurances—that should be about four thousand—to reduce the overdraft. I'll take out a straight Drop Dead Insurance—a large sum for you and John should I Drop Dead—no endowment. Say two hundred and fifty. Pension scheme—well, I want to put seven-fifty into that if I can—next to sinking in a swamp, it's old age penury that gives me the biggest creeps. What else? Booze, your fags, clothes, books, out and about—say five hundred. Accountant—two hundred and fifty. What are we up to? Plus ten per cent contingency."

He need not have asked. He had done the sum many times over, during the past few months. He had a list of plans. This was Negative Cut-Back Stage One, based on selling the cottage.

Negative Cut-Back Stage Two involved selling the London place and moving into a flat. Negative Cut-Back Stage Three—which depended on a successful and calm continuation of the marriage—was to sell the London place, come back to the cottage and batten down the hatches. Negative Cut-Back Stage Four was to get rid of all he had, rent a hovel in the hills and live rather like a land-locked Robinson Crusoe for a while. All four were on the cards at the moment. There was a Total Negative Switch-Off, which was to disappear and leave Mary with some loot and peace.

"Five thousand plus ten per cent equals five thousand, five hundred."

Even though he knew the sum, Douglas whistled in appreciation.

"Amazing, isn't it? Call it six thousand. Plus provision for tax. For us two and a child living in what any petty bourgeois Victorian would have described as squalor. On the other hand, living in a way in which my grandfather would have thought of as princely—central heating, good food, travel, fags, booze, etcetera. Let's see—he earned fifteen pounds a quarter on his first job. At that rate it would take him—about a hundred years to earn what we need—minimum—for a year."

"How will we get your basic minimum if I stop teaching?"

"Why should you do that?"

"I want another child."

"Not that again." He paused. "Sorry. But—not *now*, Mary, not when we're trying to re-group for going out to a hail-fellow night with lots of half known old half-friends—it's too hard." She accepted his decision to go down to Thurston. Argument seemed utterly pointless.

"I just think you ought to know I'm going off the pill."

"Oh hell!"

Mary smiled. It was a friendly, open smile. She had said all she wanted to say.

Douglas read it as a sarcastic reaction.

"Why do you always make me feel like horse manure?" he asked.

"Perhaps you are." She giggled.

"O.K. So I am."

"That's another trick."
"Would it satisfy you if I slowly castrated myself, bought a briar pipe, went for walks with a rucksack and did the competitions in the 'New Statesman'?"
"That's another trick." Again she laughed.
"She laughed!" He paused. He knew she was laughing at him, but pretended he made her laugh. "Take note, note-takers—she laughed."
"I'm serious," she said abruptly. "I want another child."
She stood up and stretched herself fully: a vague memory of the morning crossed Douglas' mind, but he could not catch it. He watched her appreciatively.
"Mine?" he asked, surprising himself by the question. Why had he thought to ask that?
"Yes." She took her time before repeating the word, unemphatically. "Yes; even after all—yes—I'd still want it to be ours—if we're sticking together as a family."
"If not mine—somebody else's?"
"If you push me, Douglas, yes."
"Anyone in mind?" His throat was dry; his stomach suddenly dissolving.
She paused for long enough and he knew the answers: her pause inoculated him against too severe a reaction.
"Yes, Douglas." She spoke gravely, standing now looking down on him sprawled in his chair. She was white faced and serious, somehow pitying, like the madonna on a stained glass window in his childhood church. She had often reminded him of Her—especially—sacrilegiously—when she had been strewn naked in bed in low light, dawn light, dusk, white, white skin, spread red hair, the expression of pity mingled with piety, after they had made love.
"I see." He was brisk, to get it over with. "Do I know the lucky donor?"
"I'll not answer that."
"Putting all our friends on the list of suspects. Clever move, Inspector."
"I'll answer anything else."
"Well?" He would not ask her if she had been "unfaithful" or "betrayed him". The phrases were—to his credit—stoppered

by his realization of their hypocrisy. But he longed to know.

"No. He wanted to. Very much. And so did I. Perhaps equally as much. It was so nice to be wanted and loved for a change, without all this unhappiness and distrust coming between."

"So why didn't you?" Douglas hoped he sounded merely curious: the panic was held down hard.

"Don't you know?"

"I want you to tell me."

"Reassurance? Again? Again?"

Her scorn thudded into him. He did not acknowledge her taunt.

"I won't be unfaithful to you until our marriage has 'broken down'. I couldn't be."

"Thanks for that," he said. His sense of relief surprised him. "I mean it. Thank you."

"Though why what's sauce for the gander shouldn't be sauce for the goose, I do not know."

"You have no need to say that."

"You mean I have insufficient evidence?"

"Perhaps—"

"You did have an affair, you know. You did admit it." She blushed at the memory. "I was in love with you. When you are in love with someone you know when they betray you. Without any doubt—ever. I had two alternatives. Either I could accept you were 'on the town'—which was demeaning and trivial—or I could imagine I was going mad and not the person I thought I was. I could have one explanation which wounded me terribly but left me sane and the others—*yours*, repeatedly lied about—which supposedly left me whole but feeling as if I were going out of my mind. I'll not put you through that."

When he did not reply, she took out of her pocket the piece of paper the American woman had given him on the plane. He looked at it and waited.

"While you were sleeping in the car on the way up I stopped for petrol," she said. "I hadn't enough change—as usual; you never allow enough for these trips—and so I went through your pockets looking for a couple of pounds. This felt like a note so I pulled it out." She handed it back to him. "Sorry."

He took it, glanced at it again, screwed it up and threw it into the fire. He had kept it out of an old feeling of adventuring. But there was nothing to be said.

"It's an easy name and address to memorize," Mary said.

Douglas nodded.

"Now, I don't mind if you've been screwing in L.A.—'abroad is different', that's what you say, isn't it? Let's say it is—but what I want to know, and what I hope we can work out soon, is whether you love me enough for us to stay together. Because one of the things—you're *so* typical, Douglas—"

"You and your bloody amateur psychology!"

"One of the characteristics of men like you is that you become so guilty that you take it out on your wives. You can't either be a true bastard or a true husband. So while you have a 'good time', I have to have a 'rotten time' to prove that your 'good time' is tough on you as well. Or rather, there has to be a victim and, as it isn't going to be the scarlet woman, it's either going to be Douglas or it has to be me. Well, I'm announcing the end of that role from today. I am not willing to carry the can, take the dirt, be the nursing-home or the analyst's couch or the whipping boy or whatever other object you need me to be so that you can keep your balance and your sanity. I am no longer your *thing*, Douglas."

"Can I say something?"

"Let me finish."

"I didn't—you know—Miss St John's Wood—I just met her on the plane."

"Oh, forget it."

"It's true."

"You don't read shorthand, do you? Of course not! Like all the other practical and sensible things you don't do. Well, underneath her address, Miss U.S.A. had scrawled quite a pornographic little come-on."

"*Had* she?" Douglas—inexplicably, and, he knew, reprehensibly—was delighted. "*What?*"

"You're not wriggling out of this, Douglas. I'm going to

finish. Oh, what the hell." Mary leaned on her chair as if suddenly faint. Douglas got up, came to put his arms around her. She shook her head, violently, and, offended, he stepped back.

"We can talk this out tomorrow, can't we?" He was tired. It was not the time for this.

"Why not now?"

"Well, for one thing I'm exhausted, I think, I must be, musn't I? All that non-sleep, jet lag, booze etcetera? And for another—we'd better be on our way down to the Rugby Club for the jig."

"Must we?"

"We have promised."

"Promised whom?"

"Friends."

"Your friends. I don't mean that to sound spiteful—but they are. Sometimes I don't know why you knock yourself out so much to keep things going. You're often embarrassed; you know you're a target; you're forever being hauled away to talk to people you never knew; you drink too much to get over your nerves. You end up as the caricature of yourself that you most detest. And yet you go on with it. Why is that?"

"'I do not know. I cannot say. I have not had. My — today.' The question now is, are we going or not? It's after nine—if we don't get down there before ten we won't get a seat and we needn't go."

"When you're sober, you're so terrified of showing off that you say nothing at all about the life you lead in London. When you're drunk, you seem so worried about not living up to their fantasies that you hint at things which never happened—you don't *quite* lie—it twists you up completely and yet you rush down to it as if you were going to be suckled in mother's milk. I don't understand it."

"Neither do I." Douglas could add to the list of discomforts and inadequacies. "I like those people, though," he said. "I screw it up because we always meet up in a hectic context—it's a party or a dance or some sort of celebration—and so I'm way behind on the quiet bits, on the gossip that continues to keep them together as friends. But I'm prepared to take the bashing I get because I like them."

"You romanticize them."

"No, I don't. It's just that when I look at them—there's what?—about a dozen fellows my age—schoolteachers, accountants, that sort of thing; one or two small shopkeepers—most—the vast majority—with, apparently, stable marriages, apparently a secure domestic life, satisfying jobs. They seem integrated. They have time for hobbies and sports. They put a lot into the community. That club for a start: and the sports teachers take the kids to Away matches and big games in Edinburgh or London, some of the others lay on Christmas treats for pensioners—that sort of thing—or they're on the council or in the Civic Trust. And besides, they've stuck together, they have the friendship of knowing each other inside out. The old pattern has changed. Once upon a time, the story went, provincial boy—or girl—left for the big lights at least partly because of the lure of a better social life and for metropolitan plunder. But over the last twenty years the social life of the younger lot has arguably been better outside the big cities than inside: just as many car-jaunts, parties, nights out, trips, clubs, dinners—and houses which are better, same generally with schools, hospitals, all amenities. Wages much the same. And information centralized through the newspapers, radio and television, so that except for the chance to pop up to the West End theatre—and how many in London can afford *that*?—they are better off. It's *we*, the pirates, those who struck out—for the first time, perhaps, we're the losers. We should have sat tight. Probably I do romanticize them, but only a little. It's more envy, I think. I've got out and got on—so it seems and so *they* say—but, in fact, I've missed out on what's been ten or fifteen years' solid achievement and companionship and good times. They're always telling stories about each other's misadventures here, there and everywhere—we never tell stories like that in London. The reason I say so little here—to them—is that I have so little of real interest to retail. Then the reason I say too much is because I want to pay back what I feel has been given. They cancel each other out."

"So you're neither one thing nor the other. Again."

"As usual. Yes." Douglas hesitated and then came to a decision. "Why don't we sit here and get gently drunk and be nice to each other in front of the fire of this snug little cottage we're going to have to get rid of? Eh? Quietly. Yes? It's ironic, isn't it, that my grandfather had to start out his married life in a cottage such as this, which he would regard as about the bottom of the pile, and now his so-called affluent grandson can't cope with a similar place. The pattern isn't *quite* that neat, but there's something in it. We could stay—we could spend a long night making love—that would be a change, wouldn't it? Could we summon up the desire now? We could . . . But somehow I'm geared to go down to that noisy, crowded club, crashing with rock music, to shout platitudes at strangers and then traipse around the town after midnight desperately keeping up a custom of First Footing whose origin nobody in the entire district could be sure of. Destinations—Headache, Frustration and probably Drunkenness." He finished his whisky. "I'm sorry," he said, "we have to go."

Mary sat down and held out her glass.

"Just a small one. Then I'll get changed." She smiled. "The women are always so smart. Never mind. We used to have the excuse of being broke and couldn't-care-less. Now we're supposed to be better off, my lack of even an attempt at a glamorous outfit looks a little odd. Enough." He stopped the flow of whisky and poured in water. "Right to the top. Thanks. Some of them are wearing dresses costing sixty or seventy pounds or more."

"Just nerves," he said. "Cheers."

"Cheers." She was relaxed now. "You could be right," she said, taking the lead. "It could be that up here you would lead a steadier life. There would be fewer temptations. That would help. Opportunity's half the trouble."

"Come on, Mary."

"You're always on about your family—well, look at them. Your grandfather: old John's a man—he stuck to what he was given. Joseph annoys you at times—but only because he flusters you by taking your pretensions seriously—he's kept some sort of shape to his life. Harry, of course—and even poor old Lester in his shipwrecked fashion. But you—you're all over the place."

"Yes. I am." Douglas dropped all games, all pretences and spoke as truthfully as he could. "And that's my way, Mary. Sorry. That's it. To you it looks like a mess and to me it looks like a mess—but I'm not going to run for cover into other models, past or present. I want to keep in touch up here because I love my family and friends—not because I have any silly yearning for a golden past, or any wide-eyed admiration for them as types. They're my family and friends, that's all; in a place I also love, that's all; and I want to keep up with them because my life's here as well as all over the place, as you so rightly say. But when I envy the men at the Rugby Club, I don't want to *be* like them—or rather, only when I'm *weak* do I want to be like them. I admire my grandfather and my father—but their lives are not mine. My grandfather was given a spade, a pick or a gun—labourer, miner, soldier—low wages, bare living; large families encouraged, little education, expectation ground down. I don't pretend that is what I have. My father got a little more, but too late in his life. His childhood was just as circumscribed as his father's and so he drifts in the straits of possibilities he never had the opportunity to learn to navigate."

He paused for a moment, then: "I think I've got choices. I can find ways to be more free and more fulfilled. Some of these are illusory. Some already appear to be no more than alternative methods of self-destruction. But what I have the chance to do is to try to weigh up the balance of a number of things and come to my own conclusions about them. If this includes taking chances with personal loyalties as well as a career—then so be it. I am in a mess, yes, up to my eyeballs! I'm bred to lust after security and yet I'd think myself a coward if I did not try to be totally freelance and attempt to ride on the back of the world's whims. I'm trained to all the routines and virtues of domestic fidelity and yet up come the questions—what is it worth? What is its strength? There's a decent, even a very good education been given and yet the temptation to act out of stupidity and even to act in conscious knowledge of doing myself harm is sometimes too tantalizing to resist. The very idea of resisting temptation has been one of the most powerful strictures in my social training—and yet why? What *is* wrong? All the—to you—silly, immature, self-indulgent, spoilt and blindly selfish acts of wilfulness are *not* part of a plan or a pattern—I wouldn't claim that—but they are to do with the way I live in my time now—which is a mess in a mess. My business, I think, is to live through it, and I'd be even more of a failure, I think, if I built a little Ark and sailed out of it! I don't know how to build the Ark and I don't want one anyway. So there you are and here I am."

Mary sipped, she hesitated, and then, speaking softly, she said slowly: "And yet, after all that, I still don't know whether you're behaving like a child or whether there really is something in what you're doing." She puzzled to be fair to this man she had once loved so much and still felt responsible to. "Because, besides being reckless, you have got guts—you take risks; besides being self-deluding, you try to be honest; you're spoilt but you're also serious. You try to think life through for yourself. You're brave in that. I don't know, Douglas, what you're worth. I just don't know."

"Neither do I."

"We'd better set out for the Rugby Club dance," she said, gravely. "I'm a little drunk."

"Do you want to go?"

"No."

"Neither do I."

"I'll wear my black dress. I can hang some of that cheap Arab junk on it you brought back from Israel. That looks quite sexy, doesn't it?"

"It does."

She stood up. So did he. They put down their glasses and embraced tightly, keenly, lovingly it would seem. Their hands caressed each other. They rocked slightly on their heels.

"I mean it about the pill," she whispered. "I want another child."

"So it's my responsibility."

"It is."

"Kid or bust?"

"That's about it."

"I'll have to work it out."

"Take your time." She kissed his ear and then bent her lips to that tender part of his throat; he looked down onto the glossy deep red hair and buried his face in it to draw in the scent and the comfort. His hands were on her breasts, her hips were locked tightly against his—and yet, in this poised moment of pleasure some demon ignited him with despair: for his disloyalties and failings, for his weaknesses and cowardice—the litany rose again but there was no appeal, no "Good Lord Deliver Us". Mary pulled back, tugged off his jacket, looked him full in the face and grinned—as she used to.

"Don't panic," she said. "It just finished a couple of days ago." She tugged at his shirt. "Have this one on the house."

(3)

And so the New Year came in.

Roving reporters took television audiences to Scotland for "the real, the authentic Hogmanay", where tipsy Celts and grinning Picts waved at the cameras on which the Northern sleet fell steadily. From there the armchair celebrants were whisked about the planet, images bouncing off the satellites which circled the earth remorselessly, and everywhere people were cavorting and cheering, either participating in a huge confidence trick they were playing on themselves or truly caught, for the moment, in the notion that there was a witching hour, a turning point, a pause for change.

In Thurston the church bells rang out, the pubs emptied out their rooms and people swarmed up the street to the church square as if they were hurrying to the summons of a mediaeval war. A gigantic circle was formed around the Christmas tree and smaller circles set themselves up like mere planets around this huge cheerful group, which somehow hit on a common note and chanted in faltering unison the hearty words of Robert Burns.

"Should Auld Acquaintance be forgot
And never brought to mind
Should Auld Acquaintance be forgot
For the sake of Auld Lang Syne."

Most mumbled, not knowing whether it was "should" or "would" or even "let", but no one stumbled on that great emotive trio "Auld Lang Syne". As the chorus was repeated, the circle advanced to its centre like a slow-motion rose crumpling; back again to the perimeter and then in once more, with the men happy to barge and be barged, the women saying goodbye to ladderless tights and nylons, those kids let up for the event caught up in the totally untypical circumstance of hundreds of adults prepared to be knocked around, toes trodden on, drizzled on, hustled about and embraced by strangers whose password was no more than "A Happy New Year!"

The bells rang, "A Happy New Year!" Men and boys went around shaking hands all about them, searching for relatives, making do with acquaintances, diving in to kiss attractive women, snatching the willing hands of men they had nodded to for years but never addressed—for some minutes there was a happy bedlam and Douglas, who relished these few minutes more than he cared to say, missed it.

He tried to fit in the Rugby Club's own "Auld Lang Syne" and then belt down to the church. But the greetings and mutual good wishes at the club had taken much longer than he had anticipated—spoiled, too, by the nag in his mind of that date he had made for himself with the event at the church. And so they came too late. The church square was by now empty save for two or three drunks and two young policemen. Douglas walked over to the Christmas tree and tried to imagine the scene of half an hour ago. He had taken in a large load of drink during the evening, failed to remember four or five people whom he was sure he had thereby offended, discovered himself dancing too closely to a pretty woman he'd never met before, had nothing to say while the rich banter on the last rugby tour had built up between the half dozen leaders of the pack—and generally swung between self-disgust and bare acceptance of his conduct. (A cooler, sterner voice told him, rightly, that nobody bothered much what he did.) Mary was well liked and followed her habitual routine, which was to begin talking to the person next to her and be quite content to stay there all evening.

The two policemen decided that the odd couple gazing at the Christmas tree were not about to tear it to the ground, and set off on their "low profile" walk through the town, glad of the regulation boots to keep out the slush.

"Grandad," Douglas announced, "on our way."

Mary had drunk sparingly at the club and drove carefully. As they went up to the old man's flat, they passed groups coming out of houses, going into houses, linked arm in arm, totting up the number of places they went First Footing. In the course of the evening, Douglas and Mary had received more than a dozen invitations—"any time till about five o'clock". There would be a cupboard full of drink, pyramids of sandwiches, platters overcrowded with cakes and cold meats of all sorts. Douglas—unable to say no—had equivocated—guaranteeing, he knew, that this would cause some offence—but what could you do when faced with a point-blank invitation which was the social equivalent of a hold up? If you said no—then even greater offence would be caused. If you said yes, you were committed. You had to equivocate. But he was such a bad equivocator; even in his equivocations he was not firm.

But he had his routine. First his grandfather—so that the old fellow could get off to bed. Then his mother. Then his oldest friend, who could not come to the Rugby dance because of baby-sitting complications. Then a couple of other good friends. By that time it was, generally, almost dawn. In the car, he sang:

"When that I was and a little tiny boy,
With a heigh-ho, the wind and the rain,
A foolish thing was but a toy,
For the rain it raineth every day;
With a heigh-ho, the wind and the rain,
The rain it raineth every day.

Too true. Toooo true. The rain it never stoppeth." He turned to Mary, who was peering through the drizzle-smudged windscreen. He was now well and truly drunk—the fresh air around the Christmas tree had finished him off. "I know we're here. I am looking for Grandad's bottle of scotch, purchased in Los Angeles. Got it!"

The flat was in complete darkness. Indeed, in all the block there were only two very dim lights—which might have been nightlights. Mary cut off Douglas' attempt to barge in and see if his grandfather was awake. They argued, Mary quietly and determinedly, Douglas loudly. She won. They left and the carton of scotch was propped against the door with Douglas' scrawl saying "A Happy New Year" and then "love" which was badly crossed out. "I forgot myself," he explained to Mary. "I can't start saying 'love' to my grandfather. It would never do." He printed his name in wayward letters which trekked around the seal and placed it carefully by a small parcel and then they went to round out the morning's celebrations about the houses of the town.

Old John had heard every word. He could not quite distinguish the voice—it could have been Joseph, it could have been another of his sons—but he guessed it would be Douglas, who had made a thing out of coming up First Footing on New Year's morning. It was difficult for him to concentrate on anything outside his own head; it throbbed with fear. He had woken up by the dead fire—been awakened by the cold—and, seeing the time, made shift to sort himself out for the night, knowing there would be visitors. He had stood up, and collapsed, cutting his head, as he fell, on the back of a chair. It was not a bad cut but it bled a lot. John had tried again to stand, resentful and furious at being laid low: but he could not. In his frustration, as he lay there, the blood warm on his cold skin, he had felt tears come once again to his eyes, but he had forced them back. He resolved he would not cry again as he had done in the afternoon. He was determined not to repeat that weakness. Whatever else happened—and clearly, for he saw it all—there would be a swift decline into senile infancy—there would be incontinence and bedsores, there would be forgetfulness and the stealing hopelessness of irreversible decline—but whatever else happened he would not cry.

Feeling a fool, though he had no reason on earth to feel so, but feeling a fool, he crawled to the sink as—he remembered—exactly as he had been taught to crawl in the First World War. He gripped the side of it tightly and began to haul himself up. The sink came away from the wall. He let go and rolled aside, looking up at the cheap fitment which jutted out from the wall now, like the prow of a ship. He waited for the water to pour out, but the pipes had not been damaged.

Lying there, on his back, staring at the white ceiling, crippled, bleeding and very old, he heard the church bells peal out twelve and knew he would have to hurry if he was to avoid being seen.

He crawled over to the door and locked it. Using the door handle as an aid, he reached up and knocked off the light. Then he scuffled himself through to his bedroom, undressed, pulled himself into the bed and only then realized that he had done nothing about the cut on his forehead. On the bedside table there was a glass of water: he wetted his fingers in it and dabbed the cut, which felt quite nasty to his fingertips. He kept doing this until he felt the wound grow cold. The spilt blood coagulated on his cheek.

His first visitor was Mrs. Fell from the flat next door: she knocked once politely, a second time timidly and then left her gift, a chocolate cake which she had baked that afternoon, beside the door and shuffled back to her own flat.

Then Douglas and his wife came. John could not remember her name. There were so many new names. He heard the car start up and leave and wondered how many others in these old people's flats were as wide awake as he, how many suddenly overtaken by life, quite bewildered that they should be at the end of it when they could so easily reach back to the beginnings and see themselves young and fresh and strong, how many knowing they were waiting, as he was waiting.

(4)

Harry and Aileen had been to one or two pubs, then, of course, to the Rugby Club, where Aileen had talked to Douglas, whom she liked and trusted (despite his compulsive tendency to run himself down)—and they had left in time to get to the church for the big circle. Lester had been at the church, looking as if he had been in a fight—but he had sworn not and his friends had backed him up with virtuous indignation. Aileen was not too happy about these town friends of Lester's: they egged him on, she thought, and brought out his worst side. She preferred the few friends he still had in the country, those he had met when he used to be a fell runner—farm labourers or mechanics at small garages—men, did she but know it, who were greatly envied by Lester himself—in his "down" times, such as this. For, though they would never believe it, these men were better off than him—certainly at the present time. And in his rare moments of insight Lester would guess they would always be so. More importantly, though, they lived in the country, which Lester knew about and genuinely loved. Much more than Douglas or Harry, he was a country boy; he had poached and been shooting, built camps, dammed up rivers, snared rabbits, tackled rock faces—he was never happier than when he was in the country—it was a tribute to the power of the metropolitan poison he so greedily sucked in that the fantasies he chased so clumsily and ineptly should stand in the way of the real, acknowledged pleasures and rewards he had chosen to abandon. He was not morose, though, Aileen was relieved to see: he had met up with some men: "big smart fellas," he confided, "where the money is, 'Gentlemen Farmer' types!" They were up from the Midlands with a pack of beagles and after chatting with him they had invited him to join them in their sport on the fells behind Skiddaw the following morning. "My luck," he announced, "is in again."

She kissed him and wished him a "Happy New Year" with her usual sisterly fervour. She found her father, George, pleasantly piddled; and her mother on the arm of her latest fancy man. Harry had gone around pumping hands as if clearing a flood off the decks. Then he took her to Betty's, where he always went immediately after the church square "do"—and Aileen had been glad of the chance to sit quietly for a while. Joseph had whirled in with two or three friends and half a dozen strangers, decimated the sandwiches, attacked the drink, turned the place upside down looking for a bottle-opener—and left on his own route around the town. Aileen and Betty had talked town gossip.

In the car, she leaned her head on Harry's shoulder and felt deeply comfortable. He took care, she noticed, as much as he could, to ensure that her head was not jarred nor jolted. She loved his care for her and for others. It was altogether marvellous, she thought, how sure she felt about Harry and how innocent he still was of her set intentions. She knew nobody as unassuming and as inviolably good. In his reliability, his modesty and his fidelity, she had basked for about three years now, knowing that the unspoken, unofficial arrangement they had would be more binding to him than all the rings, certificates and vows in the world to anyone else. Aileen had learned to value what was sure. Her own early life had almost been ruined by neglect from irresponsible parents. She had taken refuge in food and silence. Even today, she could be surprised at how she had managed to escape from that tired, soporific, sullen, fat, passive body and lazy mind. She was proud of the way in which she had pulled herself together, but still aware of how near a thing it had been. Only the intervention of a sympathetic schoolteacher had pulled her through. One consequence was that she was wary of everyone but Harry. Only her own efforts mattered; other people would surely do her some damage. Except Harry. This fearful self-dependence had made it hard for her initially but then, when she had got interested in her work at the college, it had been the best possible ally. She had worked alone, set out and stuck to her own standards, was now secure in her job and about to take on a new career, she hoped, in politics. But first she wanted to get married. She would tell Harry that evening. New Year's Day would be the right time to set it all in motion.

They went up to see old John. The thought of him had nagged Harry all evening. He saw that the lights were off and bit his lip in annoyance.

"We've hung about down there too much," he said. "He must have packed in and gone to bed."

"We could knock," Aileen said. "People expect that tonight."

"No. If he's put the lights out he'll want to be on his own. I hope this car hasn't woken him up."

"You can come up in the morning."

"I will, yes. But I hope somebody was with him tonight. I've just realized. Maybe nobody was."

"Why is it important?"

He told her, glad to be able to tell someone.

"I'll come up with you tomorrow," she said. "We might have

to get him into a hospital and you'll never be able to persuade him yourself."

"Of course, he could be all right," Harry said. "It could just have been a turn."

"We'll see."

"I'll take him his present."

Harry took the crate of Guinness from the back of the car. Old John appreciated whisky, but it was a bottle of stout a day that "kept him going", he said. Harry put it down beside the whisky and the cake and laid a bottle-opener on top.

Then he left and took Aileen back to his flat where they talked until he found he was about to be married and they went to bed about the same time as Joseph finally reached his father's flat. He banged on the door several times and then sat on the crate, worn out with his evening's pilgrimage, and opened a bottle of Guinness to settle his stomach. As always when alone and almost drunk, he thought about how he would have liked his retirement to be. A certain comfort—not much, peace of mind, books to read, long, interesting conversations, above all, security. Instead, what they had saved, which had seemed so huge to their mid-War minds, was just a drop in a pool. Without his part-time job as school-caretaker (which was a grand title for sweeping up the classrooms in the Comprehensive every evening) and Betty's few pounds from the lunch-time work she did in the bar of the King's Head, they would be unable to manage. Money, he concluded, had become senseless: and, with the deliberation of the very tired, he took out a five pound note, folded it up and tucked it inside the whisky carton before replacing the empty bottle in its slot and setting off for his bed.

Even later, grey with weariness, Mary and Douglas reached their cottage. He had slunk, drunk, from house to house, occasionally lurching into coherence—intense, grandiloquent, or confidential—always brief. Mary had kept going and not pressed him to give up. On the way back he had fallen deeply asleep after declaring: "Do you know that Tennyson was inspired to write about Excalibur on the shore of Bassenthwaite—two miles from us—what a thought! That hard shaft shooting up from that flat lake! Why are shords so symbolic? Sorry. Shords are. So . . . I learnt that in Hollywood!

Tennyson. Hollywood!" In his sleep he muttered broken sentences. Mary stayed in the car and smoked a final cigarette, looking out to the grey which was slowly rising against the darkness. She had given in again and she would give in again, but she had also made up her mind. If Douglas did not want a family and if he was not prepared to be stable enough to enable her to devote more time to John and to any others she might have—then she would, indeed, leave him.

He was slumped on her shoulder. His hair was dirty: it stank. He breathed like an old man and was white with exhaustion and drink. Somehow he reckoned that the world would take care of him and let him dry out, return to normality, go on as before. There was nothing about him now, as she looked down on the ageing face, which touched her, let alone moved her to love. Even his helplessness wearied her: it was such an indulgence. Yes. She would have to make the decisions. She threw the cigarette out of the window and nudged his head with her shoulder quite brutally. "We're here," she said. "Get out." It was still dark. The First Day.

(5)

Old John had not slept at all. Time stretched so far when you did not sleep. The night had gone on for so long.

His legs, useless to him now, ached and burned, while the rest of him was cold, despite the blankets. He had heard the comings and goings and almost called out to Joseph, who would have understood—but by that time his mind was set. He knew that they would take him to a home or a hospital and he did not want it done in the middle of the night with all the fuss. He would wait.

There was a feeling of vigil about the watch he kept over himself and yet the waiting lacked a point of arrival. For what was he going towards? He would not see another New Year, that was certain. He might just make the summer, though he doubted it. Maybe the spring: he would like to see one last spring. But what would he see from a hospital bed? He would like to see the new lambs—most of all the lambs—and the leaves and the flowers, yes, those too. His first wife, who had died so long ago, and his second, who had gone five years before—both had been keen on flowers. He mixed their faces up now; an expression here on a face there; and the children, *their* children, friends, Mrs. Fell with her kind cakes. He would like a drive around the places he had been hired—to see the fields he ploughed and dug and worried over. Just to see them again. That was all.

For what else was there? As the terrible long night went on so very slowly, the old man tried to ask and answer the question which was now so urgent. What had it all been *for*, this life? Would there be another life, another chance, another birth? He thought not. No. But, even so, it could not be quite meaningless, could it? What had it been for? He clenched his teeth to stop his tears as the humiliation of incontinence overcame him and he wet the bed. At last there was a bit of grey outside. They would break the door down—no—they would get the spare key from the Warden. It would be good if he could close his eyes, now, now, this moment, knowing it was over. But that was not allowed. Another car went by. He heard some children playing on their bicycles, ringing the trilling bells. They would find him soon.

3
"London Bridge"

(I)

The church clock struck six. He could hear it when the wind was in the north-east. It was odd, somehow, in London, to hear so clearly the toll of a church clock; especially such a one as this, which was tinny, unresonant, villagey, like an alpine bell. He had been awake since about four—as usual whenever he had too much to drink. The pattern never varied. A brief, slugged unconsciousness, a startled awakening, the whirling head, the pint-of-milk-and-three-Paracetemols cure and then the difficult decision: back to bed or try to read? Bed won. He had learned to stop fussing about alcoholic insomnia: he lay on his back, settled himself comfortably, and rummaged around in a mind now made companionable by the drugs.

Mary slept deeply. It was still dark outside but he could "see" her clearly. She slept face down, legs splayed, arms hoisted up onto the pillows, hair obscuring her face. He reached out his hand and let it trail gently down her back until it reached the rise of the buttocks. She stirred; he did not persist. Despite his inebriated lust, he did not want to disturb her.

They had been back from Cumbria for three months and she was not yet pregnant. Sometimes he tried, sometimes he did not. Mary was still not quite sure whether his behaviour was based on fine calculations or excusable obstinacy. So far she gave him the benefit of the doubt, choosing to ignore his unspoken but clearly felt resistance to this demand of hers. For she had got him to agree to it, but only through a manoeuvre quite close to blackmail: for if he did not, she said, then she would indeed think of seeking to have a child by someone else. She knew how violently jealous and possessive he was.

Douglas would not explain his reluctance. For if he was thinking of breaking the most serious bond in his life—his marriage—how could he ever think of tying them both together with more flesh? It was cowardly to hesitate but perhaps also he was giving the marriage a last chance. Chance was the word—for they *did* make love: maybe, before leaving, he was throwing out a last challenge to the luck which, in his pagan state of mind, seemed to have so much power.

His lack of contentment disconcerted him. At the very least it felt like selfish ingratitude. As a boy he had never imagined that he would lead such an outwardly pleasant, easy and entertaining life. His discontent made his existence appear indulgent, as well as negligible. Yet there it was, squatting like a toad in the middle of his mind and immovable, it seemed. No appeal to Third World poverty, to Calcuttas of the body and spirit, to Gulags of the mind and conscience, to lost Empires, domestic injustices—none of this could goad his self-soaked mind to stir into that bracing activity traditionally guaranteed to dissolve selfishness and destroy this boring misery. Hedonism had ended in the cul-de-sac of responsibility. Ambition was suspect. And mere accumulation vulgar. And he had blown family life, hadn't he? He had broken a trust which, like a broken egg, could never be mended; or, like a sacrificial cock, could only be killed the once. Perhaps life was not the answer: perhaps it would be better to read. Just to settle for a bed-sitter and a clutch of library tickets and read all the best books written. Leave it at that. Let what happen come. Life would crowd in fast enough: it always did. Or he could go to the U.S.A.—West Coast—pretending amnesia, and start again as a literary hobo. Why not? Infantile fantasies were the stuff of real change and revolution. Or settle down to Write The Big Play. Or work for the Labour Party. Or go into the church (which he would have done if he could have believed in God): or jump off Brighton Pier: or Blackpool Tower: or wherever was convenient. Non-existence seemed sweet and drink was the nearest substitute.

How the hell had he got into that state?

The alarm rang. He leaned across Mary and banged it shut. "I'll get up first," he announced, and the glow of virtue rose up to be quelled by the renewed pressure of the hangover.

He made the breakfast—cornflakes and scrambled eggs on toast—and saw John and Mary set off for school together. John had a cold and looked pinched, orphan-like, Douglas thought, guiltily. Mary was almost silent in the mornings; the two of them, mother and son, went off to school as if embarking on a penitential pilgrimage. So much for family life.

Douglas worked at the story.

The mail brought him an invitation from the Arts Council to go on a writers' tour of Cornwall and Devon for one week, with three other writers, for a hundred and twenty pounds plus travel expenses: he accepted. A tax account, which he stuck with the others and resolved to sort out soon, when he answered the pile of correspondence. An invitation to a lecture in the House of Commons, Committee Room Eleven, on "Censorship in Contemporary Society" by Richard Hoggart. A couple of circulars and a picture postcard, for John, from Betty, which read, "Thought you'd like this. We're glad you like your school now. Love and kisses. Grandma. XXXXXXX."

The phone rang but he had made a rule not to answer it while he was writing. Another rule allowed him to ring out whenever he wanted to.

As usual when he wrote, he would think either that it was the most satisfying and enjoyably difficult thing he ever did, or that it was utterly useless and completely unreal, sitting there scratching his ink out on narrow lined paper.

For about three hours he worked as hard as he could on something which would probably not make him a penny. He was quite happy. The invented world kept out the real world and here he ruled, a harmless tyrant.

Then he answered some letters and let others rot away in the pile—the difficult ones, hoping that somehow they would change nature, like dead cut grass ending up as live manure. Occasionally that did happen. A couple of phone calls, a desultory trot around the Canadian Air Force Exercises course (twenty push-ups—*quite* enough, and, each time his nose touched the floor, it was rubbed in the badly frayed carpet, like a symbol of his lack of husbandry), cheque book, credit cards, keys, book to read in emergency, out onto the street, making for the Underground. No coat, no scarf, no gloves, walking fast in the cold; as usual buoyed up to be diving into London—free to loot the capital.

As he waited for the tube, on the empty platform—it was a comfortable time of day to travel—he read the introduction by Gide to James Hogg's "The Confessions of a Justified Sinner". Gide had clearly been enraptured by the book's concern with good and evil. Douglas had picked up the book after he had re-read "The Immoralist".

Gide quoted from "The Doctrine of All Religions" (1704) on the heresy known as Antinomianism—founded in 1538. "Antinomians, so denominated for rejecting the law, as a thing of no use under Gospel dispensation. They say that good works do not further, nor evil works hinder salvation: that the child of God cannot sin, that God never chastiseth him, that murder, drunkenness, etc., are sins in the wicked but not in him."

The silver train shook the red tiled walls as it bolted out of its tunnel. The guard waited while a fat woman tugged at the sweets machine and finally extracted her bar of chocolate.

Into Soho at forty-five miles an hour, a day's freelancing before him. First, lunch with Mike Wainwright of the B.B.C. He looked forward to that. He read another page or two of Gide. "The child of God cannot sin!" Think on that!

(2)

There was something about the look of Mike Wainwright which said he had come through. He had. The look represented the reality.

He was in his early fifties, squarely built, neither stout nor slim but firmly muscled, light on his feet, physically poised and secure. That security had been earned and yet needed attention, you felt, for there was both evidence of past strain on his wary face, and a feeling of frailty, as if a sensitive set of features had been superimposed on a tough base, or vice versa. For there was a flickering interplay of alertness and achieved calm, of vulnerability and tranquillity. He looked experienced and yet still open to experience, as if he had learned hard lessons the hard way but, despite that, was not afraid to be open to what came. He had the look of a wise fighter, whose mind and life had raked over too much, but managed to gather together some fragments to shore up an independent personality, which existed in its own right. For that, most of all, was what Wainwright gave off: the smack of being independent, self-sufficient, self-resolved—not the self-satisfied and islanded complacency of the very rich or very powerful, whose poise depends on their distance from the rest and the maintenance of that distance by fair means or foul, by loot or by crook. Nor was it the anarchistic arrogance of the man who does not give a sod for the world, secure in the knowledge that the world does not give a sod for him—in short, the mere reckless pose of the brazen self-destructor, who can always claim a passing regard because of the chord of pointlessness he touches in us all. Wainwright had earned his independence, you felt, had been tested and not found wanting, had fallen and picked himself up again, accommodated weaknesses and wounds and carried on, selflessly. For he was, to a few like Douglas, a touchstone, incorruptible, a man to whom the word "integrity" could be applied without a twinge of embarrassment or a grain of pomposity.

He had caught the last two years of the War and seen a bit of action. If you don't get shot, he said, and you think you're on the right side and the whole business *means* something, then war for an eighteen year old is all they once said about it. There is the unblushing talk of courage, endurance, even heroism. And eighteen was a time when most men unselfconsciously wanted to be brave, to show courage in Hemingway's sense and prove themselves. War could soon seem very natural.

Mike had been on hand when the concentration camps had been "liberated" and such notions had been blown away like euphoric frost. That sight, he thought, though it was only to his wife he had admitted it, had been so devastating and yet so strange: for at first he had felt only detached natural human pity at those skeletal men. And then the mass graves were discovered and at first there was a kind of wonder at it all, as if his world were being turned upside down in very slow motion. Finally the settlement had come, the meaning of it had hit him. In 1945, aged twenty, the day the War was over, Michael Jeffrey Wainwright from South London out of the West Country,

Raleigh's country, playing football to celebrate victory, suddenly trotted off the pitch, went behind the huts they had taken over from the Germans and found himself crying helplessly but with no feeling of relief: for there was a great weariness and burden suddenly on him: a vision of the hell of the world fixed in his mind.

There followed a time of listlessness which he thought might becalm him for ever. He went to university and drifted: he had no real heart for games, although he had once enjoyed playing rugby and cricket; he was interested in his work—Modern History—but not interested enough to satisfy himself— tutorials with a man a few years older than himself dwindled into gossip about the War, lectures were soon cut, reading digressed into vacant daydreamings or private discoveries such as Camus or T. S. Eliot's "Waste Land" and "Prufrock", which shot into his system like insulin into a diabetic. He drank quietly and consistently. He was chaste. His parents had died during the War and his vacations were spent around the Mediterranean, wandering among the remainders of other lost civilizations. He failed to go back after his second year and left on a whim for America.

He read extensively, feeding on modern literature, hunting through it for certainties and clues. Like tens of thousands of others, he criss-crossed the continent, looking for a lodging place. The tiny inheritance from his parents soon gave out. He got whatever work he could, lived rough, went up to Canada where he was asked to run a lumber yard and "get on the ladder to be a millionaire", went to Mexico, where he lived for six months with a young neurotic German sculptress who finally abandoned him for an insurance salesman from Chicago. Wainwright ended up in Greenwich Village, where a short ironic account of some of these adventures introduced him to one of the small magazines of the day. In that predominantly immigrant Jewish intellectual community, where ideas and their expression were declared the most important matter in life, he flourished. He wrote little, but what he wrote was respected and encouraged. His interest in films began, caught flame and rapidly developed into the compulsive passion he had been seeking. He made his first documentary in Canada

—returning to the lumber camp in which he had worked and making a fine piece of work on the men who had been teased and drawn out into that wilderness. On the promise of a possible feature film, he returned to England.

The film was "well received" but made no money. About two years later, a second film was even better received and made less. On the back of the good notices, however, he was whisked off to Hollywood, where he spent eighteen months trying to do a film he wanted to do. He failed and walked out of his contract. Libel suits cleaned him out of the modest amount of money he had. Back in England, he set up a film too quickly and failed to make it to his own satisfaction. It did quite well at the box-office and he was bankable, in a modest way. But the five or six years had churned up a reasonably balanced marriage, left a small daughter stranded with an entrenched mother who drank far too much. Wainwright, after the divorce, devoted himself to setting the two of them up in a decent house, well appointed, with regular monthly cheques in the bank. For himself he took a small, plain service flat, just north of Soho. That was where he still lived. He had never remarried.

Throughout the Sixties and Seventies he had freelanced. His basic work was making documentaries, chiefly for television. He did some journalism. There had been one published collection of semi-autobiographical essays, which had not done particularly well. At present he was setting up two new series for the B.B.C. He liked Douglas and had arranged to meet him in Bianchi's for lunch.

(3)

Elena brought them a second carafe of red. The first floor of this little Italian restaurant was packed, as usual, while downstairs, though the food came from the same kitchen, the tables were comparatively undisturbed. It was Elena's welcome, an elegant Italian mamma who swooped like a swallow—and a consistent and loyal link with the literary/film/television/theatre younger crowd which kept the upstairs full. At times it was like a club. That helped. And the prices were reasonable.

Douglas had nodded to the half a dozen people he

knew—from vaguely to quite well, a tricky but well practised scale of nods—and been amused to watch the transparent barometer of feelings on the face of one young trendy critic in particular—a very clever chap, recently down from Oxford, much given to scorn, garlanded with recondite epithets and contempt, which he implicitly justified by comparisons with the All Time (Dead) Greats, beside whom all contemporaries were as midgets, etcetera etcetera. In fact he was following the usual and safely worn trail set by many young men in a hurry to capitalize on the energy garnered during three years in a university. The rules were simple—hit out at prominent figures, thereby getting yourself talked about, thereby getting some of the spotlight on yourself, thereby becoming a "name", thereby acquiring a market value (on a market which, naturally, you despised). Said young person—quite a cheerful, shy, decent fellow, under the twin terrors of failure and not being in fashion which currently had him by the throat—had given a brisk no-nonsense nod in response to Douglas' brisk no-nonsense nod but then, seeing that Douglas was with Wainwright, he had missed no opportunity to bow and wink and leer knowingly throughout the meal. It was so blatant that it was comical: a self-abasement Douglas had never come across in his youth, or anywhere at all. It was the sort of craven bum-boot-licking he had been told to expect but rarely encountered in Big Corporations. It was most odd. The explanation was simple. Wainwright could introduce him to the beginnings of a television career (which, naturally, he despised). He knew Douglas slightly from one or two literary cocktail parties (which he despised) and, sure enough, over he came after his unfattening veal—dragging his rumpled and lovely girlfriend—to struggle through a few banalities and at once assume and, as he thought, initiate a relationship with Wainwright. Finally, with much, much nodding, he left. "He'll do well," Douglas said. "But why does he want to do well in that way?"

"We do need a hand at the start," Wainwright said. He had registered Douglas' reaction to the young man and thought it too harsh. "Or most of us."

"Agreed."

"You didn't."

"I was lucky," Douglas said, fittingly averting any opportunity for a compliment. He hated them.

"I believe you." Wainwright took out a cigarette. "What are you doing?"

"Trying to finish some work."

"Do you still have the same system?"

"Which one was that?"

Wainwright laughed.

"You used to go and get some 'loot'—your phrase—and then simply wrote until you had used it up."

"That was one of the better systems," Douglas said, "but it's changed lately." He looked around: the place was almost empty: he still felt the guilty privilege of sitting about while others were working—yet that was the prime benefit of his "freedom", wasn't it? "How did *you* keep your nerve?" he asked. "As a freelance?"

"Desperation's a big help," Wainwright said, "or success."

"I pass on both," Douglas said. "At present."

"What are you doing now?"

"Looking for work."

"Any ideas?"

"One or two. One worthy but not necessarily dull."

Douglas outlined his idea for a series of programmes in which writers would take a region of the U.K. and produce a script which would work through from the geology to the present self-awareness of the place. He had prepared a document based on Yorkshire. Cumbria would have been too obvious. Yorkshire included great industry as well as a tradition of sport, public life, the arts, and that self-conscious "Yorkshireness" which often filled indifferent outsiders with feelings of bored desperation. This document had been sent to Mike a few days previously and he had read it. Nevertheless he let Douglas make the case: slightly resenting this, Douglas semi-deliberately made a mess of it. There was a self-destructiveness in him on such occasions which was out of his control. He stopped talking.

"It was a better idea on paper," Wainwright said.

"Most ideas are."

"Not all. Sometimes . . . You don't like singing for your supper, do you?"

"No."

"But that's the freelance life."

"Not necessarily. You can duck a lot of it. You don't do as well. That's all."

"You do it to avoid being bossed about?"

"Partly. Yes. A good part. Silly really."

"Why?"

"Well," Douglas was beginning to be muzzy: the plonk felt as if it were seeping corrosively across the runnels of his bare brain. "Well, unless you're lucky or a genius you work for *someone*. The attraction of writing is that you work for yourself. But—here's the catch—'yourself' can be a lousy boss. Still, we're free, aren't we? That's the point, isn't it? We've done with 'perfect service'."

"Do you think this freedom is something you have to have?"

"Not really. It's probably just another face of selfishness. Though what isn't?"

"Do you think much about it?" Wainwright asked.

"Why?"

"It would seem to me that your lot, even those of you who started out as provincial puritans in that good old British tradition of earnestness—plain living and high thinking—most of you simply don't concern yourselves now with what used to be called 'fundamental issues'—indeed such a formulation would make you flinch. I thought the approach nowadays was cynical, pessimistic, elliptical and somehow sapped of the moral energy that keeps those considerations alive."

"I don't know. I don't think it's an age *of* anything much. Perhaps what they say is true: the atom bomb and the concentration camps between them make a pair of inescapable pincers. We've got the stuff to blow us all to smithereens and we've got the proof we're evil enough to try it. So why bother?"

"You bother." More wine was poured.

"But I don't know why I bother to bother. And I don't bother much. Maybe it's just for something to do."

"I don't think so. But you *do* need work?"

"A fix?" He paused and sobered up in that part of his mind which needed to see sense. "Yes. Work could see me through whatever it is I'm in. I'm not complaining, you know." Douglas added this anxiously. He wanted Wainwright to be absolutely clear. "I'm not begging for work. I'm not on my uppers." He was. He took a large drink and pronounced, "I still find it incredible, sometimes, you know, to be six or seven miles high in an aeroplane with a plate of food and a glass of Beaujolais. And now—just the same—a working day—what is it?—about three o'clock—and here we are—I am babbling on in this pleasant place, swigging booze, just being here. There's some sort of fluke in it. Got to be. Millions starving, millions slaving away, millions dying, millions in factories, in sheds, in pain, in noise, in filth, in terror, in depression—what have I done that I should be living the life of Reilly? Nothing at all is the answer. It's enough to drive a man to drink." He poured himself the rest of the carafe. "Nothing!" he repeated. "Nothing at all!"

"Cheers!" said Wainwright.

"No wonder the rich and mighty worship the past—their old houses and ancestors and connections and clubs and schools and collected clutter of ages of looting and buying—the past is the only thing that possibly sustains them in this privilege with any validity whatsoever. That's why the self-made men are always such a threat. They say, 'We deserve what we've got because we've got it by our own endeavours and we owe the world nothing.' They inhabit their own moral universe. In a way they are our chiefs and heroes, but as most of us want to nobble chiefs and trip up heroes in the greater cause of making sure nobody gets too much power. We don't like them much. We prefer the luck of the past or the luck of the draw. That's real life. It's some ridiculous quirk of fortune that has me here with the time and leisure and education and drink and food and interests which would be the envy of an eighteenth-century nobleman and a grandfather who mourns for a past when eight brothers slept toe-to-tail on a mattress on a damp cottage floor which can still be found in any rural community from Pakistan to Mexico and back again. And there will be retribution. Got to be. Unless, that is, we redeem our privilege by courage. Unless we stand up and are counted—Oh God! Sorry."

"Why?"

"Boring."

"I didn't find it so."
"That's because you're a pal and I'm half drunk."
"No. I was interested. There was nothing new—"
"Thanks."
"But I was interested. Is being boring a cardinal sin?"
"Yes. *The* cardinal civilized sin."
"Your regional notion," Wainwright said, "is very worthy."
"Worthy *and* uncontroversial *and* dull," Douglas corrected him. "Carefully composed for the market."
Wainwright grinned. "I like that."
"But not the idea."
"Not much."
"I thought that was the idea."
"What?"
"Not to like something much. Liking something much might introduce that gypsy strain of passion or commitment which the B.B.C.—'on the one hand—on the other hand be our motto and we have as many hands as any goddess in Bali'—stands to stamp on. If you get my drift. On the other hand. It is *quite* a decent idea you know and if we get the right writers—say that again—and we do *have* good writers who actually *live* in regions and know a lot about them and would do this sort of thing, I'm convinced, out of a nice sense of commitment—it could work very well."
"I agree."
"Well then?"
"It'll have to take its place in a queue."
"How long?"
"About a year."
"Sod it."
"Relying on it?"
"I've just this second realized that I was. Coffee?" It was ordered.
"What'll you do?" Wainwright asked. "Anything on the stocks?"
"Nothing that would make money. Ah well." He drank the scalding coffee in two or three gulps and felt better. "I've been avoiding a crunch by an inch here and there for years. Like Jerry in those Tom and Jerry films, you know, where he walks

through one potential disaster after another, missing them by a whisker. Now it's here."

"And how do you feel?"

"Quite calm," Douglas said. "Have to change that. Give me an hour for it to sink in."

"You'd banked too much on it."

"Yes and no. The more important fact is that I've no other iron in the fire at the moment. No play on the hoof—I'm too involved in this story. No other television. Not a tickle from feature films, of course. One or two reviewing possibilities—yes. That could, perhaps, be worked up. It's as if I'd sorted it all out so that it would *have* to depend on one throw of the dice."

"'Regionalism'?"

"I agree. Not exactly Dostoevskian daring. And you see—it didn't come up. Well. There we are. Your lunch? Mine? Ours? Or Theirs?"

"Ours," Wainwright said.

It cost them nine pounds fifty each.

They went down the steep and narrow stairs and into a bright spring Soho day. "I'm going to Parliament," Douglas said. "Friend from back home—oop North—making his maiden speech."

"I'll walk along with you."

They went through the packed, village-narrow streets of Soho. Sex shops, food shops, strip clubs, and the remorseless crowd of voyeurs, visitors and villains: through Gerrard Street, Chinatown now, though once, Douglas remembered, used by Dickens to house that wonderful lawyer in "Great Expectations"—strolled down through Leicester Square, now become a "pedestrian precinct" and consequently a cul-de-sac for loafers and alcoholics, wriggled around the National Portrait Gallery and entered Trafalgar Square in a blaze of sunshine, fountains playing, tourists chasing the hundreds of fat pigeons, motor vehicles circling three deep, Big Ben dominating the middle distance and Nelson—

"What would he make of us?"

"He'd have given us all up years ago," Wainwright said.

"Who would be put up on a phallic plinth now?"

"Footballer? Pop star? *Intelligent* pop star—who writes his own stuff: Dylan, Lennon, McCartney."

"Raven?" Douglas asked.

"Most of all."

"What about him?"

"For a programme?" Mike was clearly interested.

"Yes." Douglas caught the chance.

"I thought he was uncontactable." They were now walking down Whitehall: on their right a pornographic farce was playing to a packed house on this perfect spring afternoon—Oh to be in England—while on their left the massy mausoleum of ministerial offices administered away, enscripting Britain into a legislative maze apparently as complicated as that which was spun out from the Escorial when the Spanish Empire declined and fell: farther down, on the right, two soldiers in scarlet and white with plumes in their hats confronted an inordinately large gathering of amateur photographers as they stood guard —over what? A last full stop for the Empire. And out of all the imperial past came—the Pop Star.

Merlin Raven. Life like a fairy story. Brought up in an orphanage in Widnes: "everybody" in the U.K. and the U.S.A. knew the songs about Widnes: ran away to sea. Jumped ship in Panama—bummed around America like a late beat—and that journey too was eventually turned into songs. Taken up by an austere poet in New England who educated him, loved him and, when Raven left with a woman, broke down into drink and remorse. Then Raven came to Liverpool, formed a group, let loose his songs and became one of the biggest Superstars in the Business. "Thus Spake The Raven", his first L.P., sold nine million copies and the others almost matched that. His wealth was estimated between ten and thirty million pounds. His name was associated now with poets, now with minor royalty, now with the drug-bug clique, now with a woman, now with a man: but, despite the publicity, he managed to retain an elusive quality. The associations which were said to be certain often turned out to be nothing but rumour; those who claimed friendship were discovered to have no more knowledge than a passing acquaintance; the glamorous jet cum arts cum smart set he was alleged to inhabit rarely saw him. And so an alternative legend grew up, alongside the plodding mass-media descriptions. In this, Merlin was a strange loner; someone who could walk out and put on a false beard and hitch a lift coast to coast; a man who sought out pals from the past and spent days with them just around the place, the pub, the streets, the cafés; someone who wrote and rewrote his songs and was working on a play or a script or a book . . . There had been a massive charity concert in Newcastle. Tens of thousands of fans had come to the football ground to hear him. Fights had broken out. Two teenage girls were stabbed to death. Raven had disappeared.

"Two years ago, wasn't it?" Douglas said. "Then—there was talk of a Greek island of course: and the Coast—of course. He hasn't done anything—released anything—since that concert. Lester knew him."

Wainwright knew about Lester.

"He claims he met him and even managed him for a while in Liverpool. Then lost him. Of course."

"Would he know where Raven is?"

"Are you really interested?"

"Yes."

"Another documentary on another pop star?"

"Raven's spoken to no one since the early days."

"When he spoke to everyone."

"He's interesting. He goes his own way."

They had reached the bottom of Whitehall and turned left to face Westminster Bridge. The day glittered more and more brightly: the row of tacky souvenir shops seemed cheerful: the Gothic pile where legislators sat and stood and ate and drank and talked and shouted and often made sense, that again seemed cheerful enough, as if it had been given a polish by the sun; one or two policemen stood about rather like Gilbert and Sullivan characters, aimlessly waiting to be prompted into song; the steady traffic was reassuring in its evidence of movement, even of industry.

"I enjoyed that lunch," Douglas said.

"Do a film on Raven," Wainwright said.

"Why?"

"He's worth it. You need the work. The film could be good."

"Regionalism, Mike: regionalism. The coming and going thing. Back to the Seven Kingdoms. Bring on the churls."

"Next year."

"I'll see."

"What are you thinking about?" Wainwright asked him and there was, in the unexpectedness of the question—unexpected, that is, from someone he knew so well and with whom he had been talking for two to three hours—something that forced Douglas to focus on the answer. But first he stalled for time.

"Why do you ask?"

"I've had the impression that your mind has been fixed on something else all the time we've been talking. It was as if you'd turned on an automatic pilot: the words came out, but you weren't there."

Douglas considered this carefully, not so much in order to counter it or answer it but because he scented that there was a much more important question or statement which this query was masking.

"Anything wrong?"

"Oh, that." Douglas laughed. "You worry too much, Mike. Everything's wrong and nothing is. The usual."

"Mary?"

"Fine."

"Drink."

"Under control."

"Writing?"

"Is this my ten-year test?"

"Don't you need one?"

"Why?"

"You're in a mess, aren't you? You can't focus on anything. You've talked to me endlessly without once seeming to me to understand there were two people there. Now you're headed off—for what? I can guess. Why? I can't guess that. You're sliding away somehow, Douglas: nothing matters enough to you. I'm worried."

"Save it for a worthier cause."

"Are you still fooling around?"

"I've never talked about any of that, Mike. Why do you ask?"

"Because I care about you. When I first knew you, you had a lot of optimism and balls: you didn't say so, but you were going to do your best, attempt great things, take on the world, make a mark: you had all that innocence and wide-eyed power that fools take for foolish naïveté. Now look at you."

"Yes."

Wainwright paused: and then did not resume. Douglas felt the sting on his cheeks of alcohol coming out to meet the sun. It was time to go.

They had walked onto Westminster Bridge and leaned against the parapet. Behind them Westminster Pier and the river boats, already taking trippers down past the city and the Tower and the awesomely derelict wasteland of warehouses to the spacious symmetries of Greenwich: before them Millbank Tower, glittering greenly in the sun, and the domestic skyline following the river to the vast parks and commons around the west of London.

"When I first came to London I got up at dawn just to be on this bridge at the time of Wordsworth's poem," Douglas said. He smiled ruefully: the whole telling was in some way suspect, he thought, smacking of the Innocent Abroad or the traditional Provincial Up For The Day To The Big City: yet what he said was true. "Just to be here when he was. 'Earth has not anything to show more fair'—I recited it. 'Dull would he be of soul who could pass by'. I stood—smack in the middle looking towards St Paul's. 'Ships, Domes, Towers, Temples'—did I get the order wrong there? Why should you know? And I recited it." He paused and then looked keenly at Wainwright, met, as often, by the calm force of the older man's interested and experienced look, aware that he was being shepherded and resenting having to acknowledge it. "And I remember—very clearly—that I felt brimful of pleasure—all sorts of pleasures—I cannot imagine what that sort of happiness is like any more. 'Open to the earth and to the sky'. You see, I have to be half-drunk, prepared to embarrass myself and be with somebody like you—no—*specifically* you, to use those lines or refer to that occasion. Anyway." Douglas made a last effort to make sense of it for himself and to somehow include it in the exchange he had been having with Mike. "The point is that I am certain that there will be no more times like that and that was a very good time."

"You'll talk yourself into something you'll regret," Wainwright said. "Age. Responsibility. Tiredness. Limitations. Drink. Guilt. Slows you down."

Douglas wanted to reach out and grasp Wainwright by the hand, he wanted to tell him, not that he agreed with him, but that there was something he was thankful for: but that instinct was checked by an apprehension which he could not articulate. And so the moment passed by and the two men turned to look down the river, like two sailors looking out to sea from a boat.

"There's a story I'm working on," Douglas said. "I think that matters. I was at it all morning. I won't be able to do any more today but it goes on in my head and while we've been talking I've been making notes about certain words that are wrong, particular sentences I want to re-write. I suppose that's been ticking away. I hope it has."

"Call me," Wainwright said. "Look after yourself."

The men nodded to each other. Wainwright left. As he walked away, Douglas as it were realized him as a physical presence for the first time. What Wainwright had said was true: while they had been talking he had not "noticed" him: taken no care of what his friend was wearing or how he looked. It was true. He was sinking inside this metropolis. He felt a sudden lurch of gratitude towards Wainwright for caring so much: he wanted to run after him. But . . .

So. To what was left of the day. (a) Listen to his friend be sturdy and admirable in Parliament. Then (b) go to see a film producer, a cockney who had gone to Hollywood and reputedly made a fortune, but still managed to owe money to several of those who had trustingly worked with him in the old days when there was idealism and "the great adventure of making a British Movie". Douglas was owed £2,500 and was going to attempt to beard him: he had heard he was back in London, installed, inevitably, in the Dorchester. Then (c) he would go and see Hilda. This would be melancholy. All the excitement, indeed the furore of the affair was over, but they still needed to see each other regularly, perhaps for some sort of reassurance or perhaps because they still had some hope—or perhaps out of habit. For whatever reason, he would go there and be under strain: be polite, think of Mary, feel guilty as a choirboy stealing altar wine, fumble around and then, perhaps, miraculously, discover a true feeling set alight or rekindled. Then (d) he would creep home and lie and lie again.

As he went along the railings to the Houses of Parliament, he described himself and tried to work out a story line on his future.

A rather drunk, rather untidy, no-longer-young man, unwilling to face up to Great Issues, unable to devote himself to Profound Issues, distrusting both: unbelievably luckily married and slowly screwing that up, despite a clear preference for monogamy; likewise poisoning other drops of good fortune which had come his way. And someone sucked into a weary acceptance of all this, or determined to test the strength/weakness of his position, unable to summon up the moral energy to rectify these faults, or unwilling. Unwilling or unable, often, to accept them as faults, although they were disabling. But nothing was anybody's fault any longer, was it? He went down the cold corridor of busts and into the lobby of Parliament. "The child of God cannot sin." Right? And if God were dead then the very concept of sin was destroyed. Either way it was nobody's fault any more.

Inside the Gothic pile the democratic process continued: and Jack, Douglas' friend, a not-so-young man who had given up hundreds of nights to work for his party and to help and as he saw it educate and politicize people, a man who had left a safe job with a pension and gone through a rather dirty bye-election campaign, someone who was truly pained at the lack of time he could devote to his family but had decided, after a lot of thought and a lot of discussion with his wife, to do what he thought right and help the community, got to his feet, glanced nervously at his proud parents in the gallery, nodded at Douglas, who came in at that precise moment, as if on cue, and began his maiden speech.

(4)

And all the day, the story of Alan throbbed inside his skull. On the streets of London he found himself slipping into the patch of woodland in which the man had gone to his end—willingly? Hopelessly? Or—as Douglas believed—in order to find some order, some satisfaction in life, some connection with his beginnings, a shape, and release the pain and drag of the past. The gauzy oil fumes of the city gave way to the sweaty tang of sodden leaves. The buildings would dissolve and he would see the disordered ranks of beech and spruce and pine. The noise would cease and he would hear—most of all—the remorseless sound of the man's feet trudging through the undergrowth, moving, seeking, ill, and yet, in Douglas' story, perhaps within sight of an illumination which might, might just, be some compensation for the compacted miseries of a life meaninglessly blocked, uselessly unheeded, brutally unused. For, in Douglas' story and in Douglas' memory of the man, there had been a pure love of scholarship in him and a clear, easy, unstrained talent which had been sunk in the psychological and social confusions and limitations which came upon him as an adolescent. Waste, waste. Yet, careful: no propaganda. Just the man, the story, the words, the weather, scraps of knowledge rising from old text-books, warming his mind, lines from Virgil, theorems, a sudden scroll of dates from English history, quotations from the Bible. And not a mile away was the road, buses, cars, the bustle, the business, the real world. Real.

Douglas was now in the grip of this man. However exaggerated that might seem, the fact was that the man drew him on. He dreamt of him. His story was the most consistent thing in Douglas' present life. Of course, marriage, earning a living and so on—these—in their crucial phases—were more important: but, as far as his thoughts went, they centred now far away from London, in that lonely strip of woodland, with a young man walking to his death.

4
Three Women

(1)

It had taken her more than a month. That is, a month of active searching. Before then, she had waited and hoped. She had taken herself to pubs which she and Lester had used and once or twice she had been to the Marquee in Wardour Street in Soho, when there were groups in which she thought Lester might have an interest. She had never encountered him.

Emma knew so little about Lester's daily routine. He had come into her life out of this city, out of the provinces, out of a class and background as strange to her as hers was to him. They had made contact a few times and then he had gone away, back into the anonymous metropolis, perfectly camouflaged by the crowd. He was not the sort of man to be in a telephone directory or to have a regular job or even to have regular haunts for long. He had once had a pad in Queensway. She remembered him saying that—"pad" sounded grand. Emma had never been allowed to visit him there. But that was where she began her search, hopefully walking about the area after work, after dark, peering in restaurants, slowly dragging her feet past the acres of grand town houses now converted into flats or bed-sitters. Where once the Imperial English rich had reigned, a cosmopolitan pot-pourri teemed in all-mod-cons warrens. The colonialists had been colonialized. Occasionally she went into a pub, well protected by her pregnancy. As she grew bolder, or more desperate, she began to ask around. Again, her pregnancy induced civility.

It had changed her. Curiously, in the four months in which she had carried the child, she had lost weight. The wodges of puppy fat which had outstayed their time had almost entirely disappeared. She was still firmly built but those pouches of fleshly self-indulgence were also gone, replaced by a purposeful ripeness, an attractive fullness of body. Even the life-long double chin was vanishing, and, with her hair drawn back neatly in the Emily Brontë style affected by many of her artistic contemporaries, her face had a shapeliness never before revealed. Even more curiously, she felt healthier; lighter on her feet, less lethargic, stronger. She drank less. She walked to and from the job she had found. She was a receptionist in a newly opened Information Centre, which served part of the City of London. It had been set up at considerable public expense and in considerable style. Very few people used it and the staff spent a lot of time inventing ways to become essential to the community which, they all admitted, did not really exist. Emma, who found she could regain her poise in such a do-gooder outfit, observed it all with a certain amusement and sat comfortably in her swivel leather armchair behind a teak-topped reception desk, catching up with her reading. Her back was supported by a plump purple cushion bought her by the staff to celebrate (and/or commiserate with) her "condition". She read the classics.

That was the feature of her new life. She had reverted towards the type of person her parents had always expected her to be. She was neat—the room in Kentish Town was now barrack-room bright; she was conscientious—in her visits to the doctor, her care over dosages, her attention to the job which, though easy, indeed nearly a sinecure, was yet proof of a disdain for the lack of responsibility in her earlier life. She read more, and inside her mind she was calm and determined. For the first time in her life she had a single definite goal which she was going to attain.

All this was duly noted by her friends from the theatrical world, that gang of hangers-on, of whom she had been one. It was a desperately cheerful flotsam which had sustained itself throughout endless work-droughts with stalls in antique markets, interior decorating, odd-jobbing, waiting on, not unlike the unemployed baggage train of an unextended mediaeval army, scouring the place for sustenance, longing for an engagement. She became known as "the vicar's daughter". A fine irony, they all thought. Irony was a word they relished: most things in their theatrical half-lives were "ironic".

A sweet earnestness replaced the defensive jokiness which had been her habitual expression. When caught reading a classic she would hear herself explain, "I'm thick, I have to catch up. Anyway, George Eliot's *good*." When friends stepped into her stunningly tidy flat, she would say, "It's not because I'm a fetishist or anything. It just makes it all less boring if you know where things are." When complimented on how well she looked, she would reply "Pregnancy's good for you. Like Guinness." And they would all laugh.

But these achievements, and the future she felt within her, were little compared with the love she had for Lester. She was now absolutely certain of that and nothing would budge her. The constancy of this affection was the foundation of her life. She respected herself through this love. It was extraordinarily (though not unusually) humble. She did not expect Lester to feel the same way about her.

She had no hope of marriage and little hope of living together for more than the odd few days here and there. She could see clearly Lester's shortcomings and, in one part of her, even deplore his faults. None of this had the slightest effect on what was now settled and resolved in her mind as her constant love. She was even, in one way, proud that she did not want this feeling analysed and that it resisted explanation: she wanted it to be a grand passion—something which existed "in itself"—the phrases came back to her from the romantic novels she had raced through under the sheets in the dormitory of her mean boarding school—"beyond reason", "came from where she would never know", "a love that would never die", "a love born to live forever". And indeed, it was all true.

Slowly across the metropolis she moved towards him. There was little panic—and then only momentary— for she felt certain that she would see him to tell him what had to be said. Only for one fortnight was she thrown, and that was when she returned from an evening in Queensway to a message from the old lady downstairs that "Your young man's been and gone. Didn't want a cup of tea. Didn't say when he'd be back." A few questions confirmed that it had been Lester. She stayed in for the next dozen nights, to be there, in case. But he did not turn up again.

She met someone she recognized as an acquaintance of Lester's, although at first the man denied all knowledge of him. Emma's vicarage look was again a help, though: the man thought she was some sort of social worker and passed on the possible location. It was a drinking club. She found a café just across the road and watched it as she sipped very milky coffee and occasionally risked glances at her novel—"The Mill On The Floss". A novel accompanied her at all times now, like a bible. Still, though, she did not see Lester and it was another acquaintance who gave her another address—just east of Soho—she could walk to it from her office, which she did, that afternoon, taking off a half-day.

It was a strip club. Hard core, specialist, nasty. To get to it you first went into a pornographic bookshop and either intimated your inclination to the manager or, if he thought you "safe", were approached by him and led through to the back where a couple of dozen wooden chairs, in rows of four, faced a minute stage. Curtainless, undecorated, bleak, the whole room was as camouflaged and conspiratorial as a clandestine chapel.

Emma finished her second tour of the shelves in the main shop, wincing a little at the hectoring, full-frontal display of bared breasts, bushy vaginas, rubbed nipples, splayed thighs, limp cocks, gaudy undies, whips, masks, other expensive sexual aids and ejaculative exclamations. All wrapped up in cellophane. Not to be dirtied by hand that would not pay the price.

The man, who prided himself on being good at "not-looking"—he had to be: many of his nervous customers probably suspected (rightly, as it happened) that he was a criminal, a pimp and a rough-house merchant—now turned his gaze on her and picked his teeth carefully with a match. He, too, thought she must be a social worker. You had to be careful. The police could be paid off: these do-gooders could be trouble.

"You writin' a book?"

His voice, sudden and loud in the empty shop, startled her. She had expected Lester to be working in the shop. She did not know of the existence of the strip club through the door marked Emergency Exit.

"What sort of book?"

"I thought you looked that type."

He took out the matchstick and tried his gruesome "come on" smile.

"No, I'm not."

"Sometimes you can tell. What people do. From the way, you know, they, you know ..." The smile finished the sentence. Emma felt constrained to return it. As soon as she did so, his expression changed.

"So what do you want, lady?"

"I was just looking around."

"No you wasn't."

Clearly, she had been. On the other hand, he was right. Emma would have buckled under in the face of such a dilemma only a few months before. Now, however, the resolution seemed clear.

"I'm looking for Lester Tallentire."

"Are you?"

He waited. She could be looking for Lester for a hundred and one reasons, a hundred of which would be unacceptable to Lester. The man moved the match from his left hand to his right and gouged it into his molars. Above him, a blue plastic sign went on and off, advertising a rubber penis.

"I'm a friend of his."

"I see."

"Does he—work here?"

"You're a friend of his. You should know where he works, lady, you know what I mean?"

"We've got out of touch."

"I see."

"How can I convince you?"

"What of, lady?"

"I could wait, I suppose, just wait here until he came."

"You can't hang about without buying anything."

"Is it illegal?"

"You can't do it, that's all."

"I see." Unintentionally Emma echoed his tone and smiled. Which made things worse.

"You'll have to go, lady." He stood up. He was very big.

"Please tell me where he is. He won't mind, I promise you."

"You'll have to go, lady." He moved towards her, deliberately menacing. She felt a clutch of alarm in her stomach and instantly, fearing for the child, retreated.

"That's a good girl," he said.

He watched her go out. He came to the door and he supervised her as she walked along the street. A couple of men went into the shop and only then did he leave her be.

She walked up and down, keeping her distance, for about twenty minutes. During that time nine men went into the shop. None came out. Just before five o'clock, Lester arrived—from the other end of the street. She shouted. He turned to her. She was sure he recognized her. She waved and began to run. He went into the shop.

It was empty but for the man. Only now there was rock music coming from another room.

"He said he'd see you after, you know what I mean."

Now that he knew what was what, the man had lost interest. It was an effort for him to look up from the Greyhound edition of the "Evening Standard".

"Where is he?"

"Working."

"Working?"

"S'what I said, lady. Working. Now then—hop it—don't crowd the place out."

The music stopped and she heard a few thoughtful handclaps—as at a village cricket match.

"How long will he be?"

The man looked up, and with cruel insight jabbed as hard as he could into this relationship which was obscure to him.

"Depends how long it takes, don't it? You oughta know that. Scram."

Outside she leaned against the wall and breathed slowly, counting to ten, while she inhaled, holding it and then exhaling just as slowly.

Eventually the men popped out, one by one, like parachutists taking their turn to jump, and each one moved away smartly, shoulders back, brisk and even military in bearing. Lester came out with a couple of girls. One of them left him, the other took Lester's arm and wrapped it around her own. She was rather under-nourished, disturbingly white faced and wore a chestnut wig which had slid slightly to the left. Emma took the initiative when she saw that Lester was about to slip from embarrassment into surliness.

"Hello, Lester." To the girl she said, "Hello." Unexpectedly, the girl smiled warmly and nodded. "We generally get a cup of tea at Alf's," the girl said, "and a sandwich. To build us up." She giggled. "I like that dress."

It was a sweet gesture. Emma's dress was a painfully plain folksey brown smock, picked up in a superior Oxfam shop.

"Thank you."

Although the sun was hot, the girl shivered and clutched Lester's arm even more tightly. "C'mon then, darlin'. Tea and a sandwich."

Lester nodded.

They went to Alf's, a small sandwich bar on the edge of Soho. It was as narrow as a railway compartment and about as long as a bus. Big Maltese Alf filled half the space behind his counter, which was piled high with sandwiches, biscuits and fruit cake. All wrapped in cellophane—like the dirty magazines, Emma thought. The girl ordered and tactfully left Lester and Emma alone for a few minutes, insisting that she would "bring it over". Emma could see that Lester felt humiliated and her pity momentarily overwhelmed her. She reached out and squeezed his hand. He withdrew it, sharply, and looked at her antagonistically.

"So what do you want?"

"Nothing."

"You've been following me around for weeks."

"Yes."

"So?"

He leaned back to give himself poise. But his aggression was false. Emma saw that he was miserably down on his luck and all she could do would make it worse. Alf was methodically stacking the sandwiches on the plate. There was no point in trying to win Lester back or do anything but deliver her message. But she could not resist an attempt to restore old ties through gossip.

"I was beginning to think you'd gone back to the Midlands—with those rich beaglers—do you call then beaglers? —the huntsmen you took up with in Cumbria over the New

Year—you told me about them. They were very rich, you said. One of them wanted to set you up in your own business . . ."

"He turned out to be a bastard. Like everybody else." Lester lit a cigarette and the action made his face appear gaunt. She knew how successfully he had so far managed to dodge his way through even the most desperate circumstances. He would never tell her what had driven him to this, she thought—but, as if he read her mind—and as proof to Emma for lonely weeks afterwards that there really *was* "something special" between Lester and herself—he said, abruptly, "He fucked me up rotten. I have a lot of debts. I pay them off by the week. It's cash they want."

She nodded and with an effort resisted the recurrent desire to reach out and comfort this forlorn and hapless man she loved so much.

The girl was now glancing over to them—the tray being laid by Alf was almost complete. Emma took a deep breath. She had to keep her voice neutral: she remembered that just in time.

"I just want you to know this, Lester. It is—the baby—yours. You see, there wasn't anybody else after you. After we did it. Or in the months before. I only pretended I'd had lots of men. I hadn't. After you I didn't want anybody else. No. Please. I want you to know. And I'm happy. Everything's fine. I'm having it. I'm living in the same flat. And you'll always be welcome there. Always." She paused and made the final effort, which was to subdue her tears.

"Tea up," the girl said. "I got corned beef and tomato."

Emma felt weak and shaken. She took the thick white mug of tea between her hands and warmed herself. Her throat grew constricted at the thought of a sandwich and it lay across the small white cardboard plate, its wrapping undisturbed, gaping at the mouth with ripe red tomato.

The girl was pleasant and chatty. Either she was used to gossiping away the times or she sensed the difficulties between Emma and Lester and talked in order to help: either way, Emma was grateful. She wanted to ask the girl's name but that moment had passed. Lester, she thought, was merely glum.

She was wrong about that, as she discovered when she made

her excuses and left. For he followed her, promptly. They walked together in silence a little way down the Charing Cross Road, already lit with street lights. At the gap between the two buildings of Foyle's, he took her arm and led her towards the archway into Greek Street. He stopped after a few yards and while she waited for him to speak she looked at the windows full of books. New novels: none of which she had read.

"So it's mine," he said, over her shoulder. She saw his reflection in the window, among the glossy books.

"Yes, it is, Lester."

"I'm supposed to have another one or two around the place, you know." This pathetic boast only served to stir her sympathy the more.

"You told me. But you said you couldn't be sure." She turned to face him.

"You can never be sure."

"This time you can." Emma was afraid to say any more: he stood there so tensely: like a hare just before it gallops away. Thin and fit as a hare, too, she thought: too thin though.

"I might . . ." He paused and took in her loving glance: he dropped the lie. "I'm no good for you."

"I think you are."

"Not me. Not my sort. I couldn't settle down. I couldn't put up with all that—not me."

"Are you sure?"

"You know me."

"I don't. Not enough. I think you might like to settle down."

"What sort of job? In a factory like the peasants back home?"

"You said you'd enjoyed it in Cumbria at Christmas."

"Only because I knew I was getting out in a week. It's desperate up there."

"Are you happy?" Her confidence was now building up rapidly. Lester shook his head: not in answer but in disapproval. She had trespassed on the area he held to be inviolate: his feelings. He took out a wallet and handed her three five-pound notes.

"I'm a bit short or I'd give you a bit more."

"You needn't . . . I . . . thank you."

Her gratitude came just in time and helped him rediscover something, an echo, of his old swagger.

"I might drop in from time to time. Don't count on it."

"O.K." She would not cry, she said to herself, very firmly. She would not lose him that easily.

"Take care," he said, lightly. He looked around as if he wanted to make sure he was not being followed and left her.

She watched him to the corner—too short a distance for her want to see him as long as she could. She felt the three five-pound notes in her hand and squeezed them in her palm. She would put them towards a cot for the child.

(2)

For John's sake, Mary tried hard not to appear to be afraid, but her apprehension was transmitted to the boy despite herself and he held her hand very tightly.

She had been there often enough before. No one had ever molested her. There had been nothing but kindness shown to the attractive white woman who brought her little boy to the illiteracy classes.

The Inner London Education Authority had introduced night-classes for those who could neither read nor write. Those fell broadly into two groups: the middle-aged immigrants who had first arrived in London after school-leaving age and never received an education in English, and the teenagers who had slid through the school system without picking up any proper knowledge of the language. There were about a dozen in Mary's class, the oldest a Jamaican—Fairbright Anderson was his name—in his late fifties, who reminded Mary of the Uncle Tom in her childhood illustrated version of that book; the youngest, a flash Barbadian, Alan—"El-Al" he called himself—of sixteen, who wore a butcher-boy cap and wanted to get "really into it, now, Miss, this education bit". Between them were two Indians, three Pakistanis, two Moroccans, a Nigerian and two other Jamaicans, one of whom was a telephone operator. He had conned his way into the job and "remembered" the connection between name and number on his board by a network of tricks and bluffs which he was delighted to explain to anyone who wanted to listen. Unfortunately the firm was expanding and his nerve was giving way. Mary, whom he regarded with a doggy affection which embarrassed her, had a particularly difficult time with him, as it was impossible at first to break him of the habit of finding a way to memorize the words without actually being able to read the letters or spell it out. His system was so highly developed that it was uncanny at times. It had taken her all the first term to make him realize what he was doing: now, towards the end of the second term, he was beginning to put the letters together, one by one, and, most important of all, Mary thought, he was starting to think that it was a smart thing to do.

There was great satisfaction for Mary in this voluntary work.

John, too, seemed to gain a lot from it. She had taken him along once or twice at first simply because there was no way to solve the baby-sitting problem. Douglas had been in—as he had promised—for the first few weeks and then he had been away filming. Reluctantly she had taken John with her—but he had enjoyed it instantly. Instead of feeling patronized, as Mary had feared, the group were delighted to see her son and (she suspected) they liked her more because she trusted them enough to bring in her child. The marvellous thing, though, from Mary's point of view, was that John was a help. He would sit quietly beside one of the class and talk away, drawing the letters, bringing his own recent learning to bear, often more effective than Mary herself. Soon they would compete to have him sitting beside them. And, accordingly, he bloomed. Mary brought him every time now. She was frightened that she was losing touch with her son, frightened that the strain between Douglas and herself would damage the boy, over-anxious about John's silences and capacity for isolating himself, troubled by the conflicting loyalties of her own life, her husband and her son. To see him happily employed was a great comfort.

She was not a timid woman and yet as they walked along these decomposing west London streets, she was as apprehensive as a scared child in a dark wood. She had taken her washing to the launderette, asked the woman to see it through for her and then, because the night was bright and cold and clear, she had decided to walk to the school in which the night-class was held.

She kept a steady pace so as not to encourage her panic. On one side were the houses: on the other, a corrugated iron fence which protected the railway. The fence bore scores of posters—every one ripped or defaced.

Mary looked down at John's small white face. (Why did it look so under-nourished?) Was this concrete, brick and litter all that she could give to her son? What effect was it having on him, she worried, as he walked under pale lighting, the world tinged with orange. What would he know about life, about the cycle of nature, about things that grew and unfolded, bloomed, gave fruit, stayed awhile and then died to be reborn? In her good moments she thought that the cosmopolitan zest of London life was a fair substitute; in her realistic moments she thought that—well, life will become, increasingly, city life and so he might as well get used to it; but at times like this all she wanted to do was to follow her deepest instincts and run away.

John's hand tightened on her own and he looked up, carefully. He said nothing. She wished he had not grown to be so firmly in control of himself and his emotions. She glanced back and noted again that a couple of men were still following them; about sixty or seventy yards back, dim under the weak street lighting, but steadily walking along this lonely road—behind them. It was final proof, she thought later, of her tiredness and tension that her heart instantly did a sickening somersault. She almost stumbled and when a man came unsteadily out of a side street and bumped into John, she snatched the boy to her as if he were in danger of being kidnapped. She broke into a run and then stopped, counted to ten, walked on. Looked back. The two men were still there.

Walking faster now, she turned into her badly lit side street and faced a totally empty vista. Half-demolished houses to the left; half-completed flats to the right: the only bright spot a big notice which read DANGER: GUARD DOGS.

She thought of asking John to glance back, but his set face dissuaded her. He had caught her fear and all his effort was bent to controlling it.

Her throat was strained with nervousness but she decided

that she must not run. The men drew nearer, walking more quickly than ever; John edged closer to her. But she stood her ground.

They came up.

They glanced at her, deliberately, and then moved even more rapidly and broke into a race for the pub, laughing and jostling each other. One of them shouted, "Cock a doodle do!"

Mary was shaking.

"The school's that way." John pointed it out, urgently. A lit-up refuge.

She clutched him to her, tightly, for a moment and then went in.

(3)

As he lay asleep beside her, Hilda stilled her restlessness by going over in her mind what had just happened between them. Sex was like unwrapping a secret present, she thought, knowing there would be pleasure, knowing it would be unlike anything else.

Even to herself she was shy of recollecting the details and yet she wanted to go over each moment, to be able to luxuriate in them in the voluptuous knowledge that Douglas was beside her. She was completely in love with him, as she had never been with anyone else—this she had told him solemnly and earnestly—but she could not put into words the "rightness" she felt about Douglas.

Hilda lived alone in a small basement flat in South London. She was, to a month, the same age as Mary. Douglas recognized much about her background and admired the way in which she had worked her way out of it without repudiating it. Her family had been very large, very poor and at war with each other. Deprivation, a thin gruel of affection, illness, broken schooling, neglect, a world of indifference: she had landed in the labour market aged fifteen, withdrawn, upset, unwell, barely educated and, as a result of yet another painful and abrupt parental move around the Midlands, isolated. Yet within her, not buried quite and always flickering, however feebly, was a self-generated sense of the fun of life. You could see it in the sly peeps of amusement with which she regarded the pompous and the bullying and the bureaucratic—many of those who ruled over her early working life in cold offices, sandwiches in the drawer.

Slowly she had built a life for herself. Gone to night-school and then taken a correspondence course, taken herself abroad, gone to museums, caught onto learning at its fringes and held on tight.

This had taken up her twenties. By the end of them she had re-created herself. She had got an interesting job at the British Film Institute, where she could do research as well as earn her keep by her designated job, which was still that of an "assistant"—or a superior typist. The energy she had put into constructing a life for herself had left little over for the manipulation of a career.

In her emotional life she had been unlucky. Her looks were fine rather than obvious—the blonde hair, the pale grey eyes, the shy walk. There had been one real love affair and she had spoiled it by asking too much from it. All the excuses were good ones: she was too young, she was extraordinarily nervous about committing herself, he was too young, he was unsure, he was not interested in music or books or paintings, as she increasingly was. She had mourned him for three years: pride had stopped her going back to him although she had wanted to do so several times. When she heard, eventually, that he had married, she felt sick to her stomach. Since then there had been a number of boyfriends but only one affair.

Hilda was not promiscuous. But nor was she puritanical. What she believed in was not sex or success or serenity or money or even marriage—but Love. What she wanted was a single great love which could be served by her and could be the nucleus of her life. It was her misfortune to fall in love with Douglas. It was made intolerable by the fact that he had fallen in love with her. Yet now, she knew, he wanted to get out of it.

Any time she wanted she could remember the stages of this love and, in the bed, curtains open, bright late-winter moonlight whitening his skin, she traced her fingers up and down his spine and, to comfort herself, recalled what had passed between them.

At first very little—for a long time—for almost two years.

Douglas had been in and out of the film offices proposing or completing various projects. They had exchanged some words, some glances, nothing more. Once, after an office party into which he had strayed, half-drunk and by accident, with someone with whom he was having a bitter row, he had made a clumsy pass at her. The rebuff had been accepted instantly. He had telephoned to apologize the next morning.

Then she recalled, taking it carefully out of her mind, opening it slowly, the time when they had declared themselves. In a small café, where they had gone for a cup of tea, after he had done a long day's editing and she had typed up the transcripts. They had caught each other's look. He had taken her hand, held it, and it was as if her life, all she had, went from her body into his and then returned, accompanied by his love. She also remembered, although it always gave her pain—but she was strict with herself—his first words after that silent communion.

"It's no good," he said: but he did not let go of her hand.

"I agree," she had replied, hearing this voice so familiar to her speaking brightly, even chirpily, above the numbing force and pull of her feelings. "It's hopeless," she had added, and yet she had to smile.

"Hopeless."

"So let's go no further," he said. He too was smiling. But they were not joking.

"My point exactly," she said.

Still he held her hand. They beamed at each other.

"Stupid, isn't it?"

"Very stupid. Very stupid indeed." She paused and took away her hand. "But one of the things I will not do is to have anything to do with a married man. I've seen my friends get too hurt that way."

"And I've seen my friends screw up their lives."

"Maybe our friends know each other," she said.

"So. No-go?"

"That rhymed."

"Speak Chinese fruentlee."

"I knew you were clever."

"You're lovely."

Again she felt herself wanting to rest in him, to give herself—all the clichés, all the truisms, all the truth. She felt that she had found whom she had been looking for. That the journey from overcrowded, over-hurtful, rejected and anonymous life had been aimed at this—unknown until now, but now revealed. And he was unobtainable. "You're lovely," he repeated.

"You musn't say that," she said, grimly. She pretended to busy herself. "You musn't say that."

For more than a year they had left it so. He saw her only occasionally, and then never alone—in the office, in the pub for a quick drink, once at a party. His life went on: hers too. But when they did meet, they knew that a life was waiting for them if they chose to take it.

It was strange. There was no doubt in the minds of either of them. They did not even flirt. What kept them together was as invisible as air. It was, Hilda thought, looking back on it, one of the most perfect times in her life. There was a loving security in it which she had never known before and the knowledge of it would overwhelm her with gratitude, happiness and hope: which she spiked as hard as she could.

She had a boyfriend whose intentions were serious, whose attachment was close, whose affection was genuine. They slept together. What began to happen, though, was that she would imagine he was Douglas. She did not will this on; to the contrary, when it happened she did all she could to beat it away. It was unfair on her lover, unfair on herself and unfair, in its assumptions, on Douglas. Yet it would not be beaten away. She tried to drive it off by the exercise of that willpower which had enabled her to do so much, make so many efforts—but it would not be driven off. She stopped seeing the man for a time. Then resumed: it was worse than ever. She broke off the relationship, to the astonishment of her friends, who had anticipated an engagement or at least an announcement of intent, and to the surprise of the man, who had suddenly lost what he had thought he was sure of, without any explanation which made sense.

Then Hilda was isolated, alone once more as she had so often been. Alone once again in mundane surroundings, in a mundane way. Nothing, she thought, was special about her at all. She did not mind that—but at times she questioned why it had been such a hard struggle for her to achieve the normality so many of her present friends had effortlessly inherited. She rented the tiny flat; the furniture had been in when she arrived and she had added only a few ornaments—any spare money going on books and records. Just living her life took every pound she earned: there were no savings, there was no back-stop, there was no hidden treasure, there would be no inheritance. Rather, there would be an increasing responsibility and liability for ageing parents. She did not want much out of the ordinary. A husband, two or three children, adequate provision—she could make do without luxuries, without any frills. She wanted a proper family life with someone she loved. But she loved a man who was committed to another woman.

On an impulse she had eventually sought out Douglas, found him, and said it was about time they got together.

"You know what that means," he said.

"I'll find out."

"You know it can't work."

"Let me be the judge of that. Not just you."

"Tomorrow?"

"Yes."

Both of them, she remembered with an onrush of sweet nostalgia, had been nervous, guilty and at a loss for words. They had gone out to a restaurant in the West End.

"Aren't you afraid of being seen?" she asked, protective and anxious for him.

"I'm not going to skulk about. There'll be enough deceit without that."

The restaurant was overcrowded, over-noisy and they were so placed that any conversation had to be shouted out. Afterwards they had walked back to her flat, so reluctantly that, for a while, each had thought of bolting. But they had gone in, then hovered about each other while a cup of coffee was made. A quarter-full whisky bottle was found, music put on: each move was heavily punctuated by silence.

And then, in a cathartic onslaught of self-pity and self-indulgence, but also of confiding honesty, Douglas had told her about the death of his daughter a few years before. Its effect on Mary, on John and on himself.

"And after the first year or two when all the effort went into just keeping us going, when I saw, or thought I saw, that things were at least, at least functioning again—I went berserk. I drank like someone who wanted to poison himself. I would end up drunk in strange beds, alone or not, impotent or not, but betraying Mary. There was something—I'm not proud of it, I'm not trying to excuse it—but something terrible—like a lust for sensation—to have everything—drink, sex—and a licence to roam around the city like someone unfettered. I couldn't get enough of it. All was excused—despite my claim to be without excuses—by the—by her death. Disgraceful. But I must tell you about that. And all the time there were two things—no—more. Firstly, I would try to square this behaviour by trying to fool myself that it was 'all experience', that writers—not just writers—people—anybody with guts—needed to go to the limit. I took seriously—bloody fool that I was!—the idea that unless you were straining yourself and testing yourself and on the edge of destroying yourself, you were not, in a full sense, alive. I fell for that fallacy and acted on it. Of course, all I did was to hurt myself and those I lived with. Then there was the deceit, the lies which became another drug, the inability to stop and rest and build. Finally, the self-loathing, which even began to turn towards the convenient exit of self destruction. And so in the three or four years when I should have been consoling my wife and comforting young John and consolidating my marriage and my work—I blew it. And here you are."

They had made love and it had been as extraordinary then as it always was. Hilda had slept with very few men and rarely found much satisfaction: she had sometimes found excitement; mostly she had to be content with the fact that the act was at least being done; and sometimes it had been terrible.

Douglas was strong, he was sometimes violent, but although she saw him above her, drawing his hands up her legs, stroking her shoulders, kissing her breasts, her belly, her thighs and then clutching her tightly, almost desperately until she felt that she would—she could not put it into words. Not even when he came into her and she, light, ready, felt the thrust going deep—he would stop, sometimes, and stay inside her and touch her until she came, or kiss her gently or, as if in kindness, slowly move her about him so that she moaned out and he whispered her name. It was no good. For it went on, longer than she had known or thought possible, and she would be lifted, turned, thrown, penetrated like a sheath to the hilt and then rocked as in a cradle, while she licked his skin and behind her closed eyes lived in a time outside the time spent. And he would bring her ready before he came—this, too, this wonderful coincidence worked for him—until she was ready, and then he came and she, spread beneath him, felt the cascade and was entirely his.

But what had now become of it?

To ask that question brought Hilda up against a fear which she dared not face. Douglas asked and answered it almost every time they met, forever prevailing on her to expect little, to rely on nothing and to trust him not at all—until she cried out against the injustice and inhumanity of this.

"You say that you want it to be just as it is," Douglas answered her, "and yet you act as if I am entirely at your disposal."

"What do you expect me to do? I love you. You say that you love me."

"I do."

"Well then. I can't just sit and wait. I would like to, but I can't. I want to see you," she said plainly. "What would you think of me if I didn't?"

"But look, Hilda, I have a wife, a son, a family, which I am not going to split up for anyone."

"I know that. You're always telling me that. It doesn't alter the fact that I love you. And you say you love me."

"But I can't give you what you want."

"Nobody else has. You give me more than anybody else. I just want to see you more, that's all."

They made rules. And broke them. They made plans. And broke them. The time they had together was eaten up with regret for the time they did not have together. Lately, they had come to the point of agreeing that each meeting would be as if it were a "one-off". There would be no promises and no recriminations. The affair would have no future.

This filled Hilda with panic. She needed security, she realized, for dear life.

"I'm not complaining," she said. "I'm not blaming you. I'm not blaming me, either. But I just keep saying to myself—why has it got to be so hard? Why couldn't I have met you years ago? I know it's stupid. I know all that. I feel silly saying it, but if I can't say what's on my mind to you—who can I say it to? I love you, that's all."

"And I love you."

But there was a remorselessness in Douglas which led him to reiterate incessantly the uselessness of relying on their love or allowing it to attract any expectations at all. Until, in the end, Hilda had burst into tears and Douglas had to apologize. Yet, within a couple of days, he was once more on that theme.

"What's happening is that I see you more and more, I make excuses, 'practise deceit' as they say, tell lies and perjure myself—and the more I see you the more I want to see you and yet the weight of wrongness just gets heavier. Because I'm never where I should be. When I'm with you I think I should be with Mary: when I'm with Mary I want to be with you. I don't know which of you I'm betraying. Neither of you is happy. Each has every right to think I'm a shit. But that gets me nowhere, because I admit I'm a shit."

"What you're saying is Eternal Mistress or it's over."

"Am I?"

"Yes."

"Oh Christ!"

To both of them it slid between dream and nightmare. For there were times unlike any other: they smuggled themselves away to the coast and walked along the cliffs one day and the next on the downs: the connecting night spent making love greedily. There would be times of calm, of "blessed ordinariness" when they would just read or listen to a record, have a cup of tea, refrain from making love, let it go. They had good moments. But a flick of mood could send them down.

"She wants a child? *I* want a child. I feel that I have as much right to have your child as she has. I understand why you won't leave her—but I still feel rejected. I feel it means you can't *really* love me, but I try very hard to understand. I know you feel loyal. I know that John mustn't be hurt any more. I think he's being hurt far worse by things being as they are, but I've been through all that, you know all that and you've made your decision. But you can't stop me wanting what I want and trying to get it. You *say* you love me. Well then."

"It's possible to love more than one person," he said.

"I don't think so."

"Why not? I love you, I love John, I love Mary, I love my mother, I love two or three of my friends."

"That's different and you know it's different and it's not the point."

"It *is* the point. If only it weren't."

"Not the way I mean it."

"You could call your love, then, just possessive."

"You can call it what you like, it's what I'm stuck with and so are you, or you wouldn't be in such a mess."

"You're a working class heroine, that's your problem. The man said."

"What you are is not polite to say."

"You're a love."

"I don't feel like one."

"You feel nice to me."

"Hands off."

"Private property?"

"Certainly."

It would dwindle into *babillage*, or ride to a climax of tears or loud exits soon repented.

Now he slept. They had enjoyed an unusually long evening. Despite her best intentions, Hilda clocked up the hours spent together and tonight it came to eight. He had arrived just after seven. The producer he had wanted to see had not been there. It was now just past three in the morning. They had gone out to a restaurant—choosing with care, as they always did, to find a place which had what they wanted—"separate tables that really *are* separate" (Douglas)—"plenty of people so you can trust it" (Hilda)—"somewhere new" (Douglas)—"somewhere nice" (Hilda)—"somewhere unexpected" (Douglas)—"somewhere I've just read about" (Hilda)—and they would use this choice to play the unimportant games and enjoy the unimportant arguments which were so soothing and normal. Douglas had insisted on music and they had gone to a place in St. Martin's Lane where a band popped up at ten o'clock. Then they had come back to her place and he had fallen asleep as soon as they had finished making love. She knew she was being selfish in not waking him but she had so little of his time that she ignored that. Besides, the agreement was that you were responsible for what you did, you were fully responsible for your life and dependence was out. Douglas had been fierce about that.

Yet she was a good woman and the thought that she might be getting him into a real difficulty could not be stilled, even by using his own arguments against himself. A great deal of her misery and the twisting moods in her affair was to do with the contradiction between what she thought she ought to be doing and what in fact she was doing. Her conscience pressed against her and there was no avoiding it. None. She was cheating another woman, she knew that, all her declarations were contaminated by that, all her love was shadowed by that and yet all her life was there to be given to the man who brought her to that. She was a willing accomplice. She gave herself no rest. She was doing wrong. There was no way out of it. Her only defence was that she could do no other.

She paused a moment and then kissed him awake. It was almost three thirty. He embraced her as gently as she could have imagined and came inside her so sweetly, she moaned for joy. Afterwards he made no comment about the time, but left, calmly, already inventing his lies, letting it be a good night for her. Stole out like a thief. Waited for a night taxi in the wide streets. The city was a shell now—ready to be taken over. Lights still on in some shop windows. No leaves on the few trees, no animals, the smell of petrol, empty.

The taxi went along the Embankment and swung around an empty Westminster: he saw that the bridge was deserted as it had been those many years ago. What a neat diagram he could draw if he obeyed the impulse to take the taxi to where he had once stood: then, young, he had been innocent, optimistic, full of good feeling, wanting to be useful, to do something worthwhile. Thinking warmly about the world, willing to help put it to rights, and sober. Now—half-cut, tired, corrupted in marriage, aimless, self-centred. Yet such self-criticism began to smack of inverted boasting, he thought—"Look at me! Look how *awful* I am!" It was better than that. His voyage of discovery was destined to be in this windless and mindlocked sea.

The taxi roared to a stop outside his house and the engine kept up its reverberating din, seemingly for hours, while Douglas discovered he did not have enough cash to pay for it. Mary was awake: she handed him her purse and he went downstairs aware that half the street was now disturbed by his late arrival. Paid off, the taxi driver then insisted on doing a difficult and very noisy three-point turn in the narrow street. When he left, the silence was palpable.

(4)

Mary had put on the kettle for coffee. Douglas went into the living room and switched on the electric heater. The place was chilly. As if he were decorating a set, he closed the curtains, put on the two table lights, knocked off the main light, tidied up the newspapers and puffed up the cushions on the sofa before sitting down and squashing them again. Mary came in with two mugs of Nescafé.

She was in her new dressing gown. She had given him no hint of the name of the donor and, despite his lapses, Douglas still felt secure about her fidelity. He relied on it.

They sipped the steaming coffee carefully. She smoked. Douglas felt a *frisson* of anticipation, almost as if he wanted the worst to happen. Despite himself, he had to admit this, there was a way in which he was looking forward to the quarrel, so far gone was he in his carelessness about such securities as he had. To Hilda he was far more thoughtful, because of the essential fragility of her position. Just as he was prepared to devote enormous care and time and energy to a story which would make him little if any money and bring him little if any success or fame, rather than take up the security of Wainwright's offer of a film. In his own way, he was set on some sort of important test or on a path of self-destruction: it was impossible for him to decipher which.

In the silence, Mary's presence grew stronger and it was as if his eyes were clearing and focusing on her for the first time for ages. She looked strained, older, sadder—no wonder. There was still the loveliness, the translucent patient intelligence, the honesty to what she believed in, but the lustre was going: her hair was even lank. She seemed so infinitely superior to him. Douglas felt himself morally outclassed and was both impressed and resentful.

Mary saw a man she had once loved, now out of reach. Clearly exhausted, white-faced, anxious, apprehensive—but also, and this hurt her much more—set in a wild, exhilarated obstinacy which blocked her out. For she could see that she was not to be admitted to the debate which was ravaging him. The enthusiasm and gaiety she had loved was now no more than a coarse look of boldness; the giving, the way he used to tell her about what he had read, who he had seen, what he thought about anything under the sun—that had dried up. She could accept that time and habit had performed their usual corrosive work. She could accept that love died. She could accept his sense of failure and respect his hopelessness. But she could no longer respect herself unless she confronted him and made him face himself in her mirror vision of him.

It was five o'clock. She lit a second cigarette.

"I suppose I'd better tell you," Douglas said, eventually.

"Yes. I suppose so."

There was a stiffness about them which was weary: outside it was dark and chill, the hour most vulnerable, the hour for unexpected attack. There was no traffic, a dead metropolitan stillness. And on both their faces, in both their bodies, there was a weight of pain which signalled the admission of defeat, the final realization that an end of a line had been reached: unhappiness.

"I don't know how to begin really." Douglas considered: considered the lies he had told over the past four years, the way he had evaded truth while attempting to hold onto the skirts of some approximation to integrity—which meant not much more than maintaining a balance—somehow not offending against the marriage too much, within a system which allowed it to be violated: or rather which *he* allowed could be violated. The moral superiority and inviolability of a faithful marriage was a standard against which everything else was measured. Douglas accepted that: it was the nearest he now had to a religious dogma. Therefore for some years now his life had been a failure, or a succession of failures, and his reaction had been that of a self-acknowledged sinner. Something of the stiffness of a long overdue confession also tinged his attitude now.

"Do I know her?" Mary asked, looking away, always looking away now.

"No."

"That's something."

"Not much. Still. It's serious."

"I know that. I wish you'd told me when it started."

"So do I."

"Why didn't you?"

"I suppose ..." Douglas hesitated: the only thing that mattered now was to tell the truth as faithfully as he possibly could. "Either I was frightened of the row and ducked out: or I wanted to have my cake and eat it: or I wasn't sure enough of her and wanted to let it ride out and see what happened."

"Choose any card." Mary laughed. There was plenty of misery behind her and before her: at this moment she felt a certain relief. "You should have told me. It was cruel and degrading not to."

"I know. But—it would have been like breaking faith, like destroying something."

"You made it far worse by not telling. You destroyed far more."

"We've survived."

"No." Mary felt a sudden lurch of tears and before she could stop it she was crying. Douglas watched her from across the room: he made as if to go across and comfort her but she waved him away. She controlled herself. "We haven't survived. We've changed so that we didn't split up. But it's all a sham. You don't love me, you tell me lies, you can't bear to spend time with John, you drink far too much, you play around with all this freelance business: you're nowhere near the man I married. And what do I do? Fret about you and about John: try to concentrate on teaching which seems to get harder every term: smoke far too much: mark homework, watch an hour's telly, go to bed generally well before you and never touch the piano—never. We use London so little we might as well live in Cornwall—*I* use London so little, that is. You seem to have licensed yourself to rove around like a pirate. What's she like?"

"Do you really . . .?"

"What is she like?"

"About your age."

"That seems a waste."

"She has a decent job, a rotten background and very little else."

"Ah! You can patronize her, can you? You'll enjoy that. And educate her? Did you ever . . . Did you ever—sleep with her and then come back and sleep with me?"

"No." He hesitated and repeated, "No."

"Does she want you to leave me and marry her?"

"Yes."

"Why don't you?"

"I didn't. That's all."

"You mean you needn't. Presumably she's there every time you want her and I'm stuck here. All you get is a bad conscience and all that makes you is bad-tempered to me and John. In fact, because you haven't told me and I'm here all the time like a fool, waiting for you, cooking you meals, washing your clothes, doing the shopping, trying to give our son a hope in life—because I'm here you behave as if I knew—because in a real sense I *did* know—and so you treat me with contempt for apparently accepting your behaviour."

"Well." Douglas was dry-throated. He was cold. And he could see that this was not a passing quarrel: there was in both of them a set purpose to see it through to the end. Whatever that might turn out to be. "If you *knew*—and I accept that—why *did* you put up with it?"

"Because I loved you." Mary looked at him, dry-eyed now. "Or that's what I kept telling myself. I'm not sure now. Not at all."

"I can't blame you."

"You once said you wouldn't mind if I went off and had an affair. Do you remember?"

"I've said a lot of stupid things."

"Why did you say that?"

"Maybe—I wanted us to be more even. After all, couples have mutually agreed to have affairs before now."

"But you hadn't admitted anything then. Did you hope I would do all the work—even that?"

"Yes." Douglas said. "I suppose so."

"And didn't you care?"

"I didn't know where I was."

"That's no excuse. Nor is Anne." Their dead daughter. "You gave up."

"No. I gave in. To something that was more honest than anything gained by holding out. I was trying to be honest."

"And this—woman. Was that honest as well?"

"Yes. It was."

"How many others?"

"For Christ's sake! What is this?"

"So there were others. You needn't answer. But this one—this—woman—why do you protect her so much?"

"Oh for God's sake, Mary. She exists. As a matter of truth I get no more—never mind."

". . . out of her than you get out of me. Poor her. Can't be much fun being a neglected mistress."

"You want a showdown, don't you?"

"I think I do." Mary stubbed out her cigarette and lit up instantly. She felt a lurch and a swoop of physical dizziness. But the decision was made: it had been moulded over years and months and it appeared in her mind—*set*. "Yes. I do."

"I'll make some more coffee," Douglas said. "Would you like a cup?"

"Yes. Thanks."

While he was out of the room, Mary tried to think once again, yet again, of what she had rehearsed so many times. But all she found was the memory of that curious afternoon when Mike Wainwright had brought her the dressing gown. He had met her some months before and, for a reason she still could not fully explain, Mary had found herself telling him about her unhappiness with Douglas. Mike was Douglas' friend, of course: he was also older and therefore a safe repository of confidences, but it was the quality of his sympathy which drew her on. They had begun to meet regularly, chastely, but increasingly confidentially. It was such a relief. There was repose in Mike's interest: there was also, as honesty soon forced her to acknowledge, affection and possible love. But, miraculously, it was neither forced nor strained. When she went to Cumbria for the Christmas period and made her statement to Douglas about having another child, she kept clear of Mike for two or three months afterwards—not from fear of sex—for, even up until now, there had been none, nor any but the most demure tight-lipped kisses—but in order to show to herself how serious she was. Mike did not insist but they had bumped into each other one Saturday afternoon when she was shopping in Oxford Street, trying to find a reasonably good, reasonably priced new raincoat for John, who was with Douglas, on a rare outing, at a football match. Mike had been prepared to pass on but she liked him so much and he, as importantly, gave her the feeling of being liked, likeable, even loveable. With Douglas now she felt a burden, a nag, a spent partner, a drudge dedicated to the maintenance of an obsolete marriage machine. Mike's niceness opened her up like a Chinese paper flower in a bowl of water. They talked. She relaxed. Time passed. She realized suddenly that she had only a few minutes to buy the coat. They rushed into the nearest department store and, while she sorted out her purchase, Mike, uncharacteristically, she thought at first, until she reconsidered it, turned up with this dashing dressing gown. Later she understood. It was a tribute to that particular moment, to the fun of being together, to a certain relapse, for both of them, into a welcome frivolity. She adored it and tucked her legs carefully under its full skirt. It was cold in the room. Douglas brought back two mugs of hot coffee.

"So what do we do?" he asked.

Mary felt the mug almost unbearably hot and her body seemed to grow suddenly colder: he had accepted it. He wanted a separation. He had not fought her at all. She steadied herself. "Well. We should—live apart."

"O.K. I'll move out."

She wanted to ask him where. Where? Where. But it seemed unjust. He was only doing as she asked and making it easy for her, leaving her the place. He could not be harried. "Where to?" she asked, dry-throated.

"Not with her, if that's what you're thinking. I'll get a bedsitter or a flat. Doesn't matter. I'll go up to the cottage for a few days and leave an ad. in the paper. O.K?"

"I think we should keep the cottage," Mary said, helped by having something concrete to discuss, "and sell this place. With the money we got we could just about pay off the cottage and have enough to rent a flat each. I think you need the cottage: and John does: I love it as well."

"Whereas we won't need this desirable maisonette now. Good thinking. Prices are on the up again. It could work out well. Agreed. What else?"

"I thought we'd talk about it."

"It's done. It's been talked about. We've had it in our minds for months and years. All the arguments have happened in bits and pieces here and there. But let's call it a separation."

"Why?" The start of hope in her body and her voice surprised her. "What else would we call it?" she added more sedately.

"A split up. A bust. But, let's wait a bit. For John's sake, if you like. It could work out less messily than we fear. You never can tell."

"What do you think?"

"Not much at the moment, Mary."

The sound of her own name so tenderly spoken stung her to immediate and profound nostalgia.

"What happened?" she asked.

"I don't know." Douglas hesitated. He had no more to say but she deserved more than his bare honesty. "It slid away when we weren't looking. It *was* a lot to do with Anne, whatever you say. And I behaved very badly. There's little forgiveness for that, not really, not when you hurt those you've loved. Then there's all this scrappy, half-arsed way I earn a living and the pressure that puts on you. You deserve a lot better. An older guy, maybe, someone who appreciates how marvellous you are. I can't any more. I can't see you any more—not as you are. You're hidden under a mass of deceits and disguises: it's like a fairy tale where the princess is turned into a monster. The way we've behaved has turned you into someone else in my eyes. You deserve to be seen for what you are and lead the life you *can* lead—decent, ordered, calm, happy—not this. So I don't know. Except that I think that you are right: a separation is what we're ready for. What happened was that I wasn't up to it."

"No, not that. I think you've tried. You've hurt yourself too much not to be respected. I don't think you're a shit, or greedy; and you're not weak—however hard you claim to be—you're the most determined man I've ever met. But you are determined not to make your mind up. You're a romantic, Douglas, I think, without a romantic ideal to serve. 'Love' is the nearest, and one of the reasons you ran out on me was because, inevitably, we ran out of first love. You're adrift, Douglas, but you're trying to find a course and a place. I respect that."

"So what are we doing agreeing to separate?" He paused: so did Mary. But even that reaching out, that touching, could not change what was settled. She did not reply.

"And you know," he said, "two things. While we've been talking. In my head alongside all this—and other things—two things ticking away. One—what a lovely dressing gown. Two—I want to get back to that story I'm writing because I fear it's no good. I think it isn't working."

"Oh Douglas. I'm sorry. But maybe . . ." she stopped. Polite comfort was useless.

"So I'm going up to get on with it," he said. "Take it by surprise. It doesn't expect an attack from me now in my state of mind and at this hour. Perhaps I can get it right. Can I go?"

"Yes."

"Thank you."

He stood up. He was very stiff, very tired and weary—and yet he had had a fresh thought on the story, a notion of where to trim up the development of the man's character, an idea which could restore it. He wanted to be with it.

"I'll leave this evening," he said. "After John's in bed." He paused. "Good idea to sell this place. I'll still keep up the payments to the domestic account, of course." He grinned. "If I've got the loot." Still he could not leave. It seemed that an occasion of such moment demanded more of a "mot", a statement, an acknowledgement of its gravity, a respect for its importance. "Sorry," he said, and went out.

Mary sat on for a while: the night was done. She felt the cold seep into her. Eventually she heard John's alarm clock go off and she stirred herself to begin to prepare breakfast for the three of them.

The argument had been decided long ago. In the careless rebuffs at night, perhaps, or the lack of caress and contact through the day. The lies had rotted the structure—yes—but both were capable of understanding deceits of the flesh. It was their love that had died. The fact and truth and unacceptable banality of that was something they had hid from for years. And both of them, for different reasons, wanted love. A marriage of convenience was, sadly, not enough. So there was this sorrow between them now, a sorrow which, paradoxically, bound them closely. There was this loss, this love, gone; and nothing to do but mourn.

5
Lester's Luck

(1)

He came back from Brixton market on the bus, the two carrier bags crammed full, one on each knee, squatting on his lap. When he got off, just before Stockwell Station, he had to hump the two weights—for such they had become—onto a low wall and give himself a rest. Although nobody in the wide blank streets was watching him, Lester took out a cigarette and made a fuss of lighting it in order to disguise his weakness. Spring was under way but the South London sky was still grey, the pavements like a true reflection of the spirits of those hurrying pedestrians who ducked their heads into the wind and left no prints from their thin shoes on the scruffy concrete floor of the city. Lester could not trust the plastic handles of the carrier bags and so he was forced to carry them before him, cradled in his arms, belly height, pregnant with provisions. By the time he reached her flat, having had to walk up to the eighth floor as the lift only worked between the tenth and the twentieth, he was wet with sweat and trembling from the strain.

Fiona was in a worse state. "It's only flu," she had kept saying. Both of them shared a contempt for illness, which was not generally accepted to be "real". But their refusal to yield had only made them tired and finally they had given in to it, lying in Fiona's narrow three-quarter bed in the small flat she had shared with an old friend, Janice, who had taken her in as an act of charity and accepted Lester with the greatest regret and bad grace. Lester returned the loathing. Janice, who worked in a pub, was one of those women who do not seem to be in step with themselves. Her body was large, voluptuous, altogether desirable. And yet, sitting on top of it, like a boyish, startled addition, was a small, cropped head, a face frozen in eager-to-please innocence, an expression totally devoid of sensuality, a look which seemed unaware of the forces so generously assembled below the neck. But she was shrewish and shrewd. Lester described her as a "cock-teaser" and thought no more about her.

To his surprise and gratification, he was wrapped up in Fiona. The starved-looking, cheerful, stringy-haired blonde whom Emma had seen him with had become an object of affection. He was even proud of his capacity for such a feeling. He felt protective towards her. He had even done the bloody shopping. Now he set about opening the tins, cutting the bread, "putting a meal together," as he described it, "got to build you up."

It was the mutual illness which had done it. He had talked to her as they had lain there, sweating, aching, agitated by the noises from the other flats, abandoned by the fastidious Janice, who had left them "to stew in their own juice", as she had said, charmingly. She was due back that evening. They passed the time in talking about their childhoods—something which Lester had done as rarely as Fiona. They were alike in their pride in their toughness, in the mixture of hurt and anger which had taken them from their families—hers in Deptford, dockland, his in Thurston, near farmland. It was the same story. The coincidences seemed to Lester like a stroke of fortune. To his astonishment, he heard himself telling Fiona that his mother was a "tart. I mean, she didn't walk up and down the street swinging a big black handbag—but she was after men—'fancy men' they called them up there then—and they would buy her clothes and rings—she used to tell me they were diamonds—she looked very good—she was a lovely looking woman—that's what they said anyway—a bit like you—not as, you know, good, but—still . . ." Fiona's mother had been "on the game no messin'. They used to wait outside the dock gates those days and have whoever had the price of it. She wasn't ashamed of it or nothin'. 'I'm off down the gates, darlin',' she would say to me and my brother and we'd be left with Gran, who would just curse away all the bleedin' time, except when my mum was there—then of course she daren't. My mum would just hit her. She hit us an' all. She could draw blood with the flat of her hand."

As the enfeebling flu dragged through them, they whispered and confessed the painful events of their lives—without self-pity, often with an access of scorn and viciousness—but for both of them, and particularly for Lester, it was a rare form of release and communion. Lester had detested his amiable, frightened father and still preferred to believe (which was the truth, in fact, though never admitted) that he was someone else's son. His serious sister Aileen had annoyed him because of her fatness and plainness: now she annoyed him because of her cleverness. He had relied on Joseph for a while but nowadays he felt totally displaced by successful Douglas and conscientious Harry. He missed Joseph's confidence in him. Betty had never forgiven him for stealing money from them—even though it had been years ago and even though he had repaid every penny. He would have benefited from her support, but now she could only seem to give it, and he could tell the difference. She had given him up. As for everybody else—well, in Lester's view and experience the world was made up of a few winners and a lot of losers, generally identified as the few who were lucky and the mass who weren't. Most people, he thought, were bastards or would be, given the chance: those who were not were usually cowards. The lucky ones ran the show, made the loot, got the girls, snapped up the big jobs, grabbed the headlines and had the fun. The only place to be was on top, in Lester's philosophy. To say anything else—as Aileen did and Harry and Douglas did when they had argued about it—was rubbish. And luck was the ticket to the top.

Every point that Lester made in his confession was capped by Fiona. Her hurts were deeper, her hatreds more intense. He still had a residual attachment to his background. She would have bombed Deptford, had she been able—especially the "sodding flat" in which her "sodding husband" lived with their two "rotten kids". But talk of her children would bring her to tears and she would sob, exhaustedly, while Lester comforted her, crooning meaningless phrases, "it'll be all right," and "we'll work it out," and "there, there," which had always made him curl up with contempt when he had seen them in films or books. In the two days of the worst period of the flu, he came as near to falling in love with her as he had done with anyone.

Perhaps he did love her: certainly it was "different", he told himself, and he had never fooled himself about this sort of thing. Her misery, her unhappy life, even the viciousness and the foul language all appeared to Lester to be endearing.

Now he sat on the edge of the bed and cut up her food for her. Then he lit her cigarette. He did not think of tidying up—their invalid state had rapidly brought the small flat to squalor. Fiona did not seem to notice this. Up until now Lester had automatically dismissed as a slut any woman who could not keep her place neat and tidy. All this was forgiven Fiona. She looked gaunt, unmade up, no mascara, no false eyelashes, no eyebrow pencil to contrast with the blanched blondeness which wanted constant attention; her hair needed to be dyed at the roots; her skin was bad; like Lester, she stank: and he looked at her as if she were Cleopatra. Took away the tray; washed up. Came back with a strong cup of tea. Wanted to make plans.

"The thing is to get a place of our own with a bit of class. How can you impress anybody in this dump? A council flat!" Fiona lay back and stared at the ceiling, trailing her cigarette to and from her mouth. Now that she was through the worst of the flu she was making her own calculations—but Lester did not notice. "I know I owe a bit of bread around the place, but we can do better than this," he went on. What he did not want to discuss was the prospect of their returning to work: he could no longer go on with the sex shows, not feeling about her the way he did now. He had hinted this to her and thought that from her attitude he could glean a similar conclusion on her part. "I've got this friend: he'll do anything for me." Lester was referring to Emma. "I thought I'd go and see him this afternoon—catch him when he comes in from work—he's the sort who knows where you can get these stylish little places cheap. He's good at that." He paused. It was most strange that he should be taking the trouble to lie to a woman. When he thought about it, he was confirmed in his hunch: if she was worth lying for, then she was worth a lot. "You'll be all right, won't you, if I leave you for a couple of hours?"

"Yes. Did you get those fags?"

Lester took them out of his pocket with the aplomb of a

conjuror shooting an ace from his sleeve. "Janice'll be in tonight," he said, not wanting her to feel lonely. "I might have to root around a bit."

"Janice'll throw up when she sees this place."

"She'll have something else to clean up then, won't she?"

Like a loving husband, he leaned forward, pecked her cheek and then leaned back, looking at her as if he were admiring his handiwork. He had not told her of the full strength of his feelings: nothing so direct. Not his style. And he wanted to get this one right. But, in his own mind, he had no doubt.

From Stockwell, the Northern Line took him directly to Kentish Town.

Emma had gone.

"I know she was trying to get in touch with you," the landlady said. She had most grudgingly admitted Lester into the hall, but barred him from going farther. Emma's room was still empty. The landlady was pleased to see him flounder; she had never liked him. "You needn't look up those stairs," she said, "the room's empty."

"How much a week is it?" Lester asked.

"Who for?"

"I might be interested myself."

He smiled. It was meant to be a reassuring, even a seductive smile, but the older woman was not impressed. Illness and time spent caring for Fiona had made him unaccustomedly careless about his own appearance: his clothes were rumpled, his white open-necked shirt grubby, his shoes split and unpolished. The landlady considered the state of a person's shoes as the key to his character. And his face was white and thin, bringing out an untrustworthy, aggressive expression which his smile only emphasized.

"It's already put aside for somebody," she said firmly. Lester guessed she might be lying.

"I could do a squat in it," he said. "That's what all the students tell you to do now. What if I just went up and did a squat?"

"You wouldn't do that." Squatters were her greatest fear: they had replaced burglars, for at least after robbery you could claim insurance. With squatters, all you got was filth, loss of income, abuse and, somehow, unfairly, a bad conscience. Her daily shopping outings were made uneasy through fear of squatters.

"I think I will. I'll squat this very minute." Lester made for the stairs and feebly the old lady put out an arm to prevent his progress.

"I've a letter for you," she said. "Emma left a letter."

"You're just saying that to bribe me, aren't you?"

"No. Really. You are Mr. Tallentire, aren't you?"

"The same man."

"I'll get it. Wait here." Her anxiety was comical to Lester's eyes. She had found a way to prevent him from going up the stairs—but in order to carry through her tactic—for thus he saw it, convinced she was off to telephone the police—she would have to leave him alone—rampant among her flatlets.

"I'll come with you," he said, lightly, at first relieving and then intensifying her fear. "I'll step inside with you." Still he wanted no trouble—but the desire to torment her was irresistible. Her terror of him goaded him on: did she think of him as a murderer or a thief? She behaved like it. He would teach her a little lesson—*and* keep an eye on her. "I want to keep an eye on you," he said. "I know your tricks."

"Tricks?" It occurred to her now to phone the police. If they got here fast enough before he got his friends and furniture along they might be able to stop any squat. After all, it *was* her property, left to her by her husband, a builder, who had died in early middle-age of a coronary. "What tricks?"

"It's written all over your face, ma. Now then. This letter. Pronto."

She had no alternative but to retreat into her own flat and Lester had no alternative but to follow her. Both of them went past the telephone as if studiously avoiding a massive DANGER sign. To his surprise, the letter was in his hand within seconds.

"You haven't steamed it open and read it?"

"Of course not!" She was truly outraged. "Certainly not! And I'd be much obliged if you would leave now."

"I thought you said something about a cup of tea."

"I did not."

"No? Was it sherry? I see some sherry there. I'll have a glass, yes, thank you." He made for her small, rarely used drinks cabinet.

She felt quite giddy now: before her rose up the prospect of intrusion, squatting, and worse—the man looked bad enough for anything. In her confusion she said what was uppermost in her mind. "If you don't leave I shall call the police or start screaming and someone's bound to hear."

"I'll be back," Lester said, savagely. "You listen out for me. Some time in the middle of one of these nights. You'll hear very little sound but I'll be back. I know this house up and down and inside out. I'll be back."

Her face was miserable with panic. He looked at her for a few deliberate and cruelly silent seconds and then left, closing her door and the front door very quietly.

Sometimes he was not in control of himself. The violence of his feelings towards that harmless woman had been terrible. He walked slowly to calm himself down, looking out for a café in which to read the letter. What got into him at times like that? He put it out of his mind. He had to pull something out of the hat for Fiona. He had to impress her. He had to show her who he really was.

Dear Lester,

If you read this it means I'm not here, so I'm sorry about that. Things started to get rather difficult and my mother came and insisted on taking me back with her, which I am too feeble at the moment to resist. Unfortunately it looks as if I'd be sensible to stay up there until after the birth, which means I have to give up this room here which is a nuisance. However, I'll write to you care of *this* address and I'm sure Mrs. P. will hold the letters for you. Or you could write to me! I'm at THE RECTORY, WARMINGFORDHAM, SUFFOLK. I enclose a letter from Douglas. He gave it to one of my friends who'd told him about us ages ago, an actor, anyway the gossip came in useful because here's the letter! It would be *super* if you wrote and gave me an address! Don't worry about anything at all. Good luck and all my love.

Yours ever,
Emma XXX

P.S. I've bought a second-hand cot with your money: at a local sale. It's *lovely*! Many thanks. E.

Dear Lester,

I hope this reaches you. A man called MIKE WAINWRIGHT, a B.B.C. producer, has been trying and failing to get in touch with me. He's interested in doing a big documentary on MERLIN RAVEN. I seem to recall that you were his manager once, back in Liverpool? No one else can get near Raven—they know where he lives etc. but, as usual, he's surrounded by protectors who probably don't know the alphabet. Mike Wainwright's a very distinguished producer and even Raven would be a fool not to consider any offer from him. It might do you a bit of good if you were the connection—but you know what these things are—they could use you and lose you. Your risk. Wainwright's number is 742–1373, extensions 6768 and 6350. Up to you.

Hope all's well. Good to see you in the New Year. Glad Aileen and Harry are getting hitched. About time. See you.

Douglas.

As luck would have it, Lester did know where Raven lived when he was in London. He had been connected with him, authentically though briefly. And in some obscure but definite reckoning he sensed that Raven would see him, if only to cancel out any slight shadow of a debt from the past. He would go directly to Raven, he thought: then he could bargain better with this Wainwright number.

(2)

"I'm the butler," the man said, exaggerating an accent already feminine.

Lester was drained of all strength by the force of the envy which clubbed him. He went into a massive room, a black glass window covering an entire wall, through which the London lights appeared as dainty and carefully composed as hundreds and thousands on a cake. Everywhere, Lester saw Wealth: in the chunky leather furniture, the thick glass tables, the ankle deep carpets, the unbelievably expensive Hi-Fi equipment, the paintings on the walls—real paintings—and above all the crowds of flowers—all white—which blossomed on every surface, thrusting out of the most expensive vases. Raven's collection of Art Nouveau was extensive and valuable; most of it was in his heavily guarded manor house in the country, but the few pieces here cried out "style" to Lester. He wanted all of it; he would have done anything human to get all of it; as he stood at the door he was like a poor starved hound who'd run all day without water and would die for want of a drink.

Merlin put a finger to his lips, pointed to the turntable and waved Lester in. Lester managed to sit uncomfortably on a chair which had cost £1,350 for its comfort. Merlin smiled at him and then looked up to concentrate on the music. Lester was grateful for the chance to regroup his plans: he had so often lost out by wanting things too much and too impatiently. How often he himself must have come near all this, he thought! And he had missed it, missed it—he could have broken out in a tantrum of self-pity and frustration. This was his last chance: bound to be: at this level. He would never have had the nerve to come and see Raven if the B.B.C. thing hadn't come up. He had to make it work. He had to make the best of it. He had to get it right this time. He had to pull himself together.

He would have had trouble recognizing Raven. To Lester, whose physical condition meant so much to him, Merlin was portly. The lean, whispering lad of the Sixties had not bloomed but ballooned in his retirement and the loose oriental-styled clothes only added to the impression of a grossly over-fed young man—like one of those young noblemen in ancient cultures who was selected for slaughter and spoiled for life, or a young Buddha. Lester was reassured by this. He waited and fought to expel his nerves. He did not recognize the music, which sounded to him to be classical, modern and difficult: more, he considered, to be endured than enjoyed. The sort of stuff which, in Lester's opinion, the intellectuals listened to in order to prove that they did not like what everybody else liked. Lester was totally convinced that the basis of elitist taste lay in a determination to be exclusive: he bore no grudges about this. When he became rich he too might fill in the time by pretending to like the sort of music that Merlin was now absorbed by. But no one could tell him it was any fun. Lester resolved to refuse any offer of a drink: one more stiff one—and they were always stiff in this world—would finish him.

The music stopped. Merlin paused and then, at the third go, he levered himself out of the white satin covered four-seater sofa and came over, hand outstretched, a smile on his face, more open and friendly than Lester had ever seen him in his life or on the screen. Lester jumped up, tense as a spring, and they shook hands firmly and heartily like Americans. "Good to see you," repeated twice. "How do I look?" Merlin asked, still gripping Lester's hand. Lester hesitated. "Don't tell me. You'll lie. Your touch has given me the truth. Body language can't lie. But I'm getting better. When I'm eleven stone I'll put up all the mirrors again"—he pointed at three large unoccupied panels of the walls—"Adams—never mind. Sod it! It's *dark*!" He stumbled across the room and closed the curtains—green velvet. "Windows become mirrors at night," said Merlin gravely, "have you noticed?" Lester was about to agree but Merlin had begun to talk once again, while Lester's deferential response rattled up his throat and collapsed on his tongue. "I wouldn't have seen you," Merlin said, walking the length of the curtains like someone crossing a stage, appearing to ignore his guest, "but it's time to get back. What happened to us all, Lester? Where did we make the wrong decisions? And why? Nobody asks *why* today. Everybody's too clever to ask why. Well, I can afford it. I'm asking now. Why do we live like pigs? Tell me that. Did the Sixties almost destroy us?"

Lester was bewildered but, more importantly, he was overwhelmed by the warmth of the contact coming from Merlin. For Merlin had been notorious for his "cool": he had said so little that those intellectuals who did not think him inarticulate compared him with Pinter and Beckett. His songs were praised for their economy and imitated by a generation of elliptical lyricists and lock-jawed songsters and his track record as a public figure was most unusually and impressively discreet—free of the clutter of interviews which ententacled his contemporaries. That was power. Two interviews only—to the best pop journalists—heavily controlled by Raven. Everyone respected his silence. For the old scrubbers like Lester, he was a prince, unapproachable. Now, however, there seemed to be no stopping him. Lester risked a reply although he did not know what the hell Merlin was getting at.

"Well, Merlin, I think . . ."

"Geoff! *Geoff*! Geoff Fletcher for Christ's sake! *Geoff*! That's why I let you in. I wanted to talk to somebody who knows *Geoff Fletcher*! *Geoff*! Merlin Raven is dead as the Phoenix. Merlin Raven was invented by an agent—a man I do not like. It's *Geoff*! Geoff Fletcher from 31, Harrington Road, Birkenhead. Do you drink? Do you want one?" That Birkenhead address had been his for his first six months only. His parents had been killed in a train crash: he had been moved into the Home immediately afterwards.

"Yea. Yea. Yes. Geoff. Please. Anything'll do."

Merlin put his Moroccan slippered foot on a bell which was dug into the smooth white carpet like a belly button.

"It'll have to be soft," he said. "I'm running a dry house at the moment. Gotta lose some of this *fat*. *Fat*! Disgusting. Why are fat men disgusting, Lester? I'll tell you. Because it's walking waste. I'm a mobile manure heap and that's polite! What do you think of this room?"

Lester looked around: it was Hollywood, it was fairyland, it was class, it was power and women and kicking everybody in the teeth who had hurt him, it was where he would have brought them all—to show them, to make them grovel. He worshipped it.

"Shit!" Merlin said. "Isn't it? Waste! Over-expensive chic sold to us by ponces who would strip a pickpocket."

The butler came in, immaculate in a freshly laundered and well tailored denim suit. Conversation stopped. He handed a large chunky glass of fresh orange juice to Lester, his eyes lowered, and a little Slimline tonic to Merlin. Then, noiselessly, he withdrew. Lester guessed he was about twenty-one.

"Do you know about Primals?"

Lester thought that Merlin must be referring to a new drug and in order to keep the flow going, to ensure the continuity of this great flood of words which bathed him in reassurance, he lied and nodded.

"Course you bloody well don't, Lester." Merlin drank off the tonic and made a face. "Cheers! What do you want?"

He heard himself praying inside his head, he could hear his own voice pleading in a whisper, "Oh God, help me, help me, help me God. Oh please. *Please*."

"There's this man called Wainwright," he whispered. "Mike Wainwright." The muscles were kneading his Adam's apple fiercely. He kept on.

"Know him. Go on. Don't be nervous."

"And Douglas—Douglas Tallentire—he's my cousin." Implicating Douglas was a blind inspiration.

"Your cousin! Saw a play he wrote. Go on."

"They've approached me with a proposition—a deal—not quite a deal—an idea—not worked out yet—it all depends on how you want to play it—"

"It always does. Yes?"

"You're in charge. Ha! So. Whatever you want really." Lester stopped. He had lied again and not thought it out.

"Whatever I want really where?" Merlin continued to pace about like a heavy neurotic in a significant thriller. His ruthless diet was almost driving him insane.

"This film. They want you to make—with them—they'll make it—you needn't do anything." Lester was clueless. All he knew now was that this man must not be bothered, must be approached obliquely, must be given everything he wanted always.

Merlin stopped and, with cruelty, stared at his visitor. Lester was quite clearly buggered. He looked awful, dressed cheaply and sounded beaten. He had never been bright but failure had impaired his nerve, which had always been good. Under Merlin's stare, Lester actually, physically, shivered and then smiled, as if in apology.

Then a song, one of those short, exact and poignant narratives which no one else could write, began to form in Merlin's mind: it felt right: it felt certain. It was long since he had experienced that true register. The last few years had spawned nothing but meandering tapes on philosophical themes and significant subjects—deep thought: often, shallow music. Merlin had been shrewd enough not to release any of it. The record company, whose executives neither understood nor liked the material, had paid an Arabian sum to prevent anyone else ever turning those dirges into discs. But, it was a very long time since Merlin had heard that little click somewhere deep inside his brain: that instant comprehension which told him—"it's there, it's real, use it. Click. In one. It's a song."

"You bring me luck," Merlin said. "Wait here."

He went through into his studio and swiftly wrote down about ten lines. At his white grand piano, using two fingers, he picked out a melody and put it on tape. "Good!" he whispered, eyes closed, hearing it all, overwhelmed with relief and pleasure. "Yes. That's it. Yes." The whole operation took about seven minutes and exhilarated him as nothing had done for months. The song would become a great hit and earn him more than a million dollars in the first year and about forty-five thousand dollars a year for the foreseeable future.

When Merlin returned, Lester was still standing, too nervous to sit, too intimidated to walk about.

"We'll go and eat," Merlin said. "I'm allowed one meal a day. Boiled fish, fresh veg. and fruit. We can talk there. Then we can maybe find a couple of women. You still like women?"

His old friend nodded. He did not dare trust himself to speak because he was near to tears. Just to be seen out with Merlin Raven in one of the "hot" spots—and Raven made a spot hot—would up his chances a hundred—two hundred—five hundred per cent! He really was in luck.

"I like women too," Merlin declared, seriously. "They're something else."

(3)

It was four o'clock in the morning, the dead hour, time of surprise attacks, low body temperature and intractable anxieties, the fullest stretch of the rack for insomniacs, the time when policemen stole a nap, the old witching hour; and Lester was utterly drunk and so full of happiness and love for his fellows, so brimmed up with what he would tell Fiona that, as he swayed in the gutter waiting for a taxi, it was a wonder he did not spill over onto the orange pavement which rocked gently way down at his feet.

Merlin had ordered champagne which, his doctors said, did not make you fat.

Stirred by the delicious food—he had been encouraged by Merlin to choose the most costly dishes (Merlin delighted in seeing Lester stuff himself with over-rich, over-sauced food)—Lester had begun to talk about poaching. He was led to this subject by Merlin, who had recounted with disdainful gusto his own failed attempts to "live off the land": to Merlin all this was now "phony, just another cul-de-sac, just another abortion—that's no answer—there's nothing in it. Crappy cabbages and bloody chapped hands—what does that prove?" Some phrase of his had set off Lester, though, and, for about an hour, he talked in a way in which Merlin had never heard before, nor in the least expected. Moonlit nights about the fells, gamekeepers, wardens, tickling trout, snaring rabbits, country anecdotes came out easily and naturally and Merlin shed his patronizing contempt for the man. He saw someone as lost as he was, barred from his past by a self-made debris which was impenetrable. He promised to meet Douglas and Wainwright and talk over the film "seriously".

At the well known club in the well known street where, at weekends, photographers prowled about like stray cats about the restaurant dustbins, Merlin continued to order champagne and set about picking up two women. It was so simple it was no fun at all. Lester was curious about this new development in Merlin's emotional life, but too tired and still too subserviently cautious to say anything. They returned to the penthouse flat and took their partners to separate bedrooms. Lester did it because he was too scared to break his luck by refusing. But he did not want to and felt that he was betraying Fiona: and again he was surprised that such a feeling should be able to surface through the sores and scabs of his burnt-out feelings, and again he was rather proud of himself for having such a capacity for loyalty.

When he and his partner went through to the big room, Merlin was already there, sulking, gazing at his image in the black window, now bared once more. Lester took his leave and tapped his top pocket to show that he still had the private number given him in the restaurant. Merlin scarcely noticed him. Lester's partner was pleased to see him go. She preened herself for the attentions of the superstar who continued to stare, gloomily, deep into his dark reflection, unsatisfied and building up to a characteristic explosion of irrational and violent anger which would soon scatter the hapless girls down onto the empty street and half wreck the room.

Finally a taxi came and soon Lester was bouncing over the Thames, heading for Stockwell, with the news for Fiona, still unable to believe his luck.

(4)

"She isn't here."

"Don't be bloody daft." Lester buffeted the door with his shoulder, putting no force into the action, a token assault.

"She went off just after I came. She said to tell you she's gone back to her old man and she don't want you to cause no bother."

"She's in there." Again, Lester dumped his shoulder against the door.

"Would I be sayin' this to you if she was standin' beside me, would I?"

"Why'd she go?" He could not repress the question even though he knew it exposed him.

"I never interfere."

"What did she say to you?"

"I've told you."

"She must've said more than that. You'll have talked. She must have had something else to say. Or a note."

"She didn't leave no note." Janice laughed and the cosy little tinkle of sound flew tauntingly through the thin door and into the bare corridor, lit only by a night light. The laugh made Janice real to Lester and he saw that silly little head—always so spruce and neat and well cared for—on top of the large, trussed-up body. "Fiona wouldn't leave you no note."

"So you know more about her than I do, do you?" Lester's voice rose: until now he had spoken in a strong whisper.

"I should do. I've known her longer. She's never changed. She never will."

"What do you mean by that?"

Again the burden of the answer came in that cosy tinkle of laughter—phony, Lester thought. She needed a King Kong screw, this stupid bird, to knock her out of that bloody laugh!

"There's no need to raise your voice."

"Let me in. I want to sleep."

"You must be jokin', darlin'." Safe and sound, Janice was in a pink quilted dressing gown which swept from its El Greco high collar at her pointed ears to a Cardinal's robe effect at her hidden, pink-slippered feet. She was enjoying this. The flat was finally hers once more—she would never share again, she vowed—and she had never liked Lester. Her Saloon Bar voice was designed to put him firmly in his place—as someone over whom she had complete control.

"I'll leave in the morning. Let me in. I just want to sleep."

"You'll never get in here, my son, oh no."

"I'll break this bloody door down." This time, he bumped against it more determinedly.

"Don't you swear at me. And leave that door alone or I'll scream this building down. And I mean it."

Lester stopped.

"I'll kill her."

"Charming."

Lester punched the door violently. This bumptious bar-room chat of hers was all wrong! He was in love with Fiona! Janice had no respect for his feelings. Janice was a cow with the head of a page-boy.

"I'll kill her," he repeated, feeling in that sentence a warm surge of affection for Fiona which threatened to bring him to tears.

"Listen, mate. You don't deserve this—but stay away from her, firstly because her husband's a bigger bastard than even you are and second because her brothers are back. If I know them they'll be looking for you now. In fact," Janice continued, with inspired intuition, "I wouldn't be seen around this place for a very long time, maybe never, if I was you."

He looked at the brown door: he looked up and down the murky corridor.

"Just give me my suitcase and I'll go."

"I'm not opening this door to you, Lester, not tonight nor no night."

"What about my things?"

"I'll leave them down with the warden. He has an office. Nobody'll pinch what you've got."

"Don't be bloody stupid. Just shove my suitcase out. Why the fuck should I want to touch the likes of you?"

"Don't you swear at me, mate. *She* took the suitcase. Yours'll be in a carrier bag. Now you'd better go—I want to sleep."

"I'll get you, Janice."

"You just try."

"I'll catch you. Don't look over your shoulder. Slut."

"Listen, Lester." There was not a suggestion of panic in Janice's voice, only the sternness which comes from someone who is determined that there be no mistaking her meaning. "If you touch me—I am very friendly with people who would break your legs and arms without stopping for a breath. So take your threats somewhere else. You've got enough problems with Fiona's lot, I'd say. You won't frighten me. Piss off!"

He felt very tired. Fiona was gone. "You're not worth the skin you live in," he said and kicked the door loudly. The sound boomed about the corridor. He had the satisfaction of hearing her draw away from the door. "Cock-teaser," he said. "I'll be back."

The lift was still broken; the stairs were unlit. He walked down carefully, conscious of the struggle between alcohol and temper. Not being able to explode into violent action made him feel strange. When he got out onto the street and the damp coolness of the hour before dawn hit him through his meagre clothes, he swayed and staggered for a few steps before thrusting his hands into his pockets and somehow, thus balanced, set off for the West End.

A double-decker bus, empty, lit up, moving fast, appeared from nowhere and careered away like something in a ghost story. Along the small, shop-lined and terraced empty streets of South London, there was only the occasional reminder of life: a woman, wrapped up heavily, trudging about her business, a young man with a briefcase walking briskly, one or two dogs, the occasional car.

Lester wanted there to be some grand climactic feeling within him: he wanted to be full of despair or revenge. He felt badly hurt: he would have beaten up Fiona if he could have got hold of her. But Janice's warning hand had neutralized the second course. He trekked through the empty South London streets, convinced that the one chance of a real love which might have led to "shacking up together" and even to marriage, if she had wanted it, had gone.

He would not be so soft again; that was it. Kaput. Forever.

He missed the convenience of Emma now. There was nowhere else he could turn except Douglas. Out of respect for Mary, he waited until seven before he rang. By this time he was in Westminster, seeing before him, across the road from the telephone box, the Houses of Parliament, faintly pink in the early clear sunlight. Traffic was beginning to build up and he pressed his free hand to his free ear. He did not realize how cold he was until he came into the little box and then began to shake quite violently.

"He has another number now," Mary said, reluctantly. "Is it urgent?"

"Yes. Oh yea. It's to do with the B.B.C.—a film—all that—the man—Wainwright—said I have to talk to Douglas."

She gave him the number. He dialled but there was no reply. He headed for Charing Cross and some hot tea. He would keep trying.

He stood at the kerb while a juggernaut went past. Its load was scores of tree trunks, bare and neat, parked row on row.

Lester wondered where they had come from. He'd wanted to work in the forests, once. Maybe he would have been happy. Who knows?

The thought of the hot tea surged through his mind and, simultaneously, he thought of Fiona, in bed as she had been the previous morning, asleep, spread-eagled like a child. The memory hurt him and his eyes stung with self-pity. He had loved her, but there was no way to get her back now. He had to make it first. To take this chance. And then find her again, when he was loaded. Yes. He would do that. Women went with the money. He respected her too much to go and beg and at the moment he had no other option. But it would change. Then he would seek her out. That was what you did. Came back stronger.

He trailed stiffly across the road, watched by two policemen who had been patrolling the Embankment for vagrants throughout the night. Another customer in the offing, some time in the near future, they agreed: they could always tell.

6
The End of the Day

(1)

Old John's death, just after Easter, had been so long anticipated that Joseph was surprised at his grief. It seemed indecent that a man in his sixties should seek out quiet places to cry. In public, to reassert himself, he was even more hearty than usual and one or two people thought him a little lacking in respect. Betty took it more evenly and it was she who attended to all the funeral arrangements. John had said that he wanted to be "buried not burnt": the plot was there beside the grave of his second wife, Joseph's stepmother. More than three hundred people came to the funeral.

Betty was shocked by how ill Douglas looked, but she said nothing directly: not only ill, she decided, but miserably unhappy and at odds with himself. Mary, he said, could not afford to take the time off, otherwise she would have come with him. He had come up on the morning train and intended to return in the evening, but the weight of the family dissuaded him. It would have seemed too abrupt. He stayed on. There was nothing to draw him back.

The funeral tea was pleasant. Three of Joseph's sisters were there and his youngest brother: they exchanged stories about their dead father and soon they were laughing at revised versions of their childhood. All of them had in some measure feared him: his daughters had resented his domineering and his harshness but they had adored him too and their stories were about his monstrous deeds and their perpetual survival. To them he had indeed been a lord. Now that he was gone, their memories turned towards the capturing of anecdotes and incidents which absolved and redeemed him.

The tea was in the Royal Oak: small tables placed together, making a flat-bottomed U about the room; heavy starched tablecloths; friends hired as waitresses moving across the open area with giant pots of tea and plates of cakes. It could have been an Old Persons' Outing, Douglas thought, or a break in a genteel bingo session.

He was sickeningly self-absorbed. "The spiral," he said to himself, "has come a full circle." He loathed his self-absorption and that increased it, which intensified the loathing.

They saw a man on the brink of early middle-age. They saw someone who had been offered opportunities and grasped them. They saw freedom, success, an interesting life, wealth and yet still "one of their own".

He saw old people in their best clothes: faces from past centuries—lines, strain, weather, inadequate nutrition. He saw the end of a life's struggle for common comforts clothed in chain-store affluence. It was more than most of them had dared dream—but there was an overwhelming feeling that they had come too late. They had seen their children and grandchildren grow up to a world largely without the privations and basic pressures which had been their disabling lot. He saw them left out of the feast they had funded.

They wanted him to talk, to dazzle them, to drop names and claim glamorous acquaintanceship. Had he done so, they would have been critical but delighted. He did not and they felt as if they had been found wanting.

He wanted to say, "Excuse this jaded tiredness." He wanted to be what they wanted him to be. It was not much to ask, or to give, for an hour or two. Was this the best he could do? Sit like a stooge and think his own thoughts? Why could he not bring back trophies worth winning?

But they did not question him at all. In the futility of his self-pity, he had begun to weep and the worn-out tears of exhaustion went down his cheeks as he thought of Mary, betrayed, alone now; Hilda, betrayed, alone now; John, betrayed, alone now; the story finally finished and himself weary from the effort of it. He had come to identify completely with the man who had sought death and blundered to it in those thin, wet Northern woods. An uncanny identification. It was as if he could now hear the very pitch and tone of the soughing despair in the man's head. He was drained by it. And there was the nag of Lester's plea that he make this film on Raven for Wainwright and his own need to make a living for all of them.

It was as if, as a boy, he had taken on a great pack and set out on a pilgrim's progress to find out about Learning, and then about Literature, and then about His Own Capacities and then about The Real World—and here he was, with nothing to shore up self-respect, nothing to salt intellectual curiosity, nothing to excite energy, worn to a wafer of himself by the contradictions which a certain consistency of attitude had brought about. For where you loved you followed, did you not? And yet to follow two women seemed only to split him from heart to conscience and make him either perverse or impotent. And to choose to be as free from dependencies as possible ought to bring its own reward, ought it not? Yet he hung onto his odd jobs as dependently as a beggar around the kitchen doors of Grand Hotels. To write what you felt most deeply, that was to be true to your art and to your self—surely? And yet the sad elegy he had just finished—was that any more than a sentimental gesture? And what was it worth? Why was it so tiring?

"Here." His mother pressed a small handkerchief into his fingers. It was edged with lace and bore her initials woven in blue thread. "Take this."

She looked away, but not before he had seen the respect in her glance. Joseph, too, regarded him with admiring compassion. Harry, he saw, was nodding at him, vigorous with sympathy.

Douglas realized that they thought he was crying over the dead old man. His display of deep feeling had moved them all. The party broke up and people went away to catch buses, share cars, or walk through the empty early evening town to talk about the funeral in private. In his lifetime, John had held them all together.

Douglas' tears had been a fine and proper tribute, they thought.

(2)

"But it'll have to be a church," he said.

"Why?"

"It always is. Nearly always. Up here it is anyway."

"I don't believe in all that guff."

"I do."

"I am *not* getting married in St Mary's and that's final."

Harry smiled and Aileen, thinking she had won, threw a cushion across at him. They were in his flat, Harry rather drunk, still wearing his black tie, glad of the chance to have his mind taken off the funeral, which had moved him so much that he had been forced to fight very hard not to show his feelings and upset the others—who had more right to grief than he would ever have. He caught the cushion easily and spun it back gently so that it cuffed her hair.

"We're getting married in St Mary's Church, banns, choir, and all the trimmings," he said, "and *that's* final."

"But I'm pregnant."

"It doesn't show."

"I'm an atheist."

"You only have to answer a few simple questions."

"It's expensive."

"I'll pay."

"You're on the dole."

"I've my savings."

"*Not* on a wedding in church! For Christ's sake, Harry—what are you talking about?"

She regretted the edge which had come into her voice but his insistence struck her as absurd. She had discovered herself to be pregnant and had been surprised at how happy it made her. Harry, naturally, she thought (proudly), had been pleased and instantly begun the arrangements. She had thought that his idea of a church wedding was no more than a tease and taken no notice at first. It was much more important to give attention to the problem of Harry's job. He had been made redundant.

"Harry," she said, trying hard, but unsuccessfully, to keep the lecturing tone out of her voice, "let's stop being silly about this. You are unemployed. The way things are you could be unemployed for some weeks. Even if you get a job, it will most likely be a temporary job and you'll have to wait until God knows when before you get a job you want. We're about to have a child. I shall have to give up my lectureship and come back here, which means that *I'll* be unemployed too. Besides which, I'll have to be at home for the first year or two—I have plans but they don't stand much chance—with one thing and another, darling, it is *not* the time to get married in an expensive and anachronistic ecclesiastical setting."

"It doesn't cost all that much," Harry said. "The dresses are what the money goes on and you can buy a new dress for yourself and be married in that."

"A maternity gown?"

"There's no need to joke."

"I am *not* marching up and down that aisle with half of Thurston coming to gawp."

"It might rain. Nobody would come then."

"That's hardly the point."

"What *is* the point, Aileen?"

She paused, but by now she had dug her heels in and the intransigence blunted her sensitivity. She was not aware of the new tone in Harry's voice, the unusual nervousness of his hands, the look in his eyes which pleaded with her to let him be.

"The point is that you should live by what you believe. I'm not religious—everybody knows that. I refused to go to church from the day I joined the Young Socialists, and I'd feel and look a fool if you made me go against what I stand for. I know you're a Christian and I respect that but you have to respect my point of view as well."

"I do."

"In that case—the Registry Office."

"No."

"Please, Harry."

"I didn't want to say this." He paused. "You see—it wouldn't be for you—getting married in church—it would be for Betty—for 'mother'. Douglas ran off and got married in Paris or somewhere abroad—somewhere—she never saw it. You know how much she loves weddings and how she's always wanted to be in the middle of one. Well. Here we are. This is her chance."

Aileen shook her head and tugged out a cigarette. Every time she smoked now, Harry remembered that advertisement which declared: "SMOKING CAN HARM YOUR CHILD" and showed a pregnant mother puffing a fag to its tar-soaked and cancerous tip. But he had said nothing: she could work it out for herself and if he tried to influence her—he would only make it worse.

"For Betty?" she asked.

"Yes."

She paused. "O.K."

He had won! The weight of Harry's relief indicated how strongly he had meant to hold onto his position over the wedding. Betty needed to be looked after, he felt, and there was little enough he could do: but this small thing was possible.

"No need to grin like a fat cat," she said and held out her hands to him. When he took them, she snatched at him and he allowed himself to be tugged down onto the floor where she lay on a heap of highly patterned cushions.

"I've got some news," he said. "I didn't want to say it earlier—I don't know—it would have struck the wrong note." He hurried on without giving her the chance to ask what he meant by that—her favourite conversational trip-wire. "I've got a job down at the factory. It's clerking in the loading area—about the same money as I got before."

"Not exactly professional work—or a career spangled with glittering prospects."

"I like it down there. There's plenty of the lads play for one or other of the teams. They're a decent bunch of blokes. I think I'll enjoy it."

"I'm sorry."

"No need to be sorry. I'm not."

"I didn't mean sorry for you. I'm sorry I was a bitch—all that 'not exactly professional' bit." She frowned. "It shows how infected by the bourgeoisie you can get—and how snobbish. Silly. Sorry." She kissed him on the cheek, noted the patronizing nature of such a peck, and putting her arms around him, kissed him strongly and long on the mouth. "The trouble with you is that you're so very nice, so very, very nice, and I've forgotten how to deal with people who are very honest and very nice."

"Frank Edwards works in the same shed." Harry hesitated. "We'll be able to discuss tactics."

"For the next game," she said, solemnly.

"For the next match, yes."

"You. Are. A. Lovely. Clot." The words were separated by kisses planted from his forehead down to his throat. She began to undo the buttons of his shirt. He responded immediately by loosening her clothes.

"You're not really interested in *my* plans, are you?" she asked.

"Of course I am. Put your arms up." She did as he asked and he drew off her dress.

"I'm going to try to stand for Labour in this constituency at the bye-election."

Harry continued kissing and undressing her without the slightest loss of pace or rhythm.

"It's safe Tory," he said.

"Nothing's safe nowadays."

"Tights," he said, "are an abomination."

"You could have impregnated a future Member of Parliament."

"Let me put out the light." He walked across the room naked: Aileen loved his body, its leanness and toughness and whiteness. She kept this to herself, though, for it embarrassed him to hear it.

"I meant it. I'm going to try for the nomination."

"It's handy, you being pregnant, one way, isn't it?" He turned off the light and the electric fire grinned its two scarlet bars of fire at them.

"That's nice," she said. "Harry. Harry? O.K. But I'll *not* wear white. Ssshhh. Don't say anything. Don't say anything at all."

Although he did not hurt her, he made love fiercely. All that was never said, all that would not go into words, went into actions and Aileen held on for dear life as he lifted her, turned and swung her, so easily moving her. As she began to come to him he hoisted himself onto his arms and rammed down into her again and again until her body shuddered and ached to be satisfied.

Harry shook his head and the hair, damp with sweat, tumbled over the white face she saw above her, his eyes tight shut as if in pain. "No," he said, and repeated as he had done on the last two nights, "NO! No! No! No! No!", the rhythm that of his body: the word a savage exclamation. For, since John's death, Harry had "seen" him when he was making love to Aileen. As now, as the pressure and the swoon grew stronger, there he was, the old man he had loved so much, blue eyes laughing, his face eager for life.

(3)

The truth of it all had hit Betty like a fist in the face. Douglas and Mary had parted. That was why he evaded her questions. That was why he glanced away when she asked for the usual detailed statement about John. That was why he looked so neglected. He had gone out drinking with Joseph and she waited impatiently, determined to say something which would bring out the truth and yet afraid to say anything that would make things worse or hurt him. He had looked so ill, she thought: Mary should not have let him get into that state.

To occupy herself she polished the brass as she watched television. She now had a large collection of these small brass ornaments, which hung in rows down the walls until the living room was a little like a gift shop. Cleaning them was only described as a chore for the purpose of conversation; in fact she found the activity satisfying and soothing. She worked away, sat on the edge of her seat in the same attitude of attentiveness and unease as that of her rarely worn glasses, which rested at the very edge of her nose. It was after eleven, they would surely be back soon—even though Joseph always used to tell visitors "they shut the door prompt at ten thirty in Thurston pubs—and them inside have to stay there for another two hours at least!" He was boyishly proud of things like that: out-of-hours drinking, the occasional extravagant tale of gambling—when the town presented itself as a place of Stories and Characters and Plots Comical and Tragical, then he was happy. The mundane doings of the place bored him increasingly. Douglas was drinking too much—Joseph had told her that the last time they had seen Douglas—when he had come up for two or three nights to the cottage "to see a potential purchaser"—so he had said. She had believed him then, of course: now she suspected he had come to think matters over.

The thought that her son's marriage might be over terrified her. She knew that it happened more frequently nowadays—yet the fears and the taboos remained. She knew that there was an increase in the divorce rate, she accepted that it was sometimes better for those who did not get on to part, rather than prolong what might be an agony—there was nothing but tolerance in Betty for anyone in pain. But Douglas was her son. His loss would be hers; his failure hers; the hurt he inflicted would be her responsibility in part; and there was the child. She had a feeling of sacred protectiveness about the child. He must be spared as much as possible. That would be the starting point. After that, what would be, would be. This conclusion appeased her a little.

Joseph did not come back until almost two o'clock. He was alone and tired and drunk.

"Douglas wanted to go up to the cottage to be on his own to think things over," he announced, taking care to pronounce each word clearly, taking care also to answer the question which she would most want answered and, by this act, defuse the anger which would surely be his welcome. "Sometimes you have to be alone," he added and suddenly dropped into a chair. "I'm tired," he announced.

"I'm not surprised."

"Any chance of a cup of tea?"

"You'll need more than tea to sort you out." She got up to make it and left him alone.

Joseph thought of taking off his coat and then decided against it. He would have to get undressed for bed soon enough and he could do the whole lot in one go. Besides, he was cold. He looked around the neat and pretty little room without interest: surroundings had never meant much to him. The harmony and cosiness so assiduously worked out by Betty, the polishing and painting, the re-arranging, the patient purchasing of matching curtains, carpets, cushions and the compulsive re-arranging of the ornaments which gave her a definite sense of peace—all this influenced and affected him not one iota. He would have been equally at home in a barrack room.

"Pack up your troubles in your old kit-bag
And smile, smile, smile."

He sang softly although there were no neighbours through the walls. A detached house, even though a bungalow. His own estate. Yet it gave him no feeling of achievement at all. "We're alike, Douglas and me," he said to himself, "can't settle, can't be contented." There was contentment in that observation. He wanted his son and himself to be alike and the pleasure of the evening had been in their mutual confidences.

"You are my sunshine, my only sunshine,
You make me hap-py, when skies are grey."

"Drunk and singing on the night of your father's funeral," Betty said scornfully as she brought in the tea.

"Yesterday." Joseph looked at his watch. "If you want to be nasty, be accurate." He hummed on a little, while the tea cooled on the small table beside him. Then he stopped and waited for her to ask him some questions.

"Well, I'm off to bed," she said.

"Don't you want to know what I've been doing?"

"I can smell what you've been doing."

"That's not very nice."

"Have you finished your tea? I'll take it through."

"I thought you'd want a talk. I haven't finished, no." He poured another cup, not slopping, and took up a wholemeal biscuit.

"I must say that Douglas could have *said* he wasn't staying. I made up the bed."

"We got talking," Joseph said, darkly, the biscuit blocking his mouth.

"He could have said. Still. There we are."

Again the silence started to roll up and Joseph could not sustain it. He swallowed the biscuit, washed it down with his cup and sat back comfortably, his rather small white hands crossed on the lap of his burly black overcoat in an attitude of piety.

"He and Mary have—they're having a Trial Separation," Joseph announced.

"I'd guessed something like that. Fools!"

"How did you guess?" The hands fluttered up in agitation. "What else did he say?"

"We talked a lot."

"Very well."

Betty got up, went across to Joseph, took the tray and set off for the kitchen.

"Where are you going?"

"Bed."

"Don't you want to listen?"

"I'm not going to drag it out of you, Joseph. What you have to say means a lot to me and either you say it now or I'll wait until the morning when you're sober."

"I'm not drunk."

"That's as may be."

"I'm upset, that's all. It's been a hell of a day for me, Betty. Nobody thinks I feel anything—just because I stay cheerful. But that old man meant a lot to me. And I meant a lot to him. It was always me he turned to to sort him out. He loved me, so he did, and that went for me too. And now with all this Douglas carry-on—I'm upset as well, you know. You only have to drag it out because I don't like talking about it."

Betty's self-righteousness slipped away. She saw this fuddled man, in his sixties, dumpy, exhausted, drunk, unable to define his grief, unable to control his reaction to Douglas' confidences. She understood how much it must have meant to him to have passed this evening with his son; and she thanked Douglas for that. Aware that she could not satisfy Joseph's needs, she could still see and be grateful when another could.

"We're both very tired," she said. "Perhaps it would be better to talk in the morning."

"I'll never get round to it in the morning," he said. "Anyway. There isn't much to add once you've got over the initial shock.

Sit down, though, love. I feel that you're a policeman standing there."

She could not resist popping the tray through to the kitchen so as to keep the living room tidy; nor could she resist taking up another brass and re-opening the Duraglit as Joseph unbent to describe the evening.

He went over it in detail: how they had gone up to the flats to take a drink to John's old friends, how they had called in to see a schoolfriend of Douglas', how they had landed up in The Crown after popping in the Kildare and the Lion and Lamb. He told her what Douglas had said about his work. "He's going to stick to this writing now come what may. *Come-what-may*. I admire him for that." He explained, with awe, how Douglas was stony broke and needed to sell the maisonette in London. With total recall he went through Douglas' idea for Regional Portraits: he had been absorbed in the unaccustomed confidence and caught by the detail; usually Douglas said so little and that so general that it was not worth remembering. Here, though, he had taken on the burden of their conversation and used the television idea as a way to communicate with his father. He had wanted to show the respect that was due to him on such a day, and he regretted how often he had neglected to "honour his father", how soon the filial had slid to the friendly and the friendly to the unfriendly.

For by seeing his father as a "pal"—the contemporary way—he had attempted a new relationship in his adulthood which had no guarantees of success. Pals, friends, happened by accident or mutual concerns: his connection with his father was an accident only in the cosmic sense and their mutual concerns were profound but without that surface of shared life which bred gossip and easy reference. And so it would have been sounder to have remained the dutiful son. Indeed, as Douglas delivered his life to his father in the way of a prodigal, he felt unanticipated benefits flowing from the sureness of that state. The old order worked. Both of them noticed that and relaxed. Yet both knew it would most likely be no permanent thing: Douglas had moved too far out of Joseph's range of experience. It was the father who was often the learner now. The younger who had broken new ground and the old taboos over jobs and money and risks. No old order could remain if the balance which supported the structure went out of kilter; but when it worked it gave rich sustenance.

"Then he told me all about it." Joseph finally arrived at what Betty wanted to hear. He was as shy to talk as he had been embarrassed to listen. It was strange, he reflected, an adult lifetime passed with this woman before him and yet there were still large parts of the life between them which were smothered in a mutual shyness and bled by diffidence. Still a mass of subjects which were simply not discussed because they had found no way to discuss them without embarrassing each other. Perhaps this armour was necessary for a long-term intimate life. However, it left Joseph stranded, now that he had to tell his wife about their son.

"Well?"

"I don't think it's finished, like, between them, not a bit of it. I said to him—'I like Mary. Your mother and me like Mary.' I wanted to say that."

"What's happened?" Although Betty was almost screaming to know, she realized that patience was the only course.

"Well, the thing is," Joseph sucked hurriedly on his cigarette, "he's—gone off—gone off and got himself a flat—rented."

"On his own?"

"What do you mean?"

"On his own?"

"Why shouldn't he be on his own?"

"Come on, Joseph. There's another woman involved in all this."

"Is there?"

"It's written all over your face."

Joseph could not deny it. But her insight caught him short. He had wanted to protect Betty and Douglas by retaining and concealing this information. It demeaned both of them, for he knew she would take the betrayal personally.

"What's written all over my face?"

His manoeuvre was so feeble that she did not even acknowledge it but sat, intent and alert now, tense with expectation, waiting for the truth.

"He isn't living with *her*. He assured me of that. Not that I asked. But I believe him. He's on his own. That's the top and bottom of it, Betty. He's on his own."

"He always hated that."

"He's gone up to that cottage on his own."

"That surprises me as well." She paused. "What did he say about her? Don't say 'about who?'"

"Not very much, really." Joseph relaxed into the truth. "She's not a silly young girl. That much I do know. And he's genuinely fond of her. I could see that. Mind you, you see, he's still very fond of Mary—as a matter of fact I've never heard him speak about her so much. It's hard to make out."

"Is *she* married?"

"No."

"Does he want to marry her?"

"He doesn't know. He doesn't know what he wants."

"He should by now."

"There are times when you don't," Joseph said, and although his manner was overlaid by a patina of ponderous mystery-making, there was, in his tone, a conviction that impressed her.

"At least you should know what you should do." Betty wanted to tease this out.

"You should. Yes. But it doesn't always happen like that."

"He has a wife and a little boy to keep and a family to build up. That's plain enough. It is for most people."

"Maybe so. Maybe not."

"What do you mean by that?"

"A lot of people pretend, Betty. You know that and so do I. A lot of people are quite happy just jogging along pretending. But there are those who aren't. There are those who think pretending isn't good enough."

"Douglas said that. I can hear his voice saying it."

"No. Or—maybe he did, yes. But if I am quoting from him then I'm quoting in agreement."

"Pretending what? You have to get on with it. That's all."

"Not necessarily. There's no reason why things shouldn't change. If people want them to, that's their business."

"If he's run off with another woman that's his wife's business!"

"He hasn't run off with anybody."

"Did he say why?"

"He doesn't really know."

"After all his education he can only come up with 'he doesn't really know'! I could tell him. Anybody could."

"I think he's a very unhappy man," Joseph said, carefully. He had considered the matter all evening and this was his overriding comment on it. "Very unhappy indeed."

"That's no excuse."

"Maybe not."

"You sound as if you're on his side."

"I understand him, that's all. We understand each other. After all, we ought to—father and son." He stopped. But Betty was too distressed to answer him. She had flung replies and questions at him with no real purpose, for she had guessed the true state of affairs and was badly disturbed. Joseph could see that she was near tears: he could not remember when last she had cried. When? So many years ago. He felt a surge of love for her, a pulse of spontaneous protective affection which came like a voice from the past. He wanted to reach out and take her hand—when was the last time he had reassured her? She had scorned it for so long. In that one moment he stepped back across the wilderness of habit and boredom which had been the character of so much of the second half of their life together. But he could not reach out his hand: the gesture was too sentimental and would have been rebuffed. Instead, he talked on.

"I can see that he wants to make something of his life on his own terms. He's lucky to get the chance, I know, but he wants to do things his own way and not just do them because everybody else's always done them like that. I don't approve of what he's doing—but I can see how he gets himself where he is. He wants to think things through—that's why he didn't want to come back here—no offence to you—he loves you—he always has—but he just wants to be on his own. It's a different world he's in, Betty, it's a different way of seeing the whole thing."

"What's different about where he is now?" Joseph's speech had given her time to check her tears and will herself to staunch the flow of unhappiness. "He's stuck up in the hills in a little cottage—exactly the same sort of place his grandfather was stuck in at his age. Exactly the same sort of place his grandfather was *born* in, for goodness sake—and just waiting to be hired—from what I can learn—just the same as old John used to go out to the hirings to get hired. What's the difference in that? None at all. And there's no difference in family. A wife and a child are what you have to stick by if you take them on at all and there's no way out of that."

"He takes things very hard," Joseph said, "very seriously."

"Mary would say he wasn't taking this seriously enough."

"It's all a question of how you look at it."

"No, Joseph. There are some things that are wrong and you can look at them until you're blue in the face but they'll still be wrong."

"Well, there we are."

He was tired now. He wanted to be alone now with his own thoughts of John, he wanted to remember him, he needed to think of him.

"It was Annie," Betty said, speaking of Douglas' daughter, sadly, and now there was no holding the tears. She bent forward until her head was in her lap and wept aloud. Joseph came beside her and stood, one hand gently rubbing her shoulders, unable to do more to help. "He blames himself," Betty said, "because he was gallivanting around in America when the little lass was so ill—he blames himself—which he shouldn't—it's silly—it's altogether bad—but he does—and since she died he's changed—you can see it—there's—he looks desperate. But he shouldn't."

She looked up at Joseph, who was determined not to cry. Annie had been such a lovely child, Douglas' first, their adored grandchild—such a sweet creature—to be taken from life at the age of eight by the antique Victorian affliction of double-pneumonia seemed too cruel and futile to contemplate. And indeed all thought of it wearied Joseph as nothing else did. "But he should have got over it." Betty sat up now and forced herself to behave. "You can't use the past as an excuse," she said. "You have no right."

(4)

About three weeks later, Joseph was in the cemetery at the end of a Saturday afternoon, squaring up the grave. There was little to do but he had wanted an excuse to spend some time there: to have said he had gone there alone to meditate on his father would have been as unacceptable to him as it would have been to his friends. Yet all of them would have understood that this was sometimes necessary: they too would have found a mundane excuse and hidden the deeper motive.

It was just before dusk. The cemetery was to the west of the town, firmly on the Solway Plain. Standing there, he could see the fells, Skiddaw guarding the northern entrance, now smoothly outlined, the delicate grey sky just beginning to absorb the longer reddening rays from the sun, which had been clear and solitary most of the day in the cold blue early spring sky. Beyond those fells was where his father had been hired: before them was where he had been born: to the west was where he had worked in the mines. As Joseph smoked and looked about him he could take in most of the geographical world of his father.

He had expected to have great thoughts. He had hoped to draw conclusions about life and death. Perhaps he had even hoped to recapture the keening which had swept through him the few days after the funeral and been suppressed, as usual, in his doggily jocular manner. But all he felt was a kind of every-day tranquillity. Nothing grand or profound. Nothing to take back to his own world and re-illuminate his own life. Just a plain peacefulness.

From where he stood he could see the big War Memorial to World War One—covered with so many names, two of them his own. John had gone through that and received only a slight wound in the leg. The Memorial to World War Two—less impressive, with fewer names, but again, Tallentire inscribed on it—reminded him that he, too, had been through a war—and burst an eardrum. Spread about him were the graves of friends, strangers, known and unknown, but townsfolk all, once alive in the sprawl of brick and stone now glowing in the evening sunset, once walking along the streets among the sandstone buildings which sucked in this late light as if it had been sent only to furbish the façades of this town, once as warm as the sun's rays—now six feet under, decomposing, penned into a small space by a grey wall which was green with lichens. Joseph nipped the cigarette and put the butt end into his pocket, for tidiness.

Well, there it was. He gathered up his implements. "John Tallentire"—beneath that small, neat mound. Nearby, the first green ears of snowdrops could be seen among the grass. How did they know, so deep in the ground, that they could grow, that the sun would be waiting?

Joseph's eyes smarted as he stood for a last moment there. It was difficult to leave. The sky was now lurid with the dash of the sinking sun—as if flares of life were being sent out as reminders, displays of colour and wonder—proof of the sun's power, as if it too did not want to go. About the cemetery one or two other people walked away. There was the thud of a spade. Joseph's face felt cold. What could he say? He wanted to say something. Foolish, stupid, call it what he would to himself, he wanted to say something over his father's grave. Well then. He was near to tears now. "So long, old lad," he said.

It was over. The man was dead. Joseph turned away and walked quickly home.

PART TWO

I
Setting Out

(1)

He woke up in the middle of the night and, on a sudden impulse, dressed and came downstairs into the tiny cottage kitchen. It was still very dark outside and, despite the promise of early spring, cold. Douglas made himself a cup of Nescafé, chewed through a couple of apples, and then set out.

Walking soon had its usual effect. When he was agitated, it could soothe him; when he was depressed it could pick him up; when he felt that a decision had to be clarified or a course of action resolved upon, the steady rhythm would provide the best accompaniment he had yet discovered. As now, it earthed him.

Despite the lack of light, he was sure of his course. Down from the cottage and the fells to the village and then west along the main valley road to the plain by the woods.

It was wonderfully quiet. His mind seemed to crunch against the silence as surely as his feet pressed on the surface of the lane. It was as if he swam in the quietness, tumbled and swirled and floated in it. Yet, in London, the metropolitan din was a measure of its vitality and he liked to be in the middle of that equally. He would be spending even more time there now: he had signed over the cottage to Mary and John.

There had been no need for that, but he wanted to make the gesture. They had sold the place in London for a good sum and Mary had immediately moved into the nearby garden flat she had found. Douglas had helped her with the furniture, but she had wanted no help with the arranging of it. That was to be her business. Douglas, who had inevitably felt both awkward and a little noble at joining in so heartily with the removal, had soon discovered his awkwardness superfluous and his nobility unacknowledged. Mary was brisk to the point of rudeness and clearly glad to see the back of him once the heavy stuff had been heaved into the appropriate rooms. On reflection, he had been relieved at her command over herself.

He put the residue of the money into an account in her name. This made him feel good and released him from weekly payments, should he wish it—and Mary was quite prepared to meet him on that point—but he had made a deal with himself that he would pay her the amount of the relevant maintenance allowed each week. That would keep him plugged in. He needed it.

His own ugly, bare little bedsitter, with nothing of his own in it save a few clothes and the start of a new accumulation of paperbacks, gave him an irresponsible sense of liberation. To be such a metropolitan nomad was the life which had been waiting for him, he thought. And the first few weeks had been guiltily exhilarating.

It was a cell. Those monkish qualities in Douglas which had reinforced his impulse to be a writer felt a great relief in the two-barred electric fire, white walls, utility furniture, cheap crockery, gas stove, uneasy chairs (two). All that time he had wasted with other people when there was this solitude attending him, here, in the middle of the city. Alone, anonymous, working away at re-writing the story, setting up a freelance shop as a reviewer–broadcaster: still no more than tinkering with the Raven deal.

He began reading with an avidity he thought he had lost forever. He got up early, went for a run around a nearby bleak park and then put in four or five hours at the table which served admirably as a desk. The rest of the day was his. His only tie was to check with Mary, sometimes to meet John from school (they had soon, and with surprising accord, fallen into the "weekend dad" routine of most divorced/separated couples), otherwise to rove at will.

Douglas had never belonged to any group or clique and so he had never developed or cultivated that regular pattern of pubs/restaurants/parties which keep such gangs in touch. Once he had earned enough for Mary and himself, he could be whatever he wanted all over the town.

At first he had found it difficult to believe the licence he had given himself. He would be in a new pub east of the city, or in a strange club off Kensington High Street, or find himself at a party in Wandsworth and feel—on all occasions—that he was trespassing, that he had broken bounds, ought to be the other side of that particular part of life. Then he had begun to discover that if you were on your own and unburdened by ambition, then the world was indeed an oyster for your grit. He had taken the risk of self-ridicule and gone to various exhibitions, once again revisited the Wallace Collection, the John Soane's Museum, become an instant film-buff and, above all, dropped in on all those places—however unimportant, bars, cafés, acquaintances' flats—and all those people, he had not had time for before. It was as if he had come into the promised land, for he was living off his own wits, still supporting those he owed support to, and willing and able to range all about the place.

Those few weeks, like many comparatively short periods in any lifetime which collect disproportionate significance from their intensity, seemed now to Douglas like a great blessing. But the treat could not go on. He was too committed now, in his life, to feelings of responsibility for his parents, for Mary and for John, and to feelings of responsibility over what he himself should be able to attempt, in the society in which he found himself. He could not drop out or even fly out. He was in this society and if he could not find a role to have faith in, or a faith to have a role in, then he must take from the past what served and invent something for himself to see it all through.

He had his inherited responsibility as firmly strapped to his conscience as Christian's knapsack to his back. He would go back to Mary and John. He would tell Hilda all of this and leave her. He would settle himself firmly in work and provide for all to whom it was owed. But first he would spend a long morning in that wood to collect some final details of description which he thought his story lacked. The walk had resolved everything.

(2)

It was so cold underfoot and so miserable. He had not emphasized that enough. It had begun to drizzle quite heavily and his feet were sodden. It was not surprising that the man had not survived here. The truly surprising thing was how people in the past had managed. Pre-everything except fire—and that must have been tricky in this climate—how had Iron Age man hung on? Plenty of game, yes; plenty of meat, yes. Few people—few to bother about—yes. But the misery of the elements and the boredom—or were they fully stretched merely in surviving?—that made his mind dizzy.

Or it could have been lack of food. He had traipsed about the woods for about four hours now and he was tired. He was also depressed at his lack of knowledge: he had been able to name only half a dozen of the common types of tree and the undergrowth was "just ferns". Ignorance, it was true, could be a goad: though, generally, it merely goaded you to frustration. But he had taken stock. He would re-write those parts of the story which, he had thought on the last re-reading, needed strengthening. There were some useful points to be made. And the primary point—which he had never doubted—that someone could cut himself off entirely from the contemporary world in such a small wood—was well taken. He had neither met nor seen a soul.

He had not brought a compass but he had studied the map before he set off. He reckoned he should be near the Aspatria end of the woods and should reach that town if he kept walking in the general direction he had first taken.

It was cold. Here, at the very spot, he had been unable to feel any emotion at all about the man he had written about so concentratedly over the past three or four months. Often when he was writing, he would break off and think about that lonely figure, a figure whose invented life went further and further away from the few facts known to Douglas of the real life—but he would think about him and feel sorrow, pity and sadness. Yet here, in the place itself, he could evoke nothing. Nothing of the clumsy, stumbling young man returned to his childhood paradise; nothing of the thoughts he had thought for him or of him; he did not exist in the wood.

By the time he reached Aspatria he was ravenous and he made for the fish and chip shop. It was boarded up. Douglas had been hungry in the wood and hungry on the walk into the small town: now, faced with no prospect of the nostalgic feast he had promised himself, he felt starving.

He looked up and down the street. Midday. Empty. Two cars parked. Most shops closed. No traffic at present mobile. Aspatria, born as an ancient Saxon village, perhaps from a Roman fort, and fattened on coal mines, now unworked, seemed dead. Another observation: he was the only human being on the street: and it was a long street: cruel neighbours in Thurston and other small competitive towns would talk of Aspatria as a one-street town. Cars, regulation closing hours, fridges, women working and schools had swept the centre clean of people.

There had been a restaurant, he remembered, near the cinema. There was one crucial afternoon tea—spam fritters and chips, if he remembered correctly—which he had endured for the sake of unrequited love: or, more accurately, a few reluctant kisses and half-swivelled legs on the back row and, after that, a brisk goodnight. He walked up the street in search of it.

Aspatria had been his first adolescent adventure. These things were clearly marked out. As a boy you could go to socials, church dances, A.Y.P.A parties, Scouts and Guides Christmas Revels, all this and more was in your grasp, but on every occasion the event would be supervised and subtly or not so subtly dominated by Adults. At about twelve you were too old for that. Alas, you were still too young to go off to the village dances, which would not effectively start until the pubs closed, or to Carlisle, the great city, where packs of city boys roamed like starved wolves and girls of fathomless sophistication and experience turned up at every dance hall on a Saturday night. Long trousers and more cash, height and *savoir faire* than a twelve year old possessed were essential for that leap into the big time. Aspatria filled the gap. This for three reasons. Firstly, it was not Thurston and therefore away from home and therefore an adventure, with all the dangers that implied: for it was well known that Aspatria boyos would massacre any Thurston boyo on sight (eight miles might be the distance between the towns: each side claimed that whole epochs of culture divided them). Secondly, the picture house had a coffee bar attached to it. This, in the mid-Fifties, was so racy as to be considered indecent. Methodists hurried past it with their heads averted. School-teachers singled it out for moral disapproval in their R.I. lessons. Parents built texts on it, outlining the perils and degeneration which would come to you after that first terrible step of sniffing around the picture house café in Aspatria, drinking the wicked Espresso, ordering the loose milk shakes, playing the wicked Jukebox. For there was a Jukebox. The first in the district. Sat there like Queen Elizabeth the First. A whole generation was proud of it. A whole generation lined itself up behind the Jukebox, willing to be profligate with scarce sixpences, careless of complaint, defiant of the dreadful stories of the evil consequences which came from associating with Jukeboxes—the inner city crime in America, the racketeering in Soho, the White Slave Trade in North Africa, the Drug Trade in Hong Kong and Prostitution and Assault the world over—all seemed to be accompanied by the Jukebox, which brought out the sermons of the Salvationists and the scorn of the W.I., the Rotary Club, the Church Wardens and the condemnation of all Schoolteachers. It was irresistible. And, because of this, it made Aspatria picture house café the most attractive place for miles around. And, thirdly, there were the girls. Aspatria girls were different, Douglas had reckoned and he reckoned it still. The school he had gone to had drawn pupils from an area embracing three towns of roughly the same size: Silloth, a port and seaside town; his own, light industry and a market town; and Aspatria, still connected with coal, although the miners in the Fifties had to be bussed west to dig for it, rather than finding it in their own backyards. Maybe it was something of that kick of life which is found in most mining communities—or maybe it was just the difference itself—a slight but noticeably different accent, different jokes, a tougher line on misfortune, a nimble flirtatiousness—whatever it was, Aspatria girls were different and Douglas fell in love with about four of them between his twelfth and fourteenth year. There were one or two intermissions for Thurston girls, a village girl and even, anticipating the Big Time, a brief and uncomfortable liaison with a Carlisle girl (the Carlisle theme was to come later in its fullness) but Aspatria dominated that time of his life and the girls had dominated most of his thoughts.

The whole thing had happened on two levels. At school—furtive glances (generally unreturned); awkward notes (generally returned); alternate boasts and denials. Very unsatisfactory. Then came Saturday, and after the rugby in the morning, the work about the house and the rugby watched in the afternoon, would come the preparations before clambering aboard the five-twenty-five bus. Hair, rinsed with cold water, flicked over with Brylcreem, then knocked into shape with a secret and infallible mixture of vaseline and solid brilliantine, which made it obey orders like a Horse Guard on parade. The style would be as near to Elvis Presley as he could get away with, i.e. as his mother would allow. Then off in the bus, to the café, to the pictures, if lucky with a girl, then the wary mooch around the alien town, finally homing in on the fish and chip shop and the nine o'clock bus back. Or—if gold had been struck and the heavens opened—the nine-forty. Replete and, occasionally, rewarded.

It was on that bus and in that mood he would meet and talk to Alan, who would have pursued his own solitary and, Douglas even then suspected, quietly amused path amid the Saturday saturnalia of his hot-skinned contemporaries.

The restaurant had gone. Completely. There was a hole in the street: he could see down towards the new Rugby Club and over the fields into the open country, all of which so thinly cloaked coal.

He went into the nearest pub, hoping for the best—and found it. A clean, well heated place, hot sausages, freshly cut sandwiches, decent bitter, an unpushy landlord, a comfortable chair and a table to himself. There was even a paper he could borrow from the bar: the "Telegraph". He read it with an aggressive pleasure and enjoyed the half hour greatly. He had made a settlement, he thought, and come to a necessary compromise. The rest of his life would be devoted to the attempt to make the compromise work. He could not have all that he wanted, but he could avoid all that he feared and feared he deserved. Now that he had "come through" in some way, he felt yet again the stack of luck and privilege which bolstered him up on any reasonable comparison with most of the rest . . . but, be that as it may, he had his own garden to cultivate as best he could.

The prospect, now that he thought about it, exhilarated him. He went out to catch a bus.

(3)

"You won't know me," the man said confidently, relaxed, amused.

"Of course I do," and Douglas, who saw before him a man his own age, size and shape, now dressed in a black donkey jacket and rough cords stuffed into wellingtons, instantly flicked back more than twenty years to this same person in a school blazer, short trousers and crumpled grey socks, looking every bit as confident and amused, as they had sized each other up for a fight. Joe—! Joe —! His mind scattered and fled before that surname—damn! Damn! Joe—.

"It wasn't a bad fight," Joe said. Douglas grinned at the inevitable coincidence of memory.

"Who won?"

"They stopped it," Joe said, "but I would say you were well on the way to a hammering."

"Most likely." Then Douglas jibbed at the inverted patronizing quality in his acquiescence. "It wouldn't have been a hammering, though. I was never hammered. Usually, in fact, I won."

"You were fly, I'll give you that." Joe smiled. His look was steady and pleasant. "Still are, by the look of things. You've done well."

"Oh, I don't know. What are you up to?"

"I labour for my brother. He's set up as a builder. I was at the factory. Good money but—boredom. You won't know about that in your job. It's the killer. So I walked out and ended up carrying hods, mixing cement, a bit of a brickie, a bit of a joiner, slating a speciality. Half the money, but there's some satisfaction in it. Married?"

"Yes. You?"

"Yes. Kids?"

"One. You?"

"Three. Well, that's settled." Joe looked around the small bus station. "Were you waiting for somebody?"

"No. A bus."

"Where's the car?"

"I walked here."

"From that spot I've heard you have—up in the fells?"

"Yes."

"Must be nice and quiet for you there, eh, away from it all?"

"Yes."

"I'm going near enough there to deliver some sand. I was picking up the van. You could have a lift."

"Thanks. Thanks."

They walked in step along the pavement. Joe had been one of the cleverest boys in Douglas' form at school. Immediately after O Levels—Douglas remembered that Joe had taken and passed in nine subjects—he had left to work in a garage: then he had gone into Lancashire and they had lost touch. They had played rugby together at the school—Joe was first class, played for England Schoolboys, then he had turned professional for a local Rugby League side, suffered a bad fracture of his leg and been out of the game before he was out of his teens. There was still, though, that physical confidence, the balance, belonging to all fine sportsmen. Douglas had always been a little in awe of him. Joe was someone who could pick up a tennis racquet, never having tried the game before, put in a respectable performance within half an hour and an hour later be stretching his opponent quite consistently. Any ballgame. It was a gift, people said, and in every generation two or three boys in the district came up with this talent, which was always most admired by hard-working sloggers like Douglas, who loved the game and appreciated every success and failure of a player like Joe. They walked silently for a while.

"Still got as much to say for yourself, I see," Joe said, turning to grin at him.

"Still can't shut up, yes."

"I used to be a bit worried about talking to you," Joe went on. "We would ask you a question—about homework or something—and you'd go back a hundred years to start your answer."

"You didn't need to ask many questions."

"Oh, you could always beat me at that stuff. I couldn't get interested in it. You couldn't get enough."

"Do you see many of the others?"

"A few. Quite a few's stayed around here. Those that haven't tend to drift back—like you—I don't know whether it's for local colour or roots—neither, I expect. Just to see the families."

"That'll be it."

"Norman's out at Workington—he's in Customs and Excise: I still see him down at the Rugby Club on a Saturday. He's a selector now!"

"He was good."

"He could play a bit. John worked with me down at the factory—he's still down there. A lot of them are. That new part took on a lot of those you'll know—on the scientific side, in the labs and such—Dawson and Eric, Raymond—lads like that. I worked in the old bit." Joe stopped, quite suddenly, and turned to Douglas, almost aggressively. "Do you know what I did? For nigh on three years?"

He did a brief mime, as if in a charade. There was nothing to it. He bowed or bent deeply from the waist, pulled at something with his right hand, adjusted something, stepped back, looked at his handiwork and made a lifting gesture.

"That was it," he said. "Sum total." He paused. "It nearly drove me mad. We had to have a regular wage so I stuck it—we'd managed to get hold of a little terraced cottage in the town—you'll see it in a minute—but it was in a shocking condition and I needed time to do it up. That was what kept me going."

Douglas had nothing to say. They walked on.

"There's a lot of fellas going quietly mad, I think," Joe said, resuming his cheerfulness. "Looking at those machines, performing some task the Japanese give to robots. You can see it on their faces at work—and they're on the lookout for anything to get out of it. Half the strikes are just a way of getting variety into the work, I'm sure of that. Anything. That's where *you* score."

"Yes."

"Good luck to you. Here we are."

Behind Joe's house was a neat small builder's yard. The van was already loaded. They drove directly to Douglas' cottage, chatting fairly easily about the district and people in it. When they arrived there, Douglas politely invited Joe inside for a drink.

"Oh, I could make this place sing." Joe's enthusiasm was unfeigned and it released him from any guardedness he may have felt. "If you stripped the boarding off that ceiling you'd find cross-beams. I did a cottage similar to this recently. Early seventeenth century, isn't it? And you should get a decent door for there. Those windows were just shoved in: you should get them taken out and the original size of window put back. Could I have a look upstairs?"

He went through the house, alive to every detail of it. Douglas trailed behind him, a little put out, as if a good friend of his had instantly been won over and claimed by a total stranger.

"That damp needs seeing to," Joe pointed out as they came down the stairs. "Mind you, it won't fall down and if you keep heat on it won't get wet. But you should run a damp course through there." He finished his drink and smiled at Douglas. "I don't suppose you'd know how to do that, would you?"

"No. 'Fraid not."

"Nor make a door, strip a ceiling, put in a decent set of windows and that fireplace, throw a concrete casing around that bathroom and so on."

"Sorry. No good at it."

"You would be if you tried."

"I don't think so. It once took me three years of woodwork lessons to make a key-rack. A bit of wood with four nails in."

"There you go." He finished his drink. "I'll be on my way."

"Right. Thanks again for the lift."

"No trouble." He looked around once more. "If I could live in a spot like this—you've done well for yourself, Douglas, with this and the work you do in London."

"Been lucky."

"Luck's earned. So long."

He left, briskly, and Douglas was relieved and pleased to feel that he had encountered and begun to know again someone who might, in the long run, turn out to be a friend.

It reinforced his resolution to go back to Mary and start again: tried and traditional ways were the best way through his confusion.

2

Women Alone

(I)

Superficially, Mary was in very good shape. Better shape, some of her friends told her, than she had been during the last year or so with Douglas. They told her she looked smarter, slimmer, altogether better "got together". And it was true, although another opinion could have concluded that she was not slimmer but thinner and not smarter but newly anxious about the effect of her appearance on others. She rattled through her work with an extra degree of efficiency, as if determined to prove that she was improved by the loss of a husband—and her senior colleagues noticed this and were moved to compliment her on it. One or two extra-curricular jobs soon found their way onto her timetable. With John she made very great efforts and the boy appeared to benefit from the considerations and attentions. He was encouraged to bring home friends to stay at the weekend; he was taken to the pictures regularly and encouraged in all his schoolwork as never before. And again, it seemed that things were better, for the two of them got on well, things went smoothly, there was none of the exasperating, uncertain, ill-tempered, unsettling presence and absence of a husband/father to disturb and disrupt the steady machine of a day's organization. Night brought her up against herself and each day was half spent re-grouping and half spent fortifying herself against what was to come. She could employ all her waking moments—but full consciousness, like the day itself, went only so far. There was night: there was the sub-conscious. Then her organization fell away and she was naked, alone and frightened.

It was the fear which took her most by surprise. There was the solitude of the flesh, and after many years that took getting used to, but there was a certain relief in it too and a stubborn pride in holding out on one's own, an obstinate and to some extent a sustaining conviction in the proof that she could exist alone. To that extent, the day's activities and the next day's plans reassured her. It was this fear, this uncontrollable terror which lurched into her head instead of sleep, as if it had been waiting in some cave of her mind, growing hungry on the neglect of the day, growing even more powerful through the attempts to ignore or starve it, by means of organization; growing, growing in its inscrutable ambition, which seemed to be to drive her mad. For it seized on her like a physical being: something very like actual teeth seemed to grip her brain and chew and cramp it: spasms and sweat broke out, as if some real animal were in the room, prowling about the bed, giving off a powerful odour, ready to turn on her and savage her. And there seemed to be no way of coping with it. She would be forced to sit up, switch on the bedside light and reluctantly look at the alarm clock, to discover it was no more that twenty past two or ten to four. She would swallow another pill, read another chapter. Try again.

By day she had all the comfort in the world, for the world, as usual in those circumstances, had, perhaps wisely, fallen back on the ritual behaviour of a contemporary tolerant society. That is to say, all blame attached to the man: all sympathy was extended to the woman and child: all sniping went in the direction of the mistress. Even though Douglas had not left Mary for Hilda, the reaction strayed not one iota from that norm.

Douglas kept to his word about his comings and goings, far more scrupulously than he had ever done as a husband: he was polite when they met, he was concerned for her, never lost his temper, took an interest in what she was doing, financially did everything he could without fuss, demanded nothing, stuck to the rules she made, made it as easy as he could for her, was, in truth, a friend and comforter. But often, after he had been there for half an hour or so, she could have screamed. Or she could have begged him to scream. He was like the night: he tore at what was essential in her. And she behaved badly to him, tried to spike his docile overtures, unfix his careful plans, disrupt his new laid plots with John: she tried to get him out of her life.

The fear, she decided, came from two movements: the first

was a movement away from a marriage, a passion, a love, a friendship, a husband, a family life, which had consumed her for more than fifteen years. There was an undeniable retreat from this. Something inexorable had decided that this would no longer be the way she lived. Against that was the force of regret and, within the regret, no real notion at all of what a new life would be or would lead to. Therefore there was a double fear: that something was being lost which had been proven and precious, despite its drawbacks and flaws and inadequacies: and that something would have to be found which was as yet untested and unimaginable and therefore bereft of the power of habit or the strength of adventure. This brought her little comfort. The night plundered her resources.

Mike had been a great support and yet Mary felt that she had to turn him away, before there developed a complication which would further confuse and exhaust her.

He had behaved impeccably. Once a week, Mary would go out with him to a nearby restaurant for a late supper, while John was guarded by the late-teenage daughter of a neighbour. Over the meal, she would chat about her work or listen to Mike talking about his work: there would always follow a discussion of some aspect of Douglas' character or achievement. Mike would be unwaveringly appreciative of what the younger man had done. Mary would want some specific example, put carefully in context, of the weight and worth of a piece of work, a programme, some writing, an article. It was as if they were discussing a friend who had fallen away or run into serious trouble, not of his own making. The odd thing was that, between them, no blame was ever fixed on Douglas. At some point, Mary would abruptly switch away from the subject of Douglas and there would be the awkward conclusion to the evening. For the questions—why was he asking her out? And why did she accept?—would loom up between them, unspoken but surely demanding some answer soon.

As the weeks passed, Mary in some way realized that she was moving by instinct and that she had to trust it. Her zest for the day, which had inspired her to plan it like an eager military cadet and carry it through with corresponding enthusiasm, began to wane as more and more of her life was thrown into the internal struggle which seemed forever to be demanding more recruits, as if indeed a Great War were being fought within her between entrenched and embattled forces, which called deeper and deeper for powers to sustain a struggle whose only certain end was exhaustion. So the first period passed: the time of vim and renewal, the flush of new resolution, the crisp attack of fresh endeavour, all petered away and she was left with her resources stretched merely to cover the despair which now occupied not only the night, but rose to the surface of the day and threatened to break out in public, and disrupt and sear her waking life.

What she wanted above everything else was what she also feared—to be totally alone, without acquaintances or friends, or even John, somehow to creep into a state of emotional hibernation, curl up tight over the pain which bit and gnawed at her and perhaps nurse it through, help it pass. Luckily there was a school holiday near and she paced herself towards that as a man stranded in a desert might fix his mark on a distant oasis: and like him she knew that what she would arrive at might be no more than a mirage.

Quite suddenly, simple matters appeared totally impossible. Getting breakfast was, one morning, a profoundly weary task which was performed only by dredging up scarce resources of will-power; it was as if she had been struck by an instantly disabling virus and indeed Mary did think, throughout the day, that she had "caught something". That phrase found an immediate response with her colleagues, who insisted she go home after lunch and see the doctor, who diagnosed depression.

The word itself clubbed her down. She had read about it, indeed much of the literature and drama of her contemporaries was steeped in it. It seemed to be the new Enemy, as much of a plague in its way as cancer, something that would not let go its grip of you once it had battened itself on your mind. She was given pills and advised to come again to the surgery in a fortnight if things got no better. She had a horror of these pills and yet she took them, forcing them down with large glasses of water, feeling that just by taking them she was putting herself on a road which could only draw her towards what she did not wish to be. For, as she took the pills, it was as if, she thought, she was saying farewell to independence of mind and of action, to that belief in her own capacity for living her life, her own strength of decision, her own initiative and control. Depression, Depression, Depression—the doctor's word tolled in her mind and intensified the pressures.

She had forced herself to go back to school the next day and she was glad of it, for the effort and perhaps the effect of the new pills enabled her to have the first deep sleep she had enjoyed for weeks. Yet that was the briefest of respites. Soon she was again in this claustrophobic pit of herself, battling faceless enemies who were wearing her down.

That week her meal with Mike had broken the pattern. For a while she had been monosyllabic, not rude but simply glad to be able to slump into the depths she felt without the fear of offending who she was with, or of setting off a sequence of despair which she would do anything to stave off when she was alone. Mike's strength protected her and let her be as she felt. It was after the meal was done and they had stayed an unaccustomedly long time in the place, so that it was almost empty and freer as a place in which to exchange confidences, that she began to cry. The tears were silent. At first she did not know they were there, simply felt them come down her cheeks. Mike reached out his hand. She took it. It was the first time there had been such a declaration and chaste, simple, modest as it was, Mary felt a surge of gratitude which led directly to danger. She had been talking about putting up some shelves in the kitchen when the tears had started, attempting at that stage to reclaim something from the evening for Mike, whose patience, she was sure, had been unfairly overloaded by her parched companionship. Now once again she took refuge in continuing the description of this mundane job, which had succeeded in reducing her to impotence: plaster on the floor, screws aslant, a fingernail broken and the intractable shelves still stacked against the wall, useless. Mike offered to come around on the Sunday afternoon when she was alone—John would be with Douglas—and put them up. She agreed.

He had not been to the flat. She had been fiercely protective of her new territory and even Douglas was not encouraged to stay for much longer than a decent minimum of time. She wanted to be with Douglas, she longed to be with him sometimes and would walk about the silent telephone like some animal smelling familiar prey, fighting off the ache to ring him up and quenching the pain which came from his failing to ring her up. But the flat, she had decided—and again this was a decision which came to her "ready made", from instinct rather than any reasoning, the flat had to be uninhabited by any man; it had to be free of everyone but John and herself. Without any explanation being offered or necessary, Mike had understood this and consequently the invitation was accepted with a full awareness of the possible implications.

The job was done quickly and well. He was a handyman who enjoyed such straightforward work and could turn his hand to anything, including, as Mary knew from the times she and Douglas had gone to his place for supper in the old days, cooking quite complicated meals.

It felt good to have a man in the house again. There was no doubt about that. Loneliness and liberation were not enough.

She made some tea and took it into the living room. One of the minor attractions of the place was that there was a small functional fireplace and, although it was late spring according to the calendar, there was enough coolness about the weather to make a coal fire a welcome sight.

Mike looked pleased with himself and more relaxed than he had done for ages. It would not be hard, she thought, to fall in love with him. His face was wise and strong: his manner was gentle but sure. He was everything she had hoped Douglas might become. And he too, she knew without his telling, could find her good. They sipped tea as if it were cognac, nursed it down, thoughtfully.

"That cupboard in the hall needs fixing," he said. "And the window above the sink needs attention. I tried to open it for some air. It sticks."

"I've noticed."

"They can be a nuisance unless you catch them early."

"Like everything else."

"Yes."

Mike hesitated, then he took two steps back.

"That is, I could fix them if you needed me to."

"I know."

The same intake of breath, the same dryness in the throat—she had not experienced this since Douglas had fallen for her and declared himself, all those years ago: and here it was again. She had been fancied and "propositioned" in those years—in the staff-room at school in the late afternoon, towards the end of the week, towards the end of term. But never had any overture struck home. Not once. Her fidelity had been absolute. Even the one or two pleasant friendships with men, which had sometimes been her lifeline to sanity during Douglas' bout of hurt rampaging, had been conducted with strictly platonic formality on all occasions. But now—for one reason or another—either her defences were unaware or her entire emotional life had changed or she was willing a course of revenge or merely seeking the sympathy which is sometimes essential in order to live—whatever it was, there was that stop in the flow, that pause, that uncanny recognition that a moment was here presented which could be grasped; which needed only a nod, the slightest nod, to let it through.

Before she could speak, Mary had to swallow in order to ease her throat.

"I think," she whispered, and could not speak more loudly, "I think it would be better if you did not come round again."

Mike let the implication strike into him and he repressed the surge of protest and argument and persuasion which sprang up inside him to defend his interest and win the prize he now realized was so much desired. It was at this instant that he knew how much he loved her, but also he saw before him a woman fighting for a life she could not yet see or imagine, yet determined to fight by herself. It would be possible, perhaps, to wear her down and force himself on her: it would even be possible to take her in hand and drive her to the course he wanted because, at a time such as this, a benevolent tyranny can seem a blessed release. But Mike appreciated the effort she was putting into her fight. He loved her, if that were possible, all the more because of that. And he could see how hard she was holding on, how easily she could yield, how important it was—in some mysterious way understood by neither of them—that she should not yet yield to him. At least he could give her that.

He finished his tea.

"I can mend that cupboard in ten minutes now," he said and went out to the hall.

Mary let her head slump forward, as if she were a marionette and a vital string had just been cut. Mike was a good man. Maybe she could love him.

She has had a very great shock, Mcke thought, as he unscrewed the cupboard doors. His picture of her now was complete. He saw her as brave, pure in heart, dogged, loyal, a fine ally for Douglas, willing to help him even to the point of sacrificing herself. But now the sacrifice had been made, she took the consequences hard. She took them seriously. Inside that room, literally a few feet away from him, was a woman he loved now, would always love and could cherish for the rest of his life: both of them, he knew, would be nourished by it. On all sides there would be healing. Yet because she had whispered "no", he would make no move.

(2)

They were in Hilda's flat. It was a comfortable place, Douglas thought, and he felt quite guiltlessly at home in it. Its very smallness and the earnestness of the mind which had assembled that, largely paperback, library, those often-played classical records, made him feel loving and protective to the person who had built it up. She had held to a measure of independence, a standard of intellectual satisfaction, and the cultivation of a mind which had been discarded by the school system in early adolescence. In its way, Douglas saw Hilda's achievement romantically, especially when he was in her flat, for she had made it so uncompromisingly hers. It suited him. It could have been designed by him—the emphasis on comfort and on neatness, on books and records, one or two small paintings, a few drawings and prints and, like tropical fish in an English pond, sudden splashes of gilt extravagance, small indicators of baroque impulses, capable of infinite inventiveness.

It was late. They had eaten at Hilda's place. Although Douglas had brought along a bottle of wine, he had taken no more than two glasses and Hilda had sipped at one. She had sensed something of his purpose even before his arrival and the abstemious formality of his behaviour had confirmed her suspicions. But the meal had passed cheerfully enough.

Cheerfulness, in fact, was the totally unanticipated obstacle. He had come to tell Hilda that he was going back to Mary and could not see her again. Yet no sooner had he crossed the threshold than he felt relaxed and comfortable. The meal had been chatty and agreeable, altogether neutralizing the atmosphere of drama which Douglas had carried about him all that day.

Finally, after they had washed up and he had made coffee, they sat down in front of the small electric fire which managed to make the place look cosy, and he had plunged in. It was then that her doggedness had shown itself.

"But if you say you love me," she repeated, "then I can't see what all the fuss is about. I could see it while you were with Mary and John; I understood that. It hurt me a lot but I could see that you were in a marriage and you felt a responsibility to it and you were frightened to get out of it because of what might happen. But you have got out of it. And according to you—and I've got nothing else to go by—things haven't fallen apart. According to you, when you go and take John out he seems happier than he used to. And Mary—you say—looks better and says that she feels better than she has done for years. So, although you might have been right to be frightened, they've both survived without you. They've even done well. And you say you love me." She paused and waited for confirmation.

"I do."

"So." She stared in front of her, eyebrows almost meeting as she plunged on, concentrating so hard that she was oblivious of Douglas' appreciative appraisal. He saw her long legs thrust forward, hips sunk in the seat, breasts firm and supple under a tight old sweater. He remembered the times they had slept together and knew how hard it was going to be. "Why don't you live with me?"

"I can't," he said, instantly.

"You won't."

He hesitated. But she was right. "I won't."

"Well then," she spoke slowly now, concentrating on her

line, "you seem to be forcing me to believe that you've been a hypocrite." He did not reply. She looked at him, openly: there was no use denying it. Now there was no urge to smile. Between them a sudden clarity appeared: as if, until that time, the air itself had been misty. "Well," she asked, quietly, with no accusation or irritation in her voice, "is that it? Were you lying all of that time?"

If he said "yes", it would be over. And he wanted it to be over. But he could not say "yes". To have done so would have been to have denied everything else he had said and done with Hilda. Yet this was a way. He had decided to leave Hilda and return to Mary: this, in a sense, was the easiest way—to admit or pretend that he had been a liar, a hypocrite, a fake, and at least then leave Hilda with the sustaining strength of anger, a grievance, something to help her push herself into a world without him. If he really loved her, perhaps he ought to say "yes": then at least it would be a clean and final cut, it would give her a chance. But the word stuck in his gullet.

"You see," Hilda said, softly, tenderly, "you can't lie, can you? We can't lie to each other, can we? You want to say 'yes' because it would make it easier for both of us at this present moment—but when it comes down to it—you can't do it, can you?"

Again he did not answer.

"So," she went on, deliberately, "we should live together. Either you move in here or I can move in with you or, better still, we find a new place where John can come and stay for a weekend."

He had to speak.

"That is, if you love me," she said.

"It isn't as easy as that."

"I know it isn't. I've understood that for several years. I've told *you* that, when you wanted to leave Mary and John. But now you have left them. What else can I do but want what I've always wanted. Somewhere to live with you: and a family—an ordinary family, just a family that sits around a fire and listens to the radio or the gramophone on winter evenings and plays cards and plans summer holidays and takes the bus to the Tower of London on Saturdays. That's what I want. And that's what you want, I think. Not this floating about the world, thinking you've got all the opportunities going—which you haven't; or thinking that you're well off—when in fact you're broke and rapidly approaching the age where you cease to be employable. You want an ordinary decent life, with a job that seems worthwhile and a family you can rely on, and then, if you have anything to write—it'll find a way out, but whether it does or not doesn't really matter as much as you and me being together. That's what I thought it was all about."

"I had all that with Mary," Douglas said, "in fairness. The family, the job. All that."

"Because you *wanted* it. That's my point. The fact that it didn't work with her doesn't mean that it isn't what you want. You came to me, most likely, because it *is* what you want. I've got nothing else to give you. Except that I know that it *would* work and we *would* be happy. I'm sure of that."

"How can you be?"

"Because I love you and I know you love me and because I know that we want the same things, really. It's like you said, we seem to think alike, we react in the same way, we have the same sort of—oh, embarrassment when people show off or act insensitively. You know all that. I don't need to tell you."

"Everything's so clear-cut to you."

"Because it *is* clear-cut, that's why."

Douglas laughed aloud and Hilda, released by the laughter, relaxed and joined in.

"But I *have* to go back to Mary," he said, abruptly. It was as if the laugh had cleared his mind.

"Only if you want to. You've left her now. She'll never be able to forget that. If you go back it'll just be to part again."

"Not necessarily."

"Why did you leave her, then? You've made every excuse not to for years, although it's been perfectly clear that neither of you were getting anything out of it. And now you've finally found the courage to do it you want to run back?"

"I'm not sure it *was* courage that made me leave her."

"Yes it was. Everything about you, the place you've come from, all your ideas about loyalty, all the worry about not hurting people—all that meant that you were *made* to be the sort of husband who puts up with what he's got to preserve the peace or because he thinks it's the best he'll ever get."

"Perhaps it is."

"Only if you want it to be. You can stay where you are—lots of people do that and they say it's for the sake of the children or for their career or whatever excuse it is. My parents did that and as a consequence we were all nearly driven as crazy as they drove each other. No. You can change your life if you want to. You have changed it. That's why I haven't pressed you until now. I knew what a big thing it was for you. I knew what an effort it was. But now you have to think about us."

"I think I should go back to Mary. There we are. That's what I think." He looked at her and then looked away. Finally.

In the silence Douglas felt as if Hilda suddenly fled from him—from having been close, intimate, a part of him. Suddenly she was gone, running, wanting to put as much distance between them as possible. After a long pause, she said, weakly and bravely, "You'd better go then. No. Don't say anything at all. Just go now. If you have to, you have to."

It was as if he were moving in slow motion through a heavy atmosphere. He both acted and saw himself act: saw himself get up and reach for his jacket, put it on, find his book, scan the room, seek out Hilda's eyes—unsuccessfully—hesitate while looking at the utterly dejected figure beside the electric fire, all so slowly, so portentously.

"Goodbye then," he said.

He waited for a reply but she made no sound nor any move until he was gone and she had heard his footsteps die away. Then, weary and in pain, she got up and went over to the bed. There was such a pain in her side and such pressure about her heart. She lay on the bed, her knees drawn up to her chin, trying to ease the pain.

Douglas had rejected her. She had thought, at first, that he had needed no more than some stern confirmation of what they would do. So she had rehearsed again the arguments which had become stale and unnecessary. It was only when he had said "there we are" . . . and looked at her and then looked away, that she had realized the truth of the matter. He would *not* live with her. She could not understand it. She loved him.

And he loved her, he knew that now: as he walked slowly through London he was in no doubt that Hilda was a woman he loved. But there was a force which prevented him from following that through. Perhaps for the wrong reasons and certainly belatedly there was, he felt, a right thing to do and he would do it. She had been so gallant there at the end, he thought, making no appeal, using no blackmail of tone or phrase, simply letting him be free. She had plumbed his need and made it easy for him. She had known what he wanted. She knew him better than anyone he had met. He walked very slowly, pausing now and then.

Hilda was cold, but did not want to move for fear she would break up. She had wept but even that had brought no relief. Love could kill. Men were cruel. Life was meaningless. She, for reasons beyond her, was destined to live it alone. What was she going to do? What would her life be now, without him, what was there to live for?

The city was so empty. In how many houses were couples going through the same doubts and partings and self-imparted distress? *What* was it, this conflict? What did it serve, that to achieve one right you denied another? There must be a better way, he thought.

Hilda began to shiver, a little at first and then violently. She made no attempt to stop it.

(3)

At first she had been nervous of being in the church on her own. Even though she had attended it as a child, gone to Sunday School in the front pews, passed through the period of teenage piety in the back pews of the south aisle, been married there and attended other marriages and funerals there; even though Douglas had been baptized there and she had gone to see him confirmed, to hear him read the lesson in the service of the Nine Carols, to hear him sing—the church had a place in her life like a remote friend encountered and re-encountered along the way—yet at first she had felt nervous of being in the place alone. She had taken on the job of cleaning it. For this she was paid three pounds a week. The money, said the vicar, was the best he could manage and was not important: Betty agreed. She had had enough of the lunch-times in the pub.

She had got the job accidentally. Mrs Anderson—or rather Jennie Beattie, as she had been at school—had taken care of the church for years. She was one of a large family of strong church people who had managed, unruffled, to remain strong church people through all the ebbs and upheavals of the third quarter of the twentieth century. Jennie had been at school with Betty, in the same class: and although they had never been particularly friendly, they had always been pleasant to each other. They had seen each other two or three times a week around the town, nodded, perhaps exchanged a bit of gossip about family or moaned about the weather and through that apparently slight contact a friendship had been built up, the strength of which surprised Betty: for when she heard that Jennie had been taken to hospital with suspected cancer, she felt miserable and went to see her as soon as visitors were permitted to go.

Betty was shocked to see her. Jennie had always been so calm and steady. Now she cried self-pityingly: she blamed her husband for not noticing earlier that she was ill; she blamed the work she had had to do; she complained that her children had visited her only once and were not as upset as she had expected. She spoke darkly about "not expecting it to turn out like this after the life she had led". Betty listened and nodded and was moved by the woman's distress and, when Jennie began to worry about the state of the church, Betty saw and seized the opportunity to be useful. She would clean it, she said, until Jennie was better. She would stand in for her. That was one thing Jennie need not worry about.

A few weeks after that decision had been taken and implemented, Jennie died. The funeral packed out the church. Everyone had a good word for her.

Betty was asked to continue in the job and she agreed, despite Joseph's angry objections to the large amount of work in "that cold old barn of a spot"—his concern for her health was genuine and she was touched by it, although his growing preoccupation with ailments and illnesses rather depressed her. Nor was he satisfied with the three pounds a week, but he did not make an issue of that, believing, like Betty, that, in certain circumstances, money was of no importance. Indeed he muttered that "she might as well do it for nothing and let them give it to charity" and Betty considered that, but rejected it as being too grand a gesture.

The nervousness passed as she became used to the echoes in the place and the size of it. She became used to being alone in such an unaccustomedly large area, while doing something hitherto firmly associated with extremely small areas—dusting, polishing, hoovering, cleaning. She had always enjoyed seeing places well cared for, whether it was the council house of a friend or one of the stately homes of England she had gone to on an outing. She loved things to be right for their place and in the right place and cared for, and she did not object at all to the work involved in caring for them. There was something about the complicated arrangements of objects in a room which satisfied her profoundly. Having had to struggle to create a feeling of family and having, as she now thought, failed, she still longed for domestic contentment and found that rooms themselves, certain rooms, indicated that in a way in which nothing else did. The choice of chairs, of colours, of tables, curtains, carpeting, wallpaper, photographs or paintings—the arrangement itself gave her a feeling of contentment. And very soon she began to experience and be nourished by a similar contentment in cleaning the church.

She admitted it to no one, but she began to enjoy those solitary hours in the church. It was a pleasant place, a Victorian reproduction of a Georgian church, a light and airy church with a grand organ, a gallery, a finely decorated ceiling, but—once she had got used to it—still small enough to feel cosy in. The work there seemed to steady her considerably. She slept better. She felt calmer. There was balm for that emptiness which had threatened to grow and pull her down. There was so much there.

The altar still filled her with awe. Mentally she tip-toed to it, her duster careful to disturb nothing. Passing in front of the cross confused her. As a child she had been told that whenever you were directly in front of the cross you should bow to it. The cross represented the Holy Trinity, God the Father, God the Son and God the Holy Ghost, and all earthly forces should bow down before them. This imposition had been sternly laid on her generation and now she found that it had been branded into her mind. There was no help for it. Whenever she passed by the cross, though the church was empty and she was there to clean even the cross itself, she paused and executed some sort of a bow. Yet, oddly, having tugged the cross forward and started to clean it, she just cleaned away and polished it almost like any other thing. Once back, however, in its true position in the middle of the altar under the large east window—much of which, alas, had been blocked out by an idealistic vicar in the early Fifties, who preferred the effect of a walled-up window to what had once intrigued and delighted Betty, Victorian stained-glass scenes of Christ with little children—once the cross had resumed its place, it reassumed its authority and she would bow again.

Mostly she would organize herself so that she did not have to be directly in front of it.

The church became a familiar place, the pulpit, the vestry, the font, the Lady Chapel, the choir stalls, each window with its broad sill and its stained-glass Bible-story became places, individual, particular, and all of them places in which Betty felt a different sort of emotion. For working here, doing the steady, easy cleaning, unhurried, at her own pace, released her comfortably into thoughts and speculations which nourished her. She would come out of the church feeling strengthened and consoled. Whereas when she came out of a church service she generally felt tense and a little agitated.

It had been a problem of some delicacy—whether or not to attend a service. Neither she nor Joseph had been regular church-goers since their teens. Nowadays it was the Carol Service, Easter Sunday and perhaps the Harvest Festival, to see the decorations. Betty did not fancy what would have seemed to her a rather complaisant plunge into instant piety.

On the other hand, it would have been talked about had she not gone to church and Betty would do almost anything to avoid being the subject of the slightest gossip. Cleaning the church meant that one belonged to it.

Eventually she decided to go to the Sunday morning service—what used to be called Sunday Matins, before the arrival of all that Series I and Series II business and the up-to-date Bible which never rang in her mind except to remind her that something essential was missing. No matter. The important thing was to go on the Sunday and so she did.

Curiously, bonuses followed from that decision. It gave a stem to her Sunday. She would prepare the vegetables and put on the roast before she left and come back ready for the brisk final touches without that dragging feeling of just Hanging Around for The Sunday Dinner. Moreover, it gave Joseph the chance to sort himself out in peace and quiet, after what was usually a rather fuddling Saturday night. His sabbatical surliness had evaporated by the time she returned—and her piety put him at a further disadvantage. Sundays were to some extent relieved of what had imperceptibly become a deadening pressure of the boredom that so often characterizes dutiful intense cohabitation.

Joseph would even offer to get out the car and take them for a drive to the Lakes or the coast.

In a short time, Betty was a pillar of the Anglican community. The church itself, it was hinted—no disrespect whatsoever to Jennie—but the church itself had never been so clean. It gleamed. All that was supposed to glitter glittered, all that benefited from real polishing shone with real polish, the flowers were daintily and deftly arranged, the hymn books were neatly stacked, as were the hassocks. The carpets were flawless each Sunday and this was noticed and remarked on. The other stalwarts accepted her. Jimmie, who had served the church, boy and man, for about fifty years, as choirboy, server, and now verger, as Father Christmas, boilerman, odd-job man and constant help—Jimmie, who lived alone "and very comfortably thank you very much. *I* take no harm, I'm telling you" and who was completely absorbed in the detail, history, society and daily life of the church, on which subject he was a humble but quite remorseless authority—Jimmie took his time about it, was not afraid to run a finger over a pew back in search of dust, scrutinized Betty (who had known him and liked him all her life, joked with him, and was largely unaware of how threatening her thoroughness could seem to his christianlike possessiveness) and finally capitulated. The Sunday School teacher had always liked Betty and that was no problem and the choirmaster and organist appreciated the sparkle on the organ's woodwork. Fairly soon, then, people she had known slightly for most of her life became much more important to her and she found a community there, a centre for her life outside the bungalow. And she realized this and vowed to herself to hold onto it for as long as she possibly could.

(4)

It got better and better. As the pregnancy went on, Emma felt stronger by the day. She could never remember feeling so buoyant, so fit, so clearly in tune with herself. Emma's body had, for most of her life, been a husk she was always ready to be ashamed of. From childhood she had absorbed the notion —rarely made explicit but, indisputably, there—that fatness was not only unattractive and unhealthy, it was also rather common. Vulgar people were fat. Landladies on Donald McGill seaside postcards; wives of the labourers in the village; women who trudged around the shops on Saturday morning in the nearby town—Emma's parents had unknowingly passed on a hearty but effective snobbery. For fatness—so went the implication—was to do with ignorance and self-indulgence, the two conditions—or vices—which the then confident middle classes of England attributed to the working classes more in pity than anger. Of course there was the occasional middle-class fat woman who was again either (gently) ridiculed or firmly pronounced "stout", "well made", "a good figure of a woman" *or* "jolly" *or*—finally—"troubled with her glands".

But such certainties were past—or they had gone underground temporarily, it was impossible to tell—as the working classes took on middle-class habits and proletarian militancy. Such fairly innocent snobbery withered away and that, too, benefited Emma, whose life had been made near-hellish at times because society had decided, in one of its tyrannical decrees, that it was comical and unfashionable to be fat. Dresses were not made for her, nor were clothes shops places of pleasure but little penal settlements to which she banished herself from time to time to endure the punishment of trying on what would not fit and hearing the sympathetic or politely mocking (it made no odds which) voice of the salesgirl, trying to pretend that she did not bulge out of the dress like a big parcel tied up with too little string. And Fat meant short of breath and rotten at games and excluded from the gang that took the risks and had the most fun. And Fat meant being left out when friends clicked with boys and finding excuses to save them embarrassment over the inevitable neglect: and Fat meant resigning yourself to lesser satisfactions, lesser goals, lesser expectations, lesser possibilities, even though the needs and desires and ambitions roared away inside you as fiercely as in anyone else. Sometimes there would be a fat girl who would manage to funnel this force into action and she would breeze across Emma's line of vision—only to make her feel more isolated and threaten her with being in the worst condition of all—sorry for herself: because then there would be undeniable evidence that the remedy was at hand if the will and purpose were discovered. Emma's will and purpose disappeared down a series of abortive diets, abrupt spasms of exercise and plain starvation, all of which always ended in hopeless bags of chocolates. There was no way out for her, it seemed: she had to live under this strange but powerful social curse which declared that fat women must suffer.

Then Lester turned up and banged into her without a single word about her fatness. And wanted to have her—she could tell without question, for it was unlike anything that had happened before. No kindness in it, no feeling of third best, no averted eyes and comments, no friendly reassurance and patronizing compliments—just the urgent act performed with various degrees of brisk brutality. She loved him for that.

Now the child was about to be born, and—as it were—when she least needed it, the fatness melted away. She looked like a slim young woman who was normally and even gracefully pregnant. The grace came from this unaccountable sensation of being tremendously lucky. She was lonely, she wanted Lester to be near her, she had to work quite hard to live equably with her parents, whose intentions were never less than good but, inevitably, from time to time, chafing. All this, however, faded away at the prospect of having her own baby. Her own child. She would bring the child into life, she would love the child, there would be someone lovingly bound to her and dependent on her and, despite her educated awareness of the travails and distress of unmarried motherhood, Emma wanted to clap her hands with pleasure at her own good fortune. It would be the finest thing she had done or could possibly ever do, she thought, and she was lucky to have it.

The days passed pleasantly in the vicarage. She helped her mother in the garden and, when she grew tired, she came in and read. She did not travel far from the house—there was no one she particularly wanted to see, save Lester. She wrote him many letters and posted only one or two of her briefer, breezier ones. As the time came near, though, a matter of days now, she thought that she should give him the chance to be at the birth. She had read in the paper that Douglas was going to do a film with Merlin Raven for the B.B.C. and she sent the letter to Douglas with a note asking him to forward it urgently.

Dear Lester,

I thought I'd write and tell you how things were going. Well, in a word. I'm well and, according to the ancient doctor who examines me as if I were a specimen on a slab, the about-to-be-born-baby is well, too. So you needn't worry. And don't think that this letter is blackmail or a nagging word. It isn't. Everything has been done that could be done and I have been very well looked after. No complaints! I *would* like you to be here, though. Naturally. I know that you have a lot to do but if you could make it or if you want to know where it's all happening (!) I'll be in the Maternity Ward, Ipswich General Hospital, Ipswich. From about Saturday next (the 14th), the doctor seems to think. Or you could write here of course—parents will always forward.

So. What are you up to? I read your stars regularly in all the magazines I can lay my hands on and you seem to be due for "success, excitement and unexpected rewards". I believe everything they say! Mine are quite good too.

I think about that place in Kentish Town quite a lot. I wish I'd been able to see you before I left. I know it wasn't your style but it might have been (temporarily) useful to you to have taken it over for a few months. It was very cheap and I would have liked the idea that you were there. The landlady was a bit of a grump, though.

Everything's fine here. My parents have been ace and, of course, would be delighted to meet you. They're a bit stiff and poshish, but I think that you'd like them well enough. I've told them that the baby was my fault or rather, my—what I wanted—which is correct, in a way, even though I didn't plan the accident! And that you have a busy life and there's no reason *at all* why you should be involved at all unless *you want to be*. So you are totally free. (As if you didn't know! You're the freest man I've ever met!)

And they understand all this because it makes sense and, most of all, because I'm in such good spirits. I have my downs, of course—who doesn't? And I *would* like to see you—but I'm not going to whine. What keeps me going—in fact what keeps me happy—is the thought of your baby inside me and me ready to look after it. I'm *sure* you think that's horribly sentimental and sloppy. Well—people tend to *get* horribly sentimental just before childbirth, I'm told.

There's lots I could write but I guess you hate long letters. Probably haven't even read as far as this.

I think about you a lot and love you very much. Good luck, God bless.

Love, Emma. XX

(5)

Mary had already put off two meetings with Douglas. He had phoned her the evening after his last encounter with Hilda, asking if he could come round, but she had pleaded exhaustion, which was true. They had made a date for the following night but she had asked him to confirm it and, when he rang, she again put him off. She sensed that something significant, something demanding was being prepared and she wanted to be ready for it.

She had the clear knowledge that she must tread very carefully. She had never thought that her head and her feelings could be so jangled, so liable to a sensation of break up, so hair-triggered and full of fear. Beset with a kaleidoscope of unpredictable and often new and panic-provoking feelings, she was passing through storms of the mind which left her bewildered and worn out. There were times, for example, when she would be able to think of Douglas as nothing more or less than a monster. She would recount to herself the list of his suspected infidelities; she would go over the times he had come back drunk; she would even allow herself to think back on the death of their daughter and turn *that* against him. She swung from trivial objections to Douglas, to the most profound disgust for him, and from a feeling of utter dejection at his retreat from her to some elated glimmerings of freedom.

When he did come round, finally, she was as ready as she could make herself. The flat was spotlessly tidy. John was still up, in his pyjamas and dressing gown. Douglas had not been prepared for this but appeared to welcome it, genuinely, and they played draughts for a while. It was unusual for Douglas to devote so much time in the house to John. His normal methods of executing his duty to his son and (to be fair) enjoying the boy's company, were to take him out—to a match, a film, a museum or into the park for a kick-around. Mary, while pretending to read, watched Douglas cynically: so it took a break-up and, who knew?, possibly also a breakdown, for her simple picture of family life to come true!

After John had gone to bed, Mary made some coffee. She refused Douglas' offer to make it. She did not want him pottering about the place as if he naturally belonged there. It was increasingly important to her that this flat was hers and John's, and everyone else who came to it came as guests.

They sat a little awkwardly, sipping the "real" coffee. Douglas with a small scotch; Mary was not drinking. She wanted to be as calm and controlled as possible.

The silence built up. The flat was in a quiet crescent and there was no noise from traffic. The weather had begun to turn and, although there was a cool edge to the air, there was no need for a fire, Mary had thought. She was even more careful now about every item. But she wished she had not economized on this: the longer they sat, the colder she grew. And then she thought she understood the reason for Douglas' constricted silence. She flushed with fear, shame and embarrassment.

"You want a divorce," she said. "That's why it's so formal. Isn't it?"

"No. It isn't that at all."

"Yes it is. Don't lie, Douglas."

"Oh for God's sake, Mary. I'm not lying."

"I can always tell. All the times you used to come back and say you'd met one or other of your friends and gone back to their place for a drink after the pubs had closed—do you think I'm stupid? Of course I know when you're lying! You can't help lying. You're compulsive. Do you know what it's like being lied to? And knowing you're being lied to? And accepting it because *not* to accept it would cause disruptions? You become an accomplice. I became an accomplished accomplice! Without my help, your lies would have been shown up for the tacky little cheats they were, because the funny thing is—I used to think it was the redeeming thing—that you're a rotten liar. But, because I made it so easy for you to lie, you took advantage. You take advantage of everything. I've made it easy for you to split. Oh, you've been very good about money and when I read about other poor women or hear about them I am truly grateful for that, although it's still tight—but, apart from that, it *has* been easy for you. But I can't handle a divorce at the moment. It's humiliating, you know. However much sympathy I get—and most of our friends agree that you're a prize bastard: in fact I seem to spend half my time defending you to them. But I can't—I'm not strong enough for a divorce! Not yet!"

She stopped. Lit a cigarette. She was shaking.

During her outburst, Douglas had experienced distaste, apprehension, sympathy, shame, admiration at some of her insights, but, finally, hopelessness.

"I did not come here to ask for a divorce." Say it, he urged himself, say it! "In fact," Say it! "I came to say I thought we ought to get together again." He smiled ruefully. "And that's the truth," he added.

"Just like that?"

"Yes."

"Get together? Tonight?"

"You'd have to think about it, wouldn't you?" Douglas was perturbed by his adverse reaction towards the suggestion that he stay the night. He had not thought he would be given that option so soon. He had imagined that Mary's pride would enjoin her to hold him off for some days while she thought over his proposition. Now he discovered that he retreated from the idea.

Mary seized on his hesitation, acutely sensitive to the anxiety in his mood.

"You don't want to stay tonight, do you? Do you?"

"That isn't the point."

"That isn't an answer."

Douglas took a deep breath. No. He had to go on. Nothing else made sense.

"If you would stop ranting on and scoring debating points we might get somewhere," he said, roughly. "Ever since I've walked in you've behaved like a cross between a Christian martyr and a prison governor. Besides telling me what I think all the bloody time. Now calm down. We're not talking about jumping into bed. We're talking about a life and a marriage."

"Nice one, Douglas." She puffed nervously at her cigarette. Both of them were aware that she had winkled out his evasions.

"So where does that get us?" he asked.

"Where do you want to go?"

"Don't be smart."

"I'll be whatever I want."

"Sorry."

"That's another of your favourite tricks. 'Sorry.'"

"Meaning?"

"I don't have to spell it out."

"You've got me pretty well taped, Mary. You seem to have made good use of the time—I'm Shit Number One."

After a pause, Mary began to cry. Douglas, who had been sitting opposite her, went across and took her in his arms to comfort her. For a while they sat together like that.

"You see," she said, as if picking up from a point they had reached in another conversation on another day, "I want you to come back, of course I do. I miss you terribly. But, Douglas, something's happened since you left. I still don't know what it is. But so much has collapsed and changed inside me—I'm not putting it very well: I don't want to be dramatic—it's just that it feels like that. So much has changed. I feel that in a way I'm becoming a different person. And although it scares me—I can't go back. If you come to live with me, I'd go back to what I was. I don't want that. I want to change. I'd become so horribly dependent on you for everything. I know I had a job some of the time but outside that—and even that in a way—our life—*my* life—was *your* life. I feel it now. I feel as if something has been peeled off me—something as important as a skin has been peeled off me. And it scares me so much I don't know whether I can come through. I don't know whether I can even breathe the next breath, sometimes. It's indescribably awful. And I long for you to be here—but I know that I've got to be on my own. I've got to. It's a way of becoming—I don't know—myself, I suppose—how pathetic—growing up, maybe—but I want to do it. Your mother wrote, saying she would welcome John for the holidays. He's going there to stay—he'll like that. I'm going to stay with an old girlfriend—she has a cottage in Sussex. There's a little chalet affair I can have for myself. I want to be on my own, Douglas. If you want to help me, leave me alone. That's the best you can do now. Everything else is exhausted. Somehow it's all over. Now I have to start again."

(6)

Douglas read the letter immediately.

> My darling,
>
> I know that you would prefer it if we had no contact at all but I have to write to say one thing. It's very hard to say. You know that I love you. I still think and believe that you love me. But I have grown tired of the waiting and this final decision of yours has left me without any hope. You must have known that when you made it and when you told me.
>
> I feel you must know this. I don't respect you for what you have done. I don't think it's noble of you to return to

your wife and leave me. I don't admire you for it and I don't think you've done the right thing. From what you've said and from what I can put together I think that your marriage is over. Going back will only be putting off the eventual split up. But the reason I don't respect you isn't because I think you're mistaken—it's because you seem to me to have betrayed the most important thing you were supposed to stand for.

Please don't try to see me or contact me again in any way. *Please*. It is going to be very hard for me and I'll need a lot of work to survive. I *can't* take sympathy, talk, *anything at all* from you. *Please* leave me totally alone.

I love you.
Hilda

3
A Portrait of Merlin Raven

(1)

"O.K. O.K. Understood." While Lester spoke into the telephone, he looked directly at Douglas across the mixing desk, as if he were on stage playing to an audience of one. His voice was unaccustomedly quiet, controlled and almost as business-like as he wanted it to sound. That was the new style for pop-managers: not only cool but professional, boardroom cool, and deep piled rich, international fixer confident. They had become copycats of high finance and the low profile big deal operators on the Market. Douglas refrained from smiling. "Understood," Lester kept saying, earnestly, every so often. And occasionally he would add, "No hassle" or, "You name it." He was being talked to by Merlin, who had the dictatorially eccentric habit of using the telephone precisely as if it were a person in his room; a person whom he treated rather badly. For he would put the phone down and get himself a cigarette, fix a drink, even wander off to another room—but his correspondent had to stay there, on guard, at the ready, unfazed. And the phone had not to be put down by anyone but Merlin. He had been known to keep the game up for an hour. Lester had cottoned on to this, fortunately, when he had been in Merlin's place and seen him in action receiving a call from the chief press man of the biggest recording company in the world. At one stage on that occasion, Merlin had gone for a shave. Lester had helpfully picked up the phone to explain this only to be met with a controlled, quiet, mid-Atlantic pinstripe voice saying "Understood. O.K. O.K. Understood."

The purpose of the present call was simple. Merlin was already eight and a half hours late for the first day's filming. Douglas had called the crew for one o'clock in order to set and light for a two thirty start. The crew had now been on overtime for four hours and costs were starting to soar. Douglas was working out how he would handle it when—if—Raven turned up. He was furious at being mucked about. The two thirty start had been guaranteed. Here they were in the enormous recording studio, lights rigged, microphones ready, camera positions marked out—and he had to absorb not only his own frustration but the frustration and visibly ebbing interest of two cameramen and their assistants, two sound recordists and their assistants, three lighting men, a P.A. and a researcher. They had all been on jobs involving Prime Ministers, Presidents, opera stars, ballet stars, scientists, high news-value names—and they were not very amused at being stood up by a guy whom half of them (at least) thought of as no more than the "best of that cruddy bunch of lucky little sods who can turn out the songs that get into the Top Twenty".

Douglas, who was directing the documentary as well as writing it, knew that it was important to retain the crew's interest, especially when you were dealing with individuals who could easily feel the weight of collective opinion and would inevitably react badly to the sort of disapproval now building up. So Douglas had to watch the crew carefully, staunching with a joke or a laconic rebuttal any serious sign of that snowballing discontent which could ruin the atmosphere while yet allowing, even encouraging, the sort of groaning and complaining which was therapeutic. The main thing was to keep Merlin Raven's reputation as intact as possible. This Douglas did, quite shamelessly, by two methods. Firstly by letting drop the amount of money which Raven had acquired for certain records—here he was helped by the studio's own sound crew, who had turned up to provide the technicians for an authentic studio mix. They had worked with Merlin in his great days and let drop statistics which commanded very considerable respect: a four million dollar advance for an L.P. which finally grossed nine million; a two million dollar yearly retainer from the record company with no strings attached; the full use of these studios at any time of the day or night—orchestras, other groups, whomsoever, to be displaced if necessary—discreetly, but definitely. When Merlin wanted to turn up and make a tape then the studio had to be available and so had his preferred crew. The cost of that impressed everyone, too.

Secondly, Douglas found ways to remind them how rare this occasion was: that there had been nothing on Raven for years: that there had never been a substantial interview: that he had promised them a New York concert at which they could film exclusive footage: that there was already massive American, German and Japanese interest, even before a foot had been shot: that they were, in short, on something very special which would be very big. And he had to disguise the fact that his own resentment was mounting by the minute. Who the hell did Merlin Raven think he was? (He was, of course, somebody who could keep an entire crew waiting for a week if he chose to.)

The fact that after ten o'clock the overtime began to climb into astral regions also helped, Douglas realized: and he used that too. On the other hand: he was fed up.

"Understood. O.K. O.K. No sweat. Understood," Lester said.

"Ask him when he's coming," Douglas said, very loudly. "We've had a hurried tea break and some lousy sandwiches for supper so as not to desert our post. I want to take the crew out for a bowl of spaghetti if they're going to work through the night. There's a place around the corner. Salvatore's. He can join us if he wants. We're breaking for an hour."

"Understood. O.K. O.K."

"Let's go!" Douglas bellowed, quite suddenly angry. "I'm famished."

Lester cupped his hand over the telephone.

"He might be coming along any minute," he said.

"We'll be at Salvatore's," Douglas repeated. "We'll keep a chair for him."

"Douglas. You're taking a risk, Douglas." Lester's veneer cracked. "What the hell am I supposed to say to him?"

"Salvatore's."

"You could have blown it."

"Nature calls. Food. Let's go."

He bundled the crew out and left Lester stranded with the recording crew, who looked enviously at the liberated television team.

"Understood," said Lester, making a great effort. "O.K. Er—Merlin—er—they've . . . they had to—union—the union says they have to break for an hour. No. The TV lot. Not *our* lot. Good? Oh yes. Understood. O.K. O.K."

Lester replaced the phone and smiled bleakly.

"He'll be here in two minutes," he announced. "He wants to start mixing right away. While they're not here."

"Understood," the mixer said. "O.K.?" To the others.

"O.K.," they chorused: and laughed at Lester's disconsolate expression.

"You'll get used to it, Lester."

"Don't worry, kid. Understood?"

"Understood."

Lester grinned back at them all, swore a little and went down to the machines for a coffee. He found their taunting hard to take but he had to put a bold face on it. They had discerned that his connection with Merlin was a whimsical one. They themselves, engineers, musicians, an accountant, a P.R. man, knew their worth, could always find work elsewhere in the pop business, especially after working for Merlin in this new emergent phase which was already causing a big stir in the music game and the industry. They were secure in a way which had always eluded Lester.

Yet, ironically, it was his personality which had been the catalyst to all the present activity. For Merlin had "taken to" Lester and, since that first night, he had begun to write those seemingly simple songs which were hummed by millions and treasured by minorities and worth a fortune. Some combination of the time and the man had proved perfect. Merlin had snapped out of the long tunnel of self-indulgence, self-doubt, self-absorption—and Lester was the man who had given him the final heave out of the hole. With a fine sense of judgement, though, Merlin sensed that Lester's value would be limited—and so although he was unashamedly piratical and open in looting Lester's affections—professing friendship, throwing his arms around him, hugging him, taking him out for meals, asking him (particularly) to talk about the past, his adventures, the countryside—yet he made it clear to others that Lester was not really essential. With regard to pay, for example: Lester now worked full-time for Merlin and, although the job would have been hard to describe at a Labour Exchange, it demanded all of such talents and energy as he had, and the hours were elastic to breaking point. For this, he was handed fifty pounds a week, in crisp fivers, by the haughty pretty-boy accountant who managed Merlin's money. No insurance was paid, of course, nor were there any conditions of employment—no cover at all. But fifty lousy pounds! Lester only survived because Merlin let him sleep in a bedroom in his flat—some nights.

Lester held on for two binding reasons: there was no better alternative available and he still believed that somehow he would manipulate this connection to his own unbounded glory and advantage. He would not let go this time. Already he thought he could see that his reputation was being restored around the place. A nod here, a wink there, and now and then the big hello from fellows wouldn't give him the time of day a couple of months back. Oh yes. Raven was power, no question. But how to turn it, that was the problem: how to make the first killing, do the big one, get on the trail to where it mattered.

He saw the chance in this film of Douglas', even though the idea of working with Douglas was a pain. Difficult as it was for him to admit to himself, he had been surprised and impressed by his cousin's ability. At times, indeed, he was in danger of being as overawed by Douglas as he was by Merlin. Douglas' grasp of the entire operation—the ideas in it, the structure, the final shape, the cost, the details of shooting and editing, the laws of copyright, the rights of the different unions, impressed him: most of all, though, it was the fact that Douglas was in charge which surprised him. He had always thought of Douglas as physically a bit tentative, something of a mother's boy, uncommunicative about what he did, secretive even, not to be taken for a man—and yet there he was totally dominating the lot of them. And still with the same (to Lester) unconvincing manner: that was the peculiar thing. No shouting or ordering or bulling or bullying: an occasional rapped out decision, true, but very occasional.

Yet the camera crew respected him and listened to him. The crew in the studio had soon been in much the same relationship. Merlin, who had met Douglas for a long lunch in order to clinch the deal (contracts for which were not yet signed, though a sufficient measure of agreement had been reached to enable the B.B.C. to go ahead), had declared himself "quite impressed". Yet Lester kept remembering Douglas, hesitant with his father, self-deprecating before Harry, hang-dog about his wife, grubbing about for gossip on Thurston from himself, altogether a pushover. This image persisted in Lester's mind, despite the evidence before his eyes, and he was banking on its essential truth; for, in the end, Douglas had only agreed to make the film because Lester had virtually blackmailed him into it—using as his threat the truth: that if he, Lester, did not get a job out of this, then he was finished for good. Merlin was his lifeline. And Lester knew that Douglas had been shifted, finally, by this appeal to family solidarity: the man Wainwright had confirmed it, telling Lester that without his persuasion there would have been no project, which was why Lester made an extra twenty-five pounds a week from the B.B.C. as a "consultant". Douglas had insisted that Lester get a screen credit to that effect. So Lester's reasoning was that having moved Douglas once and shifted him into something which served his own purpose, he could do it again. He had a plan.

When Douglas and the crew finally came back it was almost midnight. They had been gone for an hour and a half. They came into the control box, a noisy crew, well-fed and watered, ready to quit or bust a gut for a couple of hours to get the material.

They had ignored the red light. Merlin was recording. They quietened down.

The desk which organized the music coming up from the studio was like something out of the space programme in Houston. There were literally scores of levers, switches, buttons, lights, plugs and keys ready to mix a multitude of tracks. Even the simple songs being recorded by Merlin now were being laid out on sixteen tracks. At the moment (although his group—a couple of guitarists, a keyboard player and a drummer—were in the studio to help him) all that was being taken was his voice.

Like everyone else, Douglas was soon charmed by that voice. It was charm which was at the centre of Merlin's attraction, he thought. Charm in the older, most profound sense, of spell-binding, disarming, the siren voice, the pipes of the Pied Piper, the soothing lute, all the charm of psalms and simple songs read about in epic histories. Merlin had that for this age. He caught it in those clever, stylish, often *faux-naïf* metropolitan tales, one of which now wound about the studio like an ancient traditional air, though it had been written only a couple of days before. He was good, Douglas thought. Bloody good.

The take ended. There was a pause. The mixer pressed down the talk-back button which allowed him to speak directly to the studio.

"That was fine by me," he said. "Fine."

Merlin's voice came back out of the studio cave, rather irritable, even carping, the tone of a man engrossed in attempting to perfect something and unable, in the final stages, to find anyone to help him in that last assessment before the thing was done.

"I thought the first eight bars were a bit too soft." He thunked the strings of the acoustic guitar he used and did a witty parody of himself. "Too much like that. Needs to be harder. What do you think?"

"We could do it again."

"We've done it twenty-seven times! Is this a record, I ask myself? Did anybody else hear it? Is anybody up there receiving me?" He paused. "Was that Douglas and his mob who came in? What did they think?"

"They came in half way through."

"I thought no bugger was supposed to be allowed in half way through."

"They just came in."

"What's the use of having a red light?" Merlin hesitated. "Let's hear it back," he said, sharply.

Douglas went across to the sound engineer.

"Could I use the talk-back?" he asked.

The engineer was a little anxious after his joust with Merlin.

"He wants to hear it back," he said and pressed the button which whirled back the tape.

"This won't take a minute," Douglas said and leaned forward to press the button. "Merlin, this is Douglas—hello." It was faintly ridiculous talking into the spindly little microphone which jutted out of the control panel like a loose end. Below them, in the studio which could easily house a full classical orchestra, four youngish guys in jeans—the waiting band—swigged beer out of cans and lit up while the fifth, Merlin, entered into that long and involved system of his own, that dicing and playing ritual which was never a routine but necessary, almost as if he put himself in a trance, listening for any hint or sign which would switch him in a happier direction and give his work that final, "distinguishing" charge.

That was why he demanded to work with the same engineers, even if they had to be flown over from L.A. That was why he had used the same studio for every one of his major records. That was why a hundred and one small acts of superstition and professionalism had built up into a pattern of work which only he was allowed to be fully aware of. Merlin could always find a tune and construct a song and find words and they would work. To improve, though, to make tune, accompaniment, lyrics and performance better, needed a mixture of persistence—which he had—and this acute sense of being in the perfect mood for that particular song so that it sounded just "right". So that it could never again be done as well. It was as if he were in part a satellite returning from orbit, nudging for the absolutely correct point of re-entry. And, until he got that feeling, he was willing to keep looking for it, whatever the cost to anyone else.

"Hello, Douglas," Merlin said, with just the lightest touch of jokiness—the touch that put him above Douglas in the authority stakes in the power game they were playing. "Have a good nosh at Salvatore's?"

"Pretty good."

"It's a nice place for spaghetti. If you like spaghetti. Did you have spaghetti?"

"Merlin. It's late. We've been here about twelve hours now. The crew's tired. Some of them have a long way to travel and families waiting and so on. We've already screwed up tomorrow morning's shooting because we're so late we've run into the ten hour rule. So the question is this. We can stay and film now. For, say, two hours. Or we can go and do it again some other time. Up to you."

The words, Douglas calculated, were reasonable. So were the statements. The tone was not. Despite his admiration for

Merlin and despite his awareness that to walk off the story tonight would be to walk off it altogether, Douglas could not exclude his own annoyance at being buggered about that bit too much. Lester glared at him for presuming to call the shots.

"We're in the middle of a song," the engineer said, warningly.

Merlin took his time about replying.

"Tell you what. I'll listen to it back. Do it once more. Then we can film. How about that?"

Douglas hesitated. He knew that Merlin was quite capable of stringing them along in this manner for the rest of the night. He did not believe in his promises. He took counter-action. "I'll ask my crew." He turned to them and deliberately left the microphone open so that Merlin would "accidentally" overhear them. "Well?"

"I think we should call it a day," one of the cameramen said. He had been itching for home since seven p.m.

"I liked that song," his assistant announced. "I love that song. I think it's one of his best. I could sit and listen to it all night."

"Five minutes," said the sparks. "Give him five minutes. Then I go, I'm pissed off."

"O.K.," Douglas said and turned to the mike. "I think once you get into the record there'll be no stopping you. Fair enough. If you're going to stop you might as well stop now."

Merlin smiled. He would welcome the break. There had been two good hours and he wanted to clear his head before having a final session on the song. An interview with Douglas and larking about the studio doing a bit of filming would be just right.

"Lester!" Merlin shouted. "Go out and get us all some fish and chips, will ya? We're starving down here." Then, as an afterthought. "Right, Douglas: let's get going, man. 'The B.B.C. Int-er-view. Ho Ho!'"

(2)

"It's good," Mike said, taking care to make his words carry the weight he intended. He put the typescript of "Death Of A

Friend" back on his desk. They were in his office at the B.B.C. "It might be very good."

"It's too short." Douglas felt a little like a pupil receiving comments on an essay. But he had wanted Mike to read it. "For the publishers. '35,000 words are hopeless.' Unquote. I'm supposed to write another of the same length and they'll 'make a book of it'. Or a paper boat. So: 'Birth of An Enemy'?"

"That's a pity." Mike found it increasingly difficult, these days, to talk to Douglas about anything other than the work they had in common. "But it'll come out some day."

"Perhaps." Douglas paused for a moment. "It's the best thing I've written."

"By far."

"So. New York's on."

"Yes. The budget was agreed when I told them what it was for. They reckon that if we can get world television rights, they'll be able to sell the programme in enough places to make it worth their while. Exclusive footage of Raven's first concert for—how many years? And New York will be good for the other bit."

"The life-style stuff?" Douglas nodded. "I'm bored with all that. We've got an interview: we'll get the music—that'll do me. That's what it consists of, doesn't it?"

"Of course. And the interview was good."

"Could have been better. There's something so elusive about him that you don't see the sidestep until he's passed you by. And he *will* speak in those colloquial clichés which you have to re-interpret if you're to get the full meaning—which he intends you to get *but* he wants *the fans* to know that he's still the laddo and they mustn't be left out. He's got a double radar system: one going out to pick up the shape and size of the audience: the other is to scan his own reactions for songs. He's very clever. And when you de-code him, he's still clever."

"That comes out."

"Not enough. Why the wallpaper in New York?"

"I think it's important," Mike said. "I know you don't, but I do. He talks well—good: we hope he'll play and sing well—even better. But there *has* to be something of his 'life-style'—as you disparagingly call it. You've never been prepared to give enough value to scenes like those."

"Velvet-clad young rock-poet wandering alone through Central Park, hand in hand with a B.B.C. crew?"

"You may laugh."

"Oh no. Laugh's the last thing I do when I see 'life-style' stuff. Throw up, more like it."

"Douglas. You and I think that this man does what he does very well indeed, better than anybody alive and as good as most dead. Maybe it's an easy trade or art—maybe. But he excels. On top of that, literally millions of people, millions, think of him as a pal, a guru, a prophet, a poet, a rebel, a rocker, an idol—whatever ideal of fantasy they have is projected onto this one man. Now we'll see him sing and play—all well and good. We'll see him answer questions—fine. But we'll get nowhere near the business hassle which he's so good at. Those charts you say you'll have which will show his companies and businesses —O.K., but from what Lester says he's obsessional about money and possessions and material power—those charts get nowhere near it! And what about the sexual ambiguities which have always surrounded him? And the connections with—High Society? A few newspaper clippings? Tepid. At least this, let's see him in a suite in the Plaza Hotel or the Pierre, paying out four hundred and fifty dollars a day and being flunkied by liveried Americans. Let's see him walk through the crush bar barriers to somewhere like Studio 54 and hear le Tout New York grovelling, as le Tout that sort of New York always will at a Success. Let's see some of those magnums of champagne he sips—and many people will get far more from that than they will from the interview. You find that hard to swallow or understand, Douglas, but it's true."

"What will they see?"

"There are people who read into pictures—wallpaper as you call it—far more than you do. You're a word man. Fine. So am I. Up to a point. But words are only part of communication. Often a small and unsophisticated part compared with what we can see, the other sounds we can hear, what we can deduce from carefully edited images. *More* can be got from that. All the things that you have, frankly, failed to deliver in your film so far, can be reclaimed in the 'life-style stuff'. If he *is* the ruthless bastard I suspect from Lester's very guarded comments, then you'll catch that—if you're a good enough director and aim in the right direction. *And* the sex: it'll come out, in a disco, in a restaurant, in an unaware moment—I know he has fewer unguarded moments than most but it *will* come out and a good director would know when and where to look for that and lead to it. And there's all the rest—the social ramifications, for instance: what happened to England that a young man who got on no longer felt it necessary to ape aristocratic manners or attitudes? Up until now, the social ladder has been pretty clear for all to see and each step has counted. Who cares now? Feminists would go mad, but the fact is that a number of women still care. Do men? Do young businessmen or dramatists or television producers or whatever want to talk like or live like aristos? And, if they do, do they take it at all seriously? Here we have one of the richest, certainly the most famous, clearly among the most intelligent men of his generation, who has decided to build up his own life-style, taking a bit here, a bit there, beholden to no system yet all of a piece. How do you show that? It could be fascinating."

"O.K. New York." Douglas grinned. "Maybe American wallpaper will be better."

"You're not a film maker," Mike said, happily.

"Nope. I make programmes. A deep, dark and significant difference. But I'll try to capture the magic of Merlin on the magic of celluloid. You certainly earn your wages, Mike."

"So do you." Mike's return of the compliment disturbed him. This was not his way. It was a strain not to tell Douglas of his interest in Mary, but she had asked him not to. It was less than total openness in friendship and Mike did not like it.

"What is this?" Douglas said. "Ping-pong flattery?"

"Worrying. Let's go for a drink."

"To the B.B.C. Centre Bar?"

"There's nothing else within miles."

"When I retire, I'll take a pub outside the gate and make a mint from the likes of us."

"It's not so bad if you abandon all hope before you enter."

It was not so very bad. The problem was that it was neither

fish, fowl nor good red herring: or rather, neither pub, club nor glorified snack bar but an uncunning mixture of all three which made it rather like a trough, a place where you came to guzzle and no more. But the people were nice.

"That's the best thing about this place," Mike said, as they took their drinks over to a vacant stretch of crimson leatherette, "the people. Cheers!" They sipped in unison. "Of course, it's such agreeable work, it's likely to attract agreeable people."

"And the rest," Douglas said.

"The Rest are everywhere."

"When I first came here—it was much smaller then—it almost looked like a bar then—I used to be delighted to see that sort of thing"—Douglas pointed to three ladies in full Elizabethan costume having half of lager each—"or that sort of thing"—he indicated five men smeared in green jelly, long, lank, green ringlets drooping about their Gorgonzola faces—"or all of the Famous Face business"—Famous Faces dipped in favourite drinks. "And the odd thing is," Douglas went on, "that although the feeling of delight wore off after a year or two, it's come back. It's like getting feeling back in your fingers after they've been frozen." He drank hastily to mask the openness of the confession. "Same again?"

Mike finished his drink and considered what course to take, while Douglas went up to the long service bar for two more drinks. There must have been scores of people in this bar in an analogous position—or with experience of his present dilemma. These producers and directors, presenters, designers, cameramen, actors, actresses, researchers, production assistants, all inhabited a world just that bit more bashed below the marriage belt than most. In an age of steadily increasing divorce, separation and declared infidelity, this curious mix of public service, drama, show-business, sport, thought and art, was more used to and more tolerant of marital failings than most. Yet Mike felt as prudish as a Sunday School teacher and for this he both blamed and admired Douglas.

Over the past few weeks, as they had worked closely together and Mike had learnt again to appreciate the thoroughness of Douglas' grasp of what he was doing and the determination to do it, he had again come across the man's solitariness. It revealed itself, paradoxically, only when you got to know him well. Douglas was apparently affable and easy-going to work with, although he was liable to strong action and reaction if anyone fell down on their job. He had friends—either from way back in Cumbria or from his first year or two in London, in his early twenties. He saw them regularly and they were steady: he was liked and trusted, as indeed he was by Mike himself. But there were certain questions which would not go away. Why did he appear to be so hapless about a career which with even the slightest guidance would have been at the very least well secured, full of interest and primed with the possibilities of interesting promotion within the broad acres of this grand institution? Why did he refuse to do any of the hack writing jobs taken up by contemporaries whom he declared, truthfully, he admired? Why, though his political ideas were clear and stoutly adhered to, had he not taken advantage of the cliquish polarization which would have worked so well in his favour over the last fifteen years? Why, perversely, did he turn up with a substantial and excellent piece of writing which was, in the present market conditions, virtually unpublishable?

More important than that, Mike felt, there was a moral nerve in Douglas which it was easy to hit. The trouble was that it was not always in the same place. Yet, curiously, for someone of undoubted worldly experience, Douglas gave the impression of being disapproving when dirty stories were told or deep-throat personal gossip was being bartered or even (though he himself would swear his head off on occasions) when four-letter words flew about the place. And that was symptomatic of a general vein in his character which, unusually for the times, Mike thought, still saw most things in sternly moral terms, despite his own manifest failings. There was still a sense of sin in Douglas and, worse, Mike thought, a hopeless hope of redemption. That isolated him.

"Cheers."

"Cheers."

"Let's drink to the moving wallpaper in New York."

"Good."

"Now, this regionai business." Douglas pulled out of his bust briefcase a neatly typed half dozen sheets, which he handed over to Mike. "That's the re-think with the budget, the schedule, the structure, who I think should be in it and why, further sources and references to a couple of books and articles you might read. It's unusual, I know. Not a single man's wander *à la* K. Clark, D. Attenborough, J. Miller and all—but it's an important idea and, if it's done well, it could always be sold as a series of linked documentaries—which wouldn't scare anyone. I still think it's important." He took out another sheet. "Here's an idea for a small studio series on—well, you'll see. It's a B.B.C. 2 idea. Late night. Fun."

"Anything else?" Mike asked.

"Not at this moment."

"Why don't you sign up full time? Come onto the staff. You'll only have to work one-tenth as hard then."

"Too much else to do." Douglas paused. He was quite willing to make a confidant of Mike, but at the moment something held him back. He could not analyse it. "I'm keeping up that review spot for the World Service and there's another useful reviewing job coming up on the 'Guardian'. Fortnightly. And E.M.I. scripts have asked me to do some reading for them, plus I'm starting something else of my own. You may smile, but I need the money, with two establishments—even though mine is a ground floor garret—and the spur of honourably needed loot is, I discover, a great and revitalizing kick into honest endeavour."

"Stopped drinking?"

"Certainly not. But cut down."

"Why?"

"Hangover loses an hour a morning. Can't afford it."

"Fair enough. But you said you were going to Cumbria again after New York—something about an election, what was that?"

"My cousin's standing as Labour candidate in a bye-election. She doesn't have a hope in hell. It's one of the safest Tory seats in the U.K."

"She?"

"Lester's sister. Very unalike."

"There's a Cumbrian Mafia."

"I'm working on it. And she's pregnant. That'll help. She married my foster-brother."

"You really have an umbilical cord as thick as a rope, don't you?"

"Round my throat? Umbilical? No. People I like and know. I could cut it off and start again, say on the West Coast."

"You sound like Huckleberry Finn."

"Yes. But doesn't this—one life only business—not hit *you*?"

"Of course. It hits everybody," Mike said, matter-of-factly.

"It's extraordinary. To face that you are animate now and soon will be inanimate: no more breathing or seeing or tasting or anything. Just an end. It is overwhelming."

"Is that why you have become a workaholic?"

"Yes."

Once again Douglas would have found some relief in talking to Mike about Mary. He talked to no one at all about her and the pressure to do so threatened to spill over into this innocent conversation. But he respected his deeper instinct, which was to say nothing. There was a pause.

"What's the attraction of a bye-election?"

"It gives you a chance to ask a lot of people a lot of interesting questions." Mike nodded and Douglas went on. "That's the basic attraction of all interviewing. You get to ask the questions you would like to ask but feel too awkward to ask on any occasion but a formal interview which, after all, has been convened for the very purpose of asking such questions."

"You enjoy it. That's the point. And that makes it work."

"That too," Douglas said. Then, although he sensed that this was a move whose fullest significance he did not understand, he went on: "You and Mary get on well, don't you?"

"I always like to think so."

"You know that—you've worked all that out. Yes? We're living apart."

"I knew that."

"Well." Douglas hesitated. He detested people who brought others into their personal quarrels. On the other hand, he saw no way round this pressing anxiety he had. "The New York trip could take over a fortnight if we have all the trouble we expect. I don't like to think of her being—not so much alone—she wants that—but—without anyone to turn to." Mike was about to speak. Douglas held up a hand to silence him. "No, don't feel obliged. Just think about it. A phone call or two or maybe, I don't know, a meal out sometime. I wouldn't want to drag you into anything or compromise you. But there we are. O.K. Thanks for the wallpaper pep-talk. So long."

Douglas got up and went off immediately, leaving Mike with the convenient excuse that he had simply not had the time to tell Douglas what he believed he should have told Douglas. But he was fully aware that it was no more than a convenient excuse.

The bar was emptying as the offices and studios called back the living. The three Elizabethan ladies had long finished their lager: the Green Men had shuffled away, clutching crisps: Famous Faces, flushed salmon pink now, glanced at watches and agreed it was later than they had thought, just knock it back. The bodies which fed the machines which shot pictures into twenty-five million households trooped and traipsed and tripped back into the business of getting the show on the air.

Mike ordered himself a double scotch, added another for safety, collected half of bitter as a chaser, and, with a new packet of cigarettes, sought out a corner seat to think through, with the intention of arriving at a conclusion he would act on, the dilemma which now faced him. For he was in love with Mary and knew that they could enjoy a happy and decent life together: and he suspected now, for no reason that he could lay his finger on, that she just might have him. If he got it right.

(3)

New York, to Lester, was the playground of the Western World. The skyscrapers at the foot of Manhattan were symbols of power and riches more potent than Tutankhamun's Tomb, Buckingham Palace, St Peter's and the Stock Exchange crushed into one. The concrete canyoned streets excited him, the swashbuckling black Brummels brought the cordite of competitiveness to his nostrils, the raunchiness of the women seemed to him so much more "real" than the either tease-me-please or you-can-have-anything-for-a-price of London. He liked the loud-voiced men in the restaurants, the Brooklyn jawed and jewelled and vowelled and mawed mammas who served coffee and wisecracks in the coffee lounges. He saw 42nd Street as his kind of jungle and cruised around Harlem in a cab, eyes half-closed, weighing up the shots. In the Italian quarter he could be the tough brother in "The Godfather"; around the docks he was Brando in "On The Waterfront"; on Park Avenue and Fifth Avenue he was surprised to discover he remembered odd phrases from songs and thought he could walk into a musical any minute. When the police cars wow-wowed he was Kojak. New York was a movie and he was the whole production.

He had never had it so good. That was a phrase he had picked up somewhere and found very little occasion for. Now he could use it every day and mean it every day. He had never ever had it so bloody good!

To be in New York was enough. To be in New York when somebody else was paying—in this case a closely argued split between Raven's accountant and the B.B.C.'s contract department—was very cool, very cool indeed. To be in New York with a film crew and the open sesame that gave, not to mention the conversation starter for those evenings full of well exercised New York talent—that was very neat. But to be in New York with Merlin Raven was just something else.

New York went hysterical about the concert. Madison Square Garden was sold out within three hours of the box office opening and coast-to-coast breakfast show news bulletins carried live interviews with the plucky lucky fans who had begun to camp around the building the week before. A fierce trade in black market tickets developed, when it was murmured that among the guests for this single performance would be Frank Sinatra, Princess Margaret (who was flying up from the Caribbean), Rudolf Nureyev (who was flying in from Caracas), the wife of the President of the United States, Liza Minnelli, Francis Ford Coppola, and Muhammed Ali; Diana Ross broke an important clause in a Las Vegas contract to get there; Hal Prince re-scheduled the London rehearsals of a new opera at Covent Garden to fly back; Jackie Onassis announced that she could not make it and then changed her mind and threw the box office into a hundred per cent panic; John Lennon said yes, he would go; Paul McCartney said he'd heard most of the tunes but it was time he brought Linda to New York for a bit and he would most likely have a look in; the head of the record company hired Studio 54 for the post-concert party, fell out with its proprietor because he was manhandled at the door by the mob of youths hired to keep people out, and switched to Regine's; Nigel Dempster leaked all this gleefully; David Hockney did the poster; Edward Gorey designed the programmes; David Frost, Dempster said, had volunteered to be M.C. and was reported to be "most disappointed" when his offer was turned down.

And the only film crew allowed inside the entire place was Douglas' B.B.C. outfit. Four cameras with four old B.B.C. sweats as cameramen, four sound men and six flustered "sparks": all linked to Douglas by headphones. He directed it like an Outside Broadcast. The American TV stations were so angry that they threatened to take final and fatal action against the Garden, against Raven, against the B.B.C. and against Douglas—but he had worked out his deals carefully, spent boring and unhappy hours with the relevant and the irrelevant unions, and his contracts were watertight. The American TV stations had to take news footage at the door and no more. They burned up the lines to London for an American sale and the B.B.C. was almost alarmed to discover that it had a very hot property in its hands. Hands were rubbed. Heads were put together. Heads of Department met on the sixth floor. Nods as good as winks were exchanged and returned to sender. B.B.C. executives spoke knowingly about "Pop" and "Amazing" and "Jackie Onassis" and ". . . of the United States, old boy—*and*, would you believe it—Canada! Oh—I see," "And we *have* it all, old boy. Wainwright. Mike. *Very* bright chap. Good chap. Mike Wainwright. Producer."

The programme became a two-and-a-half-hour special, to be transmitted at peak time on Christmas Eve. Mike found his grubby, cubby-hole office suddenly become the Kings Cross of the B.B.C. with interested executive traffic and schedulers, contract men and reporters pounding through it all day. He borrowed an empty office on another floor (Religion) and was undisturbed, except by the phone calls to and from New York. For the pressures on the production had become very big and he was worried that Douglas might have no energy left to do the actual filming.

Then he saw the first four days' rushes and ceased to worry. Douglas had never directed anything better. What was more, he had adopted an interviewing style which up until now he had steadily abjured: that is to say, he asked questions as the crew was setting up, as Raven was doing other things, amid the confusion he generally so deplored. His usual method was to collect evidence, sift it, research the man or the matter as thoroughly as possible, work out a line, get the best possible conditions for thoughtful and sustained conversation and then drive it through. All this had been done in the studio that night and Mike had been delighted with the result. But it was nothing compared with this stuff.

Mike telexed Douglas to tell him as much and advise him that the budget had been increased, as had the air-time, and he could stay on another week if he needed to.

But it was when he saw the rushes of the concert that Mike knew they had a serious winner: a programme that would not only entertain and enlighten and stand for what it believed in, but something that would print itself on people's minds and leave traces found long after in all sorts of asides and recollections and impressions of the time. For Merlin was sensational.

His style was quiet, undemonstrative, intense and totally compelling. He had taken fastidious care with the band and the music balance, in that vast acreage, was almost perfect, certainly far, far better than any other similar bands had achieved there. He sang some of his old hits but, again, he had taken trouble over them: they were rearranged, sometimes subtly re-worded—which delighted the fans who knew them by heart and gave a useful stimulus to the critics who saw "development", "self-parody", "progression", "re-working" and even "re-thinking". And he sang some of the numbers which had been triggered by his meeting Lester. These, it was agreed in the serious music press, were quite simply some of the best popular songs written. They had the wit and freshness of the early songs, the unerring intelligence which hit a contemporary attitude or anecdote so accurately that it seemed to speak for a whole generation, and the intervening time had enriched the words and music. The music press had not been as interested since the early Dylan, the mid-Beatles or since Raven's own first few L.P.s. And the audience was with him all the way.

It was a nice balance. The audience was just on the edge of that berserk applause which would have wrecked the finer enjoyment of the concert. But Merlin did not let them out of his grip. That was the revelation to Douglas. Merlin's authority. He came onto the stage when the band was well into the first number and took up his song instantly, thus quenching the roar which had fired up at the sight of him. Indeed he came on so very abruptly and was playing and singing so soon that there was an element of wizardry in it. When the number ended he bowed, brusquely, turned to the band, waved, they began to play again and once more he was in harness, the lead horse, his voice racing across the famous American Garden, compelling attention.

Douglas was impressed.

The finale was spectacular. Merlin had made no concessions to show-business or to the prevailing fashion for lights, shapes, film, stills, blow-ups, eidophors and circus effects. He was a man alone, his band half unseen behind him, that was all. When the concert ended he left as sharply as he had entered. It was the audience which provided the spectacle. At first scores and then hundreds and then thousands of small points of light appeared all over the vast gloom of the indoor Garden: matches were lit, some had brought candles, lighters were fired, there were those with small lanterns and those with torches and soon the entire place was full of lights, held steadily aloft while feet drummed on the floor and a long baying cry went out. "More!" "More!" "More!" "More!"—not hysterical, not pleading, but demanding that this time of satisfaction be repeated, this revelation be played again. It was indisputably religious in its mood and in its display, Douglas thought. But what followed from that he did not know.

Merlin did not reappear.

After an hour, the crowd left the building and Douglas, having helped the crew wrap, went backstage, allowed through the massive security ring after some difficulty, despite his twenty-two carat pass. Merlin had gone to his dressing room and seen only a couple of critics, one at a time. Douglas let it be known he was there. All he wanted to do was to say "thanks", excuse himself from the party afterwards and confirm a last filming date later in the week. He fully expected not to be seen and had braced himself not to consider this to be a rebuff. The backstage scene smacked of hoods, Hell's Angels, drugs, drink, fast money, fast sex, the skid row of the instantly over-rich, over-licensed, over-exposed and over-privileged. He was surprised at how very little he cared for them all. For they were, or were often portrayed to be, the true types of the Seventies, the character of the times, at best full of hedonistic audacity and licentious aplomb: at worst full of shit. But, in either guise, this lot, this gaggle of over-dressed young men and women, were at some peak in a society which had lost sight of most peaks. It was they and their kind which dominated the new exclusive discos, the new restaurants, the flash events—world title fights, glamorous first nights, charity fairs—and though the media massage might represent very little in real terms, the whole point was that the real terms were either permanently or temporarily at a discount. "Who" (i.e. which intelligent bright young person) cared about the High Society represented in London and the Shires by the fag end of the Hickey Brigade and, in America, by the Wasp wasted pioneering Prots and their plutocratic side-riders? Some. True. But not "the people", not that moving intelligence within a society so cleverly cottoned onto by the best gossip columnists and scandal feature writers. This clustered, sparkling, shrill, champagne swigging, coke sniffing, clothes conscious, figure conscious, only semi-word conscious gaggle of youth, youth authentic, youth spurious, and youth lost but clung onto, were as people from Mars to Douglas. He had been around and about them one way and another, without really belonging, but naturally intrigued, for some years. Now, backstage at Madison Square Garden, he thought—yes, they should have their due, they are acting out that fantasy-dream-led-life which in different civilizations had been led by princes and priests and soldiers and even scholars once or twice—but the deepest feeling it aroused in Douglas now was not loathing or contempt, but tiredness. He could see no point in keeping up with it all. And more than that, it gave a kick to a puritan conscience which had been challenged and made to retreat in London—and, Douglas had thought, for sound reasons. But not so beaten as to be able to look on this compact of idle wealth, abusive liberty, narcissistic mannerisms and self-indulgent hauteur without feeling distinct twinges of disapproval at such waste, which was so ignorant of so many needs. Still, it was uncomfortable, to say the least, to moralize when you were a guest in the middle of the feast.

He waited, then, hoping for the refusal polite, and happy to think of an evening alone. He gave his messenger ten minutes. That seemed fair. He stood against a wall and watched. Need he be a guest? Why did he always think of himself as that? Even now it was no more than the other side of the coin from being the servant. And the one definite lesson he had taken from a family which did not pretend or presume to pass on "lessons from family tradition" to their offspring, was that to be an independent man, independent in as many ways as possible, was the best goal. Yet, since Douglas' hoist out of the working class, privileged through Oxford and laundered through the B.B.C. and the London middle-classless media, he had in many ways become a guest. The guest of a society which paid good money for the trained talents of an approved good education: very welcome, provided he played the established games and carried on the established traditions. A captive guest.

It was about time to quit, he thought, as the satin-clad messenger beckoned him towards Merlin's dressing room. Yes, he would quit all that. The decision came quite coolly, even coldly, but there was something in it which Douglas recognized as final. He would quit the deference.

They finally lunged through the mob, only just escaping serious injury from the security guards.

Merlin was in a chair, composed, not sprawled, a glass of champagne in his hand, the rest of the bottle in an ice bucket beside him.

"Come in," he said to Douglas. And, equally amiably, to Douglas' guide he said, "Get out, will you?"

"Drink?"

"Thanks," Douglas said. "I'll get my own."

Merlin watched him carefully and, returning the look, Douglas saw how exhausted the man was. And he realized that Merlin wanted a talk, wanted a pal, wanted something normal and friendly to balance the stupendous weight of adulation, satisfaction and triumph which he had just provoked. Yet Douglas did not want to be drawn in. There was something finally alone about Merlin which found a direct echo in himself. Douglas knew that however gently and genuinely Merlin had reached out now, it would be the preliminary to an attempt to destroy in order to control.

He poured himself some champagne.

There was the homosexual aspect. This had been successfully played down by Merlin and ignored by Douglas but he was as aware of it now as he had ever been. Merlin brought a distinctive sexual charge to every single relationship, Douglas assumed: there was no hiding it and not much attempt to blunt the discomfort of others. Part of Merlin's character was that he could, as it were, switch the mix of his personality whenever he wanted to, ensuring always that he got his own way.

"I don't fancy you, you know," Merlin said.

"Thank God for that. Cheers."

"Have you ever had—a bit of the other?"

"No."

"Been tempted?"

"No."

"Been interested?"

"Certainly."

"I'd've called you a liar if you'd said your straight-arsed 'No' to that one. What interested you?"

"The people, of course."

"Not the action."

"That strikes me as unnecessary, painful or, in its way, just the same as ours. Not the action."

"What about the people?"

"Simply that I know and like some people who are homosexuals and, as part of my interest in them, I am interested in their homosexuality. I am curious. And you, Merlin, are flirting. More champagne?"

"Help yourself."

"You were very good in that concert," Douglas said as he

topped up Merlin's glass and filled his own. "Very. I was prepared to be impressed, I suppose: or rather I was prepared to be unimpressed. I was impressed and amazed. You're some sort of balladier for our times. Good luck to you."

"'Balladier for our times'," Merlin sipped at the champagne. "Christ!"

"I'll think of a better title before the night. But that's what you *are*. *Not* a poet, though you're like a poet in some respects; not a full composer, though you can write better tunes than almost anyone; you're like some Villon—footnote follows—that's who you are."

"Was I flirting?"

"You know you are doing everything you do."

"Bothers me sometimes. I think I should be able to let go. When I did—it was just—down and out. Hell. So."

"I won't bother you. I came to say thanks. Confirm we'll do the last studio session on Thursday. And—I'll be off."

"On the town?"

"I don't know."

"There's my party to go to." Merlin held out his glass for more champagne, a knowingly infantile gesture which Douglas ignored. Merlin poured his own. "Finished. Shall we spin a coin to see who opens the next bottle? Or would you, please?"

"Sure."

Douglas went over to the fridge. It was rather misleading to call the place a dressing room. Merlin's instructions had been carried out to the letter. The place was decorated and fitted out very like the lounge in his London penthouse.

"Are you going to your party?" Douglas asked.

"Of course not."

"What'll *you* do?"

"Watch some TV." Merlin grinned happily. "Then I'll go cruising down 42nd Street, see what bum I can find. Something rough."

"Lester told me you were on girls."

"Sometimes. But they're not dangerous enough. The only risk is clap. Who cares? Or maybe I'll go into Harlem."

"Alone."

"I'd be chicken otherwise. You could come along. Or,"

Merlin paused, "I'll pass out here and be discovered intact in the morning by my gooks outside who, believe me, will neither knock nor at all disturb me until I say so."

"Careful," Douglas warned.

"I had some sex right after the show. In the corridor. But I'm restless again. Anyway, no relationship can be interesting without its quotient of sex."

"You could be right. But consummation is different."

"Lester's a silly prick!" Merlin said, viciously. "His time is up."

"Why?"

"Why?" Merlin mimicked him and got up to wander around the room, leaving Douglas beached.

Douglas finished off his champagne as Merlin pressed a button which flicked on the large colour television set. He went from channel to channel until he found a news bulletin. His concert was the number two story, following a report of a key speech by President Carter on the current almighty oil crisis, but beating news of shootings in the Middle East, riots in Pakistan, bombings in Ulster and incipient storms off Florida.

"Don't you think," Merlin said, timing his remark to coincide with the exact moment when Douglas was leaving his seat to leave the room, "when you see people's faces on television, talking about world affairs or economics, whatever it is . . . don't you think—how can they be so wrapped up in it? What about the birds and the bees and the sun and that? We'll all be dead and gone in no time. How can they all get so hooked on what they say? Look at that gook talking about his housing programme! O.K.—let's build houses. I'm not knocking him. But you look in their faces to see if there's anything else in their lives, you know? Some mischief maybe or some dirty little secret or some clean big secret but you see nothing. I can't understand it. The people I like are people who've got that kind of business going on inside them even when they're saving the universe. You can tell it by their eyes—and they're always just about to smile as if they were having trouble keeping in a very good joke."

Douglas had indeed thought that and come to a similar conclusion: so similar that he was disconcerted. He did not make any display of agreement, fearing to seem merely flattering. But it was uncanny.

"I wasn't trying to pick you up, you know," Merlin said.

"I realize that."

"I play these games." He flicked the television from channel to channel with sulky restlessness. "What the fuck do you *do* after a concert like that? You've heard of 'mind blown'? Of course you have, yes. Well, it's like that. My mind is blown. There seems no skull-case. There are a billion bits of brain drifting around somewhere like the whole galactic system after the Big Bang. Do you realize what it's *like* out there? If I said 'Do you love me?' they would yell 'We love you!' If I said 'Shit' they would send it back. And if I said 'Down with America' they would cheer. And '*Sieg Heil*'?"

"No. They might cheer but that's no more than cheering. They were there to shout and make an event of it. That was all. You have some influence, no power, little authority."

"What're you doing tonight?"

"Well." Douglas was on his feet now. "When I'm in New York or wherever abroad—Abroad being Different—after a day's work like this I always think I ought to hit the town, find a lady, get drunk, have adventures, end up ripping and roaring somewhere, leading the life I somehow think I'm supposed to be leading. What I want to do is what I usually do—have a couple of Buds in a quiet bar and go to bed. That's what I'll do."

"I'm going to take in a movie," Merlin said. "There's that 'Nosferatu' remake by Herzog. Surprise you?"

"No."

"Then I'm off up the East Side with the classy Jackie Onassis crowd. They wanted me to go to supper but I can't eat now. A movie, then the uptown party. Been there?"

"Uptown?"

"Yes. Uptown rich, very very: butler, classical this, period that, Mr Secretary of State, Ambassador, your famous violinist and conductor and sometimes writer and actress—all that High Society—still goes on, still very tasty. Know it?"

"No."

"Want to?"

"Honestly—no."

"Fool." Merlin grinned and punched Douglas very lightly on the shoulder. "I like you, Douglas. You're full of shit but I like you. You're not ambitious enough, that's your problem. You don't want enough hard enough. But I like talking with you. I'd like to talk to you a lot. You know a lot, you've made an effort to try to think about this and that. But it wouldn't work. I've got to have the edge and you don't want that. Correct?"

"O.K." Merlin sipped some champagne as he began to undress. "Lester tells me you've left your old lady but, as he puts it, haven't got the balls to shack up with the Scarlet Woman. That right?"

"Just about."

"Don't get gloomy, Douglas." Merlin was naked. He looked at Douglas and then held out his hand. "I need a stinking long bubble bath." He held Douglas' hand hard. "I've liked working with you. And what I read of yours I liked. It was O.K."

"Take care."

Merlin suddenly threw back his head, beat his chest and let out a violent Tarzan yodel. He stopped abruptly.

"So long," he said, and turned away. "Kiss my arse?"

(4)

Douglas decided to give him another half hour and be ruthless about it. The bar was crowded, even at 2.00 a.m., and the thud from the disco music upstairs, like nails going into the coffin of rock music, he thought, was pounding through his head without respecting any barriers of skull, thought or talk. Talk was minimal. He had settled down in the corner of the singles bar which Lester had denominated, and was fretting under the strain of being book-less, pal-less, partner-less and drinkful. The barman was the only safe person to talk to and he was a disco freak, clucking the beat between his teeth as he bellowed a parrot reply to your order.

It was a fashionable place up on the East Side, First Avenue, near Maxwell's Plum: once, some years back, one of the hottest spots in New York. Trust Lester, Douglas thought, to be behind the new fashions. And to choose a singles bar. And to be late.

Douglas had soon arrived back at his hotel after his talk with Merlin. He had walked through the streets, unmugged, unapproached, from the Garden to the modest, even austere little hotel into which the B.B.C. shepherded those contributors lucky enough to cross the Atlantic on its "business". It had no bar, no restaurant, no coffee shop and served no breakfast. It appealed to Douglas' sense of thrift and anonymity. Despite having the characteristics of a block of service flatlets, it seemed to him to allow him to have more of a character than he felt was ever permitted him in such grand hotels as the Plaza or such characterful places as the Algonquin. At this place, you were on your own. The B.B.C. crew liked it because it was cheap and they could claim expenses on everything else. It was also central, just two blocks away from the Avenue of the Americas in the mid-Fifties. Douglas had enjoyed walking out into the Americas for his breakfast, searching out a coffee shop in that spectacular canyon of skyscrapers, feeling the exhilaration of newness and glass and height and structural cleanliness which either intoxicates or incites all European visitors to the Big Apple.

He had planned to bath, change, eat quietly nearby—there was a Japanese restaurant he fancied—and then flick through the late night/early morning television on the way to sleep.

Lester's note had said, "See you at Ben Gunn's at about 1–1.30 a.m. It is urgent we talk together tonight because I have to go to L.A. tomorrow. So come. Lester."

So there he was. Against all his clearest wishes and desires, propped in the corner of a trendy bar which was decked out in foliage so dense as to make a Kew Gardens conservatory seem like the barren Egdon Heath, drinking Jack Daniels with Buds as chasers, avoiding the possibilities for pick-ups and trying to find ways to fend off the computered thump of the disco discs over his head.

Yet he was only pretending. He was tired, that was true, and irritated with his doggedness about family loyalties, and on the way to being drunk. He drank too much, he would remind himself, in the gaps between drinks: he ought to cut down—a resolution for the next New Year. He wondered why he was just sitting there doing nothing—was not the world his grit and he the happy oyster?—but things were coming into focus, he thought. Even as he thought it, he mentally crossed fingers and physically touched the wooden bar before him: which reminded him that he needed another drink.

He had tried to work out where the crew had gone to but then he remembered that a strip-crawl had been on the agenda. They were going to move as a herd and motor through the dirtiest bars, clubs, movies and whatever came up they could find. Excellent sport for the fourteen married men. It was as well Douglas was not with them. They would come back with enough stories for a six-month.

Douglas tried to focus on the notion that things were coming into focus. It was difficult. All around him, energetic—still, at this time of night—young Americans, at the last stop before bed, were being American. He was fascinated by them. Their difference from the English. The whys and hows of the difference. His intent look was misinterpreted a couple of times and remarkably attractive girls (what were *they* doing here?) came and asked for a light. And left soon after he had given it. He was not impolite. It was just that the deadening thump of the dead men's disco beat somehow slashed the tendons of his larynx. Smiles, however sympathetic, were not enough.

Anyway, pick-ups were out. More important, the idea that he ought to be interested in pick-ups—because that was what life consisted in if you were abroad, alone, free and virile—was out too. A great leap forward. Work was in. The previous few months had given a coherence to his life which he had forgotten about. Work was the village, the extended family, the source of all fruitfully complicated intercourse, it was stronger than marriage or friendship. He needed it. This film on Raven would set him up in work for a year or two. He would stick to it. He might even have a career.

As for the rest—Mary and Hilda—he had the hope that if he continued to try to get everything right, a solution might offer itself there too.

When Lester arrived, he gave Douglas the distinct impression that he felt he ought to be announced by the Queen's

Own Buglers. He had been to the party, sniffed coke, sunk champagne, chatted with superstars, slapped celebrities on the back, patronized other singers' managers, condescended to one or two old acquaintances, told lies to a beautiful Manhattan woman publisher, who was even now waiting for him in her expensive duplex willing to "do anything". Lester was King Kong for the New York night.

Douglas liked to see him like that. But, even so, he could not get the words out of his head. The disco beat had finished it off.

They found an empty bar a few blocks down and Lester persuaded the owner to let them drink there for a few minutes. His method was simple. He offered to pay two or three times the price of the drinks. The owner said. "English? English. You're all crazy. I had a guy in here yesterday wanted to challenge somebody to drink a bottle of vodka in one. You know? Crazy English. No—stay over there. I'll clean up around you. Drinks are house prices—no more. When I need to swab that corner—you go. Correct?"

Lester gave Douglas a wink. For a moment, Douglas was moved by it. For the wink said—what a life, eh, for two Thurston kids who wore clogs to primary school and kicked sparks off the pavement! What a life for two guys who came into late teenage thinking three pounds a week was a good start on ambition's ladder and two weeks' holiday a year a bit of an extravagance! What a journey from two halves of mild to this, from Carlisle County Ballroom to Studio 54, from provincial obscurity to Raven, from way back nowhere to up-front somebody! What a life, it said, that look, and spoke to Douglas' fondest memories of Lester, whom he had feared and loved and admired as a boy, being alternately impressed and daunted by Lester's physical powers, his trouble making, his great attempt to become an athlete, his petty crime, his pop *demi-monde* reported success. That amount of closeness meant a great deal to Douglas. The owner moved away as Douglas turned to thank him. Lester winked again.

"Sap," he whispered, happily. "If he'd've refused us, we would have jumped him."

"He seems pretty tough."

"One against two doesn't go," Lester recited, solemnly. "Why weren't you at the party?"

"Too tired."

"Too snooty, more like."

"No, not that, Lester. What have I got to be snooty about in front of that lot?"

"Exactly. So you were scared then."

"Scared?"

"I don't mean scared." With the pomposity of a man on the verge of toppling into catatonic drunkenness, Lester searched throughout his vocabulary. "Worried," he announced. "Worried you wouldn't make an impression."

"I don't know what you're on about."

"Yes you do. You do." Lester paused, drank deeply, nodded deeply. "You do."

"O.K. I do. Now then. What do you want?"

"Do you remember when we used to pinch apples?"

"Yes."

"You were worried then."

"I was. But I still came along."

"You still came along. I'll grant you that. But you were worried."

"To be totally honest, Lester, I was worried when I was with *you* because you talked about it so much I knew that Mother would get to know. When I took my own gang I was often so unworried I look back with amazement."

"Why?"

"Because I'm the worrying kind. And I'm law abiding."

"I'm not."

"I know."

"Your father was very good to me." Lester tippled a critically large Jack Daniels into his glass. Once that was inside him, Douglas knew, he would be deep in the alcoholic swamp. Lester held up the glass and glared at it, like some Norseman seeking to challenge it to do its worst. "Very good," he repeated, but before he took a gulp, Douglas arrested his arm.

"If we're going to talk, let's talk now." Douglas paused. "Before you get paralytic."

Unexpectedly, Lester saw the sense of a remark which in other circumstances and times he would have regarded as the very peak of provocation.

"My father was a bloody washout," he said. Then, unusually for him, he added, in confidence, "If he was my bloody father. You know what my mother is."

Everybody in the Tallentire family knew what Lester's mother was but, even in the late Seventies, the word did not pass their lips.

"Our Aileen's done well," Lester said, rather lugubriously. He had taken no notice of his younger sister when she was a plump, bespectacled, put upon, asthmatic and doleful child. Now that she had emerged from that sad and unpromising chrysalis as a thoughtful, educated woman, who even had not unrealizable ambitions to stand for Parliament, Lester would still have ignored her, but for the fact that she had married Harry. "I didn't think she'd manage to get hold of somebody like Harry," he said. "Now *he's* a good lad."

The implication was clear.

Was it happening all over the world, Douglas wondered. Were couples from Chicago who found themselves in Delhi discussing their back street adolescent adventures in the windy city? Were friends from Valparaiso who had met up in Leningrad talking about the days of their youth? Were students from the Sorbonne now become artists in L.A. mulling over the nights on the Left Bank? Very likely. The further we move from our past, the more eagerly we seize on the chances to revisit it. Not surprisingly. It is most of what we have.

"Lester," Douglas said, patiently. "I'm very tired. You said it was urgent. What is it?"

Over Lester's face came a look of such ill-fitting cunning that Douglas' heart sank. He had suspected that Lester was about to try to pull a dirty one: alas, it seemed that he was right. Douglas took a glum pull at his rye.

"Merlin hasn't signed his contract yet," Lester began.

"That's right."

"So—technically, technically—the thing isn't on the up and up, it isn't legal. Not yet."

"Technically you are right."

"It puts us all in an awkward position," Lester said craftily. Douglas groaned. Lester was encouraged. "I'm sorry to put it over on you, my own cousin, but it's every man for himself in this life. Agreed?" Douglas said nothing. "And you won't suffer. I'll see to it that you don't suffer. I'll guarantee that, Douglas, for old times' sake."

"What are you suggesting?" Douglas wanted it over with but for Lester this was a moment to be cherished.

"You see," Lester said, with just sufficient remaining wisdom to refrain from sinking any more spirits, "Merlin and me's built up this 'thing'. Don't get me wrong. It's nothing personal. Nothing personal. It's just that—you know," and here he became confidential, even bashful, and Douglas felt a genuine lurch of sympathy for him, "some of those songs he sang tonight—the new ones—they came out of things I told him. I couldn't tell you *how*, exactly. I couldn't put my finger on it. But they do. It could be worked out. You see. And he needs that, you see. I mean," Lester took a sip, "when I met up with him again—you know—he was just coming out of being a wreck. He'd had one of these full scale depressions. He was bumbling around. He was raving with all sorts of political stuff and messages in his songs. I've *heard* those tapes. They're terrible—what he did when he was in his depressions. But from the first time he met me—BINGO!—that was it—BINGO!—he got cracking again on the real stuff, the real hot stuff, the stuff that makes a bloody fortune. And he got thinner. Did you see him tonight? Never looked better. Looks after himself. We went to a gym together. It was in Holland Park. There was this madman . . ."

"What's this leading up to?" Douglas asked.

"I'm sorry to say this, old pal, but we won't release the film."

Lester sat back like a gangster in a movie and indeed might well have thought himself half there, with the beefy, aproned barman swabbing out the place, the chairs upended on the tables, the occasional mellifluous yodel of a police car racing up First Avenue, the Manhattan adventure just four or five yards away.

"You mean he won't sign."

"Not for the B.B.C. Why should he? This has turned out to be the biggest thing since—" Lester was no longer capable of completing such a sentence. "That's Showbiz," he concluded.

"And what do you propose to do?" Douglas heard the ice in his voice. "Although the contract is not signed there is after all a firm gentleman's agreement. I expect that would carry some weight if it came to a legal battle."

"Oh Douglas." Lester laid a sympathetic hand on his cousin's arm. "Don't come the hard man. We can always beat your lawyers to pulp. What we want is a deal."

"I'm listening."

"We want to buy all the stuff from you—we'll pay a fair price, we'll have our people work it all out—we want *you*," Lester said, graciously, "yes, we want *you*—and then we'll market the film in our own way. Look at it from our point of view. You have all that stuff. Nobody else has it. Nobody else has ever had as much stuff on Merlin in the history of the world. It's the hottest property this century. And what does he get out of it? A lousy what is it—honourable—?"

"Nominal."

"Nominal fee. And what do you get out of it? Not much more. And what about me? Sweet F.A. So we can all get rich for once and it's O.K. for the B.B.C., we'll let them have a television deal some time."

"You must do what you want but I'm having nothing to do with it," Douglas said.

"You could make a fortune. And a name. Who cares—who cares in America who directs an English TV thing? But *this*—this could make you. I've thought it all out. Listen to Lester, kid."

"I have listened. And I'm going back to the hotel."

"Think it over?"

"It won't work, Lester. I won't play. I'll advise the B.B.C. to keep hold of the material. You'll get nothing out of it."

"You wouldn't fuck it all up, would you?"

Douglas waited for that moment or two until he was certain that Lester would take in the full implications of his reply.

"Yes. If you tried it on, I'd fuck it up."

Lester hoisted himself up, drew back his arm, lunged forward and was clipped on the jaw by the barman, who then caught him as he fell, cold.

"Here," he said to Douglas. "Take him away. He's *your* pal. Get out, the both of you. Crazy English."

Douglas dragged Lester out onto the pavement, propped him up, in a sitting position, against the wall.

Lester drowsily woke up.

"One question," Douglas said, kneeling beside him. "Are you listening?"

"Yes."

"Have you sorted all this out with Merlin?"

"Merlin and me," Lester declared, eyes wide open, mind about to snap tight shut, "are like *that*!"

He held out two fingers, clearly wanting to cross them to show the rapport, the kinship, the link between himself and Raven, but he was too far gone and the fingers remained in the Churchill position as Lester crashed into inner darkness.

Poor sod, Douglas thought, you don't even know that your great pal has decided to dump you. Thus has spoken the Raven. Douglas looked around for a yellow cab to haul his cousin across the dark rock of a city to a bed.

4
Love and Marriage

(I)

When Douglas rang to tell her that he would have to stay on in New York for a few days because of the extended length of the project, Mary calmly replied that it was perfectly all right, assured him that John was about to go north to his grandparents perfectly happily, asked one or two questions about the concert and about Lester, was bright with a gobbet or two of gossip, sounded cheerful and busy, put the phone down and collapsed.

It was so unfair. She had made so many efforts and fought so many battles—yet it did not seem to be working. She despised herself for her dependence. For, even though Douglas was (at her request) not living with her, his absence in the U.S.A. pointed up how much she needed to know that he was, somehow, in a nearby zone she could retreat to when necessary. In touch. They had become—or, bitterly, she conceded, *she* had become—like one of those insects totally dependent on the immensely intimate workings of a single and delicate plant for survival: when the plant suffered, she did; when it died, she died. The plant—which had become both intricate and delicate—was her marriage to Douglas.

For, now that she had had time to think—and it seemed to Mary that she had time to do nothing else, so remorselessly did analysis and continuing analysis of her marriage pound through her mind—she saw how many, how often contradictory, how complicated and how perilous were the demands they had made on the marriage.

Yet, with all the early illusions contradicted and the attempt at an older cynicism seen to fail, Mary had discovered, in her time alone, that it was still that monstrous, useless, unsatisfactory, twisted marriage which gave her sustenance. For all its painfulness and humiliations, its deceits, shortcomings, distortions and barrenness, it was what made her live, she now found. And she wanted to be free of it. Yet a kind, thoughtful and perfectly reasonable and understandable telephone call from Douglas—the separated husband, the villain who, confusingly and unjustly, seemed to be more stable and more cheerful than she was—sent her into weak tears and turmoil.

John went to Cumbria by bus the next day and Mary telephoned Mike. Whatever happened—whether Douglas came back or not, whether she met someone else or not, whatever happened, she had to find a way to live her life without this marriage. It would have to be cast away. She needed to grow for herself and for that she needed help. The effort which went into telephoning Mike confirmed her in her determination. She hesitated and feared it and found excuses against it for some hours—confirming the very state she knew she had to get out of. He came round that evening.

When she saw him, she wished she had not invited him. Not because he was unwelcome in himself but because he would need attention and she had none to spare from herself. He stood on her doorstop like an unbidden guest and it was with a weary effort of will that she asked him in. She had made only the merest preparations for his coming: previously she would have taken care to duff the cushions, re-set anything which was out of true, put on the side lamps, do that last minute tidying up which she could do with so much flair and which clearly indicated that expectation had been keen and warm. Mike noticed this and felt the chill of neglect beginning to settle on the place. A dirty glass, a mug half full of coffee, two ashtrays teeming with butts, the "Guardian" strewn on the floor. And Mary herself, he thought, looked unwell. Undoubtedly thinner, her face white, her luscious hair drawn back for convenience and lack lustre. She did not ask him whether he wanted a cup of coffee but immediately held up the bottle of scotch and poured out two stiff ones.

They sat under the uncosy glare of the main light.

Mike was sitting in the chair which had been—still was—Douglas' favourite. An undistinguished but comfortable chair—she had seen him there so often: even though the place was different and the purpose of taking the flat had been to wipe out such associations—the chair mesmerized her.

"You seem a bit down."

"I'm sorry?"

"You seem rather down."

Mary let the repeated remark fall between them. She stood up.

"This is silly," she said, "but would you change—chairs? Oh God!"

Mike instantly understood what had led up to the request and felt drained of hope. She was in bad shape. He moved to another chair.

"It's terrible," she said.

"I thought you were doing well," Mike replied. "On your own. As you said last time."

"I thought I was. But it won't go away." Still standing, looking, poor love, Mike thought, as forlorn as he could ever imagine her looking, she held her head with both hands for a minute and then rejected the gesture as too melodramatic. "It just grows inside my head. Really. Like something growing, heavier and heavier. I keep thinking of it being a solid object, sitting there, weighing me down, dragging everything into itself, sucking on all my energy. And it's to do with loss or missing him or—I don't know. But I feel that there's nothing else except this terrible lump. The rest of me . . . never mind. I can't think about anything else. It seems I can't talk about anything else."

"You have to talk it out, I suppose," Mike said.

"Do you?"

"That's what they say. Maybe they're right. Or perhaps you need a complete change. They say that as well. Get out of yourself."

"I shouldn't have asked you round. I'm boring. People who are jilted are boring, aren't they?"

"I thought it was you who did the jilting."

"That's the strange thing. I can't seem to accept that. Even though it's true."

Again she paused and Mike let her drift into what he now saw was the beginning of a habit of reverie. Until now he had been Mr Nice and Scrupulous and Honourable until his teeth ached. Had a Senate Committee investigated his conduct they would have given him a sheet so clean it could have been used in a soap powder ad. Mary sat down, nervously, on the edge of the seat of the chair he had just abandoned.

"Mary," he said, "I think I may be in love with you. I think you could return it, eventually. Why don't we try?"

"Try."

"Yes."

She looked startled. Then she considered what he had said.

"You mean we should go to bed."

"Sooner or later."

"What would that prove?"

"That's not a question that can be answered."

"I couldn't—Douglas—I haven't. Ever." She spoke as if short of breath.

"At least we could go off somewhere for a few days. Leave this place. Leave London. Leave England. Get out."

"I'd like that."

"We could go to Paris. Tomorrow afternoon. For a long weekend."

"Paris. It sounds so old-fashioned."

"It's still a good place to go."

"We went once—Douglas . . . Are you serious?"

"Yes. We could catch the afternoon flight. I know a little hotel just off St Germain. You'd enjoy it."

"What if I didn't? What about you?"

"I'd see Paris."

"I don't know. I've never been unfaithful."

"That is not a condition. Although I intend to be irresistible! No, Mary. Let's get out. You and me. Not because you need it, or I want it, but to do something together. You and me. See what happens."

"I want to." Mary found herself weeping again and did not stop it. "I want to go somewhere else. I want to, I truly want to lose this burden of Douglas. I want to want to go to bed with—you—I must, in a way, if I'm to have any chance. You don't mind that, do you? I have to. I have to be somebody on my own. But I don't know what that is. Oh God, why is it like this?"

"Paris?"

Mary paused and then turned her head into the chair and answered him loudly.

"Yes," she said. "Yes. Yes."

(2)

Most people you worked for, Hilda had concluded, were a pain in the neck. Her boss in the film institute was typical. He was terrified of *his* boss and that governed him. When his boss threw a tantrum or demanded an explanation or passed on a grouse or a complaint he had received from *his* boss, then down it came to Hilda. She was angered at how strongly the hierarchical system based itself on shows of power and displays of fear. Surely, she thought, in the late twentieth century, and in such a milk-and-water little endeavour as this, there ought to be a feeling of ease about authority. After all, it mattered very little in terms of the work being done and it was generally acknowledged that some of the more technically (on the salary and promotion scale) junior employees did the most important work. And the work was in that apparently easy-going area somewhere between journalism, scholarship and the media where mateyness and democratic attitudes were rigorously *de rigueur*. Here there were practically no distinctions made through dress or accent or background. Here the notion of one man one equal voice (and one woman one slightly more than equal voice, at the moment, with the heightened awareness of women's rights) was taken for gospel. Here the old notions of structures of authority were daily challenged in long theoretical talks, and always decisively dismissed. Here was the all-equal society.

Yet, there was no doubt about it, Hilda thought, underneath that casual, chatty brotherhood was a rigid little power complex based on the traditional territorial premises. And that day, at the office, had been like a bad-joke day with her boss, on the run from his boss, relieving his anxiety and attempting to dissolve his fear by snapping at her and correcting her—in short, bullying her. At six thirty she invented a migraine and left. Her boss stayed on for another two hours, vainly hoping for an encouraging word from *his* boss, who always worked late.

Hilda decided to walk back some of the way. It was a fine summer evening and if she chose her streets cleverly she could pass through various garden squares, along streets with lovely shops in them, and come to the park at the perfect hour, the very end of the afternoon, before dusk began to gather. She had learnt to gather together such mundane treats and spend them carefully.

For something to do, she guessed. For a distraction.

The park was full of distractions and, Hilda suspected, just as full of people seeking them. Old men sitting on benches, sometimes smiling into an unfocused middle distance: old ladies, often with their bags of crumbs or nuts for the ducks and squirrels: solitary young people walking purposefully in a circle, looking for that big explosive meeting which would ignite their lives: she, "Lovely young(ish) woman likes films, music—all types—and books. Enjoys walking and talking. Seeks man, preferably 35–40, similar." And they would meet in a place like this—an anonymous cafeteria beside a boating lake, she with a "blue scarf", he with a "green tie" and instantly fall silent . . . It was not much use attempting to deride that sort of thing. She was very near it now and she felt ashamed.

It was difficult to bear, this shame, and even to remind herself of it gave her a stab in the brain which felt physical. She felt abandoned and rejected and humiliated.

She had been aware of the young man for some time. He had trailed her along the edge of the Serpentine as ineptly as a reluctant comic detective. He was, she thought, ridiculously young. When she turned her attention to him, she found herself rapidly spurred to imagining what he would do, what she might do. She might take him up, the Older Woman, the great layby lady of literature, the initiator of young heroes, the woman of worldly experience, teaching and moulding the virgin young, making a man of him, watching him grow and then turning him gently out into the wide world, now equipped to conquer it, herself to retreat gracefully with the wound gallantly born, perhaps to find consolation with some old flame most fortunately rediscovered. Or he could be so stoppered and pent with sexual frustration that he would awkwardly edge her into a lonely spot here in the park and fall on her, tooth and nail, insatiable. Or she would remind him of his older sister, or old girl friend, with luck, or his mother, who had died young, and they would play a scene of tender reminiscence over lagers in the metropolitan dusk until, melancholy slaked, they would ease away into the great city with hearts assuaged and a light but permanent sweet memory traced on their minds. Or she could use him. She could not be certain whether she truly missed sex or merely missed the feeling of its being always possible. Sometimes, though, she felt as ravenous as a hungry vixen. Her mind seemed to howl out for touch, contact, penetration, fondling. The loneliness of the flesh would infect her like a stinging rash. Anybody, she thought, would serve.

Yet that passed away. Another, harder fury remained: her seemingly ineradicable commitment to Douglas.

She walked over the bridge to the octagonal shaped bar with its conical glass roofs and uninviting interior. She *was* thirsty. A quick glance reassured her that the young man had stuck to his self-appointed task. She went into the bar, feeling suddenly dispossessed, as she always did when she went into a strange pub alone. The young man came up to the bar beside her. He was, Hilda could sense, almost completely knotted up with anxiety. It was the barman who undid the puzzle.

"If you sit at one of the tables," he said, in an Irish accent and not too kindly, "somebody'll come across and get your order."

By assuming they were together he helped Hilda to decide—what the hell—why not talk to a stranger for once? They sat down uncomfortably at the uncomfortable tables.

"My name's Hilda," she said.

"David," he muttered. Same initial, she thought and then thought—Oh God! "David," he repeated and then, as if remembering an ancient custom, he held out his right hand. Hilda took it. They shook, solemnly.

She felt like his mother.

But he had, after all, had the gall to—hunt her down? Something like that.

"Can I try to guess what you do?" she asked.

"Yes." His face cleared. Her attitude reassured him. He was not with a looney. And already he could feel that she was nice.

She certainly looked better close up, he decided, with the well weighed appraisal of his nineteen years. A bit too thin, maybe, and strained looking—but he did not mind that: it was her eyes, full of cheerfulness and—he hoped—promise. And her breasts, he decided—breasts were his nightly dream comforters—were much better close up. The sort you could reach out for and hold one in each hand and feel soft and firm and a delicious handful. He took his eyes off them—Hilda was wearing a thin summer dress with a shapely satin bra underneath—only when she coughed.

"Student?"

"Yes."

"That was easy." She smiled at him. He relaxed a little and his eyes dropped back to her breasts, where they landed like jump jets on target. "What do you study?"

"Er," reluctantly he drew up his irises and found it was possible to enjoy the sight of her face: he hesitated. "Engineering."

"Yes?" The barman reappeared beside them as a waiter, notebook in hand, pencil hovering, eyes scanning the twilit park for some excitement.

"I'll—what do you want?" David asked.

"Half of bitter, please," Hilda said.

"Half of bitter and—" David paused, "another half of bitter."

"Two halves of bitter!" The scorn was unmistakable. Perhaps he had dreams of running a cocktail bar with pink gins and champagne cocktails, with daiquiris and whisky sours, with all the verbal and alcoholic paraphernalia of the sunset crowd. Instead he was stuck in a glasshouse in Hyde Park serving halves of bitter to quite ordinary people.

"He thinks we're not good enough for him," Hilda said, happily. She was sure of herself now. She would chat, pay for her own drink, and then, soon, walk across the park to catch a tube.

David began to emerge from the shock of shyness which had hit him at the moment of what he now began to think of as his success. He had clicked!

"Do you make a habit of following women around in the park?" Hilda asked, amusedly.

"No." David blushed and then was vehement. "Certainly not."

"Only one or two."

"Why do you ask?"

"Because I want to know," Hilda said, calmly. "Do you?" She paused. "Or am I the *first*?"

She was afraid he would sulk: and then it would be really boring. To avert that, she smiled encouragingly.

"No," he admitted, having weighed the odds. "You're not the first."

"Clicked before?"

"Two halves of bitter!" A small dish of nuts accompanied the two halves of beer and the waiter rolled his eyes in despair as David's right hand leapt out automatically to grab a fistful. While he was grubbing in his hand, Hilda produced a pound note and the waiter took it.

"No," David gurgled, through a mass of salted peanuts. "No! It's me. I'll pay."

Frantically his knobbly hands swooped towards his trouser pockets. He was wearing no jacket and the trousers were accompanied by an open-necked orange shirt which he clearly considered dashing; the trouser pockets proving useless, he assaulted the two bulging pockets which breasted the front of the shirt. Buttons got in the way. Fingers were unable to discriminate between coins and pens and a trove of mini-junk.

By the time he had uncovered a pound note, Hilda and the waiter had completed the transaction.

"You must let me pay," he said.

"Why should you? I'm earning a wage. Your grant can't be very big. Cheers."

She held up the glass and sipped at the warm beer.

"It's very kind of you." He took a running gulp at the bitter and all but finished it off in one.

"So," Hilda said, to tease out the few minutes she would give him, "what happens with these Other Women?"

"There haven't been any," he said. "I've—tried. I'll admit that. And once or twice—but if a woman's on her own in a park maybe she's looking for companionship, just like a man. She could be. It's not a sin to ask." Again his eyes dropped to her breasts and the breasts warmed a little under his longing scrutiny. His defensive explanation had brought some animation to a face until now characterized by an intense shy wariness. He's good looking, Hilda thought, with surprise: why should he be tailing women in the park?

"Why do you do it?" she asked. "I would've thought you could have managed a girlfriend easily enough."

"It's not that easy," he replied, promptly, and then pulled back from the confession which, Hilda realized, was there to be delivered. So that was it. She was to be Mother Confessor. She relaxed a little and finished her drink. He took the hint and, after some rather frantic semaphore, indicated to the superior Irishman that the same again was required. Almost half-past eight, Hilda was thinking, stay here for about another twenty minutes, walk to the bus, trundle home by about quarter to ten, have a bath, eat a little, sink a couple of Valiums and hope for the best. Usually she took more care to organize her evenings against the kind of drifting she had indulged in this evening: it allowed too much thought, it built up regret, it signified emptiness. So she had taken a way out by taking on, as it were, this very tentative adventurer. Yet he only had part of her attention. She feared that she was beginning another of those phases where she would be drawn into an obsessive preoccupation with Douglas, with what had been, what might have been, what could be. She had beaten it off until now but she was not sure she could continue to do so.

"Good luck," she said and raised the stubby glass to the boy in front of her. He grinned rather confidently and offered her a cigarette.

"So," Hilda persisted, seeing in this line of enquiry the only interesting talk they could have, "you don't find it easy to get girlfriends."

David scowled and did not reply. Hilda ignored this reaction.

"Is it hard," she asked, genuinely, "studying engineering?"

"You have to work at it," he said, rather grimly. "And they call the place you do it in—a Polytechnic, while all the fancy boys and—women—who do any old Arts subject that anybody could do with a bit of flannel—they all go to Universities. I'm doing it and then getting out to somewhere else where engineers are thought of as something a bit more than mechanics. Even my own mother thinks that I'm studying to be a superior garage repair man. Yes, it's *very* hard. You have a lot of theory to keep up with and the practical is bloody difficult because the facilities are so second rate. The money goes on the useful citizens who are studying sociology or the Novel or the Philosophy of whatever."

Hilda's attention was engaged. The undisguised bitterness, the feeling of having to struggle against Them who had it easy: the way in which, as it often seemed to her, by some determination of history in this country, those who did the essential work were made to feel inferior—all this found an echo in her own life.

"You seem rather upset by it," she said and went on, blind but sure. "Had it something to do with why you lost your girlfriend?"

"Maybe." He paused and looked past her—out to the park now sprinkled with lights in the soft city dark. "How did you guess?"

"I don't know," Hilda lied. She knew very well; there was about him that shorn and forlorn appearance which precisely reflected her own condition. She waited.

"It wasn't the engineering," David began, almost reluctantly, "although it *could* have been the Polytechnic, a bit. No, it wasn't even that. When it came down to it, I read more books and listen to more records and certainly go to more movies than the rest of them. There's a gang of us," he explained, "most of us came to London for one reason and another and we stuck together. Until—Anne and I—split."

"When was that?"

"A month or so—a month ago exactly."

For the "exactly" her heart went out to him. He was intent now and openly unhappy. "I didn't want to see any of them, somehow," he said, and again his eyes dropped to her breasts but now the Pavlovian lusting had receded. He was no longer in the character of someone with his eye on a quick grope. The character had not suited him anyway. But frustration and unhappiness had exercised their usual distorting influence. Added to which, he had his fantasies, like all adolescents, and when the opportunity arose it was hard not to try it out. He looked up. "Anne and I had been going together for three years, you see. At school. We'd been around Europe together. We weren't engaged but that was just because our lot don't get engaged. She went off with my best friend. My best friend," he repeated, as if it were the first time in the world such a thing had happened and incomprehensible. The repetition was to reassure Hilda that she was hearing correctly. It seemed to David that it was the most unexpected thing in the world.

"It often happens like that," Hilda said.

"Your best friend?"

"Yes."

"I don't believe it." He drank some more bitter and indicated the offer of another round. Hilda shook her head. "Anyway," he concluded, withdrawing from the brink of full and true confessions, "he—my best friend—and her—Anne—they still knock around with the gang. As if nothing had happened. I can't—well. I can't go around with them pretending nothing's happened, can I? I can't see her there with him when she was with me a month ago. It isn't as if I've stopped just because she's stopped. You can't hide your feelings, can you? And so—"

So many chords had been struck in Hilda by this recital, and by its clear implications, that she felt quite hemmed in. But she helped him out again.

"You come to the park."

"Yes."

"Well," she finished her drink, "I'll have to be going now."

"Can I—we were just starting."

"I think it's better not."

"Where are you going?"

"To catch a bus."

"I've got a motorbike. It looks a bit old fashioned, I put it together myself, but it works well enough."

"I'm sure it does." Why could fifteen years not drop off her, like an old skin? Why could she not be meeting this boy-man as prepared as he was to begin something and with enough hope to see it resolved? Why were the meetings in her life always with the right men at the wrong time? "But I'll stick to the bus."

"What's your address? Can I phone you?"

He jumped up as she left the table and worried her to the door. They went out side by side and the air seemed to restore David, or rather to make him pull back to his earlier persona. His flirtatiousness momentarily asserted itself. He made a clumsy grab at Hilda. She evaded it easily and looked directly into his face.

"Why *do* you prowl around here?"

"You wouldn't understand."

"I might." In the dusk he looked fragile. His inept honesty reminded her of Douglas: perhaps, she thought, Douglas had been this fragile once, this lost in the city. "Where do you come from?" she asked, abruptly.

"Near Bristol. A little town called Thornbury."

"I see. A stranger here. And your best friend—I'm sorry but I'm curious—is he an Arts student?"

"English. Wants to do sociology."

"You shouldn't prowl around here, you know. Somebody might take you up on it, or panic and cause trouble. Either way isn't much of a life."

They were walking now, Hilda keeping a deliberately steady pace.

"What else can I do?"

"There's bound to be somebody you meet around the Polytechnic, isn't there? Or—don't you have clubs?"

"The Poly's full of men. The only decent clubs are sports clubs. We all live too spread out in the suburbs to get together much."

"Well," Hilda advised, lightly, "give it up for a while."

"I got used to it," David groaned lugubriously. "It isn't simple to give it up. I think I'll go mad if there isn't a woman to talk to. Or . . ." He left it at that. Then took up the theme again as Hilda remained silent. "I can't get interested in anybody."

"Except in a park."

"Yes." The darkness now as they went along the road, which wound, country fashion, through the trees, and the relief he felt with Hilda emboldened him. "*You* noticed me quite early on. You could have signalled that you weren't at all interested. You could have signalled that you were offended. You could've scared me off. Why didn't you?"

There was no reply Hilda could make which would not further implicate them. She decided to cut out. They would never see each other again: it had been brief, let it be a brief mistake.

Again David made a clumsy lunge for her but this time he caught her and pressed her tightly against himself uttering a little moan. Hilda wrenched herself away and, as he came back at her, she raised her hand.

"I'll scream, David, and you'll be sorry. You're right. I did encourage you—but that wasn't an invitation to rape or to a lifetime's companionship. It was the sort of thing a lonely person does without even beginning to reckon up the consequences. Now it's over. You go your way, I'll go mine. If you try anything on, I'll yell."

One or two cars swung comfortably around the bends in the road. The mild air had attracted a number of evening strollers to the park. David glanced around, apprehensively, fearing that his behaviour might already have prompted repercussions.

"I'm sorry," he said, "you've been very nice."

Hilda nodded. She felt overcome by a dizzying weariness. What had she got herself into? How could she have been so idle?

David still walked alongside her but she said no more until she reached the park gates.

"My bus-stop's over there," she said.

"Are you sure?" He sounded so sweet, she thought, so tender and companionable. "Really sure? I'm not—like that."

"Goodbye."

She held out her hand: he took it. She turned and walked away firmly, without looking back.

At the bus-stop she glanced across and saw him still watching. Then he turned and raced away. She guessed that he just might be going for his motorbike so that he could follow the bus. She waited until he was well out of sight and then walked along towards the Underground.

The weariness she had felt increasingly over the past few weeks had been exacerbated by the encounter. It could have been poignant, she thought, had she wanted to make it so, or even passionate. Women could submit to being prey in a big city: there were always hunters at large, timid though most of them were. And there would always be young men who would like advice and unfussy sex and security. There were legitimate bachelors on the go, too: she had met one or two at the occasions organized for her by one of her friends: and there was the legion of married men, more intriguing, generally, partly because they *were* married.

As she walked the last few yards to the flat and then went into the usual routine, it was the forbidden subject which crashed in on her. Douglas.

She broke her rule. As if in a daze she went to the phone, dialled his home—Mary's flat, where she thought he was now newly housed and settled—and waited. The sound of his voice would be enough. Just the "Hello". She would put down the receiver immediately.

No one answered.

(3)

Joseph had finished in the garden, or rather—he had done enough. You were never, he would say to Betty most sternly, especially when she was asking for help, you were never finished in a garden.

It was still light. The evening was warm, truly warm, with no edgy little breeze to take the pleasantness off it. And clear. The sort of evening when you could see down to Skiddaw and the fells in the south and clear across to Criffel and Scotland in the north.

He had courted Betty, he remembered, on evenings like this. Walking through the Show Fields along the River Wiza. Other couples, old and young, doing the same as them, on a summer evening in the Thirties. Nobody very well off—a chief cashier, a schoolteacher, a chief clerk perhaps being the elite: mostly working people like Betty and himself in their second best, perambulating beside the meandering stream as formally and tranquilly now, in his memory, as if they had been doing a minuet in a costume drama.

As Joseph put away his tools in the tiny shed, which he kept strictly tidy, he felt a spasm of love for that past. It was the death of his father which had encouraged his turn to the past. To his surprise, he had found himself thinking of his childhood, remembering the old man when he had been strong and hopeful and young in the other world of Britain which clung around him at Joseph's birth: the late Victorian and Edwardian age which had marked his father as if he had been a foreigner. Perhaps we each have our age and, as time goes by, become increasingly foreign to the changing world. Old John's world had altogether gone by the time he died: he must have wondered which planet he was on, sometimes.

He came around to look at the garden. Even John would have been proud of it. Harry still did much of the heavy work, of course, but the laying out and the caring for the plants and blooms was Joseph's care. He took out a cigarette and allowed himself a stroll about, bending to pluck out a minute weed here, nip off a dead leaf there. Life had certainly ended up by giving him a very good deal.

A strong feeling of gratitude surged into him on this benign summer's evening. His carpings fell away. Gone the gripe about those who did no work and those who did not know how to govern and those who were too stupid to run a football team and the councillors who were too foolish to run a fish shop and the whole dreadful world which was generally a sitting duck for the disparaging darts of Joseph and his philosophical cronies. It was not, he had to admit on a night like this, too bad.

The feeling gathered impetus. The past seemed a fine sheltered place which he could visit at will. He had spent much of his life with his nose pressed to the present. This realization of the past was like being given a new kingdom. And it rose like a tide and brought benefits into the life he lived now. He had never thought he would own a house—and such a decent, well appointed place with the garage and the garden, the central heating, the pleasant furniture, and all the knick-knacks of that bit of superfluous wealth. Nor that he would be able to have such an agreeable retirement in financial terms. The pension, plus all his small savings, together with what he got for his part-time job, kept him in very adequate comfort. His health was not so very good but not so very bad either. There were the cronies to keep interest in the world's ways alive and ticking. And there was Betty, looking after him. A full measure of contentment flooded out of his recollections and burst the banks of his usual domestic inactivity.

"Betty, Betty," he began to call as he went back to the house. It was a habit that was rooted now. Whenever he wanted anything of Betty, he would begin to call out her name— although she might be at the other end of the bungalow— and continue to do so until he came across her. He did not realize how old it made him sound—but then, he had no false vanities about age.

Betty was playing whist with young John, who had grown bored of helping his grandfather in the garden when all that needed to be done was so small and finicky. For a moment Joseph stood and enjoyed the cosy sight.

He announced his news as if heralding the principal event in a Greek drama.

"It's a lovely night for a walk," he said, and, as if expecting applause, added, "Let's up and off."

Betty had been thinking exactly the same herself and indeed she had been toying with the idea of persuading John to come with her. Just in time she caught Joseph's eye, saw the anxiety lest the request be turned down, and sensed that here was a time to drop her guard.

"Isn't that a good idea?" she said to John. "Just wash your face and put your blazer on and we'll be off."

"Along the river," Joseph put in, emphatically, as if playing a trump.

"John likes the river," Betty said, "don't you?"

John smiled and nodded. There was something a bit comical about the old pair, he thought, but he basked in their attention and liked them too much to let cruel or critical thoughts colour his love for them. He left the room for the unnecessary wash.

"He's coming on," Joseph said, expansively, as Betty tidied up the cards. "He's twice the lad he was at Christmas." He paused. "You would've thought it would've upset him—*then*—you know. I put it down to your influence as much as anybody's."

"Mary's very good," Betty said, closing further argument. "Where did he put that card box?"

"Here, mother," Joseph spotted it and all but trotted over to hand it to her. When he did so, he gave her an awkward hug. Betty looked up at him in some surprise.

"What's that for?"

"I felt like it," Joseph replied, skittishly, and the more she scrutinized him, the jollier he became. In the twilight he looked a bit like a goblin, she thought, his large red nose, the thin hair tufted up with cream, the dodging gestures. "Can't a man embrace his wife?"

"What do you want?"

"Do I have to want something?"

"Yes."

"Look." Joseph, rather dashed, stopped dancing about and spread out his hands like a salesman. "Believe me—I don't want anything. That's the point. I'm very well off. That's what I've been thinking."

"I see." Betty smiled to herself as she got up. She had sensed his mood and needed no more explanations but it amused her to tease him a little and this she did as they got ready to go out.

"You walk in the middle," Joseph said to John. "No. Walk beside your grandmother on that side and I'll be on this side."

"Like two detectives with a suspect," Betty said.

"You always take things the wrong way."

"I'm worried about your grandad's sudden urge to walk," Betty said to John and winked. "Do you think he wants to get us out of the house for some reason?"

"I've *told* you. It's the perfect night for a walk. I've told you."

Others had had the same thought. The three fields alongside the river were strewn with evening walkers. Everybody nodded a greeting at everyone else. There was a mood of satisfied amiability.

"It's just like old times, isn't it?" Joseph rejoiced. Betty nodded. She had become used to percolating all her experience into a private chamber of her mind. Sharing with Joseph had long since fallen into disuse and even when he articulated her own feelings accurately, as he did now, she found it hard to empathize with him. Yet it might still be possible.

"Your grandmother and me used to do our courting along this river," Joseph announced to John, who rather stiffly took in the information. But he was pleased to be told it, Joseph could tell.

"She was a real beauty then," he said.

"Don't listen to him," Betty said to John, but not sharply. "Your grandfather always exaggerates."

"Often enough we hadn't a penny in our pockets," he went on, enthusiastically. "And I'm speaking about old pennies. There were farthings, then, you know. I expect they teach you that in History. Things were marked up in farthings—$3\frac{3}{4}$d, $2\frac{1}{4}$d."

"He'll be thinking we've just walked off the Ark," Betty said, warmed, to her surprise, by Joseph's nostalgia.

"There seemed to be a lot of fine evenings then," he went on, encouraged to become lyrical. "Sometimes we would get our bikes out and go down to Silloth for a swim. Buy some fish and chips and then ride back—by moonlight."

"Goodness me, Joseph, the lad'll think we were daft! Moonlight!"

"We did!" Joseph maintained, stoutly and truthfully, and then burst into song: "By the light—tum ti tum, tum ti tum, of the sil-very moon—tum ti tum, tum ti tum—I heard this tune—tum ti tum, tum ti tum—Da da di da in June—"

"Those aren't the words."

"It doesn't matter. Do you think I would have made a pop singer, John?"

John grinned and Betty's heart skipped that the boy should be capable of looking so happy. Joseph was forever teasing him about pop music, which John studied fanatically and debated studiously with great expertise.

They had gone down the West Road and headed south through the fields. Joseph continued his chatting and teasing of them both. People greeted each other cheerfully; the fields were lush and dry; the hills guarding the Lake District were clear as cut-outs against the slowly darkening sky. When they came into the last field, the river swung away from the path, and John broke away to follow it along the bank, leaving his grandparents together on the path in unaccustomed companionship.

"You've helped that boy a lot," Joseph said.

"He's a brave little lad. He takes some getting to know. But when you get through to him, he has all sorts of things about him. He's a bit like your father."

"I think he's going to be very clever," Joseph predicted, rather solemnly.

"That doesn't matter as long as he's happy. Cleverness doesn't do much for you in the end." She was thinking of Douglas: it pained her to think of him, lost, as she saw it, out of true with everything that mattered.

"You mean our Douglas?"

"Of course not. He's done well. But *she's* done really well. Mary. Much better than I would have guessed. She's really given that boy what he needed. He isn't the same person he was at Christmas. I admire her for that."

"Do you think . . .?"

"I don't think about it." She glanced over at John, who was going along the bank like a bloodhound, peering into the river uninterruptedly. "We can only do so much. He needs his father."

"It happens all the time nowadays," Joseph said, trying to assuage her anxiety. "Not only in the papers. Everywhere."

"That doesn't make it any better for the children, does it?"

For some moments they walked along silently. But Joseph's euphoria would not be dashed.

"You know," he tumbled over the following words, determined to get them out, afraid that Betty would laugh and puncture his sentiment, "I've been thinking. When you get older you're supposed to get wiser—that's what they said. And I always thought that, alongside that, things got worse for you personally—that's why my own father was so reluctant to give up work. He was frightened of the workhouse still and so am I, to a certain extent. Though things are better than I could have imagined. But I don't feel any wiser. I think I know nothing at all. It's as if I've just got all the, you know, daft bits of me sorted out and what I should be doing is settling down to a life of learning things. I'm sure I would have enjoyed that. I would have enjoyed being a village schoolmaster, you know. You could have contributed something then. And there would have been time for thinking about things. What have I thought about? There's all this life to think about—what have I done about thinking about it? And mostly what I read is the newspapers. There are all those Great Books. I haven't read the majority of them. I never will now. Why have I been so stupid?" He paused. Impressed by the emphatic nature of his delivery, Betty avoided his eyes and appeared to be listening intently. "It strikes you though, doesn't it? And it all seems to add up on one or two times in your life—like tonight. Or when I took you home to meet my family for the first time. Or the day I came back out of the forces. Or when Douglas or Harry did a particular thing. It doesn't worry me, you understand, although I think that if I was cleverer it would. But I just can't make head nor tail out of it." He took a deep breath. "I'm glad we've managed to batter through together anyway. That's something."

Betty nodded. She knew he was reaching out and she would not repulse him. Perhaps there had always been a companionship between them which busyness had obscured. John had filled the gap of need: the church work enabled her to keep busy and feel tolerably useful. Between those two poles she had constructed a life, over the past few months, which had enabled her to see above the aimless despair which had begun to claim her. Sensitive to others always, she recognized that Joseph was asking for help. He had never wanted it before. She glanced at him. He was a little embarrassed by his speech and had turned away, ostensibly to watch John. He wanted to be looked after, Betty thought. He would never admit it but that was the sum of it.

"It's turning rather cooler," she said. "We should be getting back."

Joseph nodded and shouted out to John, who trailed across reluctantly.

"I saw two trout," he said.

"That place used to be full of trout," Joseph boasted. "Fresh river and sea trout. I've seen sea trout up as far as the bottom of the fields. We used to watch them jumping. It was one of the loveliest sights I've ever seen in my life. Those salmon trout struggling upstream to lay their eggs, you know. It's an amazing thing how they know and how they won't give up."

"I'd like to see them," John said, enviously. "I'd really like to."

"Right," Joseph promised. "Charlie Allardyce'll know where to look. I'll get onto him and we'll have a look-see. Mind you—you have to be patient."

"I don't mind that," the boy replied. "I just want to see them jump."

"How about a fishing rod for your birthday?" Joseph asked, struck with inspiration.

"Oh—smashing! *Smashing*!" John slipped his arm around that of his grandfather and hugged it tightly. "That's *exactly* what I want. *Exactly*." He imitated a Dalek's voice. "You — read — my — mind — you — will — not — be — exterminated."

"That was *good*," Joseph said. "*Very* good. You could be a mimic. Your dad was a good mimic. He could take off anybody in the town."

"When he was my age?"

"Yes. About then."

"What else did he do?" John spoke eagerly.

"Well," Joseph adjusted himself and decided that there was everything to be gained from telling the boy as much as he could remember. As he chatted on, John visibly squirmed with delight and then darted in with further questions to pinpoint exactly what Douglas had done, what age he had been, what others had thought of it and what they had thought of him.

The conversation went on until they were back in their street. They had walked past two of the big new estates which now encircled the town and drew the residential life out of it, and along a road full of the older cottages and small houses which Betty had known from her childhood. There wasn't a lane or alley in the place that did not bring back an image. Down that track had lived a man who bred donkeys and she had gone there with a friend one summer evening, like this, to see if they could borrow one for a carnival. Yes, he had said, if you can ride one. And the donkey had thrashed about like a bucking bronco.

Further on was the sandpit to which, audaciously, she had sneaked off one afternoon while at the primary school and later been found having the time of her life building a house in sand. There was a mission hall up the steps and the two rather grand houses with orchards the boys would steal from, and the little red-brick infants' school, like something out of a child's pop-up play book.

The images were sad, but they carried consolations. Perhaps it was better to go entirely away and just break off. Perhaps all this just dragged you down, was more of a dead weight than a ballast. She did not know. It was what she had, that was all.

As they turned into the street, Joseph, aware that some kind of domestic spell had been kindly cast over the three of them, was loath to break it. Yet the itch to return to his routine proved too compelling to resist.

"I think," he said, looking earnestly at his watch, "yes. I think they'll all be wondering where I've got to."

"In the pub?" John asked, innocently enough.

"That's where we meet, yes. For convenience's sake as much as anything else. They don't have clubs and such like in Thurston. And the Reading Room closed long ago."

"When did you ever go to the Reading Room?" Betty asked, innocently.

"We could always afford our own newspaper. But the point is made."

He hovered, edgy as a schoolboy seeking permission to leave the class. Betty smiled. She was glad he had his friends.

"What are you waiting for, then?" she asked, knowing the answer. He wanted her approval. "Give them all my regards." To pin it home, she added, "Thank George Marrs for the eggs. They were lovely. John knew they were different right away."

"I will." Joseph was very happy. "I'll do just that. There's nothing to beat farm eggs. And," he tousled John's hair, "I'll bring you a bottle of pop and a packet of crisps. Anything I can get you?" To Betty.

She shook her head. He beamed at her, turned, almost pirouetted, and puttered away down the tranquil street to his den in The Crown where the world would be shredded and reconstituted.

"Grandad likes the pub, doesn't he?"

"Men have to have some enjoyment," Betty said. "He doesn't fare too badly."

"Will he really get me a fishing rod?"

"I'll see he does."

"Who'll teach me to fish?" He paused. "I don't think Dad can, do you?"

"He was never patient enough. Your grandad'll find somebody. He knows all sorts of people. Don't worry."

John nodded, reassured, and linked arms with her. She liked that very much.

The telephone rang just a couple of minutes after they got into the house. It was Douglas.

He spent a long time talking with John and, although Betty tried to keep her eyes averted, so as not to intrude, she could not help but hear. John had been clipped in his speech, even laconic to begin with, but soon he was laughing and asking questions about the height of the skyscrapers, the lifts in the Empire State Building and the sounds on the police cars. She was relieved that he could still be so warm with Douglas. One of her worst fears was that Douglas would get separated from his son.

"He wants to say hello to you now," John said and handed over the telephone. "There was some sort of mix up at the airport and he flew back in a *Concorde*. A *Concorde*!" The boy danced about the room, clapping his hands.

"You seem to have hit the jackpot there," Betty said to Douglas. "I've never seen him so full of himself."

"He sounds very well," said Douglas. "Thank you."

"His mother's worked wonders," Betty replied grimly. She was caught in a fix. She loved to talk to Douglas and was happy just to hear him "prattle on", as she called it. But she disapproved of what he was doing. She had tried to stay on the sidelines but John had brought her into Mary's camp and, although she would never admit that out loud, it certainly coloured her behaviour and, as now, slipped into her conversation without her being able to stop it.

"She has," Douglas agreed. It would help his mother, he knew, if he had told her that he was trying to repair his marriage. But the information was too sensitive and perhaps the fear of failure was too great.

"Did you have a good time in America?"

"Very. I like it there. There's nothing depressing about—not that I see, anyway."

"What was the weather like?"

"O.K. I think. Yes. Fine."

"It's been beautiful here. John might have the starting of a tan."

"I went," Douglas searched among his souvenirs with a certain desperation, "I went up the second highest building in the world for dinner."

"The second highest?"

"Yes." Douglas laughed. "The highest's in Chicago." He swallowed his laughter. "While I was having dinner, helicopters flew past—underneath."

"I see."

"It's a marvellous city—New York."

"There's that new song about it."

"How's Dad?"

"Bearing up. Are you managing to look after yourself?" She was convinced he was living with the other woman but maintained her fiction that he was living alone: which he was. And in need of care and attention. Which he also was, though she was certain the other woman pandered to his smallest wish.

"Not too bad," he said. A glance around the dismal, littered hallway of his rooming house confirmed the accuracy of his downbeat diagnosis.

"Will you be getting up here some time?"

"I thought of coming up tomorrow and then bringing John back."

"That would be very nice for him. He would like that."

"I'll catch an early train. See you."

"Yes."

He put the phone down. She held onto it for a while. It was indecent the way her heart had leapt, physically seemed to somersault, at his news.

"Your father's coming up tomorrow to see you," she said, steadily, to John. "You can tell him all about the fishing."

(4)

Douglas had just decided to go to Cumbria on the spur of the moment. It was a good decision, though, he felt it. And he would stick to it.

He dialled Hilda's number. There had been a message left at his office and two left here. She answered immediately.

"I wanted to talk to you, that's all," she answered, in response to his first question. "I've wanted to talk to you for weeks. I know I asked you not to—but suddenly it all seemed rather silly. You can ring off if you want. Do you?"

"Don't be daft." He paused. It had been an effort to repress thoughts of Hilda and to prevent himself from ringing her up: he had made it under the impression that it was the best way, an impression which had grown firmer with time. And there had been some compensation: a feeling of simplicity entering his affairs, the sense of a single direction possible. Now it was all as it had been.

"You sound—well, nothing at all—shall I say taken aback?"

Hilda's voice danced mischievously down the phone and Douglas could see her eyes brimming with amusement at the correctly intuited assessment of his reaction.

"It is rather a turn up. After the Heavy Letter. I thought that was me executed, slam, head off, caput."

"It was. I meant every word of it—when I wrote it."

"Thanks."

"Well, you must admit it was a shitty thing to do to tell me you were going back to your wife. Although I notice you've kept your flat on. Still need an escape hatch?"

"Something like that."

"Don't we sound cross!"

"Do I?"

"Don't you want to see me then?"

"Of course."

"You don't sound very enthusiastic. When?"

"I'm going north tomorrow."

"What about tonight? Now."

"What can I say?"

"You could say no. But that would be silly because I know you want to see me too. So it's yes. Where?" She hesitated only fractionally. "Our usual place? Three quarters of an hour?"

"O.K. See you."

"Don't sound so glum. You'll love it!"

Hilda put down the receiver and Douglas went back into his room.

He had ceased to like it. The bareness and ugliness of the place depressed him now.

Once again he read the letter which Mary had left for him "To Await Arrival".

Dear Douglas,

John is with your mother. She's pleased to have him there, I'm certain of that, so there's no question of imposing. She assured me that she was well and could cope. As for John, he's delighted to go. He likes it up there. I think he may end up preferring the country.

I've gone away for a few days with a friend. I don't quite know how much or how little you have any right to be told. At this stage we've decided "least said soonest mended"—although that isn't quite what I mean. What I mean is the less said the better. I am very tired and need the holiday which I hope this will turn out to be.

I've done a lot of thinking while you've been away and I want you to know that I really did appreciate what you were trying to do, even though I might criticize the way you went about it and the assumptions you base your decisions on. (grammar!)

There's part of me that will always love you—I never thought I would write that sentence to *anyone*, let alone you, but there we are. At this moment, though, I have no idea how strong that is, or how important it is. I don't know how much it means to either of us.

What I do know is that I am very tired and need a break. I hope you enjoyed yours.

Love,
Mary.

"*We've decided*"! That was what got him. Not only was there a man, and a man who swanned in large as life when he was three thousand miles away across the Atlantic Ocean, the man had the bare face to involve himself in discussions with Mary about *him*! It was intolerable. He metaphorically clapped his hands to his ears to shut out the imagined tittle-tattle and chit-chat about whether they should tell Douglas this, when they should tell Douglas that. The idea of being talked about in that way made him angry. There was nothing he could do. He presumed she had left an address with a friend of hers, in case of emergencies: he had intended to ask John if he had an address for his mother, but pride had forbidden it. Had he asked that night—he would have been given the small hotel in Paris, the address he was given the next day when he talked with John and could no longer contain his jealousy. "*We've* decided"!

He ripped up the letter—into four—and then put the small pile on his dressing table. Perhaps if he read it later he would see more in it.

As far as he could tell, Mary had never been unfaithful to him.

Did it matter?

Of course it mattered! It stung and wounded him as if he had been unblemished. There is no fair accounting of emotions. He wanted to disable the masculine component of "*We've* decided" and win back Mary.

And yet, although this outburst of emotions did occur, it did not sweep away the complications and ambiguities of feeling. Rather, it added more intensity to what existed.

As he went towards the pub to meet Hilda, he realized how little of the solution—if there ever could be one—was in his hands. And yet with his whole spirit he longed for a solution.

The pub was on the edge of Covent Garden, still beamed and poky, still the sort of place in which you might call for a hot poker to ram into a pint of ale. Oak settles, a bar laden with good food, and, on such a warm summer's evening as this, packed out.

Hilda was already there. Douglas shrugged at her across the crowded room and she nodded and came across.

"The trouble is," he said, as they picked their way over the bodies sprawled up and down the pavement outside the two bars, "that all the decent pubs are full and if we find an empty pub it's bound to be rotten."

"We could go and eat," Hilda said. "Restaurants are easier for talking."

Douglas was still rather jet-lagged—he had only flown in that morning—and his meal-count was completely askew. All he knew was that he did not want to eat.

"Let's try Paganini's," he said.

This was one of several fashionable, expensive and reasonably good restaurants which had opened in Covent Garden since the market had moved. The whole place was inexorably escalating towards an in-town Hampstead, more-fun-than-Chelsea area. Douglas had heard Raven recommend Paganini's.

It was almost full—a good sign at that time of night—and the head waiter was an efficient young man who made no fuss, led them to a quietish table, took the drinks order and left Douglas with the impression that the drinks themselves might already be on the way. The decor was baroque pop but not offensive: Paganini himself figured in various prints and articles about the place. The only naff note, as it were, was that the menu was shaped like a violin. Still, clean table cloths and napkins and glasses, two good Pimms when they came, a menu not absurdly long and full of sensible promises such as, "Vegetables fresh from the market daily" and, "Fish absolutely guaranteed fresh daily"—not bad. It would set him back about twenty-five to thirty pounds.

"It's as if we'd never parted," Hilda said, rather uncertainly. Her vulnerable nervousness turned Douglas' confused feelings towards protectiveness. She was, he thought, defenceless and he had contributed to that.

"Cheers."

The Pimms slaked the dusty summer thirst. Hilda was nowhere near as self-possessed as she had been on the telephone. She looked thinner, Douglas saw, and fraught: she kept flicking out a hand towards his, seeking a reassuring contact.

"I thought, I'll phone, I might as *well* phone. It seemed

stupid not to. And you would have phoned if I hadn't." She gave him the opportunity to confirm this and he smiled, which did the trick. She reached out for his hand and held it firmly. "You see. It would have been one of us. We think alike. We *are* alike."

Douglas took note of the wildness which was not far from the surface of her talk and again it was her weakness which drew out his affection.

They ordered cold vichysoisse, and turbot.

Hilda glanced about her rapidly, nervously, as if pecking the air, as if reassuring herself that things were as they had been. Douglas, who had ordered hock, pulled too deeply at the chilled white wine and felt that warning chute of coarseness down his sternum which told him he was slowly toppling into exhaustion.

"I like this place," Hilda said and sipped very tentatively at the glass. They smiled at each other and held hands like honeymooners.

The fact was, Douglas reflected, that he kept falling in love. There you were. In a society so highly tuned to monogamy—and one in which the rules for breaking the rules were strict, and punishable in law and pocket—this inherently amiable characteristic was a liability. Because he meant love, not lust: not generally; not any more. And love meant worry. Or, its other face, responsibility. But such responsibility brought immediate complications, since it led to insoluble contradictions. How, for example, could he follow through his love and responsibility to Hilda and Mary simultaneously, without short-changing one or both of them?

Two bottles of wine later, over sensibly large cups of coffee, Douglas at last focused properly on Hilda. He was aware that they had gossiped. He had passed on chit-chat about Merlin Raven: everyone was interested in Raven. And Hilda had called up their few mutual friends to spin out an appearance of community. It had been agreeable, happy, the two of them harmoniously in touch, connected.

"Well," Douglas said. "Here we are."

"Yes." Hilda smiled a little over brightly. She had relaxed but clearly he wanted to talk seriously about their future and she did not. She sensed his decision before he had spoken it and tried to snap and perpetuate the present moment. If you tried, she now thought, if you really tried, you could find a way of living in the present without pain.

"I thought, you see, after your letter," he started out, rather helplessly, "that it was over. For us."

"You sound as if you wanted it to be."

"You know I don't," Douglas defended himself weakly, although in fact he meant what he said.

"I do know that." Her hand covered his and her eyes sought out his glance. "I'm sorry. I'm nervy, that's all."

"There's something I have to say. And I want it to be as honest as I can make it."

"You look terribly tired all of a sudden."

"Jet lag. Booze. And being honest." He grinned. "Hilda—listen. I can't keep going as we did. I don't know why. In its hectic way it worked. Maybe we'll all miss it and be the poorer for it. But I've had it."

It was as if Hilda's nightmare had suddenly risen up before her.

The silence between them had to be broken.

"So you've found married life gives you all you need then," Hilda said.

"That isn't it. I'm not living with Mary. She doesn't want me back. But the point is that I want to go back and I can't any longer split myself in two. We can see each other but we can't sleep together."

"Why not?"

"I don't know. Maybe it should be the other way round. We should sleep together but not see each other. That makes sense at least. It's just that if I'm going to keep things together and have some sort of coherence in my head, then I have to have everything in the same place. Splitting sex is like splitting an atom inside myself—bang! Everything scatters all over the place, destroyed. I don't know why. It's crappy and creepy in a way, but there it is."

"You misunderstood. I meant—why will she not have you back?"

"There's another fella. No. I'm sure it's not that—although there *is* another fella. She wants some air, too."

"I can't understand you."

"No?" The waiter had brought a third bottle of wine and the bill. Douglas was by now pouring down the wine like beer on a hot afternoon.

"No. You say you love me. You needn't say it actually, I know you do. And Mary doesn't want you back. And yet you still won't come and live with me." Hilda's brows furrowed—Douglas, all but drunk, was careful to notice that the word was properly applied. They furrowed.

"It makes no sense," he agreed.

"That's a cop out."

"I agree." He sank a glass of the cool wine and reached for the truth. "You say you love me and you know I love you. I don't know what love is. That is to say, I know what I want it to be but it isn't that or rather it can't be that. So I don't know what it is. I don't know what weight it carries. I know what passion is—we had that, we still have it and not only in bed. I think I know what eroticism is: this meal could have been erotic if you had not been so tense and I had not been so tired. And then there's the awful gap—love: after that I know what duty is—a bit too late—and the same goes for responsibility—again too late. But *love*—love—I'll have to do without that now."

"That's a terrible thing to say!"

Hilda was poised like a tigress threatened. He loved her when she was so intense, so devoted to an idea. Here she was defending Love as if it were her young.

"It's a tired thing to say."

"It's your own fault you're tired. Some people are *really* tired—with blooming hard work. Your 'tired' is self-indulgence."

"True, oh queen. True enough."

She smiled, confident now. "I don't think you know what you're saying, to be honest. If you want to know what I think, it's that everything's finished between you and Mary but you don't want to admit it. I'm sure you will admit it. You're in a transition period now, that's all."

"No, I'm not. I mean what I say."

"In that case tell me you don't love me."

"It doesn't follow."

"Oh yes it does," Hilda said, almost laughing now, enjoying having him cornered. "Tell me you don't love me."

"It's meaningless." And it's not the point, he thought.

"If it's meaningless say it then."

"You know I can't."

"Well, as long as you can't," she said, steadily, "I'm not going away. If you want me to vanish, just say that and I will. I've sat in my flat for nights on end, thinking I was doing something useful, I was helping you to clear up your life, taking a burden away from you, giving Mary and John an opportunity. It wasn't much consolation but it made sense of a kind. And then I began to do weird things—I'll tell you about them sometime!—and I thought—I *know*—he still loves me—whatever you say, you can't think of a better word. And if he still loves me and I certainly still love him—what am I doing alone? So I phoned. And here we are."

"Yes." Douglas still had clarity of thought, slow as it might be. "But I still mean what I said. *See*—yes. Sleep—no."

"You look as if you could sleep for a week. My place?"

"I'm going to see John." With difficulty, Douglas found and delivered his Barclaycard.

"I thought you weren't with Mary."

"Neither is he. He's with my mother. There's a sleeper I can catch."

"Where are your things?"

"Things? I can buy them up there. About time I had a batch of new things anyway. New razor thing; new toothbrush thing; new trousers and shirt thing. Advert for Oxfam. Cheers." He drained the glass and poured out a last satisfying measure. Hilda had stopped drinking long ago.

The bill came to over thirty pounds with the tip.

As they walked along the pavement, his arm affectionately, and for reasons of support, around Hilda's shoulder, Douglas incanted a favourite sum.

"Thirty pounds," he said, "was as much as my grandfather earned in his first *year* of employment—eighty-two hours a week. And thirty pounds was almost a year's wages for my father when he started although he got his keep thrown in—no, six months, six months. He was a boots boy. And thirty pounds has just slid into our organs on wined skids. Besides which, consider the starving half of the globe, about whom my more sober friends would consider it a blasphemy for me to speak in this condition: a family in the starving half of the globe could live for a year on that thirty quid. Now what sense is there in all that? Bewilderment, guilt and finally a lack of real concern. That's all. Isn't it?"

The air had spun him into drunkenness and Hilda loaded him into a taxi and, conscientiously—for John, she realized, had to be looked after—ushered him to Euston, bought his ticket and took him to the train. It was rather disconcerting how sober and perfectly self-possessed he appeared. Even when he spoke one or two words to the ticket collector the words were neither slurred nor were they nonsense.

She took him into his compartment and they kissed each other very warmly. Douglas was in the narrow bed within a few moments. His head swirled like snow in one of those tiny crystal balls. His brain seemed like a swing and sway backwards and forwards inside the stretched tent of his skull. His throat was parched. His head began to ache.

"I wanted to be a vicar," he said, abruptly, loudly. "But I couldn't believe in God. I saw eternity as two parallel lines and they never met. It used to drive me nearly mad when I was trying to get to sleep. They just kept on travelling into space."

The train jolted away. Some sort of unconsciousness descended.

Hilda stood until the train had drawn out of the station and then she turned and walked along the concrete and up the barren slipway to the gate. The main hall was like a dosshouse, students mainly, she guessed, apparently snug in their sleeping bags, between trains or holidays or lives. She envied them their licensed summer carefreeness.

Outside, London felt almost balmy. She decided to walk some of the way. She felt secure again now and she wanted to relish it. The big black city with streamers of lights and wayward strollers was just the place to savour this reconciliation.

(5)

They were playing the Eton Boating Song. Emma paused to make absolutely certain, but there was no doubt about it. In Regent's Park on a Sunday afternoon, English fleecy clouds, sunny as the weather in a rattling Wodehouse story, full of large young men in boats and pretty girls in frocks and less, strewn with ageing bodies in ageing dresses hitched up to the bare white knee for the rays of heat, infiltrated by weary-faced foreigners seeking a respite from sightseeing and collapsing contentedly onto the crew-cut lawns (no charge) patrolled by invisible park wardens and speckled by one or two gentle loonies and snoring afternoon drunks and many dogs, not to mention the famous ducks and children with ice creams and courting couples curdling their breath together obliviously, the all perspiring band in bottle green uniforms were playing the Eton Boating Song.

Emma smiled soppily. She liked to be back in London. She had come up on a very early train and gone to see her old landlady, who had a curious tale about someone who must have been Lester threatening to return and terrorize her—Emma had reassured the old lady and made a promise to herself to tick off Lester for being so wicked, although the landlady was a bigoted and prejudiced old . . . she was still a person. Then she had dropped in at the Laughing Duck and, Luck! met up with several of the gang, who oohed and aahed at her new slimness, at her post-natal "completeness", at her country freshness, and stood her gins and It. She drank only a couple and thoroughly enjoyed the tasty talk of Andrew doing well in that Granada series about the waiter, you know the one, yes, *that* one, well, Andrew was the chef, not very much to say, not anything so far, but in *every* episode, imagine the fees if it gets sold abroad! And Pris, who'd got into the National, really, the National, *Pris*, it was unbelievable and you couldn't call it the old hello-hello, not with the director *she* was working with, my dear. And Alex and Annie, always rather intense, joined a co-operative company, touring North Wales with a show about pre-revolutionary Siam (was it called that now?) anyway—*very*, you know, *intense*, voting on everything and no laughs and everybody writes the script and a tidy Arts Council subsidy, thank you very much. And did she know . . . ?

She had loved it all. Loved them for their generous gossip, loved the crowded, hemmed-in little pub, loved the stroll down towards the park. It had been a boy, almost three months old now—and the birth of the child had secured Emma as nothing else in the world could have done. Her parents had been perfect bricks. They could not be kind enough or helpful enough. Indeed, her mother swore it had given her a new lease of life and her father seemed not the slightest bit perturbed by any fear of censure from his parishioners. For three months, the four of them had been as contented as a Beatrix Potter happy family. But it would pass soon, she saw that with the clarity nowadays second nature to her. And she still loved Lester.

Needs found ways. She had heard of Douglas' involvement with Merlin Raven, contacted him at the B.B.C. and managed to engineer a phone call to coincide with a visit Lester was making to Douglas' office. Douglas was an efficient accomplice. Emma had worked out a firm proposition: would he meet her the following Sunday afternoon in Regent's Park about three o'clock near the band? No strings, no scenes, no heavy number, just a chance for a chat. Lester had agreed.

He was there before her. She could scarcely believe it and took care to take her time before going over to him. He sat, pale and sadly she thought. Dark shoes and socks, dark trousers, a white shirt wide open at the neck, his jacket on the grass behind him to be used as a pillow. He was smoking, puffing too quickly, once again, without doubt, out of luck. Emma stood there and, stupid though it was, tried to will good fortune into him, to irradiate him with good fortune. Nothing had changed in her feelings. But her will was stronger and she had a strategy. There was the child now.

At first Lester wondered who it was, this slim, sexy looking woman, very "upper" in a large straw hat with a purple ribbon round it and a basket under her arm like Cherry Ripe, coming waving across the lawn towards him, the dress fluttering erotically against her figure, long hair blowing about her face: like some posh bird in an ad., he thought. And it was all for him. Without knowing why, Lester stood up. That gesture was the first to indicate an almost subliminal awareness on his part of the indisputable superiority of her external condition. She sank into his arms and pressed herself hard against him. It was the best thing that had happened to Lester for quite a while.

When they had sat down, she took out the picnic immediately—she had not eaten lunch and Lester was always a couple of meals adrift. Her mother had packed a white cloth which she spread on the grass and loaded with fruit—home grown punnets of raspberries and strawberries; two pies, one chicken, one veal; freshly baked bread, local cheese, home grown tomatoes and rather unsuccessful lettuce, but plenty of it, large and numerous radishes and an apple cake. She had bought four cans of beer in the pub.

"There," she said. "I'm famished."

Lester flicked open a can of beer and sank half of it. Then he fell to. The food was first class and sitting on the grass eating it made conversation difficult, which suited him very well as he was suffering from a confused invasion of thoughts and impressions. He was touched that she should be so thoughtful as to bring all this along for both of them and particularly moved that there should not only be beer, but his favourite label. He was a little daunted by her attractiveness. Emma had been the big fattie, the friendly Dunlopillo in a tight night spot, the nice but really, *be serious*, handy bit for emergencies, convenient in trouble. Now she was a looker. There was no doubt about it. He had watched the men swivelling their craniums as she had floated across the grass towards him and he too had taken a keen hard look at what they were noticing. It was very good stuff.

It was also worrying. If she had changed so much outside, perhaps she had changed inside. He had turned up—although he would have denied it—because he wanted to be with someone who thought he was great and who made him feel at least a bit better than average. He had been dumped, though not nastily and with a little paper handshake, by Raven and although Douglas tried his best to pretend he was useful, it was clear to Lester that his cousin could get on perfectly well without him. Besides which, he still felt sore at being outmanoeuvred and out-drunk in New York. In short, he was back where he had started before meeting Raven. He felt lost.

Emma's bounding puppy-dog affection would be just the pick-up he needed, he had thought. Now he was faced by this very desirable, young-looking female. He waited for her to make the moves.

To occupy the time, he took up the book which Emma had brought with her to protect her against what she had more than half suspected would be an empty and embarrassingly solitary afternoon.

"'Our Mutual Friend'," he read, "by Charles Dickens. Any good?"

"Yes," Emma returned, carefully. One of the things she admired but feared in Lester was his ability to make her cast off all pretentiousness. She came clean with him and felt safer for it.

"I read some of Charles Dickens at school," he said. "I quite liked it. Then the films. Fagin. Mr Pickwick. They were all right. Are you going to read it right through?"

"Yes."

Lester nodded and eased up on the food. He had satisfied the pangs provoked by the sight of such a tasty spread and satiation, plus a feeling that he had been gobbling in rather an adolescent manner, caused him to change pace. As was his custom, he lit up a cigarette to accompany the last part of the meal, and managed, in that act, to disguise (he thought) a burp.

"I expect you talk about books in your house," he said, mildly curious.

"Sometimes," Emma admitted. "But they're such big readers that they would rather be reading than talking about it."

"I used to read a bit," Lester offered. "In Liverpool. When I was hanging around the bands rehearsing. Ever heard of a writer called Maclean? Something like that."

Emma thought she had—was he not the man who wrote adventure stories? But was it Maclean? Somehow that didn't sound right. She played safe.

"No."

"You should get hold of one. I couldn't stand Agatha Christie."

"I quite enjoy her," Emma said, stoutly, faithful to the hours of escape into her mysteries.

"She's crap," Lester said, concluding the literary discussion. "If you want a detective you have to go to the pictures. The Americans have got all the detectives." He paused. "I suppose you could get used to reading if there was nothing else to do," he conceded, out of affection. He sounded very doubtful.

Emma smiled and handed him another can of beer. Her attention had been taken by a small child—about eighteen months—naked but for a pair of briefs, toddling backwards and forwards with the index fingers of both hands placed firmly in its navel. She began to watch the performance, which resembled the entranced dance of a witch doctor, as the almost naked child stomped across the grass in patterns known only to itself. Lester caught the intensity of Emma and in a moment of inspiration found a way to repay her for bringing along the meal.

"I suppose you have a photo of it?" he enquired, rather coyly.

Emma blushed deeply. She nodded and took out a small black photo-wallet which she had prepared. It contained two photographs. One of herself and the baby, one of the baby on its own. Inside the wallet was her name, address and telephone number. She handed it over to Lester, who stared at it dutifully.

"It's a boy," Emma explained.

"Good. He looks like Edward G. Robinson. Or a Chinese."

"He looks like you."

"Does he?"

"When he relaxes."

"What have you called him?"

"I thought I'd talk to you about that."

"Harry," Lester said. "Call him Harry. That's a good name. And give him a middle name. You never know when he could need it."

"Henry Tallentire," she said.

"Tallentire?"

"Only if you agree. It doesn't mean anything. I mean, I'm not going to claim anything from you."

"I see."

He snapped the wallet shut and held it out for her.

"You can keep that," she said. "I'd like you to keep it."

Lester nodded understandingly.

This time they relaxed together. He stretched back for a snooze. Emma lazily began to gather in some of the debris and continued to enjoy the park. It was so docile here. The unhurting sun, the grass easy on the feet, people in deck chairs, apparently untroubled, white shirts, vivid summer skirts and dresses, children scampering about, the band playing—was that Elgar? Yes. She was boning up on her music, too. It had already become a greater passion than literature. She had discovered that her father had been left an immense record collection by a friendly parishioner, and that, complemented by B.B.C. Radio Three, had directed her towards a lavish pleasure ground of music and performances. It *was* Elgar. "Enigma Variations." A simple one to guess, but you had to start somewhere. The listeners offered up a discreet spattering of applause, the same polite yet grateful yet unshowy clapping which trickled across the land at this time on a Sunday afternoon, around bandstands in parks and on promenades, at village cricket matches, at horse jumping competitions, at small tennis clubs and on bowling greens, as the English led their sabbatical sporting life at leisure and warm, for a change. Lester was asleep. Emma sneaked a look at her own photograph of—Harry? Harry it was, a perfect name! She was already missing the child! Shameful. She ought to be more liberated than that.

She read her book a while and thought about Lizzie Hexham.

She was gathering her strength. There was a proposition she wanted to put to Lester. She had little doubt it would be rejected, but she had worked it out with some care and would state it, whatever happened.

Eventually he woke up, smiled beatifically at her, shivered and lit up.

"Lester," she plunged in. "I'm moving back to London. The parents are very good but I want to be in London. Daddy—my father," she corrected herself—"Daddy" had always irritated him beyond reason, she had forgotten that, "has a friend—another vicar—in North Ken. and he'll let me have what used to be the housekeeper's flat very cheap. It's fantastically lucky. There's a crèche in the Church Hall next door and I'm going to help run it so I can earn something *and* look after— Harry at the same time. Now—the address is in that wallet I gave you. If you want to come along any time . . ."

"A vicarage?"

"Yes," she whispered.

Lester unbent magisterially to ask, "What's a crèche?"

Emma explained.

"The kid'll be O.K. there? They need a lot of looking after, you know."

She reassured him.

"Sounds as if you landed on your feet," he said.

"How was New York?" she asked, in the same spirit of congratulation. "That Merlin Raven deal seems super—I mean, very good."

"Yea?" Lester looked at her as if she alone were responsible for what was to follow. "It's all over. He's a shit."

Emma was silent. She saw that yet again Lester had been used and then dropped. She wanted to cradle him and protect him from all this. She made a move but retreated at his stiffening "Keep Off". She hated Merlin Raven.

"They're all shits, aren't they?" Lester added, somehow exonerating her and putting them on the same side. "What are you doing tonight?" he asked.

She had managed to get a ticket for a concert at the Festival Hall. Rudolf Serkin. A tremendous treat—so sure had she been that, even if Lester had turned up, he would flit before the evening. She had planned to go to the concert and then catch what was called "the milk train" back, to be there for the baby in the morning.

"Nothing," she said.

"I've got to see this man about a new group. These punks! They want to do it with a light show now, as if we weren't all doing that in the Sixties. They say we're all past it—you know that? Somebody said that Raven and his lot were 'dinosaurs'. But the new guys just haven't got it. They've got the mouth and all the writers love them because they're supposed to be talking about the new generation—but who cares? The bloody tunes are no good. And the arrangements! And the playing! I tell you—I'm thinking of getting out and going into something quieter. A friend of mine's got a betting shop over your way—where you'll be—North Ken.—he says I can work in with him. Not work *for* him, more of a, sort of, partner."

"That sounds," Emma hesitated, conscious that she was walking on a stack of broken glass, "useful."

"Exactly. Useful. Could be."

Lester got to his feet and looked down on her. She was very very fanciable, he thought. But, he also thought, I've done her enough damage.

"I'm a bit short," he said, "or I'd—you know. But I've got the address." He waved the wallet at her. "I'll see you all right."

"I can—thank you."

Emma suddenly felt the pressure of tears. It was too sudden for her to hold them back. Lester squatted down beside her and talked quietly and intensely.

"Look, Emma. You've made yourself into a lovely bird. You've got looks and connections. You don't want me. You think you do now but in a few months—no. There's nothing I can give you that'll do you any good. I'll send money for the nipper if I get hold of any. That's gospel. But now I'm going to do you a big favour—and vanish. Tara."

She clutched at him but he sprang to his feet and set off rapidly through the deckchairs and sunbathers and running children. Emma wanted to follow him but knew that he would hate her for it and be cruel on that account. She tried to weep unseen.

The band played Airs from Gilbert and Sullivan.

(6)

It was surprising how soon you got used to it, Harry thought. When Aileen's pregnancy had first begun to make her look noticeably different, then Harry's pleasure and awe and, occasionally, alarm, had made him treat her as if she *were* indeed different. She laughed at the cloudburst of courtesy which showered antique attentions on her. But Harry was unable to prevent himself from leaping to open doors which were often already ajar, puff up cushions already sufficiently comfortable, make unwanted cups of tea, do domestic jobs which had been done previously and generally behave as though his wife had turned into a monster of fragility. Aileen lapped it up. And she was a little sad when his attentions began to fall off. He was just as loving—he would never, she thought happily and securely, be anything less than that: and he was still careful of her. But the fuss died down as he got used to the bulk which grew inside her. He got used to it, as she did. There were two or three months, towards the end, when it seemed as if she had been heavily pregnant all the days of her life: she could recall times without the pregnancy, of course, but they were so insubstantial compared with the solid, growing, undeniable fact of another life taking its course and shape inside her own. While, to Harry, the whole experience had so much importance that the rest of his life rearranged itself as no more than a preparation for this time—when he would incontestably root himself in the world, and join onto it by starting his own family. He wanted a large family. There seemed to him no better stake in life.

But even that profound satisfaction became absorbed and now he was fast asleep, just before dawn on a summer's morning, a Sunday, with Aileen beside him, on her back, the swell of the belly now enormous, concentrating hard. Was this a cramp or were these the first real pains? There they came again. She glanced at the electric alarm clock beside the bed. It had a second hand on it: she had put it there specifically for this moment, so that she could check on the timings. There it came again.

It was a strange moment. So, she thought, this is the time. I'm going to have a child, really to have it. It will come out of me and be itself. How very strange, she thought, in that dreamy moment which might not have lasted more than a second but which spread across her mind like a film. Some great yearning in her was appeased. There would be another human being.

Yes. The pains were definitely in the first stage. There was no panic. She knew what she had to do. She had attended the classes and Harry too had put a gallant determination before his embarrassment and done his bit. He was squeamish about her. Aileen knew that, and he had told her that he did not want to make a fool of himself or to mess things up by passing out or doing something stupid in the delivery room. The arrangement was that he could walk out if he felt that he could not take it. She had assured him that this would be all right: in fact she had helped him all the way along by saying that it might be better for her, too—because she would be worried about him! She tapped lightly on his naked back. He made no move. She looked at him in the dusky light. There was a peaceful honesty about his sleeping face which moved her greatly.

"Harry. *Harry*."

"Yes?"

"I think you'd better get the ambulance."

"I see."

It was like a double take in a corny movie. As banal as that. He turned over to steal a few extra seconds of sleep: there was a pause: and then he shot up like an electrified hare and glared at her, mouth wide open, eyes startled full awake.

"Don't panic!" he said.

"I'm O.K." Aileen felt a giggle ripple through her and somehow, comfortably, it joined itself into a pang which satisfied her, this time, like a physical relief.

"Well don't!" Harry was transfixed. "That's all!"

"Ambulance."

"Right away."

He hurled back the sheets and made for the door. Then, naked, he whirled around, came back and tucked the sheets over her.

"Keep warm," he said, still shocked. "You *must* keep warm."

"Thank you," Aileen said, gently.

"I'll get the ambulance."

Harry turned and dashed straight into her dressing table. Brushes, combs, bangles, bracelets, necklaces and perfume bottles jumped and jangled on the jarred surface.

"Sorry," he said, turning to her and bowing. Then he spun around, headed for the door at top speed and banged his foot on the leg of a chair.

Aileen burrowed under the sheets and let the laughter run up and down her body like a massage as he hopped around the room.

"An ambulance!" he said and limped out as quickly as he could.

A sense of calm must have been transmitted by the telephone operator for though Harry returned at top speed, thundering through the flat like a horse let out of the stables after a month's confinement, he was no longer quite as mind-glazed.

"Tea?" he asked. "No," he answered, before she could. "I'd better get dressed. *You'd* better get dressed. *No*. Dressing gown. That'll do. Yes. Where's my other sock?"

As Aileen levered herself out of bed she saw Harry, naked but for one black sock, crawling about the floor.

"I've lost my sock," he said, helplessly.

"You can't have done."

"I *have*. I've lost it. It was here and now it's gone."

"I'll help you."

She got down on her knees and began to travel the floor systematically in search of the sock. Harry shifted about like a pointer dog, his bare bum bobbing up and down before Aileen's eyes. Suddenly he jumped up.

"It's got to be *some*where!" He stood almost at attention. "I came in as usual. I put my shirt there—there it is. My trousers there—see—there they are. My slippers are there—*there*—yes. My underpants are—"

"Harry. Could you help me up?"

"One second. One second! *Got* it! Leg of trouser."

He made as if to launch an assault on his trousers and then spun around. Aileen, half-laughing, half-groaning, was on her hands and knees swaying from side to side.

"Oh damn!" Harry said. "I'm sorry."

The blatant evidence of his thoughtlessness cut through the nerves and restored him at once.

He helped her up. Put on her dressing gown. Saw her through to the living room where he settled her before making a cup of tea. The ambulance had to come from Carlisle, eleven miles away.

The rest of that morning was so clear and yet so hallucinatory that it seemed to inhabit a time zone of its own. The ambulance eventually arrived and they went through the deserted town along the empty familiar road to Carlisle and into the Infirmary.

Everyone was very calm. Everyone knew what to do, making Harry feel that he too knew what to do.

They were left alone in a delivery room. The pangs had eased off. Harry sat in the corner, watching.

It would take about eight hours, they said.

The room was so very bare. A bed which seemed to be made out of aluminium. His plain chair. A white bedside table. Aileen somehow scientifically displayed. Harry felt shy and tried desperately to think of something to say.

"I'm glad you're here," Aileen said, and smiled at him. "I would've been lonely on my own."

"It *is* a bit bare, isn't it?" he replied, politely. "I expect it's for hygienic purposes."

"Yes," Aileen grinned at him. "Come and give us a kiss then, before the shouting and the heaving starts."

Obediently he went across and kissed her forehead. It was a little damp. Her face had broadened during the pregnancy but she had still taken care to resist a return of the fat which had plagued her childhood so painfully.

"I'll stay," Harry said.

"You needn't."

"I couldn't leave now."

The pains began to come more regularly. Aileen shouted out. The chief nurse, a good-looking young local girl, was a little embarrassed by the shouting. As if Aileen were talking loudly in church. She asked her not to, it could upset others in the hospital. Aileen ignored her and yelled again as the pains gripped her and the calculations went through the window. The child was waiting to be born now.

Harry was decked out in a white coat, and a face mask. Stood beside the oxygen and was shown how to put the mask on Aileen's face. Helped her with the counting. Found himself joining in what became a concerted commentary of reassurance, command, instruction, congratulation, push, *push*, well done, and again, longer, there we are, push, relax now, it's O.K., oxygen, she grabbed the oxygen mask from his hands and here they came again—*puuush! puuush*—and again—and that was good, another one—no, you *must*, you must, come on, another one, wait a moment, and—yes—*puuush*—I can see the head—yes! It's nearly there—the other two nurses flanked the midwife with towels and gleaming bowls and watched Harry, who was as calm and sensible as could be and totally unaware that tears were streaming down his face and *puuush*, again! Again! *Again*! It's—*again*! You *must*!

The child slid out as comfortably as someone coming down a banana slide, just slid out; Harry felt the tension go out of both of them—it was there—a girl—she was born—Aileen was fine—the rest was uncomplicated—they wiped the baby quickly and handed it up to Aileen, who looked radiantly brisk and totally delighted with herself.

Harry looked at the two of them. Mother and child. His. Well.

"She's lovely," Aileen said, and he nodded, unable to find words.

(7)

It was Mary who had made the decision and she held to it now. After those few days in Paris, Mike had wanted Douglas to be told. It was intolerable, he said, to work with Douglas and hide this from him: it appeared cowardly and deceitful. Neither these nor other arguments budged her. She wanted it to be kept secret and again, though Douglas had pushed her hard, she had not given in.

"Why are you so mysterious?" he asked. "I come around to see you the day after you come back from your trip and clearly you've had a good time—"

"There's no need to sound so bitter about that," Mary said.

"Perhaps not." Douglas wanted to let it drop but there was something about her persistence which goaded him on. "I would have thought that it was a good time to tell the truth," he added drily.

"Listen to you!" Mary's indignation was immediate and ferocious. "Your lies wore us out."

"Do you really think that?"

"Yes, I do."

"Yes." Douglas paused. "Although you could argue that if I hadn't lied it would have come to this much sooner. Sometimes lies can staunch something or keep something going until a new skin grows. Sometimes they're a way to survive. Like mould."

"But what's left after them isn't worth having."

"There is that," Douglas agreed. "But you could argue—I think I would—that lying is, in its way, a declaration of—affection, even of love, in that you are prepared to be deceitful and run the risks of that—most importantly the risk to yourself—myself. Because lies hurt the liar most."

"You are unbelievable!" she said.

"It's true, though," Douglas protested his case the more cheerfully for her comment. "It imposes a burden on you when you lie. Its effect on the liar is probably as bad as, if not worse than, its effect on the lie-ee. It twists up your sense of reality."

"How you must have suffered!"

"I did. As a matter of fact."

"Why didn't you stop?"

"I did."

"Eventually."

"Yes."

"And now you tell no lies."

"No."

"So I'm not worth lying for now?"

"Touché."

"Are you still seeing that woman?"

"Yes."

"Do you—sleep with her?"

"No." Douglas paused only fractionally. "And you?"

"I'm not going to tell you, Douglas. Sorry."

"You have."

"Please."

"You have." He said it colourlessly. "I've just registered it. Of course you have." He paused. "Christ."

During the pause, Douglas felt as if a great deal of himself was simply draining away. Of course she had slept with him. "*We've decided*." Yes. And of course there was nothing he was in a position to say about it. But the idea of her loyalty, her purity—that was the word he would use—of all that he had both taken for granted and admired in her suddenly gone—that seemed to Douglas the worst outcome of his own behaviour. For she had cherished her own fidelity greatly, he knew that: now that was gone.

Yet, at almost the same time, the beginnings of two other responses were felt. Firstly, he realized that his reaction, given his own behaviour, was a nauseating mixture of hypocrisy, prudery and ancient male chauvinism: what was sauce for the gander was not to be sauce for the goose. Secondly, he was relieved. Quite simply, it evened the score—it entitled them to meet on equal terms again—to be, in fact, as they had been when they had first met: about equally experienced, equally prepared to say "pass" to the other's previous affairs. Yet this was a perception of future balm: at that moment, Douglas was nonplussed.

"There we are then," he said, to fill a gap.

Mary smiled. For a moment he reverted to the boyish bafflement she remembered from their first few months together. But she quickly checked herself. She had decided on a policy and was determined to stick to it.

"Yes," she said, "there we are."

She stood up and put on the light. They were in her flat, in the living room, which, to Douglas, was both uncannily similar to and at the same time different from their living room in the old place. It was sprucer than the old place. He liked that. He liked everything about it: the colours, the arrangement of the furniture and the few rugs and pictures and books, the neatness, the lack of fussiness.

"I'm sick of that place I live in," he said.

"I thought you liked it. What was it you called it? A *cell*. That was it. Like a *monk*! Yes." She smiled.

"Oh God," he groaned. "I believe I did. It sounds just like me. Yes. Well. It's a dump."

"What will you do?"

"Move in here?"

"You said that without any conviction at all," Mary observed, gravely.

"I know."

"Do you really want to?"

"I think so."

"You still *see* that other woman, you said. Why don't you move in with her?"

"I don't want to."

"Poor old Douglas."

"Not so very poor." He stood up. "O.K. You want me to go."

"Do you want to?"

"This, my dear, is how people drive each other bats."

Douglas walked across to Mary, took her by the shoulders, looked at her firmly and kissed her.

"I'll go now," he said. "I'll be back on Saturday for John. I'm taking him to see Spurs."

For a second, Douglas would have sworn that Mary was genuinely reluctant to let him go. But that could not be the case. He went to the door.

"John's been telling me all about your taking him fishing in Thurston," Mary said. "I didn't know you could fish."

"I couldn't. I made it up as I went along."

"He had a lovely time."

"He's a lovely kid. I like being with him. With your permission I intend to indulge that."

"That's fine."

"Good. Well. Back to the cell."

"Thanks for coming round."

"Thanks for the snack."

"It wasn't much."

"It was great."

"Goodnight then."

"Goodnight."

He went. Mary sat down and thought as calmly as she could. There was real hope that she would get through. No doubt about it. She felt hopeful for the first time all year. Douglas was helping her. He was better for her now than he had been for years, she thought.

5
A Matter of Conscience

(I)

It took a lot of working out. Harry felt that he needed to clear a space in his life, so that he could sit down and think through all the possible and probable consequences. But there was so little time. The dispute was by now an urgent matter, seemingly possessed of its own dynamic, which pushed and pressed it along at a rate far more rapid than most of the participants wanted or could assimilate. And Harry was very nearly in the middle of it.

There had rarely been such a strong display of political feeling in Thurston. The bye-election campaign was already under way—itself reasonably exciting, given the tight balance between the main political parties and the emotional polarization which had crept up on people, until masses of voters who would have described themselves as fairly detached now seethed with one or another fast-breeding resentment. The media were in an orgy of verbal overkill on the desperate social, economic and moral short-term and long-term straits Britain was in. The lash of blame provoked shouts and whispers up and down the island. And in Thurston the factory had on its hands its first serious industrial dispute.

Harry still could not quite believe it was happening. That was the first thing. He had appreciated, for example, Aileen's interest in politics and he would spar with her now and then when he thought she was speaking jargon or what he thought of as unrealistic theories. But it was part of her life, just as rugby was part of his life, and in the exchange market of marriage he saw them as about evenly weighted. Of course, he would concede, her interest was more serious than his: but that did not really bother him, nor did it dent his general opinion that Aileen had her Politics and he had his Rugby and it was a Good Thing because it gave them something to be independent about. He had been perturbed lately by the passion of some of her statements—but, there again, she was somebody who felt strongly and knew her own mind and he admired that in her. Yet he was relieved—and honest enough to admit it—when the birth of their daughter persuaded her not to fight the bye-election. She still worked at it, taking the child with her, carrying the burden lightly, adding provision of crèches at work-places and tax relief on home-helps who released women for work to her long list of special causes.

Harry supported her in the sense that he listened when she was tired, helped when she needed it, was, in politics as in peace, the reliable, straightforward, honest man she had spotted and wanted. She was aware, though, that he was by no means completely in agreement with her politics. She would not go so far as to think him a Tory, even less a Liberal, but there was in him a deeply obstinate complex of convictions which often opposed her position. He admired, above all, independence of mind, spirit and action in causes he held to be just. He put loyalty to his friends and family before all but the most fundamental principles and even those would be challenged in the name of his family. Politics took second place.

Like much of the rest of the country, the workers at Thurston's principal factory—which directly supported well over half the work force in the town and indirectly propped up much of the rest—were in a deadlocked dispute. It seemed endemic at the beginning of that autumn. Disputes about pay differentials, about manning, about bonus payments, new machinery, comparability rates and studies, about production targets; management-union disputes, union-union disputes, internal union disputes—all of them lumped together by much of the media and variously dubbed as "madness", "suicide" and "the end of Britain". The reaction was uniformly extreme: the solution, too, was uniform: strikes and picket lines. Instant industrial heroes and victims and martyrs were pulped into prominence.

Harry could become one of these, Aileen feared. So did he. He hated fuss. Like Betty. He avoided the least personal display. Now, to his profound embarrassment, distaste and dislike, he was the town's talking point. What would he do, they asked, would he cross the picket line?

When he had gone to the factory, Harry had taken on the job of shop steward to a small union, A.P.E.X. It was poorly represented within the works and that in itself had eased Harry into it and then helped him take on the job. He allowed himself to be persuaded because this small branch of a small union happened to include a couple of men he played rugby with, the less well-heeled members of the team, local men born and bred, irresistible to Harry. There was the clear idea around that the last in had to do the dirty job of being shop steward and it was in that compliant spirit that he had taken it on.

He resisted the, to him, over-persistent and over-angry approach from the shop steward of T.A.S.S., a union which served an overlapping number of workers but gained power far in excess of its numbers through its association with one of the biggest unions in the country, the A.U.E.W. As far as Harry was concerned, the T.A.S.S. man took himself too seriously and made too many threatening noises. It was now this man who was using Harry and, in the process, nailing him.

Both unions had gone on strike against the management's plan to introduce new machinery which would, the unions claimed, bring about intolerable redundancies. Harry had joined the strike reluctantly. Although his was one of the jobs directly threatened, he could not convince himself that a wish to improve the long-term efficiency and competitiveness of the place deserved to be met with such a blank reaction. But he came out. Other unions in the factory joined in. The place was empty. Over a thousand men were idle. The emptiness and wasted feel of the factory lay on the little town like a dead whale on the shore. There was ugliness on the picket lines—but as yet it was mimetic. As if Thurston men, having seen the television newsreels, were determined to show that they could be no less tough.

The real ugliness in that period—in Harry's opinion— concerned the threat to a man called Fletcher.

Joseph Fletcher was about ten years older than Harry; married, with four children; a pigeon fancier, with his loft along Bird-Cage Walk where he would go every evening and potter about with the pigeons or work away at the allotment, which sat beside the loft. He had never been a union man for the reason, simple as he saw it, that he did not agree with them. He did not agree with the management either, he would add, but you had to work for somebody. He had been in the army and fought in the Korean War, from which he had brought back a medal for bravery and the unshakeable conviction that *They*—i.e. *all* big institutions, bosses, unions, politicians, newspapers—*They*—were all to be looked at thoroughly sceptically and avoided if at all possible.

He thought that the strike was foolish, said so, and, despite unpleasant scenes, crossed the picket line. Harry had been on the line two or three times when Fletcher had gone over it, and, justified though he thought the union's case was, he was ashamed of the bullying taunts and threats which met the man at the gate. And impressed by Fletcher's apparent disdain.

Things had become much worse though, in Harry's opinion, when some of the wilder members of the strike committee—they denied it, but no one was in any doubt—raided Fletcher's pigeon loft and wrung the necks of all his prize racing pigeons, as well as trampling over all his vegetables. Harry had been on the gate the morning after, and he was not the only one who tried to sympathize when the man came down, alone, claiming, as he saw it, his right to go into work. Fletcher ignored them all.

Yet, despite the sympathy for Fletcher, which grew from that incident, there were still those who insisted that as soon as they did get back to work, they would operate a rigidly closed shop and Fletcher would have to go. If he did not join the union he would lose his job, and the way things were going in the district, he would find it very difficult indeed to find a job anywhere else.

In the talk over this—and there was a lot of time for talk as the management and the unions engaged in a face-to-face test of strength, aping the two super-powers—Harry came down firmly on Fletcher's side. He believed in trades unionism and saw the merits in the closed shop: but he thought that there had to be more flexibility built into it. It was not enough that the only allowable reason for objecting to being in a union was to do with conscience. Nor was it tolerable that if a man were to be spurned by the union, or even to spurn the union, he should be in a position of such weakness that his ability to gain a livelihood anywhere at all would be threatened. It seemed to Harry that for the sake of a little sense and humanity and decency a whole system was being allowed to become potentially dictatorial. He was aware, in these discussions, that the shop steward of T.A.S.S., who was wholly for the closed shop, wasted no chance to get in a dig at him.

The strike began to disturb the town. It was, after all, a one-factory town. Rumours began to move around: that it would be cheaper for the management to close down the Thurston factory altogether and concentrate on their branches in Lancashire; that they had in fact engineered the strike in order to do just this; that redundancy payment lists had been spotted in someone's car; that the top management were about to sell their houses and move south to the nearest sister-factory. People grew very worried. The Thirties depression was not erased from memory and it was not a town with any tradition of strikes, nor with any confidence in the value of its product. As in a lot of small places, there were a substantial number who thought that they were lucky to be well employed at all.

Then A.P.E.X. settled nationally. In theory, Harry and his few members could return to work. A substantial part of the work force wanted them to do that—though they would not admit it—because there was a general feeling that, once a breach was made, the factory would gradually settle all round. The T.A.S.S. shop steward, though, made an issue of it. If Harry went back, he said, then he, Harry, would be totally and personally responsible for breaking solidarity at a time when negotiations were reaching a very favourable conclusion. Although everyone knew this last boast to be a lie, they were apprehensive. Solidarity mattered. Pickets had politicized them. Harry was on his own—public opinion for him, picket opinion against him.

But Harry's union contained two men—one a cousin of Joseph Fletcher's, the other a friend of his. They had been sickened by the inhumanity shown him and were not prepared to let themselves be pushed around, as they saw it, by a union which had always bullied them, rarely supported them and was, once again, trying to lean on them.

A.P.E.X. *could* go back. Members had already returned in other plants in other parts of the country. The men were willing to follow Harry's lead. Within a day the local and national newspapers were onto it, people in the town were chivvying and persuading him wherever he went, the T.A.S.S. steward was sending an unremitting number of warnings and Aileen and himself were seriously at odds.

(2)

"It's very simple," Aileen said stonily. "Will you or will you not cross the picket line?"

"Put like that, there's no argument," Douglas said. "He's explained the position in some detail, Aileen, have a heart. It's much more complicated than that."

"Not in the final analysis," she said.

There was a resolute piety about her which made Douglas want to shake her. There she was, ironing nappies as if engaged on work of the highest worth, unimpeachable in her maternal fortress, now doubly impregnable by virtue of this inflexible call to workers' solidarity.

"It's nothing *like* as simple as you think," Douglas added, irritably.

"What have you got to do with it?"

"I asked him round to talk it over," Harry protested. "Let's not fall out among ourselves."

"He can't answer," Aileen retorted.

"The same question could be asked of you," Douglas said. "Although you rely on us not to be so ungallant as to ask it. *We're* talking—you and me—but Harry has to share the question."

"If he crossed the picket lines now—two days before the bye-election—it would be worth a thousand Labour votes to the Tories."

"Aileen," Douglas said, fully in control of himself now, "there are scarcely a thousand Labour votes available around here. This area's so Tory the Queen couldn't get in as a Labour candidate."

"It's the principle."

"And I don't know that you're right. O.K. I haven't done as much canvassing as you have—I certainly haven't done as much as I would have done if *you'd* been standing—but what I've heard convinces me that party lines are blurred on this. Even if it's useful or right to think of it in terms of party advantage—and I think it's neither—then you're wrong. *Most* people want the strike to be over. Even most of those on *strike* want it to be over by now. The real argument's over the ways and means."

"And Harry supplies both," Aileen said, sharply.

"That's not fair." Harry was ruffled and showing it. There was not enough time for him to think it through for himself. Wherever he went, other people gave him their opinions and their views. "I'm concerned with what *I* think is right and with what the members of *our* union want."

"You've never thought much of the strike anyway."

"As a matter of fact I haven't," Harry said. "But I went along with it. And I've been made redundant once already in my working life, Aileen, so it wasn't as if I was ignorant of the consequences. I just think you can't beat progress."

"But that isn't the issue here and now." Douglas cut in quickly to forestall the environmentalist anti-growth tirade which he saw that Aileen was about to unleash. Besides, he hated to see these two unhappy with each other.

"If you cross the picket lines you'll be doing what the management wants," Aileen said. "That ought to stop you for a start."

"But why?" Harry asked. "If what we want is the same as what they want—why should that stop us?"

Aileen merely stamped the iron harder on the nappy and, with an effort, held her tongue.

"For what it's worth, I think he would be perfectly justified in going back," Douglas said.

"For what it's worth I think your opinion in this matter is irrelevant," Aileen said, much more crossly than she had intended. The tiredness from the child, the tension of the election and, on top of it, this strike, in which she saw Harry spreadeagled in the middle of interests far more knowing and manipulative than himself—it was all too much for her.

"Well, I'll be off in a minute so never worry," Douglas said. "But there's one more thing. If Harry's members vote to go back tomorrow morning, he has no alternative but to lead them back."

"They've said they would take his guidance!" Aileen almost wailed out this piece of information which, in a perverse way, made her proud that Harry had become the repository of so much trust. But she was convinced that he was not up to it.

"Your trouble," Douglas said, as his parting shot, "your trouble, Aileen—and it has been ever since you got yourself into politics—is that you think that nobody else has a mind of their own. You're a bit arrogant."

She looked at him intently and then blushed. Glanced at Harry, whose embarrassment confirmed her fear that he agreed with what Douglas had said.

"I just don't want Harry to get hurt," she said. "They'll blame it all on him. They'll say he broke the strike. The next time there's trouble, then T.A.S.S. will go round saying how weak Harry was. That's what that lot *wants*. And what if the others *don't* settle and go in with him? Besides which, you can call me arrogant if you like and maybe the unions aren't a hundred per cent right but I'd rather be on their side in any struggle and that's that!"

All three of them recognized that she was about to cry.

"I said I'd be back before John went to bed," Douglas said.

"Walk him back," Aileen suggested to Harry. "I'd like to finish these and then I want to do some envelopes."

"You're tired."

"There's only two more days."

"O.K."

The two men, brought up as brothers, unalike in so many ways, walked through the deserted late-night streets of the small town.

"John looks better these days," Harry said.

"He likes coming up here. That big holiday in summer really brought him out. And I like to be up here with him at half-term. He's good company. He's teaching me to fish."

"And . . . is Mary well?"

"She seems fine." Douglas had kept a firm silence about his private life. "What'll you do?"

"I expect I'll advise them to go back. We have the meeting first thing tomorrow morning. But I'm not settled in my own mind. There's something I should do. But I don't know what it is. I'll have to sleep on it."

"What if Aileen's right and they don't follow you—the other unions?"

"We'll have to wait and see. Anyway, Douglas, you can't guarantee the future, can you? All you can do is be careful to do the best you can at the time."

"Is that the answer to everything?"

"I've no idea," Harry replied, and laughed. "I can't imagine you fishing."

"I can't imagine you still playing rugby."

"Every Saturday."

"John's a hard teacher. Tells me off if I make a bad cast."

"He's coming on well. How do you find—" Harry had always had difficulty in saying "parents" or "mother and father", much less "mam and dad" before Douglas.

"Mother's a lot perkier. The church seems to have given her a new life, if that isn't blasphemous. She seems to be busy all day. And Dad's mellowing. I'll be out for a drink with him later—in The Crown?"

"I'd like to, but I'd better not."

"He's better in the pub than at home."

"Most of us are."

"True." Douglas paused. "I think the world of Aileen, you know. I suppose we're all a bit anxious about this business. But she's quite somebody, isn't she?"

"She is," Harry said. He needed no reassurance about his wife.

When they reached the bungalow he would not be tempted in. Betty came to the door to talk to him "as if he was one of those canvassers", she said. They chatted about the baby and then John came to show him his new rod and finally Harry turned to go and went the long way round, working out his plan. He thought he knew what to do.

(3)

The next morning Harry was up early. He went down to Bird-Cage Walk. This was the old path alongside the town's minor stream and it was here that the pigeon men had one of their settlements. Joe Fletcher was working away steadily as he did for an hour every morning before work. The destruction of his loft had not set him back for more than a few days: he had immediately invested in some new pigeons and was already beginning to have hopes of them.

He was a nimble man, Joe, handy with everything, twinkle-eyed, lean, nothing mean or shifty or at all self-serving about him. The sort of stalwart man Harry could just see winning a medal and then totally refusing to talk about it.

"What's this, then?" he said. "We're up early."

"I'd like a word, Joe, if you have a minute."

Harry was standing at the gate of the allotment: Joe, in the half-light of an autumn dawn, was some yards away, on the porch of his loft.

"Come on in, then," Joe said. "Come in."

The gates were made of planks and wire netting well cobbled together. In fact the entire allotment revealed a variety of dependent skills and a wide range of materials from rubber tyres to kitchen doors, bicycle wheels, buckets, window frames, anything and everything used ingeniously to provide comfort for pigeons or repose for vegetables.

"Not interested in pigeons, are you, Harry?"

"No."

"Pity. I can't make me mind up about this one here. Looks to me like such a beauty I can't understand why they let me have it. Fellow from Maryport. I didn't ask any of the Thurston fellows in case they got themselves embarrassed and worried to death about having anything to do with me."

There was a very awkward silence.

"I'd be surprised if you didn't feel bitter," Harry said.

"Not bitter." Joe held the bird firmly and stroked it gently with his thumb. It cooed contentedly, "Mad, though."

"Yes."

"And I'm not taking it lying down either." Joe spoke evenly—without bitterness but with emphasis. "I've a good idea who was in among these birds of mine. And I'll catch up with those fine gentlemen one night and then we'll see whose feathers will fly. They'll not get away with it."

"I'm—we're going back," Harry said. "That's what I'm advising them this morning."

"You should never have come out."

"I think the fears were justified," Harry said, doggedly fair. "There had been no consultation about the machinery: there was no preparation—nothing. The unions were right to strike."

"You don't believe that. A lot of you don't. You just go along."

"I think there's a lot wrong with the union and with what it does," Harry said. "But I think the best thing to do is to try to change it from inside. Not to stand aside."

"Like me, you mean?"

"Yes. Although I think you have the right to. But yes—you should join the union. It could do with people like you."

"Is that what you came to say?"

"It is."

"Well, I'll be buggered!"

Joe threw the bird up into the air and watched it swoop into the sky.

"I thought you were coming to offer sympathy or something in that line."

"I did that before."

"You did."

"And you ignored it. I don't blame you."

"You don't like these bloody union men, do you, Harry? Look at them! Look who they are! All the arse-lickers and ferrets—you don't belong there, do you?"

"I hope not. Anyway, that's unfair."

"Well then. Tell them to drop dead."

"It's too late. I'm in it now. And, funnily enough, I see the meaning of it now."

"You see more than I do then."

"Well." Harry's throat was a little constricted: he was apprehensive of the tone of nobility which might be creeping into his voice. "The union has screwed you up. They could screw me up. If that's going to happen, I'd rather be in than out. I'd rather be trying to do something to change it."

"Good luck to you."

"I'd feel a lot happier if you were on my side—if you can put it like that."

"I'm against all the union men—all of them." Joe's fierceness felt so final that Harry was about to give up. It was a good exit line. He could say he had tried his best. Say to whom? To that part of himself which in some way had found an equation between applying himself to the task of getting Joseph Fletcher into a union and advising his own members to cross the picket lines and return to work. In that equation was the beginning of the new self-respect he would need, he now sensed quite clearly, were he to keep his head in the turbulence of the union conflicts.

"You're wrong to be against us," Harry said. "It serves you nothing to be against us. You can make us all feel small—like you did—but that doesn't do much in the end."

"What does?"

"Decent people sticking up for what they think is right."

"That's a mouthful."

"It is." Harry hesitated, as if reprimanded. Then he went on, "I'm sure we could get you into our union."

"Come off it, Harry, I *hate* the buggers."

"You know the fellows in A.P.E.X. down there. You can't hate them."

"It isn't them. It isn't you. It's the whole thing."

"The whole thing *is* them and me. That's the point."

Harry arrived at this clarity of conclusion by the accident of argument but, having done so, he experienced an enormous relief. That was it. That was his case.

"Don't you *see*!" he exclaimed. "If we get together and make it something that *we* think is O.K.—then it won't be able to do the things you object to. It's only people, Joe. There's no point in pretending it isn't. They're not monsters or dictators. I'm a shop steward and if that doesn't make you laugh, what does?"

Joe did laugh and gripped Harry's shoulder affectionately. He liked the man. He had followed what he had to say with increasing interest and even, he noticed, keenness. There was a limit to the amount of dynamic you could wrest from an isolated position—however self-justified you felt. Perhaps there would be something in going in with Harry: certainly its surprise value alone would be a tonic!

"You talk a lot of rubbish but I'll walk to the factory with you," Joe said.

Harry knew that something had caught; a grappling hook had lodged itself. He would work at it. He had made a breach.

"You don't mind being seen with a scab then?" Joe asked, as they turned out of the lane and went towards the pickets at the factory gate. The baying was already to be heard.

"They'll be calling *me* that in about half an hour," Harry said. "But they'll be wrong."

"Daft, isn't it?" Joe grinned. "The thing to be at, you know, on a morning like this, is out on the Solway doing a bit of flounder fishing. That would be the real life. Agreed?"

"Agreed!" Harry said, emphatically, as the two men, in step, came up to the massed picket lines.

(4)

Very late that night, Joseph and Douglas managed to extricate themselves from the depths of conversation, alcohol, intimacy and philosophy which had enwrapped and enraptured them in the snug bar of The Crown. Closing time had come and, fair enough, the landlord had closed the dor and locked them in. An ease and amplitude had descended on the privileged late-stayers and the central topic had been Harry's crossing of the picket lines. Contrary to the opinion which had thought that the issue was over and empty of further present passion, there had been violent scenes. Harry had come out of it more badly even than Aileen had feared. The local Tory press declared him a hero (mentioning how loyal an employee he had been of theirs before his, unmentioned, redundancy) and it was evident that T.A.S.S. and the Tories between them had used him to their best advantage.

Douglas had gone round to see them but, oddly or miraculously, he had no idea which, Aileen and Harry and the child were apparently in a state of calm and happiness. They talked about the incidents at the factory gate. Aileen, now the die was cast, surprised herself by being totally and firmly pro-Harry. Her theories fell into place behind her loyalty and love. Douglas was both moved and relieved.

Now Douglas and his father stood outside Joseph's house in a friendly, conspiratorial, boozy mood which broke down the barriers raised by so many years of different experiences and expectations; a mood in which they felt amicably towards each other and indeed as father and son. They had been talking about Harry and Joseph had been waiting for the opportunity to link this with a homily he had long thought it his duty to deliver.

"The thing about Harry," he said, in a low voice, as they stood under the street light in the sleeping town, "is that, now that he's made his mind up, there's nothing'll change it. Not if he thinks it's right." Joseph's tendency to be lyrical about those he saw as heroes was on the rampage again, Douglas could see that. But he agreed with him in this case and encouraged him by his swaying affirmation, "Yes", "That's right" and "That's Harry."

"If he thinks it's right—well then—that's that. That's that."

"That's right," Douglas said.

"And they'll be surprised," Joseph said. "He'll surprise them all because now he's got his teeth into it he'll find out all about the bloody unions and, you take my word for it, he'll be hard to beat at the game. You take my word for it, he'll be mustard. They think he's a bumpkin now but just wait, they won't do him down. And that's because he's clear in his conscience."

"Yes. Agreed," Douglas said. God, he was tired. A sleep, then back to London with John. Where was Mary tonight? With her bloke? Didn't bear thinking about. Listen. Father.

"That's what gives him the basic strength, you see. Now

then. I like Mary. I always have liked her. I think the world of her. Do you see what I mean?"

"No."

"Yes you do." Joseph smiled and in the half-light Douglas realized how very *like* his father he was. He had seen the same moony smile plastered across his own face late at night or early in the morning, as it encountered a mirror on its way from booze to bed. Was that his course? To become more and more like his father? What, then, was the man like? "Yes you do. Now then. None of my business. Haven't said a thing. Your mother's upset, of course, but she keeps it in and she gets on the telephone to Mary. And there's John between them. No, it's you. You're our son, after all. We worry about you, you know—now don't look like that—we do. It's a matter of conscience. Is it clear? There's nothing can buy a clear conscience. Harry has one. Worth all the money in the world, believe me—and I've had my failings. We all have. That's the point. That's what I wanted to say. If your conscience is clear—that's all right."

Douglas looked at him. In such a very short time they would all be dead, all the actors of the day. It was all so very strange.

"Thank you," he said. "I appreciate that."

They went in quietly and woke up Betty and John within seconds.

6
London Lives

(I)

As the calendar burrowed into autumn and London dug itself into the end of the year, Douglas, on an evening in late October, felt that the place was alive and home. The trips to Cumbria had convinced him that, if ever there were to come a day when he would be able to go back full time to the countryside which held his roots, then that time was in a future as yet unhinted at. He was not capable of drawing enough from the countryside now. It would be easy to say that the time had passed when a writer could successfully isolate himself within a rural community—but Douglas knew that, even as he thought thus, there would be someone in some remote place contradicting him by turning out fine work. No, the fault was in himself—if it could be called a fault—and the fact that he *did* think of it as a fault revealed his quasi-religious respect for the superior authority of rural life. Rural knowledge was still thought to be somehow "better", rural pastimes and pursuits somehow "purer", rural friendships more enduring and enriching, the pulse of rural life itself more direct and insistent on the bare earth than on the bare pavement. Nature was nurture.

There was something in that, he thought, but the necessities which drove him now were urban. Even in the country he had no escape from the global city. He was no farmer, no real working countryman. He loved the country, and particularly all his home part of it, and he liked to go back there and could feel alive in isolation there more comfortably than anywhere in the world. But it was here in the city that he could be all that he wanted to be. In the hard shock of late autumn when the parks rotted with dead leaves and the metropolis culled the world for films and music and shows to add to the compost of pleasure; when new night clubs opened, full of garish promises, and

Parliaments came back from an unmourned and immense absence, just as full of promises; when gossip columnists dug up the plots which would see them through the winter and television shows breezed out into the air claiming attention; when the drinkers stayed a bit longer in the pubs, rather than face the colder road home, and double-decker buses twinkled and rollocked magically through the dark streets and suburbs; when the West End seemed to speak with tom-toms from discos, strip clubs, clip joints, casinos, drinking clubs, late night stores, porno stores, family stores, delis, cafés, restaurants and private bars; this time of autumn seemed to Douglas rich indeed in the possibilities round and about him.

It was as if he stood in the middle of a tamed and humanized jungle, full of fruits and surprises, full of extraordinary transmutations and wild configurations—all the twisted and perverse developments of civilization squashed and deformed and intertwined together in this brick and concrete growth, thicketed with buildings of every kind. Here, in the middle of a giant city, the wonder of the human enterprise really came into its own: there were these deformities, these grotesque specialities, these apparently insupportable people and institutions and shops and gatherings and events—and yet they all lived, they all found accommodation in and out of the government buildings and the factories, the flyovers and museums and airports, the banks and offices and sewers, the markets and schools and homes. In this metropolis, the impact of the most generalized and the most particular, the plainest and the most perverse, the most boring and the most titillating, the dullest and the most stimulating, the lousiest, meanest, most squalid and nastiest, and the noblest, finest, most altruistic and best was there to be felt and seen and experienced every day.

And sometimes, as on this day, Douglas could imagine the whole range of it flowing through him as vibrantly as any natural impulses, as firmly as any feeling he had ever gathered in from watching a phenomenon of nature. This mouldering, dusk-filled metropolis, with its cross-cultures and dreams, its instant excitements and long disappointments, this baggage train for a hundred armies was where he could breathe most fully now: and he loved it. The question was—how to live in it.

(2)

"I'm seeing him again tomorrow," Mike said. "We're talking over the rough-cut of the Raven thing and then there's some party. He wants to eat afterwards. And talk about you, I think. He's scarcely mentioned you for weeks but I don't know how much longer he can keep it in. And if he does talk directly about you—I shall have to say something."

"Why?" Mary asked the question although she already knew the answer. Indeed it was so obvious that she was ashamed of herself. But she waited for an answer.

"Because it would be silly and hypocritical not to. As it is, I fail to see who is benefiting from this secrecy."

"I am, I think."

"And would you want me to lie to his face?"

"You needn't put it like that."

"Come on, Mary."

He was soft on her, and she exploited it, yet neither of them suffered from that. They had found a gentle, yielding friendship which gave them a lot. Mike wanted more from it than Mary but he was too wise and too schooled in disappointment to risk losing all by attempting to seize all. They were in her flat, late at night, John in bed, a bottle of wine half drunk beside them in the side-lit, dusky, cosy room; and music. She had found much consolation in music.

"How is he these days?" she asked him, as she was always asking him.

"You see him as often as I do."

"He puts on an act for me."

"Don't we all."

"Don't be silly." She smiled. She liked Mike more and more. He was so unfussed, so completed, far from the restless stretching and testing and wriggling with his fate which made Douglas, in her eyes, both fretful and disturbing.

"He's better than I've seen him for ages, as a matter of fact," Mike said. "This film on Raven is a winner, but it's very tricky work—copyright problems, Equity and M.U. problems. He had a problem with the sound on one of the mikes at the concert, his editor's playing up, the old footage he needs isn't coming through as fast as he needs it—the logistics would drive most of my other producers round the bend and Douglas just sails through it all. He's very good at his job. *And* he's back reviewing regularly and doing that World Service programme and, so he says, thinking of writing something else. In those terms he seems to me to be better than he has been all year."

"Sometimes he looks dreadful."

"So I notice."

"It isn't drink."

"No. He's cracked that. Although he still drinks hard."

"Well?"

"It could be living in that wardrobe of his and subsisting on B.B.C. canteen fodder. It could be the outward and visible sign of inward stress." Mike paused. "Or he could be missing you."

"He has his other woman."

"That's none of my business and you know it."

"He told me that someone wanted him to go to Hollywood and do a script," Mary said. "Somebody who'd heard of the—the story he's just written—"

"—'Death of a Friend'," Mike said.

"Yes. Just heard of it and wanted Douglas to transfer it to the desert in America. He said the producer thought that the idea was 'just sensational'—that was his word—and it would go down wonderfully well in America. He was going to read Douglas' book and then come back with a proper offer."

"In a way I hope he doesn't make an offer," Mike said. "I think half of Douglas' problem is that he moves from one job to another so fast he can't fix a focus on what's important."

"He's always been unwilling to stay in one place for long," Mary said. "However good the conditions. He's always had this itch to prove that he's his own boss and that he doesn't need anybody. He's quite obsessed about his independence."

"That's all very well up to a point. After that it can start to work against you."

"You should've known him when he was younger!" Mary said. "You would have thought he could have taken on everything and anything. It was like living with an army rolled into one man. He was so bold; and so funny."

"You're much better these days," Mike said, eventually.

"Some of that's thanks to you." She did feel better. Frail at times, but safely past the demoralizing anxiety which had beset her in the first months of separation.

"I'm going to tell him about us, whether he asks or not," Mike said and drained his glass. "He's probably guessed anyway."

"As long as you tell him everything," Mary said. "The whole truth. That's important."

(3)

Lester liked the back streets. They reminded him of Thurston when he was a boy. There were shops selling all sorts of bits of things, run down shops, shops which were mini-factories, shops supervised by men in ancient overcoats and a carapace of gruffness, shops where you could buy junk or metal or old hardware or wholesale lavatory pans or bargain bundles of wall paper or pre-revolutionary hosiery or pets and pet food. It was a homely little area, this west part of London, and Lester was settling into it not too badly.

He worked for a man called Latchford who owned several betting shops in that area. Lester had come across him at a party after a night at the All-In Wrestling with Merlin, in that brief period when he had been Merlin's pal about town. Lester had been in an expansive mood and included Latchford in the circle which was instantly phalanx-formed about Merlin. Latchford's red-head had been impressed and Lester had been given one of those "any time I can be of service" routines which had turned into something more substantial that same week when Lester had again run across him and again done him a small favour.

Working in the west of London while cutting the film—Douglas' editing rooms were in Hammersmith—he had bumped into Latchford—on purpose this time—and mentioned that he could do with something part time. He wanted to "look into" the bookie business, get a bit of experience, nothing like being paid while you learnt, yes, Merlin was very well, never better, old Merlin.

At first Lester had managed to play it well. Douglas had eked out his attachment to the project and he went regularly to the cutting rooms where, in the pokiest place he had ever been in, seemingly miles of black snaky liquorice celluloid spooled and swarmed all over hand-cranked machines before being cut out with a fancy razor blade and pasted together with sellotape. You could do anything with the stuff, Lester thought, disgustedly. You could make anybody look anything you liked by chopping it about. The same man could look a brain-box or a fully paid up idiot—it just depended how you played about with it. You could take a bit from here and another bit from there and pretend they came from the same place: you could find bits where he completely contradicted himself: you could cut out all the bits that were real but made him look like the creep he often was; you could put music under it and make it ten times more exciting or stuff other bits in from other people and make it seem deep: it was all a con, Lester saw that, and he was disgusted. He wanted films to be real.

But he stuck it out for the experience and also, it had to be confessed, for the increasingly forlorn hope of picking up the contact with Merlin again through Douglas. But Douglas didn't seem to care about Merlin. He seemed untouched by any consideration of what Merlin might do for him. Lester was baffled. It was not as if Douglas was doing all that well—not on the surface anyway. He lived in a single room, even smaller than Lester's own; he dressed with no great style; he seemed to organize what was left of his life after work around visits to Mary and outings with John. Nothing to write home about there. There was no push or go about him, Lester thought angrily. Still, he seemed to have a certain amount of luck and so Lester kept going to the cutting rooms and then walking back, ferreting around those little scabby streets he liked, and able for quite a while to give the impression he wanted to give: of someone looking over the business for his long-term project, not *really* concerned with the weekly wage he was lifting.

The wage kept him together. The work, too, though Lester

would not admit it, was enjoyable. He liked being in the gambling business and he liked having to do with horses and dogs and the sporting fraternity. He knew where he was in the world. He could call the odds and argue the toss with the best of them—so he boasted to Douglas, and it was true enough. As the weeks went on he began to entertain the beginnings of an ambition both sane and reasonably realistic. He would like to get a little stake together, he thought, and open a bookie's business, somewhere in the country—not in Cumbria, where he was known, somewhere he'd never been. Then he would go to the race meetings and set up his board and shout out the odds, he could be part of the crowd, he could watch the races, get to know some of the jockeys and owners, be a *real* part of that world, not the glorified typist and telephone operator you were here in London. As often happens, he had invented a convenient lie about his real intentions, but the lie had contained much of what he wished to be truth: and now he was adopting it as his ambition. Yes. He would not want to admit it yet—they would all laugh at him—what a come-down from Personal Confidant of Merlin Raven, Rock Group Manager and Associate Film Director. But the attraction of the notion had grappled itself into his mind and whenever he tugged against it he felt the pull of its power. He wanted to be a bookie.

He began to take a proper interest in the business. He asked questions. He was indeed the man who had just come in to pick up the way things worked before branching out on his own. But a curious thing happened. When he had been "playing" at it, and while he was still haloed by newness and the background presence of the phenomenally rich Raven—he had been treated well. Now that his interest was real; now that his enquiries were in earnest; now that he made notes and turned up early and stayed late—he spread unease. There was worry. A fear of possible aggravation entered the heads of the three other men who worked in the shop: it was as if Lester were casing the joint, or an informer. They alerted Latchford.

Latchford was on his guard. He dabbled in misdirected motor cars, kept an interest in a club in Fulham not best known for its clean record, employed heavies from time to time, shifted the odd few crates off the odd lorry, could always find you a real fox fur for less than a quarter the asking price, or get you a genuine Cartier watch for a song: there were connections with Amsterdam and Heathrow Airport. Latchford was a smart boy.

He waited until the place had closed and invited Lester on his own into the back room for a drink. Very civil, Lester thought, teach the others a bit of a lesson, been less than welcoming lately—not that it mattered much—he had just about got all the information he wanted. His thoughts were turning to a stake. He reckoned he needed about ten thousand pounds. It was a terrible amount of money to find. But it would set him up for life.

Lester had a lot of time for Latchford. He was about the same age, a little flabby, but only a little—tried to keep himself fit, you could see that. Dressed beautifully—three piece suits, craftily cut, the little gold chain across the almost-flat stomach, oh yes, the silk shirt and the very plushy tie, not too flashy; the beautiful boots—that thin Italian leather that cost a bomb. A gold chain around his wrist; three heavy rings—the real McCoy; hair always just washed; and always the cigar—not too big and showy but smelling perfect. And, parked on the pavement, the new Camargue with the new red-head patiently waiting inside. Latchford had made it all right, Lester thought. This was Britain working at its best. Here was an example of individual free enterprise and initiative—because Latchford's background in Fulham was every bit as poor and downtrodden as Lester's own. Fulham was maybe his one crucial advantage, Lester thought, inevitably comparing himself. Latchford had got to know the city, the ins and outs and twists and openings of the city. Lester had been left behind a bit there. But still, he would hand it to Latchford—more than to Douglas and more than to that sod Raven, who was some sort of freak—Latchford was the real inspiration.

"So how are we then, my son?" Latchford asked, offering Lester a cigar and pushing a can of beer his way. The small office was somehow made to seem tiny and shabby, Lester thought, by the glamorous presence of Latchford. There was something about the man, Lester could see that, which spelt POWER. He was a man worth sticking close by, was old Latchford. He was going places on the inside track.

"Very well, Ray, not bad at all," Lester replied, easily adopting the appropriate tone—oh yes, he still had the touch.

"And our friend Merlin? How's our friend Merlin?"

Latchford hadn't asked him to sit down and so he remained standing. Odd as that seemed, on reflection, it never occurred to Lester to question it at the time. Latchford sat in a tilted-back chair with his feet crossed on the desk in front of him—like one of the ministers in the House of Commons.

"Merlin's great," Lester affirmed. "Matter of fact, he was telling me only the other day that he was feeling better than he's felt for a long time. A very long time."

"Glad to hear it." Latchford lit his cigar and did not pass over his lighter to Lester. "The guy's a ravin' genius. Best in the world. That's what I admire. *The* very *best*." He puffed out the pedigree grey smoke dreamily. "And loaded as a ten ton truck."

"Loaded?" Lester confirmed, just a shade bitterly. "You've said it."

"What—what does your friend Merlin think of your working for me?"

"Great. He thinks it's great. He understands, Merlin, about when you want to set up a few things for yourself. He thinks it's great."

"He going in with you?"

"We haven't got round to talking about it yet." Lester's mouth was becoming dry—he could not understand it. He took a deep and noisy swig from the can of beer. That was better.

"Does he know you've been a naughty boy?" Latchford asked, very quietly.

"What's that?"

"I've heard one little bird singing out in Soho and another little bird in Brixton: and then somebody was telling me you'd done a bit in Her Majesty's."

"That was years ago," Lester said. "I was just a kid."

"I wouldn't be the man to hold a person's past against them," Latchford said fairly. "But you put me in a very difficult position."

"Why's that?"

"Don't you see? My business is very delicate. My business

is very, very delicate. There's a lot of funny people wants to know things that I would sooner they did not know. So why are you taking notes and numbers like Kojak with his tail up?"

"I told you. I want to learn. I want to start my own business."

"Yea? With Merlin Raven's money behind you? Don't make me laugh, Lester my son. You're working for somebody, aren't you? Who is it?"

"Look." Lester involuntarily glanced at the glass door behind him. Two men were leaning against it. "Honest, Ray, I'm working for myself."

"Who you gonna sell it to?"

"What?"

"The information."

"What information?"

"Don't try to be bloody clever with me, you little ponce!" Latchford jumped to his feet and the two men came into the room. "You're working for Abbot, aren't you?"

"Look. It's a mistake. I don't know what's happening. Here." He dug in his pockets. "Look at what I wrote down. Look at it. It's just tips—about rents and how you get a licence and fixing odds. Who would be interested in that?"

"That's my question. And I've got the answer. What made you think you'd get away with it?"

"It's for me. I want to start up—" One of the men chopped him on the back of the neck. Lester stumbled forward and Latchford kicked him violently in the groin and then pulled him up by his hair before smashing him in the face with his three-ringed fist. The three men slugged him around between them. They stopped before he was badly beaten.

"I'm going to be nice to you," Latchford said, standing over Lester, who was curled up on the floor vaguely trying to protect his face and his genitals. "They'll drop you off round Kingston by-pass so you can have some time to think things over away from the big city. And, listen! If anything happens to me that I can trace back to you, you'll be in at Tilbury with a block of cement up to your knees. Right? Right."

(4)

It was something Mary had thought about for weeks now. The imminent encounter between Mike and Douglas made it more urgent. In order to calm herself down, she rehearsed what she would say several times and, even in the rehearsing, felt nervous. She had tried to examine her motives for wanting to make this phone call but shied away from her own conclusions. It was enough that the impulse had endured for so long.

She decided to do it at the end of the afternoon. She would be in from school, the day's work behind her; John would be in his bedroom, supposedly getting on with his homework; Hilda, presumably, would be at the office and less pressed than at other times in the day.

Mary picked up the phone and dialled the number, as if she were embarking on an illicit gamble. She was put through to Hilda directly.

"This is Mary Tallentire here," she heard a fairly firm, even voice say. "Douglas' wife."

"Oh yes." Hilda was taken completely by surprise. She glanced around the empty office as if hoping someone would be there to give her an excuse not to talk. But what was she afraid of?

"I've been meaning to phone you up for a long time," Mary said, repeating a well rehearsed line: but where did it lead to? Her tongue was dry, mind wiped of thought.

"Yes," said Hilda, into the silence.

"I think it might be an idea for us to meet," Mary said, jumping three stages, to come immediately to her intention.

"What good would that do?"

"I don't know." Mary was trying to fit a face and a personality around this edgy, defensive voice. There were no clues. "But I think it would be more honest."

"I can't think of anything we have to say to each other," Hilda replied.

"Oh, I'm sure there would be plenty to talk about."

"But on what basis?" Hilda asked.

"What do you mean?"

"I mean—why do you want to?"

It seemed to Mary at that moment that she had been right to make the telephone call. Hilda's question seemed to signal some uncertainty. Mary's confidence, hard fought for, over the year, sometimes desperately lacking, was sure enough of itself to feel able to pass on.

"It's demeaning if we don't," Mary said. "Can't you see?"

"Demeaning to whom?"

"Both of us. It's saying—we accept that—Douglas—can come and go and keep us apart from each other while critically important decisions are being made for all our lives. I talk to him. He talks to you, I'm sure. Why shouldn't we talk?"

"It sounds very logical," Hilda admitted, rather truculently. "But I still can't see why we *have* to do it."

Hilda's sense of privacy was offended. Apart from a complex of what she would have called "natural" reasons for not wanting to see Mary, there was a reluctance bred out of a deep class-feeling. Mary's voice and manner came over to her as coolly middle class: and, to that extent, privileged and, in what she said, patronizing. After all, Mary held all the cards—what was she on about? Moreover, Hilda did not subscribe to the notion that everything ought to be in the open. She could not bear to discuss her love for Douglas with anybody. It seemed totally at odds with the mystery and uniqueness of the affair. She resented Mary's assumption that it could be discussed like a shopping list. What she felt for Douglas and what, she was still sure, Douglas felt for her, was secret and thrilling; it bound them together sexually and mystically, it existed apart from other people, it was able to survive even the competition of a marriage and a misdirected puritan conscience. Mary, typically, Hilda thought, would be unaware of all that. Her background had no respect for secrets and sex because it had no understanding of them. Her ideal was to "talk everything out", as if talking things out could even approach a solution to any real problem.

In Hilda's world and, she thought, in Douglas', due to a great number of factors, from environment through to tradition, the primacy of fine but inarticulate feelings was acknowledged. In Mary's world, Hilda suspected, if fine feelings could not be proved in dogged discussion then they did not count. Mary stood for that sort of good sense about emotions which Hilda considered to be evidence of having no emotions worth bothering about. Hilda's deep reluctance to engage in conversation seemed to Mary to be evidence of insecurity and panic.

"What can we lose?" Mary asked.

"That isn't the point," Hilda replied. "I think we could lose quite a lot." She smiled. "Our tempers for a start! But the real point is—what would we gain from it? I can't see anything."

"It wouldn't be this hole-in-the-corner business."

"It never has been. Not for us anyway," Hilda retorted.

"Hasn't it?"

Neither of them spoke for a few moments.

"It just seems so undignified," Mary said. "It's as if we're not really interested in having a say in our lives."

"I have my say."

"Do you?"

Again the silence. Mary made a last effort.

"It's quite easy to score points," Mary said. "I could do it myself. I could say that Douglas wants to come back here—I'm sure you know that. I could point out that he is not with you even though I have given him every chance . . ." she paused, "and even provocation. But there would be nothing gained from all that. I don't seem to be able to get through to you, but my only point is to try to lead a decent life. I don't want to let things pass by, unquestioned and unanswered, any more. I don't want to be just told things or faced with *faits accomplis*. I want to take things carefully. That's all. I thought it might help if we talked."

Hilda was touched by this, but her mind had been made up and she stuck with it. She was terrified of meeting Mary. She was afraid she might be drawn to sympathize with her. Then where would she be? There was a time when trenches had to be dug, when battle-lines had to be drawn, when enemies had to be named and cultivated. She *wanted* Douglas, for God's sake!

"I'm sorry," Hilda said. And then, "I can't see the point," she lied.

She would not be the first to put down the phone.

"I'm sorry too," Mary replied: and put down the phone.

She was trembling.

(5)

"It must certainly remind them of home," Douglas said.

The walls were plastered with travel posters of Greece and Cyprus. Ethnic vessels swung from the ceiling and clambered over the walls. The waiters sang out in Greek to each other and the menus were as big and as closely printed as Greek newspapers. And there was a plastic bouzouki in the background.

"There's a stage when something's so wholeheartedly—bad taste if you like—that it works. I like it here."

"Ouzo?"

"Or retsina."

"Both," Douglas decided. "Let's avoid any argument on a night like this."

"You seem better than I've seen you for months," Mike said.

"I feel it. I don't know why."

"So what are you going to do next?" Mike asked eventually, after they had gossiped for a while.

"The Raven isn't finished yet. We can't clear that early stuff of Raven in Paris, which is a damned nuisance. And the record company's suddenly decided to be very evasive about the old tour footage we were promised. I suspect Raven's moved onto something else and stopped co-operating."

"Do you see him still?"

"No."

"Why not?"

"I always felt rather uncomfortable with him," Douglas said. Then, "Lester. Is there any way you can swing a job his way?"

"Not again. We've helped him once already, Douglas."

"I saw him the other day. He's fallen flat on his face again." Douglas smiled. "I shouldn't laugh, but he does seem to walk into hammerings like Tom in 'Tom and Jerry'. If there's a loose plank, Lester'll step on it and whap! it'll flatten his nose; if there's a large pane of glass, Lester'll walk straight through it and look at you in his rags and bloody cuts as if to say, 'nobody told me about it.' But this time he seems to have lost all his bounce. There's a woman in the equation somewhere, but he keeps quiet about that."

"What can I get him that he would want?"

"I don't know. Some sort of offer—just to give him the reassurance that there's a job somewhere. I think he's come to the end of his resources. Raven kicked him out, you know. Sooner or later everybody seems to have kicked Lester out."

"That's a bit sentimental," Mike said. "Lester begs to be kicked out."

"True." Douglas motioned for another carafe of retsina. "Perhaps."

"I thought you were easing up on the booze."

"In a manner of speaking. Another, please. Thanks." He chewed at the tough lamb. "So? Any chance? He needs a job. He *got* us the Raven project, you know."

"It's where to fit him in where his pride's not hurt and then how to get him a job at all. He isn't the most employable man around, is he?"

"I thought a location driver," Douglas suggested. "He could always pretend he was just filling in until something better came up. It would get him out and about and on the set so that he could get to know everybody and do this and that. Could you try?"

"I'll talk to him." Mike said. "Then I'll see what I can do. Perhaps it could work. I'll try." He paused. Douglas clearly wanted more than that. "We should manage something."

"Thanks." Douglas nodded. "Good."

"And what about you? Are you still keen on that regionalism idea or will you take on the interviews?"

Mike had suggested that Douglas interview a dozen contemporaries—in films, the theatre, politics, businesses, show biz, the universities and sport—and make documentary portraits, rather like the Raven film, in the attempt to talk sensibly to someone about their work and show the world they lived in.

"I've been thinking that it would be very nice to come in to the B.B.C. full time," Douglas said. "It must take a lot off your mind to have a regular wage coming in and regular work lined up."

"I can understand the need for security," Mike said. "Had it myself. It's a lot easier on the inside of these institutions. You still torment yourself, don't you?"

"The days of the freelance . . ." Douglas intoned: but his glance at Mike was waiting for a different response, ". . . are over. Are they not?"

"Like other independent operators, we're told," Mike said. There was a tightness about his throat. So. The truth was already out, was it? What was needed now was for it to be faced up to. "Maybe the odds are that in fifty or a hundred years we'll all be safely tucked inside big institutions or organizations or corporations. And we'll have to make our lives revolve around that."

"Like the mediaeval church," Douglas said, "or the feudal system . . . Except ours will have a corporate head and a state policy."

"That seems to be the picture."

"And that leaves Mary," Douglas said.

There was a pause.

"When did you know?" Mike asked.

"Just a few days ago. We were in your office. It clicked. So there we are."

"I wanted to tell you much earlier."

"I know." ("*We* decided"!) "I'm still trying to work out what I feel. It's very complicated, having a friend involved with a wife you've no rights over, except most likely you're still in love with her."

"Are you?"

"Perhaps. It's become no more than a slogan," Douglas said. "I'm amazed to discover that I'm not withering away due to lack of sex. Long ago I thought I would waste away in a week if I slipped for a day. Now it seems to matter so much less." Douglas drank some more. "I trust it's a phase I'll pass through quickly. It's like the less than startling discovery that I have no career-ambition—except to do these regional programmes, that is. I've thought a lot more about them, Mike. In Cumbria, we could show the Bewcastle cross and the thirteenth-century gargoyles and features of landscape together with the menhirs and Wordsworth's verse—that would give you a new notion of the quiddity of Cumbria, for example—done all over the place, it would arrest that sort of depressing acceptance that our time is past and we're all herding ourselves gently into the asylum of institutional post-democracy. I find it painful to talk about Mary. What about you?"

"I can't think what you'd want to hear."

"You've slept together?"

"Yes." Mike hesitated. "In Paris. Not since. I think she was rather ashamed of doing it." He spoke with difficulty. "There was something wilful about it—not quite as if she were getting her own back—more—I've thought about it a lot—more as if she no longer wanted to have such an advantage over you and so she was determined to betray you physically. That's what I thought."

Douglas began to experience the peculiarly intense pleasure of talking to a man who loved the same woman as he loved.

"That sounds like her," he said. "On the other hand, it's an explanation I'm likely to welcome, aren't I?"

"If you want to live with her again."

"She must have told you that I asked her."

"She didn't think you sounded convinced. And then there's—whoever it is, you see."

"Hilda. Yes. There's Hilda."

"Mary minds about her a lot."

"So I understand." Douglas sat back while the dishes were cleared away. He ordered some more to drink. "By sitting down and trying to work out the best and right thing to do, I seem to have arrived at a state of impotence. All round. What are *you* going to do?"

"I'm afraid that depends on you."

"On her."

"On her. If it didn't happen to be you," Mike said, "I wouldn't let you have a look in." The fury and determination were undisguised.

The wine came.

"Cheers."

"Cheers," said Douglas, raising his glass.

They drank, and talked of other things until the restaurant closed.

(6)

Lester had not noticed her and yet she was sure that he had come there on purpose to seek her out. What other reason could there be for his hanging around a small, run-down shopping parade in North Kensington? Emma stopped and turned her back on him to look into the window of a shop which sold junk clothes. She had just popped out to buy some candles and turnips for the Hallowe'en party they were planning for the evening. It was to be an attempt to bring together the different sections of the community served by the church and the vicarage. The children would come first of all, and then, later, churchgoers and those who used the social enquiry service set up by the enterprising vicar. A mixture of races and temperaments; poor whites, generally, and "upwardly striving" to be mobile blacks. There would be other friends there too, those who came within the nexus of help and aid existing in the parish, and it was here that Emma was in difficulties.

There was a young social worker, an Adventure Playground and Child Care Leader called Mark, who had liked her and whom, in turn, she was beginning to like. Mark was the son of a Harley Street psychiatrist. He had been to Bryanston—a rather liberal public school—and then gone to Art College where he had taken drugs, dropped out, been salvaged by a community group and turned into a devoted helper of others. Emma felt so easy with him, sisterly and at home. They made private jokes about "The Wind In The Willows" and Toad. Mark would be there—spectacularly tall, slim, shockingly blond bedraggled hair, blue-grey eyes, now innocent, now shrewd, in most respects like a guardsman, but dressed casually, almost to the point of seeming a dosser. And charming.

Emma turned from Lester, then, in the street, because there was now a choice and a decision. Mark had asked her to go out for a bite to eat after the festivities that evening and she had not only agreed, she had revealed to both of them that she was looking forward to it. And now there was Lester. She glanced around quickly. Yes. Looking awful. He only seemed to come to her when he had nowhere else on earth to go, she thought, and then she checked the irritation. That was unfair. In one sense he did so because that was what she asked for. She turned from the window full of soiled skirts and worn shirts and half-bald coats and baggy grubby trousers and made for him. She would ask for something different now.

Lester smiled broadly. He had seen her pause and hesitate and, far from making him concerned, he had enjoyed it. It showed that he had an impact still. As she walked over to him he rocked on his heels and glanced about him like a mangy but cocky terrier sniffing the air.

"You look terrible," she said.

That was not what he had expected.

"I haven't heard from you for months," she said.

"There you go," he answered, lamely.

Although the Parade was run down, it was busy enough and it tended to be full of slow moving shoppers—old people carefully costing and comparing the vegetables from shop to shop; all ages slowly fingering the cheap knock-down SALE! SALE! furniture and the kitchen and bathroom bargains, the five-pound televisions and one-pound radios. The Parade was one of those places in London which was the last stop and prop before destitution and the dustbin. This busyness distracted Lester. And Emma, who looked better than ever and decidedly "classy" in a waisted wine-coloured velvet coat, a white crocheted scarf and dark brown boots, seemed in no mood for the acquiescent understanding he had come to rely on.

"What do you think I feel like when you just disappear?" she asked. One or two people lingered a little longer in anticipation of a good row. "You just walk off and there I am—expected to pick myself up and get on with it without the slightest help from you."

"I never promised anything."

"That's certainly true. But it doesn't excuse you."

Lester did not reply: he could not, in truth, understand the connection between his promising nothing and this not excusing him. And he wanted no public row.

"Is there nowhere we could have a cup of coffee?"

"I've got to get some things for our Hallowe'en party—I'm

only supposed to be out for ten minutes," Emma fretted. She was rigorously conscientious about her duties.

"Well, if that's the way it is, I'll bugger off."

"Don't be silly."

Emma considered for a moment or two and then sorted it out.

"There's something called DINING ROOMS just down there on the left. I'll see you there in a few minutes. I just have to buy a couple of things and then I can drop them off and come back."

"Don't put yourself out."

"What happened to you?" She reached out and lightly touched his left cheekbone, which had a bruised lump on it.

"A fracture. I fell."

"I'll just be a few minutes."

"I could come back with you if you wanted," Lester said, quietly. "If you wanted."

"It would be less disruptive if we met outside the Centre."

She nodded and left him. He watched her with some apprehension. She had made him feel as shabby as he knew that he looked. The deterioration in his appearance upset Lester, but he no longer had the nerve to steal. Or the guts—that was how he put it to himself. He was in a worse position than he had been at about the same time last year when he had sought out Emma for refuge and then gone north for the New Year. And now she seemed to be turning on him.

The DINING ROOMS were blank, shabby and already half full, half way through the morning. There were long, refectory-type tables and cheap wooden chairs. The counter at the far end announced SELF SERVICE, but signally failed to encourage it. Perhaps the much advertised SOUPS would be hot and filling and redeem the place; the mug of stewed tea and fly-catching sticky bun looked grim. The place was full of solitary people, it seemed, mostly old women staring into space.

Emma swept into it like a fairy in a fairy tale. The whole place lightened. Some of the old ladies nodded and greeted her. She seemed to know most of them by sight or by name.

"Well," she said, sat opposite him, both her hands warming on the large white mug of coffee, "it's nice to see you."

Lester grinned warily. But she meant it. She had taken the opportunity of a few minutes on her own to "get a grip on herself"

"I can remember going to a Hallowe'en do once," Lester said, "that'll be your candles and turnips, won't it?"

"Yes."

"It was at the Catholic church. In Thurston. They have nuns there. They ran a youth club—you hadn't got to be a Catholic to join, but it was mainly the Catholic lads. They used to have a football team and what they called an athletics team."

"You were good at that, weren't you?"

"Yes, I was. And they had this party. Hallowe'en. Candles and turnips." As he talked, the bruised defensiveness seemed to leave his face and once again Emma recognized the vulnerable/tough man she had fallen in love with. It was no use pretending that anything had changed. "I liked that. Mind you, I had to nick mine from somebody. But they put the lights out. All those turnip faces lit up on the inside. Amazing what you remember, isn't it?"

"Why don't you come to our party this evening?"

"I'm too old, Emma."

"I'd like you to meet some of the kids," she said. "Some of them are very good athletes, I'm sure—especially the West Indians. They've been looking for someone to start a sports group."

"An athletics team," Lester corrected her.

"Exactly. The man who looks after the kids has so much else on his plate he can't get round to it. But he says," Emma went on, improvising effortlessly, lying without a qualm, "that if somebody who knew something could get hold of those kids they could be sensational."

"You just have to look around," Lester said. "John Conteh, Maurice Hope, Viv Anderson, Cyrille Regis, Laurie Cunningham—they've got the talent." He paused. "And they're hungry for it. I was hungry for it. But I got caught up in the pro-game. In running. They never forgive you for that. That's what did it for me. A few measly quid when I was a kid."

"What about having a look at them?" Emma pressed her

case. Lester was hooked. She herself was amazed at the aptness of this impromptu inspiration. Of course—such a job would be ideal for Lester and he might even be good at it. In her imagination, the mutual benefits expanded to a bountiful shower of success all round.

"I would quite like that," Lester said. "Knocking them into shape. Of course, I wouldn't want any money for it. But I'd need facilities."

"I'm sure we could find a school that would lend us its gym. And there's St Luke's, which has a football pitch—it's not grass, it's under the motorway—but I think Mark said something about a running track being measured out."

"Mark who?"

"Mark James. He's the social worker in charge of children in this area."

"I wouldn't want any interference."

"I'm sure he wouldn't want to interfere."

"This is where the champions of tomorrow come from," Lester said, looking around at the old, tired faces. "It's from places like this that the Greats come. Yes. I'd like that."

"Good." Emma bit her tongue. She must not over-sell it or he would be suspicious. Yet it giggled in her mind. It was such a good idea—the salvation of Lester! The making of the two of them! The focus for many of the boys she saw so aimless now. He *would* sort them out, she was sure.

"Mary will be there tonight as well," she said. "Mary Tallentire. Douglas' wife."

"What for?"

"She used to do voluntary teaching around here. She gave up in the summer but she still keeps in touch. They say that she was very good. The committee wanted her to come."

"She's O.K., Mary," Lester said. He had scarcely taken a moment's notice of her in his life, but he wanted to extend a proprietorial hand.

"I must be off now." Emma was careful to be brisk.

Lester wanted to ask if he could move in with her. In his vision of the scene they were to have played, Emma was going to beg him to move in with her and he would have accepted, eventually—apparently unwillingly—to please her, retaining all his independence. Now that she was leaving he felt bereft. Her companionship, even in that brief time, had emphasized how isolated he now was.

"I'll walk you back."

"Thank you."

Those who saw them walking together through the crumbling inner city streets thought, "There goes that nice helpful girl from the Centre with another of her Good Causes." Emma thought, "I'll leave Mark a note at the enquiry office, putting off tonight's supper, so that Lester won't be embarrassed if he stays on." Lester thought, "A squad of athletes. That would be the job. I'll turn them into world beaters. They would have to do as I say, though. They would have to work—no skiving, no short cuts, no selling short. *My* rules. World-beaters!"

"How's little Harry?" he asked. The question had just popped into his head.

"*Lovely!*" Emma said—and she leaned over and kissed him.

I could do a lot worse than get married, Lester decided, and took Emma's arm.

(7)

Douglas wondered at what point he ought to tell him. As they sat facing each other he kept thinking: surely he knows; how can he not know? How can he assume I don't remember? What's he playing at? But Alfie Javitt just kept on playing. He was the film producer who owed Douglas £2,500: the man who had begun as a teenager with a fruit and flower stall and stormed up, comic hero fashion, through the tumbling Sixties to become a bright British export to the U.S. of A., where his Beatle association had boosted him into a circuit vampire-greedy for new blood. He was shrewd, fast talking, eccentric, cocksure, original, loud mouthed and full of total confidence about "the audience", "the ordinary joe", "the guy who pays for his seat in Kansas City and Wakefield" *and*, equally important, he fancied himself as a trend-spotter. "The mini-skirt is here to stay," "Jeans are on the way out, but *out*," "Health foods—forget it," "Science Fiction will never work in the big-time movies"—that kind of thing. His career had been hit and miss, rich and bust, up and down, never in or out for long.

The place at which he called the meeting was also a little disconcerting, as far as Douglas was concerned. It was in the middle of Mayfair, in a pretty street full of splendid early Victorian houses, once the town houses of the rich and racy members of English society; now offices. It was here, in this very room, that Douglas had got his first film script in the late 1960s. Paid £2,000, which was a sackful of gold then (although the going rate was at least ten times as much), and embarked on some months of a refined torment which drew out the most contradictory feelings: excitement at being in the dream machine which had blotted up so many fantastical hours of his youth, anxiety over how to do the job, bewilderment at the discovery that no one else seemed to know either, guilt at the money involved and the money talked about and the money promised and the nouveau richness of the fat-cat life of heavy lunches, heavier dinners, private cinemas, heated swimming pools, Swiss accounts and spoilt stars; disdain for the vulgarity of the operation, accreting contempt for the manners, attitudes and brains of those involved, a reluctant acknowledgement that there were Big Top Barnum skills and energies he did not possess, self-disgust at not waking up to and taking advantage of the conclusion that he was being asked to be a lieutenant in a war run by caricature colonels and mutton-headed generals, and, finally—and this was what had caused him to pull back from and out of the industry—he had found not only no satisfaction in the work but, powerfully, there had been a cold physical sensation in his stomach for weeks, as if he had contravened some basic rule within his own scheme of things and was thereby frozen out and discarded by a better and more useful self. But he remembered the room very well.

It had not changed at all, he thought. The over-large desk, the swivel chair, the two long black leather chesterfields, the yellow grassy Wilton carpet, wall to wall, the fine Victorian bookcase full of unread lengths of classics in calf, novels and biographies and stories "bought" (in a larger than usual sense) by the producer. There was still the huge photograph of Manhattan at night on the one wall and, on the other, the large blow-up of W. C. Fields holding a hand of poker close to his cunning face. And, scattered here and there, the chunky rich junk which could be found in the surrounding shops: heavy glass and gold, like ashtrays, a monstrous dice, a gargantuan paper-clip, the smaller necessities and toys of life inflated to ponderous proportions, giving an overall effect of striving for an effect which was never revealed or arrived at.

Alfie—he liked to be known by the matey diminutive—Alfie would have maintained that he was light years away from the dinosaurs of Hollywood who had inhabited this office before him. There was a brief period in the Sixties when, frightened by the competition of television in the States and in the self-constructed throes of a death agony on the Hollywood lots, several producers had shifted to Europe, further attracted by the low labour costs, the tales of permissiveness along the King's Road and a desperate search for a source of new energy to fuel the cranky monster on the West Coast. The man who had employed Douglas had been just such a dinosaur. Out of Central Europe, by way of deals and twists and turns and luck and one-reelers and "B" features and accidental deaths and meetings and then pots of gold and more gold. A loud, funny, bullying, ignorant, enjoyable, fat-faced, devious, generous, cunning, careless, big-bummed papa figure, who modelled himself on so many different picture heroes—now Big Daddy, now Wyatt Earp, now the Gent, now the Industrial Bum, now Svengali, now Napoleon—that he ended up spending most of his time outmanoeuvring himself with various opposed parties whom he thought he was playing off against each other. Working with him was like being in a very small bathtub with a gigantic manic, roistering dwarf.

Alfie would have described himself as "cool", new style, no flashy clothes—well, not *seeming* flashy, expensive on the sly. He would also have seen himself as the low profile laid back, relaxed operator, who knew the pedals on the organ. Cultural names, at which his predecessor in the swivel chair had jibbed like an unbroken horse, would slide easily across the large desk which, for some reason, had a piece of glass covering it. Douglas could not work out why. The desk was a reproduction. And

Alfie knew the in-groups: talk of trouble at the National Theatre, manoeuvres at the A.L.P., new production outfits being set up by the television companies—he would know the connections.

It took Douglas about ten minutes to work out that the old game had not changed an iota. Alfie, too, was a reproduction.

"I read your story by accident, to tell you the truth," Alfie said, smoking a thin but costly cigar, his Gucci boots firmly and coolly on the table showing off his deeply casual Molton Street cords and lumberjack shirt, for which he had paid a lumberjack's monthly wages. "Your agent had tried to sell me the usual spy-story crap." He smiled indulgently. "That's all *passé*. Spy stories are finished. What they want now—over in the Coast—is something with a bit of depth. They're looking for unusual properties they can get their teeth into. There's actors over there hungry for stretching. They've got to be stretched. They've made the money—they've got the fame and riches—you know—Jack and Robert and Richard and Al—and there are hundreds more where they came from, believe me, the Coast is crowded out with great actors. *Great* actors. Great *film* actors. On the screen. And they've got the directors. The very best. *Very* best. And *do* they know the medium? You should hear them talk, Douglas, it would amaze you, the details they go into. It amazes me, I don't mind admitting it. When you get Francis and George and—*and* the others in a room, it's like being at a fucking University, I kid you not. The *detail*. But what they have a crying need for is the story: the script: the idea: the basics. Not a *plot*! I'm not talking to you about a *plot*! That's out. Plots are finished. It's the thing itself. The Whole Thing. That's what matters. That's what grabbed me about your story 'Death of a Friend'—what a title! What an Eighties title! I tell you there are grown up men on the Coast who would sit down and weep for a title like that! I mean the title *in itself as a title* is ace. Ace. *As a title!* And the story. That *man*! What you do with him! It's brilliant. On his own. In that wood. I can see it. I can see them all wanting it. Talk about an acting role. A *role*! All it needs is to be written as a script."

"What about my £2,500?" Douglas thought. Not yet?

"What I would like to do is this," Alfie said. "I could get

up-front money here, no problem, on the title alone. But why get jerks involved? I'm going to the Coast tomorrow. I want to take that story and be in a position to set it up over there. You could come out and work on the first draft—paid in dollars, useful—I'd rather do that than set anything up here."

"You want a free option."

"Free? What's free? There's a lot needs to be done to it."

"I agree."

"Do you know what I think?" Alfie said, ruminatively, letting the creative juices squeeze through. "I think the reason he takes to the woods should be Vietnam."

"Vietnam?"

"It's the hottest thing in Hollywood now. Three years ago you couldn't touch it. Now you've got that Jane Fonda movie, you've got 'The Deerhunter', you've got 'Apocalypse' and 'Dog Soldiers'. If he's been in Vietnam you'll get Jack, Richard, Al, De Niro—any of them just waiting to get their hands on it. Just watch them. Vietnam is the business."

"In that case it would be a totally different story."

"Not totally, Douglas. Totally's going too far. I think of it as giving it recognizable motivation."

"The whole point is that the man goes to the woods for reasons neither he nor I can explain."

"That's the problem. That's perfect in a story—and, I repeat, I love the story. But in a film—motivation is the name of it. Motivation is what makes it work. We're aware of that now."

"What if the Vietnam thing is over?" Douglas asked, keeping a straight face.

"That's one of the things I want to suss out."

"I see."

"He could've been a terrorist."

"A terrorist?"

"Before he took to the woods. You need some heavy in-cut or flashback stuff for motivation."

"I see. An American terrorist."

"They have them, believe me. They have everything over there. You name it."

"Why don't we just scrap it and start from the beginning?"

"But I love the story. I've told you. The story and the title."

"They're a property?"

"You've beaten me to the post, Douglas. You've thought it through. Correct. It's a property. There are very few properties on the market now. I know that. I think I could sell this one Big. And to the right people."

"And then I would come out and change it entirely and script it."

"*With* a director," Alfie said by way of making the deal even more attractive. "With a very good director, hopefully. Working side by side at your elbow."

Douglas took a breath.

"The last thing I did for you, Alfie. A while back. I'm still owed on it."

"Money?"

"Yes."

"I don't believe it. I never owe." Alfie swung his feet off the table self-righteously and stood up, patently deeply concerned. "There must have been a mistake."

"£2,500."

"I mean a mistake—mistake. Look. I'll get onto the accountants." He shook his young head sadly. "These guys. You have to tell them everything. I mean, a simple payment. And peanuts! But, I can see, it's the principle." Douglas thought of the better flat £2,500 would enable him to rent: peanuts could taste good. "So what do you say?" Alfie asked.

"About the money?"

"That'll be through in a couple of days. Believe me. My mistake. About the property?"

"The story means a lot to me."

"Exactly. That's its strength. That's its strength. It means a lot to you. That's a very English thing. I understand it. You can feel it."

Douglas had enjoyed the bouncing around with Alfie and he was by now sufficiently in control of himself to realize that, while Alfie was not proposing anything alluring at the moment, there could be the seeds of a film project in his plans to ride around Hollywood waving the story around. There could even be interest from an intelligent actor or director. The story would be published eventually and have its own life. This was something else. There could be the fun of working in Hollywood for a short spell and, possibly, a wad of money which would bankroll him for six months—a year. It would be prissy to jib. The film could be thought of as having nothing to do with the story. Yet, before he gave it the nod, he acknowledged a passing sadness. Alan Jackson's death the inspiration for an Oscar-nominated performance by one of the new, tough American actors. Aware of the sentimentality of the gesture, he nevertheless made it.

"I'll need some time to think about it," Douglas said.

"Two days."

"O.K."

(8)

It was going to take him a long time to digest the implications of what Mary had said to him. Mike was glad that the rest of the day and the evening were full of work.

Mike sat on the jury which judged the best television of the year—in several categories, documentary, drama, light entertainment, the best actor, best actress, best factual series and so on. Mike had gradually been prevailed on to take more and more of an interest in this and eventually he had discovered that he was hooked. He found it a genuine stimulant to sit through such a selection of what was generally high quality stuff. The unexpected pleasure he had gained since his return to British television was just this wealth of work. He liked to enjoy the double satisfaction of seeing programmes and films over which so much care and intelligence had been spent, while knowing that they would be broadcast equally to practically every house in the land.

But tonight he was simply glad it was there—for occupation.

They were showing plays. Mike had seen most of them on transmission, which made it easy for him to watch them this time with half a mind, while he slowly absorbed the news and in effect, the ultimatum—though that was too threatening a word. Mary had simply stated her policy. It was unfair and ironic in several ways—not least of which was the fact that it was through Mike that she had regained sufficient strength, confidence and composure to make such a decision. But that was the least of it.

The plays went past: a drama-musical by Dennis Potter, an amoral rock-romp by Howard Schuman, a comedy of provincial manners by Alan Bennett—these and other of Douglas' contemporaries, Mike realized . . . What was the picture of the country that emerged from these works, he wondered. If, as was claimed, some of the best dramatists were writing some of their best plays for television and if, as they would likely claim, they were writing about the society they lived in—then it was not a bad piece of litmus paper, this videotape and celluloid. So. A fondness for the past, particularly the near past, something obsessive about the revisions and recapitulations of recent history, as if trying to discover what could be readjusted in order to release the present from the obsessive spell. The last fifty years came onto the screen again and again, in war and peace, rage and riches, despair and idle indulgence, politics and comedy, in bleakness and in wealth, as if the writers were saying—"We are them, look, see, they are us, aren't they? Are they? Are they?" Then you would have to admit the continued prevalence of a wry, ingrown sense of humour which got a laugh out of constipation and cocks, sexual ambiguities and social conventions—and this at all levels of class and sophistication, even within those works which strove to avoid it. There was the overall impression of a society, wealthy or quixotic, that could put so much talent into this form. A lack of passion, too, though melodrama often went on the rampage. A fondness for "character", even when the most urgent and political notions of the day were informing the piece. A nice sense of style: a strong feeling for place: a seemingly bottomless well of good actors, working hard and skilfully to the camera: a powerful air of work well rounded and completed. Nothing here for moaning or gnashing of teeth. At the most, an undefined apprehension.

The judges exchanged a few notes. The final assessments would be made in an afternoon meeting in the next fortnight. Mike declined to join a couple of the others for a quick meal.

He walked back to his flat, through Piccadilly and up into Soho—both still crowded—and onto his own pleasantly anonymous patch. He had heard that it was now being considered fashionable (what wasn't?). As long as the rents kept sane.

The flat was very cold. He had forgotten to switch on the heating. It was too late to bother now. He picked up the post—it always arrived after he had left for work—and went through into the living room. There was a small electric fire: he turned that on and poured himself a scotch. It still did not seem comfortable. He glanced around critically. There was not much furniture, but the place could not be called bare. There were books all over the place, and magazines and newspapers. One or two framed posters and prints were on the walls. He rarely gave the look of the place a thought: it was serviced and a woman came in twice a week to make sure it was clean and tidy. Mike was neat. Yet . . . it felt very empty—almost as empty as it had felt when he had first moved into it and left his family.

It was odd, he thought, having maintained and brought up a family at this distance—though no odder than a sailor in former years, or any traveller. When he had made the split, then it had been done carefully and well, but it had also seemed the best thing to do. And his wife and daughter had survived, even thriven. So had he.

But now there was a lack felt keenly. Over the past few months he had found that his friendship with Mary had opened up the potential of love. There was something erotic in meeting her, in being with her, in eating together, the fixing of small things; something which gave warmth and comfort to everything. In unseen ways he had come to want that, to assuage the lack of it which he had not noticed for many years.

She had made it clear that although she wanted to see him—she would not yet live with him. Despite what had happened. And this flat, which had seemed a refuge from one relationship, now seemed like a prison cell in which he would have to serve out his term without any real certainty.

For he knew that to force it would be to lose her. She was bound on a course of her own and as yet had no energy to share. He could only wait.

(9)

Douglas realized that time was up. The jokey phrase was deadly accurate. Mary had changed and he did not know in which direction that had taken her.

It was she who had asked him out. They had gone—the three of them—to a pleasant and calm little pizza house in Chalk Farm. Then Mary had invited him back to her place. Douglas was wary and took care. He concentrated on John. The two of them got on so much better now. Douglas had worked at it, and the first results of that were almost embarrassingly rich. John was happier, chirpier, he had found something to care about—fishing—which allowed him to feel independent. Being alone with his mother had rallied his sense of responsibility, while Douglas' new attentiveness had raised his self-estimation.

"He's a *lot* better," Mary said, when John finally disappeared into his bedroom. "I think your mother's helped him such a lot. So have you."

"You're his mother."

"He was in a bad way, poor boy," Mary said, plumping cushions, as she appeared to be setting the room for a scene. A tender enough scene, by the look of it, side lights, coffee on the bubble, an already opened bottle of red wine brought out with two glasses. "There. That looks fine, don't you think?"

"How old is this wine?" Douglas asked, feeling a spike of jealousy, for the true question he was quite obviously asking was—"Did you and Mike crack this bottle?"

"Mike and I had a glass this lunchtime," she said.

"A busy day."

"Half-term. We teachers have to fit things in when we can."

"We learners never learn that." He poured out two full glasses. "I feel," he said, "a significant moment coming on. Am I right?"

"Right," Mary said. Her tone was not solemn but it was rather sober, he noticed, carrying neither reprimand nor, particularly, any warning. Douglas had settled down in the settee beside the drink. Mary took her glass and went to the armchair which was generally his.

"You look very lovely," Douglas said. He raised his glass. "You're slimmer and it suits you. Your hair's started to look shiny as it used to when we first met. You look great."

"Thank you." She smiled. "You could do with cutting back on the drink a little. The chin," she said.

"Which one?"

"Do you remember back in the cottage last New Year?"

"Yes."

"I was thinking about it today. Although it was horrible and tense—you were exhausted *and* drunk *and* full of all your worst 'am I coming or going' symptoms—there was something about that."

"'Have this one on the house,'" Douglas quoted.

"Yes." She laughed. "And you did."

"I remember. On the mat."

He poured himself some more wine. There was knowing someone through living with them. There was all that store of just knowing them so intensely well from ten thousand observations and unknown perceptions. There was the capacity to make the finest adjustments of rhythm and mood, he thought, to let yourself be becalmed in a zoneless time, where there were just the two of you, the systole and diastole, to and fro, backwards and forwards, yin and yang, until the convergence. There was this ability to draw up from the well of commitment a deep calm, a sensuous understanding; mutual comprehension and peace. Douglas felt it lap about him.

"I'm pregnant," Mary said.

Douglas was very still. Something stopped and ended, he thought. Or perhaps nothing happened. There was this peculiar no-time. Undeniable. He waited for her to wind back, the words to return into her mouth, to be unspoken, for this not to have happened at all. It was so odd.

"I see," he said, after what seemed a very long time. Then he cleared his throat, which had become clogged and constricted. "I see," he repeated.

"It's early," Mary said, quietly. "I could get rid of it. But at my age—we talked about this, in fact I began to talk about it in the cottage—it isn't easy. We proved that."

"We—" He was going to say, "We never really tried."

"I did," she said. "But nothing happened. This could be a last chance. Anyway. I'm not risking anything; I want to have the child."

"Mike, of course."

"Yes."

It was only now that Douglas began to notice that what he had thought of as sobriety was in fact very stern determination.

"Christ," he said. He did not know what he felt. Her announcement had scooped out his normal responses and simply flung them away. But he felt it incumbent on him to keep a conversation alive. "What did he have to say?"

"He was pleased," Mary answered. "A bit surprised." She spoke on carefully. "We did it when we were in Paris for that holiday. Not since."

"Can I ask why not?"

"I don't know whether I love him," Mary said.

"How can you know a thing like that?" Douglas asked, and it seemed to him that a true answer to that question would solve the puzzle which seemed to him still at the centre of most things.

"I know it," she said. "Perhaps because I knew that I loved you."

"But you're having his child."

"Our child. My child. A child. Yes."

"I don't know what to say, Mary. What do you expect me to say?"

"I'm pleased about it—" she glanced at her belly. Without any suggestion of rancour, she went on, "Of course, you couldn't be expected to be. Not yet."

"Yet?" Douglas checked his own sharpness. But the sharpness was a superficial reaction. Jealousy had dissolved. Perhaps he had ceased to have any feelings for her at all.

"I think it must be terrible for you if you really don't know what love is," Mary said. "If you've really lost that; if you've really locked that off. But you love Betty, don't you? And John?"

"Of course. But there's no choice in that. It's where there's a choice that it seems meaningless."

"That's blasphemy," Mary said, and her voice was firm. "Where there's the choice is when it's most important."

"What does Mike have to say?"

"He wants us to get a divorce so that he and I can get married."

"I really don't know what to say."

"You don't have to say anything. It's a lot to take in." Mary held out her glass. "Could you pour me one, please?"

Douglas filled her glass.

"I ought to be yelling 'What a bloody mess!' and stomping about in a regressed and unjust but sincere war dance about my rights and your tartiness and your—sluttishness!" The word had an unintended accusing force.

"You slept with Hilda, didn't you?"

"Yes. But we were careful."

"I thought I'd been careful. It was an accident."

"I don't believe in that sort of accident."

"That's what Mike said."

"Sod Mike." Douglas glared at her. "I'm having no part of any bloody *ménage à trois*, you know. If we get together, it's you and me. He can have access or whatever, but I'm not living in a bloody little commune."

"I wouldn't want that, either." Mary paused. "I spoke to Hilda."

"What for?"

"I thought we should meet."

"Why?"

"To talk."

"Well?"

"Do you still sleep together?"

"No."

There was a long silence.

"It just seems very strange," Douglas said, finally. "That so much time and energy should go into who lives with whom."

"You think there are more important things?"

"Yes."

"Perhaps. It's very convenient to think that."

Douglas poured himself the rest of the bottle: Mary had indicated she wanted no more.

"So, after all that's happened, the old way would have been the best. One man, one wife," Douglas said.

"I think so."

"It was never that I didn't like you. Or even fell out of love with you."

"I know that now."

"It's so simple. Like self-destruction is a simple way to prove free will. I just wanted so much. I thought that with so much choice it was wrong to waste opportunities," Douglas said.

"You have no more choice than your grandfather had," Mary said. "That's your delusion."

"Opportunity?"

"He could have skipped off or opted out too."

"So I've been mistaken all along."

"In my opinion, yes," Mary said, carefully. "I once said I respected you for it. I don't now. There are commitments, not choices."

"So where do we go from here?"

"Well," Mary took a deep breath, "*we* don't go on anywhere. It's over, our living together. In one way I think you've played it gently and well, over the last year. You've been reliable where I needed it and helpful when I needed it. Given that you were not living with me, you couldn't have been much better. But there's absolutely no way at all in which we could ever live together again. None. I couldn't bear it."

Douglas took some time to digest that. Eventually, he nodded.

"Mike?"

"I think so. I hope so. But not for a while. I'm so weak at the moment. I have a chance to be on my own and get stronger on my own. I want to take it."

"Do you really think that most of what I've been saying and trying to do this last year has been a waste of time?"

"Not a waste of time, no. I'm sure you're sincere about it all."

"But mistaken."

"Yes. And," Mary added, carefully, "it's got very little to do with life as it's lived. All your worrying about being honest and truthful and loyal and believing in this but not in that and so on. Life's making the best of what you find. And that's to do with things that never seem to impinge on your 'world-view'. I mean things like putting up shelves or changing nappies or putting up with bad times. And, most of all, thinking about other people. It's all very well going around having thoughts on death! You could've spared an extra thought for our life."

"If I let you get away with that, I'd be betraying everything I believe in. It's easy to chop down those who try to take a view."

"Or to puncture those who are inflated?"

"I believe it's important to think life through. Even if you make a mess of it. There's an army of those who have failed. Better be with them than your 'making the best of it' brigade—heads down and anything for a quiet life. No thanks."

"We disagree, then. I think you've been hiding from the real facts with all your larger anxieties."

"It's got to be worth something."

"So you say."

"Perhaps you think there's no point at all in questions or answers. Let only professionally qualified people ask them. The rest of us should just get on and 'make the best of it'."

"I never thought you weren't sincere," Mary said.

"I've suspected myself regularly. I've thought I was manipulating you, me, her, them, anyone to get what I wanted."

"But you never knew what you wanted."

"That was the point!" Douglas said and they both laughed. "Don't you see?"

"Yes and no."

"Perfect," he said, feeling more warmly towards her than he had done for months.

"No it isn't," Mary continued, gravely. "Our marriage is over, Douglas. Fourteen years. It's over now. And you still don't seem to me to be facing up to it. You are upset. I can see that. You worry about John and fuss over me, I can see that. You cope very well. You write a story—Mike says it's the best thing you've done. You make this television film; you carry on with your reviewing and sell a house and get a flat and God knows what else. You cope. And I admire that. I see the strain. But what you don't do is see that our marriage has been just disintegrating."

"Maybe I saw that and decided to look the other way. Maybe I couldn't bear the sight. Maybe I thought that if I didn't look, it would go away and everything would end up happily ever after."

"Yes. Perhaps."

"Perhaps all that's been going on in my head about death has been no more than a transference. What really upset me was the death of us. Does that make any sense?" Douglas knew that, if ever in his life he was telling the truth and needed to be believed, it was now. If Mary, who knew him so well, failed to see when he had reached the bottom of his own pit of evasions and ambiguities and self-deceits, if his wife would not accept that indeed his year had been shaken and disturbed by the terrible fact of an empty marriage yawning before him, if she would not take this offering of honesty—then he was truly lost. He had so sliced through his self-confidence; he had alternately lashed and indulged himself; he had screwed up every move he made for so long that, to use the biblical phrase which often came to mind, "there was no health in him". And the salt had lost its savour. And the appetite had sickened. She had to believe him.

She said nothing.

"I love you," Douglas said, dry throated, slow, bending all his will to it. "I always will, I think, because I once did. But, the truth is," he licked his lips and forced the words through, "this last year, I've been trying all I could, not to admit to hating you. Not because of you. Not entirely. Our marriage was over, and neither of us wanted to see it. You wouldn't because of John, most probably. I wouldn't because to me the end of the marriage was the end of the world. It was shame and failure and my eternal guilt and not being able to look anybody in the eye again and spoiling John's chances of domestic security and condemning us to bitterness against each other. And it was letting parents down, giving in, joining the quitters; all that. But there was this hatred that I wouldn't even acknowledge to myself. I've chopped it out of my mind so much that it's never been articulated until now. But now I can see that it was there. All the time. I hated you as much as I'd loved you."

"Why didn't you let it out? It might have helped."

"Yes. Perhaps. Or it could have been destructive. In many ways I wanted us to go on. You know that. Not just for convenience. But because of the pain of not going on. Oh—I know I was exhilarated in those first few weeks, when I left the house. So were you, in a way. That was just to do with newness. It wasn't callous. But after that there was pain. I kept transferring it. I kept thinking it was to do with death: I kept suffocating it under that blanket expression. I put it in the story. Maybe in the film."

"Why?"

"I don't know. I suppose I didn't want to face up to it. But to admit to such a hatred would have prevented us from acting. Don't you see?"

"You mean it would have torn us apart."

"Yes. If I'd let it rise up it would have—I don't know. It would have wounded you and me so badly we could have bled to death. So maybe those useless, unrealistic thoughts you so convincingly disparage served a purpose beyond themselves: maybe they were the thousand and one strings and thin ropes that bound down this Gulliver of—feeling—which could have trampled over everything and crushed all about us."

"You should've let it out."

"No." Douglas felt deeply tired and sadder than he could remember since their daughter's death. "No. It would have spared nothing, you see. It would have stripped both of us bare. It would have said how loathsome and profoundly unlikeable each of us finds the other because it would have called on those parts—perhaps they are in everyone—which simply observe and draw on the weaknesses found in any close relationship. These are things about me you can't stand, and vice versa. If that hatred had been released it would have ignited all that and the flames would have burnt us to ashes."

"Instead of which I feel as much as a stone," Mary said.

"But you're still intact. And there's John—he's intact." He paused. "And Mike came along."

"What if he hadn't? Would you have stayed?"

"I wouldn't have gone."

"You left me long ago, Douglas," Mary said, taking yet another cigarette. "Long ago," she repeated. "You're right—you didn't face up to it—but neither did I. I let myself live, knowing that I was not loved. Loved! Not even wanted half the time, and the other half merely tolerated and only that with great efforts on all sides. There came a time when I should have rebelled against that and I didn't and the time passed. So where did that leave me? It wasn't John so much I ran away to, as work. All the extra teaching, and the voluntary overtime. You didn't know that side of me. 'Good old Mary'll do it.' And good old Mary did. If you became a monster, it was because I was a sucker. But the truth isn't so dramatic. Both of us believe in love and we fell out of it. And we couldn't accept that for several years. Finally it dawned on us and still we didn't accept it and acted as if it simply was not true. But it is true. I will always love you, too, Douglas: but the you I love is not the man in front of me now. And you don't love me, today, as I am. We've avoided stirring up the hatred against each other. Let's not sentimentalize the love. It's no more than a scar now. Maybe an honourable scar, but a scar."

There was silence for a while.

"So it *is* over."

"Yes. It is."

"It seems so very odd. I keep thinking that. Just ending."

"Will you go to Hilda?"

"No. I think not. Like you—I feel no use to anybody at the moment. Are we right?"

"Yes. I think so." Mary, too, was weary: and yet, for a little while longer, probably for the last time in this last mood of their married life, she, like Douglas, wanted to stay.

"Things can change," Douglas said. "Look at my own parents. At one time I would have said that they had got so used to living apart from each other's real feelings that they had become no more than two people who shared a house and a certain number of past experiences. Now they seem to have come together—just this year—and they seem to be getting closer all the time. So things can change. And maybe they weren't ever all that far apart, just hidden from each other by the screens of busyness and fatigue and just getting through life that surround us all. I remember my father saying once that *his* father, Old John, had once said he was always too tired to talk to his wife. We've had those chances—but there have been other barriers. And perhaps . . ."

"No, Douglas. You left me. And I let you go. That's what happened."

"But why?"

"That's either a whole history or a mystery. We met," Mary said and quite suddenly in her mind's eye she "saw" that first time: he looked so young, then, so eager and brimful of life—and the vision checked her, a treacherous view: she went on. "Now we've parted."

"John?"

"He's been better since we split. Everybody says that. And you're better to him now than you have been for years."

"I'll take him out tomorrow morning."

"Not in the morning. He's going over to the Heath fishing in the morning."

"On his own?"

"There's a few of them. I've been there. It's nice," Mary said. "It's very nice. They bring their little stools and their sandwiches and flasks and sit down beside the ponds, lost to the world. He loves it. He's quite safe."

"I'll come after lunch then."

"Yes."

Douglas stood up. It was very late. He could have slept where he dropped.

"You know, I came here fully expecting to stay."

"The night?"

"No. For ever."

"Did you?"

"I thought so."

"And now."

"I must guiltily steal away."

"Guilty, eh? In case you betray someone else by sleeping with your wife?"

"Not only that."

"Well." Mary stood up. "No doubt there'll be less happy nights than this."

"I'll go, then," Douglas said.

"Yes." Mary paused. "Goodnight."

Douglas stepped forward to kiss her but she stepped back. He did not insist. She closed the door very quietly behind him.

Outside he stood on the edge of the pavement for some time. It was as if he were still held to what was inside that flat. Quite unmistakably he felt bound to it, even lashed to it and he felt that he had to strain and pull and burst through this feeling in order to leave the spot. There was so much to leave. Wife. Child. Past. Tragedy. Past. Happiness. What would happen to that immense portion of shared life?

They had been part of each other for so long, swept in and out of each other's fantasies and pleasures and illnesses and delights and nightmares. Yes, it was no exaggeration: he felt bound to the place. He was breaking the most serious promise he had made.

From deep within the room, where he could not possibly see her, she watched him and knew why he paused, for she too felt too rooted in their relationship to want to move away and rip open the body of life they had formed together.

So, for some minutes, they stood, as close-bound as ever in their lives they had been, until finally, wearily, Douglas began to walk away. Mary let him go out of sight, out of sound, before dry-eyed, she went to her bed and crawled under the covers without undressing.

As he trudged through the dark and empty city, Douglas found that he was weeping. It did not last very long, but long enough for him to sense the regret and remorse which could well accompany many more of his solitary hours. Yet he walked on.

Tried to think of simple plans to staunch this spring of unhappiness which, released now after months, perhaps even years, of self-deceit, spilled into his mind steadily, without, as yet, either hint or promise of relief or peace. Must write to the man and accept the film offer: must buy John an aluminium rod: must write to parents, let them know how much I appreciate them—never do:—must check that Mike has got a job for Lester: must get better flat.

But these were flimsy defences, soon worn down by the relentless surge of unhappiness.

He walked to assuage it. He walked to tire himself. He walked to seek the comfort of activity. The streets were clear.

Not until dawn did he turn towards his room, his cell, and

begin the final stretch. The city began to show signs of its life and complexity. The street lights were dimmed by the lightness of the dawn and, before Douglas reached his place, they had been turned off.

Douglas needed a new line now, to set him off again into this different life. What had Mary said? Commitment. Yes. But if he had been a fool to think the world his kingdom, then the fool had seen his folly and the folly still lived. Yes, there was a kingdom he could look for, but no longer in himself. Self had been blighted in some explicable but most profound passion to survive. Now he was free. Free? Freer.

To be of some use to those he could help. Perhaps even to risk resurrecting the ideals of younger days and in some way trying to forget himself in the greater demands of others. Yes?

Inside the room, he was too tired to undress and he fell on the bed. It was sad to sleep alone. Once he had been afraid of it. As a child. And in the dark. Spells to beat off the evil spirits which so surrounded the bed . . . and prayers . . .?

"Thy Kingdom come, Thy will be done."

(10)

John got up quietly, so as not to disturb his mother.

His clothes were neatly laid out over a chair beside his bed. He had practised with his eyes closed so that he could, if necessary, dress in the dark. He did not want to draw the curtains because of the harsh sound they made.

The sandwiches were neatly parcelled: the flask stood beside them like a sentry. He put them carefully in his bag with the bait and the hooks and the flies and the tin of worms, carefully aerated. His grandfather had given him the tin—an ancient two-ounce Capstan tobacco tin.

He went out quietly. The rod and the camp-stool were behind the door. Soon he was through the streets and onto the Heath. He knew the short cuts now.

As he trekked up Parliament Hill the sun began to come up behind him. On the top of the hill he paused not a moment to look over the waking city. St Paul's, the parks, the Surrey hills, London. He was intent on his day's occupation.

Down the hill to the bridge which divided the two ponds. His heart lurched, happily. He was the first there. He could take his pick.

John chose his territory carefully and set up camp. He looked around briefly at the trees, the Heath beyond, the grand big houses backing onto the water. Then he made his first cast of the day. It was just about perfect.